THE
EZEKIEL
CODE

A NOVEL

GARY VAL TENUTA

Outskirts Press, Inc.
Denver, Colorado

The Ezekiel Code
All Rights Reserved

Outskirts Press
http://www.outskirtspress.com

ISBN-13: 978-1-4327-0650-0

To my soulmate, Julie, for her genuine enthusiasm, unwavering faith in the project, constant encouragement, and honest opinions during the many years it took to write this novel. Thanks, Jule. This one's for you.

Acknowledgments

My thanks (in random order): to Richard C. Hoagland at enterprisemission.com and Dave at AstroCentral (U.K.) for their valuable insights regarding comet trajectories; to Ian Campbell, co-author (with David Wood) of *Geneset: Target Earth*, for graciously providing me with the physical descriptions of the terrain around Rennes le Chateau and for his description of the area known as *Le Bordre de Doubt* (the edge of doubt); to Charles at Offshore Challenges for his assistance in understanding weather conditions off the coast of Cape Horn; to Joseph Turbeville (www.eyeofagiant) for his invaluable contributions concerning the geometry of the Great Pyramid; to Zecharia Sitchen, Bruce Cathie, Michael Tsarion (www.taroscopes.com), Lui diMartino (http://homepage.ntworld.com/lggl007), William Downey (www.thenewbiblecode.co.uk), Joe Mason and Dee Finney (www.greatdreams.com), Jay Weidner (www.jayweidner.com), Whitley Strieber (www.unknowncountry.com), Dr. Gary E. Schwartz (www.biofield.arizona.edu), Dr. Bruce Cornet (www.sunstar-solutions.com/AOP/esoteric/esoIntro.htm) Peter Gersten (www.pagenews.info), Joseph Campbell, Timothy Freke & Peter Gandy, Michael Drosnin, Gregg Braden, Margaret Starbird, Josef F. Blumrich, Michael Talbot, Geoff Stray, and many other authors and researchers whose works provided much inspiration and knowledge over the years; and to my friend, Susan McRae, for reading every chapter, one by one, as I finished them and who kept cracking the whip to get me to hurry up and finish the darned thing.

Note:
The "code" employed in this novel is based on the author's research and discoveries involving the English alphabet, the mystery of the number 9, the phenomenon of letter/number synchronicity and

what the author calls CryptoNumerology, essentially a form of the coding and divination technique known from ancient times as gematria. The research and findings are presented in detail on his web site, SynchroniCity, at

http://hometown.aol.com/codeufo/gematria.html.

Prologue
December 15, 1999

Frank McClintock paced the floor and watched the clock as he waited for Professor Alan Kline to arrive. *He's late*, McClintock thought to himself. *He's never late for anything. Maybe I better call him.* As he reached for the phone the doorbell rang. He moved quickly across the room and opened the door. "Alan! Glad you could make it. Come on in."

"For crying out loud," the professor complained, trying to shake off the chill. "You know I hate driving in the snow. Why couldn't you just tell me about whatever it is over the phone? And when the hell did you get back? I thought you were planning to stay in France for another week."

McClintock took Kline's coat and laid it over the back of the couch. "I got back yesterday. I could have told you on the phone but there's something I wanted you to see. Sit down here by the fire and make yourself comfortable. I'll get us some coffee."

"Great," Kline said. "I'll take a drop of whiskey in mine if you've got it."

McClintock laughed. "Of course. How could I forget?"

"What'd you want me to see?" Kline asked, seating himself in one of the pair of antique wingback chairs in front of the fireplace.

"It's on the coffee table there in front of you." McClintock answered from the kitchen.

The professor looked down. A document folder was lying on the small coffee table in front of him. He put on his reading glasses, opened the folder and took out the fragile sheet of parchment. It was yellowed with age and the writing was faded but legible. He was studying it when McClintock returned from the kitchen with two cups of hot coffee, each spiked with a touch of whiskey.

McClintock settled into the other wingback chair facing the

professor. He sipped his coffee quietly, letting the professor absorb the content of the parchment.

After a few moments Kline removed his glasses and leaned back. He looked at McClintock. "Is this what I think it is?" he asked, completely astonished.

"Yup," McClintock replied with a slight grin.

"So the story is true?"

McClintock nodded. "I believe it is."

"Where the hell did you get this? I know you told me you thought it existed but I was beginning to think the whole strange story was a crock."

"Well," McClintock started, "you remember the reason I went to France was to meet with that other researcher that I'd been corresponding with by email?"

"Yes. Jacques somebody."

"Yes! Jacques de Pereille. He claimed to be related to Raimon de Pereille but hardly anyone believed him."

"I'm sorry," Kline said, shaking his head. "You'll have to refresh my memory."

McClintock set his coffee down and leaned forward in the chair. "Raimon de Pereille," he explained, "was the lord of Montségur!"

"Montségur?" Kline asked, not yet remembering this part of the long, complex story.

For the past several months McClintock had been pursuing what he suspected to be the facts behind an old myth. It was a story so unlikely that Professor Kline doubted any of it could be true. Whenever McClintock would discover some tidbit of information about the story he would call Kline and tell him what he'd learned. But now Kline's skepticism was being seriously challenged by the evidence he was holding in his own hands.

"Montségur was a huge castle," McClintock explained. "The last refuge for the Cathars back in the Middle Ages during the so-called Holy Inquisition. They were being hunted down and slaughtered like animals."

"Oh, right. Yes," Kline said. "I remember now."

McClintock sat back in his chair. "Anyway, like I said, this guy, Jacques, claimed to be related to the Lord of Montségur."

"And you believe he is?"

McClintock shrugged. "Well, I can't say for certain but I'm damn sure about one thing."

"What's that?"

"He's the one who gave me what you're holding in your hands right now."

Kline looked surprised. "He gave you this? He just handed it over to you? Why? Why would he do that?"

"Well, it wasn't quite like that. Not exactly, anyway."

Kline looked concerned. "What do you mean?"

"Well, here's what happened. I had a conversation with Jacques at a little cafe the previous day. He confided in me that he had what he believed to be the real thing in his possession. He said he'd show it to me if I wanted to come to his home the next day. Well, I wasn't sure if I believed him or not but I wasn't going to pass it up, just in case. And then he told me he thought some kind of an agent from the Vatican had been following him around for the past week or so. Well, that struck me as a bit of a stretch and I just sort of brushed it off. I figured maybe Jacques was just getting paranoid. You know, having a little flight of fancy that was maybe getting out of hand."

"The Vatican!" Kline scoffed. "Does seem a bit extreme."

"Exactly my reaction. It was just a little too extreme. Like I said, I just brushed it off at the time. But when I got to his home the next day I found the door wide open and the place had obviously been ransacked. Furniture turned over, drawers pulled out, stuff all over the place. A real mess. I called out for Jacques but there was no answer."

"My god. So what'd you do?"

"The first thing that went through my mind was what he'd told me about someone following him around. I figured if that was true - I mean if that's what this was all about - then they were probably looking for that parchment. Fortunately Jacques told me where he'd hidden it."

"I'm amazed he would tell anyone something like that," Kline said. "Why would he do that?"

McClintock nodded. "Yes, well, I think the reason he told me was because he trusted me and figured if anything should happen to him at least maybe I could get to it before anyone else did. He'd simply hidden it inside the backing of a cheap painting that hung on the wall in his bedroom. So I rushed into the bedroom and sure enough the painting was hanging there, apparently untouched. I grabbed it from the wall and tore off the backing and there was the parchment just like he said. I shoved it under my coat and turned to get the hell out of there. That's when I saw Jacques on the floor. He was on the other side of the bed, laying in a pool of blood with a bullet hole in his head."

Kline sat straight up. "Dead?"

"As a doornail."

"Jesus! Could it have been a suicide?"

McClintock shook his head. "I doubt it. There was no gun anywhere to be seen."

"He was murdered?"

"That's the way it looked to me."

"Good Lord," Kline mumbled under his breath.

"Yeah."

"Did you go to the police?"

McClintock shook his head. "No, man. I was scared. I just got the hell out of there."

Kline looked seriously concerned now. "If this is all true, you could be in real danger."

McClintock nodded. "I know."

"Who else knows you have this?" Kline asked, laying the old parchment back on the table.

"Nobody. Just you."

"You're sure?"

"Pretty sure."

"Good," Kline replied, somewhat relieved. "If I were you I'd get rid of the damn thing and just forget about it."

McClintock swirled the coffee around in his cup a few times and looked up at his friend. "I can't," he said. "I've come so far. I'm this close. I can't let it go now. You know what I mean?"

Kline shook his head. "I figured as much," he said, getting up and walking over to the couch to get his coat. "Look, I gotta go. Got an early morning class and I promised the students an energetic lecture they'd be crazy to miss. But please, call me later tomorrow, will you? We need to talk about this. Seriously."

"All right," McClintock agreed, seeing his friend to the door.

A light snow was still falling as Kline made his way across the yard toward the street. Suddenly a black van pulled out from the curb in front of the house. The driver seemed to be in a hurry as the van fishtailed down the icy street.

Kline turned to look back toward the house. McClintock was still standing in the open doorway. Kline hollered, "Who was that?"

McClintock shrugged it off. "I don't know. Vatican spooks?" he joked.

Kline didn't laugh. "You call me tomorrow!"

"Don't worry!" McClintock assured him with a wave as he closed the door against the cold night.

But the professor was indeed worried. He shivered. A bullet hole in the head – even if it's someone else's head - should make a person worry. The next day he waited for McClintock's call but it never came. Ever.

Part 1: Turning Point

~1~

October, 2005

O nce in a while, as we go about our daily routines, something happens that just doesn't fit the program, something so out of the ordinary that it stops us in our tracks and makes us wonder. For Zeke Banyon, this was going to be one of those days.

There was a heavy mist in the air, typical for late Fall in Seattle. Out in the suburbs the fallen leaves covered the lawns. But here, in the lower end of the downtown streets by the waterfront, there were no leaves and no lawns. This was the world of old bricks and mortar, concrete and cement.

Down on First Avenue the homeless were seeking shelter. The Seattle Gospel Mission – a shelter for the homeless - had taken in just about as many as could be accommodated as one wet and bedraggled soul after another straggled in through the door.

Zeke Banyon - who once studied for the priesthood - now managed the establishment. A few of the people who frequented the shelter knew about his short stint as a seminary student and insisted on calling him Father Banyon. In truth, he was just an ordinary man who eventually earned a degree in social work and had a gift for carpentry and wood carving. He hand-carved a little sign to hang in the window of the shelter's weathered entrance door. One side read:

C'MON INN!
On this day that side of the sign had just about done its job. The other side read:

SORRY, NO ROOM AT THE INN

As evening settled in he was just about to turn the NO ROOM side toward the street when the door burst open. At first he thought it was the wind and maybe it was, but it blew in one more customer; an old black gentleman bundled up in a moth-eaten Navy peacoat. He carried a tattered guitar case in one hand and in the other hand he toted a plastic bag containing an extra pair of socks, a ball of string, and a transistor radio. They called him Old Tom.

Old Tom was a bit of a fixture on the streets around town, playing music on the corner by the Farmer's Market where passersby would typically drop a pittance of change into his guitar case. Once in a while a dollar bill would appear. On a good day he could make five dollars. Maybe six. Zeke Banyon had often been one of those passersby. Sometimes one or two of those dollars in Old Tom's guitar case were from Banyon's own pocket.

"Evenin', Father" Tom said with a voice that sounded like he gargled with gravel. "Got room for one more?"

"Hey, Tom. Sure. On one condition."

"Whaddya mean?"

Banyon nodded toward the guitar case.

"What?" Tom said. "I gotta leave it outside?"

Banyon laughed. "Hell no! Get that thing out of the case and play us a tune. If it's any good maybe I'll let you stay for a meal."

Tom looked relieved. Grinning under the dripping brim of a dirty old Seattle Mariner baseball cap, he replied, "Thanks, Father. Anything special you wanna hear?"

Shutting the old wooden door against the persistent wind, Banyon rubbed his clean-shaven chin and thought a moment. "Yeah," he said. "How about *Just A Closer Walk With Thee?*" He was joking, of course, since he was pretty sure that wasn't exactly Tom's type of music. Tom was a blues-man, *plain an' simple*, as Tom liked to say about himself.

"You got it, Father," was Tom's reply.

Thinking Tom was just putting him on, Banyon laughed and headed toward the kitchen. There he busied himself, helping a couple of the volunteers who were preparing the soup of the day and slicing the few loaves of bread donated by a local supermarket. Suddenly he heard the sweet slow sound of a true blues-man's guitar and the gravely voice of a man who'd seen it all. Banyon couldn't believe his ears. It was the most soulful rendition of *Just A Closer Walk With Thee* he'd ever heard. *Man,* he thought to himself, *they don't play it like that in church.* But the moment was interrupted by the sound of a woman's voice calling his name.

"Father Banyon?" came the voice again.

He dropped what he was doing and hurried out to see who it was.

He found her standing just inside the front door. Judging from her appearance he doubted she was another homeless person. The attractive young lady was nicely dressed in new blue denim pants with a matching blue parka zipped snuggly up to the neck. She folded her umbrella and brushed her blond, wind-swept hair out of her face. He thought she looked somewhat familiar but he wasn't sure why. He was certain he'd never actually met her before.

"Yes?" he said. "I'm Banyon. Can I help you?"

"I'm Angela Martin," she said, but she could see it didn't ring a bell. "Angela Martin. From the college? I talked with you on the phone a few days ago about working here part time. You said I should come see you today."

"Oh! Yes, I remember. I'm sorry. I get so busy around here. Come in. I have an office in the back. Let me take your coat and umbrella".

The office was not much more than a converted storage room with a desk, a bookshelf and a typewriter. It was the typewriter that first drew her attention.

"Wow," she grinned. "A typewriter!"

"What's so unusual about that?" he asked.

"Well, I..." she hesitated. "I just haven't seen one of those in a long time. Everybody uses computers now."

Banyon laughed. "Yeah, well you know. I'm just a bit out of touch with the modern age I guess. Have a seat, Miss..."

"Martin. But call me Angela. Or Angel if you like. People call me Angel all the time." Then she smiled. "But seeing as how you're a priest, you can probably tell I'm no angel!"

Settling himself down in the chair behind his desk, he feigned a rather devilish grin and looked around as if to make sure no one was listening to their conversation. "I'll let you in on a little secret," he said. Leaning slightly toward her over the top of his desk - which was covered with a pile of papers and books - he whispered, "I'm not really a priest either."

Angela wasn't sure if he was serious or not. It was the last thing she expected him to say. "Excuse me?" she said, eyebrows raised.

He reached into his desk drawer and pulled out a pack of cigarettes. "Mind if I smoke?" he asked.

The question caught her off guard. "What? No, of course not. In fact I was just going to ask you the same thing."

He smiled and held the pack out to her. "Have one of mine?"

"Sure. Thanks." She pulled a cigarette from the pack and looked at it. "Menthol?" She chuckled. "Candy cigarettes. Haven't had one of these in years."

Banyon produced an ashtray from beneath the stack of papers in front of him and set it on the desk. He offered a match but she had already fished a lighter from her purse.

"So," she said, picking up the conversation, "were you kidding about not really being a priest? I mean, you are Father Banyon, aren't you?"

Banyon studied his lighted cigarette, rolling it between his fingers. "I almost became Father Banyon. Now I'm just plain ol' Zeke Banyon."

"Zeke?"

"Short for Ezekiel. But, come on, who wants to be called Ezekiel? You think I didn't get teased about that when I was a kid? Hah! Of course it didn't help any that I was in Catholic school to boot. When my mother was pregnant with me my dad said if the baby was a boy, he liked Rick for a name. Now that would have been just great with me!"

"So Ezekiel was your mother's idea and she won the name-the-baby contest?"

Banyon laughed. "Something like that. Actually, what happened was my mom liked the name Rick just fine until the night before I was born."

"What happened?"

Banyon couldn't believe the conversation had gotten this far with a complete stranger, let alone that he was about to tell her something he'd told only three or four close friends in his entire life. *Oh, what the hell. She's smoking one of my cigarettes. We're practically old friends.* "Well," he began, "it's kind of weird." He took a drag from his cigarette. "The night before I was born she dreamed she saw me as a grown man and someone was calling me Ezekiel. When she woke up the next morning she kept obsessing about the dream. So anyway..."

he hesitated for a moment, looking a little embarrassed, "...being a good Catholic and all, she convinced herself it was some kind of a divine message - or something - and insisted that if the baby turned out to be a boy it had to be named Ezekiel. Dad wasn't real thrilled with the name but, as usual, he gave in to mom's desire."

Angela found that amusing but she was still puzzled about his background. "So, I don't get it. You mean you used to be a priest but now you're not?"

"Oh, it's kind of a long story and not all that interesting really. But how about you? Tell me something about yourself. Married? Kids?"

"I was married," she said, lowering her eyes for a moment. "My husband died a few years ago from a heart attack. It was totally out of the blue. Completely unexpected. We had no children."

"I'm very sorry," Banyon said.

Angela reached for the ashtray and crushed out her cigarette. "I thought my life was over. You know what I mean? There was just this big empty hole in my life. Believe me, I was teetering on the edge. And then one day I don't know what happened. I can't explain it. I just woke up one morning and realized I was still alive. It was like an amazing revelation."

Banyon smiled. "I think I understand."

"Well, so there I was. Thirty-three years old with a new life ahead of me but I just didn't know what to do with it. Then I had an idea. Although it seemed kind of silly at first."

"What was that?"

"I thought maybe I should go back to school. In a way, I thought it was probably the nuttiest thing I could have come up with. I mean, at my age and all. But the thing is, years ago I did want to go to college to study anthropology. I probably would have if I hadn't gotten married."

"Anthropology!" Banyon exclaimed. "That's interesting."

"Well, see," she continued, "I was a National Geographic addict. I just loved that stuff. Especially the ancient cultures. So anyway, the more I thought about it, the more I was intrigued by the possibility even though I was pretty darned nervous about going back to school. I mean, not only was I worried that maybe I couldn't cut it but I could just picture myself as the *old lady* in a class full of *twentysomethings*. That was a frightening concept."

Banyon nodded and smiled. "I can imagine! But I have to tell you, you look a heck of a lot closer to twenty-three than thirty-three!" As soon as he said it he wished he hadn't. Not that it wasn't true. She looked great. He was just afraid it sounded like a stupid attempt at flirting – something he wasn't very good at even when it was intentional.

Angela smiled, a bit embarrassed. "Well, thank you. I do what I can."

"I'm sorry," Banyon said, clearing his throat. "I didn't mean to interrupt you."

Angela shifted in her chair. "Oh, that's all right," she said. "Anyway, a friend of mine insisted that a lot of people my age were taking classes in the community colleges. So I got up the nerve, and signed up for my first two classes on my way to a two-year degree. That was about six months ago and I'm loving every minute of it. But I needed a little extra cash so I thought a part time job would be a good idea. Then I saw the help wanted notice you placed on the bulletin board at the college and so here I am." She paused and laughed. "You know, even the guy who runs the student employment office at the college thought you were a priest."

Banyon laughed. "Well, there you go. I can't get away from it!"

Now, as he sat there staring at her, it dawned on him why she looked so familiar. "Did anyone ever tell you that you look just like Meg Ryan?"

Meg Ryan was one of the few pop-culture icons that stuck in his mind. He didn't usually pay much attention to that kind of thing. He wasn't much of a TV-watcher. He'd certainly never seen *Access Hollywood* or *Inside Edition*, and he hadn't actually been to a movie since – well, since *Harry Met Sally*. In fact it was probably the famous orgasmic restaurant scene in that movie with Billy Crystal and Meg Ryan that earned Ms. Ryan a special place in the back of Banyon's mind.

The comment took Angela by surprise. "Who, me?"

"Oh, never mind," he said, thinking the comparison was probably a stupid thing to mention. *Strike two*, he thought to himself. "I admire what you've done, going back to school and all. So, hey, you're hired."

"I am? I mean... I am?" Angela stuttered at the sudden announcement. "I mean, I'm not even sure what it is you need me to do. The help-wanted notice didn't really say."

Banyon smiled. He pushed his chair back from his desk and nodded toward the huge pile of miscellaneous stuff that covered it. "If you don't mind, you could start by doing an archaeological dig through this ancient mess and see if it can be organized into some kind of order."

Angela laughed. "I'm studying to be an anthropologist, not an archaeologist."

"By the time you get through this," he said with a wink, "you'll be an archaeologist, too. You can start tomorrow." He took another look at his desk. "Maybe you should bring a shovel."

She grinned. *Tall, dark, handsome, and a sense of humor*, she thought to herself. *Not bad*. She caught herself wondering if he was married but she didn't think it would be appropriate to ask. She didn't even think it was appropriate to be thinking about it. Since her husband had died she hadn't given a second thought to the idea of another man in her life. Whenever such a thought tried to squeeze its way in she shut it out immediately. It was a guilt thing. At the moment, however, her thoughts were causing her more embarrassment than guilt. *Is that a good thing?* She wondered.

Banyon walked her down the hall to the front door where they stood talking for a few moments. They were oblivious to the presence of a man just a few paces to their left in the main lounge area. The man looked like any of the other down-and-outers off the street just trying to get warm. He was huddled over in one of the well-worn overstuffed chairs, seemingly minding his own business. But this down-and-outer had something up his sleeve. Literally. Shielding his mouth with his hand he spoke quietly and covertly into his sleeve. "Get ready. She's coming out."

"Thank you Father," Angela said, shaking Banyon's hand.

"Please," he said, "just call me Zeke."

"Okay, Father," she chuckled as she opened her umbrella and headed out the door into the mist. She turned back just briefly, peeking out from under the umbrella. "By the way," she said, grinning, "you look a little like one of the Baldwin brothers."

The moment she turned back to the sidewalk a man in a black van across the street made a quick adjustment to the telephoto lens on his 35mm Nikon. He managed to click off two good close-ups of Angela's face before her umbrella blocked his view.

Banyon called out to her. "Who the heck are the Baldwin brothers?"

But she was already on her way up the street and couldn't hear him. As he leaned out the door and watched her disappear into the night a gust of wind blew a lock of his thick black hair down into his eyes. He brushed it back and was about to close the door when the man with the wire up his sleeve quickly squeezed by him with his hat pulled down and his collar turned up to hide his face.

"Pardon me," the man mumbled under his collar as he hastily made his exit.

"Quite all right," Banyon said, stepping aside. Then he closed the door and headed off toward the kitchen. *Yup*, he thought to himself, *I love Meg Ryan. I have a feeling this is going to work out well. Who the heck are the Baldwin brothers?*

As he passed the storage room on his way to the kitchen he glanced up at the clock on the wall. He had developed a habit of checking the clock against his watch whenever he passed by. The time on the clock at that moment was exactly 9 p.m. He stopped in his tracks. *What? Wait a minute.* He checked his watch. It showed 6 o'clock. He knew his watch was right because he remembered noticing it was 5 o'clock when Angela came in for the interview. The interview, he was pretty certain, took just about an hour. That would indeed make it now about 6 o'clock. *That's odd*, he thought. *The clock must have stopped this morning.* Then he thought again. *No, that can't be. When I passed by it at noon I remember the hands were straight up at the 12, right where they should have been. So it was working fine. How could it get from 12 o'clock to 9 o'clock when it's really only 6 o'clock?* It didn't make sense. He got a chair to stand on, reached up, removed the clear plastic cover, and moved the hands back to the correct time. He stepped down, took another look at it, and shrugged it off. *Very strange*, he thought to himself as he headed off toward the kitchen. *Very strange.*

What he didn't know at the moment was that something much stranger was still waiting to happen. Pieces of a puzzle – a puzzle he didn't even know existed - were moving into place. The great mandala was in motion. The wheels of destiny were turning. And like the hands on the clock that go round and round, it was just a matter of time.

~2~

It didn't take long for Banyon and Angela to establish a comfortable work routine although that comfort zone did have a slight glitch in it. There seemed to be some sort of undefinable tension between them. It wasn't even really negative or disruptive in any way. It was just there, lurking in the background. Neither of them, of course, could be certain that the other was experiencing this feeling so they kept it to themselves and tried to ignore it.

Angela's job turned out to be a kind of Gal-Friday position, helping Banyon in nearly every aspect of running the shelter. They worked well together although they hardly ever talked about their personal lives and Angela still didn't know for sure whether or not he was married.

As far as Banyon was concerned, things were going wonderfully. For the first time in what seemed like years, he even got to see the top of his desk. That, in fact, is what triggered the first step into the strange journey upon which, unbeknownst to either of them, he and Angela were about to embark.

The actual desktop hadn't seen daylight for a long time, or so one would suspect, judging by the clutter of papers, pamphlets, and what-not that had accumulated over time. Perhaps it had been cleared off once or twice but, if so, no one - not even Banyon - had bothered to change the oversized desk-pad calendar hidden beneath the mess.

According to the current calendar on the wall, the present date was Sunday, October 26, 2005. The desk-pad calendar, however, was still at May, 2001. Apparently the former director had never bothered to change the calendar on the desk-pad and, oddly enough until this very day, it had completely escaped Banyon's attention.

Banyon didn't really know much about the former director, a Reverend *somebody*. But, whoever he was, he was a doodler. The pad was filled with quickly scratched notes and phone numbers and curious little scribbles. And something else. Another thing to which

Banyon had previously paid no attention. Not surprising, really, given that the desk had been covered with clutter for God knows how long. But now, as he studied the odd little doodles, his attention was drawn to the numbers and letters randomly scribbled all over the pad. Up toward the top of the pad someone - presumably the former director - had written the alphabet and had numbered each letter consecutively, 1 through 26, starting with A and finishing with Z. Then Banyon noticed a lot of words randomly scattered around on the pad. Each word had a number just below each of its letters. Glancing back at the alphabet at the top of the pad he realized the numbers below the letters in the words corresponded to the numbered letters in the alphabet. Apparently someone had been converting the words to numbers. *But why?* he wondered.

Now that he thought about it, he remembered seeing this before, probably in a book somewhere. *Numerology,* he mused.

Banyon didn't know much about numerology but he remembered thinking it was just a silly curiosity, something about as useful as astrology which, of course, was all poppycock and balderdash, as his mother used to say to his father whenever his father read the daily horoscope in the morning paper.

Now, looking at the scribbling on the deskpad, Banyon was amused that someone had apparently been at least somewhat serious about this numerology thing. That struck him as odd, especially if it was the former director, a man of the Cloth. At that moment something caught his eye. Off to the side of the pad he saw his own name. It wasn't referring to him personally. It was a reference to a character out of the Bible. The words, scratched out in dark blue ink, read:

THE WHEEL OF EZEKIEL = 180 = 9

Obviously, it was a reference to the book of Ezekiel in the Bible where the prophet Ezekiel recounts his vision of an object coming out of the sky. The scripture describes part of the object as a *wheel within a wheel* and Ezekiel believed it to be a manifestation of the glory of the Lord.

Using the alphanumeric table at the top of the pad, Banyon carefully did the math for himself. Sure enough, the sum of the letters in the phrase was 180. What he didn't understand was how 180 equaled 9. He studied it for a moment and it occurred to him that if the digits in 180 were added together the sum would be 9. *Maybe that's it. But, so what?* Still, he couldn't resist the temptation to see what number his own name might come to. He printed his name on the pad just below the words, THE WHEEL OF EZEKIEL, and did the math:

EZEKIEL BANYON = 144 = 9

That raised his eyebrows but his silent musings were interrupted by a knock at his office door.

"Come in," he called.

"Mr. Banyon? Am I disturbing you?"

"Angela! What a surprise! Come in, please. You don't work on weekends. What brings you in here on this beautiful Sunday afternoon?"

Typical for Seattle, the weather had changed from a week of clouds and rain to a nice, almost warm, sunny day.

With her denim jacket draped over her arm, Angela, looked amazingly attractive in a pink turtleneck sweater and blue jeans. She scooted a chair over to a spot just in front of Banyon's desk and lit up a cigarette. "I was at the main library downtown looking for some research material for one of my classes. Anyway, since I was in the neighborhood I thought I'd stop and say hi."

"Well, I'm glad you did. Hey, check this out." He showed her the date on the calendar pad. "It hasn't been changed since 2001!"

Angela laughed. "Wow. I'm sorry. I didn't notice that when I cleaned off your desk. I would have mentioned it."

"Oh, no, it's not that!" he grinned. "I just thought it was amusing." He pulled the calendar sheet out from the deskpad and was about to toss it in the wastebasket when he remembered the curious alphanumerics that were scribbled on it. He hesitated a moment and then handed it over to Angela. "By the way," he asked, "have you ever seen anything like this?" He pointed to the letters and numbers.

She studied it for a moment. "Um... well, yes. Looks like someone was playing around with numerology. Why? Are you interested in numerology?"

"Oh, I don't know anything about it, really. But look at this." He pointed to his name and the phrase about Ezekiel. "Isn't that a coincidence? They both equal 9 if you -"

"Yes," she interrupted. "If you cross-add the digits."

"Cross-add?"

"Yes, it's called cross-adding. It's what you do in numerology."

"So you know something about numerology?"

She shrugged. "Not much. I had a book on it once. Just a used paperback I happened to find in a thriftstore a couple years ago. I might still have it. I could look for it if you want."

"So what's the deal with it? I mean I imagine the numbers are supposed to have some kind of meanings attached to them?"

"As I recall, yes."

Banyon chuckled. "So what does the number nine mean?"

She handed the calendar back to him and smiled. "I don't know. But isn't this the kind of thing priests are supposed to stay away from?"

"Well, like I told you before, I'm not really a priest."

"Yes, you did say that. What happened? I don't mean to be nosey. Just kind of curious. Unless you don't want to talk about it."

"No, I don't mind. It's just the ol' twists and turns of life, you know. I started to study for the priesthood some years ago but one day I met this woman and that sort of changed everything, if you know what I mean."

Angela's stomach tensed up. *Well, now I know.* She forced a smile.

"Hey, I fell in love!" he said with a grin. "That's pretty much the long and the short of it."

"I see. So you gave up the church and got married?"

"Yup. It's funny. It was both the easiest decision I've ever made and, at the same time, really difficult. My mother was beside herself. It was mostly her idea for me to become a priest. I don't think my dad really cared that much."

"So they were both Catholic?"

"My mother was a devout Catholic and my dad converted to Catholicism shortly after they got married. But I think he did it mostly just to please her." He paused for a moment and laughed. "Needless to say, Karen and my mother never hit it off real well but my dad thought she was terrific."

"Your wife's name is Karen?"

"Was," he replied solemnly.

Angela hesitated, puzzled. *Was?* She didn't know if she should ask but her curiosity got the best of her. "You're divorced?"

Again, Banyon couldn't believe he was spilling out his whole life-story to this person he hardly knew. After all, she'd only wandered in the other day to apply for a job. Still, there was something about her. She was easy to talk to and he felt unusually drawn to her for some reason. "Karen died in a car accident three years ago," he explained. "We'd only been married for three years before it happened."

There was a sudden pause in the conversation. Not an uncomfortable one. Time just seemed to stand still for a moment as the past few years of his life ran through his mind. Angela was having her own private moment and didn't even really notice the void in the conversation.

"Anyway," he said, "The short time I spent at seminary did provide me with a direction. I went to school and got a degree in social work and eventually got a job as a counselor at a shelter for battered women. But after Karen died I just couldn't do it anymore. To make a long story short, I basically just started wasting my days not doing much of anything until an old friend of mine, Father Caldwell, came to see me and sort of gave me a motivational kick in the ass, if you know what I mean."

Angela smiled and Banyon went on. "He told me the homeless shelter here was in need of a new director and it's worked out pretty well. I like it here. I'm helping people in some small way. It's good. And, see, the deal is, a rumor got started on the street that I was, in fact, a priest." He gave a short laugh as he thought back on it. "These homeless people started coming in and calling me Father Banyon. I kind of liked it but I felt a little guilty about it at first. Anyway, the name just sort of stuck and that's why everyone around here calls me Father Banyon. It works," he chuckled. "So I just figured, what the hell."

Angela was amused by the story and felt a little guilty that she found some pleasure in knowing he was... available. She looked at him across the desk. His deep brown eyes seemed to draw her in. "I see," she said. "I'm sorry about your wife. I know what it's like. I mean I know what you were going through."

He nodded, recalling Angela's own story about losing her husband.

Angela sensed that he was feeling a bit uncomfortable. "Well," she said, graciously changing the subject. "So you want me to look for that book?"

"Book?"

"The numerology book."

"Oh! Sure. What the heck. I'm curious now."

"Okay, I'll look for it tonight."

"Great! Hey, what are you doing for dinner?" The question surprised her. *Oh my god. A date?* The very thought scared her. She shrugged, trying to appear unmoved. "Warmed up leftovers, probably."

"Oh, come on! How about having an award-winning pizza with me at Mario's down the street? My treat."

Angela tightened up. *Is he just being friendly? What's happening?* Then she shook her head. "Thanks, but I think I should probably just head home. I have a lot of homework to get done before class tomorrow morning."

Banyon smiled, trying not to show his disappointment. "All right. Maybe another time."

Angela stood up to leave and Banyon walked her out to the front door. Glancing out, they could see the evening sun had vanished behind the tall buildings leaving a sharp chill in the air.

"Oh!" she said. "My jacket. I must have left it in your office."

"Wait here," he told her. "I'll get it."

He walked into his office and found her jacket hanging on the back of the chair. He picked it up not realizing, at that moment, a folded piece of paper slipped from the pocket and settled just under the chair. He returned to find Angela waiting for him at the front door.

"Here you go," he said, helping her on with the jacket.

"Thanks Father."

"Ahem!"

She smiled, teasingly. "Zeke."

"There you go," he said with a grin. "See you tomorrow afternoon?"

"I'll be here."

He watched her walk up the street and then called out to her, "Bring the book if you find it!"

"I will!" she said, turning just briefly to wave goodbye.

Back in his office, he took another look at the curious scribbles on the desk pad. He still didn't know what to make of it. After finishing a few minutes of bookwork he decided to take himself up on his own offer of Pizza at Mario's. His treat.

He donned his coat and pushed Angela's chair back to where it had been, next to the wall. Looking down, he noticed the small piece of paper on the floor. He picked it up, unfolded it and recognized Angela's handwriting. It was a simple note:

Seattle Gospel Mission
198 Post Street

He figured it wasn't important. *Probably just a note to herself,* he decided. He crumpled it up, tossed it into the wastebasket and headed off to Mario's.

Sitting alone at a table by the window, staring out at the darkened street, waiting for his double pepperoni pizza with extra cheese, his wandering thoughts suddenly came to a screeching halt.

"198 Post Street? 198?" he muttered aloud. "One plus nine, plus eight is... um... eighteen, and one plus eight is -"

"Nine," the waitress said as she delivered the pizza to his table.

"What?" he said, a little startled. He hadn't noticed her approaching.

She laughed. "I'm sorry. I just happened to hear you doing some math."

He looked at her as if she had just said something profound. "It *is* nine, isn't it?"

"Unless they've changed it," she chuckled. "You never know with all that so-called new math and all."

He barely caught the joke. He wasn't really listening. His mind was on the address of the building where he worked. *What the hell is this?* he thought to himself. *Got to be just one of those odd coincidences, all this nine stuff.*

He removed a slice of pizza from the platter. Just as he was about to take a bite, he looked down at the rest of the pizza. He counted the number of slices. There were seven on the platter and one in his hand. *That's eight,* he smiled to himself. Then, aloud, he said, "Damn good thing!"

"Glad you like it," the waitress said as she passed by his table with an armload of dishes.

But again he wasn't paying attention. He was still thinking about that *nine thing.* He thought back to the incident with the clock on the wall... all the words and phrases with *nines* on the calendar pad...

now the street address of the shelter. He chuckled to himself, amused by the string of coincidences. *Weird,* he thought. *Why is this happening? What does it mean?*

~3~

"Hey there, Tom!" Angela said as she walked in the front door of the shelter. "How are you on this fine Monday afternoon?"

Old Tom, the African-American bluesman, was sitting on the floor putting a new string on his guitar. "What's so fine about it?" he grumbled without looking up. "It's Monday. I hate Mondays."

Angela laughed. "Really! And why is that? I would think one day is about the same as another for a free spirit like yourself."

"Free spirit? Me?" he said, still not looking up as he twisted a tuning peg on the guitar. He plucked a couple of strings and tilted his head, listening intently to see if they were in tune. "Ain't nothin' free, lady. Not even my spirit. And I'll tell you what's wrong with Mondays." He looked up at her as if he were about to let her in on something at least as important as the state of the economy or global warming. "All they serve here on Mondays is bean soup."

Angela laughed. "And what's wrong with that?" she asked. "I hear it's pretty good and hey... it's free!"

"Not hardly," he said, returning attention to his guitar.

"Not hardly what? Not hardly good or not hardly free?"

"Both," he grumbled. "Well, okay, it ain't bad but it ain't free."

"What do you mean?"

He looked up at her again. "You ever spend a night in a room full of people who all had bean soup for dinner? If that ain't a price to pay, I don't know what is."

"I see," she chuckled. "Not that I'm not enjoying this pleasant conversation but, just to change the subject, have you seen Zeke today?"

"Father Banyon? He's been holed up in his office all day. Not like him. Maybe he ain't feelin good or somethin'."

"Really? Well I'm going to go check on him."

As she headed down the hall toward Banyon's office she could hear Tom singing a blues version of the old Carpenter's tune, *Rainy Days And Mondays*. But he, of course, changed the words. She distinctly heard him crooning, *"Bean soup and Mondays always get me down"*.

She knocked on Banyon's door. "Zeke?"

"Angela! Come in!"

She walked in and found him sitting at his desk holding what looked like a beaded necklace in his hands.

"Close the door and pull up a chair," he said. He draped the object over his hand and held it up for her to see. "Do you know what this is?"

"Um, yeah, it's a rosary, isn't it? Catholics use them to say prayers or something. Right?"

"Something like that, yes," he said, staring at the rosary as he slowly rolled it around between his fingers. "You know what the address of this building is?"

"Sure," she said, puzzled as to why he would ask. "198 Post Street."

"Add that up," he said, still fiddling with the rosary.

"Add what up?"

"The numbers in the address. You know. Cross adding, like you told me."

She thought for a moment. "Um... eighteen."

He finally looked up at her but he didn't say anything.

"Oh." she said. "One plus eight. It's nine."

He stood up, rosary in hand, and turned, gazing blankly out the window behind his desk. "Remember the alphanumeric value of my name?"

"Um," she hesitated. "I don't remember. But I remember it reduced to nine. So what are you getting at?"

Still staring out the window, he asked, "You know what my birthday is?"

Angela shrugged. "You want me to guess?"

"No. I'll tell you. It's September the 9th, 1962."

"So?"

18

"So, think about it. What's September? It's the ninth month. I was born on the ninth day of the ninth month."

Angela lit a cigarette and shifted in her chair. "You're not getting weird on me, are you?"

Banyon returned to his chair. "You know what the digits in 1962 add up to? I'll tell you. They add up to eighteen."

"Reduces to nine," Angela said, beating him to the punch.

"Exactly. My birthday is nine, nine, nine."

"What are you telling me?" she asked. "You *are* getting weird on me, aren't you?"

"You know your Bible very well?"

"Not as well as you, I'm sure," she said, grinning. "Why?"

"The Book of Revelation. Thirteenth chapter, eighteenth verse. *Eighteenth verse!* Keep that in mind."

"Got it. Eighteen. Reduces to nine."

"Right. Now hang on a second." He reached into the desk drawer and pulled out a Bible. He opened it to Revelation, 13th chapter, 18th verse and read aloud. "*Here is wisdom. Let him that hath understanding count the number of the beast. For it is the number of a man. And his number is six hundred threescore and six.*"

"Oh, yeah," Angela said. "I remember. The Antichrist. Six, six, six."

There was a moment of silence as he let that sink into her head.

"Oh!" she said. "Three sixes is eighteen which reduces to nine!"

Banyon smiled. "Right. And my birthday is nine, nine, nine."

"Yes? And?" Angela replied, not sure where he was going with this.

"Think about it, Angela. Visualize those two sets of numbers in your mind. Three nines is three sixes upside down!"

She gave him a sideways glance. "Um, you're not going to tell me you're the Antichrist, are you?"

He laughed. "No, I don't think that's likely. But you have to admit it's all a bit strange, isn't it? I mean, an ex-priest with a Biblical name whose birth date is the number of the Beast upside down? I mean, what are the odds? Let me bum a cigarette."

She slid her Marlboro's across the desk. "Well," she said, "you're not really an ex-priest, remember? You have to actually *become* a priest before you can become an *ex*-priest. But I'll admit it's curious all right. So what do you think it all means? Couldn't it just be coincidence?"

"That's what I kept trying to tell myself. But as I studied that verse in Revelation I kept thinking about the coincidence of the number eighteen. You know? The eighteenth verse? So I thought, well if the number eighteen has something to do with this, maybe the number *thirteen* does too.

"Thirteen?"

Banyon nodded impatiently. "Yes!" he said. "Thirteenth chapter! So, anyway, guess what I found?"

"I can't imagine."

"Look here," he said, motioning for her to scoot her chair up closer so she could see what he was writing. He scribbled out the equation: 13 x 18 = 234. "See that?" he asked, tapping it with his pencil.

"Yeah... oh! Two plus three, plus four is nine!"

"But that's not all," he said. "I didn't know what 234 could mean, if anything. Other than being another *nine* number, it didn't seem overtly significant."

"Overtly significant," she repeated.

He glanced up at her, not sure if maybe she was mocking him. He cleared his throat and continued. "But I was thinking about the mirror images of the three sixes and the three nines. And, I don't know, it just occurred to me to reverse the *234* which of course is *432*."

"So?"

"So, guess what *234* plus *432* is?"

Angela did the math in her head. "Oh man! It's 666!"

Banyon smiled. "Bingo! The number 666 is encoded in the very numbers of the chapter and verse in which the number of the beast is mentioned! Whaddya think about that?" Before she could answer, he went on. "Then last night while looking for something in my closet I came across this." He handed her the rosary. "I've had that for years. It's a standard rosary. Nothing special about it, but check it out. Look how the beads are arranged on each strand. Every rosary is like that."

Angela examined the rosary. She found that each strand consisted of beads strung in a pattern of five groups of ten beads, with a single bead in the space between each of the five groups for a total of 54 beads.

"Well...?" Banyon said, prompting her for a comment.

"Fifty-four," she said in a rather bewildered tone. "Nine."

The look on her face made him chuckle. "Yes," he said, finally. "Nine."

"Does this mean something?" she asked.

"Hah!" he laughed. "That, my dear, is the question that kept me up all night. What the hell does this mean?"

"Oh!" she blurted suddenly. "I almost forgot!" She reached into her purse and pulled out a tattered old paperback book. "Here you go," she said, handing it to him.

"You found it!" he said excitedly as he read the title. "*NUMEROLOGY: A Beginner's Guide*. Cool! Can I hang on to this for a while?"

"Sure. Keep it as long as you want. But right now I have to get going. It's getting late."

He thanked her for the book and started to get up from his chair.

"Don't get up," she insisted with a smile. "I can see myself out."

"You sure?"

"Yup. I'll see you tomorrow afternoon."

As soon as she was gone he sensed something, something he hadn't noticed before in the comfortable confines of his shabby little office. It took him a minute to realize what it was. Rather than sensing the presence of something, it was more like the absence of something. He looked around. Nothing seemed to be missing. As he thought about it, he slowly began to recognize what he was feeling. For the first time in a long time - a very long time - he was aware of being alone. *I'll be damned*, he thought to himself as he glanced at the chair where, just moments ago, Angela had been sitting. *I'll be damned*.

That night Banyon settled into bed with a cup of herbal tea, a note pad, a pencil, and the book he borrowed from Angela. He found the book interesting but somewhat disappointing. It didn't provide the kind of information he was hoping for. He was anticipating something a little deeper, maybe even profound. Then again, it was exactly what the book's subtitle said it was: *a beginner's guide*. Still, he was left with the impression that the author of this book approached the whole subject as if it were not much more than just a form of entertainment. As recently as only a few days ago he would have agreed. But now, given his recent experience with the strange coincidences regarding the numbers, especially the number nine, he wasn't so sure. The book did, however, provide some interesting tidbits of information about the number nine and the symbolism attributed to it. He learned, for example, that the number 9 is often considered to represent the planet Mars as well as the idea of conflict or aggression and also represents male energy. Curiously - but as he probably should have expected - the number 6 was the opposite of 9. The number 6 represented female energy, love and the planet Venus.

He was starting to get a feel for this numbers thing in a way that struck him as odd. He couldn't really explain it but he was feeling as if he could almost sense if a word had some connection to this whole *weird nine thing*, as he now called it. He had that feeling when he read about the comparisons between the number 9 and the number 6 and the planets they represented. It was becoming instinctive. He was immediately compelled to calculate the alphanumeric value of the names of the planets, *Mars* and *Venus*. He was amazed at what he found. *Another one of those reversal things*, he mused to himself.

The word *Mars*, he figured out, had an alphanumeric value of 51, which reduced to 6. On the other hand the word *Venus* had a value of 81 which reduced to 9. *Interesting*, he thought. *The planet symbolized by the number 9 has the alphanumeric value of 6, while the planet symbolized by the number 6 has the alphanumeric value of 9.* As he pondered over this curiosity, he could hardly wait to tell Angela about it. He read a little more until his eyes grew tired and he soon drifted off to sleep with the book in his lap.

As he slept he had no idea that somewhere in the world men in positions of power were talking about him – and about Angela. One of those men – a man in priest's clothing – was looking at the snapshot of Angela. "Who is she?" he asked. "Does she have any connections to Densmore or McClintock?"

The man who snapped the photo shook his head. "We don't think so. She's just a college student. Good-looking babe, eh?"

The priest slid the photo into his desk drawer. "Thank you. You can go."

~4~

The next day at the shelter, Banyon anxiously waited for Angela to arrive so he could show her what he'd discovered about Mars and Venus. This business of mirrored numbers and the idea of opposites like the Mars-Male/Venus-Female thing intrigued him. He felt like he was on to something but he had no idea what it might be. He simply found it all very curious.

The morning passed slowly. There was plenty of work to be done but he couldn't keep his mind on any of it. Trying to help out in the kitchen, he found himself stirring a large pot of soup on the stove for five minutes before Jenny, one of the volunteers, pointed out to him that he'd forgotten to turn the burner on.

"Mr. Banyon," she said, trying to be tactful, "I think we've pretty much got things under control right now. You probably have other things to do."

He caught the intent of what she was implying and he had to laugh. "Okay, I can take a hint."

He was just about to exit the kitchen when he heard Jenny calling after him. He thought she may have felt that she offended him and was about to offer an apology. He turned toward her and was about to tell her it was okay but she spoke first.

"The apron," she said.

"What?"

"The apron. You're wearing my apron."

He looked down at the frilly yellow and white polka dot apron still tied around his waist. He grinned. "Ah!" he said, untying it and tossing it over to her. "Sorry about that."

"That's all right," she said, fastening the apron around her own waist. "Mr. Banyon? Are you okay? You seem... I don't know..."

"Yeah! I'm fine. Just got things on my mind, I guess. I'll be in my office. Oh, by the way..."

"Yes?"

"Think there's any chance of maybe serving something besides bean soup on Mondays?"

"Why?"

"Oh, you know. Old Tom's still complaining about having bean soup every Monday. I just wondered."

Jenny laughed. "If it was top sirloin steak and baked potato with a side of fresh green salad and a choice of wine, Old Tom would still complain."

"Yeah," Banyon nodded with a grin, "I suppose you're right."

"Besides," Jenny added, "Who's running this place anyway? You or Old Tom?"

"You, I think!" Banyon said, laughing, as he left the kitchen.

When he entered his office, He found Angela was already waiting for him.

"Angela! I didn't expect you for another half hour or so."

"One of my classes was cancelled this afternoon, so I was able to get away a little sooner."

"Great. Have I got something to show you!"

"I've got something to show you, too," she said, handing him a piece of paper.

"What's this?"

"Read it."

He read the typewritten note:

FOR SALE: COMPUTER WITH MONITOR AND PRINTER. ONLY FOUR YEARS OLD. WORKS PERFECTLY. SACRIFICE, ONLY $400.00.

He looked up at her and shrugged. "So?"

"That was on the bulletin board at school," she explained. "I think you should buy it."

He laughed. "Me? Whatever for? I hate computers."

"Actually, I was thinking of me", she replied. "I mean, since I'm doing most of the bookwork now, it would be a lot easier to do on a computer with one of those bookkeeping programs. This old ledger book stuff is a pain in the you-know-what. And you'd be surprised at what else it would come in handy for. We have the funds and the price is a steal, believe me. And besides that, we could get access to the internet."

Banyon scoffed. "The internet! You mean all that dot com stuff?

Hah! What in the world do we need that for?"

"Well, for one thing," she said, hoping to persuade him with her best sales pitch and a bit of attitude, "how about access to everything in the world you could ever possibly want to know about numerology and gematria and religion and..."

That caught his attention. "That's on the internet?"

"You betcha," she grinned, thinking she'd hooked him.

"Hmm..." he scratched his chin.

"Come on, Zeke. It's about time you made the leap from the dark ages into the modern world. Don't you think?"

"Well..."

"Great! Give me a blank check and I'll pick up the computer tomorrow."

"But," he said looking around the cramped quarters of the office, "where in the world would we put it?"

"Glad you mentioned that," she said. "That's the next thing I need to talk to you about."

"Oh no. What now?"

"You know that empty room down at the end of the hall?"

"Of course. It's another small storage room."

"But it's pretty much empty now, right?"

"Pretty much, yes."

"Well, if you can make an office out of this little room, I figured I could make an office out of that little room. What do you think? We could put the computer in there and, really, I could use the space instead of both of us trying to share this one small office. I mean, what with trying to organize the fund drives and other stuff. You know? Doesn't that seem like a good idea?"

He had to agree. It was a reasonable request and the storage room was not being used for much of anything anyway.

"You're right," he conceded. "It's actually a good idea. But you'll need a desk and file cabinets, and..."

"Got that all figured out," she said. "I have two desks at home. I only need one and I have some other things that I could bring down here. That is, if it's okay with you."

"Sure. That sounds okay to me."

"Cool!" she said with a big grin on her face. "Maybe we can do it this weekend."

"Well, okay," Banyon shrugged. "Why not?".

"Just one thing..."

"What's that?"

Angela grinned. "You wouldn't happen to have a pickup truck, would you?"

"No, but I know someone who does. I'm sure I could borrow it."

"So you'll help me move the stuff then?"

"Do I have a choice?"

"Well..."

"Of course I'll help you," he laughed. "I'll call my friend tomorrow and arrange to borrow the truck."

"All right!" she said, excitedly. "Thank you!"

"So if you're through planning my life for me," he said, "I have something I've been dying to show you."

The two of them huddled around his desk as he explained his discovery about the numbers 6 and 9 and the symbology attributed to them according to the numerology book.

"What do you make of that?" he asked. "Pretty weird, huh?"

"Wait a minute," she said, grabbing a pencil and a sheet of paper. "Let me get this straight. Nine represents Mars but Mars turns out to have an alphanumeric value of six?"

"Right."

"And six represents Venus but Venus has a value of nine?"

"Yes."

"Hmm... well, yes, that is curious, I'll have to admit," she said thoughtfully as she doodled with the numbers 6 and 9. "You know what?"

"What?"

"Look at this."

"Look at what?"

In her doodling she had drawn a 6 and a 9, fairly large, very close to each other, almost touching. The result was a large *69*. She handed him the piece of paper.

"What?" he asked, looking at her scribbles.

She reached in her purse and, after a little digging, she produced a keychain with a black and white ceramic symbol on it. She placed it on the piece of paper next to the large *69*.

"Yin yang," she said.

Banyon still didn't see the connection. "Yin yang?"

"Look," she said, pointing out the similarity between the alternating black and white swirl design of the symbol on her keychain and the *69* she had doodled on the paper. "This is a Chinese symbol representing the yin and the yang of the universe."

"Gees, you're right! Look at that! I've heard of yin and yang before but I guess I never really paid much attention to what it meant. Something about opposites, right? Balance of nature? That sort of thing?"

Angela laughed. "Well, you must have paid attention somewhere along the line because that's exactly the idea, yes. Also the interrelatedness of things. That's why in the black part of the design there's a small white dot and..."

"And in the white part," he finished the sentence for her, "there's a small black dot. I get it. Very interesting! The whole thing... amazing! How can this be? Is this all just coincidence? I mean, think about it. What are the odds of all these seemingly unrelated things all having this... this..."

"Interconnectedness?" she offered.

"Yes, exactly! That's it."

"I don't know. It's kind of exciting but it's weird!"

"What else do you know about this yin yang thing?" he asked.

"Well, believe it or not, my anthropology professor actually mentioned this symbol the other day when we were discussing differences and similarities between cultures around the world. I remember he said yin symbolizes the female energy and yang is the male energy."

"Interesting. Like the Mars-Venus thing. Male, female."

"Yes. And I remember he wrote the word, *Qi,* on the board. I think he pronounced it like the word *key*."

"What did it mean?"

"It's a Chinese word that means life force, or something like that."

"Life force?"

"Yes. It was kind of hard to understand but basically it's kind of like... um..." she stumbled around for the right word. "Man, I don't know. Kind of an all-encompassing essence that flows through everything."

"Everything?"

"Yes. Everything. You, me, this desk, the wall, everything."

"Well I guess that's not unlike some concepts of God," Banyon admitted.

"What do you mean?"

"Well, you've heard it said that God is in everything, right?"

"Oh! Yeah, that's right. Same idea, I guess."

· "And one could think of God as a *life force*, right?"

"Yes, I guess you could. Wow. Cool!"

"*Qi*, huh?" Banyon muttered, punching buttons on his pocket calculator. He scratched something down on the piece of paper. "Guess what?" he said after a few moments.

"What? *Qi* equals nine?"

"No, but something just as curious."

"What is it?"

Going on the idea that *Qi* and God are the same thing, at least maybe in some sense, I figured the value of each word just to see what it might be."

"And...?"

"And they each equal twenty-six!"

"No kidding?"

"Yeah. You know what's kind of interesting about that? The English alphabet that we're using to do all of this has twenty-six letters in it."

"How synchronistic," she said, grinning.

Banyon stood up and turned to gaze out the window. "You know what?"

"What?"

"I wonder if it's possible that the English alphabet could be a cipher of some kind."

"A cipher?"

"Yeah. You know. A tool for unlocking a code."

"A code? What are you talking about?"

He laughed. "I don't know, actually! It's crazy, I know." He paused for moment, looking down, and then turned to her. "Have you ever heard of the Bible Code?"

"No. What's the Bible code?"

He sat down again. "Well, apparently there seems to be information encoded within the original Hebrew text of the Torah."

"The Torah?"

"That's the Hebrew word for the first five books of the Old Testament."

"Oh. So what do you mean, encoded? What kind of information?"

"This was just recently discovered. The information - it could be a word or a group of related words or a phrase or even a date - is found hidden within the text by using what they call a skip code."

"A skip code?"

"Yeah. What the researchers did was to eliminate all the punctuation and all the spaces between the words in the text of the Torah. So they ended up with pages and pages of lines of text in one long string of letters. Legend has it that this is how Moses actually wrote it. Essentially, each page just looked like a big block of letters. You see what I'm saying? And the skip coding works like this." He went on to explain as well as he could, given his own limited knowledge of the subject. "You start with the first letter of the text in the book of Genesis and skip, say for example, ten letters. Now you have the first letter and the tenth letter. Then you skip another ten letters and record that. And so on, all the way through the entire Torah. Then you look to see what words or phrases may have been spelled out among those particular letters. And there are several different skip sequences that can be applied. Like you could try skipping every third letter all the way through. Or every 18th letter, and so on."

"But," she laughed, "that would take for ever!"

"Well, yeah. But they do it with a computer. They've developed a program that can process thousands of skip code functions in no time."

"See?" she grinned smugly. "I told you computers were good for something. So what kind of information have they found by doing this?"

"Amazing stuff. The guy who wrote the book about it actually discovered the name of the Prime Minister of Israel hidden in the text. It was spelled vertically instead of horizontally."

"Vertically?"

"Yeah, you know, like a word spelled vertically in a crossword puzzle?"

"You're kidding!"

"No, but wait. What's really amazing is that the phrase, *Assassin That Will Assassinate*, was also found hidden in the text and it was spelled out horizontally, crisscrossing the Prime Minister's name. You see? Like a crossword puzzle!"

"What? Come on," Angela said, with a fair degree of skepticism in her voice.

"It's true. And a year later the Prime Minister was assassinated."

"Oh, yes! I remember! But, how can that be? You mean the future is foretold in this code? That's crazy!"

"I know it sounds crazy. But mathematicians around the world have studied this phenomenon and it appears to be real."

"What else have they found?"

"Well, that's even weirder."

"That's okay. I'm sitting down. Lay it on me," she said. "This is better than the X-Files."

Banyon lit up a cigarette and leaned back in his chair. "All right. Believe it or not, it seems that nearly every significant event in history and the names of the key people involved in the unfolding of those events, and even the dates of those events, are encoded within the pages of the Torah."

"Come on! You mean..."

"The Kennedy assassination. The bombing of the Federal Building in Oklahoma. Both World Wars. The landing of a man on the moon. The Gulf War. Hitler. Watergate. President Clinton. Thomas Edison. Even the name we gave to that comet just recently, Shoemaker-Levy, was found encoded in the text. It just goes on and on."

"This is too much," she said, reaching into her purse for a pack of cigarettes. "I mean, how could such a code exist? And why?"

"Why, I don't know. But as to how it was done, believe it or not, the code actually states that it was done by computer!"

"Computer! But I thought this was written three thousand years ago! Who had a computer three thousand years ago? Are you saying the word *computer* is actually encoded in the text?"

"Yup. Of course it's in Hebrew, but it's exactly the modern Hebrew word for computer. And I don't just mean the word *computer* is in there all by itself. It was a whole phrase that said something like, *It was created by computer.*"

"But *what* was created by computer? How do they know what *it* was? *It* could be anything."

"Ah! But here's the kicker," Banyon explained. "The clue to what a

30

lot of these words and phrases refer to is found in the word or phrase that crosses it. Just like the name of the Prime Minister, Yitzhak Rabin, was crossed by the phrase, *Assassin will assassinate*. In the case of the words, *It was created by computer*, the phrase that crossed it was something like, *The writing by God on the tablets*."

"Great," Angela said, rolling her eyes. "So God's a computer nerd. Sort of a cosmic Bill Gates. Is that the deal?"

Banyon let out a good laugh. "To tell you the truth," he said, "I don't know what to think of the whole thing. But now you see why it occurred to me that the English alphabet just might be something similar to the Bible Code. I mean if there's one code, why not two? Or more? Or maybe they're all just parts of one big code. I don't know. What do you think?"

Angela didn't know what to think. Her head was spinning just trying to comprehend the implications of such a thing. It seemed preposterous. On the other hand, if there really was some kind of a code in the Bible, as these brilliant and obviously educated men seemed to believe, then maybe Banyon's alphabet code wasn't so crazy after all. She finally conceded. "Well," she said, shrugging her shoulders, "I suppose you could be on to something. I mean if the Bible Code is real then, well, why not?"

Banyon was listening but he was scribbling something down on a note pad and punching his little pocket calculator. "You know what the word, *code*, comes out to?" he asked.

"I don't know. What?"

"Twenty-seven!"

Angela caught it right away. "Two plus seven is nine," she grinned.

He nodded his head thoughtfully. "This means something," he said. "This has got to mean something."

~5~

A ngela's knack for organizing the seemingly unorganizable was put to the test the following weekend. Still, by the end of the day, she and Banyon had managed to turn the extra storage room into a surprisingly decent little office, computer and all. The room was quite small but at least it had a window that helped brighten things up.

Banyon sat down in front of the computer and stared at it like it was a piece of alien technology from a galaxy far, far away. Cautiously, he ran a finger across the top of the monitor and then quickly recoiled his hand as if he wasn't sure it was safe. Angela caught him out of the corner of her eye as she straightened the sheer white curtain she'd just hung over the window. She couldn't help but laugh as she recalled the apes cautiously poking at the mysterious black monolith in Stanley Kubrick's movie, *2001: A Space Odyssey.* The comparison was just so appropriate… and funny.

"What?" Banyon asked.

"You!" she said. "It won't bite, you know. It isn't even plugged in."

He grinned. "Yeah, yeah. Well, so now that we have this thing, how do we get on the internet?"

"Oh my! For a techno-Neanderthal you're sure jumping into things!"

"Well, I paid for this contraption! I want to see how it works!"

Angela reached for her purse and pulled out a CD. "This," she said, "is our ticket to the information super highway!"

"What is it?"

"It's everything we need to get onto the internet. We just plug in the computer, slip the disk in, and in minutes we'll be signed up and logged on!"

"Will it hurt?"

"Only once a month," she said from under the desk as she located the plug for the computer.

"What do you mean?"

Angela crawled out from under the desk. "When they ding your checking account for twenty bucks," she grinned. "You'll never miss it."

"Twenty bucks? Every month?"

"Out of my chair," she commanded, tapping him on the shoulder. "Let's get this puppy rollin!"

"You get it rollin'," Banyon said, getting up to leave.

"Where are you going?"

"To look for a second job to pay that twenty bucks a month!" He winked at her as he walked out the door.

About an hour later he returned with a cup of coffee for each of them. "Are we on?" he asked as he set her cup on what looked to him like a cup holder sticking out of the front of the computer.

"Don't do that!" Angela scolded. "You'll break it!"

"Break what? The cup holder? What good is it if it won't hold a cup of coffee?"

"It's not a cup holder!" she said. "That's the CD tray!"

"The what?" he said, cocking his head, studying the thing.

She couldn't help laughing. "It's the CD tray. You put the disk on it and slide it into the computer so the computer can read what's on it."

Banyon sat on the corner of her desk sipping his coffee. "Hmm...", he mumbled. "So, are we on?"

Angela straightened herself up in front of the monitor. "We will be in a second." She expertly maneuvered the mouse around on the pad. With a couple of clicks a colorful display came up on the screen.

"Cool!" Banyon said, peering over her shoulder.

"Shall we go surfin?" Angela asked.

"In this weather?"

She laughed. "No, silly. Surfing means..."

"I know what it means," he chided her. "I'm not completely ignorant, you know."

"Okay, smart ass," she laughed. "What do you want to check out?"

"How about numerology?"

"You got it. Let's call up a search engine and see what we get."

"Call up a what?"

"I thought you weren't completely ignorant," she teased.

"Oh!" he laughed. "Now who's the smart ass?"

She explained to him what a search engine was and what it could be used for. "So," she said, "we'll type in *numerology* and see what we get."

In just a few seconds another colorful screen came up on the monitor.

"Hoo! Boy!" Angela said. "Look at that!"

"What?"

"Says here there's four-hundred-eighty-thousand-six-hundred-and-fifty-two web sites that are in some way related to numerology!"

Banyon nearly choked on his coffee. "Are you kidding me? How can that be?"

"I guess I'm not surprised," she answered. "There are countless millions of web sites out there. This many hits on a single topic isn't unusual anymore."

The page on the screen listed the first 20 related web sites. Angela scrolled down the screen so they could read each one.

"That's only twenty," Banyon said. "Where's the rest of them? The other ten-thousand-gazillion?"

"You have to click onto the next page. That'll show you the next twenty. Each page will have twenty web sites listed on it."

"Christ! It'd take you a year to go through all those!"

Angela laughed and took a sip of her coffee. "Yup. Where do you want to start?"

"You know what?"

"What?"

"Are you hungry?"

"I guess I am," she said. "Why? What time is it?"

"It's after six. We didn't even have lunch today. How about we go down to Mario's for a pizza. We can do this surfing thing when you come in tomorrow."

"Sounds good to me," she smiled.

"My treat."

"Sounds even better!"

"Great! Let's go before it gets too busy."

Mario's was already packed when they arrived but they managed to get a booth by the window.

"I like this place!" Angela said, looking around at the decor. "It's kind of warm and cozy. And it smells great!"

"Yup. This is my hangout. Best little pizza joint in the city."

They were quickly greeted by a waitress. "Hello, Mr. Banyon!" she smiled. "Good to see you again. Your usual?"

"I'm not sure. Let's see what my friend, Angela, would like."

"What's your usual?" Angela asked him.

"Double pepperoni with extra cheese. Can't beat it. Best in town. Especially with a cold beer."

"Sounds good to me. I'll have that."

"Done, then!" Banyon said. "We'll have a large double pepperoni with extra cheese and a couple schooners."

The waitress took the order and disappeared into the kitchen.

Angela looked around. "Which way to the ladies room? I need to freshen up."

"Right down there and to the left," he said, pointing the way.

"Thanks. I'll just be a couple minutes."

While she was gone he reached for a napkin and took out his pen and his pocket calculator. Earlier in the day he had been thinking about the conversation he'd had with Angela about the so-called Bible Code. He was curious to know what the alphanumeric value of the name, *Jehovah*, might be. Or *Jesus*, for that matter. Or any of the key names in the Bible. *Would any of them add up to nine or a number that reduced to nine?* he wondered. This was the first time he'd had a chance to find out.

After a few minutes, Angela returned to the table.

"Angela," he said, looking up from his napkin full of words and numbers. "Look at this." He slid the napkin over to her.

"Oh, oh," she said lighting up a cigarette. "More numbers?"

"Yes, more numbers. No nines but check this out." He pointed to the words on the napkin. "The alphanumeric value of Jehovah is 69."

"So?"

"Remember our little discussion about Mars and Venus and the number 69 and that Yin Yang symbol?"

"Yes? And?"

"Remember we talked about the number 69 possibly representing the same concept as the Yin Yang? The idea of duality? Opposites? Two sides of the same coin?"

"I remember. What are you getting at?"

"Look at the other two names there. *Jesus* and *Lucifer*."
Angela studied the writing on the napkin:
JESUS = 74 = LUCIFER
Her eyes lit up. "My God! They both have the same number value! That's pretty weird. But what's that got to do with the 69?"

"Think about it. Could this be telling us that Jesus and Lucifer are the two sides of the one coin? Jehovah?"

Angela stared at him with a blank look in her eyes. After a moment, she shook her head. "Say that again?"

"I said, could..."

"Never mind," she interrupted, "I heard what you said. I did, really. I just... "

"Pretty cool, huh?"

She raised a skeptical eyebrow. "Pretty weird, is more like it. I mean, come on. How could that be?"

"I don't know. I agree it's very strange. I mean the whole idea is strange. But it makes sense, doesn't it?"

"Well, it does, sure. I mean I see what you're getting at. But how do you know you're not just reading something into this? Something that isn't really there? I mean you have to consider that possibility, you know."

"I know. I know. It's just so damned compelling. Of course I don't know much about that Hebrew numerology... what do you call it?"

"Gematria."

"Yeah, gematria. But I know it's been practiced by Jewish mystics since ancient times. There must be something about it for it to have survived all these centuries. I mean, who says the Hebrew alphabet has to be the only alphabet that's..." he paused, looking for the right word.

"Encrypted?"

"Yes! Exactly! Remember I suggested that maybe the English alphabet was some sort of a cipher for unlocking encoded information? I admit I didn't really know what I was talking about. I still don't, I guess, but I'm really beginning to wonder now."

For several moments neither of them said anything as they tried to sort this out in their minds. Angela was just about to say something when the waitress arrived with the pizza.

"Will there be anything else?" the waitress asked.

Banyon shook his head. "No. This looks great. Thank you."

Angela folded the napkin in half and handed it back to Banyon with a big smile on her face.

"What?" he asked. "You think I'm crazy, don't you?"

"I don't know what to think. But I'll give you this much. The coincidences are pretty amazing."

He laughed as he tugged awkwardly at a slice of pizza that was hung up with a never-ending string of melted cheese. "That's for sure. I mean even the word, *cross*, for crying out loud."

"Cross?"

"Yes. Didn't you see that at the bottom of the napkin?"

"No. Why? What?"

He unfolded the napkin and handed it back to her. "Jesus is 74 and Lucifer is 74 and, look there." He pointed with the pen.

CROSS = 74

Angela shook her head. "Oh, man," she said. "That is weird."

"Hey wait a minute," Banyon said. He wrote another word on the napkin and punched the numbers into his calculator. "Wow! Check this out." He showed it to Angela.

MESSIAH = 74

Angela stared in astonishment.

"Is that cool, or what?" Banyon beamed. "I think I'm on a roll here. Let's try this. The word messiah meant *king* to the Jewish people. Living under the oppression of the Roman Empire they were hoping for a messiah to arise and establish, or reestablish a kingship. Someone who would be the king of the Jews, right?" Not waiting for Angela's reply he jotted something else on the napkin and punched in the numbers. Somewhat stunned by the result, he slid the napkin over to her and pointed to what he'd just written:

THE KING = 74

She couldn't believe her eyes. "That's amazing!"

Banyon was having one of his moments where it seemed almost as if the information was coming to him from an outside source. He had no other way to explain it. "Give me the napkin," he said, urgently. Something else came into his mind and he wanted to jot it down before he lost it. He wrote quickly and punched in the numbers. "Unbelievable," was all he could say. He showed it to Angela. It was an alphanumeric equation.

JESUS CHRIST THE KING = 225
= JESUS AND LUCIFER ARE ONE

"Oh," she muttered, almost recoiling from the words she was reading. "I don't know if I'm liking this. This is getting too weird. We're gonna get struck by lightening or something."

"Don't be silly," he scolded. "You're sounding like my mother. It's just words and numbers on paper. But look how the idea there correlates with the fact that Jesus and Lucifer both share the same alphanumeric value. And check out that number. It reduces to nine".

She looked at him. "Did you just now come up with those phrases?"

He nodded. "Yeah."

"How? How did you do that?"

"I don't know," he shrugged. "They just sort of came to me."

Angela looked perplexed, realizing that something odd was going on. She took a swallow of beer and sat back to consider the whole thing. "Well, all I can say is that this is going beyond simple coincidence. It's more like synchronicity."

"Synchronicity?"

"Meaningful coincidence" she explained. "As opposed to just one of those odd things that happens by mere chance."

"Hmm. You mean... what? Like, planned? Predestined? Something like that?"

Angela shrugged her shoulders. "I'm not really sure. I don't know. Has to do with archetypes and all that Jungian stuff."

"Archetypes? Jungian?"

"Yeah, you know. Carl Jung? The Swiss psychologist? He coined the word, *synchronicity*."

"Carl Jung. Yeah, I remember now. A friend of Sigmund Freud, wasn't he?"

"Sigmund Freud. Yes, I think so."

"Yeah. I remember reading about him way back in college. Archetypes and all that. Man I haven't thought about that stuff in years."

"I don't think I ever really quite got that archetype idea," Angela confessed.

Banyon nodded. "Yeah, the archetype thing is pretty heady stuff. I remember some discussion about it when I was at seminary."

"Archetypes have something to do with religion?"

"Well, sort of," he said. "It's hard to explain. I should really read up on it again. Basically, as I recall, the whole notion of archetypes has to do with a kind of preexisting form of things that supposedly resides in the so called collective unconscious." He shook his head and looked somewhat surprised. "Man, I can't believe I remembered that. It was so long ago."

"Oh, right," Angela said. "The collective unconscious. More Jung stuff."

"Yeah. Like for example, angels, let's say. There's a school of thought that angels don't really exist in the conventional way of thinking. You know, like real entities living in Heaven with God. The archetype hypothesis would be that the concept of *angel* - just the concept, mind you - is somehow part of the human psyche and that the concept resides in the collective unconscious. The reality of angels, then, is of our own making. They become real through our belief in them. We paint pictures of them. We write stories and poems and songs about them and, after a while, we believe they're real. Or something like that."

"But," Angela came back, "paintings all over the world depict angels pretty much the same way. If there are no such things as angels, if nobody ever really saw one, then where did that image come from? I mean, if there wasn't some real thing that inspired the image in the first place, you'd think there would be dozens, maybe hundreds of different concepts of what angels look like and we'd see all these different images depicted in the paintings around the world."

"Well, that's just it," Banyon said. "The image, according to this archetype idea, exists naturally in the collective unconscious. And that's what people perceive in their minds."

"Pretty strange," Angela said, reaching for another slice of pizza. "Interesting, but strange."

Their conversation drifted back and forth between archetypes, Jung, angels, numerology and other related subjects. In the short amount of time since they'd first met, they'd become amazingly comfortable with each other and could talk for hours about almost anything.

"Oh man," Banyon said, glancing at his watch. "It's almost ten o'clock. I can't believe we've been sitting here for nearly three hours."

"You're kidding! Well, time flies when you're talking about archetypes."

Banyon laughed. "Apparently so. Do you want another beer?"

At the phone booth, near the cash register, a man in a black overcoat was making a call. He spoke in hushed tones. "This Banyon fellow," the man said, speaking with an Italian accent, "he might be on to something. Yes, I was sitting right behind them. I heard everything. No, I don't think so. Yes, of course I'll keep you informed."

Angela considered the offer of one more beer but decided against it. "No, I have a class in the morning so I really better get going. But thanks. It was really good. The pizza and all."

"My pleasure, Angel," he said, helping her on with her coat.

Looking back at him over her shoulder, she gave him a crooked grin. "Ha, ha." she said. "I get it. So do I exist only in your collective unconscious?"

"Well," he said as they headed for the door, "if you do, it's one beautiful archetype!" He cringed at his own words. *Gees, Zeke, how corny can you get?*

Angela didn't reply but even as she lay in the comfort of her own bed that night, those sweet words were the last to run through her mind as she drifted off to sleep.

~6~

O ver the next several days, Angela showed Banyon how to navigate the internet and use it as a research tool. Their list of keywords to plug into the search engines began to grow as they delved deeper into the strange world of numerology and mysticism.

"I've got another one for you," Angela said, arriving early for work after a fairly short day at school. She hung her coat on the rack in the corner of Banyon's office and handed him a book called *The Mayan Mystery*.

"Another what?" he asked, turning the book over to read the back cover.

"Another keyword," she said.

"What is it?"

"Mayan."

"Mayan?"

He thumbed through the pages of the book and raised an eyebrow, silently begging for an explanation.

"We're studying the ancient Mayan civilization of Central America."

"And...?"

"And it seems they were also into the number nine."

Banyon sat up with renewed interest. "Oh? Do tell."

"Yup. Seems they were very number conscious in a lot of ways. Kind of like somebody I know." She gave him a wink. "They even devised a calendar system with such accuracy it stuns the imagination. Or at least it stuns the imagination of those who understand it. But anyway, in the book, there, it mentions something about what they called the *Nine Lords of Time*."

Banyon chuckled. "The *Nine Lords of Time*? Well, now that does sound interesting. So who were the *Nine Lords of Time*, pray tell?"

"Well," she said, "If I understood it right, they were part of the ancient Mayan mythology. See, some say the Mayans were part of a large group of Amer-Indians who migrated across the Bering Strait from Asia, maybe twelve thousand years ago, and settled in Central America. But others are not so sure it's that simple."

"What do you mean?"

"Well, are you ready for this?"

He laughed. "I don't know. Am I?"

"Well, apparently, according to some researchers, the ancient Mayan writings indicate they came to the earth from another star system."

"Oh, *really!*" Banyon smiled with amusement.

"And that's where the *Nine Lords of Time* fit into the picture. They're also referred to as the *Galactic Masters.*"

"Ah! The great Galactic Masters! Of course! Please go on," said Banyon, lighting a cigarette and leaning back in his chair. "Don't stop now. This is getting good."

"Well, I've really got to get to work. There's stuff piling up on my desk. But that's why I brought you the book so you can read it for yourself."

"Okay. I'll check it out. Thanks."

Angela left the room and headed for her office leaving Banyon to explore the ancient world of the Mayans. He discovered what she said about the Mayan preoccupation with numbers was true. In fact it appeared that numbers were somehow at the root of the entire Mayan cosmology. They saw numbers as being more than just representations of quantity. For the Mayans, numbers were also living entities. He read that the key numbers, the numbers that seemed to drive everything, were 1, 13, 7, 9 and 4. He was intrigued by the fact that the number 9 was, according to the information in the book, one of the most important numbers in the whole Mayan system.

The Mayans, Banyon learned, employed a binary numbering system that used *20* as its base. This system, rather than progressing by tens as we are used to, progressed by a factor of *20.* In the first position a unit equals *1.* In the second position a unit then equals *20.* In the third it progresses to *20* times *20,* or *400.* In the fourth it equals 400 times 20, or *8000,* and continues on in that manner.

Banyon learned that the Mayans were not necessarily as concerned with the sequential aspects of numbers so much as they were with the *relationships* between numbers. To the Mayans, numbers meant far more than just a means of quantification. They believed numbers were symbols representing the harmonic values and overtones of what the book called *dynamic energies of the galaxy*. It was clear that the Mayans considered numbers to be representative of the way life and the universe work.

Suddenly he noticed the time. He'd been reading for two hours and had neglected to get his work finished for the day. Putting the book aside, he busied himself with some of the paper work that needed to get done but he couldn't get the Mayan information out of his mind. The day dragged on until finally it was time to go home.

That evening he perched himself up in bed with the book and his favorite spiced tea and continued to read well into the night. He learned that the numbers 13 and 20 were also key to the Mayan system. These two numbers, multiplied together, equaled 260 and formed the great matrix known as the Tzolkin, the basis for the Mayan calendar. It was upon this 13 x 20 matrix, or grid, that the entire Mayan philosophy was based. The other key numbers were 7, 4, and 9. Banyon was intrigued to learn that the number 9, to the Mayans, symbolized the concepts of periodicity and completeness and also represented the *Nine Lords Of Time*. Just as Angela had said, they were the original Mayan *Galactic Masters*. According to the book, some researchers were suggesting the Galactic Masters may have come to earth to present earth-humans with a key to understanding the universe and our place within it. It also cautioned that this interpretation was, of course, geared more to New Age philosophy than it was to mainstream academic thinking. But Banyon was beginning to like this New Age stuff. *Poor mom*, he thought to himself, *she's probably rolling over in her Catholic grave.*

Suddenly, given what he'd been experiencing lately, he was realizing there just might be more to *the way things are* than conventional wisdom would allow. He lit a cigarette, took a sip of tea and went on to the next chapter.

In addition to the number 9, the number 260 was of utmost importance to the Mayan system. This was the number of days in a time cycle which correlated in some way to the cycles of sun spot activity and which was at the foundation of their whole system of prophecy. It was a mystery how the ancient Mayans could possibly have known about the phenomenon of sun spot cycles.

The number 260 interested Banyon because, as he thought about it, it seemed out of place in a way. It's digits added up to 8. The book's long and detailed discussions about the complexity of the Mayan calendar revealed pages and pages of numbers. Some of them were very long numbers like the so-called *Great Cycle* number of 1,872,000. This, like so many of the other multi-digit numbers in the Mayan mathematics, could be reduced to the single-digit value of 9. In his own recent musings about the number 9 and the English alphabet, he was somewhat bothered by the fact that the alphabet consisted of only 26 letters. It just seemed like it would all be quite complete, in a neat and tidy package, if the alphabet had just one more letter to make it 27. The single-digit value would then be 9. But wishful thinking wasn't going to change anything. There was either something wrong with the picture or there was something he was just not seeing.

He pondered over the question as he got out of bed and wandered into the kitchen to brew another cup of tea. Suddenly it hit him. He grabbed his tea and his calculator and jumped back into bed with the book.

He noticed that if the first letter *A*, with a value of 1, was combined with the last letter *Z*, with a value of 26, the sum was 27 which reduced to 9. Likewise, *B*, with a value of 2, added to *Y*, with a value of 25, equaled 27 which reduced to 9. It was the same for every combination of letters working forward from the front of the alphabet and backwards from the end of the alphabet all the way to the center where *M*, with a value of 13, met *N*, with a value of 14. Like all the rest of the combinations, the sum of *MN* was 27 which, like the others of course, could be reduced to 9. Moreover, the fact that he'd already discovered the alphanumeric value of the word, *CODE*, was 27 didn't escape his attention and only added to the excitement of the moment. In his mind this validated his idea that the alphabet might be a decoding mechanism of some kind.

He was astounded. He had discovered the value of 9, by way of 27, encoded within the very structure of the 26-letter alphabet! Then he flashed on a correlation with something he'd been reading concerning the Mayan calendar. That calendar was, in essence, a system of cycles of time. Now he realized his idea of combining the first letter of the alphabet with the last letter could be seen as a circle, with *A* connected to *Z*.

"A circle!" he said to himself. "A circle of twenty six letters!"

Then he remembered something from Angela's old book on numerology. Something about what they called *harmonics*. Something about dropping the zeros. If the other numerals matched, then they were considered significantly harmonized, significantly linked in some metaphysical way. Zero was not so much a number as it was just a place holder. It was the other numbers that were important. Suddenly he realized this circle of 26 letters harmonized with the idea of the Mayan 260 day cycle. The number 26 was a harmonic of 260.

"Circle... cycle...!" he grinned to himself. "Twenty-six! Two-sixty!"

His mind was racing. It seemed as if information was being downloaded into his brain not unlike when Angela showed him how to download information from the internet onto the computer's hard drive. The idea of a circle of 26 letters kept tugging at him. Something was happening. Words and phrases seemed to be forcing their way into his brain. He'd experienced this before. It was similar to when he and Angela were sitting at Mario's writing on the napkin. But this was much more intense. It felt strange yet exhilarating. He grabbed his calculator and pen and a note pad and began writing alphanumeric equations almost as if it was beyond his control:

ENGLISH ALPHABET CIRCLE = 189
= THE ENLIGHTENED ONE
=SQUARE OF TWELVE

THE SACRED ALPHABET CIRCLE = 198
198 - 189 = 9

THE AREA OF A CIRCLE = 120
= THE MIND OF GOD

TWENTY SIX DEGREES = 222
= THE ENGLISH ALPHABET CIRCLE

His mind reeled. His attention kept going back to the first phrases that equaled 189. He focused on the phrase, *SQUARE OF TWELVE*. He punched in the number 12 and hit the button to find the mathematical square of that number.

"One-forty-four!" he said aloud. "I know that number." He had learned early on that 144 was the alphanumeric value of his own name. But it made him think of something else: the book of Revelation and the 144,000 souls redeemed. *But what does that have to do with this?* he wondered. *Maybe nothing. Am I losing my mind? Besides, 144 isn't 144,000.*

But then he remembered the harmonics and the 26 and the 260. In this case it was 144 and 144,000. The zeroes didn't matter! He felt strongly that this number, 144, was important. *Really* important. But he didn't know why. Or was he just attaching importance to it because it happened to be the value of his own name? He wanted to call Angela and tell her about all of this. But it was after midnight so he decided to wait. He was excited but he was also exhausted and what he really needed was to get some rest. Tomorrow would come soon enough. *This means something*, he kept thinking to himself as he drifted off to sleep. *This means something.*

~7~

B anyon was totally fascinated with the Mayan culture. He spent many hours over the next several days studying the book and surfing the internet for anything he could find about that mysterious race of people. He had only been vaguely aware of the fact that the Mayans, like the Egyptians, had built huge pyramids and other stone monuments. Now he wondered why? What connections could there possibly have been between the Mayans and the Egyptians? Geographically, they were on opposite sides of the planet. Archaeologists seemed to have no real explanation. It was just one more mystery to be solved.

Angela agreed the discovery of the number 9 hidden within the alphabet was a neat trick, to be sure, but she was a little more skeptical about whether or not it actually had some kind of a tie to the idea of cycles of time, or cycles of anything for that matter, in the Mayan calendar system. That seemed a bit of a stretch. After all, how could there possibly be a connection? *The English alphabet and the Mayan calendar*? The two things seemed worlds apart both conceptually and culturally. It couldn't possibly be true.

Banyon, on the other hand, was excited about the possibility. To him it didn't seem any less likely than the mystery of the connection between the Mayans building pyramids and the Egyptians building pyramids even though, supposedly, the two cultures had no means of communicating with each other. Clearly, he was beginning to understand, some things in this world are interconnected despite a lack of explanation as to the *how* or the *why* of it all.

The more he studied, the more convinced he was that something was going on here. As far as he was concerned, the common thread bridging those cultural and conceptual gaps was that mysterious and pervasive number 9.

The Mayans, Banyon learned, had a problem similar to his own when it came to that number 260 which was the Mayan counterpart to his number 26, the number of letters in the alphabet. Their number 260 – like his number 26 – added up to 8, not 9. Banyon had solved his own dilemma by discovering how to essentially fold the alphabet in half, right between the M and the N. This resulted in dividing the 26-letter strand exactly in half. This, in turn, created a strand of thirteen 2-letter combinations. Each of the 2-letter combinations equaled 27 which reduced to 9. The Mayans seemed equally uncomfortable with their number 260. The number was essential to the structure of the whole system yet it seems this system - based on the 260-unit matrix - was not particularly suited to the planet Earth, at least in terms of computing basic cycles of time. The missing ingredient was 9. So they modified the system to more closely correspond to the annual revolution of our planet around the sun. This modification brought the number 9 into the picture in a big way as it involved changing the third position number from 400 to 360, a multiple of 9. From this third position onward the base-20 progression now yielded units that were all multiples of 9. The progression was now 1 to 20 to 360 to 7200 to 144,000 and so on.

Banyon had already toyed with the idea that maybe the English alphabet and the 9-series numbering system was either a code or a cipher of some kind. *If so,* he wondered, *what secrets might it reveal? Could this be a key to unlocking some hidden messages encoded within some ancient text? Would it help reveal information encoded within certain words?* He shivered with anticipation at the very thought. He was beginning to feel like Indiana Jones on a quest to find the lost Ark of the Covenant. For a moment he fantasized himself and Angela packing their bags and heading off into the jungles of Central America, skulking around ancient stone ruins and climbing the magnificent old Mayan pyramids in search of... what? *The secret of 9? What the hell is it about this number?* he wondered. *What secret does it hold? Is it, indeed, a key?* It suddenly dawned on him that the word *key* had been coming into his thoughts a lot lately. He'd even seen it many times in his reading. Something about the word itself was now resonating in his head. Synchronicity seemed to be working overtime.

He was reminded of his conversation with Angela about archetypes and symbols. The idea of a key was definitely an archetypal concept.

Something was happening inside him. He'd never been one to experience intuitions but he somehow recognized that he was experiencing one now. The word, *key,* was practically vibrating inside his body. He shivered and tried to control the urge to laugh out loud. *Am I going crazy?* He sat back and lit up a cigarette. He was just about to put the book aside for a while when an illustration on the back cover caught his attention. He'd seen it before, of course, and there was another picture of it inside the book. But now it seemed to be attracting him like a magnet. It was a graphic depiction of the 260-unit Tzolkin, the matrix of the Mayan calendar. Basically it was nothing more than a rectangular grid of 13 vertical columns each 20 units deep, creating a total of 260 units. Each little cell, or unit, of the grid contained a number. It began with the number 1 at the top left corner of the grid and continued downward through 13. After 13 it continued on down, beginning with 1 again. Since there were only 20 units in each of the 13 vertical columns, the numbers in the first column ended with the number 7 but continued with 8 at the top of the next column. From the 8 at the top of the column the numbering continued downward again until the number 13 was reached and, once again, it continued downward beginning with 1. So it was a continuing series of 1 through 13, snaking its way all the way to the last unit at the bottom right corner of the grid where it ended with the final number 13.

1	8	2	9	3	10	4	11	5	12	6	13	7
2	9	3	10	4	11	5	12	6	13	7	1	8
3	10	4	11	5	12	6	13	7	1	8	2	9
4	11	5	12	6	13	7	1	8	2	9	3	10
5	12	6	13	7	1	8	2	9	3	10	4	11
6	13	7	1	8	2	9	3	10	4	11	5	12
7	1	8	2	9	3	10	4	11	5	12	6	13
8	2	9	3	10	4	11	5	12	6	13	7	1
9	3	10	4	11	5	12	6	13	7	1	8	2
10	4	11	5	12	6	13	7	1	8	2	9	3
11	5	12	6	13	7	1	8	2	9	3	10	4
12	6	13	7	1	8	2	9	3	10	4	11	5
13	7	1	8	2	9	3	10	4	11	5	12	6
1	8	2	9	3	10	4	11	5	12	6	13	7
2	9	3	10	4	11	5	12	6	13	7	1	8
3	10	4	11	5	12	6	13	7	1	8	2	9
4	11	5	12	6	13	7	1	8	2	9	3	10
5	12	6	13	7	1	8	2	9	3	10	4	11
6	13	7	1	8	2	9	3	10	4	11	5	12
7	1	8	2	9	3	10	4	11	5	12	6	13

On a whim, guided by this strange intuition vibrating inside him, he decided to take this 13 x 20 matrix and replace the numbers with the letters of the alphabet. The Mayans numbered the cells vertically, from top to bottom, starting in the upper left corner and ending at the lower right corner. So it seemed logical to arrange the letters of the alphabet in the same way. He grabbed a pencil and a piece of paper and a ruler and constructed a duplicate of the 13 x 20 grid. Then he inserted the letters of the alphabet, consecutively, *A* through *Z*, *A* through *Z*, *A* through *Z*, continuing all the way to the bottom cell in the lower right corner of the grid. Because there were 260 cells in the grid and 26 letters in the alphabet, the grid accommodated the series of letters perfectly, beginning with *A* in the upper left and ending with *Z* in the lower right.

Then it occurred to him to number the horizontal and vertical sides of the grid along the outside of the perimeter. Along the top he wrote the numbers 1 through 9. But since there were 13 cells across, that left four cells without numbers. He wondered if maybe he should just continue to number them from 9 through 13 but decided instead to simply begin with the number 1 again. Just as the Mayans had stuck to their series of 1 through 13 he would stick to his series of 1 through 9. *After all*, he thought to himself, *the number nine seems to be a key to this whole thing.* So the top of the grid was numbered from left to right as 1 through 9 and continued to the end with 1 through 4. He then numbered the units down the left side of the grid in the same manner. The vertical numbering then was 1 through 9 and continued downward with 1 through 9 again, and then 1 through 2, to complete the vertical count of 20 units. He had no idea what he was doing but he felt compelled to do it anyway. He lit another cigarette and studied what he'd created.

At first it just looked like a mass of letters. But it reminded him of two things simultaneously. On the lighter side, it reminded him of those *find-a-word* puzzles that he'd seen in magazines. But on the more serious side it also reminded him of the blocks of letters of the Hebrew Torah where those Bible Code researchers were finding significant words and phrases. Could that possibly be what he had here? Spurred by that possibility, he crushed out his cigarette and leaned forward to examine this puzzle more closely. Suddenly he saw it.

The word *KEY* was spelled out on the top line! Then something else caught his attention. This word, *KEY*, was right under the numbers 8, 9, 1. He recognized immediately that 891 was the exact reverse of 198, the address number of the Seattle Gospel Mission. He was stunned. *Is this just coincidence?* he wondered. *What are the odds?* This definitely called for yet another smoke. He fumbled with his cigarette pack only to find it was empty. He couldn't contain himself. He jumped out of his chair and hollered down the hall for Angela to come quickly.

Angela came running to his office, thinking something must be wrong.

"What is it?" she said. "Are you all right?"

"I need a cigarette."

"What?"

"I need a cigarette! Have you got one?"

She looked confused. She could tell there was something going on besides a nicotine fit. "You want to tell me what's happening?" she asked.

He settled down in his chair. "I will, yes. But I'd really like a cigarette."

"All right, already! They're in my office. Hang on, I'll be right back."

She returned in a moment with the smokes and lit one for him. "Here," she said. "Keep the pack. Now, you wanted to tell me something?"

She scooted the extra chair up next to his desk and listened as he explained everything to her. She sat quietly taking it all in. Then she just stared for a few moments at the grid he'd drawn on the sheet of paper. "Amazing," she said finally. She looked up at him. "This is... just amazing! Are there any other words in this matrix?"

"I don't know. When I found the word, *KEY*, I just sort of froze. You know what I mean?"

"Yeah, I bet!" she laughed. "But let's see what else might be in this magic matrix of yours."

Together they scanned the grid full of letters looking for more words.

"Um..." Angela said, "here's the word, *NO*."

"Yeah. Or maybe it's *ON*."

"Oh, right, that could be. Hmm... I don't see anything else. Do you?"

"No, I don't either. Maybe... Hey, wait... Look!" He found the word, *KEY*, again in another part of the grid.

"Yes! Of course!" Angela said. "You have the alphabet in a repeating pattern here in the grid. So there should be several incidences of the word, KEY, showing up!"

"You're right," Banyon agreed. "Yup, right there!" he pointed. "And there!"

"And here!" Angela said.

In a few moments they had found every instance of the word, *KEY*, in the grid.

"You're not going to believe this," Banyon said.

"What now?"

He circled each instance of the word, *KEY*, with a red pencil. "You know how many times the word *KEY* appears here?"

Angela counted them. "Oh, man," she said. "Nine keys! Unbelievable."

They both stared at each other for a moment in silence and then laughed.

"What the hell does this mean?" she asked, scooting her chair back from the desk.

Banyon shook his head. "I wish I knew." He walked over to the coffee maker and poured a cup for each of them. "I really wish I knew."

In the white unmarked van parked across the street, a man in a black overcoat had just recorded the entire conversation between Banyon and Angela. On a laptop computer he typed an email. The message was short and to the point:
HAVE TAPE. WILL SEND.

Two black sedans, coming from opposite directions, pulled up along side each other in the covered area beneath a bridge. The windows on the driver's side of each car rolled down simultaneously and the two drivers spoke to each other.

The first man had a slight Italian accent. "Did you get a chance to hear the tape?" he asked, tugging at the collar of his overcoat.

"Yeah," the older man in the other car responded. "This could be the guy. I don't know."

"*Could* be? What do you mean, *could* be?" the first man complained. "The prophecy says it will be a failed priest without a church and he'll be called by the name of the visionary. Right? Look, this Banyon fellow started seminary and dropped out. He no longer goes to church. And the man's first name is Ezekiel for Christ's sake. What more do you want?"

"Just keep me informed," the older man said.

Banyon took a sip of coffee. "Angela, I've been thinking."

"Oh-oh," she replied, looking up from her work.

He smiled. "No, I mean seriously."

"Okay, what is it?"

"I've been thinking about how this all began."

"How all what began?"

"This number stuff."

"And...?"

"If it hadn't been for that former director of the shelter scribbling that stuff on the desk pad I never would have known about any of this."

"Probably true. So?"

"It just occurred to me that I don't know anything about him. I want to find out who he was."

"Why?"

"Well, for one thing, why was he doing that? The alphanumeric stuff, I mean. Was he just playing around? Was it just an amusement to pass the time? Or did he know something? Or was he *looking* for something?"

Angela looked interested. "How are we going to find out who he was?"

"I think I'll call my old friend, Father Caldwell. He's back in New York now."

"Father Caldwell?"

"Yes. He's the fellow I told you about. The motivational-kick-in-the-ass guy. Remember? The one who talked me into taking this job here as the director."

"Oh, sure! I remember. Good idea. Call him. He'll probably know something."

"Do you have his number in your file?"

Angela thumbed through the card file. She found Caldwell's number and wrote it down on a piece of paper and handed it to him.

"Thanks. I'll be in my office."

He walked back to his office and sat down at the desk. He stared at the phone number on the paper for several minutes, wondering if this was a stupid thing to be doing. *What if Father Caldwell wants to know why I'm suddenly interested in the former director? What am I going to tell him? I guess I'll just play it by ear.*

He dialed the number. "Hello," he said to the woman who answered the phone. "Father Caldwell, please. Yes, tell him Zeke Banyon is calling from Seattle." He lit up a cigarette and waited. Finally a familiar voice came on the line.

"Banyon! You ol' devil! How are you?"

"Hey Father. I'm doing just fine, thanks. Long time no talk. How are things in New York?"

"Oh, you know. Just about the same. But I just returned from a trip to France. That was very interesting."

"Business or pleasure?"

"Vacation, really. Always wanted to visit the area of Rennes le Chateau."

"Ren-la-what?"

"Rennes le Chateau! You mean you never heard of it?"

"Heard of it?" Banyon laughed. "I can't even say it!"

"The place is the stuff of legend you know! Very intriguing!"

"No kidding? Like what?"

"Oh, too long to go into now. But look it up some time. You'll find it fascinating, I'm sure. But enough about me. To what do I owe the pleasure of this call from out of the blue?"

"Well, I was wondering if you knew how I could find out who was the director of the shelter here before I took the job."

"Oh yes, Densmore, I think. Yes, that was it. Reverend Densmore. Patrick, I think was his first name. Patrick Densmore. Why?"

"I was just thinking about getting in touch with him. Had some questions I thought he could answer for me."

"Well, I'm afraid that might be a bit difficult. Densmore just flat disappeared about a week before you took the job. They never did find him. I thought you knew that. That's why they needed someone to take over the position of director."

"Disappeared? I had no idea. When I was interviewed for the job they just told me the man had taken ill and couldn't handle the task anymore."

"Yes, I guess that was the line they were using at the time," Caldwell said. "The FBI was investigating his disappearance and for some reason they didn't want to bring any more attention to the case than necessary. That thing about him being sick was just a cover. But I don't think the case was ever solved. Something unusual happened, no doubt, but I never really heard much more about it."

"Well, that's quite..." he paused, looking for the right word. "...interesting."

"But if it helps any, I think his wife is still living up in Marysville just a few miles north of you. Unless she moved."

"Okay, thanks! I'll try to look her up."

They ended the conversation with promises to keep in touch more often and then Banyon sat back and wondered at this new information. He walked down the hall to Angela's office. She looked up from her work when he entered the room.

"Well?" she said, downing the last drop of coffee in her cup. "What'd you find out?"

"It's kind of weird."

Angela chuckled. "Oh, why am I not surprised? What is it now?"

"The guy's name was Patrick Densmore."

"What's so weird about that? Did you find out how to get in touch with him?"

"Well, that's the problem." He took Angela's cup and got one off the shelf for himself. Pouring some coffee for each of them, he told her what he'd learned from Caldwell.

"You mean just disappeared?" she asked. "You mean like... just vanished? No trace?"

"Apparently, yes. Caldwell thinks the case is probably still open but at a dead end."

"So are you going to go visit his wife?"

"I was thinking about it, if..."

"If what?"

"If you'll go with me."

"Hey, I'm always up for a good mystery!"

"Okay then," he grinned. "The first thing we need to do is find out if she's still up in Marysville." He paused a moment. "But how are we going to do that? I don't have a phone directory for that area."

Angela chuckled. "Never fear, the internet's here!" She turned to the computer and logged on.

"The internet? But what if she's not online? Not everybody in the world is online, you know, despite what you seem to think!"

"Doesn't matter. There's a People Search web site. I don't know how they do it, but they've got a gigantic database of names and addresses and phone numbers. Ah! Here's the site," she said after typing a few keystrokes. "Okay, now all we have to do is type *Marysville* here and... what's her first name?"

Banyon shook his head. "Caldwell didn't seem to know."

"Oh well. We'll skip that and go over here," she said, moving the curser from box to box on the screen. "And we'll just type in the last name, Densmore. Now just wait a second while it searches the database."

In a matter of a few seconds they had what they wanted.

"Ah, ha!" Angela beamed. "There we go! Patrick and Mary Anne Densmore. 171 Old Barklay Road, Marysville, Washington. And there's the phone number."

"Amazing," Banyon said. "Probably a farm. Lot's of farm land up around there."

"You gonna call her?"

"Oh man. I don't know. What would I say?"

They both sat quiet for a moment, staring at the information on the computer screen.

"Why don't we just take a drive up there tomorrow?" Banyon suggested. "You know, just to sort of drive by and see the place."

"You mean just drop in on her?"

"No, I mean just drive by. You know? Just... I don't know. I just want to see the place. Who knows, maybe that's outdated information and she doesn't even live there anymore."

"Okay," Angela said. "I'm game."

"Oh, by the way," he said, handing her a piece of paper. "Check this out."

She took the piece of paper and looked at what he'd written:

PATRICK DENSMORE = 171

"That's..." Angela started and then paused."...his address!"

"Uh huh. And the number of his name."

"And it equals nine."

"Yup."

"You were right," she said.

"About what?"

"This is weird."

Banyon nodded. "Yup. And I wouldn't be surprised if it gets weirder."

Angela laughed. "Is that even possible?"

He shrugged. "Hey, the way things are going? What do *you* think?"

~9~

D ensmore's home was easy enough to find. The Old Barklay Road was nearly a straight line running for several miles through the farm country, pretty much as Banyon had imagined.

They passed three farms along the way, checking the addresses on the mailboxes along the side of the road. The fourth mailbox was a rusty red color with **THE DENSMORE'S** stenciled in white letters above the address. A long dirt driveway led to the old, white, two-story house about five hundred feet back from the road. Between the road and the house was a field of tall, dry grass. A dilapidated antique tractor sat rusting in the middle of the field entangled in a mass of overgrown blackberry bushes.

Banyon and Angela were still parked in the middle of the road, taking in the scene, when Banyon glanced in his rearview mirror and noticed a dark green pickup truck approaching. He put the car in gear and moved over to the side of the road so the pickup could pass. He was surprised when, instead of passing, it slowed down and turned onto the Densmore property and headed down the long driveway toward the house.

"Must be Mrs. Densmore," Banyon said. "It looked like a woman behind the wheel."

The pickup came to a stop beside the house. The door on the driver's side opened and the woman stepped out. With two bags of groceries under her arms, she walked up to the house but paused a moment and turned, glancing across the field toward Banyon and Angela.

"Is she looking at us?" Angela asked, feeling a little uncomfortable.

"Yeah, I think so. She probably wonders who the heck is sitting up here at the edge of her property."

The woman turned back and walked up the stairs to the large front porch. Juggling the two bags and her purse, she fumbled for her keys and unlocked the door. Just before entering, she turned once more and glanced toward the road. Then she went inside and closed the door. In a moment, they saw the curtain in one of the windows draw back just slightly and the woman peered out in their direction.

"Let's go talk to her," Angela suggested. "She's probably worried about who we are, sitting up here."

Banyon thought about it for a minute. "Okay, maybe you're right. I wouldn't want her to think someone's stalking her or casing the house."

Banyon drove slowly down the driveway and parked behind the pickup. They got out and walked up the front steps, knocked on the door and waited. In a few moments the door opened just a crack, secured by a chain-lock from the inside.

Banyon addressed the woman. "Mrs. Densmore?"

"Yes," she answered cautiously. She looked to be in her 50s, plain but attractive, no makeup, and her graying blond hair hung loose to her shoulders.

"My name's Zeke Banyon and this is my assistant, Angela Martin."

The woman spoke slowly with a hint of a southern accent. "Yes? Can I help you?"

"Well, ma'am," Banyon searched for words. "I'm the director of the Seattle Gospel Mission."

"Oh... my," she said softly. "Won't you come in?"

The living room was tidy and quaintly old fashioned. Upon entering, one had the feeling of stepping through a time portal into the 1940s. Angela immediately noticed the intricate white doilies perfectly placed on each arm of the large brown sofa. The ornate tile-work framing the fireplace was patterned with strange geometric designs. The center tile at the top of the fireplace was slightly larger than the others and contained a complex design of interwoven triangles. Sitting next to the fireplace was an old rocking chair. One entire wall, opposite the fireplace, consisted of dark wood shelving filled with books.

"Please," Mrs. Densmore said, "won't you have a seat?"

Banyon and Angela sat next to each other on the sofa as Mrs. Densmore gracefully seated herself in the old rocking chair.

"What can I do for you, Mr... "

"Banyon. Zeke Banyon. We... well, that is, I was wondering if you would mind if I ask you about your husband. You see, I took over the Seattle Gospel... "

"What is it you want to know?" she inquired before he could finish.

"Well, this may seem like a strange request and I don't want to upset you, but..."

"You found something, didn't you?" Mrs. Densmore asked as if she sensed what might be coming.

"Well, as a matter of fact, yes. But..."

"Let me guess," she said with a slight, knowing smile. "Does it have anything to do with numbers?"

"Yes," Banyon answered, somewhat surprised. "Then you know..."

"I know Patrick was searching for something."

"What do you mean?"

Mrs. Densmore thought for a second. Glancing over at the books on the shelf, she wondered just how to begin.

Banyon could feel her hesitation. "I don't mean to pry, Mrs. Densmore. I just thought..."

"No, no." she smiled. "It's all right. In fact I suspect perhaps it's not simply by coincidence that you've come here."

"How so? I'm not sure I..."

"It's just that I don't know where to begin," she interrupted. "May I get you both something to drink? A cup of tea, perhaps?"

"That sounds good," Banyon said, getting the impression this was going to be a rather interesting visit.

Mrs. Densmore got up and disappeared into the kitchen.

Banyon wandered over to the bookshelves to browse the titles. Clearly, Patrick Densmore had been interested in metaphysics and other unusual subjects. Many of the books appeared to be quite old and ranged in subject matter from UFOs and the *I Ching* to prophetic visions and scholarly works on the Dead Sea Scrolls. An embossed design on the spine of one of the books caught Banyon's eye. It was basically two inverted triangles overlapping each other – similar to the familiar Star of David, common to the Jewish religious tradition. The triangles were enclosed in a circle. He ran his finger over the intricately embossed image as if it were a message in braille. He recognized it as the same design that was on the central tile above the opening to the fireplace. He pulled the old book from the shelf. It was titled *The Lost Scroll of Ezekiel and other Myths & Mysteries.*

"Ah," Mrs. Densmore said, returning with the tea on a silver tray. "I see you've discovered my husband's collection of esoteric books."

"So this was a hobby of his?" Banyon asked, putting the book back on the shelf.

"You could say that." Mrs. Densmore answered. She set the serving tray on the coffee table in front of them and returned to her rocking chair.

"An odd hobby for a man of the Cloth." Banyon said, smiling.

"Well," Mrs. Densmore began, "actually it was a bit more than a hobby. To tell you the truth he was obsessed with all of that sort of thing. It really began to absorb all of his attention about four years ago when he found a note tucked between the pages of an old book he found at a flea market. The book you were just looking at, actually."

Banyon's eyes narrowed. "Really? The one about... what was it? Something about Ezekiel?" He stood up and went over to the bookshelf and read the title again. News to me," he chuckled. "I didn't know there was a lost scroll of Ezekiel, mythical or otherwise." He paused for a moment and thumbed quickly through the pages. Then he said, "I noticed the symbol on the book is the same as that design there on the fireplace."

"Patrick seemed to think it was important somehow. That design, I mean. Something to do with what he called sacred geometry, I think. He had those tiles made by a local artist. You're welcome to borrow the book if you like."

"Thank you, yes. Are you sure you wouldn't mind?"

"Not at all."

"And the note your husband found inside the book?" Angela reminded her. "What was it?"

Mrs. Densmore got up and walked over to a big, oak, roll-top desk and opened one of the small drawers inside. She pulled out a piece of old, yellowed paper. It was folded in half, and slightly torn at one corner. She handed it to Banyon.

The aged paper crinkled slightly as he carefully unfolded it.

"What's it say?" Angela asked. "Read it aloud."

Banyon began to read:

Entry, December 14, 1999.
I'm now more certain than ever that it was a machine.
I believe it still exists somewhere.
I'm going to find it. The numbers are coming together.

THE WHEEL OF EZEKIEL = 180
(half of a complete circle)

SPIN THE WHEEL = 144 (light?)
THE ALPHANUMBER =144

180 + 144 = 324
REVERSE DIRECTION = 198, 198+324 = 522

THE WHEEL SPINS IN TWO DIRECTIONS = 360

Circle of Stone = 144

Reverse??? REVERSE THE NUMBER = 198

180+081=261=THE SPEED OF LIGHT IS THE KEY!

TWO SIX ONE = 144

The hub of the wheel = 171 = The Zero Point
(Counter Spiral = 171 = Reversed Spiral)

EAST OF THE HEAD = 117
= COMMUNICATE = NEGATIVE DARK
= NINE LIGHTS

THE WHEEL OF SOUND = 180
= THE WHEEL OF EZEKIEL

Sound? Light? Reverse? Stone???
TIME CHARIOT = 121 = WHEEL OF TIME
SOUTH OF FRANCE = 151

Banyon finished reading and no one spoke for several moments. He couldn't help but notice the number 144 appeared several times. It was not only the number value of his own name, it was the number he'd come across the night his brain felt like it had been barraged with a download of information. "Do you have any idea what any of this means, Mrs. Densmore?"

"I'm afraid I don't," she sighed. "Patrick and I were very close and talked with each other about nearly everything, really. But he didn't seem to want to talk much about this. I'm not sure he even knew what it meant. At least not entirely. I just don't know."

Banyon took a deep breath. "Mrs. Densmore, may I..."

"Keep the note?" she smiled. "Yes, of course. I have no use for it but apparently you do."

They thanked Mrs. Densmore for the hospitality and the information and headed back to town discussing their visit along the way.

"Well," Angela commented, "that was interesting!"

"Yeah, and some of those numbers in that note looked very familiar. Did you notice?"

"I noticed that. Let me see it again."

He took the note from his shirt pocket and handed to her. She studied it for a minute.

"Did you notice this?" she said, pointing to something on the paper.

He glanced over. "What is it?" he asked, trying to keep his eyes on the road.

"This number 522 is the only number that's underlined. And I'll bet Densmore is the one who underlined it."

"Why do say that?"

"Well, because look. The original writing is really faded. But this underline looks relatively new and it's a different color of ink. It looks like a completely different kind of pen. It obviously wasn't underlined originally."

"522?" Banyon asked.

"Yes. It's the only number that's underlined."

"Hmm..." he said, shaking his head. "I don't have a clue."

"Maybe it *is* the clue."

Banyon shot her a glance and smiled.

"What are you smiling at?" she asked with a grin.

"I don't know," he answered, evasively. But he did know. He was smiling because he couldn't believe how fond he'd become of her. His feelings for her were something more than he liked to admit. Maybe he even loved her. He thought about that for a moment. *Love? No. Well, maybe. Who couldn't love a woman who would go along with all of this and not think I'm crazy?* "Do you think I'm crazy?" he asked.

She smiled. "You think I'd be here if I did?"

He shrugged. "I don't know. Maybe you're crazy too."

She hit him in the arm.

Ah, he thought. *She likes me."*

Inside a warm and extravagantly appointed mansion on a small, remote island in the Bering Sea, nine men were gathered in the library. The room was heavy with the sweet smell of cigar smoke, brandy and expensive burgundy. They sat quietly. Waiting. The slow, rhythmic tick-tock of the pendulum on the large antique clock was amplified by the silence. Suddenly the double doors to the library opened and a tall thin man in a long dark coat entered the room. All eyes turned toward him.

"Gentleman," he began. "Mr. Banyon has read the notes."

The announcement was met with more silence. In a moment one of the members of the group - a tall, stately gentleman with thick white hair – slowly pushed his big, maroon leather chair back from the large round conference table and stood up. With a brandy in one hand and a cigar in the other, he walked solemnly over to the large bay window and stared out upon the endless gray sea. His outward expression was stoic. Inside he was smiling. "Very well, Mr. Walker," he said. "Thank you. You may go."

~10~

When Banyon and Angela arrived back at the office they studied the cryptic notes on the paper that Mrs. Densmore had turned over to them. The first sentences were perplexing. Banyon read them aloud:

"*I'm now more certain than ever that it was a machine. And I believe it still exists somewhere. I'm going to find it. The numbers are coming together.*"

"What machine, I wonder?" Angela asked.

Banyon was puzzled, too. "I don't know," he said, scratching his head. "You want coffee?"

"Yes. Thanks. I noticed that number 144 sure pops up a lot here. In these notes, I mean."

"Yeah," Banyon said, plugging in the coffee maker. "The number of my name."

"Your name?"

"Yes. Remember that was one of the first things I found when I figured out how Densmore was arriving at the number values for the words and phrases. The alphanumeric value of Ezekiel Banyon is 144."

"What about your middle name? If you include that, then it changes the number."

"Yup, it would but I don't have a middle name."

"Really? That's weird. Everybody has a middle name," she teased.

Banyon laughed. "Well, I guess I'm not everybody. So what's *your* middle name?"

"Ann. Angela Ann Martin. Most people don't ever seem to like their middle name. Ever notice that? But I like mine. Got a ring to it, don't you think?"

"Very pretty. Let's see what it comes out to."

"Okay," she said, smiling. "Where's that alphanumeric chart you had?"

"Don't need it," Banyon gloated. "I've done so much of this I've got the letter values all memorized."

He picked up the calculator and began quickly punching the buttons. When he finished he just sat there staring at the result. Finally he looked up and asked one more time, "Ann, you said, right? Angela Ann Martin?"

Angela nodded. "Yes. What's it come to?"

"Hang on. I have to do this again. I must have made a mistake."

"Why?" Angela laughed. What was it? 666?"

Banyon ran the numbers again. He looked up at her with raised eyebrows and shook his head.

Now Angela was really curious. "What? What is it?"

He slid the calculator across the desk so she could see for herself. She picked it up and stared at it. "Are you kidding me? Really? Can't be," she said.

"Figure it for yourself," he said, getting up to turn the coffee maker on. "The chart is under the paper weight there."

Angela grabbed the alphanumeric chart and the calculator and added the numbers:

ANGELA ANN MARTIN = 144

She laughed.

He looked over at her. "What's so funny?"

"Well, I mean, it's just such a bizarre coincidence!"

"Is it?"

"What? Bizarre?"

"No," he said. "I mean coincidence. Is it just coincidence? Or is it something more?"

"Come on," Angela protested. "I mean some things *are* just coincidence, you know."

"Uh huh. I know. And some things aren't. I mean go out on the street and get the names of a hundred people and how many of them do you think would add up to 144?"

"I don't know," she said, putting the calculator back on the desk. "There'd be some."

"Yeah. But I'll bet not many. And of all the people who could have come here to apply for the job like you did, how many actually came in?"

"I give up. How many?"

"One. You."

"Hmm..." she thought for a second. "Well, I don't know. So what do you think it is?"

Banyon handed her a cup of coffee and returned to his desk. He looked at her and grinned. "Destiny, my dear. Destiny."

"Gosh!" she said, mockingly. "Ya think?"

They both laughed.

"So back to the notes," Banyon said. "What else can we find to boggle our minds?"

"Well," she replied, pointing to the paper, "says here that 144 is also the value of *spin the wheel* and then in parentheses it says *light* with a question mark. What do you make of that?"

He nodded. "Yeah. That's interesting. I don't know what it means. Seems like whoever wrote those notes must have thought there might be some connection between that number, 144, and light. Hand me the calculator."

Angela slid the calculator across the top of the desk.

Banyon punched a few numbers. "Hmm... that's interesting," he muttered.

"What is it?"

"*Light* is 56."

"So? What does 56 mean?"

"Well, for one thing it means it's not 144."

"What's not 144? Light?"

"Yeah."

"So why do you think who ever wrote this note put the word *light* after the number 144? This person had to know the word didn't add up to 144. He must have had some other reason for thinking there might be a connection."

"True," Banyon agreed with a sigh. "But what was the reason?"

"Your guess is as good as mine."

Banyon nodded and took a sip of his coffee. "I came up with that number, 144, a while back, when I was studying that information about the Mayans. And I discovered how the alphabet fit into the Mayan calendar grid and the word, *key*, appeared nine times. Remember?"

"I remember. But what's the number 144 have to do with it?"

"One of the key numbers in the Mayan system was 144,000 and it's the number mentioned a couple times in the Bible. Remember I told you about the thing that numerologists call harmonics?"

"Oh, yes. 144 is a harmonic of 144,000."

"Exactly," Banyon said, pulling a notepad from his desk drawer. "Here are the notes I jotted down that night."

ENGLISH ALPHABET CIRCLE = 189
= THE ENLIGHTENED ONE =

SQUARE OF TWELVE

THE SACRED ALPHABET CIRCLE = 198

198 - 189 = 9

THE AREA OF A CIRCLE = 120
= THE MIND OF GOD

TWENTY SIX DEGREES = 222
= THE ENGLISH ALPHABET CIRCLE

"The number 189," he continued, "caught my eye because I recognized it has the same digits as the address of the shelter here, 198 Post Street. Just a different arrangement of the digits. Anyway I noticed that twelve squared is 144. That's when I started thinking about the 144,000 in the Bible and all that stuff."

"And...?"

"And... I don't know. It just struck me at that moment that this number – this 144 - might be really significant somehow. And now we see it in these cryptic frigging little notes."

After a minute of silence Angela sighed and shook her head. "I don't know what to think. It's all just so... weird. You know?"

Banyon got up and paced the room a couple times. "What's the next thing in the notes there?"

"Um... It says *the alphanumber* equals 144." Then she looked puzzled. "What's *the alphanumber* mean?"

"I'm not sure. Check it out on the calculator".

Angela punched in the number values of the letters in the phrase, *the alphanumber*. "Yup," she said. "It's 144."

"Hmm..." Banyon mumbled to himself. "Alphanumber. Alphanumber. What is an alphanumber?"

"That's what I asked you," Angela said. "Alpha implies alphabet. So I guess..."

"Yes, alphabet. Or letter. Alpha number. Letter number. Letter number. Alpha number."

"You say toe-may-toe I say toe-mah-toe," Angela grinned as she mimicked the lyrics to an old song.

Banyon groaned.

"Sorry," she muttered sheepishly.

"Wait a minute," he said. "Let me see Densmore's notes."

She handed him the paper.

"Here," he said, coming around his desk to show her. "Look here where it says *TWO-SIX-ONE equals 144.*"

"Yes? So?"

"These are numbers that are spelled out as words. T-W-O, S-I-X, and O-N-E! Word-numbers! Letter-numbers!"

"Of course!" Angela said, catching on. "Alphanumbers!"

"Yes! That's got to be it! An alphanumber is simply a number spelled out as a word! Check it out on the calculator. Punch in the number values for the letters that spell *TWO SIX ONE* and see what you get."

Angela punched in the numbers and showed it to him. The combined alphanumeric values of the words TWO SIX ONE was, indeed, 144.

"Damn, we're good!" she said. They high-fived each other and laughed.

"Got that right!" Banyon said.

"Just one thing."

"What's that?"

"What do we do with it?"

"Well now," Banyon admitted, "that's a good question. What if we calculate the values of other alphanumbers? Let's see what we get."

"Sure," Angela agreed. "But which ones? How would you know which numbers to convert into words? How would you know what you're looking for? Numbers are infinite! You could spend the rest of your life converting numbers into words and calculating their alphanumeric values. Right?"

"Yeah. Well, keep it in mind. I think there's something important there. What else can we figure out in those notes?"

"Well, there is this reverse direction thing."

REVERSE DIRECTION = 198, 198+324 = <u>522</u>
THE WHEEL SPINS IN TWO DIRECTIONS = 360

"Right," Banyon said. "And there's that 522, underlined. I wonder why he underlined it? I'm guessing it's a key to something. What's 522 plus that mysterious 144?"

Angela punched it into the calculator. "Oh, you'll like this. It's 666!"

Banyon rolled his eyes. "Not that again. The number gives me the creeps. What about 522 plus that number right below it there in the notes?"

"The 360?" Angela asked.

"Right. What is it?"

"Um, let's see... 522 and 360 is 882."

Banyon wrote 882 on the back of an envelope. "Well, that's kind of interesting," he said.

"What is?"

"What's the reverse of 882?"

"Oh!" she said. " It's 288! It's the reverse of two times 144! That's too weird."

Banyon grinned. "You keep saying that."

"Well it is!"

Banyon was scribbling more numbers on the envelope. "Here's something. Instead of adding 522 and 360, if we subtract 360 from 522 we get 162."

"So?"

"So look at the notes. It says TWO-SIX-ONE is 144. We just confirmed that for ourselves. And 162 is the exact reverse of 261! You see? ONE-SIX-TWO is 144 also! Remember weeks ago when we were talking about what I called the mirrored numbers?"

"The mirrored numbers?"

"Yes! We were talking about Revelation, 13th chapter, 18th verse, where it mentions the number 666. And I showed you how 13 times 18 is 234? Then I reversed it and added them together and found the sum was 666! Remember?"

"Oh yeah! I do remember. Hey, you were on to something and didn't even know it!"

"Well, I didn't know for sure but I suspected it. At least on some level."

"So this reversal idea is somehow important to all of this... this... whatever this is."

"It must be."

"You know we just might crack this thing yet," she said, sounding confident.

"Yeah. But that 522 has me stumped."

Angela downed the last drop of coffee in her cup. "You know what?"

"What?"

"I'm hungry."

"Marios?"

"Chinese."

"Sounds good. Let's go."

Banyon grabbed the book that Mrs. Densmore loaned him and took it along to the restaurant. During dinner they discussed the mysterious note but they were at a loss as to what any of it might really mean.

"Okay," Banyon said, pushing a couple of empty plates to the side. "Let's check out this book. Obviously it's the chapter on this alleged lost scroll of Ezekiel that the writer of these notes was interested in. Got to be some clues there."

He opened to the chapter in question and began to read to himself while Angela patiently sipped her tea. After several minutes he nudged her on the arm.

"Hey, this is really interesting," he said. "I don't know if I believe it but it's pretty intriguing."

"What is it?"

"Well supposedly there's this scroll believed to be from the hand of the same Ezekiel that's in the Bible. You remember the story of Ezekiel? He had that strange encounter with what he called the spirit of God but as he described the... whatever it was that he saw... it was unlike any description of any other prophet's vision of God."

"Oh yeah," Angela nodded. "In fact, I remember seeing on the cover of one of those supermarket tabloids that the thing Ezekiel saw was really an alien space ship!"

He turned and stared at her with a dumbfounded expression.

"What's the matter?" she asked.

"What you just said."

"What... the spaceship? C'mon."

"That's what they're speculating in this book!"

"Are you serious?"

"Yeah!"

Angela could see the wheels were turning in his head.

"You know," he said, "now as I think back on Ezekiel's whole description of that what-ever-it-was, it really was very strange. In fact... oh man, I really gotta go back and read that again."

"Read what?"

"The first few pages of the book of Ezekiel in the Bible. I mean now that I think about it... I mean from a modern perspective... I don't know, but it did sort of read like a description of some kind of a mechanical device. And it came down from the sky, too."

"Well now! Did you say a mechanical device?"

"Yes. Why?"

"Look here!" She unfolded the page of cryptic notes and pointed to the first couple of sentences:

Entry, December 14, 1999.
I'm now more certain than ever that it was a machine.
I believe it still exists somewhere.
I'm going to find it. The numbers are coming together.

Banyon's eyes lit up. "Now we're getting somewhere! Says here in this chapter that the so-called *Lost Scroll of Ezekiel* tells about another encounter Ezekiel had with another strange craft. But this craft was apparently a little different than the one described in the Bible, according to the description." Banyon suddenly hesitated.

Angela looked at him. "What's wrong?"

"I just noticed something. Here in the book. It talks about Rennes le Chateau. It's part of the story! I can't believe it! That's the place in the South of France that Father Caldwell told me about when I called him to find out about the fellow who formerly ran the shelter. Caldwell had recently taken a trip to see the place, this Rennes le Chateau. I remember he said the story of the church at this little village was really interesting in a mysterious way. He said I should look into it sometime."

"Hmm..." Angela mused. "Another coincidence? Go on. What else does it say there?"

"Okay. Well, it says the original scroll, this *Lost Scroll of Ezekiel*, eventually ended up under the flooring of the church at Rennes le Chateau where it was discovered by a priest named Saunière about 1886. How it got there in the first place is a mystery. Anyway, Saunière had just become the appointed caretaker of the dilapidated old church. He was renovating the church and when he tore up a portion of the flooring he discovered the scroll. Then at this point the story gets complicated."

"What do you mean?"

"Well, legend has it that Saunière also found additional scrolls under the floor but those scrolls are said to have had something to do with the *sangreal*, the so called Holy Grail."

"The Holy Grail? The chalice Christ drank from at the Last Supper?"

"Says here that according to some researchers the Holy Grail wasn't really a chalice. They say the term Holy Grail was actually a metaphor for the body of Mary Magdalene. They believe she was actually married to Jesus. So, rather than a mere cup containing the blood of Christ, symbolically or otherwise, it was the Magdalene who was the actual grail, as it were. She was the vessel containing the bloodline of Jesus."

"The bloodline? You mean..."

"Meaning she bore the offspring of Jesus Christ."

"Ah!" Angela said, nodding her head. "Like in that novel, The DaVinci Code!"

"Right! Anyway, supposedly those scrolls ended up in the hands of a secret society known as the Knights Templar. But it doesn't go into any more detail other than to recommend a couple of books on the subject. The author only mentions this in order to caution the reader not to confuse the grail part of the story with this mysterious scroll which apparently branches off into a story of its own, the story of the *Lost Scroll of Ezekiel*."

"Interesting. So, go on. What else?"

"Okay. Well, getting back to the Ezekiel scroll, apparently this Saunière fellow sold the scroll to yet another secret society of Christian mystics known as the Order of the New Dawn that was founded around the year 1350. The Order was based in France but it also had a branch in England. Legend has it that one of the members of this English branch of the Order - someone known only as Brother Hiram - had the gift of prophecy. The ability to see into the future. Here, listen to this."

Banyon read directly from the book:

"The Order of the New Dawn wanted the message of the scroll to be revealed to the world but Hiram, glimpsing into the future, realized the knowledge which would be gained from it, as well as from the mechanical device itself, could not even be understood until a time when science and technology were at a point where it would make sense, at least to some degree. Looking into the future, the developments in quantum physics of the late 20th and early 21st centuries seemed to be the clues alerting Brother Hiram to the idea that this would be the time when such information could most likely be understood. This mystic priest of the Order realized that the survival of the human race was going to be at a threshold in the 21st century. He foresaw a global catastrophe brought about by the appearance of a great dragon coming to earth from heaven. This had to be prevented if humans were to survive. He understood that the year 2012 would be a pivotal point in the continuation of the human race. While he did not understand the exact nature of what would happen in 2012, he understood it represented a crucial window of opportunity for the next step in the evolution of the human race on this planet."

Angela looked at him. "You recognize that date, don't you?"

"Yeah," Banyon said, thinking back to his reading about the Mayan culture. "That's the end date of the Mayan calendar!"

"Exactly. What are the odds? Or is what you just read nothing more than what most people think it is. A legend. A myth. A tale made up by some guy who knew about the Mayan prophecy of the end of a great cycle of time and he simply thought it would be clever to include the same date in his fabricated tale."

Banyon lit up a cigarette and offered one to Angela. "I don't know what to believe," he said. "It's all so... well... unbelievable."

"Understatement of the year."

"Yeah. But on the other hand look at all the stuff we've found that seems to support the whole crazy idea."

"One thing I don't get," Angela said.

"What's that?"

"Well the book you have there just has that one chapter about this so- called *Lost Scroll of Ezekiel*."

"So?"

"So that whole chapter has nothing in it that would lead anyone to write most of the things that are in the notes that were found inside the book."

"What are you getting at?"

Angela unfolded the old notepaper. "Okay, Densmore found these notes folded up inside that book you're reading from, right?"

"Right."

"Okay, look at all this. Look what's written in these notes. There's nothing in what you just read from the book that even suggests such phrases as '*the wheel spins in two directions*' or '*the alphanumber*' or "*reverse the number*' or '*east of the head*' or any of these other phrases."

"What's your point?"

"Well, think about it. How did the writer of these notes come up with these specific phrases? Where did they come from? Why was he so interested in finding the alphanumeric values of these specific phrases?"

Banyon nodded in agreement. "Good question. Maybe he had access to more information from another source?"

"That's what I was thinking. And that means if we could find out who wrote these cryptic notes we might be able to find out where the *Lost Scroll of Ezekiel* is!"

"Hmm... you just might be right. Look here," Banyon said, pointing to the bottom of the page. "There's a footnote."

"What's it say?"

"It says, *Rumor has persisted for years that there exists a short manuscript which has come to be known as the Ezekiel Code. It is said to contain encoded clues revealing the secret location of the Lost Scroll of Ezekiel. While little else is known about this manuscript, one version of the story indicates that it was penned in the English language by the same Brother Hiram. Interestingly, he did not use the alphabet or the language as it was in his time. Having the gift of foresight, he knew that alphabets and languages change, sometimes significantly, over long periods of time. Knowing this, he wrote the manuscript using the alphabet and the language as it had evolved by the 21st century. In this way, the encrypted clues (thought to be a form of gematria using the English language) could not be decoded until the time was right."*

"Well, well!" Angela exclaimed. "So now we know why the numerology stuff is part of all of this!"

"So it would seem," Banyon agreed.

"So our anonymous note writer may actually have had access to the Ezekiel Code which may have led him to the location of the scroll!"

"Exactly. Question is, does he still have the manuscript? Or, for that matter, maybe even the scroll itself?"

"Right. And who is he? How can we find out?"

Banyon had an idea. He flipped open the cover of the book. There, stamped on the inside cover, was the name of the bookstore where the book had been purchased.

"Check this out," he said with a grin.

Angela read the faded imprint:

**SIRIUS BOOKS & GIFTS
EVERETT, WA**

"Excellent!" she said. "Tomorrow we'll look up the address and pay those folks a visit. Who knows, maybe with a little luck we might even be able to track down our mysterious note writer!"

"Think so? Seems like a long shot."

"But a shot worth taking, don't you think?" The look of excitement on her face was irresistible.

"Absolutely!" he said, dumping his skepticism. "What the hell. What have we got to lose?"

~11~

A black sedan followed closely behind Banyon and Angela as they drove north along State Highway 99 toward the city of Everett in search of the bookstore.

"It should be just up ahead on the right," Angela said as she moved into the right lane.

The highway was lined on both sides with a variety of small business establishments, everything from auto repair shops to hair salons, gas stations, restaurants, supermarkets, and a giant Costco store that took up two blocks.

Banyon looked around. "I've driven by here lots of times and I don't remember ever seeing a bookstore."

"Were you looking for a bookstore?"

He shrugged. "Not really."

"Maybe that's why you didn't see it."

"I suppose."

"Hey!" Angela blurted, suddenly. "There's the sign!"

"Where?"

"Right there. That little hand-painted sign on the light pole!"

He couldn't believe she actually spied the sign. It was just a small hand-painted board attached to a wooden light pole at the entrance to a parking lot where there were several small businesses in one older single-story building. Angela pulled into the lot and they looked for the bookstore.

"There it is," Banyon said, pointing to the last shop at the far end of the building.

Parking was easy since there were no other cars in the spaces in front of the bookstore.

"Not exactly a booming business," Banyon commented.

"That's for sure. Do you have the book with you?"

"Yeah, right here."

"Well," she said, taking a deep breath, "let's see what we can find out."

They didn't notice the black sedan pulling into the lot as they walked toward the entrance to the bookstore.

Once inside they could tell immediately this wasn't exactly your modern Barnes & Noble. The lighting was rather dim, the atmosphere was quiet, and it had the musty yet oddly pleasant smell of an old attic. The inventory was mostly used books and the place had all the look and feel of a mom & pop operation. The tall rows of shelves, made of unpainted wood, were marked according to subject matter with little hand-lettered tags on colored paper.

The sales counter, toward the back of the store, was cluttered with small stacks of advertising flyers from local businesses. A young man in his mid-twenties with shoulder length blond hair was sitting on a stool behind the counter reading one of those supermarket tabloids that carry stories about three headed babies and images of the Virgin Mary on old tree trunks.

"Excuse me," Banyon said, addressing the young man. "I was wondering if you might be able to help us."

The young man looked up. "Hi. What can I do you for you?"

"Well," Banyon hesitated, "this might sound a little strange..."

"Hey," the young man smiled, "I'm reading about a lady who just gave birth to an alien baby with lizard skin. What could be stranger than that?"

Banyon laughed and was relieved to see the fellow at least had a sense of humor. "My name is Zeke Banyon," he said, handing the young man his business card. "And this is my friend, Angela."

The young man acknowledged Angela with a nod.

Banyon handed him Densmore's book. "We came across this book," he explained, "and noticed it was purchased here and - I know it's a long shot - but we wondered if there was any way to find out who might have purchased it from you."

The young man looked at the imprint of the store's name on the inside cover. Then he closed the book, smiled, and gently ran his fingers across the title on the front cover. "Well," he said, looking up over his wire rimmed glasses, "I'm afraid I wouldn't have any record of who bought the book. I mean, you know, we don't ask the name of everybody who buys a book from us."

Banyon sighed. "Damn. We kind of figured that would be the case. Well, thanks anyway."

"No problem," the young man replied. "Sorry I couldn't help."

Banyon and Angela turned to leave but stopped in their tracks when the young man spoke again. "But I can tell you who owned the book originally, if you're interested," he said, offhandedly.

They did an about-face and walked back to the counter.

Banyon looked at him. "Say again?"

"The book," the young man explained. "It belonged to my father."

Angela shook her head. "Your father?"

The young man nodded. "Can I ask why you guys are so interested in this book?"

"Well," Banyon began, but then he hesitated, not exactly sure where to start. "It's kind of a long story. See I run the Seattle Gospel Mission downtown and the man who had the job before me found this book at a flea market. Well, one thing led to another and we were just curious as to who might have owned the book before him."

The young man looked puzzled. "Why?" he asked.

"Um," Banyon started, but Angela abruptly jumped in.

"There was a note folded up inside the book," she explained. "It had information on it that interested us. I'm a student of anthropology and Mr. Banyon studied for the priesthood and..."

The young man laughed. "You guys talk like my father used to talk. He thought he was Indiana Jones or something. Always on the hunt for the next big mystery. Ancient artifacts, old books. You name it. Maybe you've heard of him. His name was Frank McClintock. My name's Jason, by the way."

"Nice to meet you, Jason," Banyon said. "No, I'm afraid we've never heard of your father but he sounds like an interesting man. You said his name *was* Frank McClintock. Past tense. I gather he's no longer alive?"

"Yeah. This was his bookstore. He passed away back in December of 1999 and my sister and I inherited the place. She handles all the bookwork. I just try to keep the place going but, as you can see, we don't get a lot of business. It's pretty tough."

"We're sorry to hear that," Angela said. "So this book belonged to your father?"

"Yeah. He had a whole mess of books like that. Metaphysics, occult, ancient mysteries, stuff like that. I put a lot of his old books out on the shelf for sale after he died. That one you've got there was one of them."

"And the note inside the book," she asked. "Would you know anything about that?"

"Doesn't ring a bell," Jason said, shaking his head. "Do you have it with you?"

Angela reached into her purse and pulled out a piece of paper. "This isn't the original," she said, handing it to him. "It's a photocopy."

Jason took the copy and examined it. "Yup, this is my dad's handwriting, all right."

"Are you sure?" Banyon asked. Several butterflies fluttered inside his stomach.

"Oh yeah, positive," Jason said. He continued to read the note. "This is weird stuff here. What the heck does it mean?" he asked, handing it back to Angela.

"That's what we'd like to know," Banyon said.

Jason pushed his glasses up onto his forehead and smiled. "My dad would have liked you guys. There weren't a lot of people he could talk to about these things."

"I can imagine," Banyon chuckled.

"Would you like to see the rest of his collection?" Jason asked, getting up from the stool behind the counter.

The butterflies fluttered once more inside Banyon's stomach."The rest of his collection?"

Jason motioned for them to come around the counter. Then he opened a door to a back room. "This way," he said.

The back room, dimly lit by a couple of bare light bulbs hanging from the ceiling, was full of books, everywhere, on shelves, on tables, and in boxes. Evidently it was inventory waiting to go out to the front shelves for sale. Jason pointed to an old leather trunk in the shadows under a table.

"This is it," he said, sliding the heavy trunk out for them to see. "This is what I have left." He opened the trunk, exposing the contents. "I sold most of his other books. Just haven't gotten around to these yet."

Banyon and Angela knelt down to take a look. There were some intriguing titles, mostly dealing with ancient mysteries and secret societies.

"Wow," Banyon said, almost in a whisper. Then he turned to

Jason. "Would you mind if we looked through some of these?"

Jason shrugged. "Go ahead. I haven't priced any of them yet but if there's something you want just let me know and we'll work something out. I'll be out front if you need me."

"Great. Thanks," Angela said.

Jason disappeared through the door and resumed his reading out behind the counter.

"Trusting soul, eh?" Banyon quipped.

"No kidding," Angela said as she slowly rummaged through the various titles in the old trunk. "Can you believe our luck? I mean, I can't believe we just stumbled into this!"

"This old trunk's been around awhile, that's for sure," Banyon observed, giving it a visual once-over. Then he noticed the tattered black fabric that lined the inside of the lid was sagging down. He tucked it back up but it refused to stay put.

"Will you forget that?" Angela said, seemingly annoyed. "Help me look through this stuff. Who knows what we might find."

"Wait a minute," Banyon said. He now noticed the fabric was sagging because something behind it was weighting it down. "There's something under this lining." He carefully tugged at the edge of the lining to pull a little portion of it free from the lid. "There's something back behind here," he said, trying to reach it with the tips of his fingers.

"What is it?"

"I don't know."

Finally, without actually ripping the fabric he managed to grasp whatever it was with two fingers and slid it out.

It was a large old brown paper envelope. He turned it over and back again, looking for some indication of what it might contain. But there was no writing on it. It was sealed only by a small copper clasp. He looked at Angela. "Should I?"

She shrugged but the look in her eyes said, *yes*. A large, unmarked envelope in an old chest full of esoteric books in the shadows of a back room of a used-book store was just too tempting to be ignored.

Banyon opened it and pulled out a wrinkled sheet of parchment, yellowed with age. He maneuvered it out of the shadows into a slightly better light. They both looked at it and then at each other, wide-eyed, as they realized what they had.

"Oh my god," Angela gasped. "That's it. The Ezekiel Code!"

"Find something interesting?" Jason asked, suddenly appearing behind them in the doorway.

Startled, and still kneeling next to the old chest, Banyon and Angela turned to face him.

"Um..." Banyon stammered. "Yes, actually. Well maybe. We're not sure. I wonder if..."

"Whatever it is you can have it," Jason said. "Just be careful."

"Careful?" Angela asked. "What do you mean?"

Jason took a couple steps toward them. "I mean I think whatever you have there might be what caused my father's death."

Angela and Banyon stood up slowly, shocked by what Jason was saying.

"What are you talking about?" Banyon asked.

"My dad was killed in a hit and run right out here on the street. They never found who did it."

A look of genuine sympathy crossed Angela's face. "I'm so sorry," she said. "You mean you think it was intentional and not an accident?"

Jason shook his head. "I don't think it was any accident. A similar incident happened to him downtown in Seattle just a week earlier but that time he managed to jump out of the way."

"Could've been just a coincidence," Banyon suggested.

"I don't think so," Jason countered. "Dad was pretty excited those last couple of weeks. Said he was close to discovering some big secret or something. I didn't pay much attention really because I'd heard him say things like that any number of times. Like I said, he fancied himself some kind of an Indiana Jones and there was always the next big mystery to go after. But he started getting some weird phone calls just a few days before he was killed."

"What kind of phone calls?" Banyon asked.

"Some guy. I don't know who it was. A couple times I took the call and the guy asked if Frank was in. Both times Dad happened to be out and I told the guy he wasn't here. I asked if I could take a message and the guy just hung up. Kind of sounded like he had an Italian accent or something. I don't know. It was just strange. One time, though, Dad was here and he took the call and I don't know what the guy said but Dad seemed pretty weirded out about it."

"How do you mean?" Banyon asked.

"I don't know. Just sort of on edge I guess you might say. I asked him what was wrong but he didn't want to talk about it."

"Did you tell all this to the police?" Angela asked.

"Yeah, I told 'em. But what could they do?"

"I see," Banyon said, somewhat at a loss for words.

"So anyway," Jason went on, "that's what I meant about being careful. I don't know what it is you found there and I don't think I want to know. Maybe it's nothing. But if it has anything to do with whatever dad was into those last few weeks then you're welcome to it. I'd just as soon not have it around here. I wasn't born with the same sense of adventure that my dad had. If you know what I mean."

Banyon and Angela looked at each other wondering what they'd gotten themselves into.

Feeling a bit awkward, Banyon cleared his throat. "I don't know what to say. That's quite a story. But I guess we will take this envelope then if that's what you want."

"Be my guest," Jason said. "In fact, why don't you just take the trunk and everything that's in it with my blessing."

That took Banyon by surprise. "You mean...? But, how much do you want for it?"

"Just take it. I'd as soon just be rid of it, really."

"No," Angela said. "We couldn't do that. After all..."

"Really," Jason said, firmly. "Just take it. I have a gut feeling my dad would want you to have it. Sounds kinda crazy I guess but if you knew my dad like I did..." He left the thought hanging.

"Thank you," Banyon said. "We appreciate it."

Jason nodded."I have to get back out front. I just heard a customer come in the door. Can the two of you get the trunk?"

"We can get it," Banyon said.

Jason turned and went to tend to the customer.

Banyon looked at Angela. "Wow," he said in a hushed tone. "What the heck have we stumbled into?"

"Something that might get us killed is my guess."

"Let's hope not. I'm guessing Jason's father probably hadn't yet found the scroll. But he was probably close to figuring it out."

"Yeah. Too close, apparently."

"I don't know. That whole hit and run thing still could have just been a coincidence, you know."

"Uh huh," Angela said, skeptically. "There sure have been a lot of coincidences the last few weeks."

"So you think we should just drop the whole thing?" Banyon asked. "Give up the chase? Hey, you're the one who said you were always up for a good mystery!"

Angela stared at Banyon for several seconds without saying anything.

"Well?" he prompted her for a response.

"I don't know," she said, finally. "Let's just get this trunk into the car and worry about it later."

"Amen to that," Banyon agreed. "Let's get the hell out of here."

They each picked up an end of the trunk and made their way through the back room door. They navigated around the sales counter and headed toward the front door. Jason was placing some books on a shelf. He turned and nodded his head as if to say goodbye – and good luck.

When they reached the front door they found it blocked by a tall dark man in a black trench coat. He stood there for a moment and then slowly stepped aside. Angela threw a quick glance at Banyon. Banyon put his shoulder to the door and pushed it open. Once outside, they managed to get the trunk into the back seat of the car and they drove away without wasting any time.

The black sedan followed just a few cars behind.

~12~

B ack at the Seattle Gospel Mission, Banyon and Angela were met at the front door by Old Tom.

"Movin' in?" Old Tom asked, holding the door open for them as they maneuvered the heavy trunk inside.

"What?" Banyon asked, nearly out of breath.

"The trunk! Looks like yer movin' in."

"Oh this?" Banyon grinned, trying to sound nonchalant. "No. Just some old stuff to go through."

"Looks heavy."

"You have no idea," Angela spoke up, straining to keep from dropping her end.

Tom moved forward. "Need some help with it?"

Banyon shook his head. "No thanks, Tom. We got it."

They made their way down the hall toward Banyon's office. The phone rang just as they got in through the door. They set the trunk on the floor and shoved it over next to the desk. Banyon paused a moment to catch a breath before answering the phone. "Seattle Gospel Mission. Can I help you?"

"Ezekiel Banyon?" the man on the other end of the line inquired.

"That would be me," Banyon said. "What can I do for you?"

"My name's Kline. Doctor Alan Kline. I'm a professor of Sociology at the Shorewood Community College. I got your number from Jason McClintock. He called me a few minutes ago."

"Jason?" Banyon asked, a bit surprised. "From the bookstore?"

"Yes. I was a close friend of his father, Frank McClintock."

"Oh?"

"We need to talk."

"I'm listening," Banyon said, now intrigued.

"Not on the phone. Could we meet somewhere?"

"What's this about?"

"Information."

"What sort of information?"

"I think you know."

Banyon hesitated for a moment, glancing over at Angela. "Okay," he said. "Where would you like to meet?"

"My office at the college. It's in the Foster building on the campus, across from the administration building. We can talk there without being disturbed."

"All right. When?"

"This evening? Say around seven-thirty?"

"We can do that."

"Good. When you come in the front door just take the stairs to the second floor. My office is down the hall to your left at the top of the stairs. You'll see my name on the door. Alan Kline."

"Top of the stairs and to the left. Got it."

"All right," Kline said. "About seven-thirty then."

"About seven-thirty. We'll be there."

Banyon hung up the phone and leaned back in his chair with a look on his face that Angela couldn't quite read.

"Okay, I give up," she said. "What the heck was that all about and where are we going?"

"That was some guy named Kline. A professor at Shorewood Community College. Says he got my number from Jason back at the bookstore. Apparently Jason called him just after we left."

"What's he want?"

"Says he was a friend of Jason's father. He wants to meet with us. Tonight. Seven-thirty."

"What for?"

"I don't know. He just said he had information."

"Information about what?"

"Whatever it is he didn't seem to want to talk about it over the phone. It's got to be something to do with what we found in the trunk."

"How do we know this guy is who he says he is?" Angela asked, recalling the fate of Jason's dad.

"Yeah, you're right," Banyon said after thinking about it for a moment. "We could call Jason and ask him."

"Good idea," Angela agreed. She got the phone directory and handed it to him.

Banyon looked up the number and made the call. "No answer," he said. He looked at his watch. "It's after five."

Angela nodded. "Maybe he's closed up and gone home."

"Yeah. Well, look, if you don't want to go with me to see this Kline fellow, that's okay. But I'm going to take a chance. The guy sounded on the level. And it's at the college. There'll be people around. I mean what could happen?"

Angela lit up a cigarette and sat in the chair across from Banyon's desk. She looked at him without saying anything. After a few moments she got up and paced back and forth. *I do like a good mystery as much as the next guy*, she argued with herself. *But I also like staying alive.* Finally she walked over and kicked the side of the trunk. "Damn it," she said. "All right, I'll go with you."

Banyon had to chuckle at her little burst of attitude. This was a peek at a side of her he hadn't seen before. "You sure?" he asked.

"No, but I'll go anyway and hope to God you're right about this guy."

Banyon smiled. "I really don't think there's anything to worry about."

"Yeah. Famous last words," she came back, still not entirely comfortable with the idea.

Banyon pushed himself back from his desk, reached into the drawer, unlocked a small metal box and pulled out a handgun.

"Would this make you feel any safer?" he asked.

"What the...?" Angela started. "Where did you get that? What the hell are you doing with a pistol?"

"I've had it for a while," he said, squinting one eye as he slowly aimed the pistol at the coffee pot. "Just seemed like a good idea, seeing as how this isn't exactly the safest part of town. I mean, you never know."

"Okay, Wyatt Earp, you can put it away now. I hate guns."

"So you don't want me to bring it?"

"All right," she relented with a heavy sigh. "Go ahead. Bring it." She crushed out her cigarette and shook her head. "I can't believe this is happening. This is all completely nuts, you know."

"Yes," he replied, leaning over the desk and reaching out to hold her hand. "But have you ever had such a good time?"

"Oh yeah," she said. "You've got a gun in your hand, we're about to go visit some strange man who calls us out of the blue, claiming to be a friend of a guy who somehow ended up with an ancient manuscript and who then got an unpleasant phone call from some guy with an Italian accent and then turned around and got run over by a car and died. Yeah, I can't recall ever having had such a good time."

Banyon laughed. "Well all righty then!" he said, getting up to make a pot of coffee. "Let the good times roll!"

The only thing Angela rolled was her eyes, wondering what she'd gotten herself into. *It'll be okay,* she tried to convince herself. *If anyone tries to get us Zeke will pull out his gun and blow their brains out.* The very thought made her laugh. Not because it was funny but because it was all just so absurd. *I only came here looking for a part-*

time job. Now I'm chasing down ancient manuscripts with a guy who thinks he's Wyatt Earp. What the hell could be next?

~13~

B anyon glanced over at Angela as they drove into the parking lot of the Shorewood Community College. "See? I told you," he said. "Look at all the cars here. Night classes. There's going be people all over the campus. Nothing to worry about. Except for a little rain."

Angela looked around, surveying the area. "All right. So far, so good."

After parking the car they walked toward the campus, huddling under Angela's umbrella.

"So how do we find the Foster building?" Angela wondered.

Banyon noticed a student sitting on a sheltered bench near the paved walkway. "Let's ask that guy over there."

"Excuse me," Banyon addressed the student. "Can you point us to the Foster building?"

The student pointed toward an older building surrounded by large trees. "See that building over there? That's the administration building. The Foster building is right behind it."

"Thanks," Banyon said.

Once under the sheltered entrance to the Foster building Angela shook the rain off her umbrella and closed it up. They entered the brightly lit building, took the stairs to the second floor and walked down the hall as Kline had instructed. The hall was lined with faculty offices. They read the nameplates on the doors as they strolled along.

"Here it is," Angela said. "Dr. Alan Kline."

Banyon rapped lightly on the door. Almost immediately the door opened and they were greeted by a short, middle-aged man with thick, wirey hair, and a salt-and-pepper beard. His wrinkled tweed blazer was about a size too big and his round-rimmed glasses were about twenty years out of style.

"Yes?" said the professor, looking up over the top of his glasses.

"Professor Kline?" Banyon asked.

"Yes."

"I'm Zeke Banyon and this is my friend, Angela."

"Ah!" the professor said, gesturing for them to come in. "Glad you could make it. Please, have a seat."

The office was subtly lit by a vintage floorlamp in the corner. The large yellowed lampshade produced a warm glow about the room. The sweet fragrance of recently smoked pipe tobacco filled the air. The place was cluttered with books and an odd assortment of small antique items like ornate wooden keepsake boxes, a couple of urns that looked possibly Egyptian, some Chinese figurines and various other little gems of interest.

Banyon and Angela made themselves comfortable on the small brown sofa across from the professor's desk.

"Miserable damp weather" the professor commented. "Can I get you some coffee? I've got the hot water going. Just instant coffee, mind you. But not bad if you spike it with a little whiskey."

"Thanks, yes," Banyon said. "Coffee sounds good. Just black, please. I'll forego the whiskey."

"Oh, you don't know what you're missing," smiled the professor. "And you, young lady?"

"Same for me," Angela replied.

While the professor prepared the coffee, Banyon scanned the titles on the bookshelf that took up most of the wall behind Kline's desk. As one would expect, the books all seemed to pertain to various areas of research in the social sciences. Then he noticed a small section of books near the far end of the shelf close to the door. He couldn't quite make out all of the titles on the spines from where he sat but clearly the letters, *UFO*, were plain to see on a couple of them. He nudged Angela with his elbow and nodded toward those books. She squinted to see what he was trying to point out.

"What?" she whispered.

Banyon silently formed the letters, *U-F-O*, with his lips and nodded in that direction again. When she caught on she raised an eyebrow and tried to hide a grin.

"Here you go," said the professor, handing them each a hot cup of coffee. He then poured himself a cup and punched it up with a drop of Jack Daniels. "Well," he said as he seated himself in the old leather chair behind his desk, "I suppose you're wondering why I wanted to meet with you."

"Information, you said," Banyon answered.

Professor Kline removed his glasses, took a deep breath, and stared into his coffee cup. "Yes. Information. Question is, where to begin?"

"Maybe you could begin at the beginning," Angela suggested.

The professor laughed. "Yes. That would be ideal. Trouble is, I don't really know where that is."

Banyon jumped in. "Obviously this must be about what we found in the trunk at the bookstore."

"That and more, yes," Kline responded. "Frank McClintock and I were close friends for many years. Frank had what you might call a passionate obsession with ancient mysteries and secret societies and that sort of thing. When he first started getting into this line of research some years ago I used to think he was going off the deep end. I had to admit some of the stuff he was telling me was amusing, sometimes downright intriguing, but I brushed it off on most accounts. I mean, you know, he started sounding like one of those conspiracy nuts. I even used him, not by name of course, but as a model in one of my classes on belief systems."

"So you thought he was just crazy?" Banyon asked.

Kline chuckled. "Well, not really crazy. Frank was, for all of his wild ideas, actually pretty much a down to earth sort of fellow. To tell you the truth, I kind of envied his open mind. Those of us trained in the sciences often get a little too attached to convention and tend to develop a bit of tunnel vision, if you know what I mean."

Angela looked puzzled. "I thought scientists were supposed to be open minded," she said. "The search for knowledge, whatever it leads to, and all that."

"Well, you would think so," Kline said. "And most of us start out that way. But science, any branch of science, relies heavily on a disciplined approach to the questions being asked. But sometimes we get stuck in the rigors and demands of the so-called scientific method and what starts out as an open mind soon becomes trapped inside the walls of the discipline itself."

"I think I know what you're getting at," Banyon said.

"Anyway," the professor continued, "one night, about three years ago, as I was driving home, I noticed something unusual in the sky."

"What was it?" Angela asked.

"Well, at first it just looked like three red lights in a triangular formation and I thought it must be three low flying planes. But as they got closer I could tell it wasn't three separate planes at all. The three lights seemed to be attached to just one plane. Or, at least I assumed it was a plane. But I also noticed it was flying remarkably slow. Not to mention how low it was. Practically tree top level. Maybe a little higher, but not by much. Pretty soon I could almost see the shape of the craft and I was a bit confused."

"Confused?" Banyon asked.

"Yes, because it wasn't a plane. I didn't know *what* it was but I knew it wasn't a plane. I'd never seen anything like it."

Angela was intrigued. "What'd it look like?"

"It was just a huge black or dark colored triangle. And I mean really huge. It must have been the size of a football field."

"A football field?" Banyon asked, trying to imagine what that would be like. "That'd be what? Three-hundred feet? Are you sure?"

"As sure as I'm sitting here." Kline said. "I pulled the car over to the side of the road and got out to have a good look. It just silently cruised right over me and off into the horizon."

"Silently? Are you saying it didn't make *any* sound?"

The professor shook his head. "That's right. No sound. Nothing. Nada."

"That's very strange," Banyon said. "Something that big, that low. You should have heard something!"

Kline laughed. "Strange? Ha! It was damned *weird* is what it was! I was stunned, to tell you the truth. I got back into the car and drove straight home wondering what the hell I'd just seen." He shook his head, again staring into his coffee cup, remembering the sight as if it happened just yesterday. "Anyway," he continued, "when I got home I jumped on the internet to see if there were any other reports of these triangular UFOs. Turns out there had been hundreds of reports of this same type of object – from various locations around the country – over the past year or two. Then I learned that some attorney in Arizona – Peter Gersten, I believe was his name - had even gathered up a couple dozen affidavits from people who had seen these things and he took the Department of Defense into court to try and get the court to force them to release any information they had about these big mysterious flying triangles."

"Something like that actually got to court?" Banyon asked, quite astounded by the idea.

"It did. Absolutely," Kline affirmed.

"What was the outcome?" Angela asked.

"Well, for a while it was looking pretty good. The judge actually found in favor of the argument that this attorney, Gersten, presented."

"Must have been a pretty good argument to get a federal judge to go along with it," Banyon commented. "What the heck did he present as evidence?"

"He had those sworn affidavits. And he argued that if such an airborne craft was flying at such low altitudes over major cities all over the country - in fact, all over the world - *NORAD* would have to have some kind of information about them. Certainly, if these things were ours, built by us, then the Department of Defense would know about them. And if they weren't ours, or anyone else's on this planet, they'd still have to have some sort of information about them even if they didn't know what they were. After all, that's what *NORAD*'s job is, you know."

"What is *no-rad*?" Angela asked.

"N-O-R-A-D" Kline said, spelling out the individual letters of the acronym. "It stands for North American Aerospace Defense. Or something like that. It's a top security command center where they have all this high-tech surveillance equipment to track everything that enters our air space, twenty-four-seven."

"So, what happened?" Angela asked again.

"To make a long story short, the court ordered the Department of Defense to run a check through their files for any and all information they might have about these flying triangles. But they came back claiming they had no information."

"Nothing?"

"So they claimed. And this time the Judge decided that was the end of it. Gersten later found out that the Department of Defense didn't actually conduct the search using the search parameters that they were supposed to be using with regard to the sort of details they were to be looking for. So Gersten filed for an appeal but it was turned down."

"That's amazing," Banyon said. "It's amazing that something like that didn't get any news coverage. I mean, I never heard anything about it."

"Exactly," the professor said. "And that's what turned me around and opened my eyes."

"What do you mean?" Angela asked.

"Well, I've come to suspect that the mainstream news is all packaged and controlled at some high level and things like this rarely, if ever, get reported. And when they do get reported it's usually with a smirk and a grin at the end of the news broadcast as a kind of light-hearted joke not to be taken too seriously."

"Now that you mention it," Angela said, "I have noticed that is the way they handle those stories. So are you saying there's actually some kind of a conspiracy of silence on stuff like that?"

"More like a conspiracy of ridicule," Kline said. "I found documented proof that a government panel was convened back in the late 1950s in which the decision was made to implement a policy whereby the whole subject of UFOs was to be ridiculed in every way possible. It was called the Robertson Panel, if I remember correctly. They definitely had an agenda to keep all of that information to themselves and to make it seem like such nonsense that the general public would be inclined to think likewise."

"And this is all true? It can be verified?" Angela asked.

Kline nodded. "Not only is it true but it's just the tip of the proverbial iceberg."

"But what's all this UFO stuff have to do with us or with the..." Angela started.

"The Ezekiel Code?" Kline finished her sentence for her. "I have to assume you had some sort of information that eventually led you to Frank McClintock's bookstore. Am I right?"

Angela gave a little smile. "You can say that again. It's been a wild ride."

"Then you must know the legend behind the lost scroll of Ezekiel."

"We do, yes," Banyon said.

"Oh!" Angela said suddenly. "I think I get the connection to the UFO stuff. The machine! Ezekiel's machine! The craft of some kind!"

Kline nodded. "Machine, craft, UFO. Call it what you will. The thing is, from my research, it seems our little planet here has been visited by some other intelligence, at least periodically, for thousands, maybe millions of years."

"You actually believe this?" Banyon asked, somewhat surprised.

Kline leaned back in his chair. "I know," he said. "It's hard to believe a college professor, a man of science, could make such a statement with a straight face. As you might imagine, I don't discuss any of this with my colleagues. But I know what I saw in the sky that night and from the research I've done, looking into this whole subject, I can honestly say it appears something very strange has been going on for a long time. Oh, there are the hoaxes, the phony photographs, the charlatans and the crackpots all right. But once you wind your way through all that, and weed out the junk, there's compelling evidence to suggest all is not what it seems. I'm now convinced there's something that we, as a human race on this planet, have been missing. Or maybe I should say we've been misled."

"Misled?" Angela asked. "By whom? That Robertson Panel you told us about?"

Kline laughed. "Well, yes. But, in a sense, that's small potatoes. The Robertson Panel was just one small piece of a much bigger picture."

"And what is the bigger picture?"

"That's not easy to say," Kline replied. "And this gets to the heart of the matter."

"You mean the reason you wanted to meet with us?" Banyon asked.

"Exactly. This is going to sound like something from the mind of a conspiracy nut but the fact is you're being watched."

"Watched?" Angela said, surprised. "Who's watching us? What are you talking about?"

The professor gave her the one answer she really didn't want to hear. "By the same people who murdered Frank," he said.

"So you don't think it was just an accident?"

Kline shook his head. "I seriously doubt it."

"But who?" Angela asked. "And why?"

The professor reached for his pipe and filled it with tobacco from a small black pouch. "Do you mind?" he asked, nodding toward his pipe.

"Not at all," Banyon said, reaching into his own pocket for his pack of cigarettes.

"More coffee?" Kline offered, as he got up to pour himself another cup.

Banyon nodded."Yes, thank you."

"You could warm mine up," Angela said, handing her cup to the professor. The conversation was making her nervous and for a moment she considered taking him up on the whiskey spike but then decided against it.

Kline filled their cups and resumed the conversation. "It all has to do with that bigger picture you asked about, Angela. The bigger picture is hard to figure out because so many of the pieces have been kept from us by a long line of secret societies - and even some not-so-secret societies - but which, nevertheless, have ties to those in the shadows, shall we say."

"And you think one of these secret societies is responsible for Frank McClintock's death?" Banyon asked.

Kline nodded. "I'm sure of it."

Banyon took a sip of his coffee and considered what the professor was saying. "Just how much do you know about what McClintock discovered?"

"Just about everything, I think," Kline replied without hesitation. "We had long talks about it. About this whole Ezekiel thing, I mean. In fact it was the last thing we did talk about the night before he was killed back in December of '99. He'd just returned from a trip to France where he managed to acquire that damned parchment."

Kline proceeded to tell them the story about the French researcher, Jacques de Pereille, whom McClintock had spoken with in a cafe one day and then found the same man dead from a gunshot wound to the head the following day.

Banyon and Angela were surprised and stunned by the gruesome tale.

"So then why haven't they come after you, too?" Banyon asked.

"Because I don't have the parchment," Kline replied. "I could talk about this Ezekiel code thing to anyone, blab about it as much as I want, but it all sounds so preposterous no one would believe me. And without the manuscript to show as hard evidence... well, I'd be considered just one more crackpot with a nutty idea."

"Jesus," Angela said, nervously. "That manuscript! We *do* have it!"

"My point exactly," Kline said.

"Just how much danger are we in?" Banyon asked. "I mean, assuming all this is true."

"Probably not much actually," was Kline's rather surprising answer.

"But," Angela protested, a bit confused, "I got the impression you were warning us that our lives were in danger."

"I said you're being watched," Kline replied. "And you are. But there's something you don't know."

"What do you mean?"

The professor looked at his watch. "It's getting late and I still have some last minute preparations to make for tomorrow's lecture. I've given you a lot to digest this evening. If you can come back tomorrow night we can continue our conversation. There's much more to tell."

"But," Angela said, preferring not to be left hanging, "what is it we don't know?"

"Please," Kline said, getting up from his chair and walking toward the door. "Tomorrow night will be soon enough. I didn't mean for any of this to frighten you. I just wanted you to know something about the background of this whole affair."

Banyon and Angela got up and shook the professor's hand.

"All right," Banyon said. "We'll be here. What time?"

"Same time would be good," Kline said, opening the door for them.

It was raining harder now. Huddling arm-in-arm under the umbrella, Banyon and Angela hurried the short distance across the campus and into the welcomed shelter of the car. Angela was shivering.

Banyon put his hand on her arm. "Are you all right?"

"Yeah, I guess."

He started the car and looked over at his shivering passenger. She was wrapping her arms around herself trying to warm up.

"You want to stay the night at my place?" he asked. As soon as the words came out of his mouth he wondered if he should have said it. At this point in their relationship he'd never so much as kissed her although he'd considered it about a dozen times. *Now*, he thought to himself, *I'm asking her to spend the night? I'm an idiot.*

"I have a class tomorrow," she said.

Banyon took that to mean no and wished he hadn't brought it up.

"You'll have to drive me to school on your way to work."

Banyon looked confused. "What?"

"In the morning," she said. "You'll have to drive me to school."

"Oh. Sure. I could probably be talked into that," he said. Then he smiled to himself. *I guess even idiots get lucky once in a while.*

"Okay," she said. "But I'll sleep on the couch."

He nodded. *Well*, he thought to himself, *maybe not that lucky.*

~14~

Banyon's home was a two-story brick house overlooking a small lake situated in the middle of a quaint older neighborhood at the north end of Seattle.

As they entered the front door, Banyon switched on a light and took Angela's coat.

"Hey, this is nice. I like it a lot," she said, taking her first look around.

"Well," he said, hanging their coats on the coat rack next to the door, "like they say, it's not much, but it's home."

The living room had a warmth to it that made Angela feel comfortable right away. The walls were a light shade of tan. The doorways and windows were trimmed in heavy, dark wood and the hardwood floor was covered with a large, and probably very expensive, oriental carpet of mostly brown and ochre tones. A brown leather couch and matching love seat were situated almost in the center of the room, facing a rather ornately carved coffee table that she was certain must be an antique. A long bookshelf, with surprisingly few books, covered one wall. On the opposite wall was a large picture window framed with dark gold pleated drapes and a matching valance.

"In the day time you can see the lake from that window," Banyon told her.

"Ah," she said. "The perfect view of bikini clad girls in the summer, I suppose!"

Banyon laughed. "Oh, I wouldn't notice anything like that!"

"Oh, of course not!" she chided.

"Something to drink?" he asked.

"Sure."

"I have a nice red wine just waiting to be opened."

"Sounds good to me."

"Great. Sit down and make yourself comfortable."

Angela took a seat on the couch and shuffled through the magazines scattered across the coffee table. Amongst the copies of *Newsweek* and *Time* there were a few issues of *Science Today*. An odd choice, she thought, for a man who until recently had never even touched a computer.

Banyon returned in a few minutes with two glasses of wine and a plate of crackers and sliced cheese. He sat down next to her.

"You read *Science Today*?" she asked.

"Mostly I just look at the pictures," he said with a wink.

"That figures."

"Actually," Banyon continued, "I like it because they always have the latest theories on the creation of the universe. You know, the Big Bang, and all that."

Angela reached for her glass of wine. "I've always wondered what was before the Big Bang."

Banyon laughed. "Exactly! That is the question isn't it?"

"So, as one who used to be a priest, do you subscribe to the Big Bang theory? Is all of this just one big accident?"

"Well, I'm no scientist, and I barely understand half of what those articles have to say, but it does look like the Big Bang believers have some good evidence to support that theory."

"I guess so. Still, it is just a theory. It hasn't ever been proven beyond the shadow of a doubt, has it?"

"It doesn't seem so, no. But even if the universe did come into being with a bang I don't think that necessarily puts God out of the picture. I mean, hey, maybe God's the one who lit the fuse."

Angela laughed. "So that would be the answer to my question of what was before the Big Bang! It was God playing with a really big stick of dynamite!"

"I guess anything's possible," he said with a smile, holding his glass up for a toast. "So here's to anything possible."

"I'll drink to that," she said, clinking her glass against his.

Banyon prepared a cracker with a slice of cheese and handed it to her. "So," he asked, "what'd you think of our new friend, professor Kline?"

Angela took a bite of the cracker and thought for a moment. "Well, to tell you the truth, that whole story freaked me out. That business about the French guy getting murdered and us being watched and all. I mean, come on. Didn't you think that was a little scary?"

"Yeah, it was a little unnerving all right."

"A *little* unnerving?"

"Okay," Banyon confessed, "a lot unnerving."

Angela slowly swirled the wine around in her glass for a moment and then looked directly at Banyon. "Do you think we're in danger?"

Banyon lit up a cigarette and sat back in the couch. He had to admit that the information from Kline did put a whole new light on the situation.

"Well?" she prodded.

"I don't know. Maybe not. Kline did say he didn't think we were in the same kind of danger that McClintock was in."

"Yeah, but he didn't exactly say why."

"I know. Apparently that's what he's going to explain to us tomorrow night."

For the next couple of hours they rehashed the conversation they'd had with the professor. They went round and round trying to put together the many pieces of the strange mystery they had so innocently stumbled into. But there were too many unanswered questions and the bigger picture, as Kline put it, didn't seem to be coming into focus.

After a while, and having had a couple more glasses of wine, Angela found herself getting sleepy. "All I know right now," she said, "is I'm tired and it's really late and I have an early class in the morning."

She got up and walked over to the window and stood looking out into the rainy night. She could see a few house lights in the distance, reflecting on the surface of the lake just a couple blocks away. Banyon came and stood beside her, putting his arm around her shoulder. For a moment neither of them said a word. The only sound in the house was the slow tick...tock of the clock on the wall. Banyon felt closer to her than ever and he couldn't help wondering if she felt the same. He thought back to the day they met in his office and how often he'd tried to push aside the feelings he knew he was having for her. And now, much to his own surprise, here she was in his home. He desperately wanted to tell her what he was feeling but he wasn't sure how to do it or even if he should. So he came up with an alternative.

"You're the only woman who's been here since my wife passed away," he said quietly, staring out the window.

Angela didn't know what to say. The moment was at once awkward and yet surprisingly comfortable. The heaviness of the conversation just a few minutes ago now seemed somehow almost non-existent. She moved slightly and he wondered if she would pull away. But she put her arm around his waist and looked up at him, smiling. "This is nice," she whispered.

In the next moment the warm embrace became a first gentle kiss and several hours later, when the first light of morning shone through the bedroom window, they were sleeping comfortably in each other's arms.

Suddenly the soft buzz of the alarm clock on Banyon's nightstand awakened them to a new day and a new relationship.

"Ohhh," Angela moaned, half asleep, "turn it off. I hate alarm clocks."

Banyon smiled, kissed her on the forehead and got up to take a shower. "Come on, sleepy head," he said, as he disappeared into the bathroom. From the other side of the door he spoke loud enough for her to hear. "You have school, remember?"

When he returned to the bedroom Angela was still comfortably curled up under the covers. *They always look so cute when they're sleeping*, he grinned to himself. He walked over to the bed and lifted her limp arm and let it flop, lifelessly, back down onto the pillow. "Are you dead or alive?" he asked.

With her face stuffed into the pillow he could hear her muffled reply: "Dead. Call a mortician."

"Come on," he said, handing her a clean towel. "The sun's out. It quit raining and, hey, this is the first day of the rest of your life!"

"Oh, puh-leese," she moaned. "I hate that."

"Oh good!" he laughed. "If you don't get up I'll keep saying it!"

"All right, all right," she groaned, finally giving in. "I'm getting up."

Banyon headed down the stairs to make some coffee while Angela forced herself to get up and take a shower.

When she came down stairs Banyon was sitting at the kitchen table with a cup of coffee and a cigarette. She walked up behind him and put her arms around his shoulders.

"Zeke?"

"Yeah?"

"Nothing."

"What is it?"

"I don't know."

He knew what was on her mind. It was the same thing he had wondered a half dozen times during the night. He turned, looking up at her. "Regrets?" he asked.

"Not really," she said softly. "I just wonder..."

"If we did the right thing?"

"Yeah."

He got up and walked over to the kitchen counter and poured her a cup of coffee. "All I know is we did what seemed right at the time," he said. "I'm not sorry."

"Yeah," she said. "Me neither. It's just that..." she paused for a moment. "I don't know. I guess it's just that everything seems different now. You and me, I mean."

"Different how?" he asked. "Different bad?"

"Oh! No, I don't mean that. Just different. Come on, you know what I mean."

"Yeah, I know what you mean. But, hey, let's not analyze it to pieces," he chuckled. "Oh for Christ's sake, listen to us. We sound like high school kids."

Angela laughed sheepishly. "Yeah, I guess we do."

"I say let's just go with the flow, baby!" he said with a swoosh of the hand.

"Oh, yeah," she laughed. "Like you would know about going with the flow! You're the one who was still stuck back in the Middle Ages with no computer before I came along! And you're talking about the flow? You didn't even know what the yin-yang symbol was. I mean, come on!"

"That's right!" he said. "See what you've done for me? I'm in the groove now, baby!"

Angela rolled her eyes. "Yeah, you may be in the groove but some of your groove is still back in the sixties, I think."

"Maybe," he said. "But at the current rate of progress I should be moving into the seventies in a week or so, don't you think? Pretty soon I'll be as hep as you are!"

"Hip."

"What?"

"It's hip, not hep. Hep was back in the 'fifties. God, you're further behind than I thought you were!"

"But I show promise, no?"

She laughed. "We'll see."

"Oh, man," he said, checking his watch. "We have to get going."

"With the flow?" she grinned.

"Yeah. But the flow's going to move on without us if we don't get out of here. Come on, let's go."

They grabbed their coats and headed out to the car. Banyon opened the door for Angela and she stopped for a moment before getting in. She grabbed his hand. "I'm not sorry," she said, looking up at him.

"Get in," he smiled, giving her a nudge. "You're going be late for school. And I don't want to have to come bail you out of the principal's office."

~15~

B anyon put on a pot of coffee, pulled the old parchment – the so-called Ezekiel Code - out of his briefcase and settled down at his desk. He was anxious to have a close look at this new piece of the puzzle. He hoped it could be the key to unlocking a mystery that so many people had tried for so many years to solve. Still, he couldn't escape the nagging thought that this could be nothing more than an elaborate hoax created by God-knows-who. But he was inclined to think that probably wasn't the case. It didn't seem likely, considering that this Ezekiel Code was apparently the reason at least two men had been murdered. First there was the French guy that McClintock found dead in the guy's house. Then McClintock, himself, turned up dead. *Hell, maybe even poor old Patrick Densmore had been killed over this thing.* A chill ran down his back as that thought crossed his mind. He relaxed a bit when he remembered professor Kline's words that the same was not likely to happen to them for reasons yet to be revealed. Apparently he and Angela would learn about that tonight.

Lighting up a cigarette, Banyon stared at the parchment. It contained nothing but a long list of enigmatic phrases, none of which seemed to make any coherent sense. Clearly, from all he and Angela had discovered so far, the key to deciphering whatever message might be here was in the alphanumeric values of these words and phrases. As he read through the list he recognized some of the phrases. They were the same ones McClintock had worked with in the notes that were found folded up in the book they had acquired from Mrs. Densmore.

He unfolded the paper containing the McClintock notes and laid it beside the parchment to make a comparison. The first thing he noticed was that there were many phrases on the parchment that were *not* included in McClintock's notes. This puzzled him for a moment but he finally decided maybe McClintock had other notes that didn't happen to get left inside the pages of the book. He also noticed the opposite was true, that some of the words and phrases in the McClintock notes were not in the list of words and phrases on the parchment. He wondered if maybe there was a missing page to the parchment. Then he realized McClintock had written some phrases entirely in upper case letters and some in lower case letters. Closer examination revealed that the phrases written in lower case were the very ones that were missing from the parchment. He couldn't figure out what that might mean, or if it meant anything at all. *But,* he thought to himself, *nothing here makes much sense at this point anyway. Obviously the first thing to do is to figure out the alphanumeric values of these strange words and phrases and go from there.*

After several minutes of punching numbers into his calculator he sat back to examine the results:

ISIS PENTAGRAM = 151
ONE HUNDRED FEET EAST = 189
FORTY FOUR = 144
THE MIDDLE IS A FIVE = 151
ONE HUNDRED FEET = 144
THE QUEEN OF HEAVEN = 171
ONE HUNDRED FORTY FOUR FEET = 288
THE EDGE OF THE CLIFF = 144
SOUTH OF FRANCE = 151
ONE HUNDRED FORTY FOUR FEET EAST OF THE HEAD = 405
COMMUNICATE = 117
NEGATIVE DARK = 117
ELEVEN DIVIDED BY FIVE = 189
FORTY FOUR FEET SOUTH OF THE MARK = 360
NINE LIGHTS = 117
THE WHEEL OF EZEKIEL = 180
SIRIUS + ISIS = 151
FORTY FOUR FEET = 180
THE WHEEL OF SOUND = *180*
HEAVENLY MOTHER = 171
KING OF HEAVEN = 117
THE THREE TONES = 162
ONE TWO SIX = 144
REVERSE THE NUMBER = 198
THE CIRCLE OF CHURCHES = 189
REVERSE DIRECTION = 198
EAST OF THE HEAD =117
THE WHEEL SPINS IN TWO DIRECTIONS = 360
RENNES LE CHATEAU = 151
THE GREAT PYRAMID OF GIZA = 234
SPEED OF LIGHT = 126

JESUS CHRIST = 151
STAR OF ISIS = 135
THE HEAD IS THE KEY= 153
DIVINE GEOMETRY = 171
THE KEY OF ISIS = 151
NINE IS THE KEY = 144
THE ALPHANUMBER = 144
ONE HUNDRED FEET EAST OF THE HEAD = 261
A ONE ON BOTH ENDS = 151
THE DISTANCE = 108
GEOMETRY = 108
POSITIVE LIGHT = 171
THE LOCATION IS HIDDEN IN THE NINE KEY = 333
FIVE FOUR NINE = 144
ISIS = 56
LIGHT = 56

At first glance it seemed to be an impossible puzzle. But it was that very thought that prompted the first move.

He always enjoyed working on jigsaw puzzles when he was a child. Thinking back, he remembered the trick his mother showed him as a way to get the puzzle started. The trick was to find all the corner pieces and then look for all the straight edge pieces and begin to construct the outer framework. He wondered if a similar strategy might work here as well. But after several minutes of trying, he couldn't identify anything in this list that might in some way equate, metaphorically, to corner pieces or even boundary pieces. A picture puzzle was one thing. But these were just words. *A picture is worth a thousand words*, he thought to himself. *Why couldn't someone just draw me a nice picture and be done with it?* He got up and paced the floor in frustration. Then a simple idea came to him. The obvious thing to do with a jigsaw puzzle is to try to fit the pieces together according to their shapes. *Is there something here that might equate to shapes?* Again, he was thinking metaphorically, not literally.

As he studied the list he noticed each of the values, with the exception of 151, reduced to 9. There was that old familiar number again. He decided to rearrange the phrases according to their number values. All the phrases that reduced to 9 would be in one group and all others would be in another group. Then it occurred to him to carry it one step further.

He decided to group together all the phrases that had exactly the same values. This way there would still be two main groups, those that reduced to 9 and those that didn't. But now there would be a subgroup in the 9-grouping. Each subgroup would be identified by the specific individual values of each phrase. But a few minutes into writing it all out by hand, erasing here and rearranging there, it seemed like a messy task.

"Hi Zeke," came a welcomed voice as his office door swung open.

"Angela!" he said, turning to greet her. "Just in the nick of time!"

She took off her coat and hung it on the back of the chair. "Why? What's up?"

"I need you to show me how to use that word processing program on the computer. Come here and look at this."

He showed her the parchment, side by side with the McClintock notes, and explained how he wanted to group the phrases. "I remembered seeing you use that program and how you could just rearrange words so easily."

"My God," she grinned. "You want to use the computer? Pardon me while I pick myself up off the floor!"

He shot her a sideways glance. "Could you not be a smart ass and just help me out here?"

"What do you say?" she asked, folding her arms across her chest.

"Please?"

"Okay. Let's go, Geranamo. Down to my office."

"Well, you're in a good mood," he said as he gathered up the parchment and McClintock's notes. "What's the deal?"

When they got to her office Angela poured herself a cup of coffee. "I aced a surprise exam in class this morning."

"Excellent! Now I hope you can help me ace this little puzzle here."

"I can't wait to get started," she beamed.

Angela fired up the computer at her desk and pulled up the word processing program. She showed Banyon how simple it was to type the words and arrange them however he wanted. She typed each phrase and the corresponding number values. Then she arranged them in the groups as he suggested:

THE DISTANCE=108
ONE HUNDRED=108
GEOMETRY=108

COMMUNICATE=117
NEGATIVE DARK=117
NINE LIGHTS=117
KING OF HEAVEN=117
EAST OF THE HEAD=117

SPEED OF LIGHT=126

STAR OF ISIS=135

FORTY FOUR=144
ONE HUNDRED FEET=144
NINE IS THE KEY=144
CIRCLE OF STONE=144
THE ALPHANUMBER=144
FOUR FIVE NINE =144
ONE TWO SIX=144
THE EDGE OF THE CLIFF=144

THE HEAD IS THE KEY=153

THE THREE TONES=162
TEN STONE CIRCLE=162
GUARDIAN PILLARS=162

POSITIVE LIGHT=171
DIVINE GEOMETRY=171
HEAVENLY MOTHER=171
THE QUEEN OF HEAVEN=171

THE WHEEL OF EZEKIEL=180
FORTY FOUR FEET=180
THE WHEEL OF SOUND=180
BENEATH THE STONES=180

ONE HUNDRED FEET EAST=189

ELEVEN DIVIDED BY FIVE=189
THE CIRCLE OF CHURCHES=189

REVERSE THE NUMBER=198
REVERSE DIRECTION=198

THE GREAT PYRAMID OF GIZA=234

FIVE STONE PENTAGRAM=252

ONE HUNDRED FEET EAST OF THE HEAD=261

ONE HUNDRED FORTY FOUR FEET=288

FORTY FOUR FEET SOUTH OF THE MARK=360
THE WHEEL SPINS IN TWO DIRECTIONS = 360

THE LOCATION IS HIDDEN IN THE NINE KEY=333

ONE HUNDRED FORTY FOUR FEET EAST OF THE HEAD=405

ISIS=56
LIGHT=56

ISIS PENTAGRAM=151
JESUS CHRIST=151
THE MIDDLE IS A FIVE=151
SOUTH OF FRANCE=151
SIRIUS + ISIS=151
RENNES LE CHATEAU=151
THE KEY OF ISIS = 151
A ONE ON BOTH ENDS=151
MIDDLE OF THE CIRCLE=151

They sat in front of the computer, staring at the list for a few minutes.

"Well?" Angela said, prompting a response from Banyon..

"You got me," was his only reply.

"This is interesting," she said, pointing to the first word in the second group.

"Isis," Banyon said. "The name of a goddess, as I recall."

"Right. Egyptian mythology. And notice the other phrases in the group that also have Isis in them."

"What in the world does Egyptian mythology have to do with any of this?" Banyon wondered. "This whole thing, from the beginning, has had only references to Christian lore."

"I don't know. And look here." She pointed to the rather oddly constructed phrase, SIRIUS+ISIS.

"Sirius," Banyon said. "That's a constellation in the stars. Is there some kind of a connection between Isis and the constellation of Sirius?"

"Actually, there is. The subject was discussed briefly in my anthropology class. But Sirius isn't a constellation of stars. It's a star within a constellation. The star we call Sirius was known as the Star of Isis by the Egyptians. It's the brightest star visible in the heavens."

"No kidding?" Banyon said, quite surprised. "I thought Venus was the brightest star."

"Well, actually, Venus isn't a star at all. It's a planet. Sirius, on the other hand, is a sun, an actual star."

"Wait a minute. Look here," Banyon said, pointing to the phrase, STAR OF ISIS. "Looks like somebody agrees with you about the Isis connection."

"Hey, do I know my stuff or what?" Angela quipped with a grin. "And look here," she said, pointing to the phrase, THE GREAT PYRAMID OF GIZA. "There's another Egyptian reference."

"It looks like we're going to have to do a little research on Egyptian mythology to figure out how these things tie in with Christianity. And how the heck does it all converge? This is interesting but confusing."

"What do you mean?" Angela asked.

"Well, the obvious connection with Egypt would be all the way back to the Old Testament. The stories of Moses and the great exodus of the Hebrew people. Moses was raised in Egypt under the rule of Pharaoh Ramses the second. Moses himself was actually a priest in the pharaoh's court."

"Moses was an Egyptian priest?"

"I believe so, yes. But it was Moses who professed a belief in a single god – you know, monotheism - as opposed to the polytheism, or belief in several gods and goddesses, which was the religious thinking in Egypt at the time. But this was all long before the days of Jesus and the beginnings of Christianity. By the time Jesus was walking the planet the story of Moses and the Egyptian pharaohs was ancient history. I'm just confused as to why these phrases almost seem to be tying the old Egyptian religious icons, like Isis, with Jesus and Christianity. It's like it's implying some sort of connection."

"I wonder if our friend professor Kline knows anything about this stuff?" Angela wondered.

"Good thought. We'll have to ask him tonight."

"Good thing we have the internet," Angela said. "It'll make doing the research a lot easier. Whatever Kline can't tell us we'll have to look up ourselves."

"I have to admit once again, the internet is amazing. I'm really glad you talked me into it."

"Mm-hmm," Angela muttered, seemingly lost in thought as she studied more of the phrases. "It's kind of curious that so many of the values reduce to 9 but only these few here that don't. Obviously that *nine* thing is somehow woven into this whole mystery. We've seen that before and here it is again."

Banyon nodded. "Agreed. There's no doubt about it. I just wish I knew why."

"I have an idea."

"About the number nine?"

"No, not exactly. I was thinking what if we arranged these phrases according to the similarities in the *ideas* they express instead of just grouping them because their numbers match."

"What do you mean? Like what?"

"Well," she said, scanning through the list, "like here. This phrase, THE MIDDLE IS A FIVE, is similar to A ONE ON BOTH ENDS. So we'll put those two together. Maybe that will lead to some ideas about what all these mean or how they correlate with one another."

"Okay, good idea. I think I already see the correlation with those two phrases. Check it out. The value of each of those two phrases is 151. That's exactly what the phrases are telling us! Look. That number, 151, is a *one* on both sides of a *five*. Right?"

"Yes, you're right. But it's so obvious. Why would someone make a clue that was so obvious?"

"I don't know. It may be obvious on one level but we still don't know what it means. Still, when you think about it, that's pretty amazing to be able to construct two different phrases exactly describing the very number value of each phrase."

"That's for sure."

"And look," Banyon said. "Here's one in the other group." He pointed to the phrase, ELEVEN DIVIDED BY FIVE. "It doesn't have a value of 151 but it seems to be *referring* to the number 151. Or at least to the phrases with that value."

"Huh?" Angela said, shaking her head. "I don't get it. What do you mean?"

"Look. The number 151 has two *ones*, like the number eleven. So you could say the eleven is divided by the five in the middle. *Eleven divided by five*. See what I mean?"

"Oh yeah. I see it. Hmm... Interesting. But what does it mean?"

"I'm guessing the fact that there's a reference to the 151 up here in the 9-group might mean that the whole group of phrases equaling 151 is important in its own right."

"Could be. And look at this. Isn't Rennes le Chateau located in the South of France?"

Banyon nodded. "Yes, it is."

"Well, can it just be mere coincidence that the phrases, SOUTH OF FRANCE and RENNES LE CHATEAU, both have the same alphanumeric value? I mean, what are the odds?"

"As well as the phrase, JESUS CHRIST," Banyon said. "Look, it has the value of 151 also. That story about Rennes le Chateau centers around the idea that Jesus and Mary Magdalene ended up living right there in that area. Remember?"

"Right. And we know that Rennes le Chateau is where McClintock met the French guy who had this old parchment in the first place. And got killed, to boot."

"Yeah, poor devil. And I wouldn't be at all surprised if Rennes le

Chateau is where the lost scroll of Ezekiel is hidden! That is, if McClintock didn't already get to it."

"It would make sense," Angela said. "But still the question would be where exactly is it hidden?"

"Well, that's supposed to be what this Ezekiel Code is all about. Somewhere in all of this is a clue to the exact spot where the scroll is located. Or so the legend goes."

Angela sat back in her chair and lit up a cigarette. "I don't think McClintock ever got that far. I mean I doubt if he found the scroll. If he did, wouldn't you think he would have made it known? I mean, really, think about it. People have been chasing this mystery for years! Don't you think he would have told somebody about it? You'd think he would at least have told his friend, Professor Kline."

Banyon had to agree. He couldn't conceive of someone discovering something like that and then never telling anyone about it. It just didn't seem likely.

They spent another half hour speculating on various aspects of the mystery but didn't arrive at any further revelations concerning the relationships between the various phrases.

"I don't know about you," Banyon said, "but I'm about ready for lunch."

"I'm with you. Mario's?"

"Hey, any time is pizza time as far as I'm concerned."

"I could print this out and we could look at it over lunch," Angela suggested.

"Sure! Good idea."

Mario's was packed with the lunch crowd but the waitress found a table for them near the back of the room. They ordered a double pepperoni with sausage and a couple of beers. While they waited for their order to arrive they sat in silence for several minutes.

"A penny," Banyon said.

Angela looked up. "What? Oh. I guess I was just thinking about us. About last night."

"Oh-oh," Banyon groaned. *Here it comes.* "Regrets?"

"Well-l-l..." she hesitated. "Not exactly. I just..."

The conversation was interrupted by the waitress as she placed the pizza and beer on their table. Banyon wasn't so sure he wanted to know what Angela was going to say anyway so he was glad for the interruption. *Whew!* he thought to himself. *Saved by the beer.*

Almost immediately the talk turned to speculation on what professor Kline might have in store for them that evening. Kline had left them hanging with the rather cryptic comment that there was something they didn't know. That, of course, was an understatement, since there seemed to be a whole lot they didn't know. But Kline seemed to be referring to something specific and they had no idea what it could be.

"There's not much point trying to guess what he has to tell us," Banyon commented. "I mean, I don't know about you but I don't have a clue."

Angela nodded. "But, speaking of clues..." she said, reaching into her purse for the printout of the phrase list. She got up and moved over to his side of the table so they could sit side by side. They both studied the list for a few minutes, trying to get back into the groove of intuiting some sort of meaning behind all the various words and phrases and numbers.

"Okay," she said. "I think I'm seeing something here."

"What is it?"

"Let's go on the assumption that the scroll is hidden somewhere in or near the area of Rennes le Chateau. All right?"

"Okay."

"So the question, like I said before, is where, exactly, is it hidden?"

"And...?"

"And I'm guessing these phrases here are clues to the answer."

She pointed out the following phrases:

THE DISTANCE = 108
EAST OF THE HEAD =117
FORTY FOUR = 144
ONE HUNDRED FEET = 144
THE HEAD IS THE KEY= 153
FORTY FOUR FEET = 180
ONE HUNDRED FEET EAST = 189
REVERSE DIRECTION = 198
ONE HUNDRED FEET EAST OF THE HEAD = 261
ONE HUNDRED FORTY FOUR FEET = 288
FORTY FOUR FEET SOUTH OF THE MARK = 360
THE LOCATION IS HIDDEN IN THE NINE KEY = 333
ONE HUNDRED FORTY FOUR FEET EAST OF THE HEAD = 405

"I see what you're saying," Banyon said. "It's like a treasure map but with words instead of a drawing."

"A good old-fashioned treasure map would have been nice," Angela said. "Which is a good question, actually. Why not just draw a map and put an X on the spot?"

"Maybe there's another level of information in this word-map that wouldn't be possible to convey in a simple drawing," Banyon suggested.

"Good answer. Makes sense. I mean, if any of this makes sense at all then I guess that makes as much sense as anything else."

Banyon gave a chuckle. "Yeah, but what's with all the different distance measurements? They're almost contradictory. One says ONE HUNDRED FORTY FOUR FEET and another says ONE HUNDRED FEET and still another says FORTY FOUR FEET. And why did you think the phrase, THE HEAD IS THE KEY, should be included here? It doesn't have anything to do with a measurement."

"I don't know about those distance measurements," Angela said. "But the phrase, THE HEAD IS THE KEY, fits with the phrase, ONE HUNDRED FEET EAST OF THE HEAD."

"Oh, right. I hadn't notice that. But the head of what? And again, look at the contradiction. One says ONE HUNDRED FEET EAST OF THE HEAD and another says ONE HUNDRED FORTY FOUR FEET EAST OF THE HEAD. There's a difference of 44 feet. I don't get it."

"Well, this might be a clue. Look here. The alphanumeric value of FORTY FOUR is 144!"

"Oh man," Banyon said, shaking his head. "If that's supposed to be a clue then I *really* don't get it."

"I don't understand it either. But that *head* idea seems to be a key to the whole thing. In fact, look here." She pointed to the phrase, THE HEAD IS THE KEY = 153.

"Yes, I recognize that number too. It's another number from the Bible."

"It is?"

"Yes. It's the number of fishes the disciples of Jesus caught after he told them where to lower their net."

"No kidding? Well, hmm... what's 144 plus 153?"

Banyon pulled out his pocket calculator. The sum was 297. "I don't remember seeing that number anywhere," he said.

"No," Angela agreed. "I don't either."

They worked at deciphering the code for a while longer but couldn't seem to get any further. They kept coming back to the question of the mysterious *head*. Finally, Banyon looked at his watch and noticed it was nearly 2:30.

"We have to get back to the office," he said. "It's getting pretty late and there are some things we need to do. I'll need your help processing some food orders and I've been letting some of the bills pile up. It'll take us a while to get all that done and our appointment with Kline is at seven-thirty."

Angela folded up the list and put it in her purse while Banyon went up to the counter to pay for the meal. As she was getting up to join him she noticed, for the first time, a man sitting at the next table. She couldn't see his face as he was turned away from her. Still, his dark overcoat and hat created a sense of recognition somewhere in the back of her mind. Suddenly she thought about the stranger who momentarily blocked the door at the bookstore as they were trying to carry out McClintock's old storage trunk. As she moved along to catch up with Banyon she purposely walked around the other side of the table trying, once more, to get a look at the man's face. But, again, he slowly turned his head the other way. Once they were outside she tried to catch a glimpse of the stranger through the window but he was gone.

~16~

Professor Kline greeted Banyon and Angela with the same pleasant hospitality as before. This time Banyon went along with the drop of whiskey in his coffee.

"Well," Kline said, settling back into the big brown leather swivel chair behind his desk, "where did we leave off last night?"

"You were about to tell us something we don't know," Banyon

said. "Something to do with why you don't think we're in the same kind of danger that Densmore and McClintock were in."

"Yes, right," Kline said, packing some black Cavendish into his pipe. "Well, I wish there was some way I could prepare you for what I'm about to tell you but, unfortunately, I can't imagine what that would be."

"Oh, great," Banyon said. "I thought this was going to be *good* news."

"Well," Kline smiled, "I guess that all depends on how you take it."

"So what is it?" Banyon asked.

Kline stroked his scruffy beard. "I'll just come right out and say it." Then he leaned forward and peered over the top of his glasses. "It's not just by accident that you've found yourself involved in this little mystery of the lost scroll of Ezekiel."

Banyon laughed. "Sure it is. I just stumbled into it by accident by getting a little too curious about the numbers and words that Densmore had been doodling on his deskpad. In fact I almost tossed it in the trash."

"But you didn't," Kline came back. "And I believe that in itself was no accident. What kept you from just tossing it away?"

"Well, that's when Angela walked in and it just occurred to me, at the last moment, to show it to her."

"And I'm telling you," Kline insisted, "it was no accident that she just happened to walk in at that moment."

"What makes you so sure?" Banyon asked.

"Because, my friend," Kline said, pausing a moment to light his pipe, "you're the *Chosen One*."

"The what?" Banyon smirked. "What the hell are you talking about?"

The professor settled back in his chair and began to explain. "When Frank McClintock died I began delving into this mystery myself. I spent weeks, months, reading and researching and I discovered some very interesting things. Every turn I took seemed to be leading me deeper and deeper into the strange world of secret societies, secret brotherhoods. First it was the Freemasons. Then the Rosicrucians, the Knights Templar, the Essenes, and on and on. And then, through a most unexpected source, I learned of one of the most mysterious groups of all. One that almost no one knows about. The Brotherhood of the Nine Pillars."

"I've heard of the others you mentioned," Banyon said. "They're all considered to be so-called Christian mystery schools aren't they?"

Kline nodded. "You could call them that."

"But," Banyon said, "I've never heard of that last group. The Brotherhood of the Nine Pillars?"

"Yes. In more recent times they've also been known as the Council of Nine. They're also sometimes known as the Brotherhood of Nine or, more often, just the Nine."

"There's that damn number again," Banyon said. "So what are the nine pillars?"

"The nine pillars are a reference to the nine planets in our solar system."

"Come on," Banyon said. "I suppose you're going to tell me it's also no accident that there are nine planets in our solar system."

"I'll tell you, Mr. Banyon, I've come to believe there are no accidents. Period. You've become familiar with the alphanumeric synchronicities, right?"

"That's for sure. Why?"

Kline reached for a piece of paper and a pen and wrote something down. "Have a look at that," he said, handing the paper over to Banyon.

Angela leaned in so she could see it, too.

THE NINE PILLARS = 162 = THE NINE PLANETS

Banyon shook his head. This was all becoming just a little too much. "You're telling me that those two phrases share the same alphanumeric value?"

"Exactly," Kline said. "You'll recall, I'm sure, the combined alphanumeric value of the words, *one, six, two?*"

"I remember," Angela said. "It's 144."

"That's true," Banyon confirmed. "But what's the significance?"

The professor gave a slight shrug. "I can't say for sure. But you've noticed, no doubt, the number 144 is everywhere throughout this whole mystery, right? It's woven in and out like a thread through a tapestry."

"So we've noticed," Banyon said, acknowledging the fact. "But why are you telling us all this? What's it have to do with that information you said we don't know about? And who is this *unexpected source* - as you put it – that told you about that secret society, the Nine?"

"I'm showing this to you just to confirm what I believe is the reality behind this ultra-secret brotherhood. And the source of this information is someone I know very well. Her name is Marie St. Claire. She's an assistant curator at the Smithsonian."

"Oh, you're not going to tell us the Ark of the Covenant is in a crate in a dark corner of the basement of the Smithsonian, are you?" Angela asked sarcastically.

Kline chuckled. "No, that's only in the movies, I'm pretty sure. Miss St. Claire, unbeknownst to her peers, is one of many who have been interested in and researching the same mystery you are involved in. She's been at it for years. I didn't know that until I decided to give her a call a few months ago. I was looking for answers to some questions that came up as I was pursuing my own research. That's when she confided in me that she had a copy of a document which, in fact, *is* kept in a locked cabinet in the basement of the Smithsonian." He smiled at Angela.

"Really?" Angela said, quite surprised. "Why is it hidden away? Why isn't it on display in the museum?"

"Because," Kline answered, "apparently no one in the mainstream world of academics believes it's genuine. Miss St. Claire, of course, believes it is."

"And this document," Banyon wondered, "what, exactly, is it?"

"It's a very old document that may have been penned by none other than Sir Frances Bacon, himself. And it tells of a mystery school, a secret society. Namely, the Brotherhood of the Nine Pillars, possibly an offshoot of the Order of the New Dawn. And more than that, it tells of a prophecy given by one of the members of the Brotherhood of the Nine Pillars."

"Hold on," Angela interrupted. "Back up a minute. Did you say the Order of the New Dawn? That's the secret society we read about in Densmore's book! The story of that Brother Hiram guy!"

Banyon nodded. He, too, had made the immediate connection.

"And Sir Frances Bacon?" Angela asked. "I know that name, too. Some of the students in my literature class were talking about the weird notion that Shakespeare didn't really write his own stuff and that it was actually written by this Bacon guy. Are we talking about the same Francis Bacon?"

"The same," Kline replied. "The Shakespeare thing is a controversial idea that can't be proven of course, but apparently there is enough circumstantial evidence to lend support to the idea."

Banyon looked puzzled. "Who was Francis Bacon?"

Kline grinned. "Well, now that's a very interesting question," he said, adjusting his glasses and suddenly taking on a more professorial persona. "Who, indeed! He was, in fact, a real person living back around the mid-fifteen-hundreds. If you look him up in an encyclopedia you'll probably find some mention of the fact that he's often considered to be the father of scientific inductive reasoning. But more interesting to us, given this little mystery we're involved in, is the fact that he was an influential figure in both Freemasonry and the Rosicrucians. According to some accounts, he was once the Grand Master of the Rosicrucian Order. But the reason your question is so interesting is that, according to legend, he's also one of the many reincarnations of Saint Germain. There's some disagreement as to whether or not he was the *final* reincarnation of Saint Germain but scholars of esoteric lore do agree that he was considered to be at least one, if *not* the final reincarnation of the great saint."

"Reincarnation?" exclaimed Banyon, ginning. "There's a concept I was encouraged to stay clear of in my household!"

"No doubt," Kline said. "It's considered heresy in the Christian religion. But there are those who claim the concept wasn't at all unusual at the time of Jesus and that the whole idea of reincarnation was purged from the books of the Bible by the early Church in an attempt to keep people from thinking they might have a chance to live another life after this one."

"In other words," Angela said, "a control tactic."

"Exactly the point," Kline said.

"I only had a brief education in the Catholic seminary," Banyon said, "but I don't recall anything about this Saint Germain. Who was he?"

"I'm not an authority on Saint Germain," Kline admitted, "but as I recall from my research, the adepts of the Mystery Schools considered him to be an Ascended Master, second only to Jesus himself. He's sometimes known as the Wisdom Keeper and they say his first appearance on earth was about fifty thousand years ago."

"Fifty thousand years ago!" Angela protested. "I haven't been at this anthropology stuff very long but, if I remember right, there were no human civilizations on earth that long ago."

"Maybe according to conventional thinking," Kline said. "But there are theories out there proposing that civilizations have come and gone many times over the ages due to large scale catastrophic events, floods and such."

"Like the flood in the Bible story of Noah," Banyon ventured.

"Exactly so," Kline said. "And even that story of Noah is older than most people realize. In fact the story of Noah is only one of many versions of that story. Several of the other versions are older than the one recorded in the Bible."

"What do you mean, other versions?" Banyon asked. "How could there be versions of the story that are older than the Bible if the one in the Bible is the original?"

"Aye," Kline said with a wink, "there's the rub."

"Meaning?" inquired Angela, becoming quite intrigued with this new information.

"Meaning," Kline went on to explain, "that the Biblical tale is not the original. It's a spin-off of another version that predates it by maybe as much as five hundred years."

Angela's eyes got wide. "Five hundred years?"

"News to me," Banyon said. "Where did the first version come from?"

"The oldest of the flood stories found so far comes from the ancient Sumerian culture which just seemed to appear suddenly about six thousand years ago."

"Appeared suddenly?" Angela asked. "How suddenly? What do you mean, exactly?"

"Well," Kline went on, "I'm not sure just exactly how sudden their appearance was. But the gist of it, at least as I understand it, is that the Sumerian culture was quite a sophisticated culture for its time. It was well endowed with the arts, literature, mathematics, architecture and so on. The puzzling thing is that, unlike other ancient civilizations, there is little if any archaeological evidence showing the evolution of the culture over time." Noticing the blank looks on the faces of his two guests he offered more explanation. "In other words, let's say you find the remnants of an ancient city somewhere and you begin digging into the layers of earth to bring up whatever artifacts you can find so you can learn more about that culture. Generally speaking, the further down you dig the more evidence you will find of the gradual progress – or evolution, if you will - of that culture."

"Sure," said Angela. "I understand that. The artifacts in the lower layers of earth strata will usually be more primitive than the artifacts found in the layers above. Like tools, for example. They'll show gradual improvements and some innovation over time."

Kline was impressed. "Exactly," he said. "But in the case of ancient Sumeria there is little if anything to indicate such a process of growth and learning. This makes it seem as though they just sort of appeared on the scene as a fully developed civilization. It's quite strange. Of course I suppose it's possible someone may eventually discover some indication of their more primitive past but so far, at least as far as I know, that hasn't happened."

"Interesting," Angela said. "And getting back to the flood stories from around the world. Are the stories all the same?"

Kline nodded. "The stories are all basically the same with only some minor differences and each one has a different name for the main character."

"You mean they're not all named Noah?" Banyon asked.

"Oh no, not at all," Kline said. "For instance, the same character in the Sumerian version is called Ziusudra. In a later Babylonian version, still predating the Biblical version, the character is called Utnapishtim."

"Well, there's a mouthful," Banyon chuckled. "Can you say that three times fast?"

Angela nudged him in the arm. "I wonder how each culture decided on a particular name for their main character?" she asked.

"Probably something to do with what the name meant in their language I would guess," Kline said. "Some researchers even suspect the name, Noah, is a masculine bastardization of the name, Nuah, who was apparently a Babylonian moon goddess who had control of the waters of the earth. Or so the story goes."

"Ah," Angela said, "I see the connection there between the moon and its effects on the tides. And I suppose you could draw a connection then between the idea of the waters of the earth and the flood."

"Well, this is all very interesting," Banyon interjected. "But aren't we getting a bit off the subject?"

"I suppose we are to some degree," Kline said. "But as you're probably beginning to see, everything is seemingly interconnected in a number of ways. It's a giant matrix, a tapestry of our reality. Some of the threads woven into that tapestry are visible as all get out. That's the picture we see on the surface. But other threads are hidden deeper within the fabric. And I'm telling you they weave a whole different picture. We can easily get back to our subject at hand from right here at the flood story."

"How?" Banyon asked. "What's the connection?"

"One of the differences between the older versions of the Flood story and the relatively newer Biblical version is that the older ones include more than just one god. The Biblical version, of course, has only the one god, Jehovah or Yahweh, depending on which version of the name you like."

"So?" Banyon asked. "What's the point?"

"So, if we go back to the original story, the Sumerian version, it's interesting to ask who these gods were."

"So who were they?" Angela asked.

"The two most prominent are named Enki and Enlil."

Banyon wasn't getting it. "This gets us back to the subject at hand?" he asked.

"Somewhat," Kline replied. "It brings us to a rather interesting but very controversial point."

"Which is?" Banyon prompted.

"Are you at all familiar with the work of a scholar named Zechariah Sitchin?"

"Can't say that I am," Banyon admitted.

"Me neither," Angela said. "Who is he?"

Kline got up from his chair. "Can I get you some more coffee?"

"Yes, please," Angela said. "Thank you."

"Sure, thanks," Banyon said.

Kline poured the coffee and returned to his desk. "Sitchin is one of the few people in the world who can actually read the Sumerian writings that have been found on ancient clay tablets. It's much too complicated to get into completely here but suffice to say his interpretation of those writings is extremely controversial. So controversial that almost no mainstream academic accepts his thesis. For the most part it's either laughed at or completely ignored."

"Why?" Angela asked.

"Well…" Kline started, taking a long draw on his pipe. "Sitchin sort of fits into the so-called *ancient astronaut* crowd."

"Ancient astronaut crowd?" Banyon asked, totally confused.

"Those relatively few folks who believe that the earth was visited by intelligent beings from elsewhere in the universe as far back as perhaps five hundred thousand years ago."

Banyon raised a skeptical eyebrow.

"Sitchin is convinced - and by the way, he's produced several books full of good evidence to support his theory - that the gods, Enki and Enlil, were actually human-like beings from another planet. A planet the Sumerians called Nibiru."

"Nibiru?" Banyon said, shaking his head. "Never heard of it."

"No, of course not. And I know it sounds off the wall, but believe me the whole idea simply can't be so easily dismissed. Sitchen has written several volumes on the subject. He's not a crackpot by any means. He's a serious scholar who's been at this for over forty years now. And he's not alone on this subject. There are others, just as serious, who have been scouring the ancient writings from all over the world, including our own Native American Indians, and nearly all of these cultures have tales about the gods who came from the sky and taught their ancestors all they needed to know in order to create viable civilizations."

"I suppose it's possible," Angela said. "But of course there's no real proof that earth was visited by extraterrestrials. Is there?"

"True," Kline answered. "But there's a lot of circumstantial evidence. You take a little here and a little there and it begins to emerge as a very intriguing picture. But there's more. Something even more radical. Or some would say downright heretical. Even blasphemous."

"Well, why stop now?" Banyon chuckled. "I can't wait to hear this one."

Kline leaned forward in his chair. "They created us," he said, tapping the spent tobacco from his pipe into the large ashtray on his desk.

Angela drew a blank look. "I beg your pardon?"

Kline nodded. "You heard me correctly. It's the most radical part of the so called ET hypothesis."

"That humans were created by aliens?" Banyon countered. "Come on."

Kline continued. "Several of the creation stories from cultures around the world indicate that these beings from the stars came to earth and created the humans in their likeness. Even the Sumerian creation story seems to imply such to have been the case."

"And God created man in his own image," Banyon muttered, quoting the Old Testament.

"Now you're catching on," Kline said.

Angela was quite amused. "So you're saying God was an alien?"

"Let me put it to you this way," Kline said, refilling his pipe. "Look how much we've learned about human DNA in just the past few years. Our scientists have mapped the entire human genome. We've cloned several animals, from mice to sheep. Some scientists say they are on the verge of cloning an entire human being. You and I know it's going to happen sooner or later. Right?"

"No doubt," Banyon admitted.

"And quantum physicists are seriously talking about the possibility of actually folding space, condensing the space-time continuum, making it theoretically possible for humans to traverse unbelievable distances through space in no time at all. Right?"

"That's true," Banyon said. "I'm always seeing articles about that in *Science Today* magazine."

"Okay," Kline said. "Now go with me on this. Knowing that all this is true, fast forward now, say, fifty years. Or make it a hundred years if you like. Now imagine by this time we've perfected the ability to clone everything we can think of including complete human beings. We have genetic engineering down to a science. No pun intended. At the same time, the advances in quantum mechanics have given us the ability to travel to planets beyond our own solar system, anywhere in the universe. Are you with me?"

"I'm with you," Banyon said.

Angela nodded.

"Good. Now imagine a crew of scientists leaves the earth in one of the latest space-time bending vehicles heading for a planet they suspect is capable of sustaining life as we know it. They reach the planet and discover, indeed, it's like a veritable Garden of Eden. And what do they find?"

"I'll bite," Banyon said. "What do they find?"

"They find that life has evolved on that planet to the point where there are what we might call proto-humans wandering around all over the place. Creatures that are, for all intents and purposes, very similar to the Neanderthals that once roamed the earth. The scientists set up a facility in the midst of a beautiful, lush green environment and proceed to capture a couple of these near-human creatures. Lo and behold, they discover the genetic make up of these creatures is nearly identical to their own. These creatures are more closely related to earth humans than earth humans are to chimpanzees which, as you may know, is about as close to being human as you can get without actually being human. As far as the genetics go, there is very little difference. Maybe as little as one percent. Of course that little difference makes all the difference but you get my point."

"Of course," Banyon said.

"So," Kline continued, "these scientists take two of these creatures, these Neanderthal types, one male and one female, and through a process of advanced genetic engineering they fuse the necessary human DNA with the natural DNA of the creatures and virtually create a couple of fully functioning, fully evolved human beings in their own likeness. That is, in the likeness of the human scientists, if you follow me."

The professor paused for a moment to let that idea sink in. Then he continued.

"The scientists teach them all sorts of things. Mathematics, art, language, writing, everything they can think of including some rules for personal and social behavior. These two new creatures - this Adam and Eve, if you will - produce offspring and their offspring produce more of the same and on it goes, generation after generation. In the meantime the scientists have left the planet to continue the same process somewhere else in the universe. Now the new creatures, virtually human in every way, begin to pass on their story of Creation. They tell of how the gods came from the stars and created them in their own likeness and taught them everything they needed to know to survive. As the population grows over time and spreads out across the planet, various groups begin to create their own cultures and the Creation stories change a little here and a little there until there are many creation stories around the planet and many different religions are built around these different beliefs. You see what I mean? Sound familiar? Now, as the ages pass, civilizations rise and fall and one day they reach a level of scientific advancement that allows them to map their own genome, engage in the science of cloning, and discover the secrets of quantum physics and space travel. Soon, a team of these scientists travels to another planet and the process begins all over again. And this scenario is going on everywhere throughout the vast reaches of the infinite universe. And in every case – on every planet - the newly created beings tell the stories of how the gods came from the stars and created them in their own likeness." Kline stopped and took a sip of coffee and waited for a reaction.

Banyon and Angela were stunned by the power of the image the professor had just projected into their consciousness.

"Jesus Christ," Banyon said, rubbing his eyes as if he'd just come out of a darkened movie theater. "That's a hell of a scenario."

"Really fascinating," Angela concurred. "So do you really believe this is the way it is?"

Kline smiled. "Well," he said, "let's just say I think there's a damn good chance that it's something very much like that."

"But what does this say about God?" Banyon asked. "Where does God fit into a scenario like that? Or is there no real God in this picture?"

"Personally," Kline said, "I don't think it eliminates God at all. But it does require a change in the way we perceive what God really is. This is where we must look to the ideas about the nature of God, ideas that already exist in various philosophies on this planet. But that's a discussion for another time, I'm afraid. The reason I'm telling you all of this is simply to get you to think about other ways of perceiving our reality and especially the idea that there are other intelligent beings in the universe and that they've been here."

"And just why is this important to us now?" Banyon wanted to know.

Kline smiled. "It's a machine," he announced enigmatically.

Banyon was puzzled. "What? What's a machine?"

"I know what he's saying!" Angela blurted. "In the McClintock notes. Remember he wrote those very words? And, besides, you know that's what it said in the book. You know. That whole story about - what was his name - Brother Hiram? I mean we discussed this idea before." She reached into her purse and pulled out her photocopy of the McClintock notes. She unfolded the paper and handed it over to Banyon. He read the writing at the top of the page:

Entry, December 14, 1999.
I'm now more certain than ever that it was a machine.
I believe it still exists somewhere.

"Of course," Banyon said. "I didn't forget. But I guess the reality of it, I mean the *real* reality of it," he emphasized, "hadn't quite sunk in until just this moment. I mean, Jesus, we're looking for a goddam space ship?"

"Not only are you looking for it," Kline said, "but I have no doubt you'll find it. Now, as to whether it's a space ship or some other type of technology, I can't say. I just don't know. What I do know, however - or let's say what I'm reasonably certain of - is that you will find it."

"What makes you so sure?" Banyon asked.

"Like I said," Kline reminded him, "you're the Chosen One."

"Oh that," Banyon said with a roll of the eyes. "Would you mind telling me just what the hell that's supposed to mean? What makes you say something like that?"

"Remember," Kline said, "earlier this evening I mentioned the Brotherhood of the Nine Pillars?"

"Of course, I remember," Banyon nodded. "And...?"

"And remember I mentioned a prophecy given by one of the Nine?"

"Oh, yeah. I was going to ask you about that but we sort of got off on to other things. So what is this prophecy all about?"

"First I should tell you I believe the Brotherhood Of The Nine Pillars still exists today and it's my guess that they just might be the ones who are watching your every move."

"Oh swell," Banyon said sarcastically. "Are they the good guys or the bad guys?"

Kline laughed. "I suspect they're the good guys if they're anything at all."

"And so what about this prophecy?" Banyon asked again.

"According to my friend at the Smithsonian, it goes like this. The prophecy foretold of a time when the *Chosen One* would come bearing the name, Ezekiel. Possibly they considered it would be the biblical Ezekiel reincarnated."

"What!" Banyon retorted. "Come on. If this is going where I think it's going, it's a little too far!"

"Hold on," Kline said, raising a hand. "Here me out on this. What they meant by the *Chosen One* is that this person would be charged with the responsibility of revealing the object of Ezekiel's vision to the world and that the future of the world, in fact, depends upon it."

"Oh, is that all?" Banyon chuckled with sarcasm. "Just the future of the world?"

"Actually," Kline continued, "there's some evidence suggesting that this prophecy was based directly on whatever is written in the lost scroll."

"Oh, I'm not ready for this," Banyon protested. He shifted uncomfortably in his chair.

"There's more," Kline continued. "The prophecy says that anyone who interferes with the progress of the *Chosen One* in his quest will suffer the ultimate consequence."

Banyon stared at Kline for a few moments. "That's it?" he asked finally.

"That's the gist of it, yes."

Banyon was temporarily speechless. He looked over at Angela. She was not surprised about the idea of the machine, whatever it might be, since it was basically just reaffirming what they already knew from reading about it in Densmore's book and as it was suggested in McClintock's notes. But she was as befuddled as Banyon when it came to the notion that he was the *Chosen One* according to some obscure ancient prophecy.

Banyon shook his head slowly, trying to comprehend the story Kline had just laid out for them.

"I knew this was going to come as a shock," Kline said. "I don't know how I'd handle it if I was in your shoes. But as fate would have it, my only job was to let you know."

"What if I don't want to continue pursuing this thing?" Banyon countered. "What if I just quit?"

"You think you could just quit now?" Kline asked. "Just give up the search? Just like that?"

Banyon thought about it for a minute. The idea of simply putting it all aside and not continuing the search for the answers had crossed his mind before and he knew he couldn't quit. Something was driving him, almost as if he had no choice. But it was crazy. *Searching for flying saucers and saving the world?* he thought to himself. *It's nuts!* Indeed, it seemed like comic book material. It couldn't be real. *Things like this just don't happen in real life.* But as the events of the past days and weeks rushed through his mind he knew it was as real as anything he'd ever experienced. It was happening all right and apparently there was nothing he could do about it. Finally he looked at Angela and then at Kline. "I think we need to go," he said, getting up and putting on his coat. "I need to think about all of this. Or forget about it. One or the other."

"I need to think about all of this. Angela put on her coat and accompanied Banyon to the door.

"Believe me," Kline said, getting up from his chair, "I understand how you must feel."

"I doubt that," Banyon replied, forcing a smile. "But I do appreciate the time you've given us."

"I'm sure we'll be in touch," Kline said. "Don't ever hesitate to call me. You've got my number."

"Thanks," Banyon replied as he and Angela left the office.

When they reached the car Banyon sat quietly for a minute before putting the key into the ignition. Staring out the window, he mumbled to himself, "The Chosen One."

Angela glanced over at him. "What?"

"Nothing," he smiled solemnly. "Let's go home."

~17~

Banyon and Angela arrived at the Seattle Gospel Mission later than usual the next morning. They had been up until nearly 2 a.m. the night before discussing everything they'd learned from Kline. Between the two of them they decided the thing about Banyon being the *Chosen One* might or might not be true. For Banyon, the idea of accepting it as fact was a little more than he was prepared to handle. The best idea, they decided, was to tuck that little tidbit of information away for the time being and just let things play out however they might. The other information Kline laid on them that night was plenty to deal with for the moment.

Banyon spent most of the morning in his office trying to take care of the business of running the shelter. He was actually glad to have some normal everyday business to take his mind off the strangeness that was consuming more and more of his life. The respite didn't last long. The intercom button on his phone buzzed just as he was about to make his second pot of coffee. It was Angela. He switched on the speakerphone.

"Hi Angela. What is it?"

"Zeke? Got a minute?"

"Yeah, I guess. What's up?"

"Come back to my office" she said. "You gotta see this."

He made his way down the hall to her office and found her sitting in front of the computer.

"What have you got there?" he asked, leaning down to see the webpage she had up on the screen.

"This is incredible!" she said.

"What is it?" he asked, scooting a chair up to the desk.

"I couldn't get that Brotherhood of the Nine Pillars out of my mind for some reason and I kept thinking about how the number nine is so much a part of all this weirdness. So anyway, I did an internet search looking for any information about that specific secret society."

"The Brotherhood of the Nine Pillars? What'd you find?"

"Actually nothing. I was a bit surprised to find absolutely nothing but then I remembered Kline did say almost no one knew they even existed."

"Well, so what is this?" Banyon asked, pointing to the computer screen.

"So I decided to just Google the *word* nine and the *numeral* nine and see what might come up."

Banyon laughed. "Google? What the hell is google?"

"Oh, it's just the name of one of the search engines on the net. When people use it they call it googling. I told you that before, didn't I?"

Banyon shook his head. "I don't know. Maybe. I don't remember."

"Well, anyway, a million web sites came up. So I narrowed the search parameter by including the word, *alphanumerics*, and this is one of the web sites that came up."

"What is it?"

"It's called *The Secret of Nine*. The guy who put it together is someone named Vince Paretti. He's just a guy who sort of stumbled onto this nine thing too, and he's even using the same kind of alphanumerics that we've been using!"

"He's looking for the lost scroll?"

"No. There's nothing on his site about that. But you're not going to believe what I did find on one of his pages! Check this out. This Paretti guy discovered something really incredible. Are you ready for this?"

"I'm ready."

Angela grinned. "I doubt it."

She clicked on a hyperlink at the bottom of the screen. When the new page came up there was a chart laid out in color-coded columns, with the numbers 0 through 9 in one column, the words ZERO through NINE in another column, the alphanumeric values of each of the words in a third column, and the reduced forms of those values in the last column. At the top of the page, in big letters, was the title: *The Remarkable AlphaNumber Table*.

"I don't believe it!" Banyon said. "*Alphanumber* is the same word that's in the McClintock notes! I remember we struggled with that some time ago. How the hell...?"

"Exactly! Remember we figured out it meant the numbers spelled out in word-form? And we thought about doing that with more numbers but didn't know what numbers to do it with?"

"Yeah, and it was so simple! This guy figured it out! The numbers *zero* through *nine*!"

Banyon studied the table for a moment. "Kind of funny he included zero, though. I would have thought it would have been just the numbers *one* through nine. Why is the zero in there?"

"He explains that in the text below. Turns out that the word *zero* is important and seems to act like a switch, turning the *nine* on and off in certain instances. And one of those instances is the Alphanumber Table itself. The inclusion of the word, *zero*, in the table just happens - are you ready for this? - just happens to answer another one of our questions from McClintock's notes."

"What do you mean?"

"Remember the number 522 that was mysteriously underlined in the notes? And we wondered why?"

"Yeah," Banyon said, waiting for the other shoe to drop.

"Look here," she said, pointing to the bottom line of the column of values on the Alphanumber Table. The bottom line was the total of all the alphanumeric values of the words *zero* through *nine*. The sum was 522.

"The sum total of the entire Alphanumber Table," Angela said, "is none other than 522."

Banyon's eyes lit up. "This is incredible! How could this guy just happen to stumble into the same sort of thing that we stumbled into? But you say there's nothing on his web site that even mentions the lost scroll of Ezekiel?"

Angela shook her head. "Nothing at all. He seems to be into something completely different. Or at least he's coming to some of the same discoveries but from a completely different starting point."

"Unbelievable."

"Well, you haven't seen anything yet."

"There's more?"

"You'd better strap yourself in. You're not even going to believe the next page."

"What is it?" Banyon asked, literally on the edge of his seat.

"Are you ready?"

"I don't know," he grinned. "You're scaring me now."

Angela clicked the link and brought up the next page. Banyon stared at it for a moment and then his eyes opened wide. He did a double take in a sudden rush of recognition.

"Holy...!" he left the exclamation unfinished. "What the...?"

Angela had been right. He wasn't ready for this. He was looking at professionally rendered, color-coded graphics of the same converted Mayan calendar matrix that he had quickly sketched out himself several weeks ago. Like Banyon, Paretti had discovered that the English alphabet fit neatly into the Mayan Tzolkin matrix. And like Banyon, he highlighted the word, KEY, as it appeared nine times within the grid.

Banyon was beside himself. "Who the hell is this guy? Is he some kind of a mind reader or something?"

"I don't know about *him*, but maybe *you* are."

"Me?"

"Well, from what I could gather from his introduction on the first page, he discovered all this stuff on his own at least three years ago."

"Three years ago? He had it before I did?"

"Looks like it. But there's more."

"I don't know if I'm ready for more. What is it?"

"You remember how you discovered the value of 9 hidden within the alphabet by folding it in half?"

"Of course. The resulting pairs of letters each had a combined value of 27 which reduces to..." he stopped short. "Oh, come on, you're not serious."

Angela clicked the link and brought up a page showing exactly the same thing, the alphabet folded in half revealing the letter pairs, each equaling the value of 27 reduced to 9. Along with it was a detailed explanation of the process Paretti went through to arrive at the discovery.

"This simply isn't possible," Banyon said, reaching into his shirt pocket for a cigarette. "What are the odds of this kind of coincidence?"

"Coincidence!" Angela laughed. "I think we're talking major synchronicity here! In fact, synchronicity is really what this Paretti guy is mostly into. That and the whole mystery of the number nine. He believes the number nine is somehow connected to the phenomenon of synchronicity at some fundamental level and he even talks about nine being a holographic number."

"A holographic number? What the hell is a holographic number?"

"I don't know," Angela said, bringing up yet another page on the screen. "But look here."

The page contained several phrases, all variously related to each other by concept. Among the phrases was NINE IS THE HOLOGRAPHIC NUMBER = 288. Banyon and Angela both recognized 288 as double 144. Then they noticed yet another interesting and related phrase:

HOLOGRAPHIC UNIVERSE = 225

Paretti included a note identifying 225 as the reverse of 522, the sum total of the entire Alphanumber Table. Clearly, Paretti was convinced that the Alphanumber Table was in some way connected to some greater cosmic picture or at least it was a tool that, if understood correctly, could enable one to catch a glimpse of the hidden layers of reality.

Banyon and Angela spent the next couple of hours reading through just a portion of the remarkable material on Paretti's website. Angela was right about Paretti coming to similar, and sometimes exactly the same discoveries that she and Banyon had uncovered. But Paretti had arrived at them from an entirely different starting point and, apparently, for entirely different reasons. Yet, in spite of the different directions, there seemed to be some sort of strange connection. It was as if two large pieces of a very big puzzle were merging. While Banyon and Angela were seeking an object - the lost scroll of Ezekiel - Paretti seemed to be looking for something more abstract. He seemed to be grasping at his own puzzle pieces trying to bring them together into a unified understanding of the universe, of all creation, the seen and the unseen, the yin and the yang. And, like Banyon and Angela, he apparently suspected the English alphabet might be a cipher that could be used to guide one's thought processes toward a clearer understanding of the bigger picture, whatever that might turn out to be.

"This is all blowing my mind," Banyon said, leaning back in his chair. "I mean, *really* blowing my mind." He was quiet for a moment and then glanced at his watch. "I can't think on an empty stomach. How about we get something to eat. It's nearly noon."

"Wait a minute. There's another page here that looks really

interesting. Actually it's a long one. A couple of pages. I'll print out a copy for each of us and we can read it over lunch."

"Sounds good to me," Banyon said, getting up to stretch his legs. "I'll wait for you out front."

After a few minutes, Angela tucked the printed copies into her purse and met Banyon at the front door.

"Let's try that little cafe just up the street," he suggested. "We can walk. It's raining but I've got my umbrella."

"All right," Angela agreed, buttoning up her coat.

As they walked huddled together under the umbrella she asked, "Have you ever heard of the eleven-eleven phenomenon?" The din of noise from a combination of the falling rain, the car tires of the noon-hour traffic sloshing down the street and the constant gusts of wind made it necessary to almost shout to be heard.

"The what?" Banyon asked, pulling the collar of his coat up around his neck.

"The eleven-eleven phenomenon!" she said a little louder.

"Can't say that I have! What is it?"

"Well, let's wait until we get to the cafe! These pages that I printed out from Paretti's web site discuss the phenomenon! It seems vaguely familiar to me! I think I heard someone at school mention it! Or maybe I saw it on TV or something! I can't remember!"

"More weirdness, I presume!" Banyon said as a sweeping gust of wind blew a blast of rain directly into his face. "Damn! Why don't we live in Florida? I hear the weather is nice down there this time of year!"

Angela laughed, clutching his arm and huddling up closer to him.

"Too many alligators!" she said, grinning.

"Yeah?" he laughed. "How many? More than nine?"

She forced a laugh and jabbed him in the ribs with her elbow. "Ow!"

Angela grinned. This was a man she could love. She'd loved Roger, her late husband, and the marriage had been a good one but it lacked two things – humor and adventure. Roger was all business all the time it seemed. He was a good man but he rarely joked, they rarely laughed and they never seemed to have the time to go anywhere or do anything out of the ordinary. Now, with Banyon, it was different. There was always laughter and there was certainly plenty that was out of the ordinary. At the moment, however, she really had no idea just how *out-of-the-ordinary* her life would soon become.

~18~

T he cafe, aptly named The Cafe, was crowded but Banyon and Angela were able to get a booth.

"Okay," Banyon said, after they'd settled into the booth and ordered the fish and chips special-of-the-day, "let's see that eleven-eleven thing."

Angela pulled both copies from her purse and handed one to him.

"Gees," he said, "it's practically a book!"

Angela laughed. "Yeah, it didn't look like that much on the computer but it took several pages to print out."

"Well," he sighed, "let's see what it's about."

The first page opened with an interesting introduction:

The Multiverse and 11:11
Part 1
By Vince G. Paretti

The following is not intended to be interpreted as "the final answer" or "the gospel truth". Some of it may or may not be literal. It may all be metaphorical. It may all be just creative interpretation of simple coincidences. However, having said that, the following is based on the hypothesis that the English alphabet is the currently activated program to be used as a gematria cipher to decode at least some of the secrets of the nature of our 3-D reality. Assuming that to be the case, for the sake of this exploration, it appears there is evidence (in terms of alphanumerics and symbolic inference) to support the suggestion that our "universe" is a computer generated illusion (via binary computer code) and that there exists a "multiverse" consisting of 144 x 144 dimensions of which our "universe" is but one of the total 20,736 (144 squared) universes. Further, the alphanumerics suggest a solution to the mystery of the 11:11 phenomenon which involves the earth as a fulcrum point between the two "elevens" which are mirror reflections of the unified multiverse.

Banyon shook his head. "Well, that's a mouthful! What's he mean, *the universe is a computer generated illusion?*"

"You know," Angela said, looking up from her copy. "Like in that movie? The Matrix?"

Banyon shook his head. "I didn't see it."

"Keep reading. I think he explains it further on."

HOW THIS EXPLORATION BEGAN:

I had been watching a John Carpenter movie called Prince of Darkness in which "the father of Satan" was attempting to manifest into our 3-D reality from "the dark side", as it was referred to in the film. This got me to wondering about that old idea of multiple dimensions and about the possibility of traversing from one dimension to another.

Toward the end of the movie it was revealed that the portal through which the entity was about to emerge was, in fact, a mirror. Not really a new idea but it was portrayed in such a way that it seemed somehow more profound than the stuff that usually gets into these kinds of films. It prompted me to explore this mirror universe idea from a slightly different point of departure, somehow inspired by John Carpenter's movie. The ideas presented here aren't new, but it's interesting to see how the alphanumerics might be interpreted as supportive of the ideas.

After about eight hours of contemplating and working with the alphanumerics in the process of exploring this idea, my brain was fried and I finally had to get some sleep. When I woke up and looked at my digital clock it was 11:11. My brain was still full of the various thoughts from the work I'd been doing just prior to going to sleep and I fell asleep again for about three hours but my mind was working while

I slept and some new ideas concerning the 11:11 phenomenon kept nagging me to get up and check out the alphanumerics.

Banyon looked up again. "This stuff is taking over this guy's life as much as it has ours," he chuckled. "Poor devil."

The previous night, after watching the movie, I was trying to get a picture in my mind of just what a "mirror universe" actually is. What does that mean? What does it look like? How does it work? What is on "the other side" of this invisible curtain? Is it the home of the archetypes which become manifest in our 3-D reality? Is it a realm of symbols? What the heck is it? And what about the notion that the universe is actually a computer program and that our "reality" is nothing more than a holographic illusion created via this program? This idea I think is best illustrated in the movie, The Thirteenth Floor and, to some degree in The Matrix, although The Matrix was too much like a comic book on steroids for my taste. In any case, I wondered, could our reality be a binary code program? Since I'm not exactly a computer nerd, all I know about binary code is that it's all just combinations of 1s and 0s. Knowing just this much, however, the alphanumerics began to get interesting right off the bat.

COMPUTER = 111 = ILLUSION = LASER LIGHT

That was interesting in that 111 suggests binary code and we know holograms are created by laser light beams.

BINARY = 69
BINARY CODE = 96, the mirror of 69

I noted that the numbers 6 and 9 come together to form the yin/yang symbol which, itself, can be thought of as a binary symbol.
We'll return to this idea of binary code in Part 2 of this paper.

"There are two parts to this?" Banyon asked. "We'll be here all day."

Angela glanced up. "We will be if you keep interrupting."

"Well, excuse me," he said, grinning.

Angela nudged him in the ribs. "And did you notice what he said about the number 69 and the yin-yang symbol? That's the same thing I showed you once before. Remember?"

"Yeah, I remember. Are you sure you two haven't been communicating behind my back?"

"Yeah, right. This is all just a big conspiracy we've cooked up to drive you nuts."

"I thought so."

"Shut up and read."

"Yes ma'am."

The rest of the paper was a long and relatively complex description of his work with the alphanumerics and the thought processes that carried him along on his own strange journey. Much of the work dealt with rather esoteric notions concerning light and dark – or *non-light*, as Paretti put it – and strange ideas about what he called a *mirror universe*. At one point they came across one of Paretti's alphanumeric equations containing a phrase they recognized:

TWO WAY MIRROR = 198, a familiar gematria number and also the value of "REVERSE THE NUMBER".

(Side Note: 198 is also the value of REVERSE THE TONES, but that would lead us into a whole different (although related) discussion.

"Hey look!" Banyon said. "*Reverse the number!* Did you see that?"

"Where?"

Banyon reached over and pointed to the phrase.

"What about it?"

"That's one of the exact phrases from McClintock's notes!"

"Are you sure?"

"I'm certain! Yes! Check it out. Do you have that copy of the notes with you?"

"No. I left it back at the office."

"We'll check it out when we get back then. But I'm positive that's the exact same phrase. How can this be?"

As they continued to read they stopped momentarily at the following section:

ZERO IS POSITIVE = 207 (a gematria number, reduces to 9)

This I had paired up with:
NINE IS NEGATIVE = 153 (a gematria number, reduces to 9)

As I pondered over these numbers and the meanings of the phrases I did see a pattern emerging. It had to do with the mirroring factor. It was about opposites joining as one. The yin and the yang of our reality. ZERO is, in fact, the mirror of NINE.

0 1 2 3 4 5 6 7 8 9
9 8 7 6 5 4 3 2 1 0
9 9 9 9 9 9 9 9 9 9

Then came an amazingly synchronistic
confirmation in terms of meaning and number:

ZERO IS THE MIRROR OF NINE = 279
= BETWEEN THE LIGHT AND THE DARK

ZERO IS DARK = 126 = NINE IS LIGHT

ZERO IS POSITIVE = 207
(seemingly opposite of ZERO IS DARK)

NINE IS NEGATIVE = 153
(seemingly opposite of NINE IS LIGHT)

However, we find this clue:
207 + 153 = 360, symbolizing a completed circle in arc degrees, the joining of the two opposites into a unified whole.
Also, "Zero is Positive" has a significant case-related equvalent:

ZERO IS POSITIVE = 207
= BINARY COMPUTER CODE

Clearly, Paretti was finding more and more evidence to support his ideas about the number 9 and it's mysterious connections to the structure of our reality. Paretti was also becoming convinced that, in some yet to be understood way, the earth was between something – perhaps between light and *nonlight* - or was in some way a kind of staging area for the proverbial battle between the powers of Good and Evil or Light and Dark, as he wrote:

EARTH IS LIGHT AND DARK = 189
= POWER OF DARKNESS
= VICTORY OF LIGHT
= REVERSE DIRECTION

Before they could finish reading, the waitress brought their lunch. They put Paretti's papers aside, enjoyed the fish and chips, and talked about what they'd read.

"This is really amazing stuff," Angela said. "Talk about - how did professor Kline put it - alphanumeric synchronicity?"

Banyon agreed. "No kidding. Especially that part about zero and nine being opposites and how the phrase values came together to support the idea! Blew me away."

"You know that business about the battle between the forces of light and the forces of dark came up in my anthropology class."

"Really? How did that come up?"

"There was a discussion about the discovery of the Dead Sea scrolls. Some of them, as I recall, were thought to have been written by the Essenes."

"I remember hearing about the Essenes," Banyon said. "It was mentioned briefly in one of my classes at the seminary. The Essenes were a religious order back in the days of Jesus."

"Right. There's some controversy as to whether or not Jesus was an Essene himself. But what I remember was that one of the scrolls talked about a final battle where the Sons of Light would fight against the Sons of Darkness. The Essenes, I think, considered themselves the Sons of Light."

"I think you're right. I do recall something like that."

"Kind of interesting how Paretti's ideas about the light and the dark seem to fit right in. I mean look at - oh, where is it...?" She leaned over her plate to look at Paretti's paper. "Oh, here," she pointed to the page. "I mean look at these phrases here. *Power of darkness. Victory of light. Reverse direction.*"

"Yeah," Banyon agreed. "Definitely phrases with a feel of battle and conflict. Interesting how it seems to indicate a victory for the side of the light but then that phrase, *reverse direction*, almost rings out a note of caution that it could go either way."

Angela nodded. "Makes you wonder what the deciding factor might be."

Banyon laughed.

"What's funny?" she asked, amused that he found some humor in it all.

"Suddenly this reminded me of the movie, *Star Wars!*"

"*Star Wars?*"

"Yeah! You remember." He tried to imitate the voice of the Star Wars character, Obi-Wan Kenobi. "*Use the force, Luke! Don't give in to the dark side!*"

"Hey! You're right! Come to think of it, that whole story was just a space age version of the Essene prophecy!"

"And what about... *the Force!*" Banyon mocked in a deep, dramatic voice. "When I saw the movie I just assumed it was a neat idea created by George Lucas. But now that I think about it, it's a lot like the things we've been learning."

Angela nodded. "That's true. I remember when the movie came out. A friend of mine, Cynthia, was really into the whole Chinese philosophy thing and told me the *Force* in *Star Wars* was a lot like the philosophy of Taoism. The yin-yang thing, where tao is the force that binds the universe together. I remember she said it's not only *in* everything, it also *is* everything. She was into that New Age stuff and her goal was to get her own personal tao in synch with the tao of the universe. At least that's how she put it."

"That's just like Obi-Wan when he told Luke Skywalker to be One with the Force," Banyon said. "Pretty interesting."

Angela laughed. "It's also like you, the other morning. You said let's just go with the flow."

Banyon smiled. "Hey, yeah. I'm a Jedi Master and didn't even know it!"

"Well, I don't know if I'd go that far," Angela smirked. "But when you think about it, you could just about replace the *The Force* with *The*

Flow. The concepts are pretty much the same. You know what I mean?"

"Yeah, you're right. I wonder what it would be like to totally live every moment of your life just going with the flow? I don't know if I could do that."

"I don't know if I could either. I don't see how you could do it while living in the modern society. Everything is so structured and we all seem to have to fit into all the little niches carved out for us in that structure. The human race just isn't ready yet to become Jedi Masters."

"Hmm." Banyon shrugged, swallowing the last bite of his lunch. "I suppose you're right. It'd sure be a different kind of world than we have now. And when the hell did you get so smart?"

Angela smiled, pushing her empty plate to the side. "You think I'm smart?"

Banyon gazed at her across the table. "I think you're pretty," he said.

She shot him a skeptical glance.

"And really, *really* smart," he added quickly.

"Correct answers, both!" she said. "You win the prize!"

"And what would that be?"

"You get to pay for lunch!"

"Oh, now you're getting *too* smart!" he said, reaching for his wallet.

The rain stopped and the wind subsided just long enough for them to make the walk back to the office.

When they reached the door of the shelter Old Tom was just approaching. He was grinning from ear to ear. "I got a gig!" he said excitedly.

"What?" Banyon asked, holding the door open for him.

"A gig, man! I got hired to play two nights a week at Charlie's Place! Ain't that a gas?"

"Yeah!" Banyon said. "You mean an actual paid gig?"

"Damn straight! I'll be makin' forty eight bucks a week!"

Angela smiled. "That's great, Tom!" She put her arms around his shoulders and gave him a hug. "When do you start?"

"Next Tuesday. It'll be Tuesdays and Thursdays, starting at nine o'clock. Just me and my guitar, you know. No band or nothin' like that. Y'all gonna come down and hear me play?"

"Absolutely," Angela said.

Banyon nodded. "Wouldn't miss it for the world."

"All right!" Tom said as his gravely voice broke into a hearty laugh. "So what y'all got to eat 'round here anyway?"

"Well," Banyon answered, "they just finished serving lunch but I'll bet if you go ask Miss Sophie real nice, she'll probably fix you up with something."

"All right," Tom said, heading toward the cafeteria. "People 'round here gonna be wantin' my autograph pretty soon!" he shouted back over his shoulder.

Angela squeezed Banyon's hand. "I'm happy for him."

"Yeah, me too. Old Tom deserves a break if anybody does."

They walked back to Banyon's office and spent the next couple of hours taking care of some routine business. About six o'clock they turned it over to the night shift and went home.

Home, for Angela, meant Banyon's house. She was completely caught up in their relationship and spending any more nights alone at her own house was something she preferred not to think about. How it was all going to play out, she had no idea. She was just going to go with the flow. As far as she was concerned their yin and yang were merging quite nicely, thank you.

What she and Banyon didn't know – couldn't know, at this point in the game – was that other forces of light and dark were also at play, deep in the background, strategically vieing for position in a bigger picture waiting to be unveiled, and a battle yet to come.

~19~

T he plan that evening was to make good use of the fireplace, fix a batch of hot spiced wine, maybe some popcorn, and just sit around reading the rest of Paretti's amazing paper.

Angela, made herself comfortable on the floor in front of the crackling fire. "I wonder where this Paretti guy lives?" she asked.

Banyon came in from the kitchen to join her. He set a hot cup of the spiced wine for each of them on the hearth. "Good question," he said, sitting down next to her. "Who knows. With a name like Paretti he could be in Italy for all we know."

"Yeah, maybe," she said, unfolding her copy of Paretti's paper. "But I doubt it. This is all in English. I'm sure he's probably an American with an Italian name."

"Could be." He took a look at his copy of the paper and lit up a cigarette. "In any case, let's see what else this ol' boy has to say. Where did we leave off?"

"I think we both left off at about the same place," she said, pointing out the paragraph.

"Oh, yeah. The power of darkness, the victory of light and all that."

"Right. And the mirror image thing."

"Yeah. I like how that idea correlates with the idea of reversals, like *reverse the number.*"

"Mm-hmm. And about the earth somehow at the center between the two opposite sides. Strange ideas, but it seemed like it was making sense in some weird way."

They both shared the excitement of making these little discoveries of the similarities between Paretti's work and the information they'd found on their own. It had to be more than just coincidence. It had to mean something but they were at a loss as to just exactly what that might be.

After a few more minutes of discussion about these ideas they settled back to read the rest of Paretti's work:

As I continued to ponder this idea of mirror images and the nature of what might lie between the two realms I was reminded of Luigi diMartino's discussions about "4.5" with regard to the numbers from his work with music, which led to more observations about the number 45 and its mirror, 54.

"I wonder who this Luigi guy is," Banyon said.

"I have no idea. Apparently somebody working with numbers related to music or something."

All of this was related to the theme of "mirror" and "middle" or "center", a point where things "cross over". It seemed obvious from both diMartino's work and my own that this 45/54 mirror/crossover idea was fundamentally important to the nature of our "reality" in some way. Then I remembered that the alphanumeric values of "FORTY FIVE" and "FIFTY FOUR" are each 126, the same as the value of the phrase, MIRROR IMAGE. I underscored this as significant.

FORTY FIVE = 126
= FIFTY FOUR = MIRROR IMAGE

Looking at 126, I remembered this:
ONE TWO SIX = 144

Something caught Banyon's attention. "Hey," he said. "Look. *One two six*. Where's the parchment with the code stuff on it?"

"The actual parchment is locked in the safe in the other room. Why?"

"Okay, then where's the photocopy of it?"

"It's in the drawer over there under the bookshelf."

Banyon retrieved the photocopy of the Ezekiel Code and returned to his place next to Angela. "Look," he said, pointing out the phrases on the old parchment:

FOUR FIVE NINE = 144
ONE TWO SIX = 144

Then he drew Angela's attention to a phrase on Paretti's paper:

ONE TWO SIX = 144

"Yes!" Angela exclaimed. "It's the same! And look here. That phrase, *FOUR FIVE NINE*. Remember when we were looking at Paretti's alphanumber table on his web site? He had the alphanumbers color coded into sets according to the number of letters in each alphanumber. The three-letter set was ONE-TWO-SIX with a total alphanumeric value of 144. And the four-letter set was FOUR-FIVE-NINE which also had a total alphanumeric value of 144."

"What about ZERO? That has four letters. Why isn't it included in the four-letter set?"

"Something to do with the zero being outside of, yet part of, the whole table. Remember, there was something about zero functioning as a switch to bring other factors into place. Something like that."

Banyon thought for a minute. "I can't believe this guy doesn't know anything about the lost scroll or even the Ezekiel Code itself. I mean look at these direct correlations! What are the odds that he would just happen to come up with the same things that are written on this old parchment?

"I have no idea. Unless..."

"Unless what?"

"Well," she paused for a second to let the thought gel in her mind. "Let's say he absolutely doesn't know anything about the lost scroll and never even heard of the Ezekiel Code."

"And...?"

"Well," she said, "assuming that's true - I mean just for the sake of argument - then what we may be seeing here is confirmation that the English alphabet is, in fact, a cipher for breaking the code. I mean, we suspected that, of course, but this would seem to be a really strong verification. You see what I mean?"

"You're right. That would explain it. I'd love to be able to talk with this guy. Is there any way we can get in touch with him?"

"I think he has his email address on his website."

"Check that out tomorrow, will you?"

"Sure," she agreed. "No problem."

Banyon got up and walked back over to the cabinet beneath the bookshelf and opened another drawer.

"What are you doing?" Angela asked.

"Got an idea," he said, coming back to her with a yellow marker in his hand. "Whenever we run across a phrase in Paretti's paper that correlates directly with one in the Ezekiel Code we'll highlight it on our photocopy. You know, just to sort of keep track and see how closely these things are related."

"Ah! All right. Good idea."

They continued carefully going over Paretti's paper:

Also, going back to the "45/Center" concept I found this:

FORTY FIVE IS THE CENTER = 252 = (126 x 2)

Also, ONE HUNDRED FORTY FOUR = 252
= CHRIST CONSCIOUSNESS
= THE ETERNAL MULTIVERSE

Now, back to 144:

Knowing that the number 144 is considered (in an esoteric sense, and especially in the incredible work of Bruce Cathie) to have a fundamental connection to the concept of "Light" and that "Light" is a significant element in this present theme, I began to wonder in what other way this important number might fit.

"All right," Banyon said. "Did you see that part about 144 being somehow linked with the concept of light? And look at this. *Christ Consciousness? Light?* Christ is known as the Light of the World. This is getting pretty deep. It's amazing how this works."

"For sure. The connection with light is what we puzzled over way back when we got the McClintock notes from Mrs. Densmore."

"Yes, exactly. According to his notes, it looked like he suspected some sort of a relationship between the number 144 and light."

Angela nodded. "And now we see confirmation of that same idea here in Paretti's paper. Just one thing, though."

"What's that?"

"Well, we have confirmation of the idea but we still don't really know what the connection is. Paretti doesn't really say."

"Yeah, you're right. He mentions somebody's work related to the idea. What is the guy's name?"

Angela scanned Paretti's paper until she found the name. "Here it is. Bruce Cathie. I wonder who that is?"

"Make a mental note to find out. If we can get Paretti's email address we could ask him about this Bruce Cathie guy."

"Good idea," Angela said. She got up to stretch her legs. "What say we move to the couch. The floor's getting a little hard."

"I'm with you. How's your wine? There's still some warm on the stove."

She handed him her cup. "Warm me up," she grinned. Then she picked up the papers and the yellow marker and moved everything over to the coffee table in front of the couch.

Banyon took off for the kitchen and returned with two fresh cups of hot, spiced wine. They settled down on the couch and continued to read through to the end of Part One of Paretti's paper.

The more they read the more opportunity they had to use the yellow highlighter. They were amazed to find more and more phrases in Paretti's paper that were identical to those listed in the Ezekiel Code. Beyond that, most of the text focused on the concept of a *multiverse* and how the concepts of light and dark play into the multiverse idea. What really caught their attention, however, was how the number 144 kept popping up as the alphanumeric value of the interrelated phrases. There seemed to be a preponderance of alphanumeric synchronicity linking the idea of *light* and a *multiverse* with the number 144. In a sense, it was all expressed neatly in a single alphanumeric equation:

MULTIVERSE = 144

At the end of Part One, Paretti wrapped it all up with a summation:

To recap what may be suggested here:

- Our "universe" is but one part of a "multiverse" comprised of 20,736 dimensions.
- The multiverse may be a programmed result of a binary computer code.
- The multiverse is divided in half between light and dark (or "nonlight").
- The concepts of "light" and "dark" here may be metaphors related more to the idea of the "1" and "0" of binary code.
- The concept of "mirror image" is fundamental to the nature of the multiverse.
- The value of "9" is fundamental to the structural nature of the multiverse as revealed by the reduction of significant numbers such as 144, 288, 432, 117, 171, 189, 270, 90, 45, 54, and others.
- The value of "0" is significant to the structural nature of the multiverse as revealed by the number 45 and its mirror 54 and their relationship to the concept of "center" (i.e., 0123-45-6789) (Note: Not only is 45 the center of the series, 0 thru 9, it is also the sum total of the series.)

Now we'll move on to Part 2 which deals with the 11:11 phenomenon and how it dovetails with this discussion of the "multiverse".

"Whew!" Angela said when she got to the end of Part 1. "Heavy stuff. My poor little brain needs a rest."

"I haven't quite finished yet," Banyon said. "Give me a minute."

"I'm going to make some popcorn while you finish reading."

"Excellent idea. There's some microwave popcorn in the cupboard above the stove."

A few minutes later Banyon joined Angela in the kitchen. She was standing in front of the microwave waiting for the popcorn to finish popping. Snuggling up behind her, he put his arms around her waist and drew her close.

"I don't know which smells better," he said, "the popcorn or your hair."

She laughed. "I take it that was intended as a compliment."

"Nope, not at all," he said. "Just making an observation."

He turned her around to give her a kiss just as the timer on the microwave signaled the popcorn was ready.

"Whew!" she said. "Saved by the bell."

"Okay," he chuckled. "You owe me one."

"You know what we should do?" she said, pouring the popcorn into a large bowl.

"No. What?"

"I think we should take the popcorn upstairs and read the rest of Paretti's paper in bed. How's that sound?"

"Hmm..." Banyon said thoughtfully, rubbing his chin. "Actually I can think of other things to do in bed."

"I knew you'd say that," she said, laughing. "But I do want to finish reading that material. Don't you?"

"Okay then, I've got an idea. Let's read it real fast and then figure out something else to do."

"You're impossible!" she said, heading up the stairs with the popcorn.

"I know," he replied with a devilish grin. "I'll get the wine."

They settled into bed, sitting up against a stack of pillows, and proceded to read Part Two of Paretti's paper:

The Multiverse and 11:11
Part 2
By Vince G. Paretti

The 11:11 phenomenon is the term generally used to describe the experience of noticing 11:11, seemingly by chance, on digital time pieces, time/temperature signs, and so on. Some people report having had this experience so often that it begins to feel like it "means something" to them. A number of ideas have emerged purporting to explain what it means to have this experience. Some say if you experience this phenomenon you are being "activated". What that is supposed to mean, I'm not exactly sure. It may mean the experiencer's consciousness is being prepared for an evolutionary leap to another level. Some say the 11:11 experience is a preparation for "ascension". This, like being "activated", is open to interpretation. Perhaps both of these ideas are correct to some degree or perhaps neither idea has any merit. Nevertheless, whatever interpretation one applies to it, the phenomenon, as such, does exist. I found the alphanumerics seemed to support the ascension idea.

One look at 11:11 and we are reminded again of the binary code discussion in Part 1:

BINARY = 69
BINARY CODE = 96, the mirror of 69
As I mentioned in Part 1 of this discussion, the numbers 6 and 9 come together to form the yin/yang symbol which, itself, can be thought of as a binary symbol.
BINARY CODE OF ELEVEN ELEVEN = 243 = TWO HALVES OF ONE WHOLE
(Side Note: The number 243 is a permutation of the number 432 which is a number that the renown mythologist, Joseph Campbell, kept running into during his research into the ancient myths and legends from around the world. See his book, The Inner Reaches Of Outer Space: Metaphor as Myth and as Religion; Harper & Row, 1986) Another permutation is 234, which is the alphanumeric value of the phrase, THE GREAT PYRAMID OF GIZA. This number 234 is also the value of the phrase, THE PHI SPIRAL IS THE KEY.

"There's another one," Angela said. "*The great pyramid of Giza.* Did you bring up the yellow marker?"

"Yup. Got it right here."

Banyon marked the phrase and they looked for more matches. It didn't take long to find them. The copy of the Ezekiel Code list was beginning to get quite a few yellow hits. The matching phrases now included REVERSE THE NUMBER, ONE TWO SIX, SPEED OF LIGHT, POSITIVE LIGHT, NEGATIVE DARK, THE GREAT PYRAMID OF GIZA, and last but certainly not least, NINE IS THE KEY.

Paretti devoted some of the discussion to the idea of 11:11 being a mirror image in and of itself. Remarkably, he even found an alphanumeric equation supporting the idea:

ELEVEN ELEVEN = 126 = MIRROR IMAGE

He noted, once again, that the alphanumeric value of ONE TWO SIX is 144. He went on to suggest that 11:11, with its obvious symmetry may represent the idea of balance. He then noted the equation, ELEVEN=63=DIVINE, and wondered if 11:11 might also symbolize a kind of spiritual balance. The alphanumerics seemed to provide him with a surprising confirmation as he discovered yet another compelling equation: ELEVEN ELEVEN IS THE DIVINE

BALANCE = 288. Banyon and Angela were quick to recognize 288 as the so-called double light number, or two times 144.

Paretti seemed to be almost obsessed with another odd notion. His alphanumerics kept implying the idea that the universe, or multiverse, was in some way similar to a hologram in an extraordinarily grand fashion. This idea was clearly indicated in his work as he wrote:

But even more relevant to the present discussion is this:
ELEVEN ELEVEN MULTIVERSE = 270
= THE HOLOGRAPHIC PROJECTION

Now with the idea of the holographic projection being introduced here, and knowing that a holographic image is an illusion, this next alphanumeric result goes to underscore the idea:
BINARY COMPUTER CODE GENERATES THE ILLUSION OF THE UNIVERSE = 612
SIX ONE TWO = 144

Banyon and Angela learned that Paretti had been in touch with another researcher by the name of Joe Mason. Mason suggested that the 11:11 phenomenon may have something to do with ascension, probably of a spiritual nature, and that 11:11 was a gateway. This prompted Paretti to see what the alphanumerics would have to say. He was not disappointed:

GATEWAY TO ASCENSION = 216
= FREQUENCY IS THE KEY
= SIXTH DAY OF CREATION

SIX DAYS = 101
= ARCHETYPE, and again the binary code idea with the 1-0-1.

SIXTH DAY = 110
= VIBRATION, and once more the binary code idea with the 1-1-0.

The 216 gives us TWO ONE SIX = 144

144 + 216 = 360, complete circle in arc degrees.

Is the divine earth fulcrum also a gateway to another dimension in the multverse?
Could there be something going on here involving "time", and "cycles"?
TIME PORTAL = 162

ONE SIX TWO = 144

ASCENSION = 99 = EARTH TIME
= THOUGHT = THE GOD MIND

ASCENSION CODE = 126
= FORTY FIVE
= FIFTY FOUR
= SPEED OF LIGHT
= NINE IS LIGHT

ONE TWO SIX = 144
= NINE IS THE KEY
= MULTIVERSE

BINARY ASCENSION COMPUTER CODE = 306
BINARY CODE OF ELEVEN ELEVEN = 243
= EARTH IS A PLANET OF THE MIND

ASCENSION CODE ELEVEN ELEVEN = 252
= CHRIST CONSCIOUSNESS
= ONE HUNDRED FORTY FOUR

Page after page, Paretti's remarkable work continued to reveal intriguing conceptual correlations. It was a *tour-de-force* into the world outside the box. In the end he finished with a succinct recap of his exploration of the 11:11 phenomenon:

To recap what may be suggested here:
• The 11:11 phenomenon may be a digital metaphor for a doorway

or portal to other dimensions within the multiverse.
- The earth may function both as a fulcrum in the balance and as the door to other dimensions.
- 11:11 may be a phenomenon unique to the digital age.
- "Ascension" (of spirit? Of consciousness?) may be a computer programmed function.
- The earth may be a hologram.

When Angela finished reading Part 2 she glanced over at Banyon and found he had fallen asleep sitting up, still clutching his copy of Paretti's paper. She gently took the paper from his hand and reached over to turn out the light. She happened to glance at the digital clock on the nightstand and was shocked to see it was precisely 11:11 p.m. *No way!* she thought to herself. *Can this be happening?* She wondered if she should wake Banyon who, by this time had slid comfortably down into the covers. *He'll never believe me if I don't show him,* she thought. She didn't know what to do. How long had it been 11:11? Did it turn just when she noticed it? Or had it been 11:11 for some time? Would it change over to 11:12 any second now? Those seconds were ticking away the longer she thought about it and she desperately wanted him to see it. The synchronicity of the moment was just too cool. She had to share it. In one quick motion she grabbed the clock with one hand and shook Banyon's shoulder with the other.

"Zeke!" she whispered loudly. "Wake up! Look!"

He rolled over. "Hmm...what is it?" he grumbled into the pillow.

She held the clock in front of his face. "Look! Check this out!"

Groaning reluctantly, and through half closed eyes, he gazed at the glowing red numbers in front of his face. It was precisely 11:12. "Uh huh," he muttered, rolling over. "It's after eleven. Let's get some sleep."

~20~

Banyon finished reading the rest of Paretti's paper in his office at the shelter. Angela told him about her 11:11 encounter but, of course, just hearing about it didn't have quite the same effect on him as it did on her. He was, however, intrigued by what Paretti had to say about the odd phenomenon. Still, he wondered, how could seeing the numbers 11:11 really have any effect on a person? Granted, it seemed the people who were really taking it seriously were those who were seeing it over and over again to the point where they felt it must mean something. That, he admitted, was a feeling he could actually relate to. He was reminded of the movie, *Close Encounters of the Third Kind*, where the fellow was obsessed with sculpting his mashed potatoes into a certain shape. He didn't know what the shape was supposed to represent but in some unexplainable way it seemed important to him. Banyon recalled how the fellow kept saying to himself, *"This means something. This has got to mean something!"* Apparently, for a growing number of people, the 11:11 phenomenon was becoming their pile of mashed potatoes much like the mysterious phrases and numbers had become for Banyon. How many times, way back at the beginning, had he thought to himself, *this has got to mean something?*

"Hey you," Banyon called out to Angela as he popped his head into her office. "Busy?"

"Not really," she smiled. "Did you get to finish reading the material?"

He walked in and sat down in the chair across from her desk.

"Yeah," he said. "Man that's some stuff, huh? I mean that Paretti guy is way into it."

"No kidding," she said, sorting through the day's mail. "Or way out of it."

He laughed. "Yeah. I guess it depends on your point of view. Anything good?"

"What?"

"In the mail."

She chuckled. "Does anything good ever come in the mail?"

"Not lately," he admitted.

"All we've got here is a telephone bill and a bunch of junk mail."

"Have you got time to check and see if that Paretti guy has an email address?"

"Sure. I think I've pretty much gotten everything in order here for a while. Let's see what we can find."

She logged on to Paretti's web site and waited a few seconds for the page to load onto the screen. "Hey! Right here at the bottom of the page," she announced, pointing it out to Banyon:

SecretOfNine@speedmail.net

Banyon took a look. "Excellent!"

"Well," she said, "now that we know we can correspond with him, what do we want to say?"

Banyon scratched his head. "Hmm. Now that it gets right down to it I don't know where to begin."

Angela thought for a minute. "Well, let's at least start with an introduction."

"Okay. Sounds good."

Angela clicked on the email address at the bottom of the page. An email form popped up immediately. Banyon pulled his chair around to her side of the desk and watched as she typed:

Dear Mr. Paretti,

My name is Angela and my friend's name is Zeke. We came across your web site the other day while doing a search for anything we might find about the number 9 and alphanumerics. We read through quite a bit of your material. A lot of what you've found in your research dovetails with quite a bit of what we've discovered in the process of pursuing our own little mystery.

She stopped typing and turned to Banyon. "Do you think we should tell him what we're doing? I mean, you know, about the lost scroll and all that?"

Banyon thought about it and decided it would be interesting to know if Paretti knew anything at all about the legend of the lost scroll. Angela agreed and continued typing:

We sort of stumbled into an old legend about a lost scroll supposedly written by the biblical prophet Ezekiel. We were wondering if you were familiar with this legend.

She looked at Banyon. "What else?"

Banyon rubbed his chin. "Hmm... I know. Ask him how he got all those phrases he uses with the alphanumerics." Then he held up a hand. "Hang on a second. Where's your copy of his paper?"

She reached into the drawer on the side of her desk and pulled out her copy of Paretti's paper.

He scanned through it looking for some of the key phrases that were the same as the ones in the list on the old parchment, the so-called Ezekiel Code. "Ask him about a few of these specific ones. Let's see... Ask him about *nine is the key* and *positive light* and *negative dark*. And ask him how he came to the idea that the number 144 has anything to do with light."

Angela continued typing and asked all the questions that Banyon suggested. "Anything else?" she asked.

"I guess not. I mean there are a million questions I'd like to ask him but maybe we shouldn't unload everything on him all at once. Let's wait and see if he even replies."

"Okay. That's probably a good idea."

"Well, maybe one more thing. Ask him where he's located."

Angela began to type and then stopped. "You think maybe that's getting a little too nosey?"

Banyon considered it for a second. "Yeah, maybe you're right," he said. "Can you erase that?"

Angela laughed. "Erase it? Okay, get me an eraser and I'll rub it across the screen."

"Don't be a smart ass," he said, rolling his eyes. "You know what I mean."

"Delete it," she said, still laughing.

"Yeah, whatever."

Angela selected the last line she'd typed and hit the delete key.

"There," she said. "It's erased."

"Okay. So that's it then? We just send it?"

"In a minute," she said, continuing to type:

We think your work is very fascinating and hope to learn more about it. Please reply at your earliest convenience.
Sincerely,
Zeke and Angela
shelter198@worldline.com

"What's that?" Banyon asked, peering over her shoulder.
"What, this? It's our email address."
"We have our own email address already?"
Angela laughed. "Of course! It's part of what you're paying for every month."
"Whaddya know. Cool. So that's it now? Just send it?"
"You want to do the honors?" she asked.
"I don't know," he said, cautiously. "Is it complicated?"
"Oh yeah," she said, getting up and motioning for him to sit in her chair. "But I think you can handle it. Come on."
"Oh, all right," he said, now facing the dreaded computer. "What do I do?"
"Use the mouse and move the curser up to the button that says *send.*"
"Okay," he muttered apprehensively. "Now what?"
"Now click the button on the mouse, one time real quick."
The computer beeped and the email vanished from the screen.
"Oops!" Banyon said, startled by the instant activity. "What happened? Did I screw it up?"
"What's the little message say on the screen?"
"It says, *Your mail has been sent!* Hey! I did it!"
"Boy," Angela grinned, "you are just moving into the twenty-first century with lightening speed!"
"No lie," Banyon said proudly. "I'm a bona fide computer nerd! So what do we do now?"
"Now we just have to wait and see if he gets back to us."

The rest of the day dragged on in anticipation of Paretti's reply.
Angela checked her email several times over the next few hours but the reply never came. She walked the short distance down the hall to Banyon's office but he wasn't there. She found Old Tom in the

cafeteria sitting at a table playing cards with some other homeless men who had come in from the cold.

"Have you seen Zeke?" she asked.

"Yup. He's back in the kitchen. Somebody had a little accident or somethin'."

Angela went to the kitchen and found Banyon attending to one of the volunteer women who had apparently slipped and fell.

"Is she all right?" Angela asked.

"Yeah, I think she's okay. Looks like maybe a slight sprained ankle. We're going to get it wrapped up here and call her husband to come take her home."

Angela was concerned. "Is there anything I can do?"

"No. We've got it."

"Okay. Well, when you get a minute can you come see me in my office?"

"Yeah, sure. Be just a minute."

After he got the woman's ankle bandaged and had her seated comfortably on one of the big old leather chairs out near the front door, he went back to see what Angela wanted.

"What's up?" he asked. "Did we hear from Paretti?"

Angela shook her head. "Nope. Maybe tomorrow."

"Then what did you want to tell me?"

She approached him slowly and pressed herself against his body until he was backed up against the wall. "How would you..." she paused mid-sentence and put her arms up around his shoulders, "...like me..." she paused again to give him a kiss, "...to fix you..." she kissed him again, "... a scrumptious home-cooked meal tonight?"

"Uh..." Banyon stammered, taken aback by the sudden rush of affection.

"Should I take that as a yes?" she grinned.

"That sounds really good!" he said, regaining his composure.

"Okay, then seeing as how I'm pretty much done here for the day, I thought I'd leave now and walk up to the Farmer's Market and get what I need. I'll just take the bus home and get dinner started. It'll be ready by the time you get home. How's that sound?"

He gave her a hug and literally lifted her up off the floor. "I think that sounds terrific," he said. "But what's the occasion?"

"Nothing, really," she shrugged. "I just thought it would be something you'd like and I haven't had a chance to try out your kitchen yet. Now, put me down!"

Banyon complied and laughed. "Well, girl," he said, "knock yourself out! My kitchen is your kitchen. God knows it doesn't see much of me other than the few minutes it takes to pop a frozen dinner into the microwave."

"That's what I figured," she said, putting on her coat. "So you'll be home about 6:30 or so?"

"Yeah, looks like it. I'll have to wait for that poor woman's husband to get here. I don't want to leave before that."

"Well, the night shift will be coming on. They can be with her if her husband is late getting here."

Banyon nodded. "Yeah. I suppose you're right."

Angela locked her office door and they walked down the hall together. He gave her a hug and she threw him a kiss as she walked out onto the street. He stood watching her through the large front window. His gaze was so fixed on her as she disappeared down the sidewalk into the afternoon crowd, he didn't notice the black sedan suddenly pull out from the curb across the street.

Back in his office, Banyon poured the last cup of coffee for the day and settled down to finish some paperwork. All the while he kept thinking about Angela. He couldn't wait to get home. *I have a feeling this is going to be an extraordinary evening!*

He had no idea how extraordinary it would turn out to be. But not in the way he imagined.

~21~

Banyon pulled into his driveway and parked the car. Before going into the house he made a slight adjustment to the bouquet of flowers he purchased on his way home. The card, pinned to the pink tissue wrapping, read:

To my favorite little code breaker.

Love, Zeke.

Satisfied that the flowers were arranged as nicely as possible, he walked up the stairs to the front door. He carefully put the bouquet on the porch in front of the door, rang the bell, and dashed quickly back down the stairs where he crouched to hide behind a bush. He couldn't help smiling as he felt a bit silly. *Who cares? I'm going with the flow.*

He waited a minute and decided she must not have heard the doorbell. He sneaked back up onto the porch to ring the bell again but noticed the door was slightly ajar. *Did she open it?* he wondered. *Maybe she's hiding behind the door. Or did she simply not close it all the way when she came home?* He could hear music coming from the radio inside the house. Picking up the bouquet, he slowly opened the door, half expecting she might be hiding behind it. She was not.

"Come out, come out, wherever you are!" he called.

No answer.

He stepped in and his heart stopped. The place was a mess. A chair was tipped over. The floor lamp was leaning against the wall. Books, magazines, and various other items were strewn across the floor. Angela's purse was upside down on the coffee table with its contents scattered about. The bouquet of flowers slipped from his trembling fingers and fell to the floor. "Oh my god!" he cried. "Angela! Angela? Where are you?"

He ran to the kitchen where he found a pot of water boiling on the stove. Several items of food were on the counter as if she had been in the middle of preparing dinner. "Oh Jesus," he muttered. He ran up the stairs calling her name but still she didn't answer.

He hurried back to the living room and looked around, trying to understand what he was seeing. *What the hell happened here?*

He tried not to panic but he had no idea what to do. He went back to the kitchen to turn the stove off. Then he felt a cold gust of wind come from somewhere. It had to be the back door just on the other side of the partition. He rushed over and found the door wide open. He stepped out and scanned the back yard hoping to see some sign of her but there was nothing. He stepped back inside and closed the door. Suddenly he stopped short. There was blood on the door. It wasn't much but it was enough to let him know someone had been hurt. In a panic, he ran to the living room to call the police. Just as he was about to pick up the phone, it rang. He stared at it for a moment, startled by the coincidence, then he picked it up. His hands shook uncontrollably as the adrenaline pumped through his body.

"Yes? Hello?" he said, nearly choking on his own words.

"Ezekiel Banyon?" It was a man's voice.

"Yes! What?" he said impatiently.

"I have something you want and you have something I want."

"*What?* Who is this?"

"Just listen to me, Banyon. I have a pretty lady sitting here and she hasn't been very cooperative. If you want to see her alive I'm betting you'll tell me what I want to know. Do we have a deal?"

"You have Angela? Is she all right? Where are you? What the hell do you want from me?"

With a sharp, angry voice the man replied, "You know damn well what I want! Tell me where it is and I'll send her back to you unharmed."

"Where *what* is?" Banyon demanded. "What the hell are you talking about?"

"Don't play dumb, Banyon. Where is it?"

"The parchment?" Banyon asked. "You want the parchment? The Ezekiel Code?"

"No!" the man yelled back. "I want to know where the craft is! Ezekiel's machine! Whatever it is! I know you've figured it out! But it seems your friend here doesn't want to tell me!"

"What?" Banyon screamed into the phone. "We haven't figured anything out! We don't know where the hell it is! We're not even sure *what* it is!"

"Your friend here tried to convince me of the same thing," the man said. "But I'm not buying it!"

"Jesus Christ!" Banyon screamed. "Just wait a minute, will you? What makes you think we know where the damn thing is? Hell, we don't even know if it exists! And who the hell are you, anyway?"

"You don't need to know who I am. You just need to tell me what I want to know or this pretty lady isn't going to end up looking so pretty."

"Listen," Banyon argued, "do you really think I would sacrifice Angela for some half-baked information about something that I'm not even sure exists? Are you out of your goddam mind? I'm telling you neither of us knows where the thing is, even if it does exist! You have to believe me for Christ's sake!"

There was a long pause on the other end of the line. In the background he could hear the muffled tones of men's voices.

Banyon was getting nervous. "Are you still there?"

"I'm still here." the man replied.

"Listen," Banyon said. "I'm telling you the truth! We don't have the information you're asking for. But you can have all the information we do have. Everything. The parchment, the notes, the computer files. Everything! Just don't hurt her! Please!"

There was another long moment of silence and again the muffled tones of men's voices in the background.

"All right," the man said. "When can you have all of that ready to deliver?"

Banyon was exhausted and sweating heavily. He sat down on the couch and tried to think. "Tonight," he said, finally. "I can have it all together tonight. How do I get it to you?"

"Do you know where Pier 34 is, down on the waterfront?"

"I can find it."

"At the end of the pier there's an old warehouse. The pier is under construction and it's blocked off at the entrance. You'll have to park your car on the street and walk down the pier."

"It's going to take me some time to get the stuff together," Banyon said. "Anything that's on computer disk is at my office. I'll have to go there to get it."

"You've got two hours," the man said. "And one more thing."

"What is it?" Banyon asked, angrily.

"Don't even think about calling the police. That would be a very bad mistake, if you know what I mean." The tone of the man's voice was dead serious and convincing. He hung up the phone before Banyon could say anything more.

Banyon looked at his watch. It was 7:30. He had two hours.

He tried to organize his thoughts. Where were the McClintock notes? Where was his copy of Paretti's paper? The parchment was in the safe in the other room. He knew that. What else did he need to find? He knew Angela had mentioned she was transcribing a lot of the stuff they were figuring out onto a computer program and she was saving it on a disk. He hadn't actually seen the disk and didn't even know what it might look like, let alone where she might have put it. *It has to be in her office*, he thought to himself. *It has to be.* Suddenly he had a chilling thought. What might he be walking into down there on the waterfront in the dark of night? Two men – McClintock and the Frenchman, and possibly even Densmore - had already been murdered over this thing. *Maybe I should call the police!* But the man's threat kept repeating over and over in his head. *Don't even think about calling the police. That would be a very bad mistake.* He checked his watch. It was 7:40. Angela had exactly one hour and fifty minutes left to live.

"Christ," he said to himself, burying his head in his hands. "What the hell am I going to do?"

He desperately wanted to tell somebody what was happening. He needed help. *What about Professor Kline?* He pulled out his wallet and nervously shuffled through several business cards until he found the one with Kline's number on it. He picked up the phone and dialed.

Kline answered. "Hello?"

"Thank God you're home!" Banyon said.

"Who is this?"

"This is Banyon! Zeke Banyon! I need your help!"

"Banyon! I didn't recognize your voice. Is something wrong? Are you all right?"

Banyon stood up and paced the floor trying to calm down while he told Kline everything that had transpired. "I don't know what to do!" he said. He was starting to panic again. He glanced at his watch. It was 7:50. "Should I call the police?"

"No," Kline advised. "This might be the same person responsible for the deaths of McClintock and the Frenchman and maybe even Densmore. If so, then this guy is too dangerous to mess around with."

"I know! Exactly! The same thing crossed my mind. But there was more than just this one guy. I could hear other men's voices in the background. Who the hell are these guys? Are they that Brotherhood of Nine you told us about? You said we wouldn't be in any danger from them!"

"No," Kline said. "It can't be. These guys can't possibly belong to the Nine. It just wouldn't make sense. Believe me. It must be someone else. Someone connected with another secret society with an entirely different agenda. That has to be it. Has to be."

Banyon sat down on the couch again, fumbled for a cigarette and searched his pockets for a lighter. Finally convinced that Kline just might know what he's talking about, he looked again at his watch. It was 8 o'clock. "All right," he said, drawing a deep breath and closing his eyes. "So what the hell do I do? Time is running out! I have to know what to do!"

"Listen to me. If I were you, I'd just get everything together and show up at the designated place and make the trade. I don't think they'll harm you."

"Why not? What makes you so sure?"

"Because these guys, whoever they are, must certainly know about the Nine and the protocol of non-interference. Remember I told you about that?"

"You don't call this interference?" Banyon argued, astonished. "What the hell do you call it?"

"What I was going to say," Kline continued, "is that they might be willing to risk breaking that rule if they think it'll gain them possession of the prize. But I doubt very much if they would dare risk harming the one man whom they know the Nine considers to be the long awaited Chosen One. They might as well call the wrath of God down on themselves. I'm serious about that."

"The Chosen One!" Banyon balked. "Why me? And what about Angela? Would they hurt her?"

"Unfortunately, yes, they probably would if they thought there was anything at all to be gained by it. I'm only assuming, of course. But you have to understand. She's not you. You're the one who really counts in this thing, not her."

"This is bullshit!" Banyon screamed.

"Calm down. You asked me and I've told you what I think. Now you have to do what you have to do."

"Jesus," Banyon said, as the reality of the situation settled over him. "I can't believe I'm going to do this."

"The way I see it," Kline responded, "you don't really have a choice. Get moving. You've only got a little more than an hour."

~22~

Banyon scrambled madly about the house gathering up the materials he needed to trade for Angela's life. The McClintock notes and the book Mrs. Densmore had given them were upstairs in the bedroom. He grabbed them quickly, stuffed them into a briefcase and tried to think. The original parchment containing the so-called Ezekiel Code was in a safe behind a panel in the wall in the closet of the spare bedroom.

He rushed to the room and opened the closet. He flipped the closet light switch but the light was burned out. He'd meant to replace it months ago. Fumbling around in the dark, he found the spot where the panel molding could be pivoted away, revealing a small notch in the edge of the panel. Fitting two fingers into the notch he slid the panel to one side. The small safe, firmly built into the casing, had a combination lock. Banyon's hands were shaking as he failed twice to get the lock to open. "Damn!" he curse loudly. Did he have it wrong? Was it 22-left or 22-right? He was sure it was 22-left. He tried it again. This time he heard the tell-tale click of the tumblers falling inside the lock. He swung the safe's door open, reached inside and pulled out the leather folder containing the old parchment. Quickly stuffing it into the briefcase, he checked his watch. It was 8:15.

He made his way back down stairs, grabbed his overcoat off the back of the couch and hurried to the front door. He put his hand on the doorknob but stopped for a moment to catch his breath. His heart was pounding. A chaotic jumble of disconnected thoughts spun wildly through his brain. He felt disoriented. He loosened his grip on the doorknob and turned around leaning back against the door. Closing his eyes for just a moment, he wished time would stop. Suddenly, almost uncontrollably, he was jolted back into the moment. He looked at his watch. It was 8:20.

Traffic was fairly light as he drove quickly down the main street. A traffic light turned yellow and he gunned the accelerator to make it through. One more light up ahead was already red. He came sliding to a stop on the damp street and pounded his hands impatiently on the steering wheel. "Damn it!" he shouted. "Come on!" He couldn't wait any longer. "Hell with it," he mumbled. He hit the accelerator and fishtailed through the intersection, nearly colliding with a pickup truck that came out of nowhere. He swerved violently around the truck. His briefcase slid off the seat beside him and slammed into the dashboard. He slowed momentarily to gain control of himself. Then, speeding up again, he was on the entrance to the freeway in just moments. He glanced at the clock on the dashboard. It was 8:29.

Moving quickly into the far left lane he was able to do 70 most of the way into town. Suddenly he realized his exit was approaching less than a quarter mile away and he needed to be back in the far right lane to catch it. In the heart of the city now, the freeway traffic was heavier and he panicked, not knowing if he could get across all four lanes in time to make the exit. He flipped on his turn signal and laid on the horn. No matter who or what was in his way, he was coming through. In a few moments he was off the freeway at the bottom of the ramp and had no idea how he did it. He checked the time. It was 8:45.

In a few minutes he arrived at the Seattle Gospel Mission and parked the car on the street in front of the entrance. He reached down, grabbed his briefcase off the floor, and ran inside the shelter. A few homeless folks were sitting around in the well-worn overstuffed chairs and no one even seemed to notice him as he burst through the door.

Hurrying down the hall, he came to Angela's office. The door was locked. "Damn!" he cursed. He'd given her the only key weeks ago and hadn't got around to having another one made for himself. He rattled the door in frustration. Knowing he had to get inside, there was only one thing to do. He stepped back and kicked the door as hard as he could. He heard the wooden molding crack. He tried again. The door didn't open but the bottom panel came loose. He kneeled down and pushed it in with his hand. Reaching in and up, he was able to grab the doorknob. With an awkward twist of the wrist the door opened and he rushed inside.

"Computer disk," he muttered to himself looking frantically around the room. "Computer disk, computer disk," he repeated over and over. "Where would she keep it? What the hell does it look like?" He rifled through the desk drawers and found nothing. He looked up at the clock on the wall. It was 8:55.

Why did I even tell the bastard about the computer disk? He would never have known if I hadn't mentioned it. Maybe he wouldn't remember! Maybe I could just show up without it!

He stopped for a moment and thought about simply leaving without the disk. Then he thought, no, it wasn't worth the risk. *The guy could be a total psycho,* he reasoned. *Just my luck he would remember I mentioned the damned disk and who knows what he'd do if he thought I was keeping something from him.* "Damn it, Angela!" he shouted. "Where the hell is it?"

He checked the shelf on the wall where she kept the paper and ink cartridges for the printer but found nothing. He plopped himself down in the chair in front of the computer and started wildly shuffling through stacks of papers and other items on her desk. Then he noticed a small plastic box with a hinged lid sitting next to the computer. He stared blankly at it for a moment. Making a sudden lunge, he accidentally knocked it off the desk. It hit the floor, the lid popped off and several disks spilled out. He pushed the chair back and got down on his knees to examine the disks, hoping she had labeled the one he needed. He flipped through them hurriedly reading the labels. Tossing them aside, one by one, he finally found what he was looking for. The label read:

Alphanumerics decoding efforts.

Progress log.

Complete entries to date.

"Yes!" he shouted, kissing the disk. He opened the briefcase, put the disk inside with the other materials and left her office. As he passed the door to his own office he stopped suddenly.

My gun, he thought to himself. *If there was ever a time, this is it.*

He ran inside his office, unlocked the safety box, took out the loaded pistol and dropped it into the deep pocket of his overcoat. He checked the time. It was 9 o'clock. He had exactly 30 minutes to find Angela.

He drove toward the waterfront, just a few blocks from the mission, but the piers identified with the lower number designations were in the opposite direction from where he was now. In this older, industrial part of town, the streets were dark, wet and quiet. At this time of night, other than a few cars parked along the curbs, there was almost no traffic at all. He passed under an old bridge and braced himself as the car bumped along over a series of railroad tracks. In a few minutes he was on the main street of the waterfront. He drove along slowly, pier after pier, passing the old buildings, the fish packing plants and warehouses that lined the street. The piers were poorly marked if they were even marked at all. The minutes were passing by quicker than he could drive.

I must be close, he thought to himself. *Where the hell is it?* Then he panicked. *Was it 34? It was Pier 34 wasn't it? Or was it 36?* The more he debated in his mind the less certain he was. *Wait a minute,* he thought. *The asshole on the phone said the pier was under construction!* He was relieved, knowing that would help him identify it. He drove on, slowly, hunched over the steering wheel looking for some sign of construction. Then he saw something: a striped barricade with two flashing amber lights. It was on the side of the street about a block ahead.

"That must be it!" His stomach tightened as he drove toward the barricade. His mouth was so dry he couldn't swallow. He parked the car and looked at his watch. It was 9:25. He had five minutes.

He took a deep breath and grabbed hold of the briefcase. He was aware of the weight of the gun in his coat pocket as he stepped out of the car.

The sidewalk had been torn up leaving a muddy mess. The flashing amber lights on the barricade reflected in the puddles. A dense fog had rolled in and the air had an eerie stillness about it. The old warehouse down at the far end of the pier looked dark and foreboding as the fog settled over it.

He walked around the side of the barricade and stepped up onto the old wooden pier. The only sounds he could hear were his own footsteps and the quiet, rhythmic sloshing of the stagnant, murky water just five or six feet beneath the decking of the pier. It had a pungent, unpleasant smell. He looked at his watch. It was 9:30 on the mark. Time was up. Suddenly, he heard a sound.

At the far end of the pier, backlit by a faint light from the opened door of the warehouse, he could see the dark figure of a man standing in the fog. Startled by the sight, Banyon froze for a moment, not sure what to do.

Standing motionless, staring at one another, Banyon and the figure at the end of the pier waited for each other to make the first move. Briefcase in hand, gun in pocket, confidence wavering, Banyon began walking slowly, cautiously toward the dark figure. As he got closer he couldn't believe what he was seeing. The man was dressed as a priest, white collar and all.

Then, without warning, two men emerged from the shadows and grabbed Banyon from both sides. Caught off guard, he was easily overpowered as they wrestled him to his knees. They grabbed him by the arms and quickly tied his hands behind his back.

"Well, look what we have here!" said one of the two thugs, removing the gun from Banyon's coat.

The man in the priest's clothing stepped forward to get a better look at his captured prey. "Bring him inside," he ordered.

They dragged him into the warehouse and closed the huge old wooden doors behind them. The place was cold and empty except for a few broken shipping crates stacked up against a far wall.

Banyon felt something warm running down the side of his face and realized he was bleeding from a wound. He started to say something but stopped short when he saw Angela. She was tied to a chair in the middle of the floor with a gag wrapped tightly across her mouth. "Angela!" he shouted. He started to rush toward her but he was held back by the two men. They shoved him into a chair and tied him securely to it. They positioned him so he was facing Angela, not five feet away. She looked worn and exhausted. He could see the frightened look in her eyes.

The man in the priest's clothes walked over and stood between them, facing Banyon. "So now I'm going to ask you, face to face," he said in a relatively calm voice. "Where is it? Where is it located?"

Banyon glared at him. "I told you we don't know. Whoever told you we solved the code was either lying or simply didn't know what they were talking about. I swear to God."

The priest's eyes flared. He whipped Banyon hard across the face with a gloved hand. "Tell me!" he bellowed.

"I can't tell you what I don't know!" Banyon shouted back.

He struck Banyon again, nearly toppling him, chair and all, to the floor. "Once more!" he demanded. "Tell me where it's located!"

Banyon's head was swimming from the blow of the man's fist.

The blood from the wound he received earlier was streaming down into his eyes. He tried to shake it away. "Please," he choked. "I'm telling you the truth!"

The priest walked around behind Angela and stroked her hair as he stared at Banyon. "Maybe you'd feel more like cooperating if we rearranged the young lady's pretty face."

"No!" Banyon screamed. "There's nothing to tell! Please! I've given you all the information we have! It's all in the briefcase! I swear!"

The priest, sweating and angry, pulled a knife out of his pocket. With a practiced flick of the wrist the blade snapped out, gleaming and razor sharp. He grabbed Angela's blouse and sliced it down the front. Terrified, Angela forced a muffled scream through the tightly bound gag.

"You son of a bitch!" Banyon yelled. He struggled to move toward them but the heavy hands of the other two men grabbed him by the shoulders and forced him to stay put.

"Tell me where it is!" The priest yelled again. Then he walked over to Banyon and grabbed him by the front of his coat, nearly lifting him and the chair off the floor. He bent down, looking right into Banyon's face, so close Banyon could see the blood vessels in the whites of his eyes. The priest screamed at Banyon once more, punctuating each word. "Tell... me... where... it... is!"

"How the hell can I tell you what I don't know?" Banyon screamed back into the man's face.

Angela managed to loosen the gag around her mouth just enough to force out a scream. "Leave him alone!" she yelled. "He's telling you the truth!"

The priest spun around and moved over to her. He grabbed her by the hair, yanking her head back. She gasped for breath. "She has beautiful eyes, don't you think?" he said, holding the knife up to her face. He shot a hellish look at Banyon. "Maybe you'd like to have one for a souvenir!"

Angela tried to move her face away from the gleaming blade but it was useless. The priest had her held tightly in his grip.

"Jesus Christ!" Banyon yelled. "You son of a bitch! Leave her alone!"

The priest yanked harder on Angela's hair, pulling her head back so far she could barely breathe. His knife grazed her eyebrow and drew blood. In the next instant all she could see was the gleaming point of the knife about to cut her eye.

At that moment a huge black, canopy-covered pickup truck came crashing through the old wooden doors into the warehouse. It squealed to a stop and three men, like guardian angels wielding automatic rifles, jumped out of the cab. The priest's two accomplices drew pistols and fired. Deafening explosions of gunfire echoed throughout the warehouse. The priest's two accomplices fell to the floor, riddled with bullets. The priest, wounded in the shoulder, dropped his knife and ran for the door but he was tackled by the three men from the truck. One of the men jammed the priest in the back with the butt of a rifle, dropping the wicked man to his knees. He gasped, trying to catch his breath and struggled to get up. Suddenly, a swift kick to the ribs took him down once more. His head hit the concrete floor with a thud and a dark pool of blood began to spread around him. Two of these guardian angels stood by the priest's body as the third one walked quickly across the floor toward Banyon. He stooped to pick up the priest's knife and turned to look at Angela. She screamed and nearly fainted. The man walked over and cut them both loose. Angela, nearly unconscious, started to fall forward. Banyon made a desperate lunge toward her and caught her just before she hit the floor. He laid her down gently and brushed the hair away from her half closed eyes. He turned and saw the man who had cut them loose was now with his two companions standing over the body of the priest.

"Damned rogue Jesuit," the man mumbled, looking down at the body. Angrily, he tossed the priest's knife onto the floor. They dragged the body over to the truck and hauled it up into the back. The canopy door slammed shut and the three men climbed up into the cab. The tires squealed in reverse and in mere moments they were gone.

Banyon was stunned, almost afraid to breathe. Still kneeling by Angela's side, he lifted her head gently. "Angela?" he whispered loudly. "Are you okay?"

She shook her head slowly, then gasped in panic as she regained full consciousness. She struggled to sit up. "Zeke!"

"Shhh! It's okay," he said. "It's over. It's all right."

He helped her get to her feet. When she saw the bloody bodies of the priest's two thugs sprawled out on the floor she grabbed hold of

Banyon. "Oh my god," she said, nearly in tears.

"We gotta get the hell out of here," Banyon told her.

His gun and the briefcase were sitting on a table by the warehouse doors that now hung in shambles, busted up from the grand entrance of the monstrous black truck. He grabbed the gun and the briefcase with one hand and held onto Angela with the other. They fled the warehouse and hurried down the long dark pier back out toward the street.

The fog had lifted and the air was even colder now. He helped her into the car and they headed for home.

The man behind the wheel of the mysterious black pickup truck made a call from his cell phone.

"The situation has been contained," he said. "Everything's okay. No. Yeah, a Jesuit. No, a rogue. I checked his I.D. He was the one we had heard about. All right. Yes. Good night."

The man on the other end of that call hung up the phone. He stood gazing out the window overlooking the vast dark expanse of the Bering Sea and lit up a cigar. In a moment he turned to address the other men in the room who were anxiously awaiting the report. "Gentlemen," he said, "we can all go home and rest easy. Everything has been taken care of and apparently the agreement has not been breached."

"Who was it?" asked one of the older men.

"It was the one we'd heard about. Just a lone wolf who strayed from the pack."

One by one the nine men filed out through the large dark mahogany doors of the meeting room, quietly congratulating themselves on their vigilance as they prepared to continue waiting patiently for the Chosen One to deliver the long awaited prize.

~23~

I t was nearly 11:30 p.m. by the time Banyon and Angela arrived home. They parked in the driveway and Banyon walked around the car to open the door for Angela. Just as she was about to step out Banyon heard another car door open and slam shut. He looked out toward the street and saw a man walking up toward the driveway. Banyon pushed Angela back into the car. "Stay there!" he told her, gripping the gun in his coat pocket.

Angela was startled by Banyon's unexpected behavior. "What is it?" she asked.

"Somebody's here," he whispered. He closed her door and motioned for her to lock it. He turned, facing the stranger who was now walking up the driveway in the dark. Banyon tightened his grip on the revolver in his pocket. *Maybe this isn't over yet*, he thought to himself. "Stop right there!" Banyon ordered, about to pull out the gun. "What do you want?"

"Zeke?" came the man's voice.

"Kline!" Banyon exclaimed, releasing his grip on the gun. "Jesus, man! You don't know how close you just came to meeting your maker! What the hell are you doing here?"

Kline walked up to him. "I'm sorry," he said. "I didn't mean to startle you. What the hell happened? You're hurt!"

"I'm all right. More or less, anyway." He nodded for Angela to unlock the door. "It's Kline," he informed her as she stepped out of the car.

"Good God," Kline said when he saw her. "You've both been hurt!"

Angela was still shaking and weak from the ordeal of the last several hours. She looked at Kline. "What are you doing here?" she asked, suspiciously.

"I tried calling a few times," Kline replied. "When no one answered I got worried. I thought if everything had gone well you would have been home sooner."

Angela didn't understand. She turned to Banyon. "What's he talking about?"

Banyon explained how he'd called Kline earlier to get some advice on how to handle the situation.

"I got worried about what might have happened," Kline said. "I couldn't sit around the house wondering, so I drove here hoping you would eventually show up."

"How did you know where I live?" Banyon asked. He, too, was slightly suspicious.

Kline shrugged. "Phone book," he said. "I hope you don't mind. What the hell happened?"

Banyon realized it was probably foolish to suspect the professor was in any way involved in the matter. He invited Kline into the house.

"Good God," Kline said as he entered the front door and surveyed the damage. Then he looked at Angela. "They roughed you up pretty good, didn't they?" His tone was genuinely sympathetic. "I'm glad you're all right. I didn't know what might happen to you."

Angela nodded but didn't say anything. She was shivering and still somewhat in shock. Banyon put his arm around her and walked her over to the couch. She sat down and began to cry despite her best effort to fight the tears. Banyon sat beside her and held her close. "It's okay," he said. "It's all right."

Kline walked over to the floor lamp that was leaning against the wall and stood it upright.

"Don't bother about that stuff," Banyon said. "We'll clean it all up tomorrow." He looked at Angela. "Are you okay?"

"Yeah," she said. She took a deep breath and wiped the tears from her face.

Taking stock of his own condition at the moment, Banyon realized he was still shaking from the ordeal. "I don't know about you guys," he said, taking off his coat, "but I could go for a glass of wine. Anyone else?"

Angela nodded.

"Sounds good," Kline said.

Banyon headed for the kitchen and returned in a moment with a bottle of red wine and three glasses. Kline grabbed the side of one of the chairs that had been toppled over and stood it upright. He turned it toward the couch and sat down.

The contents of Angela's purse were still scattered across the coffee table. She scooped it all back into her purse and made room for the bottle and the glasses.

Banyon sat on the couch beside her and poured the wine. "Well," he said, rather sarcastically, "here's to being alive."

Angela actually managed a smile. "I'll drink to that," she muttered quietly.

Over the next several minutes Banyon told Kline everything that had happened at the pier.

"Any idea who it was?" Kline asked.

"Not really, no," Banyon answered, shaking his head. "There was one thing, though."

"What's that?" Kline asked.

Banyon thought back, replaying the scene in his mind. "When the three men who arrived in the truck were standing over the body of the guy in the priest's clothing, one of them said, *damned rogue Jesuit.*"

"Jesuit!" Kline exclaimed. "That makes sense."

Banyon was puzzled. "It makes sense? How the hell does that make sense?"

Kline reached into his coat pocket and pulled out his pipe and a pouch of tobacco. "What do you know about the Jesuits?" he asked while filling his pipe.

"Not much," Banyon said. "I know they're an order of the Catholic Church."

Kline lit his pipe and took a few strong puffs to get it going. "There's more to the Jesuits than most people know." He tucked the tobacco pouch back into his pocket.

"What do you mean?" Banyon asked.

"Well, are you sure you want me to go into it now? You guys probably want to get some rest, I would imagine."

Banyon looked over at Angela. "How are you doing?"

"I couldn't sleep now if I wanted to," she said. "Maybe after another glass of wine, but not now."

"All right," Banyon, reaching for a smoke. He leaned back into the couch. "Let's hear it."

Kline thought for a moment, wondering where to begin. "Do you remember when you came to my office and we talked about what we called the bigger picture?"

Angela nodded. "I remember."

"What about it?" Banyon asked.

Kline took a sip of wine and set the glass back on the table. "Remember I said the bigger picture was always difficult to figure out, partly because so much of history seems to have been hidden from view and the truth is known only to certain initiates of any number of secret societies?"

"Like the Jesuits?" Banyon asked, anticipating where Kline was going.

"Exactly," Kline said.

"But the Jesuits are hardly a secret society," Banyon countered.

"True," Kline agreed. "But like other religious and quasi-religious groups - the Freemasons, for example - there's the public face of the organization and then there's the inner workings. The further up you go into these organizations the more secretive they get. It's a pyramid structure. The bottom level is the biggest. That's the public face of the organization with a seemingly open agenda. At that level there are very few secrets, if any, and there are many card-carrying members. Maybe hundreds, thousands. Maybe millions I suppose, depending on the organization. But the higher you go up the pyramid, there are fewer and fewer members but, ironically, more and more secrets."

"And at the top?" Angela asked.

Kline smiled and shrugged. "At the top," he said, "are the few who know things the rest of us may never know."

"Reminds me of that eye in the triangle at the top of the pyramid on the dollar bill," Angela said. "I've always wondered about that."

"There you go," Kline acknowledged. "That's a Masonic symbol. Did you ever notice that little triangle is actually above the pyramid, disconnected from it?"

"I've noticed that," Banyon said. "It's actually separate from the pyramid."

"It's a sign," Kline explained, "symbolizing that those who are in the know - the one's at the top - possess knowledge that truly separates them from the rest of humanity."

"The Illuminati," Banyon said.

"Very good!" Kline replied. "Indeed, the Illuminati. You've been doing your homework."

Banyon shrugged and glanced over at Angela. "We've learned a thing or two," he said, reaching over to hold her hand.

"What have you learned about the Illuminati?" Kline asked.

Banyon shrugged. "Not a lot. It almost seems like it's more of a myth than a reality. Lots of stories but no proof that they exist. Maybe they did exist at some time in the past, I don't know."

"Oh," Kline countered, "they existed all right. They still exist today but they've become masters at the art of concealing their true identity. In some ways they may even be in plain sight but simply aren't recognized."

"Are we talking about the Jesuits here?" Banyon asked.

Kline nodded. "Right. Here's why. And this is what most folks don't realize. The Jesuits were founded way back in the sixteenth century by a man named Ignatius of Loyola. At the time, though, they were called the Society of Jesus."

"Doesn't sound like a bad thing," Angela said.

Kline smiled. "Of course not. But what most folks don't know is that this Ignatius fellow was a high ranking officer in a secret society called the Alumbrado and he based his organization, the Society of Jesus, on the constitution and workings of that secret society."

"The Alumbrado?" Banyon asked.

"Yes. It's Spanish for illuminati."

Angela looked surprised. "You're kidding."

"Not at all. I'm dead serious."

"I see," Banyon said. "So that's the connection between the Jesuits and the Illuminati?"

Kline nodded.

"But I don't get it," Angela said. "Isn't the Jesuit organization a legitimate branch of the Catholic Church? I mean, if the Jesuits were actually some occult organization or something, wouldn't the Pope know about that?"

"Oh, the Pope is well aware of the history of the Jesuit organization. But as with so many things, politics and bribery often enter into the picture. Especially when there are secrets to be kept... or revealed, depending on which side of the game you're on."

Kline went on to explain that the Society of Jesus became very powerful and influential in Europe, gaining the friendship of many heads of state. Pope Paul III became concerned about this situation.

Not only did he perceive the popularity of the Society as a potential threat to the influence of the Catholic church but Ignatius of Loyola seemed to have access to a considerable amount of information about the Church's very secretive, politically motivated activities that the Pope simply could not risk having exposed. By an order from the Church, the Dominican faction of the Catholic inquisitors arrested Ignatius and brought him before the Pope where a deal was cut between these two powerful men. The Pope would officially sanctify the Society of Jesus as an approved religious order of the Catholic Church. And, rather than exposing the secrets of the Church, Ignatius of Loyola would be made a confidant and given immense power and authority in many political and social matters.

"So in essence," Kline continued, "The Jesuits became the secret army of the Catholic Church and Ignatius became the first Jesuit General. Literally, that's the title he was given and that's still the title of the head of the Jesuit organization today."

"The Vatican has an army?" Angela asked, completely stunned by the idea.

"In a sense, yes," Kline answered. "And I believe the Jesuits are more than just the army of the Church. I suspect they're also the intelligence arm of the Vatican. Sort of the Vatican's version of the CIA. They're a relatively independent organization."

"Independent?" Banyon asked. "I don't understand. I thought you said they were officially an order of the Catholic Church."

"Oh, they are. Yes. But unlike other factions of the Church, they're not answerable to any of the Bishops and Cardinals. They're only answerable to the big guy himself."

"The Pope," Angela offered.

Kline nodded. "Right. But remember, we're not talking about the lower levels of the Jesuit organization - most of whom, of course, are fine people with nothing but good intentions. We're talking about the top of the ladder."

"The Jesuit General?" Banyon asked.

"The Jesuit General, yes. At least to some degree. But there's a level even above that."

"Above that?" Banyon looked a little confused. "I thought the Jesuit General was the highest rank in the order."

Angela found the militaristic title to be ironic. "The Jesuit General," she said. "That's an amazing title for a religious leader regardless of where he is in the pecking order."

"I agree," Kline said. "But not as amazing as the title of the one above *him*."

"And what is that?" Banyon asked.

"The Black Pope," Kline replied.

Banyon chuckled. "The Black Pope? I never heard of such a thing!"

Kline nodded. "I'm not at all surprised," he said. "According to my information, the Black Pope is the very top of the pyramid. Higher than the Jesuit General. The most secretive enclave in the order. In other words, the real head of the relatively small cabal of Jesuits associated with the Illuminati."

"The Black Pope," Banyon said. "Does it refer to the race of the man? Like African origin or something?"

"No," Kline explained. "Has nothing to do with race or nationality. It's just a title."

"A pretty ominous title, I'd have to say," Banyon commented.

"True," Kline agreed. "And for good reason."

"How do you mean?"

Kline leaned forward and tapped the tobacco out of his pipe into the ashtray. "Well," he said, "not only does he have a considerable amount of power and influence within the decision making factions of the Church, but in the past - and I strongly suspect even now - the Jesuits have been involved in some horrendous activities. Very unpleasant stuff including political assassinations and the murders of private citizens around the world."

"You gotta be kidding," Banyon said. "How do you know this?"

"The information is there if you dig deep enough." Kline answered. Then he gave a laugh and said, "Hell, sometimes you don't even have to dig at all. Look at the reason for the whole Guy Fawkes Day in England! The so-called Gun Powder Plot and all that!"

"I've heard of Guy Fawkes Day," Angela said. "It's some kind of a holiday in Britain where they celebrate something. But I never did know what it was."

"It all happened back in the days of the reformation in England, back when King James the First was in power. King James was about as anti-Catholic as you can get."

Banyon interrupted. "This is the same King James who had the Protestant Bible translated into English?"

"Exactly. The Jesuits decided he had to go. They simply wanted to be rid of him. So a Jesuit priest by the name of Guy Fawkes led a group of like-minded King James haters in a conspiracy to blow up the House of Lords while King James and all of the important officials of the British Court were present. They had thirty-six barrels of gunpowder to do the job but they were caught in the act before they were able to light the fuse."

"That's amazing," Banyon said. "But I guess I shouldn't be surprised. I know the Church was responsible for a lot of unbelievably murderous activities during the so-called Holy Inquisition. But that was way back in the Middle Ages, the thirteenth century."

"That's right," Kline said. "At that time it was the Dominican faction of the Church that was instigating and carrying out the atrocities, torturing, murdering, raping. Truly inhuman stuff. Then, a couple hundred years later, after the Pope made the deal with Ingatius of Loyola, the Jesuits sort of took over that role as the Vatican's army."

"So the Jesuits were just as ruthless?" Angela asked.

"Oh, at least," Kline said. "As late as the eighteenth century the Jesuit organization was banned from maybe as many as fifty countries. They were despised everywhere it seemed. The French even issued an arrest warrant for anyone *suspected* of being a Jesuit! The warrant said something to the effect that the Jesuits were a dangerous political body with the single agenda of taking over the government by any means necessary including assassinations and murder."

"What's the difference?" Angela asked.

Kline looked puzzled. "What do you mean?"

"Between assassination and murder."

Kline thought about the question for a moment. "Well," he said, finally, "assassination, I think, applies more to the killing of political or religious leaders. Murder is... well, just killing anyone else who they think needs to be eliminated. It's possible the Jesuits were even responsible for the deaths of two Popes."

Banyon looked shocked. "Two Popes?"

Kline nodded. "It's possible. Can't be proven, of course, but the circumstances were suspicious."

"Which Popes?" Angela asked.

"The first one was Pope Clement the Thirteenth."

"And this was when?" Banyon asked.

"Oh," Kline said, trying to remember the dates, "that would have been sometime around the mid to late seventeen-hundreds."

"So what happened?" Banyon asked.

Kline relit his pipe and continued the story. "Pope Clement the Thirteenth was really under a lot of pressure from the various European countries to do something about the Jesuits. So he finally caved in and decided to abolish the organization. Well, not abolish it, exactly. He knew he couldn't do that. But the one thing he could do was declare a formal separation between the Church and the Jesuits. In other words, he could officially cut them loose from the Church. You see? That would absolve the Church from any responsibility for the future activities of the Jesuits. But the very night prior to the day he was scheduled to sign the order into effect he died suddenly from some mysterious illness. Now, I suppose you could chalk it up to coincidence but the Pope, himself, didn't think so."

"What do you mean?" Banyon asked.

"It's alleged that on his deathbed the Pope said something like *attacking the Jesuits is a very dangerous thing.*"

"So the Pope was convinced that the Jesuits were responsible for his death?" Angela asked.

"So the story goes. But what happened next really makes the idea of mere coincidence seem even less likely."

"What happened?" Banyon asked.

"Well, the successor to the position was Pope Clement the Fourteenth. And, of course, he just stepped into the same political pressures that the former Pope had left behind. But the new Pope had no illusions about the dangers posed by trying to get rid of the Jesuits. So he put off the whole thing as long as he could. Which turned out to be about three years. Anyway, the pressures from the other countries were closing in on him to the point where he had no choice but to attempt what his predecessor had unsuccessfully tried to do."

"But he couldn't do it either?" Angela asked.

"Oh no!" Kline said. "He did it all right! He signed an official papal brief calling for a complete dissolution of the entire Jesuit order. But no sooner had he done that than a mysterious message was found scrawled on a wall in the Vatican."

"What did it say?" Banyon asked.

"According to the way I heard it, it said *come September the Holy*

See will be vacant. Sure enough, come September the Pope died apparently from ingesting a poison."

"Interesting," Banyon said.

"Yes," Kline agreed. "But what's even more interesting, not to mention suspicious, is that this happened the same year that another Jesuit priest, in Bavaria, is said to have founded what we talked about earlier... the all mysterious Illuminati which was basically nothing more nor less than a modernized version of the more ancient Spanish Alumbrados! The agenda was exactly the same, too. The eventual establishment of a so-called New World Order. And you know what year this was? Take a guess."

"Don't have a clue," Banyon said, becoming increasingly intrigued.

"It was 1776. The very year of the signing of the Declaration of Independence of the United States. And at least eight of the signers of that document were Freemasons. Which brings us back, full circle, to the fellow who is said to have founded the modern version of the Illuminati. He was a Freemason and many of the original members that he recruited into the order of the Illuminati were Freemasons."

"I'm beginning to see the picture," Banyon said. "Jesuits, Illuminati, Masons, Declaration of Independence, and the design of the Great Seal on our dollar bill. It's all connected?"

"That and more," Kline said. "Like the lines on a dot-to-dot picture."

"How do you happen to know all this stuff?" Banyon asked. "I mean about the Jesuits."

"Well," the professor said, drawing deeply on his pipe. "I pretty much grew up with it. My uncle was a Jesuit. He was one of those at the lower level. A great guy, really. But he had an insatiable curiosity about everything. And you know what they say about curiosity."

Banyon shrugged. "Killed a cat?"

"May have killed my uncle," Kline replied. "When I was a teenager he used to tell me about this other Jesuit priest who he became friends with. He said this other priest sometimes told him things that were supposedly secrets – things he learned from members in the higher echelons of the organization. Why the other priest would actually come out and tell my uncle these so-called secrets, I have no idea, except that my uncle had this well-honed knack for extracting information from people."

Banyon looked surprised. "Did your uncle ever reveal any of this secret information to you?"

Kline shook his head. "No. At least not that I remember. What I remember most were the stories he told me about the atrocities that the Jesuits had been involved in periodically throughout their early history. He didn't know about a lot of it until later when he began to dig deeper into the history of the Order. It really began to bother him even though his superiors seemed to either claim it was all a bunch of exaggerated, baseless conspiracy theory or, in some cases, they just ignored it all without comment."

"What did you mean when you said curiosity might have killed your uncle?" Banyon asked.

"He died in a car accident about fifteen years ago. At least it appeared to be an accident although there were no other cars involved. At least not that anyone knew about. He was on the North Cascades Highway, driving back to Seattle from a visit to the little town of Winthrop over in Eastern Washington."

"I know the road," Banyon said. "It can be tricky. Lots of curves and steep grades."

"Yes, well his car was found at the bottom of one of the ravines. The guard rail on the side of the road was badly damaged as if he'd lost control of the car on a down hill curve and just went over the side."

"You don't think it was an accident?" Angela asked.

Kline shrugged. "Who can say? I don't know. It just always seemed suspicious to me. He'd driven that road dozens of times."

Angela shook her head. "Why would they want to kill your uncle?"

"Again, I don't know if they had a hand in it or not. But if they did I suppose it could be that he gained access to some information that they deemed important enough to make sure he wouldn't have a chance to reveal to anyone."

Angela sighed. "Well, now I see why you weren't surprised that the men who kidnapped me might have been Jesuits."

Kline nodded. "No. It didn't surprise me at all."

Banyon brushed his hair back and winced as his hand rubbed against the bruised wound on the side of his head.

"You should have that looked at," Kline advised. "You've got a pretty good gash there."

"Yeah. I hit my head on something when those two guys wrestled me down onto the pier. I don't know what it was. A railing or something."

Kline looked at Angela. "You were really lucky," he said, examining the mark by her eyebrow. "The knife left only a small scratch really. Enough to bleed but it looks like it'll be fine in a couple of days."

"So what do you think?" Banyon asked. "You think there'll be more of what happened tonight?"

"Well," Kline said, taking a long thoughtful breath. "Honestly? I don't think this is likely to happen again."

"Why not?" Banyon asked.

"I think when that fellow at the warehouse looked at the priest on the floor and referred to him as a *damned rogue Jesuit...* well, I think that was a pretty big clue as to what happened tonight."

Angela gave a quizzical look. "How so?" she asked.

"There can't be any doubt whatsoever," Kline said with total confidence, "that the Jesuits - those few in that upper clandestine level - are fully aware of the Brotherhood of The Nine Pillars and everything I told you when we met at my office. Remember I told you about the policy of not interfering, or in any way disrupting your progress in deciphering the code and ultimately discovering the location of the object, whatever it turns out to be?"

Banyon and Angela both nodded. "So what went wrong?" Banyon asked. "Somebody damn well interfered!"

"What went wrong," Kline explained, "is that the priest who got pummeled to the floor by your knights in shining armor – or, in this case, in a shiny black pickup truck - was just some misguided Jesuit fool whose ego and greed for power got the best of him. Sort of a Lucifer in priest's clothing you might say."

"The rogue angel who wanted to play God," Banyon quipped.

Kline laughed. "Yes, well, something like that. But the Jesuits in high places – the ones we're talking about - are anything but angels. In any case, I wouldn't worry about it happening again. I can very well imagine there's a shakeup going on right now within the ranks of the other Jesuits up there in the top levels of the Order. And you can bet the Nine will be keeping a closer eye on them. It's pretty clear that the

Nine were on top of the situation, judging from their quick response tonight."

"Not quick enough," Angela said with more than a hint of sarcasm.

"No," Kline agreed. "I suppose not. But quick enough to save you from a fate worse than what you experienced tonight. That's for sure."

Angela breathed a deep sigh and closed her eyes.

Banyon leaned closer and took her hand. "Are you okay?"

She opened her eyes slowly. "Yeah," she said. "But I'm exhausted. I feel like my head is swimming."

Kline stood up and straightened his coat. "It's late," he said. "I really should go."

Banyon got up and walked him to the door. "Thanks for coming over," he said. "This all seems so unreal. Like a dream. I can't believe it happened."

"Yes, well it happened all right," Kline replied, looking around at the chaotic state of the living room. "But you'll be all right. I'm sure of it."

Banyon put his hand on Kline's shoulder and they shook hands. "Thanks again," he said, opening the door for the professor. "I'll call you."

"Don't mention it," Kline said as he stepped out onto the porch. Half way down the steps he turned around. "Oh, by the way…"

"Yes?"

"Jason called me this evening when he couldn't reach you at home."

"Jason?"

"McClintock's son. At the bookstore?"

"Oh! Of course. Jason. What did he want?"

"Said he had something for you."

"What is it?"

"An old paperback book someone brought in as a trade."

"A book? What kind of a book?"

"Something about Ezekiel. Apparently written by a former NASA engineer. He thought you should see it."

Banyon shook his head as if he hadn't heard right. "A what?" he asked.

"Call Jason when you get a chance. He'll explain it to you."

"All right," Banyon said, still puzzled. "Good night."

"Good night," Kline replied with a final wave.

Banyon closed the door and locked it behind him.

Angela was still sitting on the couch. "What was that about?" she asked, almost too tired to really care.

"Jason. McClintock's son. He's got something for us. A book."

Angela sighed and got up slowly. Her knees felt week. "Oh, God." she said. "I don't want to think about it. I don't want to think about anything. I just want to go to bed."

Banyon walked over and held her close. She looked up at him and tried to smile. It had been one hell of a night and there was really nothing left to say. They walked up the stairs to the bedroom and soon, safe in each other's arms, they escaped into a restful sleep.

~24~

B anyon woke up early the next morning leaving Angela to sleep as long as she could. He made a pot of coffee and straightened up the mess in the living room. Thinking back on last night's conversation with Kline he suddenly remembered Kline said Jason had a book for them. Something he thought they'd be interested in. Banyon didn't feel like making the drive all the way to the bookstore so he decided to call instead.

"Sirius Books. This is Jason. How can I help you?"

"Jason, this is Zeke Banyon."

"Oh! Yeah, I tried to reach you the other day but you were out. So I left a message with Professor Kline."

"Yes, Kline gave me the message. He said you have some kind of a book for us. What is it?"

"Right. Yeah, it's an old paperback published in the early seventies. The title made me think of you."

"What is it?"

"It's called *The Spaceships of Ezekiel*."

Banyon nearly choked on his coffee. "You gotta be kidding. What is it? A novel or something?"

"No, it's not a novel. It's by some guy named Blumrich who used to work for NASA as a design engineer. I just sort of browsed through it but it looks like what he did was compare modern space technology with the descriptions of some weird object in the book of Ezekiel in the Bible."

Banyon was fascinated. "So what does he have to say about it?"

"Well, like I said, I only took a quick look through the pages but I think he reached the conclusion that the object described in the Bible resembles some of the stuff NASA actually had on the drawing board when he was working there."

Banyon was astonished. "Are you sure the author worked for NASA?"

"Yeah, just a second..." Jason paused for a moment, thumbing through the pages of the book. "Okay," he said, finally. "Says here he was chief of the systems layout branch of NASA. Whatever that means."

"Interesting. Listen, Jason, I'd really like to see the book but I was wondering if you would mind sending it to me by mail."

"Sure, no problem. I can get it into the mail this afternoon."

Banyon asked him to send it to the Seattle Gospel Mission and thanked him for his trouble.

It was nearly 8:30. He needed to get down to the shelter but he didn't want to leave Angela alone in the house. He decided to go upstairs to check on her.

"Angela," he whispered. She didn't move. "Angela", he whispered again, stroking her hair.

She rolled over and partly opened her eyes. "Hi," she said softly. "What time is it?"

He smiled. She looked beautiful in spite of the trauma of the previous night. "It's just a little past eight-thirty. How are you feeling?"

She shrugged her shoulders and sat up, brushing her hair away from her face. "Like a truck ran over me," she groaned.

He sat down on the bed next to her and held her hand. "I'm not sure what to do. I have to go down to the shelter but I don't want to leave you here alone. Do you feel up to going with me?"

"I don't want to be here alone either. I guess I'll go with you. Do I have time to take a shower?"

"Sure. No hurry. Whatever you need to do." He got up from the bed and smiled. "You're one tough cookie for such a little thing."

Angela stumbled out of bed and into her bathrobe. "Yeah right," she said with a grin. "I'm a regular Hulk Hogan. Is that coffee I smell?"

"One cup of java coming right up," he said on his way out of the bedroom.

When they arrived at the shelter Banyon made the rounds to see how things were going and Angela went to inspect her office.

"Oh, my god," she gasped when she saw the damage to the door. She walked in and surveyed the mess Banyon had created the night before. She straightened up the shelves and picked up the computer disks that were scattered across the floor. She sat at her desk and tried to imagine what he'd gone through that night in his desperate attempt to rescue her. She leaned back and closed her eyes as visions of the events of that frightening night rushed through her mind. Suddenly she was jarred back into the present by Banyon's voice.

"You okay?" he said, stepping over a piece of the broken doorframe.

"Yeah, I think so."

"I'll get someone in here to fix the door today."

Angela nodded. "Did anyone say anything? About the door, I mean?"

"No, actually. Apparently no one has noticed it yet. Amazingly, nobody seemed to hear the noise when I kicked it in last night either. In fact, nobody is even aware that anything happened here at all."

"Well, that's one good thing. It saves us from having to come up with an explanation."

Banyon gave a laugh. "True. Thank God for little favors. Hey, I have some coffee brewing in my office. You want some?"

She nodded and Banyon headed down the hall to his office. When he returned with the coffee a few minutes later he found Angela checking her email.

"Anything from that Paretti guy?" he asked, sliding the extra chair around so he could see the computer monitor.

Angela scrolled through several junk emails, deleting them one by one. "Hate this spam," she said.

"Someone selling Spam?" Banyon asked. "I always kind of liked it. Especially fried with a couple of eggs."

Angela laughed. "No, not that kind of spam. Spam is the word people use to mean junk email. You know how you get junk mail in your mailbox?

"Yeah, I get tons of it."

"Well, it's the same with the internet. People send out emails advertising everything from breast enlargement creams to real estate investment scams. For some reason people began referring to all the junk email as spam."

Banyon laughed. "I'll bet the people who make the meat product aren't real happy about that."

Angela cast him a sideways glance. "You think it's meat in that can?"

"Well, whatever it is. I still like it."

"Hey," she announced, looking at the screen. "Here we go. We got something from Paretti." She read the message aloud:

Dear Angela and Zeke,

Thanks for the email.

You wrote:

<<We sort of stumbled into an old legend about a lost scroll supposedly written by the biblical prophet Ezekiel. We were wondering if you were familiar with this legend.>>

I'm sorry, no. I've never come across that legend. Sounds interesting though. There are a lot of strange tales out there. A person could spend a lifetime checking them all out.

As to your question about how I came up with some of those phrases... well, it's a little hard to explain. But at the risk of coming off like some kind of a flake, and since you asked, I'll tell you.

Soon after I began to really get into this alphanumerics stuff it was as if sometimes my brain was doing little calculations without me knowing about it and something like a little voice in the back of my mind would suggest I try certain phrases. It was, and still is, kind of weird because when that happens I almost feel like I know ahead of time that the alphanumeric value of the phrase is going to be one of the significant numbers. If you've read through my material, you know what I mean by "significant numbers".

"Yes!" Banyon said. "I know what that's like! Remember when I told you the same thing was happening with me?"

"I remember. What is it with you guys, anyway?"

"I don't know. It's weird."

Angela continued to read aloud:

The phrases you mentioned (NINE IS THE KEY, NEGATIVE DARK, and POSITIVE LIGHT) just sort of came to mind in the manner that I just described. The phrase, NINE IS THE KEY, wasn't such a leap really, when you consider that my whole line of inquiry centered around the number nine. The further I delved into it the more obvious it became that the number 9 was, or at least might be, a key of some kind. So when it turned out that 144 was the value of that phrase I wasn't particularly surprised but I was incredibly intrigued at the same time.

The other phrases (NEGATIVE DARK and POSITIVE LIGHT) came about I suppose as a natural consequence of giving a lot of thought to the idea of light and it's importance as a metaphor in the ancient writings. Which brings me to your question about how I came to equate the number 144 with the concept of light.

Actually that's not my idea. It's something I was told by another researcher. His information was that it stemmed from the Hebrew gematria. I tried to verify this from a number of different sources, including a couple of rabbis but nothing seemed to click. Another researcher suggested it might have its roots in some Druid magic, or something along that line, but I could find no correlation there either.

Eventually I happened to hook up, over the internet, with a guy named Michael Lawrence Morton who was studying the work of Carl Munck. Don't know if you know about Munck's amazing discovery of what he simply referred to as "The Code" or "The Pyramid Matrix", but Morton was studying Munck's work and expanding on it (with unbelievable results, by the way!). It would take much too long to explain it all in this email. But the point is, when this number 144 came up in conversation, Morton suggested I might be interested in reading some books by a fellow named Bruce Cathie. Cathie's work is also too complex to get into here, but suffice to say he came up with a couple of very interesting calculations. In the course of developing his research into tracking the flight paths of reported UFO sightings from around the world he discovered what he believes is a geomagnetic grid around the earth. Again, without getting into details, suffice to say he developed a system of measurement called grid seconds based on this proposed geomagnetic grid. Using this system, it turns out that the maximum speed of light is 144,000 nautical miles per grid second. (Maximum speed, by the way, is suggested to be the speed of light in a vacuum, so to speak. Or, as Morton put it, "the speed of light in "open space" before it is 'slowed-down' incrementally by any given celestial body's atmosphere and magnetic field".)

Therefore, the number 144 is what Cathie calls the "light harmonic number". So, in a nutshell, that's the only verifiable data I have been able to find which connects the number 144 to the concept of light. Still, even without Cathie's work, the notion that 144 is the "Light Number" persists within the esoteric community. Hope that answers your question.

Thanks for taking an interest in my work. Keep in touch and take care.

Sincerely,
Vince Paretti

Angela looked over at Banyon. "Well, there you go. He answered our questions. Now what?"

Banyon gave a laugh. "I haven't the slightest idea. But the way things are going, I'll bet whatever's next is just waiting for us to stumble into it."

~25~

Other than a night out to catch Old Tom's debut performance at Charlie's Place on Tuesday which, judging from the audience reaction, was well received, the rest of the week passed without incident. Banyon tended to business at the shelter, waiting for the next shoe to drop, and Angela caught up on her studies to prepare for final exams. Then on Friday that other shoe dropped as the book from Jason arrived in the mail.

As they prepared to leave the office and head for home, Banyon handed the book to Angela. "This is really interesting," he said.

"You read it already?" she asked, a bit surprised.

"Yeah," he said, helping her on with her coat. "It's a pretty fast read. Just a little over a hundred pages I think. The last section was beyond me. I tried to read it but it's pretty technical stuff. The author was a systems engineer for NASA and he wrote the last section of the book mainly for others with similar backgrounds. There's a lot of advanced math and engineering stuff that he uses to confirm his idea that the so-called visions of Ezekiel were actually real encounters with real spacecraft. But the rest of the book is plainly written and *really* fascinating."

As they drove home he told Angela about how the book's author went into a detailed examination of the text of Ezekiel, verse-by-verse, comparing Ezekiel's descriptions of the vehicles he encountered with what we know today about spacecraft technology, or at least what was known back in the 1970s when the book was written.

"Did you know," Banyon asked as he slowed down to make the turn onto the freeway, "that Ezekiel had four different encounters with those things?"

Angela shook her head. "No, I thought it was just one. But then I never really read the book of Ezekiel. I guess I mostly just knew about it from... I don't know really. Sunday school, I suppose. And then there was that old gospel song about it."

"Oh man! Yes! I remember that! How did it go? I forget."

Angela sang a verse. "*Ezekiel saw the wheel, way in the middle of the air! Ezekiel saw the wheel way in the middle of the air! A wheel in a wheel, way in the middle of the air! Glory hallelujah!*"

Banyon shot her a glance. "Wow!" he exclaimed, nearly swerving over into the next lane. "You can sing!"

She laughed. "Well, thank you! But you don't have to get us killed over it!"

"No, really! You ought to join up with Old Tom and kill 'em down at Charlie's Place!"

Angela laughed again. It was the second time in her life someone had said something like that. She took drama in high school where she once played the part of Maria in a production of *West Side Story*. She was originally cast as one of the girls in the gang but she was also the understudy for the part of Maria. On the second night of the play the girl who was cast for the role of Maria came down with the flu and Angela got the chance to play the part. At the half-time intermission her drama teacher, who was directing the production, came up to her with a look of some surprise on his face.

"Angela," her drama teacher said in all seriousness, "you've been holding back on me. You sang very well in auditions but, good lord, your performance tonight was... well, it was stunning, really. If you would have sung like that for the audition I would have cast you as Maria. No doubt about it."

Angela grinned from ear to ear. "Yeah?" she said excitedly. "Well, I don't know what happened. I guess it was just actually being out there in front of the audience and all. It just came out of me!"

"Well," her teacher said, "whatever it was, it worked. With a voice like that you could go pro."

"Really? You think so?"

"Well, not tomorrow, of course," he said, grinning. "But yes, eventually, with a little training, sure. You have a gift. I hope you do something with it."

As it happened, however, such was not to be the case. Perhaps if she'd had some support at home things might have been different. But her mother just wanted her to get married and settle down and her father was usually too absorbed in his work to really pay much attention one way or the other. Or maybe if she'd taken the drama class in her sophomore year and continued for the next two years to gain some more experience instead of waiting until her final year of high school, maybe that would have made a difference. Or maybe it was just never meant to be. Maybe there was something bigger, something more important waiting for her somewhere down the long uncertain road.

"But that popular idea of the whole craft looking like a wheel in a wheel," Banyon explained, "is all wrong."

"I'm sorry," Angela apologized. "I guess I was thinking about something else. What did you say?"

"Maybe it was because of that song," he continued, "I don't know. But even I had the idea that the craft Ezekiel saw was shaped like a big wheel of some sort. I remember even seeing an illustration like that somewhere. Probably on the cover of one of those supermarket tabloids or something."

"You mean it wasn't really shaped like that? Like a big wheel? Like it says in the song?"

"Right. The wheel-in-a-wheel was just one part of the craft. Well, actually four parts. There were four separate units on the lower section of the craft and each unit had these odd *wheels within wheels*, as Ezekiel described them. The wheels were attached to these large perpendicular units and each one seemed to have a man inside. Ezekiel said he could see the face of a man in the front of each unit. When the craft landed these units could then move around on the ground, each apparently guided by the man inside. And it was the way the units moved that caught Ezekiel's attention."

"What do you mean?"

"I mean Ezekiel described the movement as forward and backward and side to side, almost like following a grid pattern, if you see what I mean. But it was the wheels that really captured his attention because of all the strange parts of this craft the only things he recognized as something he was familiar with were the wheels. The only problem was, he'd never seen wheels move like these ones. Any wheel he'd ever seen could only move one direction, either forward or backward. If the wheels were attached to a cart, for example, if the cart was to go any direction other than straight forward or straight backward then, of course, the whole wheel assembly would have to be turned to face the new direction. See what I mean?"

"Yes, okay. And...?"

"And *these* wheels, these wheels *within* wheels, don't have to be turned in the direction that they're moving because they propel the contraptions they're attached to in a kind of zig-zag pattern."

"I don't get it."

Banyon thought for a moment. "Okay," he said, "imagine a checker board on a table in front of you."

Angela nodded. "All right. Go on."

"Now put a checker on one of the squares on your side of the board."

Angela grinned as she moved her hands, mimicking his instructions. "Okay," she said. "I'll put it right.... here."

"All right, now let's say you want to move the checker *diagonally* toward the upper right but the rules say you can only move it forward or backward or right or left. So you move it one square straight up and then one square to the right. And then up another square and then another square to the right. Or two squares, or three, or whatever. Doesn't matter. The point is, obviously, you're moving in a diagonal direction even though you're only going straight forward and straight to the right."

"Okay, I see that. But how did these wheels make a sideways movement as well as a forward movement if the whole wheel assembly didn't swivel?"

Banyon went on to explain. "The author used his engineering expertise to figure out a way the wheels could have been constructed to allow for both forward-backward and side-to-side movement without the wheel unit ever having to be turned in the direction of the movement. There's a schematic drawing of it in the book."

Angela thumbed through the book and found the drawing. The technical solution the author came up with was very clever, indeed. It involved each wheel being constructed in a series of individually moveable sections, looking almost like a string of sausages strung together in a loop to form the wheel. While the whole wheel could move forward and backward, each *sausage* section also had the capability of rotating in such a way that the wheel unit could go sideways, right or left, as well as forward and backward. It was an ingenious solution but would obviously require some remarkable engineering.

"And he noticed something else, too," Banyon added. "Apparently it's something bible scholars have discussed for years but it lends some credence to the idea that there could actually be a lost scroll of Ezekiel."

Banyon told her how the author pointed out the fact that portions, entire phrases, of so many of the verses in Ezekiel seemed oddly mixed up, sometimes completely out of place, especially in the sections dealing with his strange encounters. Some scholars, Banyon explained, had even suggested that complete passages of the original writings were probably left out, either intentionally or by accident.

"If that's really the case," Banyon went on, "then I suppose it's *possible* the so-called lost scroll of Ezekiel could be more than just a myth. You see what I mean?"

Angela looked at him with raised eyebrows. "More than just a myth? You mean, with all that's happened, you're still not convinced? You have to be beat over the head with a hammer, or what?"

Banyon shrugged. "Yeah, I guess you're right. I don't know. I guess just reading about the possibility that entire portions of Ezekiel's writings are missing sort of makes all of this seem more real. I'm starting to become more convinced."

The rest of the way home, Angela thumbed through the book, reading portions here and there as something interesting would catch her eye. She was amazed by what the author had accomplished in his analysis. She was especially surprised to read the comment about Ezekiel's description of the so-called *calf's feet* located on the bottom of the units that Ezekiel described as *living creatures*. The actual passage read:

And their feet were straight feet; and the sole of their feet was like the sole of a calf's foot; and they sparkled like the color of burnished brass.

The author noted that he, himself, was immediately struck by this description because he had been involved in the design of such feet for the legs of landing craft some years ago. The *feet* on Ezekiel's craft could apparently be raised and simultaneously replaced by the lowering of the wheels when it was time for the units to become mobile.

All told, this book left little doubt that Ezekiel's visions were actual encounters with real spacecraft and real occupants. Who the occupants were, the author didn't venture a guess. He noted only that Ezekiel apparently found them to be fairly unremarkable in that he didn't elaborate on their physical appearance other than to refer to them, with one exception, as *men*. The exception was the occupant who seemed to be in control of the entire scenario. Ezekiel referred to him variously as *The Lord* and once as *The Lord God*. Curiously, however, he also described this entity as having "*the appearance of a man*".

"Funny," Angela commented. "Ezekiel describes the head honcho as looking like a man but also uses the phrase, *The Lord*, when referring to him."

Banyon nodded. "Yes and no."

"What do you mean?"

"The same thing occurs in other parts of the Bible where these beings referred to as *angels*, and even *The Lord,* are apparently indistinguishable from humans."

Angela looked surprised. "Really?" she said. "Like where?"

"There's a whole passage in Genesis where both *The Lord* and the *angels* are described as men. It's the story of Abraham and the destruction of the cities of Sodom and Gomorrah. I remember when I first read it I was confused. I had to read it several times to make sure I was reading it right. These three guys show up at Abraham's tent and somehow, even though he calls them *men*, he also addresses them as *My Lord.* And he invites them into his tent and they engage in conversation and he has his wife prepare a meal for them."

"Hmm..." Angela said. "Strange. I always thought of the angels as... well, you know. Having halos and wings and all that."

Banyon laughed. "Well, you're not alone. Almost everyone has that idea. I don't know where that ever came from. I don't think there's any place in the Bible where angels are described like that. Seems like, at some point, some artist had this idea of angels having wings and a glowing light around their heads and eventually that's the image everybody had in their mind whenever someone mentioned angels. I don't know. But you should read that chapter in Genesis. It's really puzzling."

When they arrived home Angela took the Bible off the shelf and sat down to read the story of Abraham. Banyon was right. It seemed as if the angels were indistinguishable from other men. Still, something had to clue Abraham and others to the fact that these *men* were different from ordinary men. Curiously, however, there was nothing in the scripture to indicate any such clue. Even when two of the angels accompanied Abraham's nephew, Lot, into the city of Sodom the townsmen clearly thought they were *men* as there was nothing to distinguish them as being anything *other* than men. But these strange *men* soon showed their true colors. Lot invited them into his house and before long several of the townsmen, apparently homosexuals, were pounding on Lot's door demanding that the two strangers come out so they could *know them* in the Biblical sense, as the saying goes. But the strangers moved Lot out of the way and let loose with a little magic:

Gen. 19:11: And they smote the men that were at the door of the house with blindness, both small and great: so that they wearied themselves to find the door.

The scripture didn't say how they managed to accomplish this remarkable feat but Angela was pretty sure they didn't just poke their eyes out with a sharp stick. Clearly they were in command of some sort of super human power even if they didn't have wings. The power they displayed in that instance, however, was nothing compared to what happened next.

After convincing Lot to gather up his family and leave the city these so-called angels proceeded to destroy both cities with one huge blast of something that turned the entire plain into a smoking wasteland:

Gen. 19:24: Then the Lord rained upon Sodom and upon Gomorrah brimstone and fire from the Lord out of heaven.

Gen. 19:27: And Abraham gat up early in the morning to the place where he stood before the Lord:

Gen. 19:28: And he looked toward Sodom and Gomorrah, and toward all the land of the plain, and beheld, and, lo, the smoke of the country went up as the smoke of a furnace.

This was also the incident where, during their escape from Sodom - just before all hell broke loose - Lot's wife turned to see the blast that destroyed the cities and she was turned into a pillar of salt.

Suddenly that verse sparked a memory in the back of Angela's mind. She remembered her old friend, Cynthia, who once told her the Force in the movie, *Star Wars*, was similar to the philosophy of Taoism. In another conversation, when they were talking about religion and how it could be that a kind and loving God could destroy all those people, Cynthia said something which, at the time, seemed quite bizarre.

"You know," Cynthia said, inhaling a hit off the neatly rolled joint, "I don't think that was the same God that Jesus talked about. I think it was a time traveler from the future."

Angela laughed. "I beg your pardon?"

Cynthia held the smoke in for a few seconds until she coughed it out. "Yeah," she said, catching her breath. "I mean check it out. The guy... this God ...whatever ...has the technology to blow up two cities in one swell foop...". She caught her own tongue-twisted mistake and began laughing hysterically.

Angela couldn't help but break into laughter too, even though she hadn't had so much as a single hit off the marijuana.

"Okay, okay," Cynthia said. "I'm serious now." But she couldn't help bursting out in laughter again.

The two of them giggled until they were out of breath and finally Angela asked her about this time traveler idea.

"Yeah, okay," Cynthia said, wiping a tear from her eye. "Seriously, I read something really interesting. You know that thing in the Bible about the lady who turned into a pillar of salt when she looked back at whatever it was that destroyed the city?"

"Vaguely," Angela replied. "I remember reading it once, I think."

"Yeah, well, I read that the word that was translated as *salt* can also mean *vapor*."

"Vapor?" Angela asked, somewhat confused.

"Yeah! Vapor! You know. Like steam or something. Vapor."

Angela still didn't understand. "And? What are you saying?"

"So, I don't know," Cynthia said. "I just read it somewhere. Thought it was kind of interesting. I could really go for a bag of potato chips."

That was pretty much the end of that conversation as far as Angela could recall. It had seemed so unimportant at the time and she'd forgotten all about it until this very moment. Now, in the context of what she'd been reading, Cynthia's bit of trivia took on a whole new meaning. She called for Banyon who had gone upstairs. "Zeke! Come here for a minute!"

Banyon came down and found her sitting on the couch with the Bible in her lap. He sat down next to her. "What is it?" he asked.

"Check this out."

She proceeded to read to him the entire 19th chapter of Genesis so he could get the whole thing in context.

"Okay," he said when she'd finished reading. "What about it?"

She told him about the conversation with Cynthia and the time traveler idea.

Banyon smiled. "Your friend Cynthia was a real hippie wasn't she? I love the idea about the time traveler. But what are you getting at?"

"Okay. Think about it. Don't they say the human body is like ninety percent water?"

"Yes. Something like that. So?"

"So what happens to water when it's subjected to high heat?"
Banyon thought for a moment. "Well, it evaporates."

"Exactly! It vaporizes, right?"
Banyon's eyes lit up as he started to see where she was going.

Angela grinned. "Lot's wife didn't turn into a pillar of salt. That doesn't make any sense. She turned into to a pillar of *vapor*!"

Banyon was intrigued by this line of reasoning. "Keep going," he said.

"I don't know what this... this *God* was," she continued. "I don't know if he was a time traveler from the future or a humanoid alien from another planet or just some meddling guy from another dimension. But whatever he was, I think he had command of nuclear weapons."

Banyon grinned. "Nuclear weapons?"

"Yes! The fire and brimstone raining down from the sky! Nukes! Missiles! Boom! Enough energy to wipe out two cities in one swell foop, as my stoned friend put it!"

Banyon got up and lit a cigarette. "Man, Angela" he said, pacing the floor. "That all makes sense! I remember those old black and white film clips from the 1950s showing the effects of a nuclear blast. You could literally see the shock wave roll out across the whole area, vaporizing everything in its path!"

"Exactly," Angela said excitedly. "And Lot's wife got caught in the wave of rolling heat and phiffft! Vaporized! On the spot."

Banyon was stunned by the revelation. It was an incredible scenario and suddenly made sense out of an ancient story that really never made much sense until this very moment. "But, wait a minute," he said, still pacing the floor. "How come Lot and the rest of his family weren't vaporized?"

"I don't know," Angela admitted. "Maybe they found shelter. An outcropping of rock to shield them from the blast of the heat wave or something."

Banyon nodded. "Yeah, could be, I suppose. In any case it's a brilliant interpretation of the events. I gotta hand it to you."

"Well, I don't think it would have occurred to me if I hadn't recalled that bizarre conversation with Cynthia. It was so many years ago. I'd completely forgotten about it."

Banyon, shaking his head, finally sat down. "This is really

amazing. I mean, man. Combine this with the stuff in Blumrich's book about Ezekiel and a whole different picture begins to emerge."

Angela agreed. "Reminds me of that scenario professor Kline laid out for us that one night, remember?"

"What scenario?"

"You remember" she said. "That whole thing about the so-called ancient astronauts who came here from another world and basically seeded our planet and taught us what we needed in order to become a civilized race of beings. And then, eventually, we get to where we are now with all of our knowledge of genetic engineering and modern technology and pretty soon we go off to other planets and do the same thing they did."

"Yeah," Banyon said, now recalling Kline's intriguing story. "We go create life on some other planet and eventually that race of humans evolves to the point where they do what their *gods* did and the process repeats itself over and over throughout the universe."

"Or the multiverse, if our friend Paretti is correct," Angela added.

Banyon grinned and shook his head. "Multiverse, yeah. Whew." He looked at Angela. "Are we crazy?" he asked. "Or is this all true?"

Angela gave a little laugh and reached into her purse for a cigarette. "Maybe a little of both," she suggested with a flick of her lighter. "Maybe a little of both."

~26~

The quiet comfort of a lazy Saturday morning was about to come to an abrupt end.

"What the...?" Banyon stood in the bedroom looking into his briefcase. "Angela!" he shouted.

"What is it? I'm in the kitchen!"

"Come up here!"

Sensing the panic in his voice she quickly made her way up the stairs. "What is it, Zeke?"

He stood there looking at her for a moment. He was clearly in shock. "Everything's gone!" he said.

She looked puzzled. "What's gone?"

He turned the opened briefcase upside down. "Everything! The notes, the parchment, the computer disk... everything! You didn't take the stuff out of here did you?"

"No! Are you sure you didn't put them away somewhere?"

"Not me. I haven't even opened the briefcase since..." He tried to think back. "...since the night you were kidnapped! I put everything in the briefcase to bring to the warehouse! But none of those bastards even bothered to open it!"

"Are you sure?"

"Absolutely! They never touched it!"

Behind an old building, in an alley near the waterfront, a disheveled, half sober vagrant hunkered down to examine the goods he'd absconded with a few nights before. He had no idea what these items were but he knew they were important or all hell wouldn't have broken loose at the pier that night. He'd been stowed away in the dark shadows of the old warehouse behind a stack of empty boxes with his bottle of Loganberry, just trying to keep warm when the priest and his two accomplices showed up with the woman. He could tell from their conversation that it was a dangerous situation and he dared not make a sound lest they discover him. All he wanted was a place to be out of the cold and to drink his wine in peace. What he got was something else altogether. How he got it was a combination of dumb luck and a rather daring spur-of-the-moment plan. When the Jesuit and the two thugs came in with Angela he got scared and quickly hid. He saw everything that happened. He heard enough to realize that whatever was in the briefcase might be valuable. When all the violence and gunfire was over and the huge black pickup truck left the building, he noticed Banyon was busy tending to Angela. That was his chance. In a rare moment of clear thinking, he knew it would be easier to simply grab the whole brief case and run. But he thought if Banyon happened to notice the briefcase was missing he might take off and go searching for whoever took it. Removing the contents and leaving the briefcase was a better idea even if it was risky. In that moment – while Banyon's attention was focused on helping Angela – the vagrant took a deep breath and quietly slipped around through the shadows toward the table where the briefcase sat unguarded. Quickly, he removed the entire contents and stuffed the various items into the large pockets of his old coat. Like a ghost he escaped, undetected, out the door and into the night.

"What the hell is this thing?" he now mumbled to himself as he crouched in the alley. Turning the computer disk over and over in his rough, dirty hands he had no idea what he was looking at. *Some kind of a... somethin'*, he thought to himself. He opened the leather folder and took out the parchment. *More weird shit.* He looked everything over, and had no clue as to what any of it meant. *Gotta mean somethin' t' somebody*, he thought. *I bet somebody'd be willin' t'pay a bunch for this stuff.* Then he remembered overhearing the man in the warehouse say something about a Jesuit. *What the hell is a Jesuit?*

The vagrant's thoughts were interrupted by a noise coming from somewhere down the alley. He quickly hid the items under his heavy coat and glanced around but there was no one to be seen. *Gotta put this stuff in somethin'* he thought. He stood up and looked around. A small pile of trash was heaped up against the brick wall of the building. He rustled through it and found a plastic grocery bag. He grabbed the bag, stuffed the precious items into it and headed out to the streets.

"S'cuse me, ma'am," he said to a lady passing by.

"Leave me alone!" the woman scolded. "Tired of you beggars bugging people for money!"

"No ma'am," the vagrant said, lowering his head and trying to look as non-threatening as possible. "Ain't lookin' for money. Just wondered if you know what a Jesuit is or where I can find one?"

The woman stopped and turned to face him. "Excuse me?" she said, not sure she heard him right.

The vagrant smiled through his scruffy five-day growth of whiskers. "A Jesuit," he said. "Need to know where t'find one."

She eyed him with suspicion, unsure of what he was up to. "Try the Seattle Gospel Mission," she said. "Maybe someone there can help you."

"Where's it at?"

"Go down here about two blocks," she said, pointing the way.

"Maybe three. I can't remember. Then walk up the hill to Post Street. You'll see it."

"Thank you. You wouldn't have a spare dollar would ya?"

But the woman was already walking away quickly and didn't bother to answer. The vagrant chuckled to himself and headed off to find the Seattle Gospel Mission.

Having stopped a couple more passers-by to ask for directions he eventually found the building. He stepped inside, clutching onto his bag of goods, and looked around. Old Tom was just leaving and stopped to ask the vagrant if he needed help.

"Ain't seen you 'round here before," Tom said.

"Ain't been 'round here before," the vagrant replied.

"Food's not bad," Tom said, "even though I gripe about it a lot."

The vagrant looked around. "So who runs this place?"

"Father Banyon, during the week. On the weekends it's sort of a part time crew."

The vagrant was stunned as he recognized the name. *Banyon! That was the name of the guy the priests were beatin' up in the warehouse!*

"Banyon?" he asked, nervously. "You sure?"

"Yeah," Tom said, noticing a change in the stranger's voice. "Why? You know him?"

The vagrant clutched tighter to his bag and stammered. "Uh, no. Never heard of him."

Tom squinted, sensing something wasn't quite right. "You lookin' for somebody or somethin?"

"Just a place t'hang for a while."

"M-hmm..." Tom mumbled.

"Uh, hey" the vagrant said, "that Banyon guy... is he a Jesuit by any chance?"

"Nope. Don't think so. Why?"

"Nothin'. Just wonderin'. Know where any Jesuits are?"

Tom thought for a moment. "Only place I know would be Queen City University."

"Where the hell is that?"

"It's a ways from here. You'll probably need to take a bus."

"Can't afford no bus, asshole. Does it look like I got any money?"

Tom reached into his pocket and pulled out a wrinkled dollar bill from the money he'd earned at his first gig down at Charlie's Place just a few days ago. He handed it to the stranger. "That'll getcha there," he said. "If ya hadn't called me an asshole I'da given ya two." With that said, Tom picked up his guitar case and shuffled out the door.

The vagrant was stunned by the undeserved gift. "Thanks," he said. "Sorry about..." But it was too late. Tom had already disappeared down the street.

The campus of the university was typically quiet for a Saturday but not totally deserted. Here and there a person could be seen coming out of a building or going in.

Queen City University was so named because in 1869 Seattle had been dubbed the *Queen City of the Pacific Northwest* by a real estate broker trying to enhance the city's image. Over the course of time a number of local businesses picked up on the name and used it: Queen City Auto Repair, Queen City Pet Shop and dozens of others cashed in on the name. The university, itself, didn't acquire the name until many years later. It began as a boy's school in the 1890s, founded by a small group of Jesuit priests. The school went through a number of incarnations over the years, changing locations more than a couple of times. Eventually it grew, always under the supervision and guidance of the Jesuits, from a small school into the realm of higher education under the name of Queen City College. It found a permanent home on Seattle's landmark Capital Hill and became a full-fledged university in 1950. The scruffy vagrant with the unusual items in his plastic bag now found himself in unfamiliar territory as he walked across the campus of this, the largest Jesuit University in the United States.

Wandering into the first building he came to, the vagrant felt uneasy in this strange environment. The old dark brick building was eerily quiet inside. The squeak of his rubber soled shoes echoed through the long hall as he walked past the endless line of closed doors. Suddenly one of the doors toward the end of the corridor opened and a man in a black priest's outfit walked out with an armload of books. The vagrant stopped and attempted to appear inconspicuous by turning to look at the notices pinned to a bulletin board. *Goddam stupid*, he thought to himself. *I can't even read this shit.*

In a few moments the priest passed by, taking only a brief notice of the unkempt stranger. The vagrant gathered up his courage and cleared his throat. "Ahem! Excuse me sir!"

The priest turned around. "Yes?" he addressed the vagrant. "Can I help you?"

The vagrant walked up to the priest and opened the plastic bag, revealing the items within. "Got somethin' here I think you'd be interested in."

The priest looked puzzled. "And just what might that be?" he asked, peering into the plastic bag.

The vagrant reached in and took out the leather folder and handed it to the priest. "Go ahead," he said. "Open it."

The priest set his own books on the floor and opened the folder. He took a look at the parchment but his expression showed no sign of recognition. "What is this supposed to be?" he asked.

The vagrant looked surprised. "You mean you don't know?"

The priest, getting a bit impatient, shook his head. "Sorry," he said. "I don't have a clue."

"But..."

"I'm sorry," the priest said as he picked up his stack of books. "You'll have to excuse me. I'm in a bit of a hurry." With that, the priest turned and left the building, apparently unimpressed and too busy to waste any more time.

The vagrant stood in the hallway with a scowl on his face. *Crap,* he thought to himself. *Somebody damn well better be in'trested in this shit.*

He was about to leave the building when he noticed a flight of stairs. *Might as well see what's up there.*

The second floor looked exactly like the first floor and just as deserted. He made his way up one more flight and stopped as he heard voices coming from one of the rooms down the hall. He crept along the wall, stopping at each door to listen for the voices.

Suddenly he heard the muffled sound of a man's laughter. It was soon followed by the laughter of perhaps two or three other men and possibly a woman. The sounds were coming from the room with a frosted glass window on the upper portion of the door just a few feet from where he was standing. The word, PRIVATE, was painted in black letters on the glass. Not being able to read, the sign meant nothing to him. He stood there a few minutes hoping someone would come out. Five minutes. Ten minutes. Nothing. *Goddam it!* His impatience got the best of him. He opened the door slowly and looked in but could see no one. Then he heard the voices again. They were coming from behind another door at the back of the room. *Damn well better be somebody in there*, he thought to himself. *Or else the place is full of fuckin' ghosts.*

He took a deep breath, tugged at his coat and spit on his hand to slick back his hair. The routine was an attempt to make himself look a little more presentable. The attempt, of course, was futile but he didn't know the difference. He checked the contents of his bag once more and opened the door. All the voices stopped as the four people in the room turned to stare at the unusual presence standing in their doorway.

The vagrant had been wrong about a woman being in the room Or if there had been a woman in the room, she wasn't there now. He could tell immediately by their clothes that the four men were priests. They were standing around a small statue of some sort that was situated atop an ornate iron pedestal. The shades on the windows were drawn and the room was dimly lit by a single desk-lamp in the corner.

"Jesus Lord," said one of the priests. "Who the hell are you?"

One of the other priests, very tall with olive skin, dark eyes and straight silver-gray hair, walked briskly up to the vagrant and surveyed him from head to foot. With a stern look, tilting his head and squinting one eye, he spoke in a low tone. "Who *are* you?" he asked. "What are you doing here? Didn't you see the sign on the door?"

The vagrant was visibly unnerved. "Uh..." he stammered. "Um, I can't read, actually."

"Well, look," said the olive-skinned priest, "if you're looking for a remedial reading class you'll have to go over to the administration building. Ask for Mr. Barton." The priest put a hand on the vagrant's shoulder and attempted to guide him back out the door but the vagrant resisted.

"No, *you* look," the vagrant said. "I ain't here t'get no readin' class. I got somethin' you oughta see."

By this time one of the other priests in the group - a shorter, younger, dark-haired fellow with a black moustache and goatee - had stepped forward to join the conversation. "I'm game," he said, reaching for the bag. "Let's see what you've got there."

The vagrant clutched the bag and drew back. "It'll cost ya," he said, sharply.

The younger priest laughed and reached into his own pocket and drew out a five-dollar bill. "If you're just looking for money," he said, holding the bill out to the vagrant, "take this and go get yourself something to eat."

"I ain't interested in your five bucks!" said the vagrant. "I want fifty grand for what's in this here bag and I want it now!"

The men broke into laughter at the absurd demand and once again the olive-skinned priest attempted to steer the vagrant back out the door. The vagrant wrestled himself away from the man's grip and stood his ground, glaring at both of the priests with a look of angered determination.

"Fifty grand!" the vagrant demanded. "People died because of what I've got here! If it's worth their frickin' lives it's gotta be worth fifty grand, you assholes!"

The olive-skinned priest had heard enough. "Look, my friend," he said in a serious tone, "if you don't turn around now and leave I'm afraid I'll have to call security. Now, take my advice and be on your way."

"Wait a minute," came a voice from the back of the room. It was one of the other priests, a short, stout, middle-aged, bald-headed man. He stepped forward. He slid his wire frame glasses down to the tip of his nose and peered over them. "I'd like to see what you have that you think is so important."

"Fifty grand," the vagrant demanded once more.

"All right," the bald priest said. "That might be something we can do. But don't you think it's only fair that you let us see what we're buying before we give you the money?"

The vagrant cast a skeptical look, not sure if the priest could be trusted. "All right," he relented. "I'll show you one of the items."

The bald priest smiled. "Well, that's a start. What do you have to show me?"

The vagrant reached into his bag and started to take out the old leather folder containing the parchment but he remembered that the priest downstairs didn't seem too impressed by it. *Probably should try somethin' else*, he thought. He pulled out the computer disk and held it up for the priest to see.

"Ah!" the bald-headed priest said. "A disk. What, pray tell, is on it?"

"On it?" the vagrant asked. "Whaddya mean, on it?"

The bald priest chuckled. "Do you even know what it is you're holding in your hand?"

The clueless vagrant tried to hide his embarrassment. "Sure," he said. "Why? Don't you?"

"Oh, I know what it is, all right," the priest said. "It's a computer disk. But it's worthless to us if we don't know what sort of information it contains. You see?"

"Information!" the vagrant said excitedly. "You damned right! Information! That's what's in it all right. Good information, too! Fifty grand worth!"

"Well, we don't really know how good the information is until we have a look at it, now do we?" The bald priest reached for the disk.

The vagrant pulled it back.

The bald priest shrugged, feigning disinterest. "Well," he said. "We certainly can't pay you for something if we have no idea what it is. So maybe you should just take your bag of goodies and leave." He turned to the olive-skinned priest. "Show our friend to the door, Mr. Salvo."

Salvo started to make a move toward the vagrant but the vagrant spoke quickly. "All right! All right!" he said, defiantly. He handed the disk over to the bald priest. "Have a look or whatever you need to do with it. But you ain't gettin' the rest of the stuff until I get my money, goddamit!"

The bald priest took the disk and noticed the label. He showed it to the other men. They looked and then looked again:

Alphanumerics decoding efforts.

Progress log.

Complete entries to date.

"You'll excuse us for just a minute," the bald priest said to the vagrant. He gestured for the vagrant to have a seat in the wooden chair next to the door. "Don't go anywhere. Just sit tight. We're just going to have a look at this."

Fearing they were going to run off with the disk the vagrant lunged forward, attempting to grab it from the priest.

"No, no," the bald priest cautioned, pulling away from the vagrant. "Not to worry. We'll just be over here." He pointed to the back of the room. "See? You can keep an eye on us."

The vagrant decided he had no choice and sat down in the chair, holding tight to his plastic bag.

All four of the priests moved to a desk at the back of the room. The bald priest took a seat at the desk and slipped the disk into a computer.

The vagrant could hear them talking amongst themselves in quiet tones as they gathered around the computer but he couldn't make out what they were saying.

After several minutes they walked back over to where the vagrant was sitting. He felt trapped as they stood directly in front of him, blocking any chance of escape.

"This is quite interesting," the bald priest said, slipping the disk into his own shirt pocket. "Are the rest of your, uh... items related to this disk in any way?"

"Damn straight," the vagrant answered. "About fifty grand worth of related, I'd say. And that's what it'll costya t'see it too, goddamit! I ain't playin' around here!"

"No, no." the bald priest said, nodding his head. "I can see you're quite serious. And I just want you to know we're quite serious, too."

"Well all right, then!" the vagrant said. "Let's do this thing, goddamit!"

The bald priest gave a friendly chuckle. "Well, my friend," he said, "you can probably appreciate that we don't have that kind of cash right here in this room. But if you'll just come with us, we'll see that you get your money."

Suspicious, but also impatient to get his hands on the cash, the vagrant agreed to go with them as long as he could hold onto the bag and its contents.

"Of course," the bald priest said. "A deal is a deal. We get you the money, you give us the bag and everything that's in it." He paused for a moment and nodded toward the door. " Shall we go?"

The vagrant got up slowly, cautiously eyeing each of the priests with suspicion. *Better not screw with me, you assholes.*

Banyon simply couldn't figure out what might have happened to the contents of his briefcase. "It just doesn't make any sense!" he said, angrily flinging the empty briefcase across the room. "The stuff couldn't just jump out and disappear!"

Angela held his hand and tried to calm him down. "Well, at least there's one good thing."

He sat on the edge of the bed, completely distraught, and looked up at her. "Yeah?" he said, "I can't imagine what that might be."

She smiled. "Why did you hire me in the first place?"

"What? What's that got to do with anything?"

"I'm little Miss Efficiency, right?"

"Yeah, so?"

"You love me?" she teased.

A look of confusion crossed his face. "What? Of course I love you! What the hell are you talking about?"

"How much?"

"How much what?"

"How much do you love me?"

"Lots! I love you lots!"

"You're gonna love me even more now," she said with a coy grin.

He closed his eyes and shook his head slowly then looked back up at her. "Angela?"

"Yes?"

"What in the hell are you talking about?"

"Don't go away," she said, leaving the room. "I'll be right back."

He could hear her footsteps going down the stairs. A few minutes later she returned to the bedroom and handed him a shoebox.

"What's this?" he asked.

She grinned. "Open it."

He removed the lid and couldn't believe his eyes. "What! How...?"

"Copies," she said. "I made three copies of everything. The disk and the parchment and the McClintock notes and even the entire chapter from the book about the lost scroll. Everything."

"You gotta be kidding me!" he said, grinning like a kid on Christmas morning.

"I told you you'd love me more," she said, sitting down beside him.

"Oh, man," he beamed, reaching over and giving her a big hug. " Oh, man."

The bald priest, led the way down the hall, followed by the vagrant with Salvo by his side.

"Where we goin?" the vagrant asked in a demanding tone.

"To get your money," the bald priest replied. "We'll take the elevator."

"I *know* we're goin' t'get the money," the vagrant said. "But where is it?"

The bald priest pushed the DOWN button and the elevator door opened. He motioned for everyone to step inside. He followed in behind and the door slid closed. "It's in a special room," he said. "We keep our large funds in a safe in a special room just for unusual situations that might come up. You understand."

"Yeah, I guess," the vagrant said. Feeling uncomfortable, he glanced up at the big olive-skinned man they called Salvo. But Salvo stood expressionless, staring straight ahead.

The bald priest pushed the button marked with an "X". The elevator jerked slightly and began to descend with a faint humming sound.

The vagrant watched the numbers light up on the panel above the elevator door as they descended. Second floor. First floor. The vagrant noticed there were no more numbered lights in front of the light that indicated the first floor and yet the elevator kept descending. He was becoming alarmed. It seemed to be taking much too long. *Where the hell is this thing goin'?* "What's the deal?" the vagrant grumbled. "Are we goin' t'hell or somethin' for Christ sake?"

At that moment the elevator came to an abrupt stop and the door opened. Salvo pushed the vagrant out of the elevator and grabbed the plastic bag in the process. He handed the bag to the bald priest.

"Hey! What the...?" the vagrant stammered, trying to regain his balance. Suddenly, he was grabbed from behind by a large burly man wearing black pants and a black t-shirt. The vagrant struggled but it was useless. The man had him in an arm-lock. The slightest movement and the vagrant could feel a pain as if his arms would be wrenched out of their sockets. He glared angrily at the two priests.

Tightening his grip even more, the man asked, "What should I do with him?"

The bald priest reached into the plastic bag and pulled out the leather folder. He opened it and made a quick examination of the old parchment "Give him his fifty grand," he said.

The vagrant's eyes lit up. The mention of fifty grand seemed to alleviate the pain in his shoulders being inflicted by the vice-like armlock. "All right!" he shouted with a grin. "I knew I could trust you!"

The bald priest and Salvo stepped back into the elevator.

"Then," the bald priest added as the elevator doors were closing, "administer his last rites and introduce him to the Devil."

The elevator doors closed and the muscular man dragged the poor vagrant down the long dark hall to his final reward.

~27~

The four priests returned to the room upstairs.

"So now that we have this stuff, what do we do with it?" the young Brother Montabeau asked, stroking his black moustache and goatee.

"We could attempt to decipher the code ourselves," Salvo suggested. "Brother Franco obviously failed in his kidnapping plan."

"I didn't agree with his plan in the first place," Beck said. "I didn't think Banyon had cracked the code and, now, having seen this material, I still doubt it."

"Yeah," Montabeau complained, "But working outside the protocol is obviously more dangerous than I thought it was going to be."

Montabeau was brought into the group for no reason other than to keep him quiet. Quite by accident he had overheard a conversation between Salvo and the bald priest, Romano, regarding the Ezekiel Code and the plan to work outside the upper echelon's protocol of nonintervention. The plan was to gain control of the mysterious object before Banyon or anyone else could get to it. When Montabeau confronted Romano with the fact that he knew what they were up to, Romano offered to bring him into the group in exchange for his silence. Romano felt he had little choice since Montabeau was related, at least peripherally, to one of the founding fathers of the University so he had a few influential contacts among the school's administrators. To make matters worse, he had a reputation as a bit of a loose-lipped gossip. Still, Montabeau agreed not to reveal anything to anyone and being accepted into the group initially aroused his sense of adventure. That sense of adventure, however, was beginning to fade in light of the recent events.

"Maybe," Montabeau suggested, "we should just turn this material over to the Jesuit General. I mean that is an option, you know."

Romano, the stocky bald headed priest and self-appointed head of the group, finally spoke up. "Not a chance," he fired back. "The good Lord has seen fit to drop this into our lap. We stick with our plan." He ran his hand across the smooth brown leather folder containing the parchment. He couldn't believe he had it in his hands. *The Lord does work in mysterious ways*, he thought to himself with a grin. "Now that we have these materials we're closer to the prize than we ever hoped to be at this stage of the game." He glared at Montabeau. "You're in this with us all the way," he said threateningly. "Remember that."

Romano walked over to the desk at the back of the room and inserted Banyon's disk into the computer. He scrolled through a couple of the pages then leaned back in the chair and looked up at the other men. "Brother Franco just went off on his own with no solid evidence to prove Banyon had cracked the code. Kidnapping the woman was a reckless thing to do. We need to be diligent, patient. With the information we have now, I have to agree with Brother Salvo. I think we can crack the code ourselves."

"Maybe so," Beck said. "But what I want to know is how the Nine found out about Brother Franco and the situation at the warehouse in the first place. I know they're following Banyon's progress but according to what we've been able to determine, they weren't exactly maintaining a round-the-clock surveillance on him. And from the old vagrant's version of how it all went down, it seems like they must have been tipped off by someone."

"Yeah?" Montabeau said with a cynical tone. "Like who? Except for that woman, Angela, Banyon doesn't really have any close associates. At least not that we've seen. And another thing, I can't believe the men who killed Franco were actually members of the Nine. I mean, no doubt they had some connection but the Nine just don't go around with machine guns, crashing trucks through warehouse doors. So who were those guys?"

Romano got up from the desk. He walked over to the large

windows and raised the old yellow shades. "You're right about Banyon," he said, staring out the window at the campus below. "He doesn't have any close associates." He turned to face the other men. "But there is that professor Kline who seems to have been feeding a lot of information to Banyon. Those men who took down Brother Franco were probably hired operatives. Like Montabeau said, the Nine never involve themselves directly with any situation like what occurred at the warehouse. Our own Order has been known to hire independent operatives to take care of unpleasant business. No doubt the Nine do the same. That Kline fellow could be a low level operative."

Salvo nodded. "It's possible. But even if that's true, how did he know anything was going on? It doesn't make sense unless he had a tap on us. Or at least," he added, "on Brother Franco for some reason."

Romano shook his head. "I don't think so. If that were the case, the kidnapping would have been stopped before it got started. If Kline is the one responsible for getting the word to the Nine my guess is he found out about the kidnapping from Banyon. Franco was clearly playing the ransom card. He kidnapped the woman and then called Banyon with an offer to free her in exchange for the information that he believed Banyon had. Banyon may have contacted Kline for advice after he got the phone call from Franco. It's the only thing that makes sense. Kline then contacted the Nine directly and the Nine put in the call to their higher-level operatives who then got to the warehouse in relatively short order."

"This Kline fellow," Beck said. "Think he'll be a problem? He could have an unfortunate accident if necessary."

Romano shook his head. "No. According to some of the notes on the disk it appears our professor Kline has provided a lot of information to Banyon. If we play this right, he might be useful."

"Useful?" Montabeau scoffed. "Dangerous is more like it."

"Dangerous only if he knows about us," Romano said, glaring back at Montabeau.

Sitting across from Banyon at the kitchen table, Angela was nearly finished with her breakfast.

"What's the matter?" she asked. "I fixed your favorite breakfast but you're not scarfing it down like you usually do."

Banyon's favorite morning meal was thick sliced French toast with a dash of cinnamon and a touch of vanilla mixed into the batter and smothered with maple syrup.

"What?" he said, looking up. "Oh, uh... no, Angel, it's great. It really is. And so are you. I can't believe you made copies of all the materials."

"Then what is it?" she asked.

"I just can't figure out how the stuff disappeared. Obviously someone had to have taken it. But I keep going over and over it in my mind and it just doesn't seem possible that it was anyone who was in the warehouse that night. The briefcase was sitting on that table by the doors over to my right the whole time. I'm sure I would have noticed someone getting into it."

"Maybe during all the gun fire," Angela suggested. "There was a hell of a lot of commotion. I mean, that part is all like a big blur to me. Someone could have taken it in the middle of all the chaos."

Banyon shook his head. "I don't think so. And besides, the priest and his two thugs ended up dead on the floor and none of them had the materials in their hands. And the guys who came in the truck didn't seem to have anything in their hands except some big freakin' guns. I just don't get it."

They sat in silence for a couple minutes while Banyon swirled a piece of French toast around and around in a pool of syrup. "Kline," he mumbled to himself.

"What?"

Banyon looked up from his plate. "Professor Kline," he said again.

"What about him?"

"He's the only other person who possibly had an opportunity to take the items out of my briefcase."

Angela looked puzzled. "What do you mean? When?"

"That night when we got home from the warehouse and he was here waiting for us. When we all got into the house I remember walking with you over to the couch. You left your coat on because you were cold. But I took my coat off and laid it on the back of the couch and I set the briefcase on the floor right next to the coffee table in front of the couch. Remember?"

Angela shook her head. "Not really. I wasn't exactly taking notes."

"Well that's where I put it, anyway."

"But I was sitting there the whole time," Angela argued. "I didn't see Kline ever reach over to the briefcase, let alone actually get into it."

"Yeah, but like you just said, you weren't exactly taking notes. What about when I left the room and went into the kitchen to get the wine?"

Angela took a sip of coffee and thought about it for a moment. "No," she said, confidently. "I'm sure I would have noticed. It would have been too obvious. And besides, why? Why would he take the material? He's interested in the whole thing but he knows how dangerous it would be for him to have possession of the stuff. People who aren't supposed to have it seem to find themselves dead sooner or later. You know what I mean? I'm sorry but it just doesn't compute."

Banyon was a little annoyed by Angela's logic because he knew she must be right. It really didn't compute. He was back to square one with no suspect. "I'm going to call him," he said, getting up from the table.

"Who? Professor Kline?"

"Yeah."

"Come on," she said. "You're not really going to accuse him of stealing the materials are you?"

Banyon shrugged. "No, you're probably right. He probably didn't take the stuff. But I'm just going to tell him I discovered it's all missing and see what his reaction is."

"All right," Angela said, clearing the dishes from the table. "Whatever."

Banyon moved into the living room to call Kline but only got his answering machine. "Alan, this is Zeke. It's Saturday morning about eleven-thirty. Give me a call when you get a chance. Thanks." He hung up the phone and returned to the kitchen. " I left him a message to call back when he gets a chance."

Angela rinsed off the last of the breakfast dishes and set them in the sink. Drying her hands on a towel, she turned and smiled. "Good," she said. "Let's go shopping."

"What?"

"Christmas shopping!" she said with a grin. "In case you hadn't noticed, Christmas is just two weeks away."

It was true. So much had been going on that Banyon had been

nearly oblivious to the fact that the holiday season was in full swing. In the back of his mind he knew it. But, despite the proliferation of decorations and lights all over the city for the past few weeks, somehow it hadn't really sunk in until that very moment.

"Oh man," he said. "Where have I been? This is usually my favorite time of the year."

Angela walked over and put her arms around him. "Well," she said, "it's not like there haven't been a few little distractions lately."

"You know what?" he said, pulling back slightly from her embrace so he could gaze into her eyes.

"No, what?"

"It's been so long since I've bought a gift for a woman I have no idea what to get you."

"Well, let's see," she said. "How about a Hawaiian vacation and a winning lottery ticket?"

"You know," he said slowly, with an unusually sly expression on his face, "that's not entirely out of the question."

She drew back and gave him a quizzical look. "I beg your pardon? Which? The Hawaiian vacation or the winning lottery ticket?"

He laughed. "Well, I don't know about the lottery ticket but the trip to Hawaii..."

Now Angela wasn't sure if he was kidding or not, although she couldn't imagine that he was serious either. "What?" she asked. "What are you talking about?"

"I have this little nest egg," he said.

"Come again?"

He gave a chuckle. "An investment."

"What do you mean, an investment? What investment? You never told me about any investment."

"It was my wife's doing. About a year before she died she inherited some money from her parent's estate. About sixty-five thousand dollars. She had this friend named Sylvia who worked for a company called CTI, Cell-Tech Innovations, and Sylvia convinced Karen that buying stock in the company would be a smart move. Sylvia knew the company was about to launch some innovative new product and she was just certain it was going go big time. Anyway, Karen bought up ten thousand dollars worth of the company stock and good ol' Sylvia apparently knew what she was talking about. It's been going up steadily. I get these monthly reports in the mail and as of last month the value of those shares totaled up to a little over a hundred and fifty thousand dollars."

Angela backed up a couple paces and swallowed hard. "A hundred and fifty thousand dollars?" she cried, nearly in shock.

Banyon couldn't help but laugh at the look on her face. "Yeah. Who'da guessed? Me with shares in a high-tech company. What's the world coming to?"

"Are you serious? You're putting me on aren't you?"

"No, really, it's true."

"You never told me about this!"

He shrugged. "Well, it just never came up."

Angela laughed. "Wow," she said. "I've snagged myself a sugar daddy and didn't even know it!"

"Well, I don't know about a sugar daddy, but it does bring up something that's crossed my mind a few times lately."

"What is it?"

"Let's sit down," he said. "Is there any more coffee in the pot?"

Angela poured the coffee. They sat down at the table and Banyon lit up a cigarette. He looked over at Angela. "I've been toying with the idea of quitting my job at the shelter."

Angela was completely taken by surprise. "What? What are you talking about? Why?"

"This whole thing we've become involved in, this code thing, it's consuming me. And trying to deal with that and running the shelter too... well, it's just getting to be too much. I mean this is some serious stuff we've fallen into and..." he paused.

"And?"

He took a deep breath. "There something else I haven't told you."

Angela closed her eyes and shook her head slowly. "I don't know if I can take any more surprises this morning. But go ahead. What is it?"

"You're going to think I'm losing it."

"Okay," she said reluctantly, "lay it on me."

"Okay. Well, I had this dream the other night."

"A dream?"

"Yeah. But it wasn't like just a regular dream. I mean, it was, but it wasn't."

"Oh, this should be good," Angela said, reaching for a cigarette.

"What was it about?"

"Well, it was like I was under water. I mean, sort of but not exactly. Maybe more like I was *seeing* something underwater. The water was really cold and dark."

"What did you see?"

"I don't know exactly. It was like... I don't know, damn it, I can barely remember. It seems like it was this tall thin thing with crosses on it or something. I don't know. But mostly what I remember was that it was really important. I mean like, *really* important. And I had this strange feeling. Really intense. Almost like I was... it's hard to explain. Almost like my whole body, every molecule, every cell, was vibrating with energy. It was incredibly intense but at the same time almost a feeling of some kind of..." he paused, trying to think of the right word. "Like some kind of *ecstasy* is the only word I can think of to describe it. Anyway, the whole point of the experience was that it had something to do with me and this Ezekiel Code business."

"Wow!" was Angela's only reply.

"Yeah," Banyon nodded. "You're telling me. Weird, huh?"

"What do you think it meant?"

"I don't know. I'd like to pass it off as just some kind of a weird dream but for some reason I can't help feeling like it was something more. I can't explain it."

Angela thought about it for a moment. "Do you believe in prophetic dreams?"

"What do you mean?"

"You know. Prophetic. Like foretelling the future."

"I don't know. Maybe."

"Could have been a prophetic dream."

Banyon chuckled. "Oh yeah. That'd be great. Have a prophetic dream but have no clue as to what the heck it was about! Wouldn't that just figure?"

Angela shrugged. "Well, it was just a thought. Maybe the meaning of it will be made known to you sometime."

"Well, I'm not going to sit around holding my breath. I guess we'll just have to wait and see."

Angela finished the last sip of her coffee. "Okay," she said. "And while we're waiting maybe we can go shopping?"

Banyon laughed. "All right," he said, giving in to her persistence.

"Let's go."

"Great! I have to change my clothes first. And when we get back I have to get busy cramming for my finals on Monday."

"Sounds like a plan," Banyon said. "And while you're studying tonight I think I'll see if I can make any more sense out of our mystery code."

Angela was about to go upstairs to change clothes when she stopped short at the bottom of the stairs. *Wait a minute*, she thought, *what about me?* "Zeke?" she called out to Banyon who was still in the kitchen.

"Yeah?" he called back.

"What about *my* job?"

"What do you mean?"

"At the shelter. If you leave, will I still be able to work there?"

Banyon came out of the kitchen and joined her at the foot of the stairs. "Well," he said, "I'm sure you could if you want. But I was thinking we could both live off my investment money for a while. I'm sorry. I should have told you. I just forgot, I guess."

Angela gave him a big grin. "Really?" she said, glowing.

Banyon shrugged. "Well, hell, yeah. Why not?"

"Wow! That's... I mean, wow! What a Christmas gift! Thank you!"

Banyon laughed. "Well it's no big deal. I mean it's not about the money. It's about... I don't know. Living. You know?"

Angela's mind was racing. "You know," she said, "This is the last week of the quarter at school. I really wouldn't mind not going back right away."

"What are you saying? You mean drop out?"

"Well, yeah. I could always go back any time. And that way we could both spend our time on this code stuff. What do you think?"

"I think it sounds great. But are you sure you want to do that?"

"I'm sure. I mean, I was only going to school for something to do in the first place. And hey, since I met you it's not like I don't have anything to do! I'm knee deep in the biggest adventure of my life! I might as well wade in up to my neck, don't you think?"

"If you're sure that's what you want to do, then I'm all for it."

"So it's settled then?"

"I guess it is."

"So," she said, grinning, "can we please go shopping now?"

Before Banyon could reply, the phone rang. He walked into the living room and picked it up. It was Kline.

"Alan! Glad you caught us. We were just on our way out."

"Is everything all right?" Kline asked. "I just got your message."

"Well, yes and no. We've got another little mystery on our hands."

He explained to Kline about the items disappearing from the briefcase.

"Hmm..." Kline said. "Interesting. Let me make a few inquiries."

The comment took Banyon by surprise. "Inquiries? What do you mean?"

"Just a hunch," Kline said. "I still have a couple Jesuit contacts. Friends of my uncle. Haven't talked to either of them for a long time and they're getting up in age but I know I have their phone numbers around here somewhere."

Banyon was somewhat puzzled and a little suspicious. "What makes you think they would know anything about the stuff missing from my briefcase?"

"Well," Kline answered, "I don't know that they do. Maybe they don't. It was just a thought. I'll get back to you if I learn anything."

"All right," Banyon said. "Thanks."

Angela joined Banyon in the living room. "Was that professor Kline?" she asked

"Yeah," he replied, hanging up the phone.

Angela sensed there was something wrong. "So what's the matter?"

"Alan said he'd make some inquiries."

"Inquiries?"

"Yeah. Remember the story he told us about his uncle who had been a Jesuit priest?"

"I remember."

"Well, he says two of his uncle's Jesuit friends are still around and he's going to ask them if they know anything."

"What makes him think they would know anything?"

"That's exactly what I asked him. But he didn't really say. He just said he'd get back to me if he learned anything."

"You're suspicious of him now, aren't you?" she asked.

"I don't know. Yeah, I guess. Maybe. Christ, I don't know."

"Well, all we can do right now is wait and see what he says when he gets back to you."

Banyon shrugged. "Yeah, you're right."

"Okay, then. Now, barring any further suspicious phone calls, vanishing items, or men in black knocking on our door, can we please go shopping?"

Banyon had to smile. "All right," he said. "You go change your clothes and I'll warm up the car."

"All right! Shopping mall, here we come!"

~28~

Within minutes of getting the call from Banyon about the missing items, Kline made a phone call himself.

"Crown Technology Systems," came a woman's voice on the other end of the line. "How may I direct your call?"

"Nathan Crown, please. Tell him professor Kline is calling."

Crown Technology Systems, or CTS, was a combination think-tank and producer of high-tech instruments. The company's primary customer was the U.S. Government by way of the secret aircraft testing facility at Groom Lake, Nevada, otherwise known to UFO buffs as the infamous Area 51. Nathan Crown was not only the billionaire founder and president of CTS, but he also held the ultimate clandestine position as the current head of the most heavily enshrouded secret society in all of recorded history, the Brotherhood of the Nine Pillars.

Kline's double life as a low level operative for the Nine began shortly after he learned of the existence of the Nine from Marie St. Claire, the assistant curator at the Smithsonian. The Nine had known about him prior to the meeting with the assistant curator because of his close association with Frank McClintock. The Nine had, of course, been keeping an eye on McClintock just as they did with anyone who was in possession of the mysterious ancient parchment. Until the meeting with Ms. St. Claire, Kline had been of little interest or concern to the Nine. But that all changed when they found out Kline had learned of their existence. They soon discovered he not only had become intensely interested in the mystery of the Lost Scroll of Ezekiel but that he had an extreme interest in other esoteric subjects as well. Knowing all of this they felt he might be a good candidate to serve them as a low level intelligence operative. The protocol of noninterference by which the Nine abided - as did the upper echelons of the Jesuit order - was a tenuous matter. It forbade any direct interference with the *Chosen One* by the members of either group. But, strictly speaking, it didn't prohibit them from employing assistance from outside the organization. It was a thin line, to be sure, but so far no negative consequences had resulted from nudging that line.

"I'm sorry, sir, Mr Crown is not available," the woman replied to Kline. "Would you like his voice mail?"

"Yes, please."

"One moment. I'll transfer your call."

Soon a recorded message came on: *You've reached the voice mail for Nathan Crown. Please leave a message when you hear the tone. Mr. Crown will return your call as soon as possible. Thank you.*

"Mr. Crown, this is professor Kline. A situation has developed. I can be reached at home."

Five minutes later Crown returned Kline's call. Kline explained the situation regarding the missing items just as Banyon had related it to him.

"Yes, sir," Kline said. "No. As far as they know I had an uncle who was a Jesuit and I stayed with that cover story. I said I would try to contact a couple of my uncle's Jesuit friends to see if they might have heard anything about the missing items. Yes, all right. I'll wait until I hear back from you. Yes. Good-bye."

Crown was puzzled by the news of the missing items. Clearly this event had escaped everyone's attention. It was a complete mystery as to who could have taken the materials and where those materials may have ended up.

After consulting with the other eight members of the Nine the decision was made to contact Crown's friend, Major Ben Corbin. Corbin had been a key figure in Project Stargate, the secret CIA program in the 1970s which was focused on developing psychic ability to locate objects, as well as information, at any distance, through a kind of exotic mental exercise known as *applied psychoenergetics*, more commonly referred to as *remote viewing*. It was the ultimate spy technology originally developed in response to increasingly disturbing intelligence reports showing that the Soviet Union was well into an ongoing program of developing such exotic technology for what was being termed *psychic warfare*. Project Stargate was classified Top Secret, yet rumors of its existence were floating around. Of course such rumors were thought to be the wild imaginings of the fruitcakes on the fringes of society and were quickly quashed by the military and aggressively debunked by the academics and professional skeptics. Nevertheless, the rumors persisted and a few people who actually did know about the project were beginning to add some degree of credibility to the stories by going on radio talk-shows and telling what they knew. None of these people had been directly involved in the project so they weren't breaking any security oaths by revealing the information. Some of them had merely happened to have a memo cross their desk now and then in the course of their duties as file clerks or other low-level administrative positions. Little by little, a few of these people began to suspect, from the rather cryptic memos, that there might be some truth to the rumors about the existence of the project. In any case, they couldn't be accused of violating security oaths because they were never officially part of the project and were never sworn to secrecy with regard to such a project.

As this continued, the military and the CIA became alarmed by the proliferation of leaks. They decided to respond by going public with some information of their own. In November of 1995 the CIA Director, William Casey, made an appearance on the ABC television show, *NightLine*. He admitted that the CIA had, in fact, engaged in this 16-year program, to the tune of many millions of dollars but, unfortunately, according to Casey, the program had to be discontinued because the results were just not reliable enough. In short, it turned out to be a waste of time and money. That was the official spin on the story and, as such, it was intended to put an end to any further rumors about the project. The truth, however, was another matter. The program was very successful, and simply continued under a new name with an even deeper cover of secrecy and security.

Major Corbin was pleased to get the call from Crown and agreed to apply his special abilities to the situation in an attempt to locate the materials that had mysteriously vanished from Banyon's briefcase. If possible, he would even try to remote view the scene at the warehouse the night of the kidnapping and see who took the items and how it was done. Crown was surprised to learn that events from the past could be accessed in this manner. Corbin explained that it was difficult but not impossible. The explanation of why it was possible was complex but had something to do with the fact that time, as we experience it, doesn't actually exist outside of our own consciousness. In a strange way, almost beyond the human ability to comprehend, all events are occurring simultaneously. Therefore, a highly trained remote viewer, as well as some gifted natural psychics, can get a glimpse of events both past and future. This, Corbin explained, was the key to the so-called gift of prophecy whereby future events could be envisioned. Corbin explained that prophecy is often thought to have failed when the foreseen events don't occur but the reason for this so called failure is that the future is malleable. It can be changed by events in the present. The past, on the other hand, is what it is and can't be changed.

As soon as Corbin received the call from Crown he was immediately flown to the Nine's secret outpost on an island in the Bering Sea and a remote viewing session was arranged. Corbin was supplied with what he needed, which was nothing more than a quiet room, a sketch pad, a pencil, and a comfortable chair. Once he was situated, he closed his eyes and focused his attention on the first target: Banyon's briefcase. He let his mind *scan the matrix*, as he put it. It was a process of protocols he'd learned through rigorous training sessions during his years with the StarGate project. The idea was not so much to see actual items - as the term *remote viewing* seemed to imply - but rather to let his subconscious mind act as a receiver gathering *information* that his conscious mind could then interpret. The universe, he later explained, is like a huge information storage unit, something like a computer that contains millions of bits of information that only manifests as pictures and words when the information is interpreted by the internal program and then displayed in visual form on the monitor. His monitor, in this sense, was the blank paper upon which he would simply let his hand sketch out any shapes or lines that would correspond to the information bits he was receiving. In some instances the information was better translated into words rather than shapes and lines. All of this would then be reinterpreted and evaluated holistically when the session was over.

When Corbin emerged from the room, several hours later, he sat down with Crown to go over the results.

Corbin ended up with several pages of sketches, a few words jotted down and a certain number that came up several times. Corbin was a master at this strange process and his sketches were relatively easy to interpret. There seemed to be little doubt, from what they were looking at, that the missing items from Banyon's briefcase were currently inside a room that appeared to be in a large brick building. One of the sketches resembled a large three-dimensional cube with several vertical rectangles along one side and one vertical rectangle on the opposite side. In the middle of the single rectangle he'd scribbled the number *306*. During the session, as this information was being received, Corbin felt compelled to write the words *education* and *teacher* inside the cube. Now looking at the sketch he was certain the cube was a classroom. The rows of vertical rectangles were windows and the single rectangle was a door. The number on the door was the room number of the classroom.

Crown was curious about who had taken the material and how it was done. Corbin said he attempted to access that information but found it extremely difficult mainly due to what he perceived as a wall of negative energy and violence that somehow tended to interrupt the clear flow of information. But he was able to perceive that there were nine people in the warehouse that night.

"Nine?" Crown asked. "But there were only eight. The priest and his two accomplices. That was three. The three men who arrived in the truck. So that's six. And Banyon and Angela. Eight, altogether."

Corbin shook his head. "I know," he said. "But there was another person in that warehouse besides the ones you mentioned." He flipped through a couple pages of the notebook and pointed to the sketch. It was not more than a few shapes and lines and a stick figure representing the unknown person. The stick figure was almost obliterated by dark shading scribbled over it.

"I think our mystery man was concealed out of sight in the shadows," Corbin said. He pointed to several small squares he'd drawn in front of the stick figure of the man. "My impression," he continued, "was that these are boxes. I suspect this fellow was hiding behind the boxes and probably had no idea who the other people were or exactly what was going on. An innocent bystander who just happened to be at the wrong place at the wrong time."

Crown thought about this possible scenario for a moment. "And," he conjectured, "our mystery man overheard enough to figure out that there was something valuable in the briefcase and somehow managed to get his hands on it."

Corbin agreed. "However it went down and whoever he was, I'm sure he was the culprit. But whoever he was, he's no longer among the living."

"What do you mean?" Crown asked. "How do you know?"

Corbin showed Crown another sketch. It looked like the same stick figure only it was horizontal, laying down, and above it were more stick figures in the same position but each one was drawn a little fainter, a little lighter than the next one until the sketches were barely visible.

"When I get an impression of a person who has died," Corbin explained, "I often end up with this same sort of sketch. I've learned from experience that these kinds of images represent the person is dying or is dead."

Crown nodded. "Fascinating. Is there anything else you can tell me?"

"Just that the materials you're interested in seem to be in the possession of a small group of men and are currently inside a classroom somewhere. The number on the door is 306."

"What about copies? Did these men make copies of any of the items?"

"I didn't get the impression there were any more than just one of each item in their possession."

Crown seemed relieved. "Well, that's one good thing. Anything else? And more details?"

"I'm afraid that's about it, my friend. I'll leave these sketches with you and I guess you'll have to take it from here."

Crown arranged for a private jet to fly Major Corbin back to his home in California and then called a meeting of the Nine to commence the following day. At the meeting, Crown presented the other members with the results of Corbin's remote viewing session and asked them for ideas about how to handle the situation.

Based on Corbin's insights and Crown's explanation of the sketches, the group was unanimous in its assumption regarding the location of the stolen items. If it was, in fact, an educational institution then the obvious choice had to be Queen City University. They also felt it was a safe bet that the man who kidnapped Angela was not quite the lone wolf they had first assumed. It now seemed likely that while he may have acted on his own behalf, he could very well have been connected with a larger renegade group of Jesuits. If that was the case, then the question now was how to find out who they were and what to do about them and, more importantly, a plan was needed to retrieve the stolen items and return them to Banyon.

By the end of the meeting, a decision had been made. Professor Alan Kline didn't know it yet, but he was about to receive instructions to carry out a seemingly simple but potentially dangerous mission.

~29~

Monday afternoon found the professor in his office grading student papers when he received a surprise delivery by courier. He signed for the envelope that bore the logo of CTS and sat down at his desk to read the enclosed letter:

Dear professor Kline,
Your assistance is hereby requested. As always, feel free to decline this request should you choose to do so.

Kline was familiar with these opening lines. He'd read them

before. The most recent was several weeks ago when he was requested by Crown to contact Banyon and arrange for a meeting at Kline's office at the Shorewood Community College. The purpose for the meeting was to begin the process of educating Banyon by supplying him with the sort of background information he would need in order to more fully appreciate the bigger picture in the middle of which he and Angela now found themselves. Clearly, the Brotherhood of the Nine Pillars was pleased with Kline's performance. The letter he now held in his hands went on to explain the new mission he was being asked to carry out.

Crown would arrange for an academic conference to take place at Queen City University, the suspected location of the missing materials. The theme of the conference would be *The Sociology of Knowledge: An Epistemological Approach* and Kline would receive an invitation to be a guest speaker. Kline had lectured on this subject several times so it would be relatively simple for him to put together a presentation for the conference. But, more to the point, it would give him a legitimate reason to be at the campus without raising anyone's suspicion. Scholars from all over the country would be attending, some as speakers and some as invited guests, and he would merely be one more academic among many. His mission, while on campus, would be to find room 306, locate the items which were stolen from Banyon's briefcase, take possession of them, if at all possible, and return them to Banyon. Obviously there would be several buildings with rooms numbered 306. Since Corbin's remote viewing failed to identify exactly *which* building contained the target room Kline would have to check them all.

He sat back in his chair and ran his fingers through his thick wirey hair. He was not surprised that Crown could pull this sort of an event together. He knew Crown could do this so covertly that virtually no one involved, anywhere along the line, would even know he had a hand in it. His contacts were many and varied and he carried a tremendous amount of influence throughout many levels of the social strata. How he could have such a widespread influence and yet remain relatively invisible to most of the outside world was a curious paradox. Nevertheless, it was a fact and, as a sociologist, Kline found that fact fascinating. At the moment, however, he was more concerned about his own ability to pull off this cloak-and-dagger mission. It wasn't the kind of thing he ever imagined himself doing although the sense of adventure, he had to admit, was tempting. Yet at the same time, thinking back on the death of his good friend Frank McClintock and the kidnapping of Angela, he recognized the possibility that this could turn into a very unpleasant situation, to say the least.

The letter ended with a final instruction:

Should you choose to comply with this request you know the procedure.

The procedure was simple. He'd done it before. He simply had to dial a certain phone number, wait for the tone, say his name, press 9, and hang up. It seemed an odd, even amusing way of communicating his decision but that's the way it was. Almost magically, that simple act would set the wheels in motion and the rest, he knew, would be up to him.

By late afternoon, Angela had taken her finals and was confident she'd done well. Banyon contacted Saving Grace Outreach, the non-profit organization that owned the Seattle Gospel Mission, and informed them of his decision to leave his position as director of the shelter. He told them he would be willing to stay long enough for them to find a replacement and he would be happy to spend a few days training whoever might take his place.

Making the decision to leave was not difficult but he knew the actual act of leaving would not be quite so easy. There were people he would miss, not the least of which was Old Tom. He felt a tinge of guilt about leaving the people he had come to know so well and who had come to rely on him for help and a bit of compassion in their otherwise compassionless little worlds. He knew it would come as a shock to some of them and he really hadn't yet thought of what excuse he was going to use as an explanation for his decision. While his old comfortable concept of God was beginning to fade in light of all he'd discovered in recent months, there was still a remnant of it left somewhere deep inside. It was that remnant that he was now relying on to help him through this transition and to give him the right words when it came time to say goodbye to everyone at the shelter.

There was no question in his mind that leaving was the right thing to do. Everything in his life had led to this. Everything. As he thought back, he could see it: his decision to leave the seminary, his marriage to Karen, the accident that took her life... *Accident?* Now he wondered if it had been simply an accident, a chance occurrence without rhyme or reason. *What was it Kline said? There are no coincidences? Had Karen's death been part of the bigger picture too?* He knew it was certainly just an accident in conventional terms but now he wondered, *had that devastating event been somehow written into the program?* Looking back, it did seem like every incident had been set up along the way: his friendship with Father Caldwell, his getting the job at the shelter, his hiring of Angela who, he now recalled, was the only person who even responded to his help-wanted ad. And then, of course, there was the deskpad on which he just happened to notice the alphanumeric doodling. All of it now seemed so clearly laid out, step by step, like following breadcrumbs along a path. With every step, he'd taken the bait. *Did I ever have a choice? Do we ever really make any choices? Or do we just think we make choices?* It was the old question about free will and the fork in the road. *Do we go to the left or to the right? If we choose one can we ever know for sure that we could have chosen the other? Or was the so-called choice already written into the program?* Whatever might be the case, he knew philosophers had been debating this puzzle for centuries and he certainly wasn't going to solve it now.

He checked his watch. It was 5 p.m. Angela was home by now, waiting to tell him about her final exams and he was anxious to tell her that he'd arranged to leave his job. So much was changing so quickly and even the end of the year was closing in on him. Christmas was less than two weeks away. He shuddered with a sudden quiver of anticipation. *What a way to start the new year,* he thought. *I can't imagine what's next.* There was, however, one thing about which he was quite certain. It was something concerning Angela. Now, smiling to himself, he knew that, too, was rapidly approaching.

~30~

A ngela was up early Christmas morning making coffee and preparing a big breakfast of baked ham, sliced peaches in cream, and Banyon's favorite cinnamon-vanilla French toast. It wasn't long before the aroma wafted up the stairs and caused Banyon to awaken with a grin and a growling hunger. By the time he sauntered into the kitchen in his bathrobe and slippers, breakfast was on the table. Angela was running some water at the sink. He moved up behind her and wrapped her in his arms.

"Oh man," he said, giving her a big squeeze. "Christmas never smelled so good."

She twisted around, facing him, and smiled. "Yup," she said, wiggling out from his embrace and handing him a napkin. "A breakfast fit for the Chosen One!"

"Oh, please," Banyon protested, sitting down at the table. "You know I hate that."

"I know," she smirked, kissing him on the forehead. "That's why I said it."

After breakfast they went into the living room to enjoy a traditional morning of opening gifts. With all that was happening lately they hadn't bothered to do much decorating but they did put up a tree and garnished it with white twinkling lights, a few shiny ornaments and tinsel. Angela put on the CD of Bing Crosby's Christmas songs that she'd found in the cabinet drawer under the stereo. She opened the drapes and they were both surprised to see that a soft dusting of snow had covered the world outside during the night. By contrast now, the sun was shining and the sky was clear. The temperature outside was icy cold. But inside, with a cozy fire crackling in the fireplace, they were comfortable and warm.

The few gifts they'd gotten for each other were wrapped and waiting under the tree but, unbeknownst to Angela, the biggest gift of all was in the smallest package. Banyon handed it to her after they'd opened all the others.

Sitting next to him on the couch, she pulled off the little red bow, tore off the wrapping, and opened the tiny box. "Oh, my god," she muttered, finally after a moment of shock. Then in full voice, "Oh, my god!"

Banyon gently took the box from her trembling hand and removed the diamond ring. Her wide-eyed expression made him laugh. Holding her hand in his, he said, "Well?"

"Well what?" she asked innocently, even though she knew very well what he was asking.

"Come on," he grinned, sheepishly. "You know what."

"Tell me!" she laughed.

He looked at her glowing face for several moments. "Will you marry me?" he whispered.

"I'm sorry," she said, cupping one hand to her ear. "What was that? I couldn't hear you."

He grinned. "*Will you marry me!*" he shouted, loud enough for the neighbors to hear.

Angela laughed and cried at the same time. She was barely able to speak. "Yes," she said softly.

"I'm sorry," Banyon said, mimicking her. "What was that? I couldn't hear you."

With tears filling her eyes she shouted, "Yes! Yes! Yes!"

The ring slid easily onto her finger and the moment seemed suspended in time like a photograph that neither of them would ever forget.

The curtains were still drawn in Kline's living room. As a Jew his only interest in Christmas was purely academic. To him it was little more than a cultural phenomenon with some questionable, yet intriguing historical roots. He found it fascinating that of all the millions of Christians in the world almost none of them were aware that the date of December 25th was not the day Jesus was born but was, in fact, the birth date of several god-men of ancient times, pre-dating Jesus. Mithras, Dionysus, Buddha, and others were all said to have been born on the 25th of December. It was the winter solstice, the time of the *rebirth* of the sun. Even the idea of the virgin birth, at least according to several researchers, was not unique to the Jesus story. Dionysus, Mithras, Buddha, Krishna, Osiris, and other religious icons from cultures far and wide were all thought to have been born of virgins or, if not of virgins, at least they arrived by some sort of miraculous birth. Kline was convinced that the famous Old Testament verse in Isaiah 7:14 was not a valid argument to support the idea that Jesus was born of a virgin nor that the virgin birth of Christ was foretold several centuries before Jesus was born. The Old Testament verse in most Bibles reads:

Therefore the Lord himself shall give you a sign; Behold a virgin shall conceive, and bare a son, and shall call his name Immanuel.

It was true that the New Testament author of the book of Matthew quoted this Old Testament verse as proof of the prophecy when he wrote:

Now all this was done, that it might be fulfilled which was spoken of the Lord by the prophet, saying,

Behold, a virgin shall be with child, and shall bring forth a son, and they shall call his name Immanuel, which being interpreted is, God with us.

But it was also true that Matthew used the Greek Septuagint for his reference and therein lay the problem, at least as far as Kline was concerned. The Septuagint was the Old Testament translated into Greek from the original Hebrew by Jewish scribes for the benefit of their Greek-speaking Jewish brethren. The scribes, however, translated the original Hebrew word, *almah*, meaning *a young woman* into the Greek word, *parthenos*, meaning, literally, *a virgin*. So while the Old Testament book of Isaiah spoke of a child being born to a *young woman*, who may or may not have been a virgin, the New Testament book of Matthew claims in no uncertain terms that the woman was, indeed, a virgin. Some scholars even went so far as to point out that the verse in Isaiah was concerned with immediate events of the time rather than a prediction of something to occur hundreds of years into the future. The question in Kline's mind was who to blame for this error? *Surely*, he reasoned, *the Jewish scribes would have known that Isaiah could have used the Hebrew word, bethulah, which does mean virgin if that's what Isaiah had intended.* But, clearly, that wasn't the case. Isaiah used the more ambiguous term, *almah*, with no indications that it was meant to infer or imply virginity. Why would the scribes, who must have known better, make such an error? Or was it more than just an honest mistake? Could it have been an intentional mistranslation for the purpose of helping to perpetuate the Jesus myth? If so, just who were these Jewish translators? And was Matthew aware of this? After all, at the very time when Jesus was preaching his version of the Truth, he had another diety-in-the-flesh to compete with; the popular god-man, Mithras, who was said to have been born of a virgin with the predestined duty of bringing salvation to the world. Mithras was not just native to a realm beyond the earth and separate from the cosmos but he was the sole lord of the realm, just as Jesus is alleged to have claimed his *kingdom* was not of this earth. *It's no wonder*, Kline mused, *that Matthew would be tempted to embellish his gospel account with attributes that would go head to head with Mithras.* This, Kline reasoned, would have been especially important to Matthew because he was writing his gospel account nearly ninety years after Jesus died and at a time when Mithraism was near it's height of popularity in the region. Also, there was the fact - as Kline later learned - that the Mithras legend was intimately tied to the twelve signs of the Zodiac and the Jesus story was so intimately tied to the twelve apostles whom many researchers had postulated may have each been born under a different sun sign, thus representing the Mithras Zodiac. It was all just too *coincidental* for Kline's taste. *And*, he wondered, *how many of these pre-Christian gods had their births announced by a bright star and were visited by astrologers bearing gifts?* He couldn't recall for sure but it seemed to him there were several. Some of these god-men were said to have performed the same miracles that were later attributed to Jesus. And some of these god-men were even referred to, in their time, by the now familiar titles such as the *Son of God*, the *Good Shepherd*, the *Light of the World*, and so on. According to some sources, a number of these *gods* in human form were said to have died violent deaths only to rise again from the tomb three days later. So even the idea of the Resurrection was old hat by the time Jesus appeared on the scene.

It wasn't so much Kline's Jewish heritage that precluded his belief in Jesus. If the evidence of Jesus' special divinity was anywhere to be found then he would probably believe with the best of them. But the more he researched the historical records the more it seemed obvious to him that the early Christians - especially two of the gospel writers - had borrowed many of the fundamental aspects of the other god-men and applied them to this new savior, Jesus of Nazareth, in order to win the so called Pagan worshippers over to the new god-man in town. In fact, Kline learned, the town of Nazareth didn't even exist when Jesus was born and that most likely the early Christians considered Jesus to be a sun god, as many of the pre-Christian gods were thought to be, and that the word *Nazareth* was probably a confusion of the Hebrew word, *Nazaroth*, meaning the twelve signs of the Zodiac. He found it curious also that the root verb, *nazar*, translates as *to surround*, which seemed to reflect the idea of Jesus being surrounded by the twelve apostles. Truly, there seemed to be no shortage of deities in those days, all of them sharing several of the same attributes, and the early Christian Church was determined, come Hell or high water, that this would be the end of the proliferation of such god-men. The buck stopped with Jesus as far as they were concerned and they made sure of it by employing a reign of brute force and terror in the name of the Lord. You were either a Christian, by God, or you were a dead Pagan.

As consumed by the curiosity of it all, as Kline indeed was, this particular Christmas morning found him much too busy with the present to bother with the past. Digging through his rather disorganized filing cabinets he searched for the notes related to his previous presentation on the sociology of knowledge. He'd given that lecture just three years ago at a special symposium held at the University of Washington and it was well received by his peers. However, there had been some recent developments in the field, some new theories proposed by a visiting German professor at Stanford and everyone interested in the subject was talking about it. If Kline's presentation was to be as well received this time as it was the last time he would have to know this new material forward and backward and incorporate it into his lecture. He realized, of course, that the lecture was just an excuse for him to be at the Queen City University campus. He'd committed himself to the request of the Nine and this covert mission was foremost in his mind. Still, he couldn't help feeling a bit excited about actually presenting his thoughts on one of his favorite academic subjects to an audience of his peers. There was much to do in preparation. He had no idea when his invitation to the conference would arrive but he assumed it would be soon and he had to be ready.

~31~

K line's invitation to speak at the conference arrived in his mailbox just four days into the New Year. Now, a week later, he found himself in the Lemieux Memorial Conference Center on the Queen City University campus with nearly a hundred of his peers from around the country. He was fully prepared for the presentation he was about to give but apprehensive about his true purpose for being there. The conference would begin with a luncheon at noon and the presentations would begin at 1:00 p.m. His was the last of six presentations scheduled for the day, thus assuring plenty of activity as people moved about - chatting amongst themselves when the conference was over - giving him an opportunity to leave without attracting attention.

He arrived early enough to familiarize himself with the layout of the campus. There were four 3-story buildings. Three were adjacent to one another and one was located on the opposite side of the campus, about five or six minutes from the others at a normal walking pace. He wished he had psychic powers and could somehow zero in on which of the four buildings contained the items he was after. His intuition told him it was the single building across from the other three but his intuition had never been very reliable.

The series of presentations by the other professors were interesting enough to hold his attention on and off for the better part of the afternoon. They served to at least temporarily distract him from the anxiety he was feeling about his ability to carry out the real mission at hand. When he was finally introduced as the last speaker, he was acknowledged by his peers with an applause. With a smile and a nod he approached the podium.

In another building, the door to room 306 burst open and Brother

Montabeau walked briskly over to the computer where Romano, Beck, and Salvo were continuing their attempt to make some sense of the mysterious phrases and numbers on the old parchment.

"He's here," Montabeau said, as he thrust a copy of the conference program into Romano's hand.

Romano glanced at it and seemed annoyed by the interruption. "What's this?" he asked "Who's here?"

"Professor Kline, that's who. There's been a conference going on all afternoon and Kline's name is right here on the program. Look!"

Romano looked at the program. "Conference? I didn't hear about any conference. What the hell is this?"

"It was news to me too," Montabeau said. "I just now found that program crumpled up on the walkway outside."

Romano pushed back from the computer and read the roster of speakers. "Christ," he said, quickly checking his watch. "Kline was scheduled to speak at five o'clock. It's nearly six now. I wonder if he's still here?"

"There's no way he could possibly know anything about us," Salvo said. "It's got to be just a coincidence that he's here."

A look of concern crossed Romano's face. "I don't know. I don't like it."

"Brother Salvo's right," Beck said. "How could he possibly know? There's no way."

Romano got up from his chair and paced back and forth, rubbing his hand across the smooth contour of his bald head. "I know, I know," he said. "But I still don't like it." He looked at his watch again. "Montabeau!" he ordered. "You gather up these materials, take it all down to the basement and lock it up in the safe. Salvo, Beck, come with me."

"But..." Montabeau began to protest.

Romano glared at him. "Don't argue with me! Just do it!"

Romano and the other two priests hurried out of the room and down the hall toward the stairs.

"Where are we going?" Beck asked.

"I want to see this guy," Romano said. "I want to make sure he leaves the campus as soon as he's finished with his presentation or whatever the hell it is he's doing here."

"We've never actually seen him," Beck countered. "We don't

know what he looks like. How are we going to know which one is him?"

"I'm hoping he's still giving his talk," Romano said. "He's the last one on the roster."

When they got to the Conference Center a number of people were already coming out of the building.

"Damn!" Romano cursed. "Damn!"

The three priests pushed their way through the crowd and into the main room where the presentations had been delivered. The conference was over but several dozen people were still milling around shaking hands and discussing the afternoon's events. Even if Kline was still in the room they had no way of recognizing him. There was only one way to find out.

"Excuse me," Romano said, addressing a man with a beard and a full head of wirey brown hair. "I'm looking for one of today's speakers. His name is Alan Kline. Would you happen to know him?"

Kline smiled. "Why yes," he said. "I'm..." suddenly he froze, staring at Romano. *Oh shit,* he thought to himself. *What if these are the guys that have the stuff?*

"Yes?" Romano said.

"I'm, uh," Kline stuttered. "I'm pretty sure I saw him heading toward the parking lot a few minutes ago."

"I see," Romano said, trying to sound as casual as possible. "We've never actually had the opportunity to meet the man. What exactly does he look like? Perhaps we can spot him outside if he's still on campus."

Kline was sweating and had to think quickly. "Tall fellow. Very tall," he said, gesturing with his hand. "Dark complexion. Quite a dapper dresser, actually. I believe he was wearing a pin-striped suit and walked with a slight limp."

Romano grabbed Salvo by the arm and the three priests hurried out of the building.

Kline took a breath and tried to gather his composure. *Now what do I do?* He looked around for another way out and noticed an exit sign above a door at the back of the spacious conference room.

Instead of immediately gathering up the materials and taking them to the basement as he was ordered, Montabeau couldn't resist the temptation to take advantage of this time alone with the precious parchment and Banyon's notes. He thought maybe with a stroke of luck he might be able to see something the others had missed, some key, some hidden clue. Romano and the others had made what they believed was at least a small amount of progress toward deciphering the code but, having almost no trust in Montabeau, they shared very little of it with him. In fact, right at that moment, outside near the parking lot, Romano was having second thoughts about the wisdom of having left Montabeau alone with the goods. Still, there was nothing he could do about it now.

It was nearly 6:30 and the darkness of the late winter evening had fallen over the campus. The only light was provided by old-fashioned globe lamps on tall, antiquated pole standards. The lamps lit most of the paths and concrete walkways that crisscrossed the campus from building to building but everything else was shrouded in darkness.

Romano and the other two priests watched carefully, scanning the few attendees from the conference who were still coming out of the building. But they were losing hope of finding Kline. So far, no one matched the description of the tall dark man in a pinstriped suit.

Kline made his way, undetected, into the first of the three buildings that he'd identified earlier in the day. Rushing up the three flights of stairs he quietly walked down the hall until he came to a room numbered 306. The frosted glass window on the door was aglow, revealing that the lights were on inside. Putting his ear up to the door he could hear the muffled sound of voices but he couldn't make out what they were saying. Suddenly the door burst open, nearly striking him in the face, and several students came pouring out in a din of chatter and conversation. Glancing into the room he could see several more students gathered around the professor's desk. The professor noticed Kline standing in the doorway and addressed him. "May I help you?" he asked with a pleasant smile.

"Oh, uh, no," Kline stuttered. "I think I just got the wrong room."

The professor smiled again, nodded his head, and resumed his conversation with the students.

Kline walked a few steps down the hall. If the materials were in that room, he had no idea how he could find out. Something told him the best thing to do was to go on to the next building. *If the gods are on my side*, he thought to himself, *they'll give me a sign.* At least he hoped that would be the case.

The next building, curiously enough, didn't have a room 306. The last room on the even-numbered side of the hall was 304. The rest of the wall, all the way to the end of the hall, had no doors or windows at all. *Apparently*, he reasoned, *room 304 must be one long room. Maybe it's a study hall or something.*

Finally he got to the third building. It did have a room 306 but it was locked. *Damn it!* he swore to himself. He hadn't anticipated any of the doors being locked. *So what the hell am I supposed to do? Break the door down?* He shook his head in frustration and glanced up and down the hall. He couldn't see anyone but he could hear a muffled voice coming from one of the rooms down the hall. *Probably someone conducting a class.* He nudged his shoulder up against the door and pushed as if testing its strength. It was solid. He set his briefcase on the floor and grabbed the doorknob with his left hand. He leaned back, took a deep breath, and thrust his full weight against the door. Rock of Gebralter. It was pointless to try again. The gods had either abandoned him or this was a sign that it was the wrong room. Whichever was the case, there was only one option left: the older building across the campus. Quickly, he scurried off in that direction.

It was five minutes to seven and the priests figured they had missed Kline altogether. Then Salvo nudged Romano's arm and pointed toward a grassy area just beyond one of the lighted walkways. In the shadows they could see the figure of a man with a briefcase moving suspiciously fast toward the older 3-story brick building.

It was difficult at this point to know just whose side the gods were on but it wasn't looking too good for the poor professor.

~32~

W hat time is it?" Banyon asked Angela as they pulled up to the curb in front of the Seattle Gospel Mission.

She glanced at her watch. "Five minutes to seven."

He smiled. "Perfect! Wouldn't want to be late for my own going-away party!"

They walked in the front door to find the place filled with familiar faces. Most of the volunteer staff was there, as well as several of the homeless regulars that Banyon had come to know so well. The new director for the shelter, this time a real honest-to-goodness priest by the name of Father Girard, was present also. Banyon and Angela had barely stepped inside when Old Tom led the group in a rousing rendition of *For He's A Jolly Good Fellow* and one of the kitchen staff wheeled out a beautiful cake with the words **We Will Miss You!** scrolled across the top. Everyone knew he was leaving his position at the shelter but no one yet knew exactly why and he had been wondering for days just what he would tell them. Tonight he would get that opportunity.

As Kline raced across the dark campus he stopped short when he noticed the three priests staring in his direction not a hundred feet away. If he had run just another few feet before stopping he would have been completely in the shadows. As it was, he found himself caught in the light from one of the lampposts. The light was dim but just bright enough for the priests to recognize him as the man they had spoken to inside the Conference Center.

"Gentlemen," Romano said, "I believe we were lied to. That's him."

Beck wasn't so sure. "You think that's Kline?"

"One way to find out," Romano answered.

Kline couldn't hear what they were saying but he suspected he'd been recognized. His suspicion was confirmed within seconds as the priests began walking quickly toward him.

Shit! he thought to himself. *They know!* He was tempted to turn and run for the parking lot, jump into his car and get the hell out of there. But if he was fast enough, maybe he could lose them in the dark, trick them into thinking he'd left the campus, then double back with enough borrowed time to check out the last building. It was worth a try. He hoped. With that decision made, he took off running toward the parking lot. The priests made a sudden lurch and took off chasing him into the darkness.

Banyon and Angela were enjoying the party when they were approached by Old Tom.

"You know, Father," Tom said in his familiar gravely voice, "You've been one of the most important people in my whole miserable life. I can't believe you're leavin'. Didja get an offer you couldn't refuse or somethin'?"

Banyon sighed and smiled. Old Tom had been one of the first people he met when he came to work at the shelter. How many dollar bills had he dropped into Tom's battered old guitar case whenever he passed by a corner where Tom was playing? How many times had Tom livened up the shelter with his unique brand of the blues and a gospel song or two? How many times had Tom complained about the food but kept coming back for more? Banyon had often looked at Old Tom, a poor, aging, black man with nothing but a beat up guitar and a song and he would think to himself, *no matter how hard things might get there's always hope for something better to come the next day.* That seemed to be the way Tom lived his life and it served as a daily lesson for Banyon and anyone else who might be paying attention. This was a sad moment but, not being very adept at sentimentality, Banyon decided to take it another direction.

"Tom, my man," Banyon said, putting an arm around the old blues singer, "you've been one of the most important people in my life too." Then he shook his head and grinned. "But to tell you the truth, I'm leaving because I just can't take anymore of your constant complaining about the damn food!"

That rattled Tom for a brief moment until he realized it was a joke. "Yeah, well," Tom fired back, "the food still stinks. Except for that cake over there. That ain't too bad. But I've already told that new guy... what's his name?"

"You mean Father Girard?"

"Yeah, that's right. Girard. I've already told him I ain't comin' back here if he don't change the menu pretty soon! And that's a damn fact!"

Banyon laughed and gave Tom a friendly hug.

"Ah, knock it off," Tom grumbled. "I'm gonna go get another piece of that cake. It's the only good thing there's been to eat around here for months."

"Bring us a piece too, would you, please?" Banyon said.

"You got it, my friend," Old Tom replied.

Banyon looked around at all the people enjoying themselves. "This is great," he said to Angela.

"Yeah. Too bad you didn't think to invite Professor Kline."

"Actually I tried to but he wasn't home. I left him a message. You know, I haven't heard from him since the day we talked on the phone. Remember? I told him about the stuff disappearing from my briefcase. He said he'd make some inquiries or something like that. Remember?"

Angela nodded. "Yeah. I remember. That is odd. I wonder where he could be?"

Banyon shrugged. "I don't know. I hope he hasn't gotten himself into some kind of trouble."

Running blind through the dark, Kline stumbled on the cement curb at the edge of the parking lot. He cursed out loud, brushed himself off and glanced back toward the campus. He couldn't see the priests but he knew they must be close behind. His pulse was pounding. He scanned the lot for his car. It wasn't hard to find. The old 1979 Buick V-8 stood out like a sore thumb. It was at that moment he realized the parking lot was so well lit that he was sure to be seen. *But maybe that's a good thing*, he thought. *They'll see me getting into my car and driving away.*

"There he is!" Salvo shouted.

Kline turned around and saw the three men approaching quickly. He ran to his car and struggled with his keys to open the door. The keys had become entangled in the ring of the key chain. "Damn it!" he swore. "Don't do this to me now!"

The three priests were fifty feet away and gaining quickly. With adrenaline pulsing through his entire body Kline grabbed the key tightly and somehow wrenched it back through the ring. He opened the door, jumped in, fired up the engine, slammed it into reverse and hit the gas. He nearly smashed into the car behind him and then quickly shoved the gearshift into drive. He cranked the steering wheel hard, and burned rubber peeling out of the parking lot.

The festivities at the shelter were in full swing as Father Girard stood up on a small platform that someone had built just for the occasion. He raised a hand and called for everyone's attention. The crowd quieted down. "You know why we're all here," he began.

"Yeah!" someone yelled. "Because we're not all there!"

A roar of groans and laughter filled the room.

Girard grinned. "Speak for yourself," he retorted with the quick wit of a professional who's used to dealing with hecklers. Again, everyone laughed. "We're here tonight to say farewell to Mr. Zeke Banyon who has done a marvelous job during his time here at the Seattle Gospel Mission." He turned to Banyon and held out his hand. "Now the man of the hour would like to say a few words. Zeke! Come on up here!"

Kline squealed around the corner and out onto the street. Thinking quickly and with amazing clarity, given the situation, it occurred to him that he could drive to the south parking lot which he knew was right next to the only 3-story building remaining to be searched. He realized the three men chasing him were as exhausted as he was and they would probably take their time walking back to the main part of the campus. If he hurried he could be at the south parking lot in less than a minute, park the car and probably have at least a few minutes to check out the building before the three priests returned. If the gods were with him they'd open the door to room 306, hand the materials over to him personally and apologize for making it such a rough evening.

Driving furiously, he swerved the big Buick into the south parking lot and noticed the building was even closer than he'd thought. In fact, the back of the building actually bordered one entire side of the lot. *It's about time I had a little luck on my side.* He pulled into a space next to the building, grabbed his briefcase, and jumped out of the car. A janitor, carrying a large bag of trash, was just coming out of one of the doors at the back of the building. When he came out he left the door open behind him. The timing couldn't have been better. Kline straightened his jacket and tried to catch his breath. Then, looking as casual as possible, he walked past the janitor on his way toward the opened door.

"Evenin'" the janitor said.

Kline smiled and nodded and kept walking. He took a brief look back. The janitor was busy dumping the trash into a dumpster. Kline held his breath and slipped in through the door.

"And so," Banyon said, "I know you're all wondering why I've decided to quit my job here at the shelter. The reason is simple. I just couldn't take any more of Old Tom's complaining about the food!"

Everyone got a good laugh as Tom's complaints had become legendary.

"I never complained about nothin' that didn't need complainin' about!" Tom shouted from the back of the room. That brought an even bigger round of laughter.

Banyon smiled. "I'm kidding, of course," he said. "This place wouldn't be nearly as colorful without the likes of our good friend with the guitar and a song in his heart." He paused for a moment as a few people actually applauded for Tom. "No," Banyon continued, "the reason I'm leaving has nothing to do with any of you or with this place that I've become so fond of. It's been... well, interesting, challenging, and even fun at times. I've enjoyed it all and I've enjoyed getting to know so many of you who have so graciously honored me with this party tonight. The reason I'm leaving is strictly for personal reasons. None of them bad, mind you. In fact one of the best reasons is standing right here next to me." He reached for Angela's hand and held it up for everyone to see the ring. "Angela and I are engaged to be married!"

The announcement brought a cheer and a round of applause.

"I knew there was something going on back in that office!" shouted one of the volunteer staffers. Everyone laughed again.

"Yes," Banyon smiled. "Well, don't believe everything you hear! Only half of it is true."

"Which half?" someone shouted. More laughter.

Banyon grinned. "I'm not telling! Anyway, so that's one reason for my departure. Not that I couldn't work here and be married, too. You've all come to know Angela and it's obvious she, too, has good feelings about this place. The point is, some other things have come into my life besides Angela and it just seems like the right time to make a change. I trust you'll understand that I don't want to go into it all right now as it is quite personal. But maybe one day I'll be able to come back with a great story to tell about what I've been doing. Like the younger generation is fond of saying these days, *it's all good*. And with that, I want to thank you for this farewell party and for being such good friends while I've been here. I know you'll like Father Girard. I've had the opportunity to spend some time with him and I can tell you now they couldn't have made a better choice for someone to take over where I left off. So I guess that's about it. Thank you all again and God bless everyone of you. Now party-on, people!"

Once inside the building, Kline hurried down the long, dimly lit hall and found a staircase leading up to the main floor. With a new surge of energy he made his way up the flights of stairs heading for the third floor.

"Oh to hell with it," Montabeau muttered in frustration as he ejected Banyon's disk from the computer. "None of this makes any sense." He checked his watch. *They'll probably be coming back anytime. I better pack this stuff up and get it down to the basement.* He put all the items into a box and carried it out of the room.

Kline rounded the top of the third floor stairs and stopped short, just in time to see Montabeau closing the door behind him with the box under his arm. Kline quickly ducked back around the corner.

Montabeau locked the door and started down the hall, heading away from Kline, toward the elevator. Kline watched for a moment and when Montabeau was far enough down the hall he advanced a few paces. Then a little further. Quietly. Slowly. In a moment he was able to see the number on the door that Montabeau had just locked. It was room 306. Kline realized he wouldn't be able to get into the room but he had a feeling he didn't need to. It was just a hunch but something told him the objects of his intention were walking down the hall in front of him. He didn't really know why he thought that. Maybe the gods were speaking to him. *It's about time*, he thought to himself. Then it suddenly occurred to him. *That priest doesn't know me from Adam. He's never seen me before. I could be just another professor as far as he's concerned.* There were several non-Jesuit instructors employed at the university so it was a perfectly reasonable idea.

Montabeau stopped at the elevator, pushed the button and waited for the doors to open. Kline swallowed hard, gripped his briefcase and began walking quickly down the hall in Montabeau's direction. He had no idea how he was going to handle the situation if, indeed, his instincts were correct about what was in the box under the priest's arm. Kline was operating on autopilot without a flight plan. There was nothing to do but improvise. *I'm not cut out for this*, he thought to himself as he hurried down the hall a little faster with every step.

The elevator doors slid open. Montabeau entered without hesitation and the doors began to close. Kline rushed forward, thrusting his briefcase between the two doors just in time to keep them from closing. He stepped inside. "Sorry," he said, feigning a complete lack of interest in either the priest or the box under his arm. "Too tired to take the stairs."

Montabeau said nothing but stared straight ahead. The elevator doors closed. Kline felt trapped and still had no idea what to do next. A string of thoughts raced through his mind. *Okay, what now? What floor is he going to? Probably the first floor and then he'll leave the building. Shit, I'm just standing here. He's expecting me to punch a floor button. I better do something...*

At that moment, Montabeau leaned forward and reached toward the panel. Kline thought it looked like he was about to press the button for the first floor. *Good*, he thought. *I'll just say thanks, that's my floor too*. But Montabeau's hand reached lower and pressed the button with an X on it. Kline was puzzled. *What? What the hell is the X Floor?* The elevator clunked and began to descend.

"Thanks," Kline tried to smile. "That's my floor, too".

That comment caught Montabeau's attention and he immediately became suspicious. *Why would this guy be going to the basement?* Something was wrong. Montabeau could feel it. Out of the corner of his eye he glanced over and lowered his gaze toward the briefcase in the stranger's hand. What he saw shocked him. The name *A. KLINE* was clearly engraved on a small brass nameplate on the top edge of the briefcase.

Without hesitation Montabeau reached out and hit the EMERGENCY STOP button. The elevator jerked to a sudden halt. Montabeau dropped the box and lunged at Kline, knocking the poor professor backward against the side of the elevator. Kline dropped to his knees, shocked and disoriented by the sudden burst of violence. The contents of the box spilled out onto the floor. Kline, still on his knees, eyed the goods with a look of desperation. The computer disk rattled off into the corner. The leather document folder containing the parchment lay just inches from his hand.

Montabeau looked down. "Don't even think about it!" he warned Kline. "Your business here is finished!"

Montabeau, thinking he'd intimidated Kline into staying put, kneeled down to recover the items. Kline took advantage of the moment. He jumped to his feet and swung his briefcase with all his might, striking a brutal blow to the side of Montabeau's head. Montabeau fell backward, dazed and bleeding but he managed to get to his feet. Kline staggered sideways preparing to swing his weapon once again but Montabeau suddenly stopped and stood motionless with an odd look on his face. In the next moment he stumbled backward against the wall. He moaned as his knees buckled under. With a look of confusion in his eyes, he collapsed completely, striking his head on the steel handrail as he fell to the floor.

Kline was in a state of shock. The adrenaline was still surging through his body. He couldn't stop shaking. *Got to get the hell out of here!* He pressed the button for the main floor. The elevator jerked once and began to move. Suddenly he realized the items he came for were still scattered at his feet. He got down on his hands and knees and began gathering up the materials. He put the last item into his briefcase and closed it up when the elevator stopped and the doors slid open. Before he could even get to his feet he looked up in disbelief. Standing at the opened door were the three priests. His option of fight or flight had run out. He didn't have enough energy left to do either one. He simply lowered his head and sighed.

"Well," Romano exclaimed, genuinely surprised. "Look who's here!"

Kline's ploy had worked and yet backfired at the same time. He'd fooled the priests into thinking they'd been outrun and that he had left the campus. Now they realized they'd been duped and the tables were turned.

"Grab him!" Romano ordered.

Beck and Salvo took Kline by the arms, pulled him to his feet and dragged him out into the hall. Romano stepped into the elevator to check on Montabeau.

"He's dead," Romano said, looking up at the others.

Kline was shocked. "What!" he cried. "He can't be dead! I only hit him with the briefcase! I just knocked him out!"

Romano checked Montabeau's body again. "He's not breathing and he has no pulse." Then he added, sarcastically, "That usually means you're dead." Examining the body, he turned Montabeau's head to the side, revealing a deep gash at the temple.

"I didn't do that!" Kline protested. "I couldn't have done that!"

Romano dragged Montabeau's body out into the hall and instructed Beck and Salvo to bring Kline back into the elevator.

"Where are you taking me?" Kline demanded.

"A nice cool place where you can rest," Romano replied. He left Montabeau's body laying on the floor and joined the others in the elevator. He pressed the X button and they began their descent.

When they reached the basement Beck and Salvo ushered the professor from the elevator out into the cool dampness of the basement.

Salvo turned to Romano. "What about Montabeau?"

Romano pulled Salvo aside and whispered, "Montabeau is still alive."

Salvo looked confused. "What? But I thought you said…"

"I just wanted Kline to think he'd killed him," Romano grinned.

Salvo acknowledged the ruse with a nod and stepped back to rejoin Beck who still had a firm grasp on Kline's arm. Salvo grabbed Kline's other arm and repeated the question to Romano. "So what about Montabeau?"

"Leave him up there," Romano answered. "We'll let someone else find his body. We don't know anything about it."

Beck and Salvo both nodded in agreement.

Romano grabbed the briefcase and checked the contents. "It's all here," he said. "Take our friend to the storeroom. I'll catch up with you after I wipe our fingerprints from the elevator."

The two priests took Kline by the arms and walked quickly, nearly dragging the exhausted professor along with them, down a long dimly lit concrete corridor. At some point they turned left down another hallway that led to a large metal door secured with a padlock. Romano joined them a few minutes later. He reached into his pocket for the key, unlocked the door and flipped the light switch. Two bare light bulbs - dangling at the ends of electrical cords hanging from the ceiling – flickered briefly before coming on.

Kline looked around. If this was in fact a storeroom it didn't seem to be storing anything at the moment except three priests and one frightened professor. A long row of small, rusty, steel hooks of some sort were sticking out from one of the concrete walls. Another wall was completely made of brick with a small window up near the ceiling. Kline supposed it might be the back wall of the building next to where he'd parked his car. He thought he could make out the shape of a narrow door in the darkened corner of the brick wall. *It could lead to a stairway going up to the parking lot*, he thought. But he knew he had no chance of escape as long as they were with him.

On Romano's order Beck and Salvo released their hold on Kline and shoved him up against the wall.

"Have a seat," Romano said.

With his back up against the wall, Kline slid down and sat on the cold cement floor while Romano paced back and forth in front of him.

"We figured you probably work for the Nine," Romano said.

Kline didn't look up. "I don't exactly work for them," he mumbled.

"Hmm. What exactly would you call it then?"

Kline drew his knees up against his chest and didn't answer.

"Never mind," Romano said. "I think I understand. You do them a favor now and then in hopes of a reward, shall we say, somewhere down the road. Yes?"

Kline remained silent, his eyes fixed on the floor.

Romano stopped pacing and stared down at his prisoner. "You're obviously an intelligent man," he said. "And we know you know a lot about Banyon's activities." He paused for a moment and began pacing again. "And obviously you're aware of the power and influence behind our side in this little game, yes?"

Kline shot a quick glance up at Romano.

"Of course you do," Romano said. "Whatever little reward you've been promised by the Nine can't be much. What is it? Maybe a little security in the coming *new order*? A low level administration position perhaps? Whatever it is, we may be able to offer you more if you were to, shall we say, switch sides? What do you say, professor? Otherwise I'm afraid your future might be rather bleak, if you understand what I'm saying."

Kline looked up and gave a short, sarcastic chuckle. "Bleak," he said. " That's an interesting way to put it. Why don't you just say what the hell you mean?"

"Well," Romano answered, "my friend here, Brother Beck, once thought you should have an unfortunate accident. I didn't agree at the time. I thought you might be of some value to us. But now I'm beginning to think maybe he was right."

Beck, who had been quietly leaning against the wall, stepped forward. "I can arrange for it right now," he said.

Romano was just about to reply when something came crashing through the small window near the ceiling and landed with a *klunk* on the floor.

"What the hell is that?" Salvo shouted, as all eyes watched the small object roll across the floor. Suddenly a short popcorn burst of automatic gunfire from the window shattered the two light bulbs and cast the room into total darkness. A noxious cloud of smoke quickly filled the room, burning everyone's eyes and making it difficult to breathe.

"Tear gas!" Romano yelled, choking out the words as he stumbled blindly around in the dark.

Kline panicked and jumped to his feet, gasping and choking with every breath. He raised his arm to cover his face with his coat sleeve. *What the hell is happening?*

In less than a minute the door in the corner of the room flew open. A flurry of flashlight beams zigzagged back and forth like lasers cutting through the darkness. Someone grabbed Kline, shoved the briefcase into his hand, and pulled him into the shallow stairwell just outside the door.

Kline's throat kept closing up as he tried to ask what was going on. "Just get the hell out of here! Now!" a man shouted.

The man pushed the professor toward the short flight of cement stairs and quickly returned to the room to assist his partner.

Through blurry, burning eyes Kline could see the stairs led to the parking lot just as he had suspected. He wasted no time getting to the top where he was met by yet a third man. The stranger was dressed in black with a stocking cap pulled down to his eyes. He took Kline by the arm and led him to his car.

"You'll be all right in just a minute," he told Kline. "From what they tell me, your job isn't quite finished. Better get going." The man turned and headed back to the building before Kline could ask any questions.

Romano, Beck and Salvo were easily overpowered by the two men who had burst into the room. The tear gas slowly ventilated out through the open door and the priests found themselves standing immobilized, backs against the wall, with their hands tied to the wall-hooks a foot or so above their heads. A faint light was now coming in through the open door. Groggy and with blurred vision, the priest's could see their assailants: two large men wearing gasmasks and night-vision goggles. They looked like monsters in the dark - an intimidating sight that the three Jesuits would not soon forget.

The impairment to Kline's vision was minimal due to the short amount of time he was exposed to the gas. After a few minutes in the fresh air he was able to drive. He quickly maneuvered the big Buick around and left the parking lot. As his thoughts cleared he realized what the man meant about his job not being quite finished. He had to get the materials back to Banyon. *But how? I can't just waltz in and personally hand the stuff to him.* He didn't want Banyon to know about his connection with the Nine or even to suspect such a connection. He had nearly decided to wait until the next day to work out a plan when he suddenly recalled the message Banyon left on his answering machine. *The farewell party! It was tonight wasn't it?* He was certain Banyon had said the party was this very evening. *Maybe there is still time*, he thought. *Maybe they're not home yet.* He looked at his watch. It was just nine o'clock.

Angela and Banyon left the shelter and walked out to the curb where their car was parked.

"It was a great party," she said, giving his hand a squeeze.

"Yeah, it really was," he said as they got into the car. "It was great." He looked at his watch. "Hey, it's only nine o'clock! The night is still young! You want to stop and rent a movie on the way home?"

"Rent a movie?"

Banyon shrugged. "Yeah. It was just a thought."

"Well, okay. That sounds good. A comedy maybe?"

Banyon nodded. "Sure, I could go for that."

"Okay," she said. "Let's do it."

As Kline drove toward Banyon's home the events of the day ran through his mind like a movie. Now safe in his car, several miles from the campus, it all seemed so surreal. It was just at that moment he realized he was breathing rapidly and was still shaking. He took a long deep breath and let it out slowly. *The worst is over*, he kept telling himself. *What more could happen?*

"Oh!" Angela squealed, taking one of the videos from the rack. "I love this one!"

Banyon didn't find anything that particularly struck his fancy so he moved over to see what Angela was going on about.

"What is it?" he asked, looking over her shoulder. She handed him the box cover. He read the title. "*Young Frankenstein?*" he said, obviously not recognizing the title. "I thought you wanted a comedy, not a horror flick."

"You never saw this?" she asked, a little bewildered. She'd just assumed everyone had seen it. "It *is* a comedy!" she insisted. "It's a parody on the old black and white Frankenstein movies. It's hilarious! You'll die. Seriously! Like there's this one part where..."

"That's okay. Don't tell me. If it's half as funny as you are, then it'll be worth the money. Come on. Let's pay for it and go home."

Kline glanced over at the clock on the dashboard. It was half past nine. On the one hand he wanted to step on the gas and get to Banyon's as fast as possible. Yet, at the same time, a touch of paranoia was making him exceedingly cautious. Speeding might attract attention from a cop. From anybody. He just didn't want to be noticed by anyone. *I just want to get there and get this over with and go home.* He began to relax but then suddenly panicked. *Shit!* he cursed to himself, slamming the steering wheel with his hand. *If Banyon's not home how the hell am I going to get this stuff into his house?* With a loud sigh he pushed his glasses up and rubbed his tired, burning eyes. He was too exhausted to think. It was all he could do to drive. *I'll worry about it when I get there,* he decided as he exited off the freeway. Banyon's house was just ten minutes away.

When he arrived at the house he could tell no one was home. The porch light was off. The windows were dark and Angela's car was the only one in the driveway. Obviously they had taken Banyon's car to the party.

Kline parked his car about half a block down the street. He looked around to see if anyone might be watching. The street seemed quiet and the curtains were drawn on the windows of most of the neighbor's homes. It looked safe enough. He grabbed the briefcase and walked up the street to Banyon's house. He decided he might as well try the front door but he wasn't surprised when he found it locked. Going around to the back, he tried opening the two windows on the side of the house but he couldn't budge either one. *Damn!* he swore to himself. He continued around the perimeter of the house, feeling his way through the dark, until he came to the back door. It was locked. Grabbing the doorknob, he shook the door several times in frustration but only succeeded in rattling the glass window on the upper part of the door. *The window!* He couldn't believe what he was thinking. He glanced down at the briefcase in his hand. He could never have guessed, when he left home with it this morning, that it would serve to get him out of a tricky situation. Twice.

He lifted the briefcase and tapped it gently against the glass a couple of times to get an idea of how much noise it was going to make. He looked around. He seemed to be quite alone in the dark. He tapped the briefcase against the glass a couple more times. Then he looked away to shield his eyes and smashed out the lower corner of the window. The broken glass falling to the floor inside the house made more noise than the actual impact. He looked around once more and reached his arm through the window trying to feel for the doorknob. His probing fingers located a chain bolt that he easily slid open. He had to stretch his arm into the window all the way up to his shoulder to reach the doorknob. Giving it a quick awkward twist, the door opened and he quickly slipped inside.

He couldn't see where he was going but he didn't dare turn on a light. Feeling his way along the wall he made it into the kitchen without bumping into anything. Having been in the house before, he remembered he could see the kitchen sink from where he had been sitting in the living room. Now he turned his back to the sink and walked straight ahead. The streetlight in front of the house brought a bit of illumination into the living room through the front window. It was enough to help him see where he was going. He quickly walked over to the coffee table and opened the briefcase.

"I don't know," Banyon said as he turned into the driveway and parked behind Angela's car. "The Frankenstein monster dancing in a top hat and tails sounds pretty silly to me."

Kline was startled by the sound of the car doors slamming shut. He froze and listened. He recognized Angela's laugh. *Oh Jesus!* he cursed to himself. *Shit!* He turned the briefcase upside down and dumped the contents onto the coffee table and hurried into the kitchen. He froze in place again when he heard the sound of a key unlocking the front door.

Banyon flipped on the light in the living room and hung his coat in the closet.

"I'll make us some popcorn," Angela said, handing her coat to Banyon. She went to the kitchen and turned on the light. "There's a draft coming through here!" she called back to Banyon.

"What'd you say?"

"Never mind. Looks like we must have left the back door..." she stopped cold. "Zeke! Come here! Quick!"

Banyon ran into the kitchen. Angela was petrified, pointing to the back door. "The window!" she said. "Somebody broke into the house!"

Banyon couldn't believe what he was seeing. She was right. Someone had, indeed, broken in. He walked over to inspect the damage and then closed the door.

"Oh God," Angela whispered. "Somebody could still be in here."

"Stay with me," he said, taking her by the hand. He led her back into the living room to the cabinet where he kept his gun in a locked box.

Kline was silently moving along the outside of the house. He paused briefly, peering into one of the side windows and saw Banyon taking the revolver out of the box. Angela turned suddenly toward the window. Kline quickly ducked back out of sight.

"What?" Banyon asked.

Angela shook her head. "Nothing, I guess. I'm just scared."

"I'm thinking we should check upstairs."

"I don't know," Angela cautioned. "I think we should call the police."

Banyon glanced down at the gun in his hand and considered the consequences of actually having to shoot someone. "All right," he said. He picked up the phone and dialed 911.

"Nine-one-one," said the dispatcher on the other end of the line. "What is your emergency?"

Banyon was just about to reply when something caught his eye. "What the...!" he said aloud.

"Sir? Can you please state your emergency?"

"Uh..." Banyon said, squinting his eyes in disbelief. "Nothing. I'm... sorry." He hung up the phone with the most baffled look on his face.

"What's the matter with you?" Angela asked. "Why did you hang up?"

Banyon pointed to the coffee table. "What the hell is this?" he said.

Angela looked to see what he was pointing at. She couldn't believe her eyes.

They moved toward the coffee table and stood staring at the familiar items. Banyon reached down and picked up the leather folder and opened it. "The parchment," he said, staring at Angela. "What the hell?"

She kneeled down and picked up the computer disk. "It's all here," she said. "The disk, the book, all the notes... everything!"

Banyon shook his head, totally confused. "Somebody didn't break in to steal anything. They broke in to *leave* something!"

"Oh, this is too strange," Angela said. "This is just way too strange."

At that moment Montabeau, still lying on the floor, regained consciousness and let out a long groaning sound. He slowly opened his eyes and sat up. Glancing down, he saw his own blood on the floor and raised his hand to touch the side of his throbbing head. He felt the gash and suddenly it all came back to him. Still dazed, he looked around and wondered about Kline. Had he escaped with all the materials? And what about Romano, Salvo, and Beck? Where were they? He struggled to his feet and pressed the button to hail the elevator. In a few moments the doors slid open. Stepping inside he expected to see some sign of the struggle, perhaps even more of his own blood as he now recalled the blow from Kline's briefcase and the shock of falling against the handrail. But there was nothing. It didn't make sense but he was too groggy to think about it. He made his way back to the office upstairs and tended to his wound.

Outside Banyon's house, Kline crouched below the windows to avoid being seen as he made his way to the front yard and down the street to his car. After fastening the seat belt, he leaned forward, resting his head against the steering wheel for a moment. He let out a long deep sigh. His job was done. *Hell of a day*, he thought to himself. Then a sudden realization sat him straight up in the seat. "Oh my god," he said aloud as the elevator incident flashed into his mind. "I... killed a man."

~33~

L unch is ready," Angela announced. "You want to eat here in the living room?"

"Wait a minute" Banyon said, turning up the volume on the TV. "Listen to this news story."

"I'm here, live, at Seattle's Queen City University where a bizarre incident occurred just last night. A janitor discovered the priests tied to this wall and immediately cut them loose. According to police, the victims were visibly shaken from the ordeal but otherwise unharmed. The priests told police their assailants wore black hoods over their heads and were probably members of some sort of satanic cult. According to police the attackers subdued the priests with tear gas. Nothing was stolen and no one was physically harmed, leading police to suspect the motive may simply have been to terrorize the priests. According to a detective we talked to, this may have been some sort of an initiation ritual although, at the moment, there are no suspects in the case. John Villanova, KGOT News, live from Queen City University. Back to you, Brenda."

"Thank you John. In Iraq today, three more..."

Banyon clicked off the TV. "That's totally weird," he said.

Angela could tell by the look on his face that his wheels were turning. "You think it has something to do with our materials showing up last night?"

Banyon shook his head. "I don't know. They were Jesuits, you know. I mean it could just be coincidence, but..."

"Professor Kline says there are no coincidences," Angela reminded him, only half joking.

"Yeah. Dear ol' Professor Kline. We still don't know where he was last night."

"Come on. You're not suggesting he had anything to do with it, are you? He hardly seems the type to be involved in anything that violent."

"Mm-hm," Banyon nodded. "Still..."

"Well, why don't you try calling him again. See what he has to say."

Banyon thought for a second. "I'm not sure I want to know."

"Oh come on. You know it's going to eat at you if you don't at least talk to him."

"Yeah, you're right. Okay, I'll call him."

"Why don't we have lunch first? You can think about what to ask him."

"Yeah. Good idea."

He followed Angela out to the kitchen and was just about to sit down at the table when the phone rang.

"I'll get it," she said, heading back to the living room. "Sit down and eat your sandwich."

In a few moments she returned to the kitchen. "It's for you."

"Who is it?"

"Guess."

"Kline?"

Angela nodded.

"Unreal," Banyon said, shaking his head. He got up and went to the phone. "Hello?"

"Zeke! Sorry I wasn't able to make it to your party last night. Had a prior engagement. How'd it go?"

"It was great," Banyon said, wishing he'd had more time to prepare for this conversation. "But we had quite a surprise waiting for us when we got home." He waited to hear what Kline's response would be.

"Really," Kline said, after a short pause. "What sort of a surprise?"

"Would you believe all the missing materials?"

"You're kidding!" Kline came back, trying to sound surprised. "You mean just sitting there on your doorstep, or what?"

"Not exactly. Somebody broke in through..." he stopped short and had an idea.

"Yes?" Kline said, waiting for Banyon to continue.

"I mean," Banyon said, hoping to catch a reaction from Kline by changing the facts, "somebody broke in through the front door. We found it wide open when we got home and all the stuff was just sitting there on the coffee table."

Kline knew, of course, that wasn't the case and figured Banyon must be fishing for a reaction. "Broke in through the front door?" he inquired, keeping up the charade.

"Yeah," Banyon answered, listening carefully for any hint of guilt in Kline's voice. "Can you believe it?"

"The front door?" Kline asked again. "Are you sure?"

"Sure, I'm sure. Why do you ask?"

"I don't know," Kline said. "If it was me I don't think I'd break into the front door right out there where someone could see me."

"Oh?" Banyon said, suspecting Kline may have just put one foot in the trap.

Kline laughed. "Well yes! I mean, would you?"

Banyon hesitated. It was a good point. Now the tables were turned. Either Kline was on to him or he was completely innocent.

"So," Kline continued, "you mean it was all there? Everything? The disk, the original parchment? Everything?"

"Everything," Banyon said, still unsure of Kline's possible involvement.

"That's amazing! I can't imagine who could have done it or why. You know what I mean?"

"Yeah, I know what you mean. We're just glad the stuff was returned." He decided Kline just might have no knowledge of any of this. But there was still the matter of the news report. *How would Kline react to that?* he wondered. "I was going to call you this afternoon," Banyon continued. "Did you happen to catch the news on TV today?"

"No," Kline replied. Of course he had heard the news but, the way the conversation was going, he decided it might be better to feign ignorance. "What news?"

Banyon related to him the story he'd just heard on the television. "It just seemed like a strange coincidence, what with the break-in here at the house and all."

"Good lord," Kline said. "This was on TV?"

"Just a few minutes ago, yeah."

There was a brief pause before Kline spoke again. "Wow," he said, finally. "That's a strange story, for sure. You're right. It's awfully coincidental. Although I can't figure out exactly what the connection might be. If there is one, I mean."

"Well, there's the obvious connection with the Jesuits."

"Right, of course," Kline agreed. "Still, it could be just a coincidence."

Banyon laughed. "Aren't you the one who told us there are no coincidences?"

Kline was becoming increasingly uncomfortable with the conversation. The memory of last night's struggle in the elevator came rushing vividly into his mind. "Indeed I did," he said, attempting to return the laugh. "You got me on that one!"

"So what do you make of it all, anyway?"

Kline thought for a moment. "Well," he said, "even if there is a connection it's not likely we'll ever know for sure. It is a strange and unexpected turn of events to have your materials returned, I'll give you that. I guess we should just accept it at that and you can continue on with the work of decoding the parchment. Don't you think?"

Banyon sighed. He really had no reason to suspect Kline. Even if the old professor was involved in some way, what harm had been done? Nothing, other than a broken window on the back door. And the original materials were now safe and sound in the house. "Yeah," Banyon said. "I guess you're right."

"Well, look," Kline said casually, "I have to get going. But I just wanted to call and apologize for not being able to attend your going-away party. Tell Angela I said hello."

When they finished their conversation Banyon returned to the kitchen and sat down at the table with Angela.

"So?" she prodded.

"Well," Banyon said, taking a bite of his sandwich, "he was calling to say he was sorry he missed the party. Prior engagement or something."

"And?"

"And, I don't know. I guess maybe he didn't have anything to do with the materials being returned. He seemed totally surprised. And he didn't seem to know anything at all about that incident at the university. He hadn't heard the news on TV or anything."

"Told you so," she said with a wink.

Banyon smiled. "Yeah-yeah."

"So what'd he say?"

Banyon shrugged. "He just said we'd probably never know for

sure if there was any connection between the incident at the university and the return of our stuff and that we should probably just get on with trying to figure out the code. I suppose he's probably right."

"I'm all for that," Angela said, finishing the last bite of her sandwich.

Banyon sat back in the chair and lit a cigarette. "Me, too. Trouble is, I really don't know where to begin."

"Begin? What do you mean, begin? We began a long time ago! We just need to keep going."

"I know, but I mean it's been a little while since we've really studied it. It's all just kind of a mish-mash of random information piled up in my brain somewhere."

"Well, what we need to do is sit down and review all the notes and try to organize it somehow. Look for patterns. Put things together."

Banyon smiled as he thought back to the day he hired her to help him organize his office. "Well, that's what you do best," he said. "You lead. I'll follow."

Angela looked surprised. "What, right now?"

He laughed. "It's not like we have anything else to do. I guess now is as good a time as any." Immediately he could see something was on her mind. "What is it?" he asked.

"Well," she said thoughtfully, "if we're going to pursue this thing... I mean really do it right..."

"Yes? What?"

"We could really use a computer. You know how much we relied on it at the office."

Banyon sighed. "Yeah, I suppose you're right. What do you suggest?"

"I was thinking we don't need to spend a lot of money. Just something to run our programs and give us internet access. I bet we can get a used laptop for under a grand at a place I know of by the mall. They sell refurbished computers."

Banyon's eyes opened wide. "A grand! A thousand dollars? For one of those little laptop thingies?"

Angela laughed. "*Under* a grand! Probably around eight-hundred would be my guess."

"Oh! Only eight-hundred dollars!" Banyon came back sarcastically. "That's much better."

That was Angela's cue. She gave him *the look*.

"Oh god," he sighed. "Please. Not *the look*."

But it worked and soon they were out the door on their way to buy a laptop. Angela was dead-on about the price and she somehow managed to get the dealer to throw in a printer for free.

When they returned home Angela went straight to the kitchen table and began setting up the equipment.

"It's going to be a little while," she said, paging through the manual. "I have to figure this out."

Banyon stretched his arms and yawned. "Okay. Call me when you're ready. I'm going upstairs to take a nap. Writing that check for eight-hundred dollars completely wore me out."

Angela shook her head. "Whatever."

As he walked up the stairs he turned once more to catch a glimpse of her through the kitchen door. He had to smile. Now that the materials had been returned, he had a funny feeling they were about to embark on a new leg of this strange journey that began so unexpectedly, so many months ago.

~34~

Later that evening, after his nap, Banyon came down the stairs and walked into the kitchen with all the materials. Angela was sitting at the kitchen table playing with the new computer.

"So we're online and everything works?" he asked.

"Yup. We're ready to rock."

"Great!" he said, handing her the disk. "Here. See if this works."

Angela popped the disk into the slot. "There you go," she said. "Works like a charm."

"For eight-hundred bucks, I should hope so," he said, scooting a chair up next to her. "So, can you bring up that list of the phrases we transcribed from the parchment? I remember we categorized them somehow."

Angela brought the document up on the screen and printed out a copy. The phrases were grouped according to their respective alphanumeric values:

THE DISTANCE=108
ONE HUNDRED=108
GEOMETRY=108

COMMUNICATE=117
NEGATIVE DARK=117
NINE LIGHTS=117
KING OF HEAVEN=117
EAST OF THE HEAD=117

SPEED OF LIGHT=126

STAR OF ISIS=135

FORTY FOUR=144
ONE HUNDRED FEET=144
NINE IS THE KEY=144
CIRCLE OF STONE=144
THE ALPHANUMBER=144
FOUR FIVE NINE =144
ONE TWO SIX=144
THE EDGE OF THE CLIFF=144

THE HEAD IS THE KEY=153

THE THREE TONES=162
TEN STONE CIRCLE=162
GUARDIAN PILLARS=162

POSITIVE LIGHT=171
DIVINE GEOMETRY=171
HEAVENLY MOTHER=171
THE QUEEN OF HEAVEN=171

THE WHEEL OF EZEKIEL=180
FORTY FOUR FEET=180
THE WHEEL OF SOUND=180
BENEATH THE STONES=180

ONE HUNDRED FEET EAST=189
ELEVEN DIVIDED BY FIVE=189
THE CIRCLE OF CHURCHES=189

REVERSE THE NUMBER=198
REVERSE DIRECTION=198

THE GREAT PYRAMID OF GIZA=234

FIVE STONE PENTAGRAM=252

ONE HUNDRED FEET EAST OF THE HEAD=261

ONE HUNDRED FORTY FOUR FEET=288

FORTY FOUR FEET SOUTH OF THE MARK=360
THE WHEEL SPINS IN TWO DIRECTIONS = 360

THE LOCATION IS HIDDEN IN THE NINE KEY=333

ONE HUNDRED FORTY FOUR FEET EAST OF THE HEAD=405

ISIS=56
LIGHT=56

ISIS PENTAGRAM=151
JESUS CHRIST=151
THE MIDDLE IS A FIVE=151
SOUTH OF FRANCE=151
SIRIUS + ISIS=151
RENNES LE CHATEAU=151
THE KEY OF ISIS = 151
A ONE ON BOTH ENDS=151
MIDDLE OF THE CIRCLE=151

"Oh right," Banyon said, lighting up a cigarette. "I remember when we did this. And you suggested we might also try grouping them by their similarity in meaning or something like that."

Angela nodded. "Yes, by the ideas expressed in the phrases. We never did that. But we did notice the similarities in some of them." She pointed out some of the relevant phrases:

A ONE ON BOTH ENDS
THE MIDDLE IS A FIVE
ELEVEN DIVIDED BY FIVE

There were others, such as those that mentioned the word *key* and those that seemed to allude to measured distances. Several of the phrases mentioned Isis, the name of the Egyptian goddess. They noticed the phrases, HEAVENLY MOTHER and QUEEN OF HEAVEN, were not only similar in the ideas they expressed but they also shared the same number value. They found that to be an interesting coincidence. Banyon commented that both of those titles, HEAVENLY MOTHER and QUEEN OF HEAVEN, were often applied to Mary, the mother of Jesus. Then Angela surprised him with something she'd learned in her cultural anthropology class.

The Egyptian goddess, Isis, was also referred to by these same titles. This, then, was at least part of the esoteric connection between ancient Egypt and the religion of Christianity; a connection Banyon had been curious about from the first time he saw this list of puzzling phrases. A little research on the subject proved enlightening but confusing. They learned, for example, there were several pre-Christian goddesses of the ancient world who shared nearly identical attributes: Ishtar of Babylon, for example, or the Sumerian goddess, Innana, among others. It was interesting information but what did it have to do with the lost scroll of Ezekiel? Neither of them could come up with the answer. They decided perhaps it had no direct connection but was merely a side glimpse into a history that seems to have been intentionally ignored by the primary mainstream vendors of the Christian religion.

"You know," Angela said, "there is one thing that seems obvious to me from what I can see here. It's the same thing we discussed the last time we poured through this stuff."

"What's that?" Banyon asked.

"Look at all these phrases. I can't figure out how some of them are supposed to connect. But several of them are obviously directions, like pointers to a location. And the only actual geographical place mentioned in any of these phrases is the South of France."

"And specifically Rennes le Chateau," Banyon added.

"Exactly. And so we're back to where we were several months ago with the same question. Where, precisely, in or near Rennes le Chateau is this alleged scroll located?"

"One-hundred and forty-four feet east of the head," Banyon said. "Or one-hundred feet east of the head. Or the edge of a cliff. Take your pick."

"Yes, but the head of what? And what cliff? There's nothing here to tell us! It's so frustrating!"

"Well, okay," Banyon said. "I agree that Rennes le Chateau is the general location. Even if we don't know the precise spot, at least we know that much. That's something, anyway."

Angela sighed. "Yeah. It's something."

Banyon got up and walked over to the kitchen counter. "So," he said, putting on a pot of coffee, "let's stick close to that and work from there. The next thing we need to figure out is..." he thought for a moment. "Well there're two things actually. We need to know what that reference to a *head* is and we need to figure out which of the two distance measurements is the right one. A hundred feet? Or a hundred and *forty-four* feet? And why are there two of them anyway? It just confuses things."

Angela's face lit up. "Wait a minute! Maybe that's the point!"

"What do you mean?"

"Maybe some of those phrases are nothing but red herrings."

"Red herrings?"

"You know. Put there with the intention of confusing the issue. To make it all the more difficult to decipher. To insure that whoever tackles this puzzle is diligent enough to figure out the key."

"And the key is...?"

She shook her head. "Hey, you're the *Chosen One*. You tell me!"

Banyon took it in good stride and shrugged. He poured a cup of coffee for each of them and returned to the table. "Okay," he said, with a look of renewed determination. "All right."

He reached across the table and grabbed the leather document pouch. He pulled out the old parchment and laid it on the table. The old paper crackled as he smoothed it out with the palm of his hand. Angela sat there watching him as he stared blankly at the parchment.

"What are you doing?" she asked.

"Waiting for a little divine intervention."

"What?"

He looked up at her. "A little divine intervention. If I'm the *Chosen One* you'd think I'd get a little help from a higher source somewhere."

Angela took a sip of her coffee. "That'd be nice," she said, rolling her eyes. "Getting anything?"

He returned his gaze to the list of phrases on the computer screen and smiled. "One-forty-four," he said confidently.

"Huh?"

"The key," he said. "One-forty-four. That's the key."

"Oh yeah? What about this?" She pointed to the phrase, NINE IS THE KEY.

"Yes, but look at the value of that phrase," he replied. "It's 144."

"Yeah, but it says *nine* is the key!" she protested.

"Well," he countered, "144 reduces to nine."

"Yeah, but so do all these other numbers. Except for 151."

"Okay," he shrugged. "So maybe there's more than one key. But something tells me the key to unlock this particular door is 144."

Angela chuckled. "Okay," she relented. "What the hell do I know? After all, you are the *Chosen One*."

"So they say," he grinned. "But seriously, something in my gut tells me 144 is the key to this door."

"Okay, I'm game. Are you saying, then, that the correct distance measurement is 144 feet?"

"That's my guess."

"But what about this here?" She pointed to the phrase, ONE HUNDRED FEET = 144. "Seems to me if 144 is the key, then that would indicate the correct distance is 100 feet rather than 144 feet. How can we know?"

"Red herring," he said.

"What?"

"The 100 feet is one of your red herrings."

She gave him a skeptical look. "How come you're so confident about this all of a sudden?"

He shrugged. "I don't know. Just a feeling. Seriously. I just opened my mind up to receive whatever help I could get and I just had this... epiphany."

Angela laughed. "Epiphany?"

"Yeah."

"Okay," she sighed. "I'll go with your epiphany. But it'd be nice to know for sure. How can we test it?"

"Hand me the calculator."

Angela slid the calculator over to him. He pointed out the phrases on the computer screen:

ONE HUNDRED FEET EAST OF THE HEAD = 261
ONE HUNDRED FORTY FOUR FEET EAST OF THE HEAD = 405

"Okay," he said. "Here goes. We're going with the *hundred-forty-four* feet, right?"

"Right."

"Which means we're eliminating the *hundred* feet, right?"

"Right."

"So, in math terms, to eliminate means to subtract, right?"

"Well, that's one way to think of it, yes."

"All right. Look at the alphanumeric values of those two phrases." He pointed to them again:

ONE HUNDRED FEET EAST OF THE HEAD = 261
ONE HUNDRED FORTY FOUR FEET EAST OF THE HEAD = 405

Angela nodded. "Yes?"

"So," he continued, "let's see what happens when we subtract 261 from 405." He took a deep breath as he prepared to put his gut feeling to the test. He punched in the numbers and was visibly shocked by the result.

"Well don't keep me in suspense! What is it?"

He handed the calculator over to her. With her own eyes she saw the remaining value was 144.

"Oh my god!" she blurted. She looked up at Banyon. "You *are* the *Chosen One!*"

They both laughed.

"Wait," he said. "There's more."

She looked surprised. "More? Okay, lay it on me."

"In terms of just the words alone," he said, "what's the difference between those two phrases?"

Angela looked at the two phrases. "Um... oh! The words *forty-four.*"

Then he directed her attention to the phrase, FORTY FOUR = 144. "Oh my god!"

Banyon laughed. "You keep saying that!"

"I know! But it's brilliant! How did you...?"

He shrugged. "Hey, I'm the *Chosen One!*"

"No divine intervention?"

"Well, maybe a little."

Angela took another sip of coffee. "Now we're getting somewhere."

"So it would seem," Banyon said, thoughtfully. "But it does beg the old question. Where, exactly, are we getting *to*?"

It was the one thing that seemed to be a major stumbling block. Without knowing what the reference to the *head* might be, they had nothing to go on.

"We need to learn more about that whole mystery of Rennes le Chateau," Angela suggested. "Let's do an internet search and see what we can find. Maybe we can figure out what this *head* business is all about."

Banyon agreed and Angela logged on to a search engine. She typed in the keywords, *Rennes le Chateau,* and waited to see what came up. Not surprisingly, the search engine returned hundreds of websites that had at least some amount of information about that mysterious place in the South of France. They spent hours checking out several of the websites that seemed most promising in terms of credible information. The book they'd acquired from Mrs. Densmore told them a little about the mystery of Rennes le Chateau but now they learned the story was more complex, and certainly more bizarre, than they could have possibly imagined.

The tiny village of Rennes le Chateau, they learned, may have become the depository of an enormous amount of treasure sometime near the end of the 5th century AD. The treasure was a combination of gold and artifacts plundered from various locations such as Greece, Rome, and Jerusalem over a period of many years going back to AD

70 when Jerusalem was taken by the Roman Emperor, Titus. The treasures of Jerusalem were taken to Rome where they remained until 300 years later when a Visigoth king, Aleric, marched his armies into Rome, sacked the place, and made off with Rome's entire fortune. Legend had it that the amount of the booty was so large it took Aleric's army six days just to load it all up for transport. *But transport to where?* That question had never been answered definitively. There was much speculation, however, that the final resting place of this tremendous treasure was the place that later became known as Rennes le Chateau in the South of France.

All of this was interesting history but, aside from the question of where the treasure ended up, there really wasn't much in the way of mystery, *per se*. The real mystery of Rennes le Chateau began much later, in the 19th century, with the arrival of a newly ordained priest by the name of Bérenger Saunière.

Saunière was appointed to be the caretaker of a dilapidated old church in the village and he was to be paid a monthly stipend that was just barely enough for a person to survive on from one day to the next. At some point he somehow befriended a wealthy countess who gave him a fairly large sum of money with which to begin restoration of his church. The roof of the church was in such bad shape that the rain and weather had actually damaged much of the building's interior including the altar.

When Saunière began repairs to the altar it cracked apart and broke into pieces. Much to his surprise, he found, hidden within the altar itself, three old wooden cylinders each containing mysterious parchments that he could not decipher. This was just the beginning.

A while later, some of his hired workers discovered a clay pot hidden beneath the stonework in front of the altar. The pot contained a treasure of its own: ancient gold coins, a golden chalice, and some fine jewelry of Visigoth design. But there was more to come. Sometime after much of the restoration had been completed, the church bell-ringer noticed something gleaming in the sunlight at the foot of a pillar. It turned out to be a very small glass vial with a piece of paper rolled up and tucked snuggly inside. The bell-ringer brought the vial and the paper to Saunière. Whatever was written on that piece of paper apparently caused Saunière to begin a mad search for *something*. He began digging holes in the grounds surrounding the church and even began excavating inside the church. Legend had it that he carried on much of this digging and searching in secret, at night, when no one else was around.

Whether or not Saunière found what he was looking for was not known, at least according to the various websites that Banyon and Angela visited. What was known, according to most researchers, was that Saunière suddenly became exceedingly wealthy to the tune of the equivalent of at least five million dollars; an incredible amount of money back in the 19th century. Some believe it wasn't treasure that he found but, rather, it was information; information so important to someone or some group that they were willing to pay a hefty sum in return for Saunière's silence. The information may have been derived from the parchments he found in the wooden cylinders. The parchments - of which only two have ever been actually seen and examined - were not only written in at least two different languages, Greek and Latin, but they were also ingeniously encoded. Information was encoded within information in a manner so cleverly conceived that to this day even the best cryptographers in the world have not been able to decipher the entire contents. Even this, however, was not the end of the mystery of Renne le Chateau.

The place seemed layered in mystery. Added to this was the persistent story of Mary Magdalene and Jesus having arrived at this very location following the crucifixion not to mention the equally persistent story that the Knights Templar may have deposited their own treasure here. *What sort of treasure might that have been?* Again, it was a matter of speculation, but some evidence suggested it was none other than the coveted Holy Grail. But even that became part of the mystery. What, exactly, was the Holy Grail? Was it the silver chalice from which Christ drank at the Last Supper, as many suppose? Or is this part of the story somehow confused with the idea that Mary Magdalene and Jesus were married and had at least one child in this village, thus beginning the royal bloodline of the famed Merovingian Kings? To some researchers, the Holy Grail was, in fact, the womb of Mary Magdalene, the Sangreal, the bloodline of Jesus the Christ.

"This is all incredibly interesting," Banyon said after they'd spent a considerable amount of time exploring the subject. "Some of it is the same as we read in Densmore's book. But I notice none of these websites even mentions anything whatsoever about the Lost Scroll of

Ezekiel. Remember in Densmore's book it says Saunière found the alleged scroll under the floor boards of the church and sold it to some secret society."

Angela reached over and picked up Densmore's book. She turned directly to the marked page. "Yes," she said. "Here it is. The secret society was called the Brotherhood of the New Dawn."

Banyon nodded. "Right. And nothing even remotely like that is mentioned anywhere on these websites."

Angela sighed. "You're right. Nothing. It's weird. Almost like none of those researchers ever heard of that part of the story."

"Or maybe it's just such an unlikely scenario that serious researchers have long since abandoned it as nonsense."

"Could be, I suppose."

"And also there doesn't seem to be anything on any of those websites that gets us any closer to understanding just where the heck we're supposed to look for that scroll."

"That's for sure. Unless we're supposed to go digging in and around that church itself, like ol' Saunière."

Banyon gave a laugh. "Yeah, right. I can just see whoever manages the church now letting us tear the place up. *So what is it you think you'll find here, Mr. Banyon?* Oh, uh, well, we don't really know but I'm sure we'll recognize it when we find it!"

Angela grinned. "Okay, I see your point." She hesitated a moment and then had an idea. "I know. Let's email that Paretti fellow and see if he has any information that might help us."

"You think he might?"

"I don't know. Just a hunch. He sure seemed to know a lot about all kinds of unusual stuff."

Banyon agreed it couldn't hurt.

In the email Angela reminded Paretti of who they were in case he'd forgotten and she asked if he had any information about Rennes le Chateau. She added that they were interested in anything regarding measurements and compass directions.

Banyon looked at his watch."Well," he said, stretching his arms above his head. "It's nearly midnight. I doubt if he'll get back to us tonight."

Angela, feeling the lateness of the hour, agreed. "You're probably right. Let's get some sleep. Maybe we'll hear from him tomorrow."

He looked at her. "You get the feeling we're on to something here?"

Her only response was a kind of enigmatic Mona Lisa smile and a peck on the cheek before heading up the stairs for bed.

That night as Banyon drifted off to sleep he thought about that funny feeling he'd had earlier in the evening about embarking on a new leg of the journey. That funny feeling was more accurate than he could possibly have imagined.

The great mandala was still in spin and the wheels of destiny were about to shift into high gear.

~35~

Angela awoke about 9 a.m. to find herself alone in the bed. "Zeke?" There was no reply. "Zeke?" she called louder. "Down here!"

She got up and slipped into her robe and slippers and went downstairs.

Banyon was sitting at the kitchen table with a cigarette and a cup of coffee. She could tell he seemed a bit disturbed.

"What's wrong?" she asked, pouring a cup for herself.

"I had that dream again."

"What dream?"

He looked tired as he took a drag off his cigarette and crushed it out. "The same one I had... I don't know... some time ago. Where I saw that thing... that sort of thin object... kind of like a rod or something... with some kind of crosses on it... and it was deep under the water... cold and dark." The thought made him shiver.

Angela sat down across from him at the table. "I remember you telling me about that. It was the same dream? I mean, like, exactly the same?"

He thought about it for a moment, trying to recall any details. "Seems like it was the same, yeah. And the number 144 kept impressing itself on my mind over and over again. It was weird."

"Was it a scary dream? You seem upset about it."

He shook his head. "No, not scary. Just... intense, I guess is the word. *Really* intense. I don't know how else to describe it. What the hell could it mean?"

Angela was at a loss for any sort of interpretation. "I don't know. You think it has something to do with the Ezekiel code?"

"I'm sure it does but damned if I know how. I can't make any sense of it."

Angela got up and walked around to his side of the table. Standing behind him, she massaged his shoulders for a minute.

"How about we forget the silly ol' dream and have some breakfast," she suggested. "You'll feel better."

She fixed a quick breakfast of ham and eggs.

When they finished eating, Banyon was in a better mood and seemed anxious to talk about continuing their work on the code. "I wonder if we got a reply yet from Paretti?" he asked.

"I don't know," she said, clearing the dishes from the table. "Shall we see?"

She retrieved the laptop from the living room and brought it back to the kitchen table. In a minute she was online and checked the incoming email.

"Yup," she said. "Got something."

Banyon scooted his chair around so he could see the computer screen. Angela opened the email:

Hello Zeke and Angela. Yes I remember you. Good to hear from you again.

Yes, I'm familiar with the story of Rennes le Chateau. Quite a mystery, eh?

You asked about measurements and compass directions. Sounds like maybe you'd want to check out the work of a couple of British researchers named Ian Campbell and David Wood. Check out a book called Genisis. How do you like that for a title? Pretty clever, eh?

Hey, here's something you might find interesting. I just came up with it a few days ago. I was reading a book about royal bloodlines and it mentioned that idea about Mary Magdalene being the actual Holy Grail or the Sangreal. If you're into the Rennes mystery then you must have come across that idea. In this book the authors refer to the book, Holy Blood Holy Grail, where it says the word Sangreal could be a combination of two words, Sang and Real, meaning Blood and Royal. In other words, royal blood. Well, anyway, I found this:

SANGREAL = 77 = CHRIST
JESUS = 74 = GRAIL CODE
JESUS CHRIST = 151 = JESUS SANGREAL (or "Jesus Royal Blood") = HOUSE OF MAGDALENE

How about that? And you probably know about that verse in the Old Testament (Isaiah, chapter 7, as I recall) that is thought by some to have been a prophecy of the coming of the messiah. It says his name shall be Immanuel. Many have thought it odd then that Jesus wasn't named Immanuel. But I found a connection through the numbers:

IMMANUEL = 88 = BLOODLINE
MARY MAGDALENE = 119 = STAR OF DAVID = ROYAL BLOOD
JESUS BLOODLINE = 162 = IMMANUEL+JESUS = THE HOUSE OF DAVID = THE ROOT OF DAVID = THE CODE OF THE BLOOD
ONE SIX TWO = 144 = CHURCH OF MAGDALENE = FEMALE PRINCIPLE
Interesting "coincidences", don't you think?
Keep in touch. Always good to hear from you.
Best,
Vince

Banyon couldn't help but grin. "This guy is amazing. He comes up with some of the most intriguing stuff. Look at that. I mean he's found alphanumeric correlations between significantly related biblical elements! Jesus is, in fact, said to be of the bloodline of King David. And there it is. The House of David. And he's even got the name Immanuel in there connected to Jesus! And then he finishes it off with the church of Magdalene? I read on one of those Rennes le Chateau web pages that Saunière's church was known as the Church of the Magdalene! That's just amazing!"

Angela was in total agreement. "And the sangreal thing," she added.

"How cool is that?"

"Very cool. But what about that book he recommended. What was it? Gen...isis?"

Angela scrolled back to the top of the email. "Yes, here. *Genisis*. Let's google it and see what we can find."

"Google," he said, chuckling at the word. "Cracks me up."

Angela pulled up the search engine and typed in the title of the book. In a moment it returned a number of related websites. The first thing they found was that there were actually two books of interest. One was *Genisis* but it was authored by David Wood alone. The other book was called *Geneset*, authored by Wood and a fellow researcher named Ian Campbell. Fortunately they were able to find a few reviews and some excerpts from the books online. What they learned from these sources was extraordinary.

David Wood was a cartographer, well-practiced in the art of map making. He spent many years researching one of his favorite subjects: the mystery of Rennes le Chateau. He came across some information from another researcher, Henry Lincoln, co-author of a highly controversial book called *Holy Blood, Holy Grail*. Lincoln had studied a strange painting called *Les Bergers d'Arcadie* or, in English, *The Shepherds of Arcadia*. The painting itself was part of the mystery of Rennes le Chateau mainly because of its depiction of some men inspecting a tomb that resembled an actual tomb near the church at Rennes le Chateau. But perhaps more importantly, there seemed to be a specific pattern to the layout and composition of the various elements in the scene. The geometry underlying the composition seemed to be a pentagram, a five-pointed star. The pentagram, a key design element in the esoteric art and science of sacred geometry, was a relatively common symbol surfacing again and again throughout various aspects of the Rennes mystery. Lincoln wondered if the similarity of the painting's scenery to the actual area surrounding the village of Rennes le Chateau - combined with the apparent fact that the painting involved this sacred geometry - might indicate that some similar pattern could be discovered in the *geographical* layout of the village itself. Lincoln, too, was a skilled mapmaker, and he found this idea too intriguing to pass up. Eventually, through a long series of trials and errors, he found what he was looking for, and more.

Using a map of the area, and employing his mapping tools,

Lincoln discovered the distances between three significant castles in the area formed an isosceles triangle with two angles of 72 degrees and one angle of 36 degrees, a perfect 180 degrees. These castles, he learned, were perched upon mountaintops. He was amazed that these natural mountainous upwellings were aligned in such a way as to form this perfect triangle. It seemed an unlikely coincidence. Wondering if more triangles might be found in the same manner, he continued his investigation. Sure enough there were more. Eventually he noticed, when connected by straight lines on the map, they intersected in such a way as to create a pentagram. The more he experimented with this idea of a sort of hidden geometry in the lay of the land the more he found. He produced a television documentary about the Rennes mystery and showed his discovery to the world. One of the people who saw this documentary was David Wood.

Wood had been making his own discoveries of a similar nature by connecting various places of interest within the area of Rennes le Chateau. He, too, discovered a pentagram in the lay of the land but his pentagram was unique in all of geometry and revealed something most extraordinary, something that, for Banyon and Angela, would become a key element in deciphering the Ezekiel Code.

~36~

As Angela continued to read through the immense amount of material about David Wood's work, Banyon got up to brew a pot of coffee. Just as his thoughts were beginning to drift back to the strange dream he'd had last night he was startled by a sudden outburst from Angela.

"Oh! My god!" she cried, sitting bolt upright in her chair.

Banyon nearly dropped the coffee pot. "What? You find something?"

"Read this!" she said, excitedly.

He sat down and read the words on the computer screen:

Examining the topography of the area around Rennes le Chateau, Wood identified fifteen features (churches, ancient chateaux, and significant rock formations) that formed a perfect circle some six miles in diameter. This has now become known as the Circle of Churches. Upon further examination of the spatial relationships between these features he eventually discovered they could be connected in such a way as to produce a most unusual pentagram. This pentagram, rather than being contained within the circle (such as the symbol often seen related to so called satanic rituals) was constructed in such a way that the uppermost point extended out beyond the perimeter of the circle. When drawn out on a map of the area, this extended feature rises northward, the tip of which is located at a geologic feature called *Le Bordre de Doubt* (the edge of doubt) which might best be described as a cliff. The entire extended pentagram covers an area of more than forty square miles.

Oh my god, is right! Banyon thought to himself. "Angela!"

"I know! I know! Can you believe it?"

Banyon grabbed the printout of the Ezekiel Code phrases. "Here! Right here!" he pointed to the phrase, THE CIRCLE OF CHURCHES = 189.

"And here!" Angela said. She pointed to the phrase, THE EDGE OF THE CLIFF = 144. Then she noticed something else. "Look here," she said, pointing to the text on the website. "It says the entire pentagram covers an area of more than forty square miles. Now look here." She pointed to another phrase on their list: FORTY FOUR = 144. "What do you want to bet the area covered by the geometry is actually forty-*four* square miles?"

Banyon was impressed. "Brilliant deduction, my dear Watson!"

"Why thank you, Mr. Holmes."

Banyon could hardly contain himself. He turned to Angela with a huge grin on his face. "This is it!" he said, bursting with laughter. "We found it!"

"By Jove, Mr. Chosen One," she said, reaching over and squeezing his hand, "I believe we've got it!"

The revelation was made even more extraordinary when they discovered the fact that Wood had reason to believe this unusual pentagram was a symbol for the Egyptian goddess, Isis. This became clear to Wood from a number of clues gleaned from his extensive research into the many elements of the Rennes mystery, including Saunière's strangely encoded parchments and a peculiar text entitled *Le Serpent Rouge*. Even the so-called Circle of Churches contained a clue. The circumference of the circle was marked by 15 distinct features. The number, 15, was the clue. The god, Osiris, the consort of the goddess, Isis, was attacked by his brother, Set. Set killed Osiris and cut up his body into 15 pieces. Isis hoped to find all the pieces and put them back together to resurrect her slain companion but she was only able to find fourteen of them. The missing piece was, unfortunately, his phallus. Being a resourceful goddess, however, she fashioned one out of gold or clay or stone, depending on which version of the story one prefers. Banyon eventually settled on stone because of the alphanumeric value it produced: STONE PHALLUS = 162. This seemed the most likely to him because he already knew the alphanumeric value of ONE SIX TWO was 144. The number 144, he had already determined, was emerging as an important key in this complex puzzle. As the story goes, Isis then reassembled the body of Osiris from the fourteen pieces and attached the magical phallus in its proper place and lowered herself upon it. It was a magical phallus indeed because, in an unprecedented act of penile prestidigitation, she miraculously conceived and gave birth to the sun god, Horus.

Wood identified the portion of the pentagram outside the circle as the *head* of Isis. Below the head were her two outstretched arms and below the arms were her two legs, spread to receive the *seed* of *Osiris*.

Banyon, now sensing a sort of intuitive nudge, grabbed the calculator and punched in some numbers:

OSIRIS = 89
ISIS = 56
89 − 56 = 33 = SEED

It was almost too much to believe. Nevertheless, since he was on a roll, he decided to try one more:

SET = 44

He was astonished. This number, 44, was the same number they had just discussed as the probable number of miles covered by the entire pentagram. Here were the goddess and the two gods that were intimately connected with the Rennes geometry and the numbers fit like tailor-made gloves.

So much was now coming into focus. The pieces of the puzzle were beginning to fall into place. Certainly this geometric image could be called the *Isis Pentagram*, a direct hit on yet another of the Ezekiel Code phrases:

ISIS PENTAGRAM = 151

It was an exciting moment for both of them. Stunned at what was happening, they felt like proud parents witnessing the birth of their first child. Lacking a good cigar, Banyon settled for a cigarette and offered one to Angela. They sat back admiring the fruits of their labors.

"Okay," he said, trying to gather his composure. He stood up and began pacing the floor. "Okay, what do we know? I mean, what do we really know?"

"Well," Angela said, "I think what we know is that whatever we're looking for is located 144 feet east of the head of Isis."

Banyon nodded. "Right. The tip of the pentagram. And how do we know where the tip of the pentagram is?"

Angela looked back at the information on the computer screen. "*Le Bordre de Doubt*. The edge of doubt."

"The cliff."

"So it would seem."

Banyon stopped pacing and looked at Angela. "You know what this means, don't you?"

She knew what he was thinking. "It means I need to go shopping." The comment caught him off guard. He shook his head. "What?"

She crushed out her cigarette and sauntered up to him with a teasing grin. "If we're going to France," she whispered in his ear, "I'm going to need a new outfit."

~37~

The rest of the day was spent talking about the trip neither of them ever dreamed they'd be taking.

"You know," Angela said, as she slipped a frozen pizza into the oven for dinner, "I have no idea what the weather is like in the South of France this time of year." Then she laughed. "Maybe I'd better hold off on that new outfit until we know what the heck we're getting into."

They moved into the living room and settled down on the sofa. "We also don't know what the terrain looks like around there," Banyon said. "Your new outfit might have to be some wool pants and a pair of hiking boots."

Angela frowned. "No bikini?"

Banyon laughed. "I don't think so. Besides the natives go topless on the beaches there you know."

"Oh that's right," Angela grinned. "The land of topless babes with hairy armpits."

Banyon laughed again. "Well, yes. Or at least so they say."

"Hmm... well, I'm sure you'd enjoy that."

"True," Banyon said. "I am a big fan of hairy armpits."

Angela grinned and hit him in the arm. "You know what I mean, smart ass."

Banyon shifted his position on the couch. "Hey, I've got an idea," he said, changing the subject.

"What is it?"

"Well, if you'll stop hitting me, I'll tell you."

"Gee, and I was just getting warmed up."

"I was thinking maybe I should call Father Caldwell."

"Caldwell?"

"Yeah. Remember? He's the priest I called a couple months ago to see if he knew anything about that Densmore fellow."

"Oh, sure. I remember. Why do you want to call him?"

"I remember during that conversation he told me he'd just returned from France. He mentioned he'd been to Rennes le Chateau and said I would probably find it interesting. It was the first time I'd ever heard of the place."

"I remember you telling me that, yes." Then it hit her. "Hey, right! He could tell us what its like there!"

"Thing is," Banyon said, "I don't know if I should tell him why we're going there. How the hell would I explain all of this without coming off like some kind of a nut case? Come to think of it, that's the same problem I had the last time I called him. Remember? I didn't want to tell him why we were interested in finding out about Densmore."

"Well, you could just tell him we're planning to take a trip there. Just a vacation."

"I thought about that but I'd like to ask him if he has any idea what the terrain is like out away from the village. And, specifically, if he happens to know the location of that cliff."

"Oh, I see what you mean. If you ask about the cliff he's going to want to know why the heck you're interested in some obscure cliff out in the middle of nowhere."

"Exactly."

"Well, then I don't know."

"Oh the hell with it. I'll tell him if he asks. What's the worst that can happen? He'll just tell me I'm losing it and suggest we change our vacation to a relaxing week in the Bahamas."

Angela laughed. "Are you sure?"

"Yeah. What the hell."

She shrugged. "Whatever. It's your call."

Banyon checked his watch. It was 5:30 p.m. *Three hours difference between here and New York. It's only 8:30 there.* "Yeah, I'm going to call him."

Just then the oven timer started buzzing.

"Pizza first," Angela said. She got up and headed for the kitchen.

Banyon joined her and nibbled at his pizza while he tried to imagine how the conversation with Caldwell might go. *The lost what?* he could just hear Caldwell saying. The more he thought about it the more bizarre the imagined conversation became. He nearly changed his mind about calling but decided to bite the bullet and go ahead with it.

Caldwell's phone rang several times and Banyon was just about to hang up, thinking perhaps it was too late in the evening. Maybe Caldwell was asleep. Then a familiar voice came on the line.

"Hello?"

"Daniel? It's Zeke Banyon. I hope it's not too late to be…"

"Zeke! You ol' devil!"

Banyon laughed. "You always call me that!"

"Yeah, well, nothing personal, you know. I call everybody that! How are you? What the heck have you been up to? I heard through the grapevine that you left the shelter and got married or something!"

"Well, not married but there is a lady in my life and we are engaged. Her name is Angela. You'd like her."

"That's great. Really glad to hear it."

"Thanks. Well, the reason I called is because Angela and I are thinking about taking a trip to France and I remembered you mentioned to me once about that place called Rennes le Chateau."

"Ah, yes! The village of mystery and romance! You've signed up for one of the guided tours, I presume?"

"Uh, well…the truth is…"

Banyon barely got started with his explanation about the lost scroll of Ezekiel when Caldwell interrupted. "The lost what?" he said, unsure that he'd heard Banyon correctly.

Banyon took a deep breath. "Okay, maybe I'd better start all the way back at the beginning. Are you sitting down?"

Angela could only hear one side of the conversation, of course, but she could tell from Banyon's last comment that it was going to be a long phone call. She couldn't help but chuckle as she tried to imagine the look on Father Caldwell's face. She had never met the man but Banyon had told her enough about him that she had a pretty good mental image of what he looked like. He was a tall, rather dark complected man now in his early 60s. He had inherited his mother's handsome Italian facial features and his father's barrel-chested physique. According to Banyon, Caldwell was a bit of a walking contradiction in that he was a totally devout Catholic but was much more open-minded than any religious person he'd ever met. *There are more things in heaven and on earth, Horatio, than are dreamt of in your philosophy*, Caldwell was fond of saying. Banyon had heard him quote the Shakespearean line so many times he began to think of it as Caldwell's mantra. But, Angela wondered, would he be open-minded enough to refrain from having Banyon committed? One could always hope.

A half hour passed and, from the other room, she could overhear parts of Banyon's side of the conversation:

"...the desk pad ...thought it was just silly numerology but ...to the number 9 ... alphanumeric value is 144 ... so Angela suggested ...internet, believe it or not ...we met with Densmore's wife ... he had this book ... note paper with ... then these amazing number correlations ... these phrases ...Yes, I know, but ... rosary has 54 beads ... the number 9 that even the ancient Mayans called ... Bible Code so maybe the English alphabet has ...then that number, 144... the lost scroll of Ezekiel...the 9-thing again ... then Professor Kline told us... Yes... No... Yes, the Jesuits ... No, I'm serious! Egyptian ... Jesus and Mary Magdalene ... book was called The Spaceship's of Ezekiel and ... this fellow, McClintock was killed... when I got to the warehouse Angela was tied to a chair and ... guys in this big black pickup truck ... Yes! They killed the... I don't know... our back door was busted into... Illuminati as far back as... ancient astronaut theory... genetic manipulation just like we're experimenting with now... name is Paretti... weird, I know, but ... at Rennes le Chateau... I know you know about that but I'm telling you it's ...No, not *Genesis*. Gen-*isis*... this odd pentagram ... decided on 144 because ... east of the head of Isis ... over 40 square miles ... translated means the edge of doubt ...

Two hours later the conversation ended. Angela had retired to the bedroom with the laptop and was searching the internet for photos of Rennes le Chateau and the surrounding countryside. Banyon walked in looking like he'd been through the wringer. He stood there in the doorway with a rather dazed look on his face.

"Well?" she said. "Did he suggest we go to the Bahamas?"

"Not exactly."

"Oh, oh. Worse? He's having you committed?"

"Actually," Banyon said, still looking a bit dazed, "he's going with us."

Angela gave a laugh. "What. To the looney bin?"

Banyon shook his head. "No. To France. To Rennes le Chateau."

"What!"

Banyon nodded. "Yeah."

"You're kidding, right?"

"I know. I couldn't believe it either."

"He's going with us? What did he say? You mean he believed the whole story?"

"Well, I wouldn't say he believed it, exactly. He found it all really fascinating and finally admitted the lost scroll thing could be true. He just didn't know. He'd never heard of it before so it was all new to him. But he did believe what I told him about all the things we've experienced over the past few months. He knew I wouldn't just make all that up."

"Make it up?" Angela laughed. "If you could make up a story like that you could be writing movie scripts in Hollywood. But why, exactly, is he going with us?"

Banyon shrugged and sat next to her on the bed. "Well it turns out he was familiar with most of the Rennes mystery. The stuff about Saunière's strange little church and the encoded parchments and the Templar connection and all of that. He knew it all because he'd signed up for the package tour where a guide takes people in small groups through the church and the courtyard. He even knew a little about Henry Lincoln's original discovery of some geometric patterns to the layout of the land. But he'd never heard of Wood and Campbell or their books, *Genisis* or *Geneset* or even the Isis Pentagram. When I explained it to him he was fascinated. He said the Egyptian goddess connection made some sense to him when he stopped to think about it. The lost scroll thing he wasn't so sure about. He thought it sounded more like an urban legend. But I reminded him of his favorite saying. There are more things in…"

Angela took up the mantra. "…heaven and on earth, Horatio, than are dreamt of in your philosophy. I know, I know."

Banyon looked surprised. "You remembered!"

"Yes, I remember you told me he was fond of that quote. But I still don't get why he's coming with us."

"He just sort of offered. He said he could help us find our way around when we get there. He knows a great place where we can stay and then he admitted that if we do, in fact, locate what we think is hidden there he sure as hell wants to be there when we find it."

"So the old guy does have an open mind, like you said."

"Yup."

"What'd he say when you told him you were the Chosen One?"

Banyon chuckled. "He about choked on his brandy."

Angela laughed. "So what's next? How are we going to coordinate all this? I mean, he's all the way over in New York, right?"

"Yeah, well, that's something we have to work out. Most likely we'll fly to New York, stay with him for a day or two so we can get organized and then we'll catch a flight out of New York for France."

"I can't wait!" Angela said, excitedly. "When do we leave?"

Banyon laid back on the bed and folded his hands behind his head. "The day after tomorrow."

Angela snuggled up next to him. "Really?" she said, sounding concerned. "Gee, that presents a problem."

He glanced at her. "What is it?"

She sighed. "I just don't have a thing to wear."

~38~

The next day Angela got her wish. Banyon tagged along while she browsed through the clothing stores at the mall. They had no idea they were being followed at every turn.

"Ooh!" Angela squealed. "Let's go in there!"

Banyon recoiled and backed away. "Oh no," he said, shaking his head.

"I'm not going into Victoria's Secret! You go. I'll wait."

Angela laughed. "Just kidding. I don't think they have quite what I'm looking for."

Too bad. I was kinda hoping... Banyon relaxed. "Okay, what the heck *are* you looking for? We've been to every clothing store on the mall. You've tried on a half dozen outfits."

"Hmm... I don't know. Maybe I don't really need anything."

"What!" Banyon rolled his eyes. "You drag me all over the mall for two hours and decide not to buy anything?"

"Well," she said coyly, "a girl's gotta look, you know."

Banyon threw up his hands. "Women!"

Angela squeezed his hand and gave him her pitiful doe-eyed look. It was a trick she'd learned as a little girl. It worked so well on her father she added it to her arsenal of man-manipulation techniques that came in handy as she developed into her teenage years and beyond.

"Angela!" her dad would say in his booming voice. "I thought your mother told you to clean up your room!"

"But daddy..."

"No *but daddy*, Angela! You're grounded for the rest of the week!"

Then she gave him *the look*. The look she'd spent so much time perfecting in front of the mirror.

"Well..." her father would relent, "for the rest of the day, anyway."

Banyon sighed, helplessly. "Well, as long as we're here, let's get something to eat. I'm starved."

"Me too. How about that little place at the other end of the mall."

They strolled arm-in-arm past the shops toward the Hole-In-The-Wall Café, still unaware of the man following close behind.

The tiny café was quite literally not much more than the hole in the wall for which it was named. It was crowded but they managed to get a table near the back. The man following them took a seat just two tables away and ordered a coffee.

As they ate lunch they chatted about their recent breakthrough with the code and about their plans to go to New York and on to France. The man with the coffee strained to hear what they were saying. The music from the jukebox and the din of chatter from the lunchtime crowd made it difficult to listen in on a conversation six feet away. He couldn't catch it all but what he did hear was enough. *Jesus! France? They've done it! They've broken the code!*

Finally, they got up to leave. As they wound their way around and between the small dining tables where others were enjoying their meals, Angela accidentally bumped the arm of the man with the coffee.

"Oops! Sorry," she apologized as the hot brown liquid sloshed over the rim of the cup and dribbled onto the man's lap.

Instinctively, the man jumped up and bumped the table with his own knee, spilling even more of the coffee. Somehow his hat toppled off his head in the process.

Angela gasped. "Oh!" she said. "Are you all right? I'm *really* sorry! Please let me buy you another cup of coffee! It's the least I can do." She reached down, picked up his hat and handed it to him.

He snatched it from her hand, glared at her momentarily, then quickly looked away. "No. It's nothing," he mumbled as he covered his fat bald head with the hat.

She started to insist but before she could say anything more the man turned and headed quickly for the door and disappeared into the swarm of shoppers on the mall.

She looked at Banyon with a perplexed expression.

Banyon shrugged his shoulders. "People are weird," he said. "Can we go home now?"

~39~

The flight to New York took six and a half hours. It seemed like six and a half days.

Angela shifted uncomfortably in her seat next to the window. "We should have splurged for first class," she groaned. "Gees, we can't even smoke."

Banyon reached into his coat pocket and pulled out a pack of gum. He offered her a piece. She rolled her eyes but accepted it anyway.

"Thanks," she said, holding it up between two fingers. "Got a light?"

He smiled. "Some traveling companion you are. We're only thirty minutes into the flight and you're already complaining."

"How long before we get there?"

"Another six hours."

"Lovely."

In another window seat, just five rows behind them, Romano was sweating. He hated flying. It terrified him. *But this will be worth it*, he thought as he stared at the back of the woman who only yesterday had spilled coffee on his best pair of beige Dockers. *This will be worth it.*

They were due to arrive at New York's Kennedy International Airport at 6:38 p.m. The weather was cloudy all the way but the flight was smooth and uneventful. By 5 p.m. Banyon and Angela had both drifted off to sleep. At 6:28 p.m. they were awakened by the warm baritone voice of the captain on the intercom. He was announcing their immanent arrival.

Angela opened her eyes and smiled sleepily. She looked at Banyon "Are we there yet?"

"Look," he said, pointing out the window.

It was already getting dark and the view of the lights of New York City below was a sight to behold.

"Oh my god," Angela whispered, spellbound.

Banyon nodded. "Yeah."

Just as they had planned, Father Daniel Caldwell met them at the airport when they arrived.

"Banyon! You ol'…

Banyon grinned and cut him off short. "Don't say it!"

"…devil, you!"

They walked briskly toward each other and met with a handshake that quickly morphed into a bear hug and the obligatory pats on the back.

"God, it's been a long time!" Caldwell said, stepping back to get a good look at Banyon. "You look great!"

"You don't look any worse for the wear yourself," Banyon returned the compliment.

"That's a lie if I ever heard one," Caldwell laughed. "But I'll forgive you." He turned to Angela. "And this must be the Angel you told me about."

Angela smiled and held out her hand. "Pleased to meet you, Father. I've heard a lot about you."

Caldwell shook her hand and grinned. "Please, call me Daniel. And don't believe everything you hear."

"But it was all good," she said.

"Really!" Caldwell replied. "Well, in that case…!"

Caldwell looked almost exactly as Angela had pictured him in her mind except for the hair. For some reason she pictured it being thick and black and maybe graying a bit at the temples. Instead, it was quite the opposite: thick and silver with a small wisp of black at the temples. And he wore glasses; stylish, expensive looking horn-rimmed glasses. She hadn't pictured him with glasses at all.

"It's stiffling warm in here," Caldwell said. "Let's get the heck out of here. You kids hungry?"

"Famished," Banyon and Angela chimed in unison.

"Well," Caldwell said, "I can see you two are a perfect match."

Angela put her arm around Banyon's waist and gave him a squeeze.

"Okay, look," Caldwell said. "I know you must be tired from that long flight. So we can either go get a bite to eat at a little restaurant I know of or we can just head straight to my place and toss a frozen pizza into the oven. It's up to you. Whatever you want."

Banyon was quick to answer. "Well, to tell you the truth, I'd just as soon do the frozen pizza thing and relax." He looked at Angela. She nodded in agreement.

Caldwell looked pleased. "Home it is then! Let's get your luggage and head on out of here. We've got a lot to talk about."

After retrieving their luggage they made the long walk to the main entrance. Once outside the door Banyon lit up a cigarette. Caldwell nudged him and pointed to the no-smoking sign. Banyon grimaced, inhaled a quick drag, and dropped the cigarette on the cement. Crushing it out with his foot, he mumbled, "Damn."

"I'll second that," Angela said.

Caldwell laughed and hailed a cab.

"Where to?" asked the cabbie, as they settled into the back seat.

"Bronxville," Caldwell answered.

Frank Romano was right on their tail. He stepped quickly into a waiting taxi and slammed the door shut. "Follow that cab!" he ordered.

~40~

The ride from the airport to the community of Bronxville couldn't have been more than twenty minutes by Banyon's estimation. As they turned into Bronxville proper Angela's eyes lit up. "This isn't anything like I pictured for a New York neighborhood. This is beautiful!"

Even at night the village community of Bronxville was, indeed, an enchanting sight. As they passed through the central business district the immaculately clean streets were lined with quaint shops, specialty boutiques, hair salons, art galleries, a supermarket, antique shops, book stores, just about everything a person could want all in one small community. All of this and more in an area covering just one square mile.

"You got an address?" the cab driver asked.

"125 Parkway Road," Caldwell answered. "The Avalon."

"The Avalon?" Banyon asked.

Caldwell nodded. "The name of my apartment."

The driver took a right at the next corner and within a minute or two they entered into the residential area.

"Oh my god," Angela said. "Look at these homes!"

The well-lighted streets were lined with elegant homes

representing several classic architectural styles. The yards were all meticulously landscaped. Clearly this was a place for folks with rather hefty bank accounts.

As they drove along the streets, Caldwell pointed out some of the homes with interesting histories. "That one over there," he said, "was where the Kennedy family lived from around 1930 to about 1940. The neighborhoods all have names. We're passing through Crownlands right now."

The driver made another turn. "Ah!" Caldwell said. "This is Sagamore Park. You know the great composer, Jerome Kern?"

"Kern?" Banyon asked. "Umm... let's see..."

"American composer," Angela jumped in. "He wrote Broadway musicals. Famous for his work in *Show Boat*. Two of his most famous compositions are *Old Man River* and *The Way You Look Tonight*. I think he died sometime in the mid 40s."

That sudden little burst of encyclopedic information took Banyon by surprise. He shot her an inquisitive glance.

"Music appreciation class," she shrugged. "It was an elective."

Caldwell laughed. "Well, you're absolutely right. He lived here in this neighborhood for a time."

Banyon folded his arms and struck a pompous look. "Well," he said, "That's nothing. If you come to Seattle I'll show you where Jimi Hendrix lived. He was a great American composer too, you know."

Angela gave him a sharp jab in the side with her elbow.

"So I've heard," Caldwell said, laughing.

Within minutes they came into view of a huge, stately apartment building.

"The Avalon," the driver announced.

"Well, here we are," Caldwell said. "Home sweet home."

Romano's cab pulled over to the curb a block behind them.

Caldwell's two-bedroom apartment was huge and decorated in a much more modern style than Banyon would have expected. *The rent for this place must be astronomical*, Banyon thought to himself. *I'll bet the Pope is footing at least half the bill*. He knew Caldwell was currently assigned to the local Bronxville Catholic Church. That was his officially sanctioned job. He was also teaching comparative religion three nights a week at Bronxville's local college. Banyon suspected that the teaching job was probably not approved by the local diocese. *They probably don't even know about it. Be just like Daniel to do something like that*, he thought with a grin.

Caldwell showed Banyon and Angela the room where they'd be sleeping for the next few nights. After acquainting them with the rest of their new surroundings he ushered them back to the living room and lit a fire in the fireplace.

Above the fireplace was a large framed print of Salvadore Dali's strange and strikingly dramatic painting of Christ on the cross. It wasn't the kind of art Banyon imagined would be in Caldwell's home. He pictured Caldwell having more of a taste for the classic religious art of Michaelangelo, Rembrandt, or DaVinci. Dali's *Christ of St. John of the Cross* was anything but classic in that sense. It depicted Christ on the cross but the perspective was from an aerial view, looking down onto the top of Christ's head. The cross itself looked as if it was constructed of polished bronze, smooth and geometrically balanced, and it took on an elongated perspective as it got progressively smaller from the top to the bottom. The image of the cross appeared to be floating, weightless, out in the inky blackness of space. Far below the cross were the golden clouds of a sunset and below that was a dark body of water, perhaps the Mediterranean Sea, with a single large rowboat tied up on the shore. As Banyon studied this part of the painting he noticed the tiny figure of a man standing in the water just behind the boat. Another man stood on the shore holding a rope that was attached to the boat. The entire scene, like most of Dali's work, had a weird dream-like quality about it. *Definitely an example of surrealism at its best*, Banyon thought, *but the last thing I expected to see in Caldwell's living room.* Clearly there were aspects of his old friend's personality that Banyon had never known.

"So," Caldwell said, "how about that pizza and a cold beer?"

Banyon grinned. "Now you're talking."

Angela agreed.

Banyon noticed an ashtray on the table. "Mind if we smoke?"

"Be my guest," Caldwell said, heading for the kitchen. "I've taken up smoking a pipe lately, myself."

Glancing again at the Dali painting Banyon wondered just what

Caldwell might be smoking in his pipe.

Angela was busy browsing the titles on the bookshelf. "Check this out," she whispered.

Banyon joined her in front of the bookshelf as she pointed out the titles: *The History of Zen Philosophy, The Gods of Ancient Egypt, The Way Of The Buddha, Christian Mysticism, The UFO Abduction Phenomenon: Case Studies, Religion and Quantum Physics, The Miracle at Fatima, Catholic Controversies, The Book of Mormon, Symbolism in Christian Art, Is The Pope Catholic?*

It was not an altogether unusual set of books given the fact that Caldwell was currently teaching a course in comparative religion at Concordia College right there in Bronxville. The books on UFOs and quantum physics seemed a bit out of the ordinary but, Banyon reasoned, Caldwell was a bit out of the ordinary himself. What really seemed out of the ordinary was that Caldwell, a Catholic priest, was contracted to teach at Concordia, a college that was founded by the Lutherans in the early part of the 20th century. Banyon was quite aware of Martin Luther's role in the history of Christianity. Luther was the rebellious German priest who broke from the Catholic Church in the 16th century with his famous *95 Theses,* a flaming criticism of papal policy and Catholic dogma. It was, in fact, Luther who virtually founded the very anti-Catholic Protestant movement. Now here was Caldwell, a Catholic priest, teaching at a Lutheran college. *God does work in mysterious ways*, Banyon mused.

Caldwell slid the pizza into the oven and set the timer. He opened three cold Budweisers and brought them out to the living room where Banyon and Angela were seated comfortably on the couch near the fireplace. Caldwell relaxed in his recliner across from them. After a few minutes of small talk, Banyon found himself describing how he and Angela met. At some point, somehow, the conversation jumped forward all the way to his going-away party at the shelter. In the middle of a story about Old Tom's antics, he was interrupted by the timer on the oven. Caldwell excused himself and disappeared into the kitchen. A few minutes later he returned with the pizza on a platter and set it on the glass-topped chrome coffee table between the couch and the recliner.

"Dig in," Caldwell said. "And explain to me again that whole story about this lost scroll and this code business."

Over the next couple of hours Banyon and Angela told him the whole story from the very beginning. They explained the idea behind the system of alphanumerics and the ancient form of divination known as gematria. They showed him the book they'd gotten from Mrs. Densmore and the notes that were on the piece of paper folded up inside the book. They read from the chapter in the book about the Lost Scroll and the possibility that it was hidden somewhere in or around the village of Rennes le Chateau. They reminded Caldwell that the scroll wasn't the final goal. The scroll, itself, holds the key to the location of the real pot of gold at the end of the rainbow, the craft or some sort of technology of profound importance to the very survival of the human race. They told him about Frank McClintock's attempt to unravel the code and about his apparent murder. They told about discovering the parchment, the so-called Ezekiel Code, in the lining of the old trunk in the back of McClintock's bookstore. They showed him the book by the NASA engineer who suggested the possibility that the thing Ezekiel encountered was actually a spacecraft of some kind. They showed him the copies of their own work and their attempts to crack the code. They explained their relationship with Professor Kline, his information about the Jesuit involvement and the Brotherhood of the Nine Pillars and how Kline had been an important asset in their understanding of what he called *the big picture*. And, of course, they recounted that unbelievable night Angela was kidnapped, the dramatic eleventh hour rescue by the three unknown men in the black pickup truck, and the disappearance - and mysterious reappearance - of all their notes and other materials.

Caldwell sat spellbound and mostly silent throughout the two hours it took his guests to tell their story.

"And then," Angela told him, "there was our contact with that fellow, Paretti, and that's how we sort of came full circle back again to the mystery of Rennes le Chateau. It was Paretti who told us about this researcher named David Wood and Wood's discovery of the huge, oddly shaped pentagram formed by linking certain significant features in the lay of the land around that area."

Caldwell remembered. "Ah, yes," he said, turning to Banyon. "The Isis Pentagram that you told me about when we talked on the phone the other day."

"Right. Exactly," Banyon said. Then he laid the copy of the parchment on the coffee table so Caldwell could take a look at it. He handed him the printout of the phrases and showed him how they had grouped them according to their alphanumeric values. "You can see here," Banyon explained, "how all these numbers reduce to the single-digit value of 9. That number, like I told you on the phone, seems to be extremely important when it comes to matters of spiritual and cosmic mysteries. All of these groups fall into that category except this group here. They're all 151."

"That reduces to 7," Caldwell commented.

"Well," Angela said, "it does, but we don't think that has any significance here. At least not so far as we can tell. What does seem to be significant is simply that this group stands out from the others. And it's the group in which some of the most important clues are found."

Caldwell picked up the paper and examined the phrases from the 151 group:

```
ISIS PENTAGRAM = 151
JESUS CHRIST = 151
THE MIDDLE IS A FIVE = 151
SOUTH OF FRANCE = 151
SIRIUS + ISIS = 151
RENNES LE CHATEAU = 151
THE KEY OF ISIS = 151
A ONE ON BOTH ENDS = 151
MIDDLE OF THE CIRCLE = 151
```

"Did you notice," Caldwell pointed out, "that there are nine phrases in this 151 group?"

Banyon looked surprised. "You're kidding. Let me see that."

Caldwell handed the paper over to him.

"Interesting," Banyon said, showing it to Angela. "I can't believe we missed that."

"Think it means anything?" Caldwell asked.

Banyon shrugged. "I don't know. Wouldn't be surprised."

Caldwell examined the other phrases on the list. "Hmm...this is interesting." He pointed out the phrase, STAR OF ISIS = 135. "The Egyptian goddess. As I recall, it was Venus that was known as the star of Isis wasn't it?"

"Well, yes," Angela said, "but also Sirius. Zeke and I had a discussion related to this some time ago. Venus isn't technically a star. It's a planet. Sirius, on the other hand *is* a star. I did a little research on this later and learned that the Sirius-Venus-Isis thing gets a little confusing. Seems that Venus and Sirius were both considered to be Isis, depending on whose version of the ancient mythology you wish to go with. But one thing that's known for sure, and is really interesting, is that the planet Venus traces out a huge pentagram in the sky over the course of its eight year journey as seen from earth. "

"Interesting," Caldwell said. Then, half jokingly, he asked, "So what's the alphanumeric value of Venus?"

"Well, why don't we find out?" Banyon said. He pulled out his pocket calculator and punched in the numbers.

"Don't just sit there grinning," Caldwell chided. "What is it?"

Banyon looked up. "It's 81."

"Ah ha!" Caldwell exclaimed. He was getting the gist of it. "It's a *nine* number! So what's the alphanumeric value of 81 if you spell it out as a word?"

Again, Banyon punched in the numbers. "Oh, this is good!"

"What is it?"

"It just happens to be 108."

Caldwell was clearly amused. "Another *nine* number!"

"Not only that," Banyon said, "but 108 also happens to be one of the numbers the ancients attributed to the goddess energy in general. And I just now made yet another connection. I remember somewhere in my notes I jotted down the alphanumeric value of the word, *geometry*. It's alphanumeric value is 108."

"Uh," Angela started with a little hesitation, "there's one more thing. Not to get too graphic, but I remember seeing a diagram of Wood's unusual pentagram noting the degrees of the various angles." She blushed a little. "The angle between the two spread legs of the Isis Pentagram - what some people call the vulva point - is exactly 108 degrees."

"You gotta be kidding," Caldwell said.

Banyon laughed. "Now you see the kind of thing Angela and I have been dealing with. That's how it's been since day one. It's like one thing leads to another. It's all interconnected."

Caldwell smiled. He was beginning to like this game. "Isis Pentagram," he said. "Star of Isis. Venus. Sirius."

"There you are," Banyon said. "See, this whole alphanumeric

thing, this Ezekiel Code, it's like a map. On a map, not all the roads lead to your destination. But some do. On *this* map, the trick is to figure out which roads take us where we want to go and which ones go somewhere else."

Caldwell lit up his pipe and took a couple of thoughtful puffs. "Kind of makes you wonder where the other roads go, doesn't it?"

Banyon and Angela both gave a laugh.

"One destination at a time, thank you!" Angela said.

Caldwell nodded. "And so we follow the road to the South of France in two days. I can't wait. Whether you're right about this whole thing or not, it's still going to be a great little adventure."

"Yup," Banyon agreed. "And I've been thinking. My guess is we're going to have to literally dig for this treasure. Which means we're going to need shovels and who knows what else. Maybe even a pick-ax of some kind. But I doubt if we can bring those things with us on the plane."

"Well," Caldwell said, "why don't we wait and just buy the tools we need when we get there?"

Banyon agreed. "Good idea, actually. And another thing. You've been to the area. What do you think we can expect as far as the weather goes? And what's the area like? Are we going to need hiking gear and stuff like that?"

Caldwell thought for a moment. "Well," he said, "this time of year there's a good chance we could hit some wet weather. Probably not very cold but possibly a bit of rain. It's hard to say but we should be prepared. We'll want some backpacks and we'll need some good hiking shoes. Did you bring anything like that?"

"Not at all," Angela said. "We didn't know what to expect. So we decided to wait and see what you thought."

"Well," Caldwell explained, "there's some fairly rugged country around there. But we have a little advantage I haven't told you about yet."

"Oh?" Banyon said. "What little advantage is that?"

"I contacted a friend of mine who lives not far from Rennes le Chateau. He's a helicopter pilot and he's agreed to fly us from Rennes le Chateau to the area where that cliff is. How about that?"

"No way!" Angela said. "Really?"

Banyon was just as surprised. "Are you serious?"

Caldwell laughed. "Yup. He's an American fellow. Michael Taylor. Used to be a Methodist minister and flew choppers in the Viet

Nam war. I met him at a religious studies conference in Chicago a few years ago and we became pretty good friends."

"I don't get it," Banyon said. "How'd he end up in France?"

"Somewhere along the line he met this French girl and got married. They lived in Chicago for a while. Then they went to France so she could visit her folks. Long story short, they ended up staying there. Now he has a small business selling helicopter rides to tourists. Runs his business right from his little farm just a stone's throw from Renne le Chateau."

"Well," Banyon said, "that's just too cool. I can't believe it! Thanks for setting that up."

"No problem at all. Actually he owed me."

"What do you mean?" Angela asked.

Caldwell grinned. "I loaned him the money to get to France in the first place! I knew that between he and his wife they were just making enough money to carry them from month to month. So I told him not to worry about returning the loan. I said maybe one day I'd need a favor and if he could help me out then that'd be good enough. So I called in my favor. Pretty good coincidence, eh?"

Banyon and Angela smiled as they recalled professor Kline's words about no coincidences.

As the conversation wound down, they made plans to spend the next day shopping for the clothing items they would need. On the list were some good hiking shoes, backpacks, and some sort of rain gear, just in case. Any hardware they might need could be purchased in France.

Later, in the warm surroundings of Father Caldwell's luxury apartment, Banyon and Angela retired to the extra bedroom, exhausted yet excited about the adventure ahead of them. *Hiking boots and a backpack. Hmmph. Some outfit*, Angela thought as she drifted off to sleep. Banyon fluffed his crisp clean pillow and closed his eyes. *The Pope's gotta be footing some of the rent for this place.*

Frank Romano remained parked at the side of the road only long enough to make sure he knew where Banyon and Angela would be staying. Tomorrow he would rent a car and return to the Avalon early in the morning. But for now, in his own hotel room near the airport, he, too, drifted off to sleep and waited for the next leg of the adventure to begin.

~41~

The next two days passed in a blur and they soon found themselves boarding the plane for France. Angela was excited about the destination but she was less than enthused about spending another six hours on a plane. To her surprise, however, the time passed quickly as there was so much to discuss and the conversation between the three of them seemed nonstop.

Caldwell couldn't seem to make up his mind about the idea of the English alphabet being somehow encoded. He thought the idea was bizarre on the face of it, yet he found himself strangely drawn to it. He knew about gematria. He was well aware of the fact that the original Greek versions of the New Testament, for example, contained certain phrases constructed in such a way as to produce numerical sums that were symbolic of certain spiritual and esoteric ideas. He recalled reading about the number 276, for example. Some researchers had discovered many phrases in the New Testament pertaining to the notion of obeying the *Laws of Moses* all of which had gematria values that were multiples of 276. The number 276 was, in fact, the sum of the phrase, *LAW OF MOSES*. There was no denying the fact that the Bible was loaded with gematria from the Old Testament Hebrew through the New Testament Greek. It was a method of transferring information to *those in the know*, the *initiates*. But the idea of using the English alphabet as a gematria tool, a conveyance for the transfer of secret information was something he'd never considered. Yet, as he studied the Ezekiel Code and the rest of the notes accumulated by Banyon and Angela over the past several months, the proof seemed to be staring him in the face. *How likely was it*, he kept asking himself, *that the phrases RENNES LE CHATEAU, SOUTH OF FRANCE, ISIS PENTAGRAM and JESUS CHRIST, all intimately related, would each equal 151?* In their conversation during the flight he played the role of the Devil's Advocate trying to find a way to dismiss the whole idea. But for every argument he could come up with Banyon and Angela simply pointed to the words and phrases and the amazing synchronicity of the matching number values. That evidence in black and white, combined with the strange story about the priest of the Order Of The New Dawn was overwhelming. Caldwell was satisfied. There was something going on here that was beyond mere coincidence. There had to be something to it.

Once again - unbeknownst to Banyon, Angela and Caldwell - Frank Romano sat silently like a dark shadow just a few seats behind them. Patiently. Waiting.

The sun was setting as their plane began its descent. Banyon and Angela stared out the window, amazed at the size of the historic city sprawled out on the earth below.

"Oh my god!" Angela gasped. "I had no idea!"

"Nearly a million people in Toulouse," Caldwell said. "One of the biggest cities in France."

The plane landed smoothly at the airport and taxied down the runway. The weather was chilly but clear and the stars were just beginning to appear in the sky. A shiver of sheer excitement ran through Banyon's entire body as he stepped off the plane. *The Chosen One has arrived*, he smiled to himself. Angela, too, felt a quiver of anticipation as she wondered what might be waiting for them. Caldwell, having been here before, was simply curious.

They rented a van and drove to Chateau de Cavanac, a rustically beautiful hotel that looked like something out of the seventeenth century. Caldwell had reserved two rooms for them before they left New York.

"Let's get our luggage into the rooms," Caldwell suggested, "and then we'll get something to eat in the restaurant."

"I can't wait," Angela said. "I'm starved."

Romano dined on junkfood and orange juice from a vending machine and spent the night outside the hotel in his rented car.

Early next morning Caldwell drove them to the Toulouse town center to purchase the equipment they would need the following day.

Considering the medieval ambiance of this ancient town, Banyon and Angela were shocked to see there were actually several shopping malls in the area. They were equally shocked to learn this area, so totally drenched in esoteric lore and religious history, was also the site of Europe's growing aerospace industry. *Strange bedfellows*, Banyon thought to himself.

Caldwell motioned to his left as they drove through a parking lot. "There's a bank where we can make a currency exchange. And look, there's a hardware store. We can buy a shovel and probably whatever else we might need."

After finishing their business at the bank they strolled over to the hardware store. It seemed as well stocked as any good hardware store back in the States. They wandered up and down the aisles discussing what items they might need. Apparently they must have looked somewhat confused as a clerk approached them.

"Bonjour! Vous cherchez quelque chose?" he asked.

Caldwell stepped forward and smiled at the clerk. "Je regarde, merci," he said with a certain nonchelance.

Banyon looked at Anglea. They both looked at Caldwell. "You speak French?"

"Just enough to get me in trouble most of the time," he grinned. "The clerk wanted to know if we were looking for anything in particular. I told him we were just browsing. It's easier than trying to explain what we're looking for. I have no idea how to say shovel or pick-ax in French."

Banyon laughed. "Good strategy."

It didn't take long to gather up what they needed: a couple of shovels, a pick-ax, and some work gloves. They even found a hand-held compass and a measuring tape marked off in inches and feet.

"How about this?" Angela asked, pointing to a huge reel of nylon rope.

Banyon wasn't sure. "Why would we need rope?"

"I don't know. Just seems like it might be a good idea. Who knows?"

Caldwell agreed. Using the knife conveniently hanging next to the reel, they measured out what they estimated to be about twenty feet of the rope and gathered it up into their shopping cart.

"If we find what we're looking for out there," Banyon said, "we'll need something to put it in."

"Good idea," Caldwell agreed. "Any suggestions?"

"Why not just bring a briefcase?" Angela suggested. "After all, it's probably only going to be a sheet or two of parchment."

"That should work," Banyon said. "I brought my briefcase. It's back at the hotel. We'll use that."

"Looks like this is about it," Caldwell said. "Can you think of anything else we might need?"

"Just a helicopter," Banyon quipped.

Caldwell laughed. "Yes. Well, fortunately we don't need to buy one of those. My friend, Michael, will be waiting for us tomorrow about two o'clock."

"So what's next on the agenda?" Angela asked.

"How about we pay for this stuff and then have lunch somewhere," Caldwell suggested. "Then I'll take you around and show you some of the sights."

"I'm up for that!" Angela said.

Banyon agreed. "Sounds like a plan."

Caldwell took them to the *Cave au Cassoulet* where they enjoyed a casual lunch. Later they strolled the various shops and markets along the old narrow cobblestone streets of the ancient city. Angela noticed the odd but beautiful pinkish color of many of the old buildings and cathedrals. The entire town seemed to glow with a dusty rose hue. Caldwell explained that Toulouse was known as *la ville rose*, the rose red city, because of the pinkish coloring of the bricks and tiles used in the construction of the buildings.

They spent the rest of the day seeing the sights, thrilled to be walking through living, breathing history.

With every step they took, every corner they rounded, every doorway they entered, Romano followed close behind. *Perhaps I missed my calling*, he mused to himself. *I should have been a private detective.* He was, in fact, cunningly stealthy in his pursuit. Several times he managed to position himself within earshot of the trio, close enough to catch snippets of their conversations from which he gathered enough information to know every move they planned to make.

~42~

Banyon was awake even before the alarm clock sounded at 7:30 the next morning. He wasn't sure he'd slept at all that night. Angela groaned and flopped an arm over to shut off the alarm. It took her a few moments to realize what was happening.

"Oh man," she said, rubbing her eyes. "This is it, isn't it?"

Banyon was already getting dressed. "Yup," he said. "This is it. Today's the day."

A quiet knock at the door was followed by Caldwell's voice from out in the hallway. "You guys up?"

"Barely," Banyon answered.

"Okay. I'll meet you downstairs in the restaurant!"

"All right," Banyon answered back. "Give us a few minutes."

He looked over at Angela and smiled. "Come on, sleepy head. Today we make history."

She grinned but the grin quickly turned into a frown. "I have to put on those stupid-looking hiking boots today, don't I?"

Banyon chuckled. "Think of it as a fashion statement."

Angela rolled out of bed and wrinkled her nose. "Yeah," she yawned. "I'll be a real trend setter."

There was surprisingly little conversation as the three of them sat at the table consuming a light breakfast and a few jolts of espresso. Everything had been discussed. The plan was in place. The time had come. Now they were each simply filled with a nervous anticipation of the adventure that lay ahead. An hour later they were in the van and on the road to Rennes le Chateau.

Along that same road Romano was following close behind but he cursed as a large produce truck cut in front of him and completely blocked his view of the van. There were too many curves in the road to risk passing the truck yet he didn't want to risk losing track of the van. Even though he knew they were planning to make a stop at the old walled city of Carcassone, he couldn't stand the thought of not having them in his sight every minute. His sleuthing had been faultless to this point. *Damn it!* He laid on his horn but the driver of the produce truck responded by sticking his arm out the window and flashing the international hand sign that required no translation. Romano's face grew red. *You son of a...* In a fit of anger, despite the curve ahead, he stepped on the gas and swerved into the other lane to pass the truck. The driver accelerated, trapping Romano between the side of the truck and the guardrail. The curve ahead was fast approaching. Romano had to decide quickly whether to tempt fate by trying to get ahead of the truck before another vehicle came at him from the other direction or drop back and risk losing sight of the van altogether. In a sudden flash of sanity he realized the risk of a head-on collision with another vehicle wasn't a good choice. But it was too late. Before he finished the thought, a large tour bus rounded the curve with nowhere to go but through him.

~43~

A ngela's eyes grew wide as she stared out the window at the sight coming up over the hill. "What in the world?"

"Carcassone!" Banyon announced excitedly.

"Indeed it is," Caldwell said. "I'd hoped we could take a couple hours to walk through it and take it all in but we're running a little late."

"It looks like a giant medieval fortress or something," Angela said. Then she sighed, "I can't believe we're this close and can't take the time to see it."

Banyon reached into his briefcase and pulled out a travel brochure. He handed it to Angela. "Here you go," he grinned. "At least you can look at the pictures."

"Thanks," she said, sparing no sarcasm. She grabbed the brochure and began her own private tour through the colorful photos. "Looks like something out of an old Robin Hood movie."

"The place was originally constructed by the Romans," Caldwell explained. "Changes and additions were made to the original construction ages ago but today it's pretty much the same as it was all the way back in the thirteenth century. The Visigoths took it over sometime back around the fifth century. I swear the damn place is still haunted by the violence. You can feel it."

As they continued to drive along the winding road past the ancient walled city, Angela took a virtual tour of the colossal old fortress and tried to imagine the bloody, violent battles that took place there between the Visigoth invaders and the mighty Roman army. Minutes later, when she looked up from the brochure, the mental image faded and the real city, with its towers and lingering ghosts, was now a couple of miles behind them.

Romano's car and the tour bus were about to collide at a combined speed of nearly 80 miles per hour. Sudden death was imminent. Realizing what was about to happen, the driver of the produce truck moved over just enough so Romano could share the lane in a tight squeeze between the truck and the bus. The bus swerved, nearly out of control, careening along the side of the metal guardrail. Romano hit the brakes and his tires squealed as he skidded to a stop at the side of the road. The produce truck vanished around the curve up ahead. The bus disappeared around the curve behind him. Suddenly there was nothing but silence. He sat, staring blankly out the front windshield for several moments as the dust cleared. His sweaty hands were still gripping the steering wheel. *Jesus Christ!* he thought to himself. *What the hell just happened?* The last time he checked, he was a split second from death. He got out of the car and paced back and forth a few times to make sure he was actually still alive and functioning. Regaining his composure and realizing he'd lost precious time, he climbed back into the car and sped off toward Carcassone.

~44~

A s they drove along, Banyon noticed the sky was beginning to darken. The small clouds that once dotted the morning sky were beginning to close in. *Don't rain*, Banyon prayed, *just please don't rain.*

A few minutes later, Caldwell spoke up. "There she is," he said, pointing toward the barely visible village on the hilltop in the distance. "Rennes le Chateau."

Like an apparition in the mist, the large conical shaped hill appeared and disappeared from view several times behind the trees and scrub-covered cliffs as the van snaked its way back and forth up the narrow winding road. About fifteen minutes and a half dozen hair-pin turns later, they reached the top. They passed a crumbling stone wall on the right that seemed to be buttressing the edge of someone's property that was situated several feet above the road.

Driving slowly, they approached the entrance to the village. In an instant, the 21st century was gone. The weathered cottages and other structures were relics of ages past, untouched by - and totally oblivious to - the modern world beyond the foothills of the Pyrenees Mountains.

Angela was mesmerized, wide-eyed. "This is unreal," she whispered under her breath.

Caldwell smiled, recalling he'd had the same thought upon his first visit.

"Sleepy little place, isn't it?" Banyon commented.

"Sleepy and creepy," Angela added. "Where is everybody?"

"Well," Caldwell answered, "it's not exactly the height of the tourist season."

"I know," Banyon said. "But Angela's right. The people who live here - the villagers - where are they?"

Suddenly, as if on cue, two of the town's older citizens - a man and a woman - came walking around the corner only to vanish again as they entered a small shop in the purple shadows along the cobbled walkway. But more signs of life began to appear as Caldwell drove slowly along the narrow road further into the village.

The anthropologist in Angela was bubbling to the surface. "Can we spend a little time here?" she asked, still disappointed that they had to pass up a chance to explore the walled city of Carcassone. "This is so fascinating."

Caldwell checked his watch. "Plenty of time," he said. "At least enough to see a few things before we meet with Michael."

"The church," Banyon said. "Sauniére's church. We have to see it. Is it far?"

"Just a few minutes away," Caldwell answered as he rounded another corner of the village. "Just down this road a piece, if I remember right."

As they drove through the village streets toward the strange church dedicated to the Magdalene, Romano was frantically searching the streets of Carcassone looking for the Chosen One and his two companions. He soon realized they had already left, or maybe hadn't even stopped there at all. Angered by the circumstances and bad luck he got back into his car, slammed the door and hit the gas. His car fishtailed on the dirt road leaving a cloud of dust in its wake.

~45~

There was absolutely nothing about Sauniére's old church that would make anyone feel welcome. The rugged stone exterior seemed cold and dead. Angela shivered as they approached on foot through the small church yard. They passed by a weathered statue of the Virgin Mary perched atop an ancient pillar carved in Visigothic style.

"Notice anything peculiar about that pillar?" Caldwell asked.

Banyon shrugged. "Not really. Why? What's wrong with it?"

"Nothing," Caldwell said. "Except that it's upside down."

Angela stopped for a moment to consider it. "Really?" she said. "Why?"

"Nobody knows!" Caldwell said with hearty chuckle as they continued along the narrow path across the churchyard.

When they reached the entrance they stopped and stared at the inscription carved into the stonework above the doorway:

Terribilis est locus iste

"What does it say?" Angela asked.

Banyon answered without hesitation. "Terrible is this place."

Caldwell looked impressed. "Well, I see you still remember your Latin."

Banyon smiled. "Not really. I read it on the internet."

Caldwell gave a laugh. "Shall we?" he said, motioning toward the door.

Banyon stepped forward and pushed on the heavy wooden door. As it opened, the old hinges creaked and groaned. "A creaking door," he muttered as he entered the darkened chamber. "How appropriate."

Just inside the door was a small box with a sign asking visitors to drop in a donation of money. Banyon reached in his pocket and pulled out some change. He dropped the coins into the box. That action somehow triggered a light switch. Now the church was lit, but barely, by a few light bulbs.

Angela followed close behind but stopped short with a frightened gasp.

Banyon spun around to see what happened and found her staring at a most hideous, evil-looking, life-sized statue of the Devil himself. Its posture was bent into a crouching position. Its neck was craned, stretching to gaze upward, glaring back at the observer with the whites of its eyes bulging from the sockets. It was, in fact, the first thing that greeted any visitor who walked through the door. Incredibly, Banyon had missed it when he walked in. His attention was drawn to the strange arrangement of the Stations of the Cross. Now, however, seeing the statue of the crouching demon with its long curling horns, he too was taken aback.

Caldwell chuckled. "Asmodeus," he said, patting the thing on the head.

"Ass-what?" Angela said, backing away. Her body shuddered.

"It's the demon, Asmodeus," Caldwell explained. "Or so I've been told. Like most everything around here there are different stories about it. I've heard it's supposed to represent the demon that was tamed by King Solomon."

Curiously, as Caldwell was quick to point out, the church's baptismal font was literally perched upon the muscular back of the hunched-over demon.

"Pleasant way to have your first born child baptized, eh?" Banyon joked.

Angela cringed and went off to find something less disturbing to look at.

As they wandered through the church, taking in all the garishly painted statues and unusual artwork that adorned the walls, Banyon was still puzzled by the way the Stations of the Cross were arranged.

"Angela, do you have your camera with you?" he asked.

"Sure," she said, reaching into her coat pocket.

She handed him the camera and he proceeded to get as many shots of the enigma as he could.

Caldwell grinned. "I knew that would pique your curiosity."

Angela was puzzled. "What are you guys talking about?"

Banyon explained to her the concept behind the Stations of the Cross. "After the crucifixion," he said, "word began to spread about this man, the Christ, his life, his teachings, the crucifixion, the resurrection, the whole story. Soon people were making pilgrimages from far and wide to see the place where Jesus was crucified and to visit the locations where the various events of his life were said to have taken place. They literally wanted to walk in his footsteps. But for many people, who lived very far away, it was just not possible to make the journey. Still, they wanted a way to remember the key events of Jesus' life and to meditate on these things. Finally, maybe around the twelfth century, Christianity was becoming hugely popular across Europe, what with the Crusades and all. As I recall, it was the Franciscan monks who finally came up with the idea of creating paintings and sculptures representing the last days of the life of Jesus."

Caldwell took up the explanation from there. "You see, Angela,' he said, "these shrines – the paintings and sculptures that Zeke just mentioned - were placed inside churches and sometimes out in the churchyard. Each shrine is called a station. People could then walk the stations from one to the next, stopping at each one to meditate on the particular scene or event depicted at the station. It was an act of prayer and devotion."

"And I take it," Angela said, "that there's something different about these stations here in this church?"

Banyon chimed in. "Exactly. Back in the Middle Ages, when this idea was first beginning to catch on, there wasn't any real protocol as to which events should be depicted or even how many stations there should be. Eventually, around the eighteenth century, the Pope declared that the official number of stations would be fourteen."

"Why fourteen?" she asked.

"Don't know," Banyon said. He looked to Caldwell for an answer but Caldwell admitted he didn't know either.

Angela scanned the church and made a quick count of the stations. "Well, there seems to be fourteen stations here. So what's the problem?"

"The problem," Banyon explained, "is the way they're laid out."

"What do you mean?"

"I mean traditionally the stations are arranged into two rows of seven stations each. So you'd begin at station one and continue down the line to station seven. Then walk across the floor to the other row where you'd begin at station eight and continue up the line to the final station number fourteen."

Angela immediately caught the glaring difference here. Sauniére had arranged the stations in a circular pattern. Not a perfectly round circle because the church was pretty much rectangular and the space wouldn't accommodate a perfect circle. But the arrangement was, nevertheless, circular in that a person following the stations ended up back at the place where he began.

Caldwell pointed out another anomaly. The stations here didn't follow the traditional and logical sequence. Instead, they seemed to be situated in pairs of odd combinations. Station 5 was paired with station 10. Station 4 with 11, 3 with 12, 2 with 13, 1 with 14, 6 with 7, 8 with 9. Strange, also, was the fact that the station of each pair was situated so they faced each other. That is, with the exception of the 6/7 pair and the 8/9 pair. The stations of those two pairs stood side by side. It was all highly unorthodox and no one had ever come up with an explanation for this unusual pattern.

Angela turned to Banyon who was still snapping pictures. "And you think you're going to figure it all out, I suppose."

Banyon laughed. "Well, I don't know about that. But it's damn curious, that's for sure. I mean, it's so obviously intentional. One has to suppose Sauniére had some reason for laying it out like this."

"So one would think," Angela said. "But on the other hand, look around you. Does anything in here make sense? Maybe Sauniére was just nice man with a few loose screws."

Caldwell chuckled. "If that were the case then it could all be easily dismissed. The whole Rennes le Chateau mystery, I mean. By all accounts Sauniére was anything but a nutcase. Don't forget, it all began right here where we stand with his unexpected discovery of those coded parchments."

Angela nodded. "I suppose. It's just that it's all so…"

Caldwell looked at his watch. "Oh man," he said, "we'd better be going if we want to see any more sights before meeting with Michael."

"Just a few more pictures," Banyon said. He was focusing the camera on the beautiful stained glass window depicting Mary Magdalene anointing Jesus.

The whole interior of the church was laden with a bewildering display of strange statues and mysterious symbols. If the odd arrangement of the Stations of the Cross wasn't enough to cause one to engage in a bit of head scratching, the statues of the Virgin Mary and Joseph certainly were. They were perched high up near the vaulted ceiling, on either side of the gaudy, yet beautifully ornate alter. Joseph was on the left and Mary on the right. The puzzling thing was that each of them held an infant in their arms. *Why are they each holding an infant?* Banyon wondered. It was a question many had asked but no one was quite sure of the answer. Some were convinced it was Sauniére's attempt to confirm the persistent rumor that Jesus had a twin brother. This, of course, led to speculation that it was Jesus' twin who died on the cross, leaving Jesus with the opportunity to escape with Mary Magdalene to find refuge here in the South of France.

When Banyon finished taking pictures they left the church and drove back into the main section of the village. They parked the van and walked along the cobbled streets. As they passed in front of a bookstore Banyon noticed the display in the front window.

"Hold on a second," he said, turning to Angela. "There's that book!"

"What book?" she asked. There were several books by various authors in the window. All of them seemed to be about some facet or another of the mystery of Rennes le Chateau.

"That one!" he said, pointing to the book that had grabbed his attention. "It's one of those two books by those researchers Paretti told us about."

He was right. Among the various titles on display was *Geneset*, by Wood and Campbell.

"I have to buy it," he said. "We really need to have it, don't you think?"

Angela agreed and they entered the shop. Fortunately, the young lady behind the cash register spoke very good English and the purchase was made without having to resort to silly gestures and Caldwell's rusty French.

Back out on the street, Banyon took another look at the cover of the book. "That's odd," he said.

"What?" Angela asked.

"The subtitle."

Angela looked at the book. Below the main title, *GENESET*, was a subtitle: *Target Earth*. A photo of the earth as seen from space was depicted on the cover. The earth, however, was shown to be in the crosshairs of a targeting mechanism.

"I don't get it," she said. "How does that pertain to the mystery of Rennes le Chateau?"

Banyon shook his head. "I have no idea."

"It does seem odd," Caldwell agreed, looking over Banyon's shoulder. "But we don't have time to ponder it now. We've got just enough time to get a quick glimpse of the *Tour Magdala* before we go."

The words were unfamiliar to Angela. "The what?"

"Sauniére's amazing Magdalene Tower," Caldwell explained.

"Oh, yes!" Angela said. "I saw a picture of it on a website!"

They returned to the van and drove a short way to a location just outside the village, overlooking the valley below. Caldwell pulled off to the side of the road and pointed out the window. Across the vast expanse of rolling green and brown hills they could clearly see the unusual structure situated high up on the side of a sparse, shrub-covered hill. The old stone structure looked like a single corner tower of a medieval castle with a huge, slightly curved stone wall attached to one side. The curve of the wall, which must have stretched several hundred feet, followed the contour of the hill. This gothic-styled tower was where Sauniére stored his voluminous library. Whatever else it may have stored was a matter of speculation. Rumors persisted that its odd location was the key to its real mystery. It may have been built on that particular spot to hide the entrance to an underground cave wherein may lie hidden the legendary Cathar treasure. Still, if that were true, no one had yet claimed such a discovery.

As they sat, spellbound, gazing across the land at the historic site, the clouds began gathering, ever darker, in the distance. Against the darkening backdrop the ancient tower took on an even more ominous appearance.

"We'd better get moving," Caldwell said. "We've got some digging to do."

~46~

Having reached the bottom of the hill, they drove along the main road into the countryside. After about 20 minutes Caldwell made a left turn onto a smaller unpaved road where they bumped along maneuvering through a virtual obstacle course of road ruts. Just about the time Angela thought she was going to lose her stomach, Caldwell brought the van to a sudden stop.

"Whoops," he said. "Just about missed the turn!"

He put the van in reverse and backed up about 20 feet, pointing out a small handwritten sign tacked to a post:

HELICOPTER TOURS, THIS WAY

Following the sign, Caldwell drove down the long narrow dirt drive leading to Michael Taylor's farm.

The farm was small but quite beautiful, especially the area immediately surrounding the cozy cottage-styled home. Michael's wife, Renée, had a way with plants as the lovely gardens demonstrated. Her hearty herb and vegetable garden provided some extra income as she periodically sold selected varieties to the village market. Around to the back of the house was a small field where a barn had been converted into a workshop and doubled as a reception area for people who came to pay a reasonable fee for a 30-minute helicopter tour of the countryside.

Michael, wearing his favorite old baseball cap and faded blue sweatshirt, was performing a last minute safety check on the helicopter when he heard the van coming down the drive. Grabbing a rag and wiping the grease from his hands, he hurried from the barn to greet his visitors. "Father Caldwell!" he shouted as he sprinted toward them, waving his hand.

Caldwell waved and pulled the van to a stop at the side of the house. "Michael, my old friend!" he shouted back, as he stepped out of the van. "We made it safe and sound!"

"So I see!" Michael said, giving Caldwell a friendly bear hug. "And this must be our two mysterious treasure hunters!"

Banyon laughed. "Well," he said, shaking hands with Michael, "not exactly treasure hunters. And not exactly mysterious either. But maybe a bit off our rockers, I'm sure some people would say. I'm Zeke Banyon and this is my fiancé, Angela Martin."

"Really pleased to meet you," Angela said.

Michael tipped the brim of his hat. "Ma'am."

The four of them exchanged pleasantries for several minutes before Michael led them around back to his office in the converted barn. "So you want me to take you to the cliff they call the Edge of Doubt, is that right?" he asked.

Banyon nodded. "That's what we're here for."

"And if memory serves me, Father Caldwell told me you're searching for a lost scroll?"

Banyon nodded again. "The lost scroll of Ezekiel. Ever hear of it?"

Michael lifted his cap and ran his fingers through his hair. "Can't say that I have. And living 'round these parts, I've heard about every lost this-that-and-the-other-thing that you can imagine. I asked one of the old timers up in the village if he'd ever heard of it but he just sort of laughed and shook his head. He'd heard plenty of tales, but that was a new one on him."

Banyon shrugged. "Well, I guess I'm not too surprised. We just stumbled onto it in a book."

"A book?"

"Long story," Banyon said, grinning.

"Well," Michael said, "I wish I had time to hear it but if we're gonna go then we'd better get started. Are you ready?"

"I can't wait," Banyon replied. "How about you guys?"

"I'm with you," Caldwell said.

They looked at Angela.

"Is it safe?" she asked with a tone of apprehension.

Michael grinned. "I haven't crashed yet! You wanna see my baby?"

"Your baby?" Angela asked.

"My whirlybird. My chopper."

"Oh! Of course. Where is it?"

By the time Romano reached the village of Rennes le Chateau he realized he had missed them once again. *Probably only by minutes,* he thought to himself, cursing. His plan had been to follow them to Michael Taylor's home, hijack the helicopter at gunpoint, and order them to take him along with them. At the site where the scroll would be found he would take possession of it and do whatever was necessary to make his escape with the precious artifact. But things were not going as planned and he didn't know exactly where Michael Taylor lived. Even if he found out where Taylor lived he knew they might already be gone by the time he got there. He hadn't come this close only to be discouraged now.

He drove down the main street of the village wracking his brain for a solution to his problem when he noticed the bookstore. He stopped the car. *If there's one place on this God-forsaken hilltop that Banyon couldn't have resisted, if he'd seen it at all, it would be the bookstore.* Romano reasoned that if someone in the bookstore had seen them he might be able to find out how long it had been since they left. At this point any little bit of information could help.

"*Bonjour,*" Romano said to the young lady behind the counter.

"*Bonjour*," she replied.

"Uh," he stammered, "*Parlez vous*, uh, *Anglais?*"

The lady smiled. "*Oui.* Yes, I speak English."

Romano was relieved. "Ah! Good! I'm looking for some friends. Perhaps they might have stopped in here."

He provided a description of the three travelers. Yes, she had seen them about an hour ago. No, she didn't know where they were heading. Yes, she knew of Michael Taylor's helicopter tours. She pointed to a small poster pinned to a bulletin board on the wall. It was a handmade advertising poster promoting Michael's service. It included a telephone number. Romano's eyes lit up.

"May I use your telephone, *s'il vous plait?*"

"Well…" she hesitated. "A local call?"

"Yes," he said, pointing to the phone number on the poster.

"*Oui,*" she smiled, handing the phone to him over the counter.

Romano dialed the number. A recorded voice instructed him to press 1 for French and 2 for English. He pressed 2 and waited. A woman answered.

"Taylor's helicopter tours. This is Renée. May I help you?"

Within just a few moments he learned that, yes, three Americans were just about to leave on a tour. However they had requested to be dropped off at some location, apparently to be picked up sometime later. She didn't know why. But the next tour was not booked until 4 o'clock that afternoon. If he would like to reserve the helicopter for a tour anytime between now and then it would be no problem at all since she expected Michael to return within the half hour after dropping off the Americans. Romano recognized a window of opportunity. All was not lost. Thinking quickly, he explained that he was short on time but would love to be able to see the region by air before he had to leave. The woman was understanding and booked Romano for a tour, scheduled to leave as soon as possible, pending the expected early return of the helicopter.

Romano got directions to the Taylor farm, thanked the bookstore clerk, and returned to his car. He fastened his seatbelt and sat quietly for a moment to gather his thoughts. Then he reached over, popped open the glovebox, grabbed the gun he'd purchased underground in Toulouse, and dropped it into his coat pocket. He inhaled deeply, holding it for a few seconds then let it go. Mentally prepared, he slid the key into the ignition and started the engine. "All right!" he said, putting the car into gear, "Let's do it!"

Michael led his guests out to the back of the barn where the helicopter sat in all her rustic splendor. His baby. His whirlybird. His chopper. Angela didn't know anything about helicopters but this *baby* looked like it had been around a long time. An awfully long time. She couldn't tell if the body color was painted rust red or if it was really rust. She feared the latter. *Good lord,* she thought. *We're going up in that?*

"Whatcha think?" Michael asked. "She was built back in '87 and still going strong. Ain't she something?"

"Oh she's..." Angela hesitated, "...something all right."

Michael walked up to the helicopter and slapped it on the side panel. "I know she doesn't look like much but she purrs like a kitten."

Angela tried to think of something positive to say. "Well," she forced a smile, "I love kittens."

Banyon noticed some writing painted in small script on the side. He walked over to get a better look. It read, ***"Maggie"***. "You named her Maggie?" he asked.

"Yeah," Michael grinned. "You know. Short for Magdalene."

"Ah," Banyon said. "Of course."

Michael helped them get their gear out of the van and into the helicopter. Caldwell took the seat beside Michael. Banyon and Angela occupied the bench seat just behind them. When everyone was situated and seatbelts were secured, Michael started the engine and Maggie's rotors began to turn, gradually gaining momentum. In a few moments the blades were cutting through the air with a loud *whomping* sound.

Doesn't sound like a kitten purring to me, Angela thought, grasping tightly onto the hand-strap hanging next to her.

Banyon could see she was nervous. He held her free hand and leaned close to her. "Not to worry," he whispered in her ear. "You're with the Chosen One."

She gave him a sideways glance. "Yeah," she said. "Lucky me."

Abruptly, Maggie jerked and jostled back and forth and before Angela could catch her breath she realized they were eye level with the roof of the barn. Then suddenly higher still. The next moment Angela felt almost weightless as the chopper hung in mid-air and spun like a top, making a 180 degree turn to the left. With a slight dip and a stomach-churning swerve they took off heading north over the valley just as Romano was coming down the drive toward the barn.

~47~

Michael was well aware of the famous cliff. Other visitors, familiar with the work of David Wood and his discovery of the huge invisible pentagram over the landscape, had requested to fly over the theoretical tip of the head of Isis at *Le Bordre de Doubt*. Having studied Wood's diagrams, and equipped with GPS units, slide rules, and yes, even psychically channeled information from cooperative but long since deceased Visigoth warriors, some of the visitors had determined the exact location of the tip of the geometric figure. Curiously, by coincidence or by design, they all seemed to agree it was located exactly in line with the apex of a large V-shaped crevasse notched into the edge of the cliff. No one, until now, however, had actually requested to be dropped off at the site. For the previous visitors it was enough just to say they'd hovered over the head of Isis and apparently none of them had any reason to suspect there was anything down there worth investigating. Banyon and Angela had reason to suspect otherwise.

The current destination was a mere 7 or 8 miles, as the *Maggie* flies, and they reached it in a matter of minutes. Michael circled the helicopter around the site a few times so they could get a good look at the cliff. It was difficult to determine the height of the cliff but it appeared a bit higher than Banyon had pictured it in his mind. If one were to tumble over the *Edge of Doubt* there would be no doubt about the results. Severe injuries, if not certain death, was Banyon's guess.

Michael explained to his passengers that because of the various outcroppings and uneven terrain there were not a lot of choices for a secure landing.

"I'll have to put you down right over there!" Michael shouted over the loud *whomping* of the rotors. He pointed to a flat clearing about 50 yards back from the edge of the cliff nearly in line with the V-shaped crevasse.

"All right!" Banyon said loudly, leaning forward to make sure Michael could hear him. "But could we circle around a few more times? I'd like to study the view a little more!"

Michael nodded. "Roger that!"

As Michael expertly handled the chopper, Banyon scanned the area below looking for some indication as to where the scroll might be buried. He tried to estimate an approximate distance of 144 feet east of the V-shaped crevasse, the head of Isis, but all he could see was a mass of small scrubby bushes, tangled groundcover and a few trees. He reached into his shirt pocket and unfolded a copy of the list of phrases from the Ezekiel Code. The mysterious coded phrases had taken them this far, he reasoned. Maybe they would provide yet another clue at this crucial moment of the journey. He scanned the list but nothing in particular stood out. *What the hell am I looking for? Come on! Speak to me!* Gazing down out the window again something suddenly grabbed his attention. *Those two trees near the edge of the cliff!* Something clicked. He felt a rush of recognition and then panicked. Distracted by his own excitement he thought he'd lost his mental connection. *What was it? What was it?* He went back to the list, frantically scanning the phrases. His eyes fell on two of them, one above the other:

TEN STONE CIRCLE = 162
GUARDIAN PILLARS = 162

He looked out the window again just as Maggie was coming around for the best view. *Could it be? Is it possible?* He tapped Michael on the shoulder. "Michael!" he said loudly. "Can you hover in this position for minute?"

Michael nodded, affirmative.

Angela could tell Banyon was onto something. "What is it?" she asked.

He didn't hear her. His synapses were firing full throttle, connecting dots. The two very tall trees near the edge of the cliff, about 10 to 12 feet apart, were the only two trees within a good fifty yards of the cliff. As he gazed down at them he didn't even have to look back at the list. In his mind's eye he saw the phrase, GUARDIAN PILLARS. The phrase just above it was TEN STONE CIRCLE. He put on his sunglasses to cut the glare from the window and squinted his eyes.

"What is it, Zeke?" Angela prodded.

Banyon raised a hand. "Hang on a sec," he said. He could see a fairly large stone boulder peeking up from a clump of bushes near one of the two trees. "Hand me the binoculars!" The motion of the helicopter made it difficult to keep the binoculars steady but once in focus he could see what he was looking for. There was another large boulder a few feet away from the first. Then he spied another beyond that. "Angela," he said, handing her the binoculars, "look down there by those two trees. See those large stones? One there, one over there, and another not far from it?"

It took her a moment but she finally saw what he was pointing to.

"Do you see any others?" he asked.

"I think so," she responded. "Looks like maybe one over by the other tree. You can just barely see the top of it above the tall grass."

The more they studied the ground between the two trees the more boulders they could make out, all of them nearly hidden by the overgrowth and all of them apparently forming a large circle, maybe 9 or 10 feet in diameter. Banyon was betting on 9 feet.

"How many of those boulders do you see?" he asked, talking loud enough to be heard over the noise of Maggie's motor.

"Hard to say! Ten, I think!" Angela said, still not sure what he was getting at.

He looked at her and grinned. "I think that's it!"

"You think that's *what*?"

He pointed to the two phrases on the list. "The *guardian pillars* and the *ten-stone circle!*"

Angela's eyes grew wide. "Wow! Yes! I can't believe it!"

It seemed obvious now but anyone could have missed it. In fact, apparently everyone had indeed missed it. It was really only noticeable from the air and even then it wasn't likely to be seen, if one had no particular reason to suspect it in the first place.

They shared the revelation with Caldwell who was patiently waiting to be let in on the cause of all the excitement. Michael, not knowing anything about the list of phrases, was completely in the dark but he was getting a kick out of what seemed to be a good time being had by all.

Banyon leaned toward Angela and pointed out another phrase:

FIVE STONE PENTAGRAM

"Look here!" he said. "You know what you can make by connecting certain stones on an evenly spaced *ten- stone circle?*"

"Yeah!" Angela replied. "A five-stone pentagram!"

"You got it!"

"That's great!" she said, But does it tell us anything about where, exactly, to dig for the scroll?"

It was a good question. Would they have to turn over every stone? Or would the Ezekiel Code yield yet another clue? Banyon went back to the list. Perhaps his synapses had overheated. Nothing was coming to him. Angela saw him shaking his head.

"Let me see it," she said.

He handed her the list. It didn't take her long to come up with something. "Well," she said, "We're in the south of France, right?"

Banyon nodded. "Right!"

"At Rennes le Chateau, right?"

"Right!"

"At the Isis Pentagram, right?"

"Right! What are you getting at?"

"Those three things are in the 151-section of the list, right?"

He looked at the list. "They are! Yes! But I..."

"Then I'm guessing the clue is right there in that section! My money's on this one!" She pointed to a phrase:

MIDDLE OF THE CIRCLE = 151

Banyon thought for moment. "I was assuming all along that it referred to the circle of churches!" he said. He looked at the list again and his attention was drawn to the 144-section of phrases. "But you could be right! Look here!"

In the 144-section, two phrases now stood out as clues to their question:

CIRCLE OF STONE = 144

THE EDGE OF THE CLIFF = 144

Banyon had to admit it seemed like she'd connected the right dots. The place to break ground was the center of the ten-stone circle between the guardian pillars. He reached forward and tapped Michael on the shoulder. "Take us down!"

Michael acknowledged the request and *Maggie* swooped around in a fluid motion as she prepared for descent. Angela gripped the hand-strap and braced herself to land with a thump. But when *Maggie* touched down with the grace of a floating feather Angela quickly released her grip on the strap, hoping no one noticed her unnecessary anxiety.

Caldwell stepped out of the helicopter, followed by Angela and then Banyon. Michael stayed at the controls and waited for them to unload their gear. When they had everything out, they walked around to the pilot's side of the chopper. The tall grass and shrubs rippled violently in the waves of air currents from the deafening rotor blades. Angela's hair thrashed around in wild confusion, whipping her in the face as she ducked low and backed away.

"I gotta go!" Michael shouted from the cockpit. "I'll be back to pick you up in about an hour!"

Banyon and Caldwell both nodded and gave a thumbs up. Michael returned the gesture and took *Maggie* back up with a flourish. They watched the chopper until it disappeared beyond a distant hill.

Suddenly there was silence.

Looking around, it was impossible to imagine anything more serene, more peaceful. A light rain began to fall but somehow it didn't matter. In a way, it added something to the mystique of their surroundings and their reason for being there.

Banyon walked toward the edge of the cliff and stopped at the V-shaped crevasse. He looked up and grinned like a kid. "Hey!" he shouted to the others. "Look at me! I'm standing on the head of Isis!"

"Don't move!" Angela said, reaching into her pack for the camera. She snapped a shot of the Chosen One standing on the head of Isis at the Edge of Doubt. "That's a Kodak moment if ever there was one!" she said, laughing.

Knowing the hour would pass quickly they wasted not another moment and immediately set to work on the mission at hand.

Michael landed the helicopter at the usual spot behind the barn and walked in to see if his next customer was waiting. Through the window between his office and the adjoining reception area he could see a stocky, bald headed man pacing back and forth. Renée always filled out an information form for each customer, leaving it on Michael's desk. As usual the form was completed and waiting for him. Romano, however, had signed a phony name to the document.

"Mr. Girarde?" Michael said as he walked into the reception area.

Romano looked up and smiled. "Uh, Yes! I'm Girarde! You're the pilot?"

Michael nodded. "That I am," he said, shaking hands with the man. Michael introduced himself by name and then glanced down at a note Renée had written in the comments box. He turned to Romano. "Says here you're pretty short on time but would like at least a quick fly-over of the area. Carcassone is an amazing sight from the air. Should we put that on our list of sights to see?"

"Yes, yes, that sounds great. How soon can we leave?"

"Maggie's all warmed up and ready to go. We could leave right now if you'd like."

"Maggie?"

Michael explained the name.

"Ah," Romano said. "I see. Well, then, yes. I'm ready."

"Right this way then," Michael said, leading Romano out to the back of the barn. "Ever ride in a helicopter before, Mr. Girarde?"

Romano shook his head. "No, never have."

"Well, I think you'll find your first time to be a rewarding experience."

"I'm sure it will be," Romano replied.

Once they were buckled into their seats *Maggie* lifted up and turned toward the direction of Carcassone. Immediately and without warning, Romano reached into his coat pocket, pulled out the gun, and jammed it into Michael's ribs.

"What the...?" Michael shouted, shaken by the sudden action.

"Change of itinerary," Romano said. "Take me to the cliff!"

"The what?"

"Don't play stupid with me! You know what I'm talking about! The Edge of Doubt! Move it!"

"But..." Michael stammered, not quite sure what was going on.

Romano jabbed the gun into Michael's ribs again to emphasize his impatience. "Now!" he shouted.

Banyon was certain they had correctly identified the spot where the scroll - if indeed there was such a thing - would be found. Still, he wanted to be sure. With the measuring tape they began measuring eastward from the point of the V-shaped crevasse. The tape only extended to 20 feet and it was difficult trying to get a flat measurement over the shrubs, and rocky terrain. They could clearly see the two tall trees, the guardian pillars, standing majestically just a short distance away. They knew it would take seven lengths of the 20-foot tape plus an extra four feet to reach the mark of 144 feet. By the time they measured out the seventh length they were past the first pillar. The three large stones they had first seen from the helicopter were now clearly visible. Banyon used the tape once more to measure off the final four feet.

"Well, there it is." he said, marking the spot by stomping his boot heel into the ground.

The end of the measured distance appeared to be exactly midway between the two trees. Their attention had been so focused on the tape that it was only now, as they were gathered around his boot print in the soil, that they looked around and found themselves surrounded by a circle of ten large stones the size of basketballs. Most of them were covered in moss and overgrowth providing such camouflage that it made them nearly impossible to see from a distance. The moment was totally surreal. No one spoke for the longest time.

"There's an energy here," Banyon said, finally. "I can feel it."

"There's *something* here," Caldwell agreed with a shiver. "But I don't know what it is."

Angela walked over to one of the ten stones and sat on it. "Just out of curiosity," she said, "I wonder which five of these ten stones are supposed to form the pentagram?"

"Well," Banyon said, "technically, I guess it wouldn't matter. You could actually use all ten of the stones and create two pentagrams."

The ground was soft and moist from the light mist. Banyon picked up the shovel and began to scrape straight lines in the ground from one stone to another until he'd created a pentagram. Then he created a second pentagram using the remaining stones. Immediately he noticed the result was that each pentagram was the reverse of the other. Depending on where you stood, one was pointing upward and one was pointing downward. He recalled the alphanumeric value of the word, *pentagram,* was 95. He gave a little laugh.

"What's funny?" Angela asked.

"The value of the word, *pentagram* is 95."

"So?"

"Here we have two pentagrams," he explained. "One is right side up and the other is upside down." He chuckled again as if he couldn't believe what he was about to show them. "If you look at the number 95 upside down it's 56."

Angela got it immediately. "Ah!" she said "Fifty-six! That's the alphanumeric value of the name, Isis!"

Banyon nodded. "Yes! And that's not all. Add 95 to 56 and what do you get?"

Angela did a quick calculation in her head. "Oh my god," she said. "It's 151!"

"I'd say we must be at the right place, wouldn't you?" Banyon said with a grin.

Caldwell was beside himself with all of this. He shook his head as if it was too much to believe. "Something tells me you'd better start digging, my friend. I'm guessing there's something under that boot print in the dirt and it's been waiting a long time for you to come dig it up."

With those words all the events of the previous months came together, compressed into the moment. Banyon looked over at Angela. She smiled and simply nodded knowingly. Without ceremony or even another word, Banyon positioned himself directly over the boot print in the soil. With the blade of the shovel, he inscribed a three-foot diameter circle on the ground around the center mark. He shot a quick glance once more toward Angela. Her eyes were bright with anticipation. Then, placing his foot atop the shovel blade, he shoved it in and dug out the first mound of dirt.

Beginning at the edge of his three-foot circle he worked his way around and down. Suddenly, only about a foot of the way into the dig, the shovel clanked on something hard. Stunned for a moment, he hesitated. Angela and Caldwell rushed closer to see what it could be. Banyon tapped it again with the shovel. *Could this be it?* Carefully he manipulated the shovel, trying to find the edges of whatever it was that those few inches of dirt were hiding. Finally the shovel slid down beside the object with a scraping sound. Cautiously, he pried upward.

Caldwell leaned down to grasp the object by hand. Giving it a good tug, it flipped upward.

"Christ," Banyon said, both relieved and disappointed at the same time. "It's a freakin' rock."

He continued to dig. Mound after mound was piling up beside him. The pit was now easily three or four feet deep and the shovel had hit nothing more, not even another rock. He'd worked up a pretty good sweat and stopped for a moment to rest. "There damn well better be something down here," he groaned. Once again he shoved the blade into the dark soil.

Then, *CLANK!* The shovel struck something and the wooden handle vibrated in his hands. He tapped it again. *Clank-clank!* This time it sounded different. He didn't think it was a rock. He looked at Angela and then at Caldwell. All three of them dropped to their knees and began scraping the dirt out with their hands. Then they saw it. Something flat. Metallic.

"Jesus," Banyon whispered. With his gloved hands he brushed away the thin layer of dirt covering the object. It appeared to be rectangular, about 4 inches wide and 10 inches long. Working his hands into the dirt along the edges of the object he managed to hook his fingers around the bottom of it. Slowly he lifted it out. Angela couldn't believe what she was seeing.

"Oh my god," Caldwell said, nearly choking on his words. "That's no rock."

Banyon set the object on the ground and brushed off the rest of the dirt.

Angela ran her fingers over the top of the shiny metallic box. She looked up at Banyon. "Is it...?

"Gold?" he said, finishing her question. "Looks like it to me. What do you think?" he asked, looking at Caldwell.

"Looks like it to me, too," Caldwell replied.

The gold box was ornately adorned with engraved borders and detailed scrollwork. The lid was hinged on one side, and held closed by a small silver ring passing through two gold u-shaped loops. The small ring itself was an intricate piece of work. Examining it closely, Banyon could see it wasn't a completely closed circle. It was actually two half-rings. The two halves came together on one side so closely it was difficult to see the split between them. Directly opposite the split the two halves were joined by a tiny, ingeniously designed, fitting which allowed the ring to be opened by twisting the two halves in opposite directions. Banyon held the box in his hands and shook it. Something rattled inside.

Angela couldn't contain her excitement. "Come on!" she said. "Open it!"

Banyon twisted the ring and it came loose in his hand. He put it in his coat pocket and set the box back down on the ground.

"Come on! Come on!" Angela prodded. Her heart was pounding.

Slowly, carefully, Banyon raised the lid of the gold box. Inside was a copper cylinder. He hesitated. This was the most exhilarating moment of his entire life. He could feel his own pulse racing. He took the cylinder out of the box and wondered, for a moment, if he was dreaming.

Caldwell put a hand on Banyon's shoulder. "Go on," he said with an assuring tone. "This is what you came for."

Banyon looked at Angela.

Biting her lip, she nodded encouragingly. "Yes," she whispered, trying to choke back her emotion. "Do it."

Banyon removed the wooden plug from one end of the cylinder and looked inside. A long, slow grin crossed his face. He cast a glance at Angela and then back to the cylinder. Just as he was about to remove the parchment the sacred moment was shattered by a loud, familiar, but unexpected sound.

~48~

Startled, all three of them jumped up and spun around to see the helicopter hovering above the trees. They'd been so lost in their moment of discovery that they hadn't heard it approaching.

"It's Michael!" Caldwell said. He looked at his watch. "What's he doing back already?"

They stood watching as the chopper hovered over them.

"What's he doing?" Banyon asked.

Caldwell shook his head. "I don't know."

"Right there!" Romano ordered, his gun still pointed at Michael's side. "Put us down right there!"

"I can't!" Michael complained. "It's not a good spot!"

"Just do it!" Romano shouted, again jabbing the barrel of the gun into Michael's ribs.

Now, more frightened of the gun than of a bad landing, Michael looked down to consider his options. The only small portion of ground he could see that was even marginally safe was too close to the Edge of Doubt for comfort but he had no choice. He brought *Maggie* down to the precarious spot, not 50 feet from where Banyon and the others stood watching.

When the chopper touched down, Michael shut off the engine and climbed out.

Caldwell hollered and waved. "Michael! You're early!"

But Michael didn't move.

Angela looked perplexed. "Why is he just standing there?"

Caldwell, equally perplexed, shook his head. "I don't know." He was about to call out again when another man came walking around from the other side of the helicopter and stood directly behind Michael.

"Who the heck is that?" Banyon wondered.

Caldwell shrugged. "Can't tell from here."

In a moment, Michael began walking slowly toward them with the other man following close behind. The closer they got the easier it was to see something was wrong. Caldwell had rarely, if ever, seen such a solemn expression on Michael's face. Clearly the man behind him was the problem.

Suddenly Michael came to an abrupt halt and finally spoke. "I'm sorry," he said to his three friends.

"Shut up!" Romano bellowed, stepping out from behind with the gun still pointed at Michael. The others were paralyzed with a mix of fear and confusion. Romano shoved Michael forward. "Get over there with them!" he ordered.

Michael stumbled over and stood with the others near the middle of the ten-stone circle. Frank Romano's eyes narrowed in on the prize clutched firmly in Banyon's right hand.

"I'll take that!" Romano shouted, motioning with his gun.

Shaken by the sudden action of the gun being pointed directly at him, Banyon accidentally dropped the cylinder into the freshly dug pit and the scroll slid part way out.

"Pick it up!" Romano ordered. "Tuck the scroll back into the cylinder and toss it over to me!"

Banyon retrieved the cylinder from the hole and stood up. "Who the hell are you?" he demanded.

"Doesn't matter," Romano said, defiantly. "Just toss the cylinder over here and no one gets hurt."

"Wait a minute!" Angela said. "I know you! I've seen you before! You're the man at the mall! I bumped against your table and spilled your coffee!"

Banyon did a double-take. He couldn't believe what she'd just said. "What are you talking about?" he asked.

She reminded him of the incident but it wasn't registering in his memory.

"Shut the hell up, lady!" Romano shouted angrily. "Just tell your friend there to give up the cylinder or somebody's gonna die!" He had no intention of killing anyone, really. It wasn't in him. Shouting and verbal intimidation had been the only weapon he'd needed throughout his life to get him what he wanted. It was a tactic he'd learned from his own father growing up in Brooklyn. However, he seemed to overlook the final lesson that he should have learned from his father. Shooting off at the *mouth* could sometimes get one killed when someone else responds by shooting with a *gun*. In a barroom confrontation his father's final shout proved that point beyond the edge of a doubt, leaving the young Romano fatherless. "Now!" Romano shouted at Banyon. "I don't have all day and I'm losing patience! Toss it over here!"

Banyon did as he was ordered and tossed the cylinder toward Romano. But instead of aiming for a spot at Romano's feet he lobbed it a bit further. It flew just over Romano's head. Tumbling end over end it landed a foot or two behind him. The one remaining wooden plug popped off and the scroll slid completely out of the cylinder. Romano backed up and crouched down awkwardly, trying to retrieve both the cylinder and the scroll with one hand while his other hand waved the gun around wildly and dangerously out of control.

Taking advantage of Romano's awkward moment, Banyon lunged forward, with the intention of knocking Romano down and grabbing the gun. With any luck at all, Romano just might stumble backward far enough and tumble off the edge of the cliff. Instead, Romano turned and looked up just in time to dodge the tackle. He fired off a shot and the bullet struck Banyon in the shoulder. Banyon yelled out in pain and slumped to the ground. Bleeding, he struggled to get to his feet but fell again to his knees. Angela screamed and started to run toward him but Caldwell grabbed her by the arm to stop her from getting herself killed.

Romano quickly picked up the cylinder and the scroll. He rushed toward Michael, grabbed him by the shirt, and pushed him toward the helicopter. Michael reluctantly climbed into the cockpit. Romano, still waving the gun around, climbed into the seat next to him and shouted his next order. "Take me back to your place!"

Michael shot him a rebellious look.

"Just do it!" Romano threatened.

Within moments the helicopter lifted off and disappeared over the hill leaving the others stranded with Banyon lying on the ground, bleeding.

~49~

Michael landed the helicopter behind the barn and Romano forced him, at gunpoint, into the office.

Romano, agitated and desperate, shoved Michael into a chair and looked around for some rope. Finding none, he grabbed a heavy-duty electrical extension cord that was hanging neatly coiled on the wall and used it to bind Michael to the chair. He thought about knocking

Michael out with a blow to the head with the butt of the pistol but decided against it. For all his bravado Romano really had no stomach for inflicting pain. Shooting Banyon had been an accident. But what was done was done. His only thought now was to get away as fast as possible. He walked up behind Michael and put the barrel of the gun to Michael's head. Michael's body tensed up. After several long moments Romano lowered the gun and leaned down. He put his mouth next to Michael's ear and whispered, "This is your lucky day." With those parting words Romano left the barn and hurried to his car.

As soon as Michael heard the car drive away he struggled to free himself. After several minutes of twisting and turning he managed to loosen the cord and wriggle out of the restraint. Exhausted, he ran to the phone to call the police but the phone was dead. It took him a moment to figure it out. *While I was still at the cliff with Caldwell and the others the bastard must have cut the outside line!* Then he panicked as he remembered his wife had been alone in the house. *Jesus! Renée!* He sprinted out of the office and rushed to the house calling her name. There was no answer. He ran to the front door. It was locked.

"Renée!" he shouted. Still no answer.

He pounded on the door. Nothing. Moving around to the other side of the house he found the back door unlocked. He entered and shouted again, "Renée!" Then he heard a muffled scream. He worked his way through the house, moving toward the sound and found her tied up and gagged, lying on the bedroom floor. She was crying. "That son of a...!" Michael cursed. He lowered the gag from her mouth and untied her hands. "Are you all right?"

"Yes, I... I think so," she said, choking the words out.

Gently, he helped her up and sat her on the bed. "Thank god," he said.

"Michael," she sobbed, looking up at him. "I was so scared! Who was that man? What's happened?"

Michael brought her a glass of water and was torn about what to do next. He wanted to stay and comfort his wife but the longer he waited the more of a lead Romano would have. If he jumped into the helicopter right now he could track Romano down and ram him off the road. He could cause enough damage to the car that it would be impossible for Romano to go any further except on foot. *That would allow me enough time to get to the village and call the police.* It was worth a shot.

"Renée," he said, "listen. I can't explain right now. You'll be all right here. He's gone and I have to go after him. You understand? I can't let him get away."

"But," Renée protested, "you should call the police! Don't do this by yourself!"

"I tried but the phone is dead. The son of a bitch cut the phone line. I have to go. Lock the doors after me and stay inside. You'll be all right." He hated to leave her but he felt he had no choice. Half way out the door he stopped. "Oh god," he muttered. "Damn it!"

Renée reached out and touched his arm. "What is it?" she asked. "What's the matter?"

"Banyon!" he said.

"Who?"

"Father Caldwell's friend! He's out there in the middle of nowhere bleeding from a bullet wound. Hell, for all I know he's dead by now!"

Renée was completely in the dark. "Michael," she cried. "I don't understand. What's going on?"

Shaking his head in frustration he looked at her. "I don't know, exactly. I just know I have to get out there and help them."

"And the other man? He'll just get away?"

Michael tried to think. "I don't know. We'll have to deal with it later. Maybe call the police from the village. I just know I have to get moving. That Banyon fellow might be hurt bad." He held Renée close and kissed her. "It'll be all right. Lock the doors and stay inside. I should be back within the hour."

~50~

The bullet had passed through the soft portion of Banyon's shoulder, ripping away a good-sized piece of flesh. Fortunately,

Angela had packed a first-aid kit and she managed to apply a temporary dressing to the wound. When Michael arrived he was relieved to see Banyon was all right. He helped them get Banyon and their supplies into the helicopter. As they lifted off, he told them what had taken place back at the barn. "But who the hell was that guy?" he asked.

Banyon started to say something but was too weak to talk over the noise of *Maggie*'s engines. Angela explained that they didn't know the man's name but that she'd seen him once before at a shopping mall back in the States. She described the episode where she bumped the man's table and spilled his coffee.

Michael was confused. "And so now he just coincidentally pops up here in the South of France? He must have been pretty pissed about that coffee! I don't get it!"

"Seems pretty clear to me!" Caldwell said, shouting over the roar of the rotors. "He must have been following Zeke and Angela all the way from Seattle!"

Angela thought about it for a moment. "You're right!" she said. "He must have! But I can't figure out how he could have known what we were doing!" She paused and then added, "Unless..."

"Unless what?" Michael asked.

"Jesuit!" Banyon interjected, trying to be heard from the back seat of the helicopter.

"What?" Michael asked. "What did he say?"

Caldwell knew exactly what Banyon said and he knew it was exactly what Angela was thinking. He wondered if she would even attempt to explain it to Michael. From the front of the helicopter, he turned to glance back at her. Banyon was slumped over, resting his head on her shoulder.

"It's a long story!" she said to Michael. "Some months ago, when we were beginning to get somewhere with this code stuff, I was kidnapped by..."

"What!" Michael interrupted. "Kidnapped? Are you serious? By who?"

Angela hesitated. "You wouldn't believe me if I told you!"

"Try me!" Michael encouraged her.

"Apparently by some rogue Jesuit priests!"

Michael nearly choked. "Rogue what?"

"I said you wouldn't believe me!"

Michael shook his head. "Lady, after today I'm just about ready to believe anything! But come on!"

"Like I said, it's a long story! To tell you the truth, when I think about it, I can hardly believe it myself! I can hardly expect anyone else to believe it!"

"And these…" Michael paused, "…these Jesuits! This guy today was one of them?"

"We don't know for sure! But it's the only thing that makes sense!"

"Well," Michael said, pointing to his property now coming into view, "unfortunately I guess we won't have time to hear the whole story! We're almost there! When we touch down I think we should drive up to the village and call the police! And Mr. Banyon needs to get to a hospital!"

Banyon stirred and sat up. "No hospital," he groaned. "I hate hospitals. And no police either."

When they landed and were safely inside Michael's house, Renée attended to Banyon's wound. She'd had some past experience as a nurse's aide when she worked in a small clinic in Carcassone as recently as a year ago. The dressing Angela had applied was soaked with blood and needed to be changed. After cleaning the wound with an antiseptic and applying a professional dressing, Renée gave him a codeine tablet for the pain and dropped a couple more into his shirt pocket. She got him a pillow and had him lie down on the living room sofa. While she was taking care of him there was still an argument going on about Banyon's reluctance to go to a hospital and especially about not involving the police.

"Okay," Michael said, getting a bit frustrated with the whole affair. "I get that you don't want to go to a hospital. But what's your problem with calling the police? I mean, the bastard assaulted me and my wife! And you! Look what he did to you! Not to mention that he stole that *whatever* it was from you!"

Banyon nodded. "I know. I understand. Believe me. But if the police got involved, and managed to catch that guy, they'd want to know all about that cylinder and the parchment. Unless we all lied our asses off they'd sure as hell confiscate the artifacts and claim them as the property of France. It would all end up in the back room of some curator's office and we'd never see it again."

"But it *is* the property of France," Michael argued, pacing the floor.

Banyon struggled to sit up and looked at Michael. "Michael, listen. I know how you feel but you don't know the whole story. Not that I'd expect you to believe it even if we told you. But it's much too long, and to tell you the truth, we still don't understand it all completely ourselves. I'm asking you please just try to understand that this is all incredibly important. Not just to me and Angela. If that's all it was, I'd probably be more likely to call the police myself. But people have died in the pursuit of that scroll. It holds the key to something I believe is somehow profoundly important to everyone on this planet. There are powerful people behind the scenes, people we've never even seen, who are somehow involved in this."

"What are you talking about?" Michael pleaded angrily for more of an explanation. "What kind of people?"

Banyon wasn't sure how much to tell him. He looked down and sighed, then looked up again. "Would you believe people that reach all the way to the Vatican? Would you believe the Society of Jesus? The Jesuits? Would you believe a secret society called the Brotherhood of the Nine Pillars? Would you believe…"

Michael interrupted with a skeptical laugh. "Come on! You expect me to believe that?"

Banyon shook his head. "You see what I mean? I said you wouldn't believe it. But I'm asking you to at least give me the benefit of the doubt. Look. You saw the gold box we dug up. You saw the cylinder and the scroll. Would you have believed any of that if you hadn't seen it?"

"No. Probably not," Michael admitted. "But why you? What the hell is your role in all of this? Assuming that it's all true. Which I find pretty damned hard to believe."

The last thing Banyon wanted to say was that he was the *Chosen One*. He'd have no credibility left after making a statement like that. He looked over at Angela. Her eyes met his and she knew what he was thinking. She very subtly shook her head, *no*. Banyon nodded. *Of course not.*

"Well?" said Michael, pushing for an answer.

Banyon looked him in the eyes. "Do you believe in fate?" he asked.

"Fate? You mean like predestination?"

Banyon nodded. "Yeah. Like that."

Michael thought for a second. He looked over at Renée and remembered when they first met he thought it must have been fate. "I guess so," he relented. "Sometimes it seems like some things are meant to happen. Why? What are you getting at?"

"You wanted to know *why me*. That's what I'm telling you. I have plenty of good reasons to believe fate has chosen me to play this out. I know that sounds crazy. But I believe it's true."

"Oh yeah? Well, considering that the asshole with the gun has possession of your precious scroll, it sort of looks to me like fate has chosen somebody else for the job. Wouldn't you say?"

Banyon winced at the thought. It did seem now like it had all been for nothing. The man who stole the scroll had probably made it all the way to Toulouse by now and could even be on a plane leaving the country. He couldn't imagine a worse turn of events. Suddenly his mind was spinning in a kaleidoscope of confused thoughts. *Is it possible this is the end of the road? Who the hell was that guy? How did all this happen? Why do I... feel so...*

Angela noticed him beginning to lean sideways. She went over and knelt down in front of the sofa where he was sitting. "Are you okay?" she asked, brushing his hair away from his eyes.

He shook his head and sat up again. "Yeah. Must be the codeine. Just felt a little dizzy. I'm all right."

Michael looked at Caldwell. "You go along with all this?" he asked. "You think this is all true?"

"All I can say," Caldwell replied, "is that, from what I've seen and from what I've heard of their story, and knowing Zeke as well as I do, yes. I can't say I understand it all. But I'm convinced there's something to it."

Michael threw up his hands and sat down. "Well," he said, giving in with an exasperated look on his face, "I guess I've heard it all now."

Caldwell chuckled. "Oh, believe me. You haven't heard the half of it!"

"Yeah," Michael said, with a nod. "And I'm not sure I want to, either."

Glancing out the window, Caldwell could see the sky had cleared and the sun was going down behind the barn. He looked at his watch.

"It's getting late," he said. He looked over at Banyon. "Are you up to heading back to the hotel?"

"Yeah. I'm all right. I can make it."

Caldwell spoke with Michael and Renée out in the kitchen for a few minutes to make sure everything was okay and to apologize for bringing so much trouble into their beautiful home. Michael had relaxed by now and had pretty much accepted the outcome of the day's events. It wasn't difficult to forgive his old friend. Shaking hands and giving Caldwell a friendly hug, he grinned. "Next time you call in a favor," he said, "could you make it something a little less violent?"

Caldwell smiled. "I promise."

That night in the hotel Banyon took another codeine and fell asleep within minutes. Angela and Caldwell stayed up for a while and talked. There seemed to be nothing left to do now but return home empty-handed, save for one small gold box and a book with a picture of *target earth* on the cover.

~51~

The next morning Angela was already up and dressed by the time Banyon finally stirred. "Did you sleep all right?" she asked. "How's the shoulder?"

Banyon groaned and tried to sit up in the bed. The effort caused a pain to shoot through his shoulder. "Ohhh..." he moaned. "Jesus. I feel like a truck rolled over me." He looked around to reacquaint himself with the hotel room. "I barely remember even getting back here last night."

"The codeine," Angela reminded him. "You were out in nothing flat."

He sat in silence for a few moments, still groggy from the drug-enhanced sleep. As the cobwebs cleared, the events of the previous day came flooding back.

Angela was sitting at the window looking out at the French countryside.

"What are you looking at?" he asked.

"Nothing."

He sighed deeply. "That's about what we've ended up with, isn't it?"

"Pretty much."

It was easy to see she was as disappointed and depressed as he was about the way things turned out. He swung his legs over the side of the bed and sat in silence, staring at the floor. Finally he spoke. "I can't believe it ends like this," he said. "It just doesn't make sense. Not after all we've gone through to get here. I mean, we were so close. Hell, we had it in our hands!"

"I know," Angela said, still staring blankly out the window. "I know."

"I didn't even get a chance to really look at the scroll," Banyon lamented.

Angela didn't respond. There seemed to be nothing else to say about the matter.

Banyon glanced over at the table next to the door. The small gold box was sitting there, empty, a reminder of what almost was. It just didn't seem possible.

"Have you seen Father Caldwell yet this morning?" he asked.

She replied without turning around. "He knocked on the door about an hour ago. Asked how you were doing. I told him you were still sleeping."

"He went back to his room?"

"I think so." She turned to him. "Are you hungry?"

"Starved."

"Feel like going down to the restaurant?"

"Not really. Can't we get room service?"

She nodded. "Sure."

"Okay," he said, struggling to get up and dressed. "Go get Caldwell and bring him back to our room. We'll eat here and figure out what we're going to do."

By the time room service delivered a light meal, it was nearly noon. The conversation amongst the three of them was mostly about what had happened the day before. The more they talked about it the heavier the depression weighed on Banyon. "So," he sighed with a shrug, "I guess there's nothing left to do but go home, yes?"

"Are you really ready to travel?" Caldwell asked, nodding toward Banyon's injured shoulder.

Banyon nodded. "I just want to get the hell out of here."

"It could have been worse," Angela offered, trying to lighten his mood.

Banyon snorted sarcastically. "Yeah? How?"

"Well, for starters, you could have been killed."

The words rang in Banyon's ears. It was true. He knew it. He rubbed his wounded shoulder. "Yeah," he said, smiling for the first time that day. "There is that."

~52~

Banyon slept most of the way on the flight from Toulouse back to New York's JFK International Airport. At the same time, Romano was far ahead of them already leaving New York on a flight bound for Seattle.

Anxious to finally have a chance to study the mysterious ancient document, Romano removed it from his carry-on bag and began to read. There was just one problem. It was written in Hebrew and Romano's Hebrew was not up to par. Most of it meant nothing to him. Frustrated, the best he could hope for was to find someone to translate it for him.

At that moment, somewhere over the Atlantic, Banyon awakened abruptly.

From the adjoining seat Angela turned to him. "You all right?"

"Yeah," he said, clearing his head. "I had that dream again. About that strange object that seems to be surrounded by dark, cold water. Sometimes I almost think I've got it. Like it's about to make sense. And then, I don't know. It seems like..." he paused, "something's missing".

Gazing out across the Bering Sea through the large plate glass window in the meeting room of the Nine, Nathan Crown lazily rolled a lighted cigar back and forth between his fingers. "We've just received word from our contact in Paris," he said to the man standing in the doorway behind him. "Seems like we have another situation."

"What sort of situation?"

"Breach of protocol."

"Jesuits?"

"Just one."

"Romano?"

"Of course."

Crown turned from the window and sat down at the large round conference table. The other member of the Nine approached and sat across from him. Crown explained what had taken place between Banyon and Romano at Rennes le Chateau.

"What do we do?" the man asked.

Crown laid a large envelope on the table. "Dispatch three of our operatives," he said, sliding the envelope over to the other man. "Inside the envelope are complete instructions, a photograph of Romano, and a transponder tag that's keyed to one of the electronic lockers at the airport in Seattle. Give this envelope to the operatives. They'll know what to do."

~53~

Clutching his carry-on bag, Romano grinned as he walked out of the main terminal at the SeaTac airport in Seattle. He had pulled off a major *coup d'état*. Even though he couldn't read most of the ancient writing, he knew he now possessed an artifact of immense importance, a prize that other men had died trying to find. He was reminded of the poor vagrant who showed up at the university some months ago trying to unload Banyon's entire cache of materials for an enormous sum of money. *Poor devil*, he smirked, remembering the fate of the old fellow. Of course Romano hadn't carried out the deed himself. That sort of business wasn't in him. His forte was ordering other people to take care of things that he would rather not handle personally. Suddenly he wondered about the fate of Banyon. He had no way of knowing whether Banyon survived the shooting or not. It would be just fine with him if Banyon were completely out of the picture although he never intended to do the man any harm. *It was, after all, just an accident.* Either way, there was nothing he could do about it now. What was done was done and none of them – not even Angela who had spilled coffee on him at the mall - had any clue as to his identity. He was home free and, at the moment, that was all he cared about.

Lifting the carry-on bag up to his chest, and clasping it closely, he laughed silently to himself and hailed a cab. The taxi rolled up to the curb and stopped. He was just about to open the door when a black limousine pulled up behind the cab. Three men in dark suits stepped out and walked toward him.

"Mr. Romano?" one of the men asked.

"Yes?" Romano replied, nervously. He tried to step back but there was no escape as the three men gathered closely, surrounding him.

"This way, please," said the first man, grabbing Romano firmly by the arm. They escorted him to the limousine.

"What the…?" Romano protested as he was forcefully ushered

into the back seat.

The three men then climbed into the limousine and closed the doors.

The car remained at the curb for several minutes. Inside, behind the black tinted windows, one of the men held a moist handkerchief against Romano's face. Romano struggled only briefly before slumping down into the seat, unconscious.

When the door of the limo opened once again, one of the men stepped out with the cylinder in hand and walked into the terminal. Reaching into his pocket he pulled out the transponder tag that was keyed by a corresponding number to an electronic security locker. A few minutes later he returned to the limousine. The window slid down. He leaned in and spoke to the other two men.

"It's done," he said. "I'll wait here for Banyon." Then he looked at Romano, still slumped and unconscious in the seat across from the two men. "You know what to do with him."

The man then turned and reentered the terminal as the limousine drove away.

A few hours later a gentle nudge in the ribs brought Romano back to consciousness. He was lying on his stomach. He groaned as his eyes opened slightly. It was nearly dark. Then came another nudge in the side from a well-shined black shoe.

"Hey you!" came a man's voice.

Romano rolled over and looked up at the uniformed police officer towering over him.

"Hey you!" the officer said again. "You can't sleep here. Move along."

Romano struggled to sit up. Looking around, he found himself in an alley between two buildings. "Wha...? Where am I?"

"If you need to sleep it off, there's a homeless shelter just two blocks away."

Romano got to his feet, still confused. "A homeless...?"

"The Seattle Gospel Mission," the officer said.

The words echoed inside Romano's head. Even in his barely conscious state the irony was not lost on him. *Christ, you gotta be kidding!*

Now that Romano was on his feet the officer got a better look at him. He seemed to be dressed a little too well to be just another down and out street person. "You got any I.D.?" the officer inquired.

"Huh?"

"Identification."

"Oh, uh, yes." Romano reached for his wallet but it was gone. He checked his inside coat pocket for his passport but it was also missing. "But I... I..." he stammered.

Now somewhat suspicious, the officer noticed the carry-on bag still lying on the ground. "What's in the bag?"

"The bag?" Romano replied. "Oh! My bag. Nothing. Just personal stuff."

"Mind if I have a look?"

"Um, well," Romano started, stooping down to retrieve the bag, "there's nothing in it, really."

"I think maybe you should let me have a look," the officer insisted.

Romano knew if he took off running the officer would catch him and that would only mean more interrogation. He didn't need any more trouble. At this point he was only just beginning to realize what had happened to him. *The limousine!* He suspected they'd taken the cylinder and the scroll but he didn't know for sure. Reluctantly, he handed over the bag, trying to think of an explanation for the cylinder and scroll if they were still in there. The officer unzipped the bag and looked inside.

"I thought you said there was personal stuff in here."

"Well, like I said, it's nothing."

The officer turned the bag upside down and shook it. "I can see that."

Romano gasped. "What!" he said, grabbing the bag from the officer. As he feared, the bag was indeed empty. A hollow feeling came over him. His knees buckled and he nearly collapsed.

The officer grabbed his arm and steadied him. "You don't look so good. You want to tell me what's going on? How did you get here? Where's your identification?"

Romano knew the truth was not only too unbelievable, it was dangerous. It was the last thing he needed to reveal. "Look," he said, trying to think quickly, "my name is Frank Romano. I'm a Jesuit priest at Queen City University. I was on my way to, uh, that homeless shelter you mentioned. And I guess I was mugged. All I want to do is go home now."

347

The officer eyed him with suspicion. Romano was dressed in a casual, light brown suit with a pale yellow shirt, opened at the neck with no necktie. "You don't look like any priest to me," he said.

"Yeah, well," Romano responded, beginning to lose patience, "when you're in your street clothes I don't suppose you look like a cop either."

The officer considered the comment. "You want me to fill out a report?"

"A what?"

"A police report. Do you want to report the assault? You were mugged, right? Somebody robbed you?"

Romano shook his head. "No. I don't want to file a report. Can't you just let me go? I have business to take care of."

"I thought you said you just wanted to go home."

"That's right."

"Well, which is it? Business or go home?"

Romano was reaching the end of his patience but struggled to maintain a civil attitude. "Both," he said. "I have to go home and take care of some business."

Having no good reason to detain him any longer, the officer relented. "All right. Go on, then. Get the hell out of here."

Romano turned and headed down the street, still somewhat dazed and completely distraught. *Christ almighty!* he cursed to himself. *I don't believe this! This isn't happening! Fuck!*

The officer stood watching him for a few minutes. *Jesuit priest*, he thought, shaking his head. *And I'm the Pope.*

~54~

On the flight back to Seattle from Kennedy International, it was Angela who slept while Banyon was wide awake. He couldn't seem to quiet his mind. It was impossible for him to accept the idea that they'd reached the end of their journey in vain. There had to be a reason for this most recent turn of events. Although, for the life of him, he couldn't guess what it might be. Finally he decided to have a look at the book he purchased from the bookstore back at the village of Rennes le Chateau. He was still curious about the enigmatic subtitle: *Target Earth*.

Once he began reading the book he found it so captivating he couldn't put it down. The information it contained was stunning. When it came to the subject of that mysterious little village in the South of France, the authors, David Wood and Ian Campbell, had uncovered clues and connected dots that no one else had even thought of. He was fascinated to learn that Wood and Campbell often found themselves at dead ends during the course of their investigation. When this occurred, despite their meticulous mathematics and dogged research, it was good old intuition, seemingly out-of-the-blue hunches, that came to the rescue. Banyon could relate to that.

Much of the first part of the book dealt with the history of Rennes le Chateau as the authors introduced the reader to the related mysteries. Banyon was able to skip over most of it but he was intrigued by the abundance of related information interspersed throughout that section of the text. There seemed to be no end to the connections with ancient Egypt and its pantheon of gods and goddesses. Isis, of course, played a major role as her story weaved in and out of the Rennes mystery like threads through an intricate and ancient tapestry.

As interesting as the material was, he nevertheless caught himself speed-reading through much of it. Then a certain paragraph jumped out and stopped him cold. Some writers, the paragraph revealed, had speculated that a device of some sort - *which can only be described as a 'Time Portal'*, to use Wood's words - may be hidden in the area of Rennes le Chateau. *Time portal? Time portal?* He repeated the words over and over to himself. It struck him as a bizarre notion. Still, there was something hauntingly familiar about the idea. As he puzzled over it, two thoughts hit him almost simultaneously. First, the strange recurring dream flashed through his mind followed by an urge to go back and read the McClintock notes. He reached into his briefcase and pulled out a copy of the notes. Near the bottom of the old notepaper was the phrase: TIME CHARIOT = 121 = WHEEL OF TIME. *What the...?* He tried to recall the strange object in his dream. All he could conjur up was a vague image of something like a rod with what seemed like crossbars on it. Now that he thought about it, it almost seemed like an antenna. He shook his head. *That doesn't make any sense. Why would there be an antenna under the ocean?* Suddenly the question became the answer. *The ocean?* This was the first time he'd actually understood the dark cold water in the dream. *Yes! It's an ocean!* Unfortunately, it didn't help clarify matters and he certainly couldn't see any connection between the object in his dream and a *time chariot* or a *wheel of time*, for that matter. He did find it very curious, however, that McClintock had even written such phrases in his notes. They weren't part of the Ezekiel Code. *Had McClintock also come across Wood and Campbell's book?* He turned to the front of the book and found it was published in 1994. *Hmm... I suppose it's possible*, he mused. *Another coincidence?* He smiled as he recalled, once again, Kline's admonition that there were no coincidences. He pondered the matter for a few minutes then turned his attention back to the book. He was anxious to find out something that would explain the strange subtitle. He skimmed quickly over several pages dealing with some fairly heavy mathematics and geometry that he barely understood. A couple chapters later he found what he was looking for.

"Angela," he whispered. She didn't move. He nudged her gently in the arm. "Angela?" he whispered a little louder.

She squirmed in her seat and rolled her head sleepily toward him. With half opened eyes, she muttered, "Hmm? Are we there yet?"

"Not yet. But check this out."

"What? What is it?" she asked, a little annoyed at being awakened from a good sleep.

"A comet."

Angela furrowed her brow and squinted toward the window. "What?"

"No. Not out there. Here." He tapped the page of the book with his finger. "The reason for the subtitle, *Target Earth*. These guys figured out the geometry of Rennes le Chateau is a warning that a comet is going to hit the earth!"

Still half asleep, she said, "A comet?"

"Yes! It says here..."

She slumped back into the seat and turned her head away. "Maybe you can tell me about it later, okay?"

"But…" he started. It was too late. She had already closed her eyes and was gone.

He looked over at her and smiled, knowing how exhausted she must be. He probably shouldn't have tried to awaken her. It could wait. But he couldn't.

The idea that the Rennes mystery had anything at all to do with an impending comet impact was a complete surprise to him. Of all the information they'd read about the mystery of Rennes le Chateau they had never seen this mentioned. Yet there it was. Wood and Campbell had seemingly discovered something no one else had even come close to finding. *Hell,* he thought, *no one else even suspected it was there to be found in the first place!* In truth, Wood and Campbell didn't know it was there to be found either. Not for a long time. It was almost by an act of divine inspiration that they were led to the discovery.

For Wood and Campbell, the sequence of connecting the right dots began innocently enough. One night, exhausted from a day of intense research, Wood was interrupted by his daughter when she brought him a cup of tea. Under her arm she carried a book by the 18th century French author and science fiction visionary, Jules Verne. For some strange reason that even Wood could not fathom, the name Jules Verne seemed to jump off the cover and lit a spark in his otherwise rather fatigued mind. He suddenly found himself drawn to the name and wondered if Jules Verne had any connection to the mystery of Rennes le Chateau. It was an odd thing to consider but he felt compelled to look into the matter.

Wood soon learned, with the help of his friend and fellow researcher, Ian Campbell, that Verne had apparently been well connected with various members of certain occult groups such as the Theosophical Society and even the Order of the Golden Dawn which, at one time, was headed up by none other than the infamous occultist and self-proclaimed *Beast of the Apocalypse*, Aleister Crowley. Wood discovered that, according to one writer, Verne's works were loaded with hidden codes which, to the initiated, were seen as clues to the fact that he had some specific knowledge about the secret of Rennes le Chateau. Moreover, Wood learned that Verne's famous book, *Journey to the Center of the Earth*, contained hidden references to Set, the ancient Egyptian god of destruction. As fate would have it, Wood and Campbell had already made a connection between what is known as the Paris Meridian and this same god, Set. The meridian, like the north-south meridian that today runs through Greenwich, England, was at one time used as the zero point of longitude by ancient mariners. This particular meridian, running through France, had acquired a strange connection to religious matters and also to the color red. These two facts, for a number of reasons, provided the clues that eventually led Wood and Campbell to suspect a connection between the meridian and the Egyptian god, Set. Wood had already suspected a connection with Set because the legend of Set cutting Osiris into 15 pieces seemed to fit with the 15 points that defined the circumference of the circle of churches in the area surrounding Rennes le Chateau. They also discovered the Paris Meridian just happened to intersect with the ground geometry of the Isis Pentagram at a particular angle. As they worked out the resulting geometry, more clues began to unfold. Now, with the information from Jules Verne regarding Set, the brother of Osiris, they had confirmation of their suspicions from yet another source. Set seemed to be playing a very important part in the mystery. That much was known. The question now was, *why?*

~55~

I t was after 2 o'clock in the morning by the time Banyon and Angela arrived at the airport in Seattle. Having retrieved their luggage they were making their way through the terminal when a man clumsily bumped into Banyon. Banyon stumbled backwards, dropped his luggage, and landed on the floor, nearly knocking Angela over in the process.

"I'm terribly sorry!" the man said as he grabbed Banyon's hand to help him up.

By the time Banyon regained his composure and looked around, the man had disappeared around a corner and down a flight of stairs.

"Idiot!" Banyon said, angrily. He bent down to pick up his suitcase when he realized he was holding something in his hand. "What the...? he said, looking at the object. "What is this?"

"Let me see," Angela said.

The flat plastic object was about the size of a credit card. He handed it to her.

"It's a transponder tag," she said.

"A what?"

"A transponder tag. An electronic key to a locker here at the airport. Look, here's the locker number."

She handed the tag back to him. He looked at it. Sure enough there was a number imprinted along the side of the tag: 000144.

"You gotta be kidding me," he said. "Look at that number! What the hell's going on here?"

Angela was as confused as he was. "Where did you get it?"

"I don't know. That guy bumped into me and..." He paused, mid-sentence, and mentally replayed the incident that had just taken place.

"And what?"

"He must have put this in my hand when he helped me up."

"On purpose?" she asked. Or didn't he realize it? Maybe it belonged to him and now he's wondering what happened to it."

Banyon considered that for a moment. "Yeah, maybe."

"Maybe?"

"Well, look at that number!" he said. "Is that just a coincidence?"

"Hmm... well, I know someone who wouldn't think so."

He nodded. "Yeah, so do I."

"So what do you think? What should we do?"

Banyon turned the transponder tag over and over in his hand as he thought about it. "I say we see what's in the locker."

Angela agreed.

When they located the bank of lockers they began looking for the number that matched the transponder.

"Here it is!" Angela said, pointing to the top row of lockers.

"All right. Now how do we work this thing?"

At the end of the bank of lockers they found a computerized Pay-Point terminal.

Banyon stood back, surprised. "I'm going to have to *pay* for this?"

"No," Angela explained. "It's already paid for. Just insert the tag and the locker will open."

Banyon slid the tag into the slot on the terminal and a small green light on locker number 000144 began to flash. They walked back to the locker and pushed the button. The door popped open a fraction of an inch. Banyon reached up and opened it further so he could see inside. He stepped back in shock. "What the...!"

"What is it? What's the matter?" Angela asked. Even standing on her toes the locker was too high for her to get a good glimpse.

Banyon couldn't believe what he was looking at. "It's the cylinder," he said, incredulously.

"What? No way! Let me see!"

He reached in and took it out. They stared at it in disbelief.

"Oh my god," Angela said. "Is that really it? Open it and see if the scroll is inside."

Banyon was almost afraid to open it for fear that maybe an empty cylinder was all he was going to get.

"Come on!" she prodded.

Banyon twisted the wooden plug back and forth until it popped out. Suddenly his face lit up with a grin. He tipped the cylinder upside down and the ancient parchment slid forward. Grasping it gently, he slid it the rest of the way out and handed the cylinder to Angela. Carefully unrolling the parchment he recognized the writing was in Hebrew. For a moment he was speechless. This was the one thing he thought he'd never see again. "How...?" he started to ask.

"One guess," Angela said.

Banyon looked at her. "The Nine."

"Gotta be."

"The guy who knocked me over."

Angela nodded.

"Unbelievable," he said. "But what about the guy who stole this from us in the first place? The bastard who shot me! Where the hell is *he*?"

Angela shrugged. "Good question."

A sudden paranoia ran through Banyon's entire body. "Oh man," he said, looking around. "We gotta get this out of here. Now!" He carefully slid the scroll back into the cylinder and tucked it into his suitcase. "Let's get a cab and get home before this dream turns into a nightmare."

As if on cue, a taxi was waiting just outside the door. In a few minutes they were situated comfortably in the back seat and the cab rolled out toward the highway. Almost immediately a black limousine pulled up into the now vacant parking space and sat there, ominously, silently, waiting.

The man who knocked Banyon over, and who had been watching them all along, emerged from the shadows, climbed into the limo and made his phone call.

"Misson accomplished," he said. He closed his cellphone, nodded to the driver, and the mysterious limo headed off into the night.

~56~

Banyon looked out the window of the cab. Even in the dark it was good to see familiar streets again. He reached out and held Angela's hand. "Can you believe any of this?" he said. "I mean, I can't believe we've got the scroll!"

She gave a little laugh. "I'm ready to believe just about anything anymore."

Banyon nodded. He knew exactly how she felt.

After a few minutes Angela turned to him, "So what's this about a comet?"

"You really want to hear about all that now?"

"Good a time as any," she shrugged.

"Well, ok then." He took the book out of his briefcase and told her some of what he'd learned.

She raised her eyebrows. "Wow! That's really interesting. But why was Set so important to all of this?"

He explained that Wood and Campbell had uncovered several clues in ancient legends about major cataclysmic events brought about by great celestial dragons or, in modern terms, meteors and comets.

The Greek god ,Typhon, seemed to be connected with such events and the Egyptian version of the same god was called *Set*. There was even a Hebrew version called *Seth*. In every case this Typhon-Set-Seth was the *destroyer god*.

"And look at this," he said. He pulled a folded piece of paper from his pocket and handed it to her.

While reading through the book on the plane Banyon had noticed Wood and Campbell's mathematics were revealing the number 56 as something significant. They also found the same number mentioned, by an ancient historian, in association with Typhon. The number came up again and again. It was the number of post holes in the ground surrounding Stonehenge in England, and it was the number of face stones on a tomb near Rennes le Chateau which was pictured in the famous painting by Poussin which, itself, was yet another part of the mystery. And last, but not least, it was the alphanumeric value of the name, ISIS. And, if that wasn't enough, 56 was 95 upside down, as he and Angela had noted at the place where they dug up the scroll. Combined, 95 plus 56 came to 151, the very alphanumeric value of the phrase SOUTH OF FRANCE and the name of the village, RENNES LE CHATEAU.

Angela reached into her purse and took out a small penlight. She unfolded the paper and read what Banyon had scribbled while she'd been asleep on the plane:

ISIS = 56 = COMET

"That's a pretty good hit," she said. "But from what you've told me, Isis isn't associated with a comet or anything like that."

"No, you're right" he said. "But it did seem fitting that Isis would figure into the picture with the number 56. And check out the stuff below that. Considering that the Hebrew god, Seth, was the same as the Egyptian god, Set, the god of destruction, the numbers just fell so neatly into place."

Angela focused the penlight a little further down the page. He was right. The phrase correlations were remarkable and the numbers were certainly familiar by now and each one was a multiple of 9:

COMET SETH = 108 = GEOMETRY

THE COMET OF SETH = 162 = THE DESTROYER

THE RETURN OF THE DEATH STAR = 279 = RETURN OF THE DESTROYER

Angela shook her head. "Those are amazing correlations!"

Banyon nodded. "I thought so too."

"So this is it?" she asked. "This is the answer to the whole mystery of Rennes le Chateau? That the earth is going to be destroyed by a comet?"

The taxi driver couldn't help overhearing their conversation. *What kind of nuts have I picked up this time?* He cast a glance at them in his rearview mirror. Banyon caught the glance and nudged Angela with a nod toward the driver. She grinned and got the message. They continued the conversation in low whispers.

"I don't know if that's the whole answer," Banyon said quietly. "This Rennes le Chateau thing seems like mysteries layered upon mysteries. Some of which may not even be related to the others. I don't know. It's very strange. But from what I can see here," he said, tapping on the image of *Target Earth* on the cover of the book, "I think these guys, Wood and Campbell, are spot on. There's no doubt in my mind that they're right about the message of the comet encoded in the geometry of the Isis Pentagram. When you read it you'll see what I mean. And there's something else, too."

"What's that?"

"Are you ready for this?"

"I don't know. Give me a try."

"Some researchers have speculated that some sort of a time portal or maybe a dimensional vortex, or something like that, exists in the area around the village."

"The village? Rennes le Chateau?"

Banyon nodded. "Weird, huh?"

"Yeah. A time portal? What makes them think so?"

"I don't know. The book didn't really elaborate on it. But when I read that, I had a weird feeling. It rang a bell and then I remembered."

"Remembered what?"

Banyon reached into his briefcase and handed her the copy of the McClintock notes. He pointed out the phrase: TIME CHARIOT = 121 = WHEEL OF TIME.

"Well," she smiled, "It might be pretty weird, but at least now these two phrases make some kind of sense. I mean, if any of this makes sense. At least now it's in a context with something else. But gees, it's getting a little Star-Treky, don't you think?"

Banyon laughed. "Yeah, but there it is. You know what I mean?"

The driver, now curious about all the whispering, gave them another quizzical look in his rear view mirror. Banyon stuffed the book and the notes back into his briefcase and they didn't say anything more during the rest of the ride home.

Home, Banyon thought to himself. Just the thought of it made the cold night seem a little warmer. *I can't wait to get home.*

~*57*~

After his encounter with the police officer in the alley, Romano staggered on down the road. Just as the officer had said, the Seattle Gospel Mission appeared just two blocks away on the other side of the street. Even now, at this time of night, a light was on inside the building. The night staff, of course, was on duty. Without his wallet or a dime to his name, Romano felt helpless but defiant. *I'll be damned if I'm going in there!* he thought to himself. *I'll call a taxi to take me home. I have money in the house. I can pay the driver when we get there.* He looked around for a phone booth but couldn't find one. He walked another block past the shelter. Still no phone booth. He thought about walking a few blocks back the way he had just come but hesitated. He didn't want to see that officer again. It was getting cold and the fog was beginning to settle in. He was shivering now. *Damn!* There seemed to be no option. He would have to swallow some pride and ask to use the phone at the homeless shelter.

As soon as he approached the front door another figure came walking down the street toward him. The man was bundled up in a heavy coat and seemed to be carrying some kind of luggage. As the man passed under a streetlight Romano could see now it wasn't luggage. It was a guitar case. The two men met at the door.

"Evenin'" said Old Tom, returning from a gig at *Charley's Place*. "Don't think I've seen you 'round here before. Looks like you could use a hand up. Come on in." He pushed the door open.

Romano hesitated.

"Well," Tom said, "don't just stand there lettin' the heat out! You comin' in or ain't you?"

Romano took a deep breath. The last thing he wanted was to be seeking sanctuary in the enemy's camp. It was secular sacrilege. Worse than that. It was a blow to the ego. "Yeah, all right," he said, stepping inside the door. "Just so you know, I'm not one of your street people. I'm actually a Jesuit priest who ran into a bit of trouble. I just want to use the phone. That's all."

Tom looked the man up and down. He didn't know for sure what a Jesuit priest should look like but for some reason it didn't seem like this fellow was lying. Tom had a sense for that sort of thing. Just a sixth sense one picks up after years on the street. "Jesuit, eh?" Tom said, resting his guitar case up against the wall and hanging his old peacoat on top of it. "Funny."

Romano looked at him. "What's funny?"

"All the time I've spent hangin' 'round here I've never heard anything about Jesuits. Now it's come up twice in just the last couple weeks."

"What do you mean?"

"Oh, it ain't nothin'. Just some ol' geezer came wanderin' in here a while back, askin' me if I knew any Jesuits." Then he laughed. "Like I would know any Jesuits! Ha! What do I look like? The Pope?"

"Not exactly," Romano said, anxious to cut the chitchat and get to a phone.

"To bad you weren't here then," Tom said. "Maybe you could have helped the poor guy out."

"I'm sure," Romano said. It never occurred to him that the old geezer Tom referred to was the vagrant whose greed and ignorance had gotten him killed at Romano's behest. In an incredible twist of fate it was also this same vagrant who was ultimately responsible for Romano ending up here, now, at the shelter where the poor vagrant had once come searching for a Jesuit! The irony, unrecognized by either Old Tom or Romano, was thick enough to cut with a knife.

Romano was running out of patience. "Where's the phone?" he demanded. "I need to call a cab!"

~58~

The porch light at the front of Banyon's house had burned out while they were away. Fumbling around in the dark, Banyon finally got the key in the lock and swung the front door open. They stepped in and Angela flipped the light switch.

"Oh, *yes!*" she cried with a burst of orgasmic enthusiasm. She dropped her luggage in the middle of the floor, plopped herself down on the sofa and let out a long sigh. The comfortable, warm surroundings of their living room were a welcomed sight. "I didn't know how much I missed it!"

Banyon smiled and sat next to her. "Yeah," he said, surveying the room. "I guess I didn't either."

Angela reached over and held his hand. "How's your shoulder?"

"You know, with everything that's happened tonight I'd really forgotten about it." He rotated his shoulder a few times and stretched his arm. "It hurts a little but it's a lot better."

"You know what you ought to do?"

"What?"

"Call Father Caldwell first thing in the morning and tell him the good news."

Banyon looked at his watch. It was nearly 5 o'clock in the morning. He chuckled. "It already *is* the first thing in the morning!"

Angela laughed. "I know but give the poor guy a few more hours."

Banyon agreed and glanced over at his suitcase. "What do you say we have a good look at our hard earned prize?"

"Absolutely!"

Banyon got the suitcase and flipped it open. He took out the old copper cylinder and set it on the coffee table in front of them.

"Well, come on!" Angela said. "Aren't you going to open it?"

"Just savoring the moment," he said, smiling. He rubbed his hands together, slowly, as if he were about to perform a surgery. Then he picked up the cylinder and twisted the wooden plug off the end.

Reaching in with two fingers he slid the ancient scroll out and carefully flattened it on the table. He expected it to be quite fragile but it seemed to have a suppleness about it. "What do you think this is made from?" he asked.

Angela examined it, rubbing her fingers across its surprisingly smooth surface. "I don't know. Some sort of animal skin? But like really well preserved? I don't know."

"Wish I knew how to read Hebrew," he said. "I'm dying to know what the hell this says! We have the key to our whole mystery right here in our hands and we can't read it!" He sat back. "God, this is frustrating."

"Do you know anyone who can read Hebrew?"

"Not personally."

"Maybe Father Caldwell can recommend someone."

"Good idea."

"Or even Professor Kline. He seems to have his finger in just about everything. Maybe he knows someone. You should call him anyway. He doesn't even know we've been gone! He'll be blown away when he finds out what we've done!"

Banyon grinned. "You're right. I do need to call him." He ran his fingers over the old scroll like a blind man reading braille. "One way or another we're going to find out what the hell this thing says."

~59~

The next morning the phone woke Banyon and Angela from a sound sleep. Banyon looked at his watch. It was 11:14 *a.m.* He reached over and picked up the receiver.

"Hello?"

"Zeke! You ol' devil you! Just calling to make sure you guys made it home all right."

"Daniel? Hey. Yeah, we're here. I was going to call you."

"You sound a little groggy. You all right? How's the shoulder?"

"We were sleeping when you called. Didn't realize it was after eleven already. The shoulder's much better, thanks."

"Still sleeping? Sorry ol' man. Didn't mean to wake you up."

Angela rolled over. "Who is it?"

"Caldwell," Banyon whispered.

"Hi Daniel!" she said loud enough for him to hear.

Caldwell laughed. "Tell her I said hello."

"I will," Banyon said. "Listen, are you sitting down?"

"Should I be? What now?"

"You're not going to believe this."

"Try me. What is it?"

"We have the scroll."

"What!"

"Yeah."

"But how…?"

Banyon related the whole incident about getting knocked over at the airport and how it led to the discovery of the scroll in a locker.

"My god," Caldwell said. "That's great! But I don't understand."

"The only thing we can figure is that the guy who bumped into me, and passed the transponder key to me, must have been somehow connected with the Nine. I don't know how he or they or whoever managed to get the scroll, but there it was and here it is. The only thing is, I can't read Hebrew. We were wondering if you knew anyone who could translate the writing for us."

"Unbelievable. Well, unfortunately the only person I know who could translate the writing is here in New York. A rabbi I happen to know. But that won't do you much good way over there on the other side of the continent. And listen, if you go looking for someone near you, be careful. If what you have there is truly authentic, it's probably worth a fortune. You'll have to find someone you know you can trust."

"Yeah, we thought about that. We do have a friend here who might know someone. Professor Kline. We told you about him, remember?"

"I remember. I wish I could offer some more help but… well, just be careful. And keep me posted. You hear? This is incredibly exciting!"

"You'll be the first to know when we find out something."

"All right. Excellent."

They finished their conversation and Banyon hung up the phone. "Well," he said, turning to Angela, "he couldn't help us find a translator."

Angela nodded. "I kind of figured that from the conversation. So let's hope our professor friend knows someone."

"And if he does," Banyon cautioned, "will it be someone we can trust? Like Daniel said, if this thing is what we assume it is, it's probably priceless."

Angela got up and put on her robe. "Well, we could just sell it and buy an island somewhere and let someone else be the Chosen One for a while."

Banyon laughed. "There's a good idea."

"You want some coffee?" she asked on her way down the stairs.

"Sounds good. I'll be right down."

Banyon got dressed and joined Angela at the kitchen table. After a cup of coffee and a light breakfast he walked into the living room and called Kline. Kline had already been informed of the situation in France and the recovery of the scroll at the airport. The Nine had kept him updated but now he was doing his best to feign great surprise as Banyon recounted the entire journey.

"So," Banyon said, "we were hoping you might know someone who could translate the writing on the scroll."

"As a matter of fact, I do," Kline said. "His name is Rabbi Feld. He teaches a course in religious history at the Evergreen State College."

"The Evergreen State College?"

"Yes. You know. They used to call it *that hippie school in the woods.*"

Banyon remembered. It was an alternative college tucked away on a secluded wooded campus down by Olympia, the state capital, about an hour and a half drive from Seattle. Because of it's unconventional and controversial educational philosophy it didn't take long for the school to become populated with the young hip crowd from every part of the country. Long hair, beards, bell-bottoms, and hippie love-beads seemed to be the uniform of the day on campus for the first few years. But, as with so many things that come along and cause a big stir at first, it eventually subsided into the background noise of daily life in the society at large. These days Banyon, like most folks, had completely forgotten it was there even though it continued to quietly receive many awards for its high standards and academic achievements.

"Ah! Yes, of course," Banyon said. "The ol' hippie college in the woods! How could I forget? So this Rabbi Feld, he can be trusted to keep this confidential?"

"Not to worry. I'll explain the whole situation to him. He'll understand, I'm sure."

"You're going to tell him everything?" Banyon asked, not really sure that was such a good idea. "How do you know he won't think it's all a bunch of nonsense? I mean, it's a pretty wild tale, you know."

"Yes," Kline agreed, "but you don't know Rabbi Feld."

"What do you mean?"

"I mean he's very much into the old Jewish mysticism. A student of the Kabalah and, of course, he's familiar with gematria in the Hebrew tradition. You two should get along quite well, actually."

"Gematria. No kidding. How convenient."

"Indeed."

"Well, when can we meet this Rabbi Feld?"

"When would you like to meet him?"

"The sooner the better."

"Excellent. I'll call him this afternoon and get back to you."

Banyon hung up the phone and lit a cigarette as Angela walked into the room.

"Well?" she asked.

"Well," he said, somewhat surprised at how easily the pieces seemed to be suddenly falling into place, "apparently we've got our translator."

~60~

In the small meeting room behind the door at the back of room 306 at Queen City University, Salvo, Beck and Montabeau sat silently stunned as Romano rolled out the story of his failed escapade over the past several days. They'd been wondering where he disappeared to. A few inquiries revealed he'd arranged for a short leave but they had no idea why.

Salvo couldn't believe his ears. "You had the scroll in your possession? You actually saw it?"

"Saw it?" Romano exclaimed. "I had it in my damn hands! All the way across the Atlantic Ocean! Then at the airport I was accosted by these bastards who knocked me out with chloroform, stole the scroll and dumped me in a goddam alley."

Beck shook his head. "Unbelievable. Who did this?"

A grim look crossed Romano's face. "Banyon's guardian angels. Who do you think?"

Beck shook his head knowingly. "The Nine."

"But how did they know?" Montabeau asked.

Romano sighed. "They always know. Somehow they always know."

"You suppose Banyon has it now?" Salvo asked. "The scroll, I mean."

"Of course he does!" Montabeau snapped with his typical cocky attitude. "After all he is the *Chosen One!*"

Romano glared at Montabeau. Even several days and thousands of miles wasn't enough to make Romano's heart grow any fonder of him. But he knew Montabeau was right. He didn't know how the transfer was made but there was no doubt in his mind that somehow Banyon had ended up with the precious scroll. With resignation, Romano acquiesced to Montabeau's outburst with an affirmative nod.

"So what now?" Salvo asked.

Again Montabeau cut in. "I say forget the whole thing. I mean, what's the point? The Nine have eyes everywhere. Sooner or later somebody's going to get killed over this thing and it sure as hell isn't going to be me! I can tell you that!"

The comment drew a disgusted glare from Romano. "Nobody's asking you to do anything," he said. "Except to keep your damned mouth shut."

Montabeau returned Romano's glare but said nothing. Then Montebeau turned abruptly and walked out of the room slamming the door behind him.

The fact that young Montabeau had personal, if tenuous, connections to a couple of important people in the upper levels of the university's hierarchy was a constant concern for Romano. If Montabeau should happen to drop a word to the right people about the group's covert agenda it would immediately reach the desk of the Jesuit General in Rome. Romano, Beck, and Salvo hated to even think what the consequences would be if that should happen. Romano shot a look of concern to the others. "That boy's beginning to worry me," he groaned.

"Well then," Salvo said, "you'll be pleased to know what I learned while you were away."

Romano looked puzzled. "About Montabeau?"

"Yes. About Brother Montabeau."

Romano sat up in his chair and leaned forward. "Well? What is it?"

Salvo's face slowly contorted into a grin that would have put the devil to shame. Reaching into the inner breast pocket of his jacket he pulled out a Polaroid photo and handed it to Romano.

Romano stared at it, trying to reconcile in his own mind what his eyes were seeing. In a few moments he uttered, almost in a whisper, "Oh, Jesus."

~61~

The door was wide open when Banyon and Angela arrived at Rabbi Feld's office on the second floor of the main library on the campus of Evergreen State College. The unmistakable scent of sandalwood incense wafted out into the hall.

"Come in!" Feld called out to them from inside the office.

The office was small, just big enough to accommodate a desk, a bookshelf, and a couple of rather plain wooden chairs pushed up against the wall opposite the desk.

They walked in and found the rabbi sitting behind his desk apparently playing a game of chess with an invisible partner. For some reason Banyon had imagined the rabbi would be a younger man. This man appeared to be well into his sixties. He was perhaps a little more than five feet tall, a bit on the stocky side, dressed in dark pants and a black knitted sweater over a wrinkled white shirt. His graying hair, had it been just bit longer, would have given Einstein a run for his money. Either he was having a bad hair day or he was just another one of those eccentric intellectual types that Banyon had observed on occasion, the type of men who never seemed to learn how to use a comb.

The rabbi spoke again without looking up from his chessboard. "Make yourselves comfortable," he said. Slowly stroking his salt-and-pepper beard, he contemplated his next move against his invisible opponent.

"Thank you," Banyon said. "I'm…"

The rabbi held up a hand, cutting Banyon off in mid-sentence. "One moment, please," he said in a hushed, self-absorbed tone.

Banyon and Angela looked at each other and shrugged. They seated themselves in the two chairs facing the desk.

The rabbi continued to concentrate on his game, all the while stroking his beard. It reminded Angela of how, as a child, she used to watch her grandfather gently petting his favorite long-haired cat as it laid comfortably stretched out across his lap.

"Oy vey!" the rabbi burst out, throwing his hands into the air. He was clearly frustrated. He pushed the chessboard to the side, leaned back in his old leather chair and finally looked up to address his guests. "So what's the use?" he said. "I can't even beat myself! You must be Mr. Banyon and you must be Miss Martin."

Banyon smiled. "Yes. Zeke Banyon. This is my fiancé, Angela."

Rabbi Feld sat silently for a moment, rocking slightly back and forth in his chair. Banyon wasn't sure if he was praying, or sizing them up, or still trying to figure out how to protect his last bishop from being taken by either one of his alter ego's two knights. Finally the rabbi leaned forward, folding his arms on top of the desk. "Our mutual friend, Alan Kline, tells me you've come into possession of a rather interesting artifact."

Banyon reached down and opened his briefcase. "Yes," he said, pulling out the cylinder and removing the ancient papyrus. "We believe it could be the...'

Feld finished the sentence for him. "The lost scroll of Ezekiel. Yes, yes, so I've been told."

"You know of it?" Banyon asked, surprised.

The rabbi shrugged. "There have been rumors. Usually considered nonsense by most scholars."

"Then you don't think...?

"I don't know," Feld said. "Let's have a look."

Banyon got up and gently laid the old manuscript on the rabbi's desk. "We were hoping you could tell us what it says."

Feld studied it for a moment then briefly glanced up at Banyon and then back to the scroll. He mumbled under his breath. "Mm-Hmm. Mm-Hmm." He sounded like a medical doctor examining a patient. After several minutes he finally spoke. "Very...", he hesitated a long moment, "... interesting."

"Well?" Banyon said, anxious to hear the rabbi's opinion.

"The phrasing, the terminology... very interesting indeed. It does suggest the possibility...the *possibility*, mind you... I can't say for sure, but...", he paused again, "I'm going to need a few minutes."

"Of course," Banyon said. "Take all the time you need. Do you want us to leave? Should we come back later?"

Feld waved him off without looking up. His attention was glued to the parchment. "No. No, that's not necessary. Just give me a few minutes. There is a coffee dispenser just down the... hall... if you..." his voice trailed off as he became absorbed in his examination of the ancient text.

Banyon looked at Angela. She nodded. "Sounds good to me," she said. "Why don't you wait here. I'll go get it."

She returned in a few minutes with the coffee and they sat quietly, waiting. The pendulum on the wall clock ticked off the minutes as Feld studied the writing on the scroll. Ten minutes. Fifteen. Twenty. The rabbi seemed to be off somewhere in another world, oblivious to everything around him. He pulled a couple of reference books from the shelf behind his desk and thumbed back and forth between pages. He jotted some notes on a yellow legal pad. "Mm-Hmm. Mm-Hmm." Twenty-five minutes. Thirty. Suddenly the clock chimed. Banyon glanced up. It was 11:30 a.m. Angela shifted in her chair, swirling the last drop of coffee around in the bottom of her paper cup.

Finally Rabbi Feld put down his pen and sat back, staring at his own handwriting on the yellow note pad. "Just another minute," he said. He swung his chair around to access the computer on the small table beside his desk. In a moment he began typing the translation, referring again and again to his notes. When he'd finished he printed out two copies. "Very interesting," he said, handing a copy to Banyon and one to Angela. "If this is as authentic as it appears it might be – and again I stress, *might* be - then it is very interesting, indeed."

Banyon and Angela each read their copy of the rabbi's translation:

I looked, and behold, the glory of the Lord appeared in the clouds like a chariot and I was not afraid. It descended with grace and speed coming as it were from the direction of the morning star. And as I stood before the miraculous vision I saw it was as a wheel sideways within another wheel sideways and they gleamed like burnished bronze. The two wheels turned in opposite directions, one within the other as they turned. A dome with the appearance of polished copper sat upon the top of the wheels like a crown with nine eyes all about it's rim. And above the dome stood a staff with six crosses, one above the other.

And a voice spoke unto me saying, this miracle is for a generation yet to come. Here is a great mystery for which you have no understanding. But you, Ezekiel, will write these words and preserve this vision for a generation yet to come. A son of man bearing your name will come in the days of that generation and to him will be given the knowledge to understand the mystery.

And when the voice had spoken I saw, as in a vision, a number. And the number was a hundred and forty and four. And the great wheels did spin in two directions at once, one within the other, and the chariot of the Lord lifted up and entered into the clouds. And I fell to the ground and was overtaken by sleep. And I dreamed I was taken to a distant land where I saw the chariot fall from the sky like a serpent and descend into the sea and it was swallowed up by the deep and I saw it no more.

Banyon's heart jumped to his throat. A chill shot through his body like a jolt of electricity. "Oh Jesus," he muttered. He looked at Angela. "The dream. It's the object in my dream! The object in the deep water! The rod with the six crossbars! The number 144!" His hands began to shake. Angela reached over to calm him.

"Are you all right?" Feld asked, peeking over his glasses.

Angela nodded. "He'll be okay. This is a bit of a shock."

"So I see," Feld said. "Not that it's any of my business, but you want to fill me in here?"

Trusting that the rabbi would hold all of this in confidence, Angela launched into a condensed version of the long story. Feld had heard much of it already from Kline. As a student of the ancient Hebrew gematria, Feld was skeptical about the idea of an English language version of this method of divination but he had to admit this case was compelling. The part about Banyon's dream was new. If Kline knew about it, he'd failed to mention it. The rabbi was fascinated. It certainly added another level of intrigue to the story.

Banyon was not hearing any of the conversation. The voices of Angela and Rabbi Feld were just muffled sounds in the distance.

His entire focus was on the words of the translation as he read them over and over again. The images of the recurring dream burned into his mind now more clearly and more detailed than ever. It was exactly as described in the scroll. His eyes kept returning to one particular part of the translation:

A son of man bearing your name will come in the days of that generation and to him will be given the knowledge to understand the mystery.

He could no longer dismiss what he now knew was the truth. *I bear the name of the ancient prophet. I am...* he paused, barely able to think the words, *...the Chosen One!* Not that dismissing it had been much of an option for quite some time but it was only now, at this very moment, that it came weighing down on him with such gravity. He wished he could feel elated. After all, it was a privilege. Wasn't it? Instead of elated, he only felt an enormous pressure. One question now loomed over him. *What the hell am I supposed to do about it?*

Suddenly the rabbi's phone rang and jarred Banyon back into the moment. The rabbi took the call and apologized for the interruption. "Something's come up that I must attend to right away," he said. "I'm sorry."

Banyon and Angela were disappointed that they couldn't spend more time with him. There were so many more questions. They thanked him for taking the time to provide the translation and left the office.

As they walked across the campus to the parking lot, Banyon handed the keys to Angela. "You drive."

She gave him a concerned look. "You okay?"

"Yeah."

They drove all the way home with hardly a word spoken. Angela could tell he was feeling burdened by the implications of the translation. She was beginning to feel the same way. The frightening episode at the warehouse. Banyon nearly getting killed at the site where they found the scroll. All of it had been plenty serious, almost deadly so. But now this. The revelation of the contents of the scroll was, in its own way, even more unsettling. Suddenly, her own future seemed uncertain. *My future?* she thought to herself. She almost laughed at the absurdity as it dawned on her, at that moment, that her future was just a tiny part of something much bigger. Something so big it was beyond comprehension. If all of this was what it appeared to be, then the real uncertainty was not just her future or Banyon's future but the future of the rest of the unsuspecting world. She laughed to herself again. *This is insane. It's crazy. What could possibly be coming next?* The question scared her. She only knew one thing. Whatever *it* was, it *was* coming.

~62~

As Banyon and Angela were on their way home from Feld's office, a meeting was taking place in a building just outside Vatican City. Bernard DuPont, the Jesuit General, was speaking with a small elite group of Jesuit priests.

"So, gentlemen," he continued, "I've just been informed that Mr. Banyon has met with a certain Rabbi Feld in the States. According to our American operative, the Rabbi successfully translated the contents of the scroll. This took place only minutes ago. Banyon and the woman, Angela, are on their way home at this moment. I immediately ordered the operative to arrange a delay in their arrival. This should provide enough time to get an audio surveillance unit in place at their home before they arrive. We need to know whatever they know."

"But the protocol," protested one of the priests. "What about the protocol? Direct intervention is prohibited by the prophecy."

"I understand your concern," DuPont responded. "But this intervention is not technically *direct*. It's being carried out by operatives unaffiliated with the Order of the Jesuits."

"But…" the priest tried to object.

"I understand," DuPont said again. "Believe me. I understand. However, the terms of the protocol are apparently malleable. We now know the Nine have been using outside operatives to influence events that have come to pass due to the involvement of Romano and his group. The Nine have suffered no negative consequences as a result of employing outside operatives and we simply cannot allow them to have an advantage over us. There is too much at stake here."

Another priest voiced a concern. "So what about Romano and Salvo and the others? They're intervening directly and nothing has happened to them either. Perhaps the protocol was merely an invention tacked onto the prophecy for reasons that no longer apply. Or perhaps never did apply."

DuPont nodded in agreement. "It's possible."

"And what about Romano and the others?" asked yet another priest. "They've come close to ruining everything. Shouldn't they be stopped? At least reprimanded in some way?"

DuPont paused a moment before answering. "I've decided to leave them alone for the time being. Given the extent of their involvement at this point they may turn out to be useful informants. They have a traitor amongst them. The young Montabeau has been in contact with me."

At that moment, a lone gunman sat poised in a shadowed camouflage of shrubs on a small hill in Seattle just above a freeway on-ramp. As soon as Angela made the turn and entered the on-ramp the sniper raised his rifle and squeezed off a shot. Angela swerved to the side of the ramp. The sudden movement startled Banyon out of his dazed thoughts. "What is it?" he asked. "What's the matter?"

Angela shook her head in disbelief. It was the last thing they needed on this already disturbing evening. "Looks like we've got a flat."

The gunman now had a stationary target. His orders were simply to delay Banyon's arrival home. The mission would seem to have been accomplished. But the gunman gave a cynical chuckle. *I could really delay his arrival. Permanently.* He raised his rifle and took aim at the window on the passenger side of the car. He now had Banyon's head directly in the crosshairs of his scope. He tightened his grip on the rifle and began to squeeze the trigger. The sound of a police siren broke his concentration. He froze for a moment and listened. It seemed to be coming closer. On the freeway ramp below, Banyon stepped out of the car to change the tire. The gunman had to make a decision. *It's now or never,* he told himself. Nervously, he brought the rifle up to his shoulder and locked Banyon in his sight once more. Suddenly the sound of the siren came to a dead stop just on the other side of the bushes from where the gunman was situated. He had no choice now. *Damn!* he cursed. With no other option he scrambled to his feet and scurried through the bushes, disappearing into the night.

~63~

B anyon sat up in bed, unable to sleep. "You awake?"

Angela rolled over in the dark and looked at the glowing red numbers of the digital clock on the nightstand. It was 3:15 in the morning. "I am now," she said rubbing her eyes. "What's the matter?"

"I almost wish we'd never gone to see the Rabbi yesterday. What the hell am I supposed to do now? I've got a million pieces of this puzzle swirling around in my head and I don't know how to put it together."

Angela sat up and switched on the light. She sighed, "Sort of like being back to square one isn't it?"

"Yeah, sort of. But something's missing. Some... I don't know. Some key piece of information that will bring it all together. I just know it. And that dream."

"About the thing in the water?"

"Yeah. What the hell is that? And what's up with that number 144? Why is that number so important in the dream?"

Angela thought for a moment. "You know who seemed to know a lot about that number?"

"Who?"

"Paretti."

"Paretti?"

"Yes, remember in his email? We asked him about that number and why he said it was associated with the concept of light. Remember?"

"Yeah, you're right. What was it he said?"

"Something about some guy. Some researcher investigating UFOs or something. We were going to follow up on it and never did."

"Do we still have a copy of that email he sent us?"

"It's in the briefcase with all the rest of the stuff."

"I have to see it."

"Now? It's after three in the morning!"

Banyon slid out of bed and into his slippers. "You can go back to sleep. But I have to check this out."

He left the room and returned a few minutes later with the briefcase and the printout of the email from Paretti. "I thought you were going back to sleep," he said, getting back into bed.

"You've got me wide awake now," she yawned. "What's it say? Read it aloud."

Banyon read the email and saw the name of the researcher Paretti referred to. It was Bruce Cathie. Banyon continued to read:

"*Suffice to say Cathie came up with a couple of very interesting calculations. In the course of developing his research into tracking the flight paths of reported UFO sightings from around the world he discovered what he believes is a geomagnetic grid around the earth. Again, without getting into details, suffice to say he developed a system of measurement called grid seconds based on this proposed geomagnetic grid. Using this system, it turns out that the maximum speed of light is 144,000 nautical miles per grid second. (Maximum speed, by the way, is suggested to be the speed of light in a vacuum, so to speak. Or, as Morton put it, "the speed of light in open space before it is 'slowed-down' incrementally by any given celestial body's atmosphere and magnetic field".)*

Therefore, the number 144 is what Cathie calls the "light harmonic number". So, in a nutshell, that's the only verifiable data I have been able to find which connects the number 144 to the concept of light. Still, even without Cathie's work, the notion that 144 is the "Light Number" persists within the esoteric community. Hope that answers your question.

Angela rolled out of bed and put on her bathrobe.

"Where you going?" Banyon asked.

"To get the laptop."

He grinned. "You read my mind."

Side by side, sitting in bed, they googled Bruce Cathie.

They only found little bits of information about him scattered throughout several websites dealing with UFOs. They were starting to get a little disappointed, jumping from site to site, when suddenly Banyon's eyes lit up. He blinked twice, completely stunned by the image on the screen.

"Holy shit!" he said. "There it is!"

He was staring at a photograph of an object under water.

Angela leaned in for a closer look. "What is that?"

"That's it! That's the thing I've seen in my dream!"

"Are you sure?"

"Yes! Jesus Christ! Yes! That's it!"

Angela squinted, trying to make some sense out of the blurry old black and white photo. She shook her head. "But what is it?"

"Here. What's this say?"

Angela read aloud the text accompanying the image:

The Mystery of the ELTANIN ANTENNA
Several years ago Capt. Bruce Cathie made a study of tracking UFO sightings. He noticed a pattern in the data. The UFOs seemed to frequent certain locations and flight paths. This led him to suspect the

possibility that the UFOs might be following some sort of magnetic ley lines. Eventually, through a series of mathematical calculations, he believed he had discovered a magnetic "world grid". What he needed now was to find a point position on the earth upon which to "orientate the geometrical pattern" (p.16, Cathie, The Bridge To Infinity). Synchronicity came to the rescue.

Cathie stumbled onto a news article about an American survey ship, the *Eltanin*, that was conducting a sweep of the seabed off the southern coast of South America. Apparently the project had something to do with investigating what was thought to be the site where an asteroid slammed into the sea at some time in the ancient past. The research vessel was photographing the bottom of the sea with a camera attached to a long cable. At a point in the ocean about 1000 miles south of Cape Horn, which is located at the southern tip of South America, the camera recorded a most unusual object (pictured here) about three or four feet tall and sticking straight up out of the sea floor. The ship's crew admitted that it appeared to be an artifact of some kind. It did appear as if it might be made of a metalic material and there was a symmetry to its construction. It had the appearance of a pole or a rod with six cross bars, one above the other. Although some researchers insisted it must be some sort of a strange undersea plant, to Cathie's eye this looked more like a sophisticated antenna of some kind.

As Cathie studied the photo it occurred to him that the orientation of the six crossbars on the object corresponded with an aspect of the geometry of the grid system he'd developed. In a flash of intuition he found out the precise latitude/longitude coordinates of the object. He then decided to see what would happen if he used this "antenna" as the zero point upon which to position his theoretical "magnetic world grid". When he'd finished mapping this out on a globe of the earth the result was extraordinary. His complex grid system now lined up nearly perfectly with the magnetic field of the earth as he'd calculated it in his previous research. From this point his work took on new dimensions as, even today, he continues his efforts to discover the secret of UFO propulsion through combining electromagnetism and gravitational force. His work is highly technical and steeped in mathematics. His books, therefore, are probably best understood by people with backgrounds in these areas. Still, they do make fascinating reading even for the relatively non-technical lay person.

The rest of the article went on to briefly describe more of Cathie's work but the author of the article was right. The mathematics and technical jargon left Banyon and Angela about a light-year behind. Clearly, though, that didn't matter. What mattered was the obvious. The Eltanin Antenna was the key to their own quest and the answer to Banyon's baffling dream. The whole thing also fit like a glove with Ezekiel's vision as translated from the scroll by Rabbi Feld.

Angela shook her head. "Just when I thought it couldn't get any weirder."

"Tell me about it," Banyon said. For a moment he wasn't sure that he wasn't dreaming. "I need some coffee," he said, reaching over to the nightstand for a cigarette.

"I'm with you there. It's not like we're going to get any sleep after this anyway. I'll go brew us a cup."

While she was downstairs Banyon had *one of those feelings.* "Angela!" he shouted down to her. "Where's the calculator?"

"Right there in the briefcase!" she shouted back.

He found the calculator and began punching in some numbers.

"Un-freaking-believable," he muttered to himself. "I should have known. Angela! Come here! You won't believe this!"

In a few moments she returned with two cups of hot coffee. "What is it?" she asked, setting Banyon's coffee on his nightstand.

He grabbed a pencil and a sheet of paper from the briefcase. He scribbled something down and passed it over to her. She did a quick double take and then stared at it for a moment. It was, as Banyon had exclaimed, un-freaking-believable:

ELTANIN ANTENNA = 144

"No way!" she said. "Are you sure?"

"Sure as I'm sitting here."

"What does this mean?"

"Pretty obvious, isn't it? It's confirmation."

"Confirmation?"

"Of my dream. The antenna, the cold dark water, the number 144. It couldn't be any clearer.

"Well," Angela said, "one thing could be clearer."

"What's that?'

"How did that thing...that antenna...whatever it is...get there in the first place? And what the heck is it for?

It was a good question, of course, and Banyon was stumped. He ran his fingers through his hair and massaged the back of his own neck as he tried to think of a good answer. The trouble was, his brain felt like it was closing up shop. The excitement, the stress of dealing with the recent revelations, and the long night were all catching up with him. He suddenly felt too tired to think anymore.

"I don't know," he said, crushing out his cigarette. "I guess all I know right now is I have to get some sleep. Maybe it'll all come clear in the morning."

"Sounds good to me," said Angela, trying to stifle a yawn. She glanced at the coffee still steaming in the cup. "Well, that was a waste."

He chuckled. "That's all right. It was the thought that counts."

She leaned over and gave him a kiss. "I guess."

They shut off the lights and within minutes they were both asleep. But it didn't last long. Banyon shot up in bed.

"The asteroid!" he blurted.

His sudden outburst startled Angela. She sat up and switched on the light. "What?" she said, rubbing her eyes. "What's the matter? Are you all right?"

"The asteroid in the article! It said the survey ship was investigating a site where an asteroid was thought to have splashed into the sea!"

"So?"

"So, what if it wasn't an asteroid? What if..."

"What if what?"

"What if it was a UFO? An extraterrestrial craft!"

"A space ship?"

"Yes, don't you see? You asked me how that antenna thing got embedded into the ocean floor!"

"Yes, but what are you saying?"

"It's all coming together now. Think back. You know that book we got from Mrs. Densmore?"

"What about it?"

"That chapter about the Ezekiel Code. The author was speculating that the thing Ezekiel encountered was actually an alien spacecraft. We talked about all this before. Remember?

378

"Oh, wow. You're right. Yes."

"Hang on," Banyon said. "There's more." He jumped out of bed and got the briefcase. He opened it and rifled through the stack of papers inside. "Here!" he said, holding up a sheet of paper. "Look at this."

He got back onto the bed and showed Angela the copy of the text from the scroll that Rabbi Feld had translated for them. "Right here. Read this part."

Angela read the words:

And I dreamed I was taken to a distant land where I saw the chariot fall from the sky like a serpent and descend into the sea and it was swallowed up by the deep and I saw it no more.

Banyon emphasized what she'd just read. "*I saw the chariot fall from the sky and descend into the sea*! There it is! Old Ezekiel called it a chariot. Oh, man. If he only knew."

Angela was shocked. "So, the antenna…"

Banyon jumped on top of her words."Maybe that antenna is just *part* of the craft! You know? Like attached to the top of it and the rest of the craft is buried under tons of sand on the ocean floor!"

"Or…" Angela said, stopping to think for a moment.

"Or what?"

"Or maybe it's not part of the craft at all but part of something that the craft planted down there. It might be attached to something but not the craft itself. Here, wait a minute." Reaching into the briefcase she pulled out the McClintock notes. "Here," she said. "Look what it says here:

Entry, December 14, 1999.
I'm now more certain than ever that it was a machine.

Banyon considered it for a moment. "Hmm… yes. McClintock was definitely on to something. But it almost doesn't matter whether it's the craft itself or something the craft planted there. In either case, you know what that would mean?"

She knew what he was thinking. "Oh god," she whispered.

Banyon nodded. "Yeah. Oh god is right. It means we know where the smoking gun is. Proof of alien intelligence on our own planet. And it arrived here thousands of years ago!"

"My god," she said as the ramifications began to sink in. "What does this mean for us?"

"I guess it means…" he hesitated, then he began to laugh.

His laughter took her by surprise. "Something's funny?"

He got up and walked back and forth across the room. "Nothing… nothing's funny," he choked the words out. Taking a sip of coffee, he regained his composure, plopped himself down in the chair across from the bed and let out a deep sigh. The look on his face was a rather comical combination of resignation and bemusement. He looked over at Angela and shrugged his shoulders. "I guess it means we're going to go deep-sea diving off the southern tip of South America. What else?"

Angela closed her eyes and shook her head slowly. "This is insane."

Banyon nodded in complete agreement. He crawled back into bed and they talked a while longer. Finally he turned off the light. "Let's get some sleep. Maybe it'll seem less insane in the morning."

"Somehow I doubt that," Angela said, under her breath. Then, after a few minutes of silence, she whispered in the dark, "We're going to South America?"

Banyon was nearly asleep, "Mm-hmm. I guess," he mumbled into his pillow.

Another few minutes of silence, then Angela whispered the final words of the night. "Zeke?"

"Hmm."

"What am I going to wear?"

Inside the white van, parked across the street from Banyon's house, two of the Jesuit General's hired operatives had captured the entire conversation in digital format and transferred it directly to the Jesuit headquarters in Italy. After listening to the recorded conversation, General DuPont had just one comment. "Holy Mother of God."

Part 2: Revelation

~64~

Several days after their meeting with the rabbi, Banyon called his good friend Father Caldwell to tell him about the translation and about the Eltanin Antenna and how it was all beginning to make some sense.

Caldwell was both astounded and elated by the news. "Listen, ol' boy," he told Banyon, "if you decide to go ahead with this - um, this salvage mission and you need an extra hand - I wouldn't mind coming along on the trip. This could be history in the making. And if it is, I'd love to be there! Seriously, if you figure out how to get this all together – you know, put together a team – count me in!"

Banyon promised to count him in and that's pretty much where the conversation ended. There wasn't too much more to be said because it was early in the game and Banyon had no clue as to how he was going to manage any of this *salvage mission*, as Caldwell put it.

Knowing the location of the mysterious Eltanin Antenna was a revelation but it was only the beginning of a new chapter in Banyon's appointed task. Many new questions arose from that revelation, not the least of which was how to reach the object. And even if they could reach it how were they going to bring it to the surface? Or were they even supposed to bring it to the surface? And what if Angela was right? What if the thing was only part of another object? What was the other object? And how big was it? The size of a breadbox? Banyon chuckled to himself at the thought. *A breadbox. Nobody uses breadboxes anymore.* The last time he'd seen one was in his grandmother's kitchen when he was a child. His brief nostalgic sidetrip into his grandmother's kitchen quickly dissipated as his mental image of the breadbox morphed back into the image of the strange object protruding from the ocean floor. *What if the thing it's attached to is bigger than a breadbox?* His imagination began conjuring up the unimaginable. *What if it's something the size of...* he hesitated ...*a railroad car? Hell, a Boeing 747!* Whatever the case, he knew it was probably useless to speculate. Moreover, his quip about going deep-sea diving was just an off-the-cuff attempt at a joke. Not only did he know absolutely nothing about deep-sea diving but he was pretty sure that a depth of 13,500 feet must be way beyond the capability of such a task. The only thing he could think of was a submarine. He'd seen those small one-man submersibles in a couple of television documentaries. He recalled one documentary about exploring and photographing the sunken remains of the Titanic. *This is nuts!* he thought to himself. *Where the hell am I going to get a mini-submarine? And who's going to operate the damn thing? What am I? Jacques Cousteau?*

The more he thought about it the more improbable this whole search-and-retrieval mission seemed to become. Forget the mini-sub. He didn't even have the slightest idea how they were going to get to a location a thousand miles south of Cape Horn in the first place. It was crazy.

He pulled his World Altas off the bookshelf and looked up the location of the Eltanin Antenna using Cathie's latitude and longitude coordinates. *Why does it have to be there?* he sighed. *Why couldn't it be in the nice tropical waters off the coast of Bimini or something?* But that was definitely not the case. The Eltanin Antenna was at the bottom of the freezing Antarctic Ocean off the tip of South America. To make matters worse, according to some information he found in an article on the internet, the location was smack in the middle of one of the most treacherous navigation routes on the planet. Waves could reach heights of 65 feet or more. Furious storms with gale force winds 200 days out of a year. Not exactly the place for a pleasure cruise. From what information he could gather, the picture only got worse. There was also the possibility of large ice flows in the area. The only type of vessel really adequate for this mission would be an icebreaker, a ship designed especially for operating in such an environment. How he was going to get access to a boat like that, he had no idea. *Might as well be asking to hitch a ride on the Space Shuttle.*

"Zeke?"

The sudden sound of Angela's voice brought him out of his frustrated contemplation. He put the atlas back on the bookshelf and went into the kitchen where he found her sitting at the table musing over a cup of coffee. She looked worried. "What is it?" he asked.

"Something wrong?"

"I was just thinking about Rabbi Feld."

"Feld? What about him?"

"Well, wouldn't you think someone like that – I mean, he's a rabbi, after all – wouldn't you think he'd be like really excited about..."

"About an ancient scroll apparently penned by one of the most important prophets of the Old Testament?"

"Took the words right out of my mouth."

"I know," he said, sitting down across from her. "It occurred to me too. I sort of expected we'd hear from him again. A phone call or something. But it's been what - a week or more? It does make you wonder. Although," he said, getting up to pour himself a cup of coffee, "Professor Kline did say the guy could be trusted to keep it under his hat. Or his yarmulkah, as the case may be."

Angela forced a grin. "Yes, but still. I mean, how do we know he isn't blabbing about it to all his rabbi buddies?"

"I guess there's no way we could know that. We'll just have to trust him."

"I suppose. But it still seems odd to me. Like you said, it seems like he'd call us to see what else we'd found out about it."

"I don't know. Maybe he thought about the whole thing and just decided it couldn't possibly be authentic. You know?"

Angela nodded. "Maybe. By the way, don't you think it's about time we called Alan?"

"Kline? Yeah, I was thinking the same thing. Don't know why I've been putting it off. I guess I thought he would have called us to find out how it went with the rabbi."

"Gees, you get the feeling we're being avoided?"

Banyon gave a laugh. "Well, on second thought, I suspect he's heard all about it from Feld by now. But I should call him. Who knows, maybe he can pull some other tricks out of his bag."

"What do you mean?"

"Well, I mean he did hook us up with someone who was able to translate the scroll. Maybe he can point us to some resources that will help us figure out how the heck we're going to get that thing – whatever it is - off the bottom of the ocean."

"Hmm, yes, that will be a good trick."

Banyon chuckled. "Yeah, a really good trick, seeing as how we have no idea of the size or the weight of the thing. Seems like that would have to be a known factor in order to be able to plan some way to salvage it."

Banyon moved into the living room and placed the call to Professor Kline. Just as he suspected, Kline had indeed heard from Feld. The rabbi faxed Kline a copy of the translation the day after he translated it. Also as Banyon suspected, Feld had expressed some skepticism as to the authenticity of the scroll. When Kline pushed for a reason, the rabbi's only reply was that he *"just couldn't get his mind around it"*. Banyon thought this was an odd turn of phrase for a rabbi but according to Kline it was a direct quote, straight from the rabbi's mouth. Kline, on the other hand, expressed no doubt whatsoever.

"I believe you've got the real thing," he said to Banyon. "I think the good rabbi is just experiencing a serious case of denial."

"What makes you so sure it's the real thing?" Banyon asked.

Kline laughed. "C'mon! After all you've been through and after what I've been through? Don't tell me you still have doubts!"

Banyon hesitated. Something Kline just said was still resonating in his head. *What he's been through? What did he mean by that?* "What do you mean, what you've been through?"

"What?" Kline asked.

"You said, *what you've been through.* What did you mean by that? What have you been through?"

Kline suddenly realized his slip of the tongue. He paused a moment before answering. "Well, you know…"

"No, I'm not sure I do."

Kline tried to think fast. "Well, I mean like the time you called me for help because Angela had been kidnapped. And then that night when I came over to check on you and found out what had taken place at the warehouse. You know. It was all quite upsetting. That's what I mean."

Kline's explanation made sense, of course, and Banyon found himself a bit embarrassed for having put Kline on the defensive for no good reason. "I'm sorry," Banyon apologized. "Don't know what's the matter with me. Maybe this whole thing is just starting to make me a little paranoid."

Kline breathed a silent sigh of relief. It wasn't that he wanted to keep anything from Banyon. Not really. But he was pretty sure the Nine would not want him to let on to Banyon about his covert relationship with the Brotherhood. For Kline, however, it was becoming an awkward situation. "Well, a little paranoid, especially in your situation, is probably not such a bad thing," he told Banyon. "After all, you've been through a lot. Christ's sake, man, you even got shot. You could have been killed. I'd be a little paranoid too."

Banyon rubbed the area on his shoulder where the bullet had struck. The entire frightening incident flashed through his mind in an instant. "Yeah," he said, "I guess you're right. But now I've got more information and, of course, more problems. Angela and I were wondering if maybe you might be able to help."

"Whatever I can do," Kline said. "What is it? What new information?"

"Well," Banyon began, "are you ready for this? You remember I told you about that recurring dream I'd been having?"

"Yes. The strange object with the crossbars in the water. And something about the number 144. I remember."

"Yes. Well, we now know what it is and we know *where* it is. The thing in the water. The thing with the crossbars."

It took Kline a moment to process what Banyon just said. "Excuse me? You know *what* it is and *where* it is?"

"Well, we sort of know what it is. No, that's not quite right either. What we know is what one person has decided to call it."

Kline was confused. "One person? Someone else knows about this?"

"Sort of, yes."

Banyon explained the whole thing to Kline, about how their search for information about the esoteric associations with the number 144 had led them to information about Bruce Cathie and the photograph of the object that Cathie dubbed the Eltanin Antenna. He told him about the latitude/longitude coordinates and how that translated into a point in the Antarctic Ocean about a thousand miles south of Cape Horn. He explained how it tied in with the text of the ancient scroll as translated by Rabbi Feld and, of course, he included the real bombshell: that this thing, whatever it is, is probably an extraterrestrial artifact of some kind.

Kline was stunned by this revelation. In his mind this moved the whole scenario ahead several notches. It occurred to him that he should probably inform the Nine of this news as soon as possible.

"Good God, man," Kline said. "I don't know what to say. This is incredible. What are you going to do?"

Banyon couldn't help but give out a laugh. "Yes, well, that is the question, isn't it? I guess I'm going after it. Which brings me back to what I said about more problems and hoping perhaps you might be of some assistance."

"Of course. I'm listening."

Banyon recounted the list of problems and questions that had been plaguing him earlier. How were they going to get a boat capable of making the trip? What would they do about a crew? And the thing that baffled him the most, for some reason, was how were they going to reach the thing 13,500 feet under the Antarctic Ocean? And how the *hell* were they going to bring it to the surface? Perhaps even more perplexing, daunting, in fact, was the question of just what was he supposed to do with the thing even if they did manage to bring it to the surface? What exactly is this thing and how is he supposed to know what to do with it? *Would it come complete with an instruction manual?* Somehow he doubted that. Like everything else that had happened up to this point the whole thing was crazy. But at least, up to this point, there had been clues to follow. Now, as this leg of the journey was about to begin, Banyon feared the trail of clues had run dry. What was he supposed to do now?

Almost without hesitation, Kline offered a suggestion. "I think this calls for a meeting of the minds."

Banyon didn't understand. "What do you mean?"

"I mean between you and Angela and me, I think we have enough intelligence to figure this out. My gut tells me the clues have not run out. If this is all what it appears to be, the fulfillment of a prophecy, and if you are, in fact, the Chosen One..."

"Oh God," Banyon interrupted, "we're back to that again."

"Well, are you going to deny it? *Can* you deny it?"

Banyon, of course, couldn't deny it. As much as he'd like to, at this point in the game, with all that had happened, it was all but impossible to deny his apparent role in whatever it was that was unfolding. "Okay," he gave in. "So what was your suggestion?"

"What I was about to say is that if you are – forgive me – the

Chosen One, and with all the information and knowledge you've gathered so far, I'm betting the answers to your questions are probably closer at hand than you think. The problem of the boat and how to get to the location and all of that? I have no doubt it will all fall into place. Don't ask me how. At the moment I don't have a clue. As crazy as it sounds, I have to think something beyond our understanding is guiding you along this strange path. I can't imagine it would leave you hanging now at the moment of discovery. What do you say we get together soon and start from the beginning. Go over everything. All three of us. Remember what I told you about the bigger picture?"

"Yes, I remember. What about it?"

"It's time to add more pieces to it. I'm betting the answers to your questions will be found among those pieces. What do you say?"

Banyon was a bit stunned by Kline's sudden outpouring of optimism and his apparent enthusiasm for taking on the challenge. He couldn't help but wonder what Kline's motivation was. Was there an ulterior motive behind his offer to spend the time and energy it would take to go over everything and expand their perception of the bigger picture, as he put it? *What's in it for him?* But he felt guilty as these thoughts raced through his mind. After all, Kline had done nothing but help them along the way. He offered his knowledge and advice freely, never hinting at an ulterior motive. It was the damn paranoia creeping in again. *I need to get over this*, he thought to himself. "Okay," Banyon said. "You're on. And you're probably right. What about this weekend? Saturday maybe? At our place?"

"Saturday would be good," Kline said. "But I'd like to suggest another location. This information you've told me today is incredibly valuable. My guess is if the bad guys haven't gotten wind of it yet they soon will. They could be listening to us right now. Just because you can't see them doesn't mean they aren't there. Remember that."

"Okay. Where, then?"

"Not over the phone. Come to my office Saturday, say about ten in the morning. I'll meet you there. I have a plan."

Banyon gave a little chuckle. "Sounds like cloak and dagger."

"Just a little precaution."

"I know. You're right. Okay then. Saturday, ten o'clock, your office."

"And bring everything. Well, everything except the actual scroll. I don't want to be even partially responsible for that little artifact. I assume it's in a safe place?"

"It is. Don't worry about that."

"Good. Saturday it is then."

"All right. And Alan?"

"Yes?"

"Thank you."

"Don't mention it. Let's just get this done."

Banyon hung up the phone and went into the kitchen to tell Angela about the plan for Saturday. She thought it was a great idea.

"Where are you going?" he asked as she left the kitchen and headed upstairs.

"This is Thursday," she grinned.

"Yeah? So?"

"So I've only got today and tomorrow to figure out what I'm going to wear for the big meeting of the minds!"

Banyon laughed. "You're impossible!"

"I know!" she shouted back from the top of the stairs. "That's why you love me!"

That night Banyon had another strange dream about the object on the bottom of the ocean. Again there was the strong impression of a number. But instead of 144 it was 162. And there was a peculiar sound, a discordant tone emanating from somewhere. And the object was moving... slowly... upward.

~65~

On any typical morning Angela would wake up about 7:30, an hour or two before Banyon. It just seemed to be their natural pattern. Then she would roll over, facing him, drape her arm around him and doze off for a while before getting up. This morning was different. She woke up as usual and looked at the clock. It was just a little after 7:30. She rolled over for her morning cuddle but was surprised to find Banyon apparently wide awake, lying there with his hands behind his head, staring at the ceiling.

"Well," she yawned. "I can see this is going to be an interesting day."

He barely heard her as he was deep in thought. "Huh?" he said, turning to look at her. "What?"

She smiled and brushed the hair away from her face. "You're awake before me. This could affect the entire planet, you know. A world gone mad. Confusion. Disorientation. And it'll be all your fault."

He was momentarily befuddled by the comment. Then he grinned, finally getting the joke. "Very funny."

"I thought so."

"I was just laying here thinking about the dream I had last night."

"The antenna thing in the water again?"

"Yeah."

She sat up on the edge of the bed and slid her feet into her slippers. "Well, what's the big mystery? I thought we had that dream all figured out."

"That dream, yes. But this was different. The whole thing was different but it had the same..." he paused to think of the right words. "...the same *feel* as the other dream."

"Okay," she said. "Lay it on me."

He sat up and thought about it for a minute. "Okay. Well, I saw that same object on the ocean floor. I mean it looked exactly like it does in that photograph. You know, the one we found on the internet. That antenna thing. And there was this sound. I don't know how to describe it. It was like... well, imagine somebody just holding down a bunch of random keys on an electric organ, creating a weird tone. Kind of like that. And it lasted the entire duration of the dream. And as I was trying to understand the source of the sound - you know, like where it was coming from – I looked at the antenna and it was moving. I mean like it was beginning to rise up from out of the ocean floor!"

Angela was transfixed by the vision he was describing. "It started to move? Was the sound coming from the antenna?"

"No, it didn't seem to be coming from the antenna. But I couldn't tell where it *was* coming from. That's what really puzzled me. And check this out. Remember how you wondered if maybe the antenna might be attached to something else buried under the ocean floor?"

Angela nodded. "Yes. Why?"

"Well, it looks like you were right."

"What do you mean?"

"When the antenna began to raise up I could see it was attached to something."

Angela was now all the more intrigued. "What was it?"

"I was only given a glimpse before the dream ended. And I could only see a couple inches of it poking up through the sand. But it was pointed and it seemed like it was shiny like gold or something."

Angela's eyes brightened. "Really! What could it be?"

"I don't know. But there was something else too. Remember in my other dreams how the number 144 was important?"

"Yes, of course. Was it in this dream, too?"

"No. This time it was 162. The whole thing was as weird as those other dreams. And just as powerful. If that's the right word. I mean these dreams leave an almost indelible impression in my mind. The memory of them doesn't fade away like most dreams usually do. They're like branded on my brain. Just thinking about them brings them into focus as clearly as when I'm dreaming them. It's weird."

Angela thought for a moment as she slipped into her bathrobe. "You know what? I think maybe Kline was right about the trail of clues not having run out."

Banyon was still lying in bed. Looking over at Angela in her flowing white bathrobe was like looking at an angel. A sexy angel, but still an angel. He smiled to himself. In the middle of a serious conversation the only thing he wanted to do at the moment was pick her up and bring her back to bed. "What?" he said, trying to shake the fantasy out of his mind.

Angela recognized the look. "Oh, come on," she smirked. "I know that look and it ain't gonna happen."

Banyon tried to feign surprise. "What look? I'm listening. The trail of clues...something."

She put her hands on her hips and shook her head. "And you think *I'm* impossible!"

He knew he'd been caught. He gave a sheepish grin and tried to look serious. "Okay. I'm listening. Really. The trail of clues hasn't run out. What do you mean?"

"That number. What was it?"

"One-sixty-two."

"Yes. That's probably a clue right there."

As soon as she said it he knew she was right. It was one of the numbers in the Ezekiel Code. "By Jove, I believe you're on to something, Watson. Let's check it out. Go get the briefcase and bring it back to bed here."

Angela laughed. "Nice try, Sherlock. But it ain't gonna work. You get up and get the briefcase," she said as she headed down the stairs, "and I'll go put on some coffee. I'll meet you at the kitchen table."

"We could do it on the kitchen table," he said quietly.

"What was that?" she shouted up the stairs.

"I said, okay, I'll meet you at the kitchen table!"

~66~

I t didn't take long to find the first clue.

"Well, there it is," Angela said. "Right on top." She pointed to a section in the list of phrases:

THE THREE TONES = 162
THE STONE CIRCLE = 162
GUARDIAN PILLARS = 162

Banyon sipped his coffee and lit a cigarette. "Hmm... Yes, *the three tones*. The other two were the clues to help us find the scroll in France. I wonder if *the three tones* could relate to the odd sound I heard in the dream?"

"That's what I was thinking. I know a little about music theory and the three tones makes some sense."

"How so?"

"Well, a musical chord is typically made up of three notes."

"Three notes?"

"Yes. For example, the notes called C, F, and G make up the C-chord. The chord is usually named after the first note in the series. It's the foundation note for the chord."

Banyon scratched his head. "I don't get it. How do you know what three notes to use? I mean if you start with C, for example, how do you know what the other two notes are?"

Angela thought for moment. It had been many years since she'd had a few music lessons when she was a teenager. "I remember it could get really complicated," she said. "But the fundamentals were not so hard to understand. Believe it or not it's all mathematics."

Banyon looked surprised. "Mathematics?"

Angela got a piece of paper and a pencil and wrote as she talked. "Okay," she said. "Here are the notes."

She wrote the word, <u>NOTES</u>, at the top of the page and underlined it. Below that she wrote the names of the notes:

A B C D E F G

"That's it?" Banyon asked. "It only goes to G? There are only seven notes?"

"Yes, just seven basic notes. That's it. After G it starts all over again with A. Of course," she added, "there are more if you include the sharps and flats.

Banyon scratched his head. "Great. We've just gotten started and already it's getting complicated."

Angela laughed. "Well, with my limited knowledge of this stuff, it won't get too complicated."

"I'll bet," Banyon said skeptically. "But let's hear it."

For the next hour Angela launched into a rather detailed explanation of music theory, how scales are constructed, how chords are constructed, half steps, whole steps, sharps, flats – everything she could think of – and how the mathematics plays into it through the phenomenon of harmonics and tonal frequencies. Clearly, she remembered a lot more than she at first thought.

Banyon struggled to keep up with her but eventually it began to sink in and he actually understood most of it. One thing that puzzled him, however, was the odd sound of the tone he heard in his dream. With all this talk of harmonics, the tone in his dream seemed very unharmonic. If the tone in his dream was composed of three notes they certainly didn't seem to be in what he would call harmony. It was at that point in the conversation that he happened to glance back at the word, <u>NOTES</u>, that Angela had written and underscored at the top of the paper.

"Hey," he said. "Check this out. The word, *notes*, has the same letters in it as the word *tones*!"

"Hey, yes! You're right! Coincidence?"

They looked at each other. "No coincidences!" they chimed in unison.

Banyon laughed. "Now that's harmony!"

The moment called for a high-five, a kiss and a fresh cup of coffee and then it was back to work. They tried everything they could think of to come up with three notes that might somehow in some way relate to the phrase, THE THREE TONES = 162. They tried every 3-note combination that could be created from all the notes in the scale but they seemed to be getting nowhere.

"Wait a minute," Banyon said. "We're looking for three notes, right?"

"Right."

"Maybe that's the wrong track."

"What do you mean?"

"Look. The phrase we're working with refers to three *tones*, not three *notes*. What if, just maybe, the tones it's referring to are actually chords? Don't you see? Each *tone* might be a whole *chord*, not just a single note."

Angela thought about it for a moment. "Hmm… not a bad idea."

Banyon had a feeling he was on to something. "I'll bet my calculator on it. In fact, slide that calculator over here. Something just came to me."

Angela slid the calculator across the table.

He punched in some numbers and quickly wrote something on the piece of paper. "Ah ha!" he grinned. "Check this out." He showed her what he'd written:

ONE TONE IS ONE CHORD = 198

"Good number," Angela said. "Reduces to 9. But what does 198 refer to?"

They checked the Ezekiel Code phrase list:

REVERSE THE NUMBER = 198
REVERSE DIRECTION = 198

Angela was puzzled. "Reverse what number? Reverse what direction?"

Banyon shook his head. "I don't know. Maybe it doesn't refer to these phrases. But I'll still bet my calculator that this one-tone-one-chord idea is right."

Angela had to admit there was no good reason why it couldn't be the right idea. "Hey, why not?" she said. "I'll go along with that."

"So," Banyon said, really beginning to feel the flow, "now with three chords, that means we've got nine notes! Right? Three notes per chord? Nine notes."

No sooner had the words come out of his mouth than another phrase flashed into his mind. He grabbed the calculator, punched in the numbers and wrote the phrase:

THE NINE SACRED TONES = 198

Even he was shocked. "Well!" he said. "That didn't take long, did it?"

Angela arched her eyebrows in surprise. "No way! It's a match for the one-tone-one-chord phrase!" She shot him a puzzled look. "How do you do that?"

Banyon shook his head. "Damned if I know. It just comes to me. Like I've said before, sometimes it feels like it just gets downloaded into my brain. It's weird. I think Kline was right again."

"What do you mean?"

"On the phone. He said he believes something beyond our understanding is guiding all of this. Maybe he's right."

"Well," Angela said, "whatever it is, it's weird. But I kind of like that *sacred tones* thing. Kind of adds a nice spiritual touch."

At that moment something outside the living room window caught Banyon's eye. It was the flashing blue lights of a police car that had just pulled up behind a white van parked next to the fire hydrant in front of the house. He got up and moved to the living room to get ma better look. A man stepped out of the van and was talking with the officer. After a few minutes the officer appeared to be writing a ticket for the parking violation. After another moment of conversation the man got back into the van and drove away. Banyon returned to the kitchen.

"What was it?" Angela asked.

Banyon shrugged. "Nothing. Just some guy getting a ticket for parking in front of the fire hydrant."

As the van headed off down the street the driver cursed. "Damn it!"

The operative in the back of the van echoed the driver's sentiment. He shut down the audio surveillance equipment and transferred the recorded conversation between Banyon and Angela to the Jesuit headquarters. Within minutes a cell phone rang in the back of the van. It was the Jesuit General, DuPont.

"Is that all there is?" DuPont demanded. "I just listened to the transcript! It doesn't seem like they were finished with their work! What you've recorded here is just enough to be interesting but not enough to be of any use! Why did you terminate the surveillance?"

The operative explained how the cops had interrupted them in the middle of their surveillance. "We're just lucky they didn't search the van!" he said, trying to add some positive spin to the situation. "It could have been worse."

The General, obviously angry, hung up the phone without another word. The audio equipment operator moved from the back of the van to the passenger seat beside the driver. "Somebody's not happy," he said.

"Piss on him, Montabeau," the driver growled. "He's never happy."

As Banyon and Angela continued trying to figure out just exactly which chords and which notes they were supposed to be dealing with, Banyon's mysterious guiding force seemed to be taking a break. Nothing was working out and no other miraculous phrases were downloading into his brain. Desperate to come up with a solution they decided to have a go at the internet. With a few choice key words they finally came to a website that had some promising information. A musician with an interest in ancient sacred numbers had discovered something unique. Extraordinary, actually. It would prove to be not only the solution to the their present musical question but would soon serve to expand the entire vista of the bigger picture.

The white van pulled into the faculty parking lot at Queen City University and Montabeau stepped out. He said something to the driver and closed the door just as Romano was coming out of one of the buildings. He watched the van drive away and confronted Montabeau.

"Who was that?" Romano asked.

"Nobody. Just a friend," Montabeau replied, turning to walk away.

Romano looked agitated. "Where are you going?"

Montabeau spoke without turning around. "To get something to eat. Is that all right?"

Romano watched him walk across the campus toward the cafeteria. Rubbing his hand across his bald head, Romano thought for a moment and then walked back into the building. He couldn't escape the feeling that something wasn't right – and he didn't like it.

~67~

I t was easy enough for Banyon and Angela to at least get the gist of the information on the website. The musician was experimenting with compositions using something other than the standard tuning. It was all about frequency in terms of cycles per second. Standard tuning protocol for the music of the western world called for the note of A above middle C - on a piano keyboard for example - to vibrate at a frequency of 440 cps, cycles per second. The vibration rate of each of the other notes in the scale then increased or decreased in various increments relative to the 440 cps of the A-note. That much, at least, Banyon could comprehend. The 440 cps of the A-note was the key to the whole system of standard tuning.

This musician, however, was experimenting with the A-note at 432 cps instead of 440. This rather unorthadox departure from the norm resulted in something quite remarkable. Not only was 432 a number familiar to anyone who had studied the ancient canon of sacred numbers but, almost as if by magic, it resulted in many of the other notes in the scale having cps values that were also part of the sacred numbers! That these numbers were reducible to the single digit value of 9 did not escape the notice of Banyon and Angela. The first ones that popped out at them were those that fell below middle C. They were D with a cps of 144, E with a cps of 162, and A with a cps of 216. That's when they noticed the key that unlocked the door to their dilemma.

The notes A, D, and E - at every octave up and down the scale - were the only three notes with cps values that reduced to the number 9. Banyon's invisible guiding force had once again brought them to where they needed to be. If there was any room for doubt, that doubt was erased when they discovered this musician was apparently a friend of Vince Paretti, the same man who had provided them with so much valuable information already. Their own friend, Professor Kline, would surely have agreed this was no mere coincidence.

The website offered up yet another piece of information. These three numbers, 144, 162, and 216, as well as many of the other numbers generated from this A/432 scale, could be found in the geometry of many ancient monuments and sacred sites around the world including the Great Pyramid of Giza. The website also mentioned that the cps of the G-note, at one position on this musical scale, was 48.034717. According to the musician, this was a precise decimal harmonic of the height of the Great Pyramid which, it was pointed out, was 480.34717 feet. Banyon found this to be very interesting. He had always been fascinated by the mysteries of the Great Pyramid.

What Banyon didn't realize at the time was that this information would expand the bigger picture even further in the days ahead. At the moment, however, it was enough that they'd found their three tones: A, D, and E. Or was it three *notes*? That was their first question. The work on the website was clearly referring to the individual notes of a scale rather than chords. But since they'd already settled on the idea that the word, *tones,* in the Ezekial Code, referred to *chords* rather than individual *notes*, they were not sure exactly what to do with this new information.

"Wait a second," Angela said. "I just noticed something."

"What is it?"

"Using the alphanumeric values of these three letters, what do we find? We find A equals 1, D is 4, and E is 5. Right?"

Banyon nodded. "And...?"

"And I just remembered that 1-4-5 is a standard chord progression. So maybe we should be thinking of these letters as the names of *chords* rather than as the names of individual *notes*."

Banyon was once again at a disadvantage. The only musical training he'd ever had was when his mother taught him how to whistle. "Slow down," he said. "Chord progression? What's that?"

Angela explained that most songs, especially in popular music and folk melodies, had only three basic chords. These three chords typically progressed through the song in a repeated pattern with the notes of the melody following suit. The process of figuring out which three chords to use in a song was similar to the process of figuring out which three notes to use in a chord.

Banyon was still shaking his head. "Show me."

"Okay. Typically the key of the song is determined by the first chord in the song. So let's say the first chord in the song is A. So A is our *one*-chord. Count upward four steps from A."

Banyon counted. "Okay. A, B, C, D. Four steps up from A is D."

"Right. Then count *five* steps up from A."

"That would be, um..." he counted on his fingers, "A, B, C, D, E. Five steps up from A is E."

"Right. So the chord progression for the song would be A-D-E. Or one-four-five. Get it?"

Banyon thought about it for a moment. " I get it. So you're saying we should be thinking of our A, D, E as the names of *chords* instead of the names of individual *notes*?"

Angela shrugged. "Well, I don't know for sure. I'm just saying when I noticed that A-D-E was alphanumerically 1-4-5, it seemed like a possibility. I mean, everything else so far seems to be keyed to the alphanumerics. I'm just guessing that might be the clue."

"You're right," Banyon said. "Makes as much sense as anything else. And it confirms our initial idea that the word, *tones*, in the Ezekiel Code phrases actually refers to *chords* rather than individual

399

notes! I love it. You've nailed it."

Angela grinned. "Hey, I'm getting pretty good, ain't I?"

Banyon gave a laugh. "As good as they come, sweetheart. What else have you got?"

"Well, the next thing we should do is figure out which notes make up the A-chord, the D-chord, and the E-chord."

Angela conjured up a piano keyboard in her mind and imagined herself as a young girl fingering those very chords. It all came back to her in a flash and she quickly came up with the three notes for each chord. She jotted the information down on the paper:

The notes for the A-chord are: A, C#, E

The notes for the D-chord are: D, F#, A

The notes for the E-chord are: E, G#, B

Banyon looked at what she'd written but, lacking a background in music, he had no sense of what these notes would actually sound like.

"So," he said, "if we're right about this, and these are the nine notes that make up the three chords, then..."

"Yes?"

"Well, I'm assuming each of these chords makes a pleasing sound, right? Harmonic?"

"Sure, of course. Why?"

Banyon looked a little perplexed. "I'm just wondering because in my dream the sound I heard wasn't all that pleasing."

That aspect of Banyon's dream had completely slipped her mind. She considered the three chords for a moment and then it dawned on her. "Well," she said, trying to hear the chords in her mind, "the sound of all three of these chords – if they were played simultaneously - would be a little hard on the ears. I think hitting all of those nine notes at the same time would produce quite a cacophony."

Banyon laughed.

Angela looked surprised."What's so funny?"

"You said cacophony!"

"That's what it would be. What's so funny about that?"

"Nothing. It's just that..." he laughed again, "...nobody says that!"

"Says what? Cacophony?"

The fact that she was so serious about it made him laugh all the more. "Yes! Who says that?"

"I just did!" she countered, trying to stifle her own grin.

"Cacophony! Cacophony! Cacophony!"

Banyon covered his ears. "Okay! Okay! Okay! You can stop now!"

She leaned back in her chair and folded her arms. It was hard not to get caught up in his infectious laughter. Putting on as serious a face as she could muster, she glared at him for several seconds. "Are we done making fun of my vocabulary now? Can we get back to work?"

Banyon wiped a tear from his eye. "Okay," he said. "I'm sorry. I must be getting tired."

"That's all right. I'm glad I could provide some comic relief. Maybe I should quit this day job and do some stand-up. I could kill 'em with my cacophony routine."

"No doubt. But don't quit your day job yet. I still need you here."

"Oh, all right," she sighed. "So where were we?"

"You were telling me that if all of those notes were played at the same time it would cause a cacophony."

She shot him a look. "Don't start."

"Hey," he said. "It's *your* word."

"Yes, I know. Let's just say it would produce a really bad sound. All right?"

"Okay. Well, I guess that does answer the question then," he said, trying to get serious again. "So where do we go from here?"

"Hey, you're the Chosen One with the invisible guiding force. I shouldn't have to come up with *all* the answers."

"You're right," he conceded. Then he lifted his hands up over his head, striking a biblical pose. "Come on, o' mighty invisible guiding force! Show me some stuff!"

Angela pursed her lips. "You know," she said, "somehow I don't think it works that way."

"I suppose not," he said with a sigh. He stood up and stretched. "I think my brain needs a break. I can't think anymore. Especially on an empty stomach. What time is it?"

At that moment the pendulum clock in the living room sounded the hour of nine. The nine tones of the chime seemed to vibrate through Banyon's entire body.

"Hey!" Angela said, getting up to fix breakfast. "Talk about *ask-and-you-shall-receive*! At the tone the time will be nine o'clock."

Banyon barely heard her. His head was cocked to one side as if he was listening to something. The clock had stopped chiming but he was replaying the series of tones in his mind. Then, in a delayed response to Angela's comment, he said, "Not tone. *Tones.*

"Say again?"

"Tones, plural," he said. "At the *tones* the time will be nine!"

"Oh. Correcting me on my English now, are we?"

Banyon grabbed the pencil and paper and scribbled something down. Then he reached for the calculator and tapped away at the keypad. "Look at this," he said.

Angela came back to the table and looked at what he'd written:

NINE TIME TONES = 162 = THE THREE TONES

"Wow!" she exclaimed. "Where the heck did that come from?"

He shook his head as if he'd been in a mild trance. "I don't know."

"Another one of your downloads from the invisible force, I suppose."

"Sort of. But different. The clock... the chimes. It was weird."

"Yeah, well, weird is one thing. But this is getting spooky."

Banyon couldn't have agreed more. It was getting damned spooky.

Angela fixed a quick breakfast of toast and fried eggs and they talked about what they'd put together so far.

"Well," Angela said, between bites, "one thing I don't get is what these tones are supposed to do. What's the whole purpose of all this?"

Banyon wiped the last bit of yolk from his plate with a piece of toast. "If I'm interpreting the vision in my dream correctly," he said, attempting to eat and talk at the same time, "I'm thinking the tones somehow activate the antenna. Because..." he paused to take a sip of coffee, "...when I heard that sound in my dream I could see the antenna start to move. And I could swear it seemed to be moving upward. You know? Like starting to come up out of the ocean floor."

"Levitation?"

"Exactly! And that would answer the question I had about how we were going to ever get the thing - that antenna, or whatever it is – up from the bottom of the ocean!"

"Is that even possible? Levitation by sound?"

Banyon nodded. "It's not only possible, it's been done."

"Are you kidding?"

"Seriously," he said. "Wait here. I'll show you." He disappeared into the living room and returned in a few minutes with a back copy of

Science Today. "Here, look at this." He opened the magazine to an article called *Acoustic Levitation: From Science Fiction to Science Fact.*

Much to Angela's surprise, the article told of levitation research and experiments being conducted in the physics departments of major universities in various countries around the world. Even NASA was jumping onto the bandwagon. Some successful experiments had indeed produced the phenomenon of levitation using sound waves and resonant frequencies. So far the objects that had been levitated were just small things like coins and even small frogs. But as the research progressed the results were becoming more dramatic. The most recent of these experiments, using the latest technology, not only levitated the object but was also successful at maneuvering the object in horizontal directions while it was suspended in the air. The scientists claimed they were certain that the technology would one day be able to lift larger, heavier objects.

Angela was shocked. "Amazing!" she said. "I've never heard about this before!"

"You think that's something? Have you ever heard of a place called Coral Castle?"

Angela shook her head. "I don't think so. What is it?"

"Here, check this out." He turned the pages until he came to a sidebar article that the editors probably only included for it's amusement factor. "Read this," he said. "It'll blow you away. And it's all true, too. I was so intrigued when I first read it that I went to the library to check out more information. It's one of the biggest mysteries of all time but practically nobody's ever heard about it! And it's right here in our own country!"

Angela picked up the magazine and began to read.

Coral Castle, she learned, was the name given to an extraordinary stone structure in Florida. It was built single-handedly, in the early part of the 20th century, by one man with a rather odd name: Edward Leedskalnin. Because it was constructed out of giant blocks of coral rock, some weighing as much as 30 tons, it has been compared to the great wonders of the world such as Stonehenge and the pyramids of Egypt. It was a fact that some of the stone blocks in the castle weighed nearly twice as much as the largest blocks in the Great Pyramid. Leedskalnin, himself, weighed barely a hundred pounds and had tuberculosis, yet he somehow managed to quarry the huge stones, transport them to the site and move them into place by himself. Since he worked only in the dark of night - and even then only when he was sure no one was watching - no one can say for certain how he did it.

To make the story all the more incredible, he built the entire structure twice. The first location of the castle was a secluded place that suited him just fine. But after several years, more and more development was encroaching on his privacy. So he decided to move the entire castle to another location ten miles away! Again it was all done in the dark of night and, while some people did see big flatbed trucks hauling some of the giant blocks of stone, no one knew how he managed to get them onto the trucks. One of the truck drivers claimed that he was called to the site where he drove the truck up next to one of the huge stone blocks. Then Leedskalin ordered him to close his eyes until he was told to open them again. The driver claims that he did as he was instructed and within a few minutes, when he opened his eyes, the stone block, weighing several tons, was sitting on the flatbed! Another story told of two teenage boys who peeked over the tall fence one night when Leedskalnin was working and they saw one of the huge stones raise up off the ground while Leedskalnin effortlessly maneuvered it into place with nothing more than the touch of his own two hands. One bit of information, apparently confirmed, is that Leedskalin was once asked by a reporter how he was able to do these things. Leedskalnin's reply was short and sweet: "I have learned the secrets of the pyramids."

"My god!" Angela said. "That's unbelievable! I wonder if he was using *sound* to raise the stones?"

"That's a good question. As far as I know, nobody ever reported hearing any strange sounds coming from the site. But who knows? Maybe he used sound frequencies above or below the level of human hearing."

"Maybe," Angela said as she considered the possibility. "Then again, what do I know? This levitation by sound is all news to me. But apparently it's at least *theoretically* possible. There's just one thing."

"What's that?"

She pushed her plate aside and leaned forward, looking directly at Banyon. "Let's say you're right. That the way to raise this thing out of the water is by this acoustic levitation idea. Just how do you propose to create the tones? What sort of apparatus would you need? I mean, I doubt that a boombox from Radio Shack would do the trick. And the tones themselves. Would they have to be prerecorded, or would you need some kind of a device that would produce the sounds right there at the site?"

The more she tried to envision the whole scenario, the more questions came to mind. They were the same questions that had been plaguing Banyon and he had no answers.

"I don't know," he said, shaking his head. "I'm just hoping the good professor will be able to come up with some answers when we meet with him on Saturday."

~68~

Banyon and Angela arrived at Kline's office at precisely ten o'clock Saturday morning as the clouds were giving way to what was expected to be an unusually warm day for early summer in Seattle.

Professor Kline greeted them with a look of anticipation. "You brought everything?" he asked.

Banyon held up his briefcase. "It's all right here,"

"And I've got the laptop," Angela said.

"Excellent. Do you think you were followed?"

Banyon shook his head. "Not as far as we could tell."

"Well," Kline said, "just to make sure, I've parked my car behind the building. There's a back exit downstairs. The car is right next to the door. We'll take the maintenance road to leave the campus."

"All right," Banyon agreed.

"Just where is it we're going, exactly?" Angela asked.

Kline grabbed his coat and his own briefcase. "I'll tell you after we get in the car."

Once they were off campus it was only a matter of minutes before they were on the freeway heading north.

"Where are we going?" Banyon asked.

"Lake Cavenaugh," Kline replied. "I have a little summer place there."

"Never heard of it," Angela said. "Where is it?"

"About an hour and a half from here. It's a nice little mountain lake up in the Cascade foothills. I inherited the house from my father. Just a small place. Nothing fancy but right on the lake. You'll like it."

A half hour later they were off the freeway and heading into the foothills of the North Cascades. Kline was right about being able to tell if anyone was following them. The deeper into the forested territory they drove the fewer cars they encountered. Eventually they seemed to be the only car on the road.

Angela marveled at the natural beauty surrounding them on all sides. Every bend in the road brought a new perspective into view. The road, enshrouded by towering evergreens, followed the winding path of a sparkling, shallow river for several miles. For a moment Banyon flashed on the alleged accident that took the life of Kline's uncle – the innocent but much too nosey Jesuit priest - on a curvy section of the North Cascades Highway not far from where they found themselves now. He tried to let the thought pass. *Just another coincidence*, he thought to himself. He glanced over at Kline and then back to the scenery whizzing by. *I know. I know,* he mused. *No coincidences.*

The conversation along the way consisted mostly of Banyon and Angela explaining their idea about the three tones. Kline was not just intrigued by the idea but he also happened to be familiar with the research being conducted in the area of acoustic levitation. He explained that his friend and colleague, Alec Rajani, a physics professor at the college, was interested in the subject and was apparently conducting such experiments on his own time. He and Rajani had once discussed the subject over coffee in the faculty lounge. In fact it was Kline who initiated the conversation by asking Rajani if he had ever given any serious thought to the UFO phenomenon. He half expected Rajani to blow the question off as a joke. To his surprise, however, he learned that Rajani actually had an interest in the subject. Rajani, of course, didn't share this interest openly for fear of ridicule but he was fascinated by the idea and often wondered if the crafts that people reportedly witnessed might be using some form of antigravity in their propulsion systems. It was during this conversation that Kline learned about vimanas.

"Vimanas?" Kline asked, giving Rajani a puzzled look.

"Yes," Rajani replied. He still spoke with the lilting accent of his native India. "The flying vehicles described in the ancient Hindu writings."

Rajani was now an American citizen but, as he explained to Kline, he was born in India and lived there until his relatively recent arrival into the United States. "When I was much younger," he said, "my father introduced me to the strange stories from an ancient Vedic text called the *Ramayana*. It contains elaborate tales of a secret society called the Nine Unknown Men and the priest-kings who flew through the skies in flying machines called vimanas. What is amazing to me," he went on, "is that some of these tales describe these crafts as disk shaped, very much like what we now call flying saucers. And even more amazing, they describe the weapons that these vehicles had! And I am telling you they seemed to be very much like what we would think of as laser weapons. And the descriptions of the battles! I am telling you they seemed too much like nuclear warfare to be mere coincidence."

Kline was astounded by what his friend was telling him. "And these texts were written when?"

"Many thousands of years ago. I do not know for sure. Maybe it is all just tall tales made up by ancient storytellers. Or maybe not. Who can know? But the similarities between the technology they describe and the technology we have today, not to mention the similarities to some of today's UFO reports, well..." he left the sentence hanging.

"Is there anything in those texts that tells just exactly how these things flew? What sort of propulsion systems they employed?"

"Some say there were texts with that information but I have not seen them myself. That secret society I mentioned..."

"The Nine Unknown Men?"

"Yes. It is said that each of the nine men wrote a book dealing with the sciences that had been developed at that time. Remember, this was thousands of years ago! One of the books, the sixth book, is said to have been called *The Secrets of Gravitation*. Or at least that would be the rough translation. This book is supposed to have described exactly how the ships were able to fly."

"Anti-gravity?" Kline was clearly intrigued.

Rajani shrugged. "So it is said. Unfortunately, that one book is apparently the only one of the nine volumes that no one has ever been able to find."

Feeling confident that Kline would keep the discussion in confidence, Rajani went on to elaborate on his own ideas about antigravity. The topic soon steered the conversation toward the subject of acoustic levitation and the current research going on in that field.

Kline slowed to maneuver a sharp curve in the road and glanced over at Banyon. "Rajani might be someone we should think about bringing into this project," he said.

"Can he be trusted?"

Kline gave a little laugh. "Oh yes, I'm sure he can. After all, if word got out that he was involved in something as..." he paused a moment. "How should I put it? As *unconventional* as this, he could probably kiss his career goodbye. If you know what I mean."

Banyon understood. According to what Kline had told them before, scientists were pretty much confined to working within the system, within the parameters of currently accepted theories. In this case, the acoustic levitation aspect wouldn't be considered too much of a stretch in terms of exploring the fringes of accepted science. That was probably safe territory. But if anyone found out about the rest of the story it would surely mean professional suicide. *Funny,* Banyon thought to himself, *if Rajani did join our little group, and people found out about it, he'd be ridiculed. But if, after all was said and done and the mission was successful, he'd be awarded a Nobel Prize.*

The tree-lined road they were traveling on was old and barely wide enough for two cars to pass. Quick glimpses of the lake could be seen between the trees as they drove along. They soon noticed old rural mailboxes along the narrow road marking the driveways to the private residences situated around the lake.

As the car slowed down, Kline gestured with a nod. "There it is," he said. "The big yellow mailbox. That's my place."

They turned down the long driveway next to the yellow mailbox and stopped at the back of small A-framed house. Kline's description had been accurate. The house wasn't fancy but it appeared to be a comfortable place situated just fifty feet from the water.

As they got out of the car they were greeted by the sun breaking through the clouds.

"This is it," Kline said, leading the way to the back door. "Home sweet home away from home." He fumbled with a ring of keys until he found the right one and opened the door. "Come on in and make yourselves at home."

The back door opened into a small utility space and a short hallway. The place had a musty smell as if it had been closed up for some time. The only bedroom in the house was at the immediate right as they entered the hall. It was barely big enough for a double bed, a nightstand, and a chest of drawers. A few feet down the hall from the bedroom they came to a small but adequate kitchen and then into the living room. The living room was cozy with wood-paneled walls, a sofa, a couple of chairs, and a potbelly woodstove in one corner. In another corner, next to a large window, was a vintage 1950s dinette table and matching chairs. A narrow flight of stairs led to a loft that could comfortably accommodate at least two overnight guests. Angela motioned for Banyon to come over to the window.

"Check this out," she said.

He walked over and stood next to her. The window provided a panoramic view of most of the lake and the tree-covered hills behind it. The clouds had all but vanished now and the lake reflected the pastel azure of the sky.

"This is incredible!" Angela said.

Kline was back in the utility room turning on the electrical switches. "Yes!" he said, from the back of the house. "Go on out to the front deck and get a good look!"

The front door led directly out to a wooden deck. The view was spectacular. From the deck one could walk down a small flight of stairs to the lawn. The front yard extended fifty feet to the shore of the lake. "So," Kline said, joining them on the deck, "what'll you have? I've got coffee, tea and beer."

"A cold beer would suit me fine," Banyon said. "Thank you."

Angela nodded. "Sounds good to me too."

Kline smiled. "That makes three, then."

Soon they returned to the cozy front room of the cabin and settled down to the task at hand. They spent the next couple hours recapping everything Banyon and Angela knew to this point. For the most part, Kline just listened and took notes.

"And so," Banyon said, "what with the stuff Angela and I put together the other day, about the tones and the levitation idea, that pretty much brings us up to date. The big questions now are how do we produce these tones and how the heck do we get from here to the Antarctic Ocean? The whole thing just seems overwhelming."

"Indeed," Kline agreed. "It does seem overwhelming. But you know, something you said about the tones reminded me of a strange story I read a few years ago. It had something to with an archaeologist back in the 1920s, I think. He claimed he witnessed a group of monks in the Himalayan Mountains who used sound to levitate a huge boulder. I wish I could remember the details."

"Do you think we could find that story on the internet?" Angela asked.

"Yes!" Kline said. "Excellent idea. It's worth a shot anyway."

Angela set the laptop on the dinette table and began a search.

"Ah!" she said, finally. "This looks like it!" She clicked on the link and a page came up with the exact story that Kline had mentioned. Unbelievably, it was a page on Vince Paretti's website.

"Oh my god," Angela said. She looked at Banyon. "Wouldn't you just know it?"

Banyon shook his head. "That guy. We can't seem to get away from him!" Then he laughed. "Not that we'd want to."

"Who is he?" Kline asked.

Banyon explained that Paretti was the fellow with whom they'd communicated by email a few times and who had provided them with so much of the information they were seeking. "He's really into the English gematria thing," Banyon said. "In fact, he'd come up with several of the same phrases and numbers that were in the Ezekiel Code. Is that crazy or what?"

Kline looked surprised. "This fellow knew about the Ezekiel Code?"

"No," Banyon explained. "That's what was so shocking to us. He was working on other things, completely independent of anything we were doing. Anyway, it was Paretti who led us to the work of Bruce Cathie which led us to the story about the Eltanin Antenna and the connection to the number 144. It's almost as if Paretti is on a kind of parallel path in his own research. And now here he is, completely unawares, giving us more information. It's really weird."

Together, the three of them read what Paretti's web page had to say about the monks:

There's a story about an archaeologist who once visited a monastery high up in the Himalayan Mountains. There, according to the story (which was published in a newspaper), the archaeologist witnessed a group of monks as they levitated a huge block of stone. The stone lifted into the air and floated into place, high up on a cliff. They did this by making a lot of noise with some sort of drums and with horns. A quote from the article reads:

"Then 19 musical instruments were set in an arc of 90 degrees at a distance of 63 meters from the huge stone slab."

Apparently the monks started chanting and tapping on the drums and blowing on the horns, gradually increasing the rhythm and the volume. Eventually the stone began to rise. One researcher believes that if this story is true, the chanting probably had little, if anything, to do with the actual levitation. He thinks the chanting was simply part of the ceremony and that it was actually the tonal frequency of the drumming and the horns that caused the levitation.

The key things to note here are the 19 musical instruments, the 90 degrees of arc, and the 63 meters. First, notice 90 and 63 are both "9" numbers. That is, they reduce to the single digit value of 9.

Now, notice the mention of "an arc of 90 degrees". The word "arc" implies "circle". A complete circle is an "arc" of 360 degrees. An arc of 90 degrees is one quarter of the complete circle (360/4 = 90). Notice 360 is a decimal harmonic of 36, the reverse of 63, which was the number of meters in the distance from the instruments to the stone.

90 + 63 = 153 (a key Biblical number)

THREE SIXTY = 153

360 + 153 = 513

513 + 153 = 666 (a key Biblical number)

63 meters is the equivalent of 207 feet. Notice 207 is another "9" number. Now watch:

360 − 153 = 207, the number of feet equivalent to 63 meters!
Now, here's something interesting:

153 + 63 = 216 = FREQUENCY IS THE KEY
360 − 216 = 144
= CIRCLE OF SOUND
= CIRCLE OF TONES

Is this all just coincidence? I think not! And there is more:

The number 216 is a decimal harmonic of 21600. It just so happens that 21600 minutes of arc is equal to 360 degrees of a circle. Moreover, two times 216 is numerically equal to the square of the speed of light in miles per second with only an insignificant margin of error:

216 x 2 = 432 = sq. rt. of 186,624 (0.18% error)

Notice 432 is the Kali Yuga cycle-of-time number and also the reverse of 234 which is the gematria value of the phrase: THE GREAT PYRAMID OF GIZA. I mention this because we're dealing with numbers generated by the story of the monks levitating a giant stone and no one really knows how the giant stones of the Great Pyramid were raised and maneuvered into place. Perhaps it was by the same technique? Levitation by sound?

Now, regarding the number 19
(the number of musical instruments)

First we notice this:
SOUND = 73 = TONES = NOTES
= STONE = NUMBER

73 − 19 = 54 = TONE = NOTE

HARMONIC TONE = 288 = 144 x 2
288 is the CPS (Cycles Per Second) of the note "D" at a specific point in the musical scale when the note of "A" is tuned to 432 CPS (see the work of Jim Furino).

From Furino's work I discovered the following gematria:

THE HARMONIC FREQUENCY TONES ARE A, D, E, G = 342

Banyon nudged Angela. "Do you see that?" he said. "Those tones – A, D, and E – they're the same as the ones we came up with! But he has a fourth note, G. What's up with that?"

Angela nodded. "The G-note is more of an incidental. In a chord progression of A, D, and E, for example, the G note could be added to the A-chord. Since G is the seventh note up the scale from A, that would turn the A-chord into an A-7th chord. That would produce a kind of transitional sound as you go from the A-chord into the D-chord."

Banyon was completely lost. "Come again?"

Angela shook her head. "Never mind. That extra G in there is incidental. For our purposes it doesn't matter."

Banyon shrugged. "Whatever you say."

They continued to read through Paretti's work:

Now divide that 342 by the alphanumeric value of TONE (TONE = 54):

342 / 54 = 6.3, a decimal harmonic of 63, the number of meters in the levitation story.

So, we have identified the number 342 as being associated with the harmonic tones, A, D, E, G. Now, referencing back to our number 19 we find this:

342 / 19 = 18

EIGHTEEN = 73 = TONES = NOTES = SOUND = STONE = NUMBER

HARMONIC = 81, the reverse of 18.

81 − 18 = 63, the number of meters in the story!
63 x 2 = 126 = THE CAPSTONE (another reference to the Great Pyramid?)

TONE = 54

FIFTY FOUR = 126 = THE CAPSTONE

"Well, professor," Banyon said after everyone had finished reading the page, "what do you think? Bet you didn't expect to get all that in addition to the monk story, eh?"

Kline sat back and shook his head. "That's a lot to take in all at one time!"

Angela laughed. "Now you have some idea of what we've been dealing with."

"I do, indeed. And you know what I have to say about coincidences."

"Yup," Angela said. "We're constantly reminding each other of what you said."

Kline grinned. "Well, then," he said, "that being the case, I'm inclined to think the information in this story of the monks holds another key to the puzzle. Wouldn't you agree?"

"What part of the story?" Banyon asked.

Kline thought for a moment. "Judging from what your friend, Paretti, has laid out here, I'd say there's something to be learned from the way the monks situated themselves with their instruments in front of the stone. The idea of the quarter circle and the specific distance from the object of their intention. Clearly, they had some reason for this."

"Wait a second," Angela said. She got out the copy of the phrase list from the Ezekiel Code. "I thought so!"

"What is it?" Banyon asked.

"Look here," she pointed to a phrase on the list:

CIRCLE OF STONE = 144

Then she pointed out the phrase on Paretti's web page:

CIRCLE OF TONES = 144

"See that?" she said. "It's just a rearrangement of the letters in the words *stone* and *tones*."

Kline wasn't sure what she was getting at. "So what are you saying?"

"I'm saying maybe this *circle-of-stone* phrase is a double clue. Maybe our project requires a full circle rather than just a quarter circle. Literally, a *circle of tones*."

Banyon considered the idea for a moment. "Hmm. You may be right. I think you might be on to something. Question is, how big of a circle?"

"Well," Kline offered, "according to that story about the monks, it appears that the stone they levitated was situated 63 meters from the circumference of their quarter circle. If we extrapolate from that information we could assume the stone marked the center of what would have been a *full* circle."

"What are you getting at?" Banyon asked.

Kline continued. "You wanted to know how big the circle should be, right?"

Banyon nodded.

"Then," Kline went on, "let's suppose that object, that antenna - like the stone in the story - marks the center of our circle. Simple geometry. Here, let me illustrate."

He drew a circle on a piece of paper and put a dot in the middle of the circle. "The dot is the antenna, " he said. "Now draw a straight line from the dot to the edge of the circle. The distance from that dot to the circumference of the circle is the radius. In this case -if we're using the information in the story as our model - the radius of the circle is 63 meters. From this radius of 63 meters we can calculate the actual diameter of the entire circle."

"Meters," Banyon said. "I have no idea what a meter is. What is that in feet?"

Kline thought for a moment, trying to do the conversion in his head. "That would be... uh...that would be about 207 feet."

"Exactly!" Angela exclaimed. "Look, it's right here in Paretti's paper."

Banyon's eyes lit up. "Really? I like that number!" He could tell Kline didn't get it. "It's a *nine-number!*" he explained. "It reduces to the single digit value of nine. It fits right in with all the rest of this stuff! So then, if the radius is 207 feet then the diameter must be 414 feet, right? Two times the radius?"

"Exactly," Kline said. "Our circle of tones would be 414 feet across."

"Or," Angela said, "126 meters."

Not having a great love for the metric system, Banyon was about to brush her comment off when he glanced at the portion of the text she was pointing to on the computer screen:

63 x 2 = 126 = THE CAPSTONE (another reference to the Great Pyramid?)

"As we should know by now," Angela said, "it's not always about the *unit* of measurement. Feet, inches, meters..." She looked up at Banyon. "Sometimes it's just the *number* that's important."

"That's true," Banyon conceded, staring at the words on the screen. "And I can't help but notice the pyramid and the capstone keep sneaking into the picture." Then he groaned, "I hope this doesn't mean a trip to Egypt. That's all I'd need on top of everything else."

Kline gave an understanding nod. "The capstone thing is interesting, isn't it? There's a school of thought that the missing capstone has some alchemical symbolism about it. Something to do with transformation. There's a legend that says the capstone will appear when the earth is about to transform from a state of relative spiritual ignorance to a more enlightened state. When you think about it - from what you told me about the message of that prophecy... who was it? Brother..."

"Brother Hiram," Angela said. "What about it?"

"Yes, thank you," Kline continued. "That prophecy of Brother Hiram did imply some sort of a major change was coming."

"What are you trying to say?" Banyon asked.

"Not sure, really," Kline admitted. "But it couldn't hurt to just keep it in the back our collective mind. It could be an important part of the bigger picture."

They continued to talk and eventually the discussion came back around to the circle of tones. Giving the idea even more thought, they realized if the monk's *quarter* circle required 19 musical instruments then their proposed *full* circle would require four times that many sound devices, all situated around the circumference. Doing the math, Banyon found 4 x 19 equalled 76. Getting *one of those feelings* again, he checked the gematria:

SEVENTY SIX = 162 = THE THREE TONES

ONE SIX TWO = 144 = ELTANIN ANTENNA = CIRCLE OF TONES

Kline was visibly stunned. "How did you know that?" he asked.

Angela gave a laugh. "You haven't seen anything yet. Wait'll he really gets warmed up."

Banyon was hardly paying them any attention. He was thinking about the three tones. According to what he and Angela had figured out, the three tones were actually three chords and each chord consisted of three notes. "So," he said, "if we have 76 sound devices then each one will actually be broadcasting three chords or nine individual notes simultaneously. What does that give us?" He did the math on the calculator: 9 x 76 = 684. Again, he went for the gematria:

SIX HUNDRED EIGHTY FOUR NOTES = 333 = THE VIBRATIONAL FREQUENCY OF NINE

Angela leaned over and whispered to Kline. "See what I mean?"

Kline was completely taken aback. But it was just the beginning. As their discussion continued into the late afternoon, certain words and ideas seemed to trigger the gematria downloads into Banyon's consciousness. When the conversation got around to questions about just exactly what sort of device could generate the necessary tones, they found themselves at a loss for answers. Again, Kline suggested it would be a good idea to bring his friend, Alec Rajani, the physics professor, into the group. They all agreed it was probably a wise decision. They really had no other source for such expertise. Nevertheless, Banyon felt something coming. He grabbed the calculator, punched in some numbers and wrote:

TONE GENERATORS = 176

The number meant nothing to him until he felt another download coming. The pendulum was about to swing right back to the mysteries of ancient Egypt. They were about to make the disturbing discovery of just how precious little time they had to figure this all out and, with any luck, to prevent the most catastrophic disaster the modern world had ever known.

~69~

Nathan Crown stood gazing patiently out the window at the unusually blue sky stretching endlessly over the great Bering Sea. One by one the other eight members of The Nine arrived and seated themselves around the large round conference table. When everyone was present, Crown took his seat at the table.

"Gentlemen," he said, "thank you for coming on such short notice. Since the information I have to share with you is brief I would have preferred to phone each of you rather than have you make the trip. However, I can no longer be certain that our communications are entirely secure."

This news, alone, caused a brief buzz of concern among the members. These were men whose lives and reputations, outside the walls of this secluded room, would be jeopardized if the world outside discovered who they really were. Two of them, Sam Delaney, the gray-haired U.S. senator from the Midwest and Oscar Hart, the executive editor of one of America's most influential newspapers, were old friends. Sitting on opposite sides of the table, they exchanged worried glances. Several of the members shifted uncomfortably in their chairs as they waited for an explanation. Crown raised a hand to ease their apprehension.

"I don't want to cause undue alarm," he said. "I have no direct evidence of anyone trying to penetrate our security or monitor our communications. I simply mentioned it as a precaution."

The senator cleared his throat. "Come on, Nathan," he said. "What's going on?"

Nathan Crown scanned the uneasy faces of the other men. "Simply this," he said. "Our man in Rome informs me that something has been causing a bit of a stir at the Jesuit headquarters. Not among the rank and file but at the top."

"So General DuPont's got his panties in a knot," said Hart. "That's not exactly news."

The comment raised a few knowing chuckles and several heads bobbed in agreement.

"True," Crown smiled. Then his expression became more serious. "But this is different. As you know it's extremely difficult to learn much about anything going on at the top levels of the Order. What we do know, however, is that recent chatter suggests DuPont has hired someone to electronically monitor Banyon's private conversations – even in his own home. Simply put, it seems Mr. Banyon may have unraveled some important information and DuPont..." he paused for a moment. "Well, let's just say DuPont may be a step or two ahead of us in the game, as a result."

Senator Delaney spoke up. "But what about Professor Kline? I thought he was supposed to keep you informed of any new developments! What's he doing? Have you heard from him?"

Crown shook his head. "He hasn't contacted me for several days. I tried to reach him this morning but there was no answer."

"I don't like it," Hart said. "Without Kline we have no close link to Banyon."

The senator chimed in. "I hate to bring this up," he said, "but is it possible that Kline is the one who's feeding information to DuPont?"

Crown shook his head. "No, I doubt that. I trust Kline. There must be something else going on."

"So what do we do now?" Hart asked.

"If I don't hear from Kline by Monday" Crown said, "I'll send someone to investigate. Until then..." he stood up to indicate that the meeting was over, "...we wait."

~70~

The warm afternoon sun finally peeked over the eves of Kline's lakeside cabin, and came streaming in through the large front window.

"Getting warm in here," Kline said, opening the front door. "Anyone for a break?" Without waiting for a reply, he stepped out onto the deck and breathed in a hefty helping of fresh mountain air. Angela got up and followed him out to the deck.

"Come on, Zeke," she said.

"In a minute," Banyon responded, still sitting at the table staring at that last phrase:

TONE GENERATORS = 176

Although the number seemed meaningless it was that very meaninglessness that somehow kept drawing him back to it. *What is it?* he kept repeating to himself. *What the hell is it?* After several minutes he was about to give up and join the professor and Angela on the deck when he started to get that familiar feeling. Suddenly the synapses in his brain were firing rapidly like a string of tiny firecrackers. He grabbed his calculator. With one finger, he could tap out the alphanumeric values of words and phrases on the keypad faster than most people could type. It was strange, this gift he'd acquired. But it worked, somehow bringing order out of chaos in an oddly, but obviously, interconnected universe. It was becoming increasingly difficult to deny Kline's comment about being guided by some invisible force. *May the force be with me*, he grinned to himself as his index finger worked its magic on the calculator's keypad. He picked up the pencil and scrawled the result on the notepad:

ONE HUNDRED SEVENTY SIX = 270

He smiled and marveled at the number for a moment. *Good hit*, he mused. *Reduces to nine. But what is it? Gotta be something.* He grabbed the copy of the Ezekiel Code phrases and scanned the list. The number 270 wasn't on it. He scratched his head. *What's it refer to?* He checked the Ezekiel Code list again. Maybe he'd missed something. No. Nothing there. But he was in the flow. It would come. He could feel it. When the pressure was on, entire phrases seemed to enter his mind from out of nowhere. Such was the case at this very moment. He was tapped into the source – whatever the source was – and the words came. After an almost frantic twenty-minute flurry of calculating and jotting down the results, he came to an abrupt stop and sat straight up. It was like someone suddenly pulled the plug and cut the power. He felt dazed, as if he'd been in a trance. He blinked hard and shook his head to clear the fog. Staring at what he'd just written, it was as if he were just now seeing it for the first time. It was a shocker. *Jesus Christ!* he thought. *What the hell was that?*

~71~

"Apparently he's not into taking a break," Kline commented. He leaned comfortably against the deck railing with the warmth of the sun against his back.

Angela watched a crow pecking at something down by the lake. "So it would seem," she said. "He's probably lost in his numbers. I'll go drag him out here."

She walked into the living room and found Banyon staring at the piece of paper with a puzzled look on his face. "Oh-oh," she groaned. "Just as I thought."

Banyon looked up. "Yeah. Oh-oh is right. Check this out."

She moved over to the table and leaned over his shoulder to see what he'd written. "What the...?" She bent down closer to get a better look. "What is all this?" she asked, nudging him out of his chair so she could sit down and study the jumble of words and numbers.

Kline returned to the living room. "Am I missing something?" he asked.

Without glancing up, Angela motioned for him to come take a look.

He peered over Angela's shoulder. "Good lord," he said. "What's all this?"

Angela gave a knowing chuckle. "My question exactly."

Banyon was as bewildered as anyone. He shook his head. "Don't ask me. I have no idea where all that came from. Hell, I don't even know what it all means. There are words in there that I've never even heard of before."

It was, indeed, a mysterious jumble of seemingly disjointed information. And yet, somehow, it seemed to have a sort of cohesive underlying thread woven throughout. One could feel it on an intuitive level but, clearly, if there was a message embedded in the noise, it was going to take some work to figure it out.

Banyon had scribbled the words and phrases so quickly that some of it was difficult to read. Angela took on the task of making it more legible by typing it into her word processing program. When she finished typing she plugged in the portable printer and ran out a copy for each of them. With his own copy in hand, Banyon sat back to have a fresh look at his latest download:

TONE GENERATORS = 176
= MUSICAL ALPHABET = FOUR POINT FIVE

ONE HUNDRED SEVENTY SIX = 270
= NORTH+SOUTH+EAST+WEST
= ISIS+OSIRIS+HORUS+SET (SETH)
= THE CAPSTONE IS A MERKABA VEHICLE
= COUNTER ROTATING MERKABAS

ISIS IS THE EAST = 162 = 9

OSIRIS IS THE NORTH = 225 = 9

HORUS IS THE SOUTH = 225 = 9

SETH IS THE WEST = 180 = 9

162 + 225 + 225 + 180 = 792

792 / 4 = 198 = THE NINE SACRED TONES
= ONE TONE IS ONE CHORD
= THE MUSICAL SCALE OF GOD
= THE GOLDEN MEAN SPIRAL
= COUNTER SPINNING
= POSITIVE + NEGATIVE

THE INNER MERKABA = 144
= INTERNAL MERKABA
= THE HOLY MERKABA
= THE PERFECT BALANCE

OUTWARD MERKABA = 153
= SPINNING MERKABA
= THE TONES OF GOD
= THE ALCHEMY OF LIFE

THE STAR OF DAVID IS A COUNTER ROTATING MERKABA = 432 = 9
THE DESTROYER = 162 = 9

ONE SIX TWO = 144 = 9
REGENERATOR = 126 = THE CAPSTONE

ONE TWO SIX = 144

THE DESTROYER REGENERATOR = 288 = 144 x 2

SET IS THE DESTROYER = 234
= THE GREAT PYRAMID OF GIZA

ISIS IS THE REGENERATOR = 243 = 9

234 + 243 = 477
= FOUR HUNDRED AND THIRTY TWO CYCLES PER SECOND

THE CORNER STONE OF THE GODDESS = 306 = 9

THE CAPSTONE = 126 = 9

306 + 126 = 432 = 9

THE CAPSTONE IS THE CORNERSTONE = 333
= THE VIBRATIONAL FREQUENCY OF NINE

ONE POINT SIX ONE EIGHT = 243 = 9

THE PHI PROPORTION OF ONE POINT SIX ONE EIGHT = 486 = 9

486 / 3 = 162 = THE TONE SPIRAL
= THE THREE TONES = THE TIME PORTAL
THE GOLDEN MEAN SPIRAL = 198
= THE MUSICAL SCALE OF GOD

THE TIME PORTAL = 162 = THE SHIFT OF THE AGE

THE THREE TONES ARE THE KEYS = 279 = 9

THE THREE TONES OPEN THE DOOR = 297
= THE NUMBERS OF THE GREAT WORK

THE THREE TONES OPEN THE DOOR INTO FOUR POINT FIVE = 531 = 9
FOUR POINT FIVE IS THE DOOR TO THE TIME PORTAL = 486
= THE PHI PROPORTION OF ONE POINT SIX ONE EIGHT

FOUR POINT FIVE IS THE DOOR TO THE NEXT DIMENSION = 522 = 9

0123...4.5...6789
FORTY FIVE = 126
= FIFTY FOUR
= THE CAPSTONE
= THE ANKH OF GOLD

TONE = 54 = 9

54 + 54 + 54 = TONE + TONE + TONE = 162
= THE THREE TONES = THE TIME PORTAL

THE TORAH MATRIX CODE = 207
= ACTIVATE THE CAPSTONE
= THE GOLD ANKH IS THE KEY

THE BIBLE CODE = 90 = 9

THE ANKH IS THE KEY TO THE CAPSTONE = 315 = 9

THE LOCULUS HOLDS THE GOLD KEY = 306 = 9

THE GREAT WORK IS THE KEY TO THE CREATION OF LIFE = 459 = 9

FOUR FIVE NINE = 144 = 9

DNA IS AN INFORMATION SYSTEM CREATED BY INTELLIGENCE = 495 = 9

FOUR NINE FIVE = 144 = 9

DNA IS A HOLOGRAPHIC SYSTEM = 261 = 9

TWO SIX ONE = 144 = 9

THE ALCHEMICAL CODE IS THE GREAT WORK = 306 = 9

ALCHEMICAL TRANSMUTATION TONE = 306 = 9

THE NINE TRANSMUTATION CODES = 306 = 9

THE CODE WITHIN DNA = 162 = THE THREE TONES

FOUR FIVE NINE ARE THE HOLOGRAPHIC NUMBERS = 405 = 9
ONE TWO SIX ARE THE HOLOGRAPHIC NUMBERS = 405 = 9

ONE TWO SIX FOUR FIVE NINE ARE THE HOLOGRAPHIC NUMBERS = 549 = 9

FIVE FOUR NINE = 144 = 9
HOLOGRAPHIC UNIVERSE = 225
= DEOXYRIBOSE NUCLEIC ACID CODE
= DOUBLE HELIX GEOMETRY

GEOMETRY OF THE DOUBLE HELIX = 279 = 9

THE TONE WAS WITH GOD = 216 = 9

THE TONE WAS GOD = 175 = 4

THE TONE WAS MADE FLESH = 203 = 5

216 + 175 + 203 = 594 = 9

FIVE NINE FOUR = 144 = 9

THE THREE HARMONIC TONES OF THE ONE VOICE OF GOD = 432 = 9

Banyon sat back with a befuddled look on his face. Then, scanning the list quickly one more time, his eyes fell on the phrases with the word *merkaba*. "I don't believe this all came out of me!" he said. "And what the hell is a merkaba?"

~72~

Angela was stumped by Banyon's question about the merkaba. The professor, on the other hand, was at least somewhat familiar with the subject.

"Well," Kline said, "I'll tell you what little I can remember about it. The merkaba is a metaphysical concept. Essentially it has to do with moving between dimensions. Think of it as a kind of space-time vehicle created out of counter rotating energy fields, male and female, positive and negative. Here," he said, reaching for a blank sheet of paper. He picked up the pencil and drew two interlocking triangles, one superimposed upon the other. One triangle was pointed upward. The other pointed down.

Banyon recognized it immediately. "The star of David," he said.

Kline nodded. "Exactly. Look here." He pointed out the phrase that Banyon had written:

THE STAR OF DAVID IS A COUNTER ROTATING MERKABA = 432

"The star of David," Kline continued, "is, of course, a flat two-dimensional image like I've drawn it here. But an actual merkaba is supposedly a three-dimensional object composed of two interlocking tetrahedrons."

Banyon shook his head. "You're losing me already. What's a tetrahedron?"

"I think I know," Angela said. "It's a three dimensional geometric form. Kind of like a pyramid shape but the tetrahedron only has four sides."

"Wait a second," Banyon said. "A *pyramid* has four sides. So what's the difference between a tetrahedron and a pyramid shape?"

"No," Angela explained. "We tend to think of a pyramid as having only four sides because that's all we see when we look at the Great Pyramid, for example. But remember, it's sitting on the ground. If you lifted it up off the ground you'd see the flat side underneath, right? That's the fifth side."

"Ah," Banyon said, now getting the picture. "So a pyramid shape really has five sides. Or four sides and a bottom side, so to speak. Right? And the tetrahedron has *three* sides and a bottom side, or four faces altogether. I get it."

"Exactly right," Kline said. "Now, the tetrahedron pointing upward represents the male energy and the one pointing downward represents the female energy. The whole thing symbolizes a perfect balance of male and female energies or positive and negative energies."

"And it's supposed to function as a vehicle of some kind?" Angela asked.

"Yes. The whole thing works as a unit where the two interlocking parts rotate in opposite directions, the male to the left and the female to the right. Amazingly, it's all indicated in these phrases. Look here." Directing their attention again to Banyon's download of cryptic information, he pointed out certain phrases such as *counter spinning*, *counter rotating, the perfect balance*, and *positive+negative.* "There's something profoundly interesting going on here, especially since this merkaba idea has a direct link to Ezekiel."

Banyon and Angela both looked surprised. "What? How do you mean?" Banyon asked.

"Well," Kline explained, "In the Kabbalist tradition, that mysterious flying contraption described by Ezekiel in the Bible is said to be a merkaba. Even the *Sefer Yetzirah* refers to Ezekiel's merkaba as a mystical chariot."

"I'm sorry," Banyon said. "The Sefer what?"

"The *Sefer Yetzirah*. It's the most mysterious and possibly the oldest of the books in the tradition of Kabbalah."

"Mystical chariot," Angela said, musing over the implication. "Interesting way of putting it."

Banyon, still confused, was left scratching his head. "But," he said, trying to make some sense out of it, "you just showed us how the merkaba is supposed to look like these interlocked three-dimensional triangle things."

"Tetrahedrons," Angela threw the word in for him.

Banyon nodded. "Right. Tetrahedrons. But we've read Ezekiel's description of whatever it was he encountered and there's nothing about it in the Biblical text that even remotely resembles this tetrahedron thing. So what's the deal? I'm confused."

"I agree," Kline said. "It would seem to be contradictory information. I'm only telling you what little I know about it. It's possible the differences might be due to varying interpretations of the merkaba coming from different esoteric traditions. Or perhaps the merkaba can take different forms. I don't know. In any case there does seem to be a direct link here to Ezekiel. That, in itself, is remarkable considering that the only reason we're even here talking about it is because of the Ezekiel scroll in the first place. Like I mentioned before, I believe you're being guided by something beyond our comprehension. This is the most remarkable thing I've ever witnessed."

"Yeah?" Banyon quipped with a wry chuckle. "You should be in my shoes. You think it's remarkable. I think it's just freakin' weird."

Kline nodded and took a deep breath. "Yes, well, I'm afraid it might get even weirder."

The comment raised Banyon's eyebrows. "What do you mean?"

"Well, there's something else I see here." He pointed out the phrases that used the terms *alchemical* and *the great work*.

"I noticed that," Banyon said. "More stuff that's totally unfamiliar to me."

Kline explained that *The Great Work* is a reference to alchemy.

"Alchemy," Angela said. "You mentioned alchemy a little while ago in connection with the capstone."

Kline nodded. "Yes. In some esoteric teachings the capstone of the Great Pyramid is an important alchemical symbol."

"Wait a minute," Banyon said. "I think I've got this merkaba business but now what the heck is this alchemy stuff?"

Angela jumped in. "Something to do with turning base metals, like lead for example, into gold." She looked to the professor for confirmation. "That's right, isn't it?"

Kline grinned. "Well, yes and no. The Hollywood movie image of the alchemist as a crazy old man with a long beard and a pointy hat, mixing potions in a dungeon, trying to turn lead into gold, is pretty much what most people think of as alchemy. But it's much more than that. Turning a base metal into gold through a transmutation of the elements wasn't the ultimate goal, despite what most people think. The ultimate goal of alchemy was really the transformation of consciousness and eventual immortality. Some alchemists were even convinced it was possible to bring a dead person back to life through a kind of regeneration of the cells."

Banyon looked skeptical. "Sounds more like witchcraft if you ask me."

Kline nodded. "I know. And it was – still is – considered by many to be a form of sorcery. But these terms, witchcraft and sorcery, are just labels that people attach to things they don't understand or that they're afraid of. It's a terribly taboo subject within the Christian community, for example, even though there were many Christian alchemists in the early days following the crucifixion of Christ. There were many Gnostic Christians who believed Christ was, himself, a master alchemist."

"Ah," said Angela. "Sure. That turning-water-into-wine thing. It could be thought of as a form of alchemy. I can see that."

"Good example," Kline said. "And, of course, there was the idea of the resurrection which would have been seen as a dramatic demonstration of the ultimate alchemical transmutation. It's all really very intriguing actually, when you think about it. And I see more indications of the alchemical process here in these phrases."

"Such as?" Banyon asked.

Kline pointed out the same phrases that he saw as pertaining to the merkaba: *counter rotating, counter spinning, the perfect balance*, and *positive+negative*. "These," he explained, "are very much in keeping with the alchemical process of combining opposites in such a way as to create a harmonic balance. It ties the idea of alchemy into the notion of the merkaba. Interesting. I hadn't thought of it in that way before. The more I look at it the more fascinating it becomes." He paused for a moment to consider all that he was seeing. Then, more to himself than to anyone else, he muttered, "I wish Miriam was here."

"Who?" Angela asked.

Kline looked up. "What? Oh. Miriam. Miriam Flamel. She's a student of alchemy. I met her a few years ago through Frank McClintock. As you might imagine, McClintock's interest in the lost scroll resulted in his coming into contact with some rather interesting characters along the way. Miriam was one of them. Nice young woman. A little too deep into the Goth movement for my tastes. You know, all the black clothing and multiple ear piercings. A little stud in the side of her nose, too, as I recall. But very likeable, actually. Not nearly as strange as she looked. Of course I haven't seen her for a couple of years. She could be covered in tattoos now for all I know."

"She was really an alchemist?" Banyon asked.

"Well, I'm not sure she would claim such a title. I only heard her refer to herself as a student of alchemy. By that I think she meant she was more interested in the history of it rather than actually practicing the art. Although she did claim to be related to Nicholas Flamel, a fourteenth century alchemist. She didn't tell me that, herself. It was something she told McClintock and I heard it from him. Anyway, after he told me about it, I looked up Nicholas Flamel in an old encyclopedia of the occult and, sure enough, there he was. One of the few who claimed to actually have succeeded in changing a base metal into silver or gold several times."

"So you think she's really related to him?" Angela asked.

Kline shrugged. "Who knows. Maybe she's just conveniently trading on the name. Or maybe it's true. I have no idea. But she might be a good person to bring into the group. Especially if I'm right about what I see here. It looks like we may be needing an expert in alchemy."

Banyon laughed quietly to himself. "Is there anybody you don't know?" he asked sarcastically.

Kline looked surprised at the comment. "What do you mean?"

Banyon shook his head. "I don't know. It's just that every time we need some sort of expert information about one thing or another you seem to be able to pull just the right person out of your hat. First there was the rabbi who was able to translate the scroll. Then there's your friend who just happens to be knowledgeable about acoustic levitation. And now you're telling us you know an expert in the obscure art of alchemy. Just seems a little odd, that's all."

"I hadn't thought about it," Kline said. "Now that you bring it up, I guess it does seem a bit fortuitous, doesn't it? Then again, as you well know by now, I don't believe in coincidence. I'm guessing I was probably destined for this role just as you were destined for yours. Don't you think?"

Banyon shrugged. "I suppose," he said, reluctantly conceding the point.

"Well, gentlemen," Angela said, getting up to stretch. "I have a suggestion. Why don't we break for something to eat? I brought bread and some cheese and sliced ham."

"Excellent idea," Kline said. "And there's more beer in the refrigerator. Or juice, if you prefer. Just help yourselves."

This time Banyon welcomed the idea of a breather. He and Kline opened another beer and stepped out onto the deck while Angela prepared the sandwiches. Banyon looked at his watch. It was nearly three o'clock and the sun was still blazing in the clear blue sky.

"You know Zane Grey?" Kline asked. "The famous writer of novels about the Old West?"

Banyon sat on the bench next to the deck railing and took a sip of beer. "Not personally," he said.

Kline laughed. "Well, he had a shack up in those hills behind my place. When would that have been? Back in the 50s? Anyway, apparently he wrote a few of his novels up there. Or so folks around here say."

"No kidding? That's pretty cool. You think it's true?"

Kline shrugged. "I don't know. I kind of like the thought though."

Then he laughed. "Actually, I'm afraid to check it out. If it turned out not to be true I'm afraid I'd be disappointed."

Angela came out with the sandwiches on a tray. "Here you go, boys. Dig in."

An hour passed and the small talk got smaller, to the point where it nearly vanished. Finally Banyon decided to crank it up a notch. "So," he said, downing his last swallow of beer, "do either of you have any idea what those references to the Egyptian gods might mean?"

"And goddess," Angela said. "Remember, Isis is in there too."

Banyon smiled. "I stand corrected. Any ideas?"

"I was looking at that," Kline said. "Interesting how they seem to be associated with the four cardinal directions, north, south, east and west. I've never seen that before. I have no idea why they might be linked together like that."

"Unless," Angela said, "it has something to do with the Great Pyramid."

"How so?" Kline asked.

"Well, it's just a guess," she answered, 'but I do remember in my anthropology class we spent a little time talking about the pyramids of Egypt. And I remember someone saying that the Great Pyramid was perfectly aligned with the cardinal points of the earth. Someone else pointed out that it was off by something like one twelfth of a degree but our anthropology instructor said that was because over time there had been a slight shift in the earth's axis."

"So in other words," Banyon said, "it was in perfect alignment when it was constructed?"

Angela nodded. "Apparently so."

Kline was impressed with Angela's contribution. "That's interesting," he said. "It does make some sense, then, that the pantheon of Egyptian deities would be associated with the four directions. Still, I don't ever recall seeing that association before. It's just odd."

"Maybe it's like some of the other things we've worked on," Angela said. "It seems that sometimes the numbers are just as important as the phrases. In some cases I think the numbers actually take priority over the phrases. What was the number connected to that batch of phrases?"

Banyon couldn't remember and neither could the professor. They moved back inside and gathered around the table with their copies of

Banyon's latest download. Kline was still a little bothered by Banyon's comment about him coming up with all the right people to help them along the way. *If he thinks that's something*, he thought to himself, *I wonder what he'd say if he knew about my connection to the Nine? Maybe I should just get it all out into the open.* This dilemma kept creeping back into his mind. He was feeling increasingly uncomfortable keeping the secret from Banyon. It was, after all, a hell of a secret. He was one of only a handful of people on the entire planet who had a connection with the most secret society in history. He realized it was an honor to be in their trust. Betrayal of that trust could have devastating consequences for him, personally, to say nothing about the entire project. But the secret was becoming a burden. He was going to have to give it some serious thought.

~73~

The sum of the numbers in the batch of phrases pertaining to the Egyptian pantheon was 792. Other than the fact that it could be reduced to 9, it meant nothing to them. The only thing that did have some meaning was where the number 792 had been divided by 4. The reason for the division by 4 was apparently because the number, itself, was the sum of the four phrases that produced it. The quotient from dividing 792 by 4 was 198. That number was at least familiar to them as were some of the phrases connected with it. The most meaningful, at the moment, were the phrases about the tones and chords. Banyon was surprised to see THE NINE SACRED TONES included. It was the same phrase that came to him several days ago when Angela was giving him a quick lesson in music theory. The phrases, COUNTER SPINNING and POSITIVE+NEGATIVE, also now seemed relevant after Kline's informative mini-lecture about the merkaba. The phrase containing the geometry term, *Golden Mean*, and the one about *God's musical scale* were still a bit baffling. The most they could derive from the whole thing was that it simply tended to confirm at least a few of the ideas they'd already worked out.

They spent the rest of the afternoon and well into the evening discussing this new download of material, trying to pull all the pieces together into some sort of bigger picture. The process was as excruciating as it was intellectually stimulating. It was a taxing procedure of connect-the-dots. Eventually they had the entire contents of Banyon's briefcase, every scrap of note paper, every computer print-out, the copy of the Ezekiel Code phrase list, the McClintock notes – everything – spread out on the table. By the time the moon was high over the lake they felt they had made some progress. Between the three of them, each reaching back into their cranial storehouses of half forgotten knowledge acquired over the years, they were able to come up with more answers to the puzzle than they otherwise would have imagined.

Kline's notion that Banyon was being guided by some mysterious unknown force was called into question when they discovered that many of the words and phrases in this latest download already existed in and amongst the cache of miscellaneous notes and papers they'd collected over the past months. It came as no surprise to Banyon and Angela that many of those words and phrases were in the printouts of Paretti's work. Paretti had no knowledge of the Ezekiel Code or anything else pertaining to Banyon's appointed quest. Paretti had been working, independently, for years, simply trying to establish a basis for a gematria system based on the English alphabet. Simultaneously he was focusing on the mystery of the number 9 and what he perceived as its intimate connection with the phenomenon of synchronicity. The fact that he'd come up with so many of the same phrases and numerical values that were found in the Ezekiel Code as well as in Banyon's own enigmatic downloads certainly reflected the synchronicity aspect. It also made them wonder if it had less to do with mysterious guiding forces and more to do with simply tapping into the archetypal realm where every imaginable – and unimaginable - idea, concept, and informational data-bit exists in a sort of shadow world just waiting to be tapped. Still, even if that were the case, it didn't explain why some people – Banyon and Paretti as prime examples – seemed more tuned in to that realm than others. Perhaps something, some word, some number, some emotion, some event occurs and sets the spark, igniting the connection between an individual human consciousness and the archetypal realm. On the one hand it seemed like a pretty good answer, at least as a way to explain the work of someone like Paretti. But it only partially explained Banyon's unique position. His case was different. It involved something more. Kline knew it for certain but he couldn't, of course, let on that he knew it. Moreover, he couldn't reveal *how* he knew it. Or could he? Should he? Again it was the question of his association with the Brotherhood of the Nine Pillars and, again, he was frustrated with having to pretend that he was merely engaging in speculation along with his two companions. *Maybe tomorrow*, he thought. He knew if he brought it up now it would disrupt the work that was progressing so well.

As they studied the material it soon became clear that much of it, especially that which pertained to DNA, as well as anything having to do with alchemy, would have to wait. Kline's gut feeling, in fact, was that the subjects of DNA and alchemy were probably intimately connected. Miriam Flamel would be their best bet when it came to this subject. Several other things, however, seemed to be falling into place.

The reference to Set/Seth seemed to square with the information Banyon had found in Wood and Campbell's book, *GENESET: Target Earth*. Rifling through the mound of material now on the table, Banyon spied the small piece of paper he was hoping to find. It was the group of phrases he'd jotted down on the airplane during their flight home from France:

ISIS = 56 = COMET

COMET SETH = 108

THE COMET OF SETH = 162 = THE DESTROYER
THE RETURN OF THE DEATH STAR = 279
= RETURN OF THE DESTROYER

Banyon laid the note down next to the paper with the new phrases for comparison:

THE DESTROYER = 162

ONE SIX TWO = 144
REGENERATOR = 126 = THE CAPSTONE

ONE TWO SIX = 144
THE DESTROYER REGENERATOR = 288 = 144 x 2

SET IS THE DESTROYER = 234
= THE GREAT PYRAMID OF GIZA
ISIS IS THE REGENERATOR = 243

234 + 243 = 477
= FOUR HUNDRED AND THIRTY TWO CYCLES PER SECOND

THE CORNER STONE OF THE GODDESS = 306

THE CAPSTONE = 126

306 + 126 = 432

THE CAPSTONE IS THE CORNERSTONE = 333
= THE VIBRATIONAL FREQUENCY OF NINE

There was no question about it. Clearly there was some symbolic notion here that the capstone of the Great Pyramid was somehow associated with the Goddess Isis. Isis was being presented as the feminine aspect to balance out the masculine aspect of this potentially frightening implication, the impact of a comet. Set/Seth, the destroyer was the comet and Isis the Regenerator was the Capstone.

Something began to stir in the back of Banyon's mind. *Could it be?* he wondered to himself. He scanned the list of phrases and found what he was looking for:

THE TIME PORTAL = 162 = THE SHIFT OF THE AGE
THE TORAH MATRIX CODE = 207 = ACTIVATE THE CAPSTONE = THE GOLD ANKH IS THE KEY

His mind began to race. Pieces of the puzzle were frantically swirling through his mind, vieing for position, shoving, shifting, exchanging places in a mechanical frenzy, each one eventually finding its match and locking into place. *Time portal...shift of the age...Mayan calendar...2012...the prophecy of Brother Hiram...global catastrophe...must be prevented...time portal...activate the capstone...activate the capstone!*

He may as well have been struck by lightening. An intuitive flash lit up his brain and nearly sent him reeling. "Oh my god!" he blurted out. "I get it! I know what it is!"

Angela and the professor were startled by the outburst.

"What *what* is?" Angela asked.

Banyon got up from the table and began pacing the floor, trying to hold the picture in his mind. "Okay. Okay." He turned to Angela. His eyes were intense. "You remember what I told you about my latest dream? About the antenna being attached to something buried under the ocean floor?"

"Sure, I remember. Why? Oh-oh. Are you saying you know what it's attached to?"

"Yes! It's the capstone! The antenna is attached to the tip of the capstone!"

Kline's brow suddenly narrowed. "Wait a second," he said. "You want to run that by me again? Are you talking about *the* Capstone? The missing crown of the Great Pyramid?"

"Yes! Exactly!" Banyon nearly shouted.

"Are you sure?" Angela asked. "How do you know?"

"I don't know *how* I know! I just know! It all came to me in a flash!"

"All?" Kline asked. "There's more?"

Banyon was so ecstatic he could barely contain his excitement.

"Okay, okay," he said, lighting up a cigarette and trying to calm himself. "Yes, there's more. I get it now. It all fits together." Still pacing back and forth, he began to explain. "I'm just going to lay it right out," he said. "There's no other way to do it. Here's the scenario as it came to me."

He paused for a moment to compose himself and then continued. "McClintock's notes indicated his conviction that it – the mysterious *It* - was a machine of some sort. He was right. Probably not in any way that he could have imagined, but he was right. The capstone is a machine. A highly advanced technological device. The year 2012? The Mayan calendar date signifying the end of an age or some turning point in the evolution of human consciousness? It's coming. The vision of Brother Hiram as recounted in the book we got from Mrs. Densmore? It corresponds with the Mayan prophecy but with a caveat, a warning."

"Yes," Angela said. "Wait just a sec." She grabbed the book. The page with the information about the Order of the New Dawn and Brother Hiram was marked with a dog-eared corner. She opened it and read the text aloud. *"This mystic priest of the Order realized that the survival of the human race was going to be at a threshold in the 21st century. He foresaw a global catastrophe brought about by the appearance of a great dragon coming to earth from heaven. This had to be prevented if humans were to survive. He understood that the year 2012 would be a pivotal point in the continuation of the human race. While he did not understand the exact nature of what would happen in 2012, he understood it represented a crucial window of opportunity for the survival of the planet."*

"A great dragon coming to earth from heaven," Kline said, beginning to see the picture. "The comet."

"Yes!" Banyon said. "Exactly! And it must be prevented if humans are to survive!"

"And..." Kline started but paused, not sure he should even ask the question, "...just when is all this supposed to happen? Is a comet impact the fate that awaits us in 2012?"

Banyon shook his head. "I only know what Wood and Campbell had to say about that in their book. They determined it would be a long while yet. Something like around the year 2085.

"The year 2085?" Kline objected, "That doesn't make sense in the context of what Angela just read to us."

Banyon nodded. "Exactly. It doesn't seem to make sense. But maybe this here is a clue." He pointed to the phrases referencing *THE TORAH MATRIX CODE* and *THE BIBLE CODE*. He turned to Angela. "Feel like googling?"

"Google the Bible Code?" she asked.

"Yes. Let's see what we can find. Try including *comet* as a keyword."

Angela brought up the Google search engine and entered the two items together: *Bible Code, comet*. In a moment they had a direct hit. The search engine located a website dedicated to all the things people had discovered by using the various computer programs available for conducting skip searches through the text of the Torah. Amazingly, several people had found references to a comet impact.

"Wow!" Angela said. "Look at this!"

A half dozen researchers, all working independently, and using different skip sequences, had hit on virtually the same information in different parts of the Torah. In each case they came across interconnected words and phrases indicating a devastating comet impact and what the researchers referred to as the "civil year" of 1566. From what Angela could determine, this appeared to have something to do with the ancient Hebrew calendar. There was agreement among the researchers that this translates into our modern calendar year of 2006.

"My god!" Kline said. "That's now! This year! But *when*, exactly? Is there anything more specific?

Angela scrolled through the entries posted on the web page. Banyon and Kline peered intently over her shoulder.

"There!" Banyon said. "Scroll back about a paragraph."

Doing as he suggested, she scrolled the page back until Banyon told her to stop.

"Right there." he said. "Look. What's that say?"

The information in the paragraph referred to something called *9 Av*. The author explained this was a date from the Hebrew calendar. The date of *9 Av* corresponded with our calendar date of 3 August. Kline had his answer. According to the Bible Code, the impact of the comet would occur on 9 Av, 1566.

Angela looked stunned. "That's…"

"August third, of this year." Banyon said.

"My god," Kline spoke softly. "That's just four months from now."

Banyon knew this was it. That old feeling was coming over him. He reached for the pencil and paper. After writing something down and punching numbers into the calculator he handed the paper to Kline.

NINE AV, THE DAY OF DESTRUCTION = 297 = 9
THREE AUGUST IS THE DAY OF DESTRUCTION = 405 = 9
405 – 297 = 108 = COMET SETH

Kline reacted with a sigh and a befuddled shake of the head. "Damn strange talent you've developed there, my friend." He passed it over to Angela.

She read it and handed it back to Banyon. "Not good," she said with a look of apprehension.

"Yes, but it can be prevented!" Banyon said, still feeling the buzz of his recent epiphany, "That's what this is all about!"

Kline looked puzzled. "And you know how to accomplish this? How to prevent the catastrophe of a comet impact?" The very idea was beyond comprehension but he knew Banyon was right about one thing. This was indeed what it was all about.

Without hesitation Banyon answered. "Yes! The capstone! It's the key to avoiding the impact!"

"But how?" Angela wanted to know.

Banyon shook his head. "I don't know, exactly. But here..." he held up the paper with the jumble of downloaded phrases, "...these phrases triggered everything for me." He pointed out the phrases he was referring to:

THE TIME PORTAL = 162 = THE SHIFT OF THE AGE
THE TORAH MATRIX CODE = 207 = ACTIVATE THE CAPSTONE = THE GOLD ANKH IS THE KEY

"These two sets of phrase equations are the Rosetta stone for a big part of this puzzle. It came to me in a flash. Remember the part in Wood and Campbell's book where it said some people believed there was some sort of a device in or near Rennes le Chateau that could open up a time portal?"

Angela nodded.

"Close but no cigar," Banyon said. "The rumor of such a thing was vague. No one really knew what it meant or how it got started in the first place. But I know. I get it!"

"Well," Kline said, "would you care to enlighten the rest of us?"

The adrenaline rush that had Banyon pacing back and forth just a few minutes ago was slowly diminishing. Feeling a bit more in control of his emotions now, he let his friends in on the secret. "There was a device all right. But it wasn't at or near Rennes le Chateau. The device is the capstone!"

Angela was stunned by what he was saying. "Are you saying the capstone is a time machine?"

Banyon nodded. "Maybe not like ol' George Orwell thought it would be, but I'll bet my trusty calculator that it has something to do with opening that so-called *time portal* that keeps cropping up in this little mystery of ours. What, in fact, *did* exist near Rennes le Chateau was the gold box containing the scroll which, as we can see now, had an intimate *connection* with the capstone!"

"The time portal device," Angela said, still wanting to make sure she was understanding Banyon's new revelation. "You're telling us the capstone is the time portal device?"

Banyon nodded. "Exactly. The rumors of such a thing existing in that area of Rennes le Chateau must be the remnant of some long lost knowledge that someone once had about the scroll. The facts – the real facts - probably got lost in the mists of antiquity until there was nothing left but misguided rumors."

"I'll buy that," Kline said, nodding his head thoughtfully. "Makes sense, I suppose. But what about this here?" He pointed to the phrase, *THE GOLD ANKH IS THE KEY.* "What can *that* mean?"

Angela jumped in. "Well, an ankh is…"

"I know what an ankh is," Kline said. "It's the Egyptian symbol for life. It resembles the Christian cross but with a loop at the top. In fact some scholars believe the Egyptian ankh was the forerunner of what became the Christian cross. But what I'm asking is *what* ankh is it referring to and what is it the key to?"

"Simple," Banyon said. "It tells us right here." He pointed to the phrase, *THE ANKH IS THE KEY TO THE CAPSTONE.* "Couldn't be any clearer."

Kline shrugged. "Well," he said, "it could be a *little* clearer. It still doesn't tell us *what* ankh it's referring to. I know that other phrase tells us it's the *gold* ankh but *what* gold ankh? It's not like there are a lot of gold ankhs floating around. You can't just go down to your local ankh store and buy one, you know."

"There's an ankh store?" Angela quipped.

Kline grinned. "All right. I'm sorry. But you know what I mean. If this thing - this golden ankh - is so important, you'd think a more helpful clue would be on the menu."

"Hold on a minute, guys," Angela said. "What the heck is a *loculus*?"

Banyon gave a quizzical look. "A what?"

Angela pointed out the enigmatic phrase:
THE LOCULUS HOLDS THE GOLD KEY = 306

The phrase had somehow slipped Banyon's attention altogether. He looked at Kline, hoping for an answer but Kline just shook his head. In their combined cranial storehouses of half forgotten knowledge, the word *loculus* had never made an appearance. At least not that any of them could recall.

Angela had a hunch. "That phrase about the loculus," she said, "just might hold the answer to the professor's question."

"Any suggestions?" Banyon asked.

Angela muttered the phrase to herself. *"The loculus holds the gold key."* She thought about it for a moment. "Well," she said, reaching for the computer, "loculus sounds like a *key* word if I've ever heard one. No pun intended."

The professor groaned at the humor but secretly appreciated it. *Puns,* he thought. *The lowest form of humor.* Or so it was said. But he didn't agree. As far as he was concerned it took a quick wit to come up with a good pun. *Really deserves a higher ranking on the humor scale,* he smiled to himself.

Angela pulled up the Google page and typed the strange word into the search engine. Dozens of suggested links appeared on the screen. She chose one and scored on the first hit. It was a dictionary of Latin terms. "Well," she said, turning toward the two men. "Not exactly a mind blower of a definition. *Loculus* is a Latin word that means *box.*"

Kline read the phrase again, this time substituting box for loculus. "The *box* holds the gold key. Oh, that's just great," he said with growing frustration. "*What* box?"

"There's only one box that it could be," Banyon said.

Kline tossed a questioning look to Angela who returned it with a shrug. Banyon got up and walked over to the corner of the room where he'd stashed his overnight bag. Reaching in, he shuffled through his personal belongings and pulled something out. When he turned around he was holding the last thing either Kline or Angela expected to see.

~74~

The ancient gold box containing the lost scroll of Ezekiel was such a priceless relic that Angela was surprised to see Banyon had actually risked bringing it along on the trip. "You took it out of the safe and brought it up here?" she asked, rather astonished.

"Yeah, well it was a last minute decision. I grabbed it and put it in my bag just as we were about to leave the house." He carefully set it on the table and ran his hand over the ornately carved lid.

Kline's jaw literally dropped at the sight. It was the first time he had actually laid eyes on it. The detail of the engraved scrollwork was clearly the work of a master craftsman. "Beautiful," he said under his breath. He reached a hand out toward it but stopped short, glancing up at Banyon. "May I?"

Banyon nodded, releasing the ringed latch that held the lid closed. "Of course. Go ahead. Open it."

In much the same way as his old friend, Frank McClintock, fancied himself as another Indiana Jones, Kline suddenly understood what that feeling was like. He recalled, vividly, the first dramatic minutes of that now classic film where Indiana cautiously reaches out to grab the precious golden idol. Fortunately now, unlike the movie hero, Kline wouldn't have to dodge poison arrows and falling boulders for the privilege of handling the treasured artifact. Slowly, he lifted the lid and was treated to yet another surprise. "Oh my god," he gasped. "Is this the cylinder containing the actual scroll?"

"The very same," Banyon said, removing the copper cylinder from the box. He slid the scroll out from its container and unrolled it for Kline to feast his eyes upon.

The professor stared at it, absorbing the moment. "Amazing," he muttered. "Unbelievable." For a man who was pretty good with words, most of them were failing him at the moment. Finally he sat back, took a deep breath and managed to get out a complete sentence. "I'm simply blown away," he said. "This is incredible. I had no idea you would bring this with you."

Banyon rolled up the scroll, slid it back into the cylinder and laid it on the table next to the box. "Well, like I said, it was a last minute impulse. But now I'm glad I acted on that impulse. This has got to be the box, the loculus."

Angela wasn't convinced. "I don't know," she said. "There's the cylinder and the scroll and here's the box. And you'll notice - surprise, surprise - the box is empty."

It was at that moment Kline had an idea. Some of the half forgotten knowledge, stored away in the deep recesses of his cranium, came from his one actual guilty pleasure: old pulp fiction detective novels. Not exactly classic literature but they did often have cleverly conceived plots. Looking now at the empty gold box on the table in front of him he remembered *The Case of the Missing Gun*. It, too, involved an empty box. Or so it seemed to everyone except Mike Ruby, the novel's crack private detective. Nothing ever got past Mike. He found the missing gun. Kline grinned and turned to Banyon. "Could be one of the oldest tricks in the book," he said.

"What do you mean?"

"Well, you're going to laugh, but I once read an old detective novel involving a missing gun. The gun was found inside an apparently empty wooden box."

"Come again?" Banyon said. "The gun was in the box but the box was empty? I don't get it."

"I said the box was *apparently* empty. *Apparently* being the operative word." He could see from the blank look on Banyon's face that he still wasn't getting it. "A false bottom," he said with a wry grin.

Angela had to chuckle. "Oh, that's good," she said. "I like that."

Banyon looked at Kline and then stared at the box. *Could that be possible?* He glanced at Angela who was quietly staring back at him. Her eyes were saying, *well, what are you waiting for?* He turned his attention back to the box. *The apparently empty box.* He picked it up to examine its construction. The hinged cover would be easy to remove. Dismantling the rest of it didn't look like it would be so simple. The four sides seemed to be held together - as well as being attached to the bottom piece - by small gold pins inserted from the top edges and through the side-pieces. The bottom piece did seem to be thicker than necessary for the size and function of the box. "Well," he said, not believing these words were coming from his own mouth, "might as well get started."

He was right about the top cover. It was a simple hinge construction and easily removed. The rest of it looked like it was going to be a little more challenging. Examining the heads of the pins he could see they were shaped like tiny hexagons. He fiddled with one of them to see if he could loosen it. It was small but because of the hexagonal shape he could actually get enough of a grip, between his forefinger and thumb, to pull on it. But it wouldn't budge. "I don't know," he said. "It's pretty solid."

"Try turning it," Angela suggested. "Will it turn? You know, like a screw?"

Banyon looked at her. "Hmm... did they have screws four thousand years ago?"

She shrugged. "Hey, somebody tossed around fifty-ton blocks of stone to build a pyramid. I suppose a screw wouldn't be too hard to come up with."

Banyon and Kline laughed. She had a point.

"Okay, let's see," Banyon said, trying to twist the head of the pin. It wouldn't budge. He turned to Kline. "Got a pair of pliers?"

"On the shelf by the back door. I'll get it."

Banyon couldn't believe he was about to defile a priceless relic with a pair of pliers. It was crazy. *Who would do that?*

"Here you go," Kline said. "I covered the teeth of the pliers with a couple layers of masking tape. Maybe it will be less likely to damage the pinheads."

The only pinhead around here is me for even thinking about doing this, Banyon thought. He took a deep breath and applied the mechanical grip to the head of the pin. Gently, cautiously, he began to twist. He stopped suddenly and dropped the pliers. "It moved! I think I can twist it with my fingers." He grasped the pin with his fingers and twisted. It was definitely moving. Another turn. And another. In a moment the head of the pin on the other side dropped to the floor. "Damn!" He looked at Angela. "Did you see where it went? Can you find it?"

Angela got down on her hands and knees and felt around in the carpet. "It's okay," she said. "I got it." She stood up and handed it to Banyon.

Upon examination Banyon saw that the fallen pinhead was exactly that. A single head with a hole in it, not unlike a modern-day bolt. Now that this piece had fallen off, the pin he was twisting simply pulled straight out of the hole which was bored through the front side panel, all the way through the length of the end panel and then through the back panel. The entire box was fitted together this way, including four pins coming down from the top edges of the side panels into and through the thick bottom panel.

Banyon picked up the pliers and tried the next pin. "This should be a piece of cake now," he said.

In just minutes he had all of the side-mounted pins removed. The side panels were flopping loosely so he set the box down on the table to remove the top-mounted pins. Kline helped steady the side panels by holding them together with his two hands while Banyon removed the last four pins.

Banyon slid the final pin out and stepped back. Kline slowly removed his hands, letting the pieces lay gently down, flayed out around the perimeter of the bottom panel.

Banyon reached down and picked up the bottom panel. "I'll be damned," he said, examining it closely.

With the sides removed, he could easily see the bottom panel was actually two panels, one on top of the other. He looked at Kline and then at Angela. They were both stone faced with anticipation. He held the bottom plate up to the light and turned it every which way to see if he could tell how the two pieces were fit together. Suddenly, without realizing what he'd done, the two panels shifted against one another, the upper section sliding in the opposite direction of the lower section as if on a tracking mechanism. The two panels only moved apart about a quarter of an inch but it was enough to reveal a small opening between them. Then it hit him. "Oh my god!" he said, excitedly. "You were right, professor! The damn thing's hollow!"

Gripping the object from the top and the bottom, he gave a tug, trying to pull the two pieces in opposite directions. No movement. He tried again. Still nothing. They seemed to be stuck. He held one end out to Kline. "You pull on the upper panel and I'll pull on the lower one. Okay?"

Kline stood up and got a firm grip on the upper piece. "All right," he said.

"Okay. On three. Ready? One... two... three!"

Kline nearly fell backward as his piece came sliding off. Banyon reeled back and was left standing, staring, mouth agape, at the piece he held in his hands. He couldn't believe his eyes. With all the care of a mother cradling a newborn child, he gently placed his half of the false bottom on the table for all to see.

"Holy Jesus, Lord," Kline muttered.

Exactly as the phrase in Banyon's download predicted, snuggly and firmly resting in a perfectly molded impression in the hollow panel, lay the key to the capstone. The golden ankh.

The three of them stood frozen like statues, staring at the prize.

Golden. Gleaming. Perfect. Untouched by human hands for thousands of years. This was truly a sacred relic. None of them, not even Banyon, wanted to be the first to reach out and actually touch it. The entire room seemed to be bathed in the warmth of it's glow. Emotions were palpable. Angela's eyes teared. She looked up at Banyon. "Go ahead," she whispered. "It's been waiting for you long enough."

It was Banyon's turn to be Indiana Jones. Taking a deep breath he reached down to remove the ankh from its ancient sarcophagus. But it fit so snuggly into its contoured encasement that he couldn't just easily grasp it and pull it out. *Playing hard to get, eh?* He picked up the entire panel with one hand, turned it over and held his other hand beneath it. With a slight jog the golden ankh dropped gently into his hand, the first hand it had touched in four thousand years. But the look on his face was not what they expected.

"What's the matter?" Angela asked.

Banyon set the panel on the table and wrapped both hands around the ankh. He stood motionless for a moment, concentrating, almost as if he were listening for something.

"What is it?" she asked again.

Banyon handed the ankh over to her. "Hold this," he said. "Am I crazy or is that thing vibrating?"

"What do you mean, vibrating?" she asked, cautiously reaching for the ankh. She felt a shiver of anticipation rush through her body as she took the object into her hands. She marveled at it's simplicity of design, it's rounded contours, the coolness of its touch upon her skin. "I don't..." she started, then hesitated. "Wait a second." She wasn't sure if she actually felt something or not. Was she just imagining it now that Banyon's question had put the thought into her head? She touched the ankh gently to her cheek. The cool smoothness of the gold was palpable in an almost erotic sense. Still holding the ankh to her cheek, eyes narrowed, she concentrated. "Gees," she said, almost in a whisper. "You might be right."

"Let me see," Kline said.

She handed the ankh over to him. He held it gently at first, then more firmly. With a look of astonishment he had to agree. "I do seem to sense something. But it's very subtle. Almost imperceptible." He handed it back to Banyon. "I have an idea. Why don't we fill a glass with water and set the long end of the ankh into it. If there is any vibration at all, we should see some evidence of it."

"Of course!" Angela said. "It would cause the water to ripple!"

"That's what I'm thinking," Kline said.

Banyon shrugged. "Makes sense to me. Got a glass?"

Kline went to the kitchen and came back with an 8-ounce glass of water and a towel. He set the glass on the table and laid the towel next to it. They waited a few seconds to make sure the water was perfectly still.

"Okay," Banyon said. "Here goes."

He slowly inserted the long stem of the ankh into the water but the water didn't seem to register any vibration at all.

Kline offered another suggestion. "Maybe the grip of your hand on the ankh is inhibiting its vibration. Why don't we try suspending the ankh by a string tied to this part here," he said, pointing to the loop-shaped portion of the ankh.

"Makes sense again," Banyon said. "Got string?"

Kline made another trip to the kitchen and returned with an adequate length of string. Once they had the string tied to the ankh they tried the experiment again.

"Oh, man!" Angela said. "Look at that!"

Clearly there was a vibration coming from the ankh. The surface of the water became agitated, quickly forming into an intricate geometric pattern swirling around the stem of the ankh like a pinwheel of liquid lace.

Spellbound, they watched in silence, mesmerized by the phenomenon.

Kline was the first to break the silence. "What the hell have we got here?" he said, stepping back and pushing his glasses up onto his forehead.

Banyon pulled the ankh out of the water, dried it off with the towel and carefully placed it back into its 4,000-year old casing. Then he reached for the list of his recently downloaded phrases. "Like I said before, I think the answer is right here in front of us." He pointed to the now familiar portion of the list:

THE TORAH MATRIX CODE = 207

= ACTIVATE THE CAPSTONE

= THE GOLD ANKH IS THE KEY
THE BIBLE CODE = 90

THE ANKH IS THE KEY TO THE CAPSTONE = 315

THE LOCULUS HOLDS THE GOLD KEY = 306

"The ankh," he explained, "is the key that activates the capstone," Kline nodded. "But how?"

Banyon shook his head. "That I don't know. Your guess is as good as mine."

"And what's causing it to vibrate?" Angela asked. "I mean, that can't be just an ordinary chunk of gold we've got here."

"Possibly the result of an alchemical process?" Kline suggested.

"How so?" Banyon asked.

"Just a guess," Kline shrugged. "For all we know this ankh began as a chunk of lead. Who knows what the residual effects of a transformation process like that might be?"

"Interesting idea," Angela said. "Or maybe it's some kind of a technology. You know, a gizmo of some sort. Like the capstone."

"All I know," Banyon said, "is that it's the key to activate the capstone to make it do whatever it's supposed to do."

"Which is what?" Kline asked.

Banyon shook his head and let out a deep sigh. "I don't know, exactly. Create a time warp? A shift in the space-time continuum? I have no idea. I just know its purpose is to somehow save this planet from being destroyed by the comet."

"Great," Kline said. "We're only ninety days from impact and we don't know how any of this stuff works."

It was a sobering realization and Banyon was fresh out of answers.

~75~

Banyon drifted in and out of sleep that night. Aside from too many loose puzzle pieces rattling around in his mind he was also feeling uncomfortable with the strange ability he had acquired. The huge download of information – from God knows where, or how – that got dumped into his brain yesterday was more unnerving now upon reflection than it was when it happened. It was the kind of thing that would happen in a Twilight Zone episode or maybe in a Steven King novel. *It's not normal,* he thought to himself. *People don't do that. Poor mom. If she could see me now she'd roll over in her grave. Poor mom? What the hell. Maybe it's all her fault in the first place. She's the one who named me Ezekiel.* Before he knew it the morning light was squeezing its way in through the shaded window in the loft where he and Angela spent the night.

"Angela," he whispered.

"Uh? Hmm…?"

"You awake?"

Her eyes opened half way. "I am now."

"Did you sleep okay?"

She nodded. "Uh, yeah," she said quietly with a slight grin.

He was puzzled by the grin. "What?"

"Oh, nothing."

"Come on," he prodded. "What is it?"

"Just a dream I had."

"A dream?"

She turned away from him and buried her head in the pillow. "Yeah."

"Well? What was it about?"

She chuckled. "A vibrating ankh."

"So what about it?" he asked, still not quite catching on.

"Let's just say it was, um… stimulating."

Now he got it. He grinned. "Oh really? Mmm… do tell."

The stimulating conversation was interrupted by a voice from below.

"Morning, my friends!" Kline hollered up from the living room. Coffee?"

Banyon rolled his eyes. "Crap."

"We'll be right down!" Angela called back.

They found Kline in the kitchen pouring the coffee. He apologized for not being able to offer much of a choice for breakfast. "Eggs and toast," he said. "That's about it. How would you like them?"

"Cooked," Banyon said.

Angela poked him in the ribs with her elbow. "He knows nothing about anything when it comes to preparing food," she said. "He likes them over easy and so do I, thank you."

Kline smiled. "That makes three of us then. Over easy coming right up."

"Nothing kosher?" Banyon asked, referring to Kline's Jewish heritage.

Kline grinned. "Gave it up for Lent."

Banyon laughed.

"Is there anything I can do to help?" Angela asked.

"Not a thing, my dear," Kline answered, expertly cracking the eggs - one handed - onto the sizzling skillet.

Sitting around the table, enjoying the light breakfast, the talk immediately turned to the events of the previous day.

"I was thinking," Kline said, as he finished his last bite of toast, "about that levitation idea. If we're right about having to have seventy-six sound devices situated around a four-hundred-and-fourteen foot diameter circle, I'm not sure how that could be accomplished. Especially if the water conditions at that location are as rough as you say they are. It doesn't seem feasible that you could simply drop them into the water and expect them to just float in place."

"You're right," Banyon said. "I hadn't actually given any thought as to how that could be done."

"But," Kline said, "what if the sound devices – I suppose they'd be some sort of resonators or something like that – what if they were attached to some kind of a huge floating donut."

"Floating donut?"

"Bad analogy, maybe," Kline said. "Okay, a floating ring. Something constructed out of a light weight material."

"Like aluminum?" Angela offered.

Kline nodded. "Like aluminum. Or maybe even a high strength plastic of some sort."

Banyon lit a cigarette and leaned back in his chair. "I see what you're saying. With the sound-generating devices evenly spaced around the ring."

Kline nodded "Exactly. What do you think?"

"Sounds like a reasonable idea," Angela said. "Except for one thing. You know how big four-hundred-and-fourteen feet is? That's huge! Even if we had something like that, how would we be able to get it there in the first place?"

"Good question," Banyon said. "I doubt if the U.S. Navy is going to let us borrow an aircraft carrier."

Kline pursed his lips and gave the matter some thought. "Well," he said, packing some tobacco into his pipe, "what about if the ring was built in sections?"

"Ah, yes!" Banyon said. "That would make sense." But then the hopeful expression on his face suddenly faded. "Only…"

"Only what?" Kline asked.

Banyon shook his head. "I don't know. I mean it's all well and good to sit around here trying to come up with clever ways to accomplish the task. But really, when you think about it - I mean really think about it - how are we going to actually get any of this stuff done? Who's going to construct this… this ring… this giant donut? And the tone devices? I don't know about you but I haven't a clue as to what sort of devices will work or where to get such things. And we still have no idea how the hell we're going to find a ship to transport this stuff and get us to where we need to go. And let's say we were somehow able to accomplish all of that, then…" he paused and let out a cynical laugh, "…then tell me, please, how the hell we're going get the capstone all the way to Egypt and then somehow talk the Egyptian government into letting us put the thing on top of the Great Pyramid?" He paused again, shaking his head. "I'd say it's pretty clear we're in way over our heads."

It was true. The more they talked about it the more they realized that they were looking at an expedition that would eventually require the enlistment of a large number of people – people with expertise in several different fields. Just having an ocean-going vessel at their disposal meant that a whole crew of people would be involved. The entire project was going to necessitate a tremendously coordinated effort and with that many people involved there was no way the operation could remain a secret. That would present a problem. If word of the operation got out the media would be all over it. And if the media got wind of it then it would soon become an international story. Before it even got that far, the bad guys – the illuminati by way of the Jesuits – would be ready to hijack the entire mission. Kline knew such plans were already in the works. The Illuminati had one ultimate goal. From the very beginning, all the way back to the Spanish Alumbrados, they'd set their sites on world control. They wanted to be at the helm, driving the New World Order. As far as the Illuminati were concerned, the time was near. The signs were everywhere if one knew what to look for. Even former President George Bush, Sr. had introduced the phrase, *New World Order*, to the great uninitiated general populace in some of his speeches. Strings were being pulled. Favors – deep favors, sometimes going back generations – were being called in. People were being put into the right places like shifting chess pieces around on the world board. Even people who would be thought the least likely of pawns were in the game, with or without their knowledge. Bill "Bubba" Clinton, the obscure governor of Arkansas was a prime example. Months before he made his bid to run for the office of President, before most of the country had even heard of him, he was invited to that year's annual secret meeting of the Bilderbergers. To this day, as Kline knew, the average man or woman on the street has never heard of the Bilderberg Group. Yet every year this clandestine organization, comprised of some of the world's wealthiest and most influential people, meet behind closed doors to discuss the current world situation and basically set the gears in motion to steer world events in whatever direction would be most beneficial to their own agendas. Clinton was a perfect candidate. Not because he was well-known but precisely because he was relatively *unknown*. Why this low-profile politician from the politically unremarkable state of Arkansas should suddenly receive an invitation to the closed-door meeting of the Bilderberg Group is a question that would baffle most people. But it wasn't as sudden as it appeared on the surface. The wheels had been set in motion some time before, when the young Bill

Clinton was awarded a Rhodes scholarship. That was his first initiation into the Plan even though he probably didn't realize it at the time. Cecil Rhodes, Kline had learned, was not just the founder of the prestigious Rhodes scholarship. He was also said by some to have been an agent for the Illuminati. Curiously – or perhaps not so curiously, in Kline's opinion - a disproportionate number of Rhodes scholars seem to end up in positions of power and influence in the upper echelons of various governments. Clinton was no exception. Kline was convinced, however, that Clinton wasn't one of the bad guys. *He was probably just one of the unwitting pawns in the game*, he told himself. Kline realized the Illuminati have no Party affiliations. They use any political party of any country in any manner they wish. The Bush vs. Kerry campaign for the American presidency was a case in point. Not only were both candidates members of Yale's secretive Skull & Bones Society – an organization with its own connections to the Illuminati somewhere down the long dark corridors of time – but they were cousins to boot. Sure the familial relationship was a few generations removed but that just showed how deeply the strands of the web were woven into the fabric of the biggest conspiracy ever conceived. It didn't matter who won the so-called election that year. One way or another, the Illuminati would be the winners. Kline knew all of this was true. He also knew Banyon had phrased it well. They were, indeed, in way over their heads. But Kline knew something else too; something Banyon and Angela were only aware of in a peripheral sense. He knew the other side of this dark scenario was represented by the most highly guarded secret society in the long history of the human race. An organization on the side of the Light. The Brotherhood of the Nine Pillars was on their side. *Maybe*, he thought to himself, *it's time to tell them the truth.*

"You're right," Kline said. "We are in over our heads. There's no way you're going to be able to go much further without a lot of help from a lot of people."

"Banyon laughed. "Oh here we go again. You're going to tell me you just happen to know all the right people who can help us out, including the Admiral of the Pacific Fleet who actually does have a spare aircraft carrier he's not using."

Kline removed his glasses and rubbed his eyes. Putting his glasses back on, he looked at Banyon. "Better than that," he said.

Banyon blinked. "What are you talking about?"

"I don't personally know all the people who can help us out but I know who does."

Banyon squinted with a skeptical look. *This ought to be good.* "And who might that be?" he asked.

Kline inhaled deeply and scratched his chin through his wirey beard. "The Nine," he said.

"Excuse me?"

"I couldn't tell you before. I'm not even sure I should be telling you now, actually, but…"

"Tell us what?" Angela asked.

Kline looked at each of them for a moment, trying to think of how to broach the subject. "Well," he said, finally, "the truth is, I've had a relationship of sorts with the Nine for some time now."

Banyon shot a glance over to Angela and then back to the professor. "Are you saying… are you telling us you know the Nine? Personally?"

Kline confessed everything. He told them how the Nine had contacted him after he'd learned about them from Marie St. Claire, the assistant curator at the Smithsonian. How the Nine had solicited, as it were, his occasional assistance in certain matters; that he was, in effect, what they called an operative; that, in fact, he'd been instructed by the Nine to set up that first meeting with Banyon and Angela in his office at the college. He told them about the night he was sent to Queen City University to retrieve the materials that had been stolen from Banyon's home and how it was he who had broken into Banyon's house to return the goods while they were attending Banyon's going-away party at the homeless shelter.

A range of emotions filtered though Banyon's mind as he tried to absorb this shocking news. Aside from a feeling of having been violated by Kline's admission that he'd broken into his home, there were other feelings welling up. On the one hand he felt somewhat betrayed by this man whom they'd befriended. Yet, on the other hand, he felt vindicated about his occasional suspicions that Kline often knew more than he was letting on.

"You mean," Banyon said, pointedly, "when I saw that report on the TV news about the priests being tied up in the basement of the University… are you telling me you were involved in all of that?"

Kline nodded. "That's why I wasn't at your going-away party."

Banyon thought about telling the professor that he'd often suspected he knew more than he was telling but he could see Kline had been placed in an awkward position so he decided to let it pass.

"One thing I don't get," Angela said. "Your mission was to go to the University and retrieve the items that had been stolen from Zeke's briefcase, right?"

Kline nodded. "Right."

"How did the stuff get taken out of the briefcase in the first place? It had to have been done that night at the warehouse on the pier. But if that priest and his two thugs didn't do it, and those guys who rescued us didn't do it, then who did? And how did the stuff turn up at the University in the hands of those other Jesuits?"

"That's still a mystery," Kline admitted. He explained how the Nine had brought in a remote viewer to ascertain the location of the stolen materials but that the remote viewer was not able to detect precisely who the culprit was. "All they were able to determine was that it was someone who had been hiding in the warehouse the whole time. In any case, the thief – whoever it might have been – apparently died a short time after the incident."

"Obviously not before he delivered the goods to someone at the University," Banyon said. "But if the Nine don't know who it was then how do they know he died?"

Kline shrugged. "That was the last bit of information the remote viewer was able to see."

Banyon shook his head. "Very weird story. That's all I can say. If I didn't know better I'd think you were making it all up. But who the hell could make up a story like that? So how are you contacted by the Nine? Have you actually ever met any of them in person?"

"No. I'm contacted by phone or sometimes by a letter in the mail. I'm not at liberty to tell you the name of the person but he's the head of the Brotherhood."

"But you know him well enough to arrange some sort of help for us in this impossible little salvage mission we're supposed to carry out?"

"I think so. I hope so. To tell you the truth I don't exactly know how they will react when they find out I've told you about my association with them. In any case, what's done is done. I'll contact them tomorrow. That's the best I can do."

~76~

E arly Monday morning, in the parking lot of the community college, Romano waited patiently in his car for the arrival of Professor Kline. When he discovered earlier that Kline, Banyon and Angela were away from home for the entire weekend he figured they were probably together somewhere for some reason. Something important must have developed and he wanted to know what it was. But he needed to be extremely careful. The incident at the University had brought him face to face with Kline. He had to assume Kline would surely recognize him now. Romano didn't know exactly how he was going to find out what went on over the weekend. *Maybe*, he thought to himself, *I'll just get lucky.*

Kline arrived within an hour. Romano watched him park the car and disappear into the adjacent building. He wanted to get out and follow the professor on foot but decided that was too dangerous. *Patience*, he thought to himself. It was one of the many virtues in which he was sorely lacking. But he had no choice. He sat and waited.

As soon as Kline got settled into his office he put in a call to Nathan Crown. He revealed every detail of the astounding events that transpired over the weekend and was relieved to find that Crown was not at all disturbed by the fact that he'd told Banyon and Angela about his relationship with the Nine. During their telephone conversation Crown said the protocol of nonintervention had run its course and that a more direct course of action now seemed inevitable.

"Destiny unfolds in mysterious ways, my friend," Crown said, ending the conversation. "You've done well. We'll keep you informed."

This *destiny*, it seemed to Kline, had been unfolding for quite some time. But over the ensuing weeks it seemed to pick up speed. Within the first week following their discovery of the golden ankh, Miriam Flamel – the student of alchemy that he'd met several years ago - entered the picture in a most unexpected way.

Kline's personal library included quite an impressive array of titles pertaining to various esoteric subjects, from the UFO phenomenon to Christian mysticism. The one thing it didn't include was anything substantive pertaining to alchemy. Since Banyon's strange download of phrases included certain references to *the great work*, it seemed like having some relevant information on hand might be a good idea. Ideally, as he mentioned to Banyon, it would be good to have Miriam Flamel on the team but, since he'd lost track of her some years ago, it was going to take a good bit of detective work to locate her. In the meantime, a good book on the subject would have to suffice and he knew just where to get one.

As the professor walked out of the building and climbed into his car Romano was watching and grinning. "Jesus," he muttered to himself as he put his car in gear and got ready to follow the professor. "Maybe I *will* get lucky."

~77~

The young clerk at the *Mystic's Choice Bookstore* had her nose buried in an inventory list when Kline walked in and addressed her with a question. She looked up from her work and smiled. "Alchemy?" she said. "Sure. That would be right over there next to the display of crystals."

He thanked her and made his way over to the shelves next to the table full of crystals and so-called *Magic Stones*. There were only five titles on the shelf that were related to alchemy. After browsing through four of the five he became disenchanted. None of them, in his opinion, appeared to be very academic in their approach to the subject. The title of the fifth book, *Become An Alchemist In Ten Easy Lessons*, assured him that it wasn't even worth picking from the shelf. Disappointed, he turned and headed for the door.

At that moment a well-dressed young woman, in her late twenties, early thirties, was approaching the door from the outside. She was carrying a briefcase in her left hand and struggling with several books under her other arm. Kline opened the door for her. She brushed by him with a quick "thank you" and hurried inside. He was halfway out the door himself when he caught part of a comment from the clerk behind the counter.

"Hello Ms. Flamel," the clerk said. "We have a table set up for..."

Kline spun around just as the door closed behind him. *What?* He peered back through the glass but the young woman with the briefcase and books had disappeared behind a stack of shelves. As he was about to reenter the store he noticed a poster taped to the window:

BOOK SIGNING!
TODAY ONLY! 2 P.M.
MIRIAM FLAMEL
Author of
BECOME AN ALCHEMIST IN 10 EASY LESSONS!

He was stunned. *How could I have missed this poster the first time? How could that attractive well-dressed woman be the same black-garbed Goth-freak I once met? And how in the world could she be the author of a book with such an inane title? If this is one of destiny's mysterious moves*, he thought to himself, *it's a doosie.*

He rushed back in and looked around. The young woman was setting her books on the table by the far wall in preparation for the book signing. Her shoulder length hair was a deep chestnut brown whereas he remembered it being jet black with a streak of day-glow crimson running down one side. The black t-shirt, black jeans, black leather wristband, and black hiking boots were replaced with a peach-colored blouse, a knee-length brown skirt, a gold bracelet, and comfortable pumps that matched her blouse. The nose stud was gone and, as far as he could tell, there was only one set of earrings dangling from her ears. Interestingly enough, the earrings were little golden ankhs.

From a distance, he watched her for a couple of minutes, amazed at the radical change. *Talk about transmutation from lead into gold,* he mused. She was sitting at the table jotting something down on a yellow legal pad when he finally approached her.

"Miriam?"

She looked up. "Yes?"

He smiled, wondering if she'd remember him. After all, other than a few more gray whiskers in his wirey beard, he hadn't changed one bit in the past few years. "You don't remember me, do you?"

She tilted her head and gave an inquisitive look. "No, I'm sorry. Do I know you?" The words had barely left her lips when her eyes widened. "Wait! Yes, I think I...you were a friend of Frank McClintock weren't you?"

Kline smiled. "Indeed, I was. Frank and I were good friends. He introduced me to you a few years ago at one of those New Age expos."

"Yes, that's right! It was down in Tacoma as I recall. I'm sorry," she blushed, "I don't remember your name."

"Alan Kline."

"Yes, now I remember! *Professor* Alan Kline, isn't it?"

"That's right," he said.

She stood up and shook his hand. "Well, this is really a surprise! What brings a mainstream professor into a New Age bookstore? Surely it couldn't have been to see me and have a book signed!"

He laughed. "Well, no. Well, I mean, not exactly. That is..." he hesitated. A dozen ways to explain the situation raced through his mind, each explanation jockeying for position at the front of the line. "Well," he said, finally, "the truth is, it's a long story. And actually I don't expect you to believe a word of it even though it's all true."

She folded her arms and gave him a knowing look. "Oh, my god. You've picked up where Frank left off, haven't you?"

He shrugged and nodded. "You might say that. It's..."

"Complicated?" she grinned.

He nodded again. "That's an understatement. And actually I was wondering..."

Their conversation was disrupted by a sudden din of voices near the door. It was nearly two o'clock and people were beginning to show up for the book signing.

"I really would like to talk with you," he said. "Would you happen to be free later this afternoon?"

"I'll be finished here about four o'clock. There's a café across the street. Will that work?"

"Yes," he smiled. "I'll meet you there." He turned and dodged his way through the oncoming crowd of Miriam's fans as he made his way to the door. "Unbelievable", he muttered to himself. He left the store and headed for the café across the street. *I can't wait to hear her story,* he thought. Then he chuckled. *Her story? Ha! Wait'll she hears mine.* He shook his head. *Can this get any weirder?*

~78~

When Miriam arrived at the café Kline was already occupying a booth with a slice of apple pie and a cup of coffee. He was completely unaware that Romano, with a great deal of stealth, had made his way to the booth directly behind him.

Kline smiled as Miriam came through the door. He waved her over.

"Can I buy you something to eat?" he offered as she seated herself across from him.

"Why thank you, yes."

She ordered a salad and an iced tea. He still couldn't get over the change in this woman. She was really quite attractive.

"You know," he grinned, "I wouldn't have recognized you at all. In fact, I *didn't* recognize you at all! We were practically face to face when I held the door open for you at the bookstore. The last time I saw you, you were... well..."

Miriam lowered her eyes and looked a little embarrassed. "I know," she said with a sheepish grin. "Let's just say it was a phase. Didn't you ever go through a phase?"

He thought for a second. "No, I don't think so. When I was your age I was already an old codger. Been an old codger ever since! Or maybe that was my phase. The old codger phase, and I just never grew out of it."

Miriam laughed. "Well, look at it this way" she offered, "you've just done it backwards. You've gone through the old codger phase so now you can move into your young whipper-snapper phase."

"Nah," he chuckled. "Nice idea but I don't think it works that way."

"Well, anyway," she said, picking at the salad with her fork, "I must say it's quite a surprise to run into you like this. What a coincidence."

The comment made him grin. *Coincidence. Yeah.* "Maybe not such a coincidence," he said. "Like someone said to me recently, destiny unfolds in mysterious ways."

"Mmm..." she nodded, crunching on a slice of cucumber. "Interesting turn of phrase."

He grinned. If Banyon were here he'd be whipping out his calculator to figure out the alphanumeric value of the phrase. "Speaking of phrases," he said, "I must confess I was a bit taken aback by the title of your book. I don't mean to be critical, but..." He paused for a second. "Well, for someone with your depth of knowledge about the subject... I mean I know you were a serious student of the history of..."

Miriam shrugged. "I still am. But a girl's gotta make a living you know."

"Meaning?"

"I published a scholarly book on the subject about two years ago and nobody bought it. This new book is a fluff piece, I admit, but it's selling pretty well. It's the New Agers. But they all think it's just about turning lead into gold. And they want to learn how to do it over a weekend. You know. Get rich quick. Have it mastered by Sunday and quit your job on Monday."

He laughed. "I see. Well, whatever works, I guess." He took a sip of coffee. "You're not going to believe this," he said, "but I was going to try to find you. And quite soon too."

She looked surprised. "Really? Why?"

"Well, I have something to ask you. Something very interesting has come up and we could use your help."

"We?"

Suddenly he realized this wasn't going to be easy to explain. But explain, he did.

By the time he'd brought her up to date, his pie was long gone and his third cup of coffee was getting cold. Miriam had barely spoken a word throughout the entire discourse. She sat quietly, mesmerized by the tale that was almost too tall to be believed. However, she was no stranger to strange tales. She hadn't stumbled into the world of alchemy by chance. It was her birthright. Or so her father, Terrance Flamel, liked to say. "After all," her father told her, as he told everyone, "we *are* related to Nicholas Flamel, the most famous alchemist in all of history!" This fact – or at least this alleged fact – had fascinated Terrance since he was a youngster when he heard the story from his own father. Terrance became obsessed with the idea. He soon began experimenting with various chemical compounds in his parent's basement. He dabbled, unsuccessfully, in the art for most of his life. But failure after failure began to take its toll on what was probably already a rather fragile ego, until finally he became more of an alcoholic than an alchemist. Instead of being on a quest for the fabled alchemical *Elixir of Life*, he was more interested in the somewhat more practical idea – at least from his point of view - of turning lead into gold. The gold, of course, could keep him in liquor for a long time. For him, Miriam was convinced, a bottle of good tequila *was*, in fact, the *Elixir of Life*. Unfortunately, it turned out to be his elixir of death.

As a child, Miriam had not really understood - nor was she particularly interested in – whatever it was her father was doing into the wee hours of the night with all of that strange paraphernalia out in the garage. Later, in her early teens, she became more curious and asked her mother about it. Her mother – a woman who, it seemed to Miriam, had been born without a curious bone in her body and had no interests outside of her Betty Crocker recipe books and how to get the brightest wash possible – simply said, "Ask your father". So she did. But the things he told her – especially the idea that by heating this and distilling that and combining something else, you could turn lead into gold – seemed crazy. After all, she was a sophomore in high school now and, if this stuff was really true, she would have learned about it in her chemistry class. Which, of course, she didn't.

Eventually the whole thing became an embarrassment to her. When her friends wanted to know what all that weird stuff in the garage was she told them it was just junk that the previous homeowners had left behind. The excuse seemed to work and no one was any the wiser.

Within a short time after that her father died of liver failure. Miriam was just seventeen and a week after his death she discovered something that would turn her father's obsession into her own.

She decided it was time to clean out the garage and get rid of all those objects of her father's obsession. It was then that she found a cardboard box filled with her father's notes. What intrigued her was the fact that much of it read almost like a kind of strange poetry and some of it even seemed as if it was written in some sort of code. Odd symbols were sketched in the margins along with words – obviously penned by a shakey, uneven hand - words she'd never heard of before. *My dad did all this?* she wondered to herself in amazement. She didn't understand what she was looking at.

As she sat there on a wooden bench, in the dim light of the old garage, surrounded by the scorched glass vials, small chunks of various metals, cans of sulphur and the various tools of her father's odd 'hobby', she began to wonder. *Are these the writings of a crazy man or a man who knew something?* She looked around and her gaze fell upon a very large old leather-bound book propped up between two smooth, white stones on a shelf above the workbench. She took the book down and read the title: *The Secret Teachings of All Ages* by Manly P. Hall. She sat down on the bench again and laid the book in her lap. A bookmarker made of white ribbon, now aged and frayed along the edges, was peeking out from a section near the middle of the old tome. The ribbon was embroidered with a red rose superimposed over a gold cross. She opened the book to the marked page. The section was entitled *Alchemy And Its Exponents*. She began to read and found it was a series of short biographical sketches of four alchemists of ancient times going back as far as the 13th century. Her jaw dropped when she saw the name, Nicholas Flamel, headlined on one of the pages. Her father, of course, had told her there was such a man but until this moment she had always suspected he'd made it up. She read the biographical stories of these strange men who had dedicated their lives to the study and practice of alchemy or, as she learned it was also called, the Great Work.

For the first time in her young life she actually found herself unexplainably fascinated by this subject that, such a short time before, had been the cause of great embarrassment for her. She couldn't stop reading. She went right on to the next section, *The Theory And Practice Of Alchemy, Part 1.* Much of what she read made little or no sense to her at all but, for some reason, she found it strangely compelling. She did recognize that some of the strange words and concepts were the same as she'd seen in her father's notes.

She went on to Part 2 and, from there, on to the sections that followed. Before she realized it, nearly two hours had passed. Her eyes grew tired and she felt both mentally exhausted and emotionally invigorated at the same time. She closed the book and took it into the house.

Up in her room she laid down on the bed with the book resting on her chest, her arms crossed over it. Her eyes felt heavy and in moments she fell asleep. As she slept she dreamed she was standing next to a dark-haired man. She and the man were both standing on a floor of transparent glass. Looking down through the glass she could see a large body of dark, turbulent water far below. There was an intense feeling of excitement as if something extraordinary was about to happen.

She awoke with a start. *Jesus*, she thought to herself, *what the hell was that all about?* As she sat up the book slipped to the floor. She bent down to pick it up and at that precise moment, as her hand touched the book, the world stopped for a fraction of a second, and she had an epiphany, a sudden intuitive flash. She knew, somehow, deep inside, that her life was about to go in a different direction. There was something she had to do. She had a purpose. She didn't know what it was and she was perplexed by the fact that she even had such a thought. *Was it something to do with the dream?* Suddenly she heard the familiar sound of her mother's electric beater rattling against the side of a glass mixing bowl down in the kitchen. Then she knew. It was a subtle thought. Silly, in a way. Yet, oddly, at this moment, it resonated with an almost profound sense of importance. *Cookies.* She ran her hand across the hard leather cover of the old book. *There's more to life than making cookies. You knew it, didn't you dad?*

Her transformation could have taken any number of directions but the path she chose, or that chose her, was called rebellion. With her father gone and her mother perpetually stuck in the land of *Leave It To Beaver*, she headed out to find her own destiny. Along the way she met others who had forsaken their mother's cookies.

They gathered in coffee houses and metaphysical bookstores and the food court at the shopping mall and hung out on the streets and tattoo parlors and listened to heavy metal and punk rock and got their noses pierced and wore a lot of black clothes and - whether the straight world believed it or not - they sometimes talked philosophy and wrote poetry and were seriously concerned about the spiritual state of the insane world that had spawned them.

"So," Kline said, taking a sip of his cold coffee, "what do you think? Will you join us on our little adventure?"

She thought about that moment in her father's garage...that moment when she knew something was waiting for her... something she was destined to be part of. Pursing her lips, she leaned back and appeared to be thinking it over. The truth was, she had already decided. Or in some way perhaps it had been decided for her. "How can I not?" she said with a shrug. "Sign me up."

Romano – sitting in the booth behind Kline and Miriam – couldn't quite catch every word of their conversation. But he wasn't disappointed. What he did hear was enough. He now knew all he needed to know.

~79~

The campus of Queen City University was quiet. Most of the night classes were over for the evening. Up in their small private meeting room - located at the rear of room 306 and sealed off by a separate door - Beck and Salvo were in the midst of a friendly game of poker when Romano entered and looked around. "Where's Montebeau?" he demanded.

"Don't know," Salvo said. "Haven't seen him all day."

"Good," Romano replied, closing the door behind him. He hung up his coat and walked over to join Beck and Salvo at the table.

"Why?" Beck asked. "What's going on?"

"Plenty," Romano said. "And I'd rather that Montebeau not get wind of this. I don't trust that little…"

"Nothing new there," Salvo chuckled, shuffling the deck of cards. "I take it you found Kline this morning. So what happened?"

Romano lit up a cigar. "Found him and learned something you won't believe."

Beck and Salvo sat in rapt attention as Romano laid out the essentials of the conversation he'd overheard between Kline and Miriam Flamel. What he didn't know was that his own conversation was now being overheard by Montebeau who was standing on the other side of the meeting room door. He'd entered the main room just moments after Romano closed the door to the meeting room.

Romano's informative report was followed by a long moment of silence as the other two men tried to absorb the astounding news.

Salvo shuffled and reshuffled the cards. He seemed nervous. "Alchemy?" he said. "Golden ankhs with strange powers? Acoustic levitation?" He shook his head. "Do we really know what we're getting into?"

Romano looked surprised. "What are you talking about?"

Salvo shrugged. "I don't know. It just seems like maybe this is getting beyond anything we're going to be able to handle. What the hell do we know about alchemy? Or acoustic levitation? And if this thing is at the bottom of the Antarctic sea… I mean, come on. If *they* don't know how they're going to create the mechanism to bring it to the surface then what chance have *we* got?"

"He has a point," Beck said. "The whole idea was that we'd find out the location of the thing and take possession of it before they could even get there. Now that we know where it is and what it's going to take to get to it, it seems impossible."

Romano appeared unconcerned. "Not if we let *them* do all the work and we show up at the last moment and take possession of the prize."

Salvo laughed. "Sure. Just like that. You and what army?"

Romano took a drag from his cigar and blew a smoke ring. "I'll figure something out."

On the other side of the door Montebeau grinned. *Not before I do.*

He turned to leave when suddenly the meeting room door opened. Montebeau froze.

"Montebeau!" It was Romano's voice.

Montebeau turned around, facing Romano.

Romano stepped forward. "What were you doing?"

Montebeau stuttered. "N-nothing. I was just..."

"Listening in on our conversation?"

"What? No! I..."

Romano stepped closer. "What did you hear?"

"Nothing!"

Romano's face turned red. He stepped up and grabbed Montebeau by the front of his coat. "You heard it all, didn't you!"

"All right! All right! So I heard a little. So what? I'm part of this little team, remember?"

Romano released his grip on Montebeau's coat and took a step back. "Oh, I remember all right. And just to make sure *you* remember our little agreement to keep all of this strictly to ourselves..." He turned and spoke to Salvo who was still sitting at the card table. "You have that photo?"

Salvo opened his briefcase and took out an envelope. He got up and handed it to Romano.

"What's that?" Montebeau asked.

"Insurance" Romano said, opening the envelope. He removed the photograph and held it up for Montebeau to see. "I can't believe you would let someone actually take a picture of you in such a compromising position!"

Montebeau was stunned. Shocked. The photo of him engaged in a sex act with another man had been taken five years ago. Now his deepest secret – and his worst fear – had been pulled from the safe darkness of the closet and into the light. In an embarrassed panic, he ripped the photo from Romano's hand and rushed for the door.

"Go ahead! Take it!" Romano shouted after him. "I made a copy!"

The door slammed shut and the sound of Montebeau's rapid footsteps echoed down the hall and faded into the distance.

Salvo turned to Romano with a look of surprise. "You made a copy? How could you make a copy? I've had the photo with me all along."

Romano shrugged. "No, of course I didn't make a copy. I wish I would have. But as long as Montebeau thinks I have a copy he'll keep his mouth shut."

Beck looked concerned. "Yeah," he said. "Let's hope so."

Once outside the building, Montebeau stopped to gather his thoughts. Suddenly the last words he heard Romano shout at him echoed in his head. *He has a copy? The son of a bitch has a copy? I have to get it!*

~80~

Professor Kline dismissed his Tuesday morning class after assigning a homework project and headed back to his office with one thing on his mind. He'd spent half the night trying to figure out how to approach his friend and colleague, the physics professor, Alec Rajani. It wasn't that Rajani was likely to think Kline was crazy. That wasn't the problem. Rajani was already privately researching and experimenting with acoustic levitation and was no stranger to the kind of subject matter that mainstream academics considered to be nonsense. The problem, in Kline's mind, was how to convince Rajani to participate in this extraordinary venture. His participation would likely require a considerable amount of time at some point and there was a possibility that if the nature of his extracurricular activity became known to the rest of the faculty, it could be detrimental to his professional career. Kline kept thinking about poor John Mack, the Harvard psychology professor whose career was nearly shattered just a few years ago when it was discovered that he was conducting serious investigations into the alien abduction phenomenon. Fellow academicians and the Harvard authorities were aghast. The firestorm of controversy resulted in an attempt to remove Mack from his otherwise prestigious position at the University. But Mack fought back, incurring the expense of a high-powered attorney, and eventually prevailed under the banner of academic freedom. Then, in an ironic and tragic twist of fate, he was soon afterward killed when struck by a car. The scenario was all too familiar to Kline. His good friend, Frank McClintock met his fate in exactly the same manner. Was there a connection? Kline didn't know but in the back of his mind there seemed to be plenty of reason for suspicion. The last thing he wanted was for the scenario to be repeated once again with Rajani as the victim. Kline realized that he, himself, was in the same position. All of this was going to require considerable stealth in order to protect their reputations as well as their lives. *Would Rajani be willing to take the risk?* There was no point thinking about it any longer. Kline left his office and walked across the hall.

The door to Rajani's office was slightly ajar. Kline rapped on it. "Alec?"

Rajani's smooth, dark features, almost boyish, belied his actual age of forty-seven years. In his customary white shirt and tie he presented a stark contrast to Kline's typically rumpled appearance.

"Alan? Come in!" he said, looking up from his desk. He closed the book he was reading and moved it aside. "How does the battle go?"

How goes the battle? Kline rephrased the question in his mind. Even after five years in the States Rajani still occasionally managed to mangle some of the common colloquialisms. Kline found it amusing, comical actually. "Can't complain," he answered. "I was wondering if you might have a few minutes. I have to ask you something."

"Absolutely, my friend," Rajani said, motioning for Kline to come in and have a seat. "What is it?"

Kline stepped in, closed the door behind him, and took a seat across from Rajani's desk. He looked at Rajani for a few seconds, wondering where to begin. He thought he had an opening line all figured out but it suddenly escaped him. He'd have to try something else. "Remember when we had that little discussion about those flying ships from the old Hindu legends?"

Rajani smiled. "The vimanas! Yes, I remember."

"And you told me you were doing some personal research into acoustic levitation?"

Rajani's expression turned to one of concern. "Yes? Is there a problem?"

Kline raised his hand. "No," he assured him. "No, nothing like that."

"Then what is it?"

"Well, the thing is, I've become involved in something... a project, you might say... and it turns out we could use your expertise if you'd be willing to take part."

Rajani's curiousity was piqued. He sat forward. "What kind of project?"

Kline paused for a moment. "When is your next class?"

Rajani looked at his watch. "Not for about two hours."

"Good. That's plenty of time. I've got quite a tale to tell you."

When Kline finished laying out the story from beginning to end, Rajani stared at the professor for several seconds without saying a word. "If I did not know you better," he said, finally, "I would think you are stretching my leg."

Kline chuckled. "*Pulling* your leg. But no, not at all. I swear, it's all true. Hard to believe, I realize. But I couldn't make up a story like that."

Rajani had to admit it was unlikely that Kline would be fabricating the whole story, as strange and unbelievable as it might be. "And these tones you mentioned. This fascinates me, of course. What were the specific notes? What frequencies?"

Kline shook his head. "That I can't recall. It all got to be quite complex and, to tell you the truth, it was beyond my comprehension. In fact, it really was even beyond the comprehension of Mr. Banyon even though it all came out of his head. But it's all recorded on paper. That's why we're hoping you'll join with us. We could use your help. We *need* your help, if you're willing. What do you say?"

"This Banyon fellow. I can meet him?"

Kline grinned. "Of course! The sooner the better."

Rajani sat back in his chair. "All right," he said. "I cannot believe I am saying this. But all right. I would at least like to meet Mr. Banyon and have a look at the material."

"Excellent," Kline said, beaming. "I'll see if we can set up a meeting for some evening this week."

Rajani was tapping his fingers on the desk. He looked as if he wanted to say something but seemed to be hesitating.

"What is it?" Kline asked. "Having second thoughts?"

"No, but...I was just wondering. Will I be able to see the ankh? If it is what you say it is or does what you say it does, well... I would just like to see for myself. You understand."

"I'm sure Zeke will be only too happy to let you examine it. I'll call you tomorrow after I talk with him. I also need to call this lady, Miriam, and find out what her schedule is. It will be best, I think, if we can arrange a time for all of us to meet."

Rajani checked his watch. His next class was about to begin. "Well," he said, reaching for his briefcase, "my students will be waiting for me. I do not know what you have talked me into but I am curious to know more. It does sound like it might be right out in my alley."

Kline chuckled but didn't bother to correct the phrase. "Yes," he said, getting up to leave. "I think you'll find it certainly is that."

~81~

About the same time that Professor Kline was leaving Alec Rajani's office that Tuesday morning, Marcel Montebeau was staring out the window of his second floor apartment near the top of Seattle's Queen Anne Hill overlooking the city. The altercation with Romano the previous evening had set his emotions on fire. He was awake most of the night, humiliated, embarrassed and totally pissed off. Getting hold of that copy of the damning photo was the only thing on his mind. The more he thought about it the more incensed he became and the more determined he was to prevent anything from getting in his way. *But where is it? Where would Romano keep it? At the University? No. Probably not. Too risky. With my access to almost every nook and cranny of the campus...no.* Then it hit him. *His house! I'll bet the son of a bitch has it stashed away somewhere in his house! It's the last place he'd expect me to be!* Montebeau watched his own reflection grinning back at him in the window. *Well, think again my dear Brother Romano.* He knew Romano taught two classes almost back-to-back on Tuesday evenings, between 4 p.m. and 6 p.m. *Perfect*, he thought to himself. *Plenty of time to break into the house, search for the photo, hopefully find it, and get out before Romano gets home.* He looked at his watch. *10:30.* He had his own introductory level economics class to teach at 12:30 but he was too hyped up to even think about going in. He made a phone call and arranged for his graduate student intern to stand in for him. He mixed himself a double Bloody Mary and stretched out on the couch to give the matter some serious thought. He needed a plan of action.

Romano's home, Montebeau recalled, was a modest ranch style house, with an attached garage, in the suburb of Mountlake Terrace. He'd been there twice before, reluctantly invited by Romano himself, to meet with Beck and Salvo. On one of those occasions the four of them rode together in Romano's car. Upon arriving at the house, Romano opened the garage door with a remote control device and they parked inside. There were two doors inside the garage. One led into the house and the other led to the back yard. They got out of the car and were about to go into the house when Romano excused himself for a moment and walked over to the door that led to the back yard. It was slightly ajar. He cursed and slammed it shut. Thinking back now, Montebeau remembered Romano muttering something about the damned door latch and how he kept forgetting to fix it.

"Aren't you afraid someone might break in?" Beck had asked.

In response, Romano had simply shrugged. "Yeah," he said, "I'll get around to fixing it one of these days."

Montebeau now hoped Romano's procrastination had persisted long enough to provide him with easy access. The door leading into the house from the garage, he recalled, had no lock at all. That thought repeated itself over and over in his mind as the Bloody Mary and the lack of sleep began to take affect. *Rubber gloves... need... to... get... rubber...* His eyes grew heavy and his thoughts began to fade.

After what seemed like only minutes he sat up with a start. "Jesus!" he said, looking at his watch. He was shocked to see that several hours had passed. It was nearly 3:30 in the afternoon. He planted his feet on the floor and shook off the sleep. *Time to go.*

The drive to Romano's house took only a half hour even with a quick stop at the drugstore for a box of surgical gloves. He parked a block away from Romano's house and walked up the street. The timing was good. Romano was still at the university and most of the neighbors were not yet home from work. Confident that no one was watching, he slipped around to the back of the garage.

The back door was still in the same defective condition as he remembered it from several months ago. He reached into his pocket and drew out a pair of the rubber gloves. *No fingerprints*, he thought with a grin as he pulled them on and gave them a snap at the wrist. *I was never here.*

Once inside the garage, he looked around. Just as he remembered, the door leading into the house had no lock. He stepped up to it and gave the knob a twist. His hands shook nervously even though he knew there was no one home. He opened the door and entered the main part of the house. He stood quietly for a moment and looked around. *Time to get to work.*

He went through everything, rifling through drawers, searching through cupboards, under seat cushions, under the mattress. He even looked behind the paintings on the wall. Nothing. Then he remembered his own mother's secret hiding place for important documents. The freezer compartment of the refrigerator. *Could Romano have been that clever?* But a thorough check revealed nothing more than two frozen pizzas, an ice cube tray with one ice cube, and a half gallon of spumoni ice cream. He slammed the refrigerator door shut. *Damn it!* There seemed to be only one thing to do. Wait for Romano to come home and confront him with a demand to turn over the photo.

Montebeau's resentment and anger grew more intense with every passing minute as he waited impatiently for his enemy to arrive. An hour later Romano walked into the house.

"What the hell...?" Romano gasped, startled. "What are you doing in my house!"

Montebeau, glaring angrily, immediately rushed Romano, pinning him against the wall. "The copy of that picture!" he shouted into Romano's face. "Give me the goddam copy!"

The adrenaline surging through Montebeau's veins doubled his normal strength. He grabbed Romano by the front of the shirt and nearly lifted the stocky man off the floor. Just yesterday the roles were reversed and it was Romano who had Montebeau by the collar. Now the tables were turned. Romano, taken by surprise, was defenseless against Montebeau's uncontrolled rage.

"All right!" Romano choked, red faced. "All right! I'll give it to you!"

"Where is it?" Montebeau demanded, ratcheting his grip up another notch.

"Please," Romano coughed out the word, barely able to breathe. "I'll get it for you!"

Montebeau eased his grip ever so slightly, allowing Romano to catch a breath. "Now!" he shouted at Romano.

"Okay! All right! Let me go! I'll get it for you!"

"Do it!" Montebeau screamed. He released Romano and shoved him into the middle of the room.

Romano reached into his pocket, pulled out a key, and staggered over to a small table that was nearly hidden by a large recliner. The table had a single drawer with a brass keyhole in the center. Montebeau looked puzzled. *How could I have missed that?* It didn't matter now. He was about to get what he came for.

Standing in front of the little table, hands shaking, Romano bent down. He unlocked the drawer, reached in and pulled out a loaded revolver. Spinning around suddenly, he pointed it at Montebeau.

Montebeau jerked backward, jolted by the surprise. His mouth fell open. He put his hands up and wondered if Romano had the nerve to pull the trigger. He recalled Romano's own confession that he hadn't really meant to shoot Banyon – or anyone else during the confrontation in France – because he didn't have it in him to do such a thing. But was that the case? Was that true? Why would Romano have a gun in the house anyway if he never intended to use it? Was it just something to give the fat little man a false sense of security? Maybe. Maybe not. Montebeau couldn't be sure.

"So, what are you going to do?" Montebeau asked, feigning a smile to hide his fear. "Shoot me?"

Romano said nothing. With the gun pointed at Montebeau, he began to move slowly forward. With each step Romano took, Montebeau took a step backward, uncertain as to how this would play out.

Romano appeared determined to do something, but said nothing. His silence made Montebeau's nerves all the more unsettled. Montebeau couldn't know that the look of controlled aggression in

Romano's eyes betrayed the confusion going on inside his fat bald head. Romano had reached the end of his rope with Montebeau and he would like nothing better than to be rid of him. One squeeze of the trigger would do it. He'd be perfectly justified, protecting himself and his property from an unwanted intruder. Still, as much as he would like to see Montebeau dead, he knew he didn't have the nerve. With each passing moment, however, Montebeau was beginning to think otherwise. Now, backed up against the wall, staring down the barrel of the loaded gun, he realized he may have finally pushed Romano to the edge. As unbelievable as it seemed, the fat little bald man with a gun might be the last thing he would ever see. He closed his eyes and drew what he thought may well be his last breath.

Suddenly the ringtone of the cellphone in Romano's pocket began to chime the first nine notes of the old hymn, *Onward Christian Soldiers*. Montebeau's eyes snapped open as the sudden distraction caught Romano off guard. Montebeau lunged forward, grabbing for the gun. Romano held on to it, tightly. Montebeau wrenched Romano's arms one way and then the other but Romano wouldn't let go of the gun. Struggling furiously in what each of them was convinced was their last chance to stay alive, they locked arms and wrestled furiously, stumbling backward.

Then the ringtone stopped.

The strange dance ended.

The two men stood locked in a frozen embrace.

Sweating, panting hot breath into each other's face, staring into each other's eyes, trying to read each other's mind - each hoping that just maybe the other would give in - there was one last moment of total silence before one of them made an abrupt but subtle move and the gun went off.

~82~

That's life!
That's what all the people say…!

S inatra was crooning out his hit tune, *That's Life*, from the oldie's station on Kline's car radio as he drove home from the college. Along the way he couldn't help but smile at how things were going. *First,* he thought to himself, *I get a pat on the back from Nathan Crown, then Miriam Flamel just miraculously pops into the picture and then Rajani jumps on board.* He shook his head. It was beyond belief. *The ol' finger of Fate is sure stirring things up,* he grinned as Sinatra brought the song to a close:

I'm gonna roll myself up in a big ball aaaaand… die!

Kline leaned forward and switched the radio off. "Not tonight, Frankie, baby. Too much to live for."

~83~

M ontebeau stood frozen, his hand still gripping the smoking gun. A look of confused desperation filled Romano's eyes before they rolled back into his head. His heavy torso went limp and slumped against Montebeau's rigid body. Slowly, Romano slid downward, melting into a lifeless heap onto the floor. Montebeau dropped the gun. *My God. What have I done?*

He knelt down to check the body for any sign of life. There was none. A crimson color was spreading outward from beneath the body, soaking into the fibers of the spotless beige carpet. Montebeau panicked. He stood up too quickly, and became dizzy. His head was swimming. His legs wobbled. He stumbled backward, collapsing into the recliner next to the small table from which Romano had extracted the gun. *The gun! Fingerprints! No. Wait.* He looked down at his own hands. He was still wearing the rubber gloves. *What if...* Without another thought, he was up and moving toward the gun on the floor next to Romano's body. He picked up the weapon, wiped it clean, and wrapped Romano's dead fingers around it. It didn't occur to him that if a person was going to commit suicide he probably wouldn't do it by shooting himself in the stomach. All he knew was that Romano's fingerprints would be on the weapon, not his. He took one last look at the body on the floor and quickly exited the house the same way he'd come in. No one had seen him enter and no one saw him leave. He was home free. It was over. Or was it? He thought about Beck and Salvo. *Would they suspect I had anything to do with Romano's death? So what if they do? What could they do about it?* Montebeau knew they had their own demons to hide and they knew that he knew every last detail. *Even if they suspect me they won't say anything to anyone. They wouldn't risk it.* He paused as a moment of doubt crept in. *Would they?*

~84~

When Kline arrived home he had a message on his answering machine from Nathan Crown. Returning the call, Kline learned that Crown had reason to suspect Banyon's house and telephone may have been bugged. He left instructions for Kline to pass on to Banyon as soon as possible. He called Banyon immediately.

Banyon answered the phone. "Alan! We've been waiting to hear from you. Apparently the Nine didn't have you assassinated for spilling your guts to us, eh?"

"No. But listen," Kline said. There was a sense of urgency in his voice. "You need to do something as soon as I hang up. Don't ask me any questions. Just do what I tell you."

"Is something wrong?"

"Do you have something to write with?"

Banyon reached for the pen and paper next to the phone. "Okay. What?"

Kline gave Banyon a phone number and told him to write it down.

"All right," Banyon said. "Got it. Who's number is this?"

"As soon as I hang up you need to call that number and order a pizza for delivery. The man on the other end will ask if you want anchovies. You say *a pizza just isn't a pizza without anchovies.* You got that?"

"A pizza just isn't a pizza without anchovies."

"Good. And when he gets to your door, ask him if he knows what time it is. I can't tell you here on the phone what his answer will be but you'll know if it's the right answer anyway. That's how you'll know it's the right guy. Trust me. After the pizza is delivered, call me."

Banyon laughed. "Come on! Order a pizza? Anchovies? Ask him what time it is? What the hell are you talking about?"

Kline didn't want to say any more. "Just trust me," he said, hanging up the phone.

"What was that all about?" Angela asked.

Banyon shook his head. "I think our friend, the professor, has gone off the deep end. He wants me to call this number and order a pizza!"

Angela gave a laugh. "What?"

"Yeah. That's what he said. What's even weirder is the way he said it. He sounded dead serious."

"I don't get it. So what are you going to do?"

Banyon raised an eyebrow and looked at the number on the paper. "I guess I'll order a pizza."

He dialed the number and waited. After several rings a man answered. "Crown Pizza," the voice said. "Can I help you?"

Banyon hesitated a moment. He'd never heard of Crown Pizza.

But the name, Crown, rang a familiar bell. Was it just coincidence? He decided to go along with it. *What the hell.* "Uh, yeah. I'd like to order a sausage and mushroom pizza for delivery."

"Would you like anchovies on that?"

Banyon chuckled, still not quite sure what was going on. "Uh…" he paused a moment, trying to remember what Kline instructed him to say. "Uh, well, a pizza just isn't a pizza without anchovies, now is it?"

"Very good, Mr. Banyon. Your pizza will be delivered in twenty minutes or less."

Banyon's brow furrowed. "Wait a minute. I didn't tell you my name. How did you…" Before he could finish asking the question, the man on the other end of the line hung up. Banyon looked at Angela. "I don't know what's going on here but it's creeping me out. I'm going upstairs to get my gun."

"What?"

"Just in case," he said, heading for the stairs. But it was too late. The doorbell rang. "Jesus. When he said twenty minutes or less he wasn't kidding. Where the hell was he? Parked in front of the house?"

Angela peeked out the front window. There was no sign of a pizza delivery vehicle. She did see an unfamiliar Volkswagon Bug. The doorbell rang again. Banyon went to the door, switched on the porch light, and looked though the peek-hole.

The man appeared to be in his thirties, dressed in a dark blazer, white shirt, no necktie and a rugged face full of 5 o'clock shadow. He had a black briefcase at his side. He smiled as if he knew Banyon was checking him out. "Pizza delivery!" he said.

Pizza in a briefcase? What the hell is this? Banyon remembered Kline's instructions. "What time is it?" he asked through the door.

Without looking at his watch, the man answered, "Exactly nine!"

Banyon looked at his watch. It was just six-thirty. Then it hit him. Was this some kind of a code? *Christ, this is like some international espionage movie or something. Okay, I'll play the game. Let's see what else he's got.* "Wrong! It's only six-thirty!" he taunted the fellow.

The man rolled his eyes but didn't hesitate for a moment. "Well, you know what they say…" he came back. His accent was New York all the way, and heavy on the Brooklyn side. "A stitch in time saves nine."

Banyon shook his head. Obviously he'd guessed right. Nine was a code word. But why all the James Bond dialog? It seemed silly. He opened the door and faced the stranger. "Okay, what's this all about? Who are you and why are you here?"

"I work for Nathan Crown. You know?"

Banyon looked surprised, even though earlier he'd suspected the name, Crown Pizza, was maybe more than just a coincidence. "Crown sent you? Why?"

"I'm here to sweep your house."

"I beg your pardon? Sweep my house? What are you talking about?"

"Mr. Crown suspects your home may have been bugged. You know? Audio surveillance? Bugs? I'm here to find out. That's all I know. You know?"

Suddenly Kline's odd behavior on the phone made sense. If the phone was tapped Kline would want to say as little as possible. Banyon stepped aside and motioned for the man to come in. "You have a name?" he asked the man.

The man stepped inside, immediately surveying the room. Without looking at Banyon, and still intently scanning the interior, he said, "Jake." Apparently that was all the personal information the fellow was willing to give out. "This shouldn't take long," he said.

The stranger knelt down and opened his briefcase. He pulled out a few odd-looking electronic gadgets. He picked one that resembled a TV remote control with a small LCD screen. He extended a tiny antenna from the top of the device and pushed a button. Something appeared on the screen. He stood up and headed straight for the telephone on the end table next to the couch. He picked up the phone, examined it, and set it down again. Then he followed the phone cord to the wall jack behind the couch. Moving the couch away from the wall he manifested a screwdriver and removed the wall plate. After a few moments he stood up from behind the couch, holding some small object in his hand. He held it up for Banyon to see. "CTX model," he said. "UHF crystal-contolled. Pretty cool. High rate packet transmission capacity. Looks like an older series. Haven't seen many of these lately. You know?" He dropped it into his jacket pocket.

Banyon and Angela exchanged glances. They had no idea what the stranger was talking about.

Jake came out from behind the couch. He didn't bother to move it back into place and - Banyon noticed, a bit perturbed - he didn't bother to replace the wall plate over the phone jack either. "Got anymore phones?" he asked.

Banyon rolled his eyes. *How about putting things back the way you found them?* "No, that's the only hard wired phone in the house."

Jake nodded and went back to his briefcase. He shuffled through a few more gizmos, finally selecting one about the size of a cigarette pack. Like the other gizmo, it had a small LCD screen. Jake switched it on. The little screen glowed green and appeared to display a grid of tiny black lines. The instrument had a numbered keypad like a calculator below the screen and a slider switch on the side. Jake keyed in a code and watched a series of numbers flit across the tiny display screen. He walked over to one of the living room walls and placed the object flat up against it. In a moment all of the grid cells on the screen filled with an array of colors. Jake seemed unimpressed and went to the next wall and then the next until he finally ended up in the kitchen where something on the screen seemed to attract his attention. He backed up from the wall and checked the instrument. He seemed puzzled. "Hmmm..." he mumbled. "Where are ya, you little bugger?" He looked around and walked over to the kitchen table. He paused to check his instrument again. Then he crawled under the table and crained his neck to look up. "Gotcha, you little bastard." When he came out from under the table, he was holding another small odd device. He looked at it, nodding approvingly, and started in with the tech-talk again. He may as well have been speaking in Greek.

"Can you say any of that in English?" Banyon asked.

"Yeah, sure," he said, as he continued to examine the device. "Neat little bug. Bertoli 44TR. Voice activated, you know? Long range transmission. Made in Italy. You never see them in this country. Well, I mean once in a blue moon. But, you know what I mean."

Banyon cocked an eyebrow. "Italy, huh?"

Jake nodded and dropped the bug into the briefcase. "Yeah. Whoever planted it must have connections. You can't buy 'em here. You know?"

"Really," Banyon said. "So how would a person be likely to get one of those if he wanted one?"

Jake looked Banyon square in the eyes and said, "If I told ya, I'd have t'kill ya." After a pregnant pause with the most serious expression on his face, he burst out with a hearty laugh and continued on through the house, checking the walls, looking behind picture frames and under tables. He didn't find anything else. "What's upstairs?" he asked.

"Couple bedrooms," Banyon answered.

Jake picked up his briefcase and climbed the stairs with Banyon and Angela following behind.

"Is this your master bedroom?"

Banyon nodded and Jake moved straight toward the bed. He made an adjustment on the detection device and smiled. "Too easy," he said. He pulled the bed away from the wall and leaned over the headboard. "Yup," he said, reaching behind the headboard. His hand emerged with yet another Italian-made Bertoli 44. "Sweet," he said. "Two in one night. How lucky can a guy get? Maybe I oughta go buy a lottery ticket. You know?" He looked over at Banyon. "Show me the other room."

When Jake was satisfied that the house was clean he simply packed up his gear and walked to the front door. He stopped momentarily, winked at Angela and turned to Banyon. "That's it. Clean sweep. Sleep tight." With that he walked out the door, climbed into his VW Bug and was gone.

Banyon and Angela were left staring at each other.

"He winked at me," she said.

Banyon shook his head as if he didn't hear her right. "What?"

"He winked at me!"

Banyon gave a laugh. "A strange guy walks into our house with a bag full of weird techno-gadgets, scans our walls and goes around finding surveillance bugs like a kid on an Easter egg hunt and all you can say is *he winked at me*?"

She shrugged. "Well, he did. Why'd he do that?"

Faking his best Brooklyn accent, sounding a little like Sylvester Stallone in a *Rocky* movie, he said, "Hey. He's from New Yawk. New Yawk guys do dat, ya know?"

She groaned and let it slide. "So aren't you supposed to call Alan now?"

"Yeah. He wanted me to call as soon as the pizza was delivered."

"And find out who the hell bugged our house," she said. "It pisses me off, excuse my language. While you're doing that I'll fix something for dinner."

"How 'bout pizza?" Banyon joked.

"Not unless you want to have one delivered."

Banyon chuckled as he went to find a screwdriver to replace the wall plate. That taken care of, and the couch maneuvered back into place, he called Kline.

By the time he'd finished his conversation with the professor, Angela was just setting dinner on the table.

"Well, that was encouraging," Banyon said, sitting down to a meal of scrambled eggs, sausage, and pancakes. "Hey, breakfast for dinner! I love that!"

Angela grinned and sat down across from him. "What's encouraging? What'd he say? Did he know who planted the listening devices?"

"Yeah. He said he got a message from Nathan Crown. It was Crown who arranged for the guy to come *sweep our house,* as they say. Crown suspected it was – get this – someone at the top of the Jesuit Order. Probably the big guy, himself."

Angela nearly choked. "The Jesuit General? What's his name? DuPont?"

"Yeah. That's what Crown told Kline. I sort of suspected something like that when the bug-man said those devices were made in Italy and you can't buy them in this country. Remember he said someone must have some pretty good connections? Can you believe it?"

"I can believe just about anything anymore. But it's a little scary, don't you think? I wonder how much they know. Do you think they heard much of our conversations? How long were those things in our house, anyway?"

Banyon shrugged. "Don't know. Hard telling. Crown thought maybe a week. He wasn't sure."

"Hmm..." Angela said, pushing the food around on her plate. "And so the plot thickens."

Banyon snickered. "Yeah."

"You said Alan told you something that was encouraging. What'd you mean?"

"Well, it turns out he ran into Miriam Flamel – you remember, that alchemy girl – and she's agreed to work with us. Not only her but that physicist fellow too."

"Really! That was fast. I thought Alan wasn't sure how to find her."

"Yeah. Well, it was another one of those weird things." He paused for a moment and then looked at her. "If you think you're ready to believe just about anything anymore, listen to this."

He told her about Kline's unlikely encounter with the former goth-chick-student-of-alchemy-turned-sophisticated-author-of-simplified-mass-market-books-on-how-to-become-an-alchemist.

Angela was surprised. "She was really that different? There was that big of a change?"

Banyon nodded as he finished his last bite and lit up a cigarette. "Apparently so."

"Wow. I still don't understand what alchemy has to do with anything that concerns us."

"I don't either. Neither did Miriam, apparently. None of us do. But hopefully we'll figure it out. Kline wants us all to get together as soon as possible so we can get acquainted and begin working on all of this."

They talked a little more before Angela got up to clear the table. She carried a couple dishes to the sink and paused a long time. A stream of disturbing thoughts and images raced through her mind: the Jesuits, the night she was kidnapped, the loculus, the scroll, the numbers, the thing at the bottom of the ocean, the incomprehensible task of raising it up, Banyon's appointed mission and – most troubling of all – the omen of the comet and it's unthinkable outcome. If she hadn't been involved in all of it from the very beginning she would never have believed any of it. But so far it had all proven true and the weight of that realization was sinking deeper into the fibers of her being at that very moment. Things were moving quickly and time was short.

Banyon noticed her standing solemnly, staring into the sink. "Angela?"

She turned around and looked at him. She wiped a single tear from her cheek.

He got up and walked over to her. "What is it?" he asked. "What's the matter?"

She lowered her eyes. "I don't know. I guess I'm just a little scared." She looked up at him. She didn't want to say what she was really thinking.

But he knew what she was thinking. *What if we fail?* It had crossed his mind more than a few times. He put his arm around her and drew her close. He wanted to say he was scared too but he knew that wouldn't sound very comforting. "Everything will work out okay," he said, hoping he sounded more confident than he really was. *The Chosen One*, he thought to himself. *Why me?*

~85~

The meeting was scheduled for 7:30 p.m. at Banyon's house the following Saturday. Professor Kline was the first to arrive.

Banyon opened the door. "Hi Alan. Come on in. Angela will be down in just a minute."

"Anyone else here yet?"

Banyon took Kline's coat and noticed he was carrying something under his arm. "No. Just you, so far. What's in the box?"

Kline sat down on the couch with the plain brown cardboard box in his lap. "Just a little house-warming gift from our friend Nathan Crown."

"House warming gift? What are you talking about? What is it?"

Kline handed him the box. "Open it."

Banyon opened the box and looked puzzled. "A clock radio? I don't get it."

"Looks like a clock radio, works like a clock radio, and as far as anyone would guess it's nothing more than a clock radio. But it's a little more than that. Here, hand it to me. Where can we plug it in?"

"Right there behind the couch."

Kline got up and pulled the couch away from the wall. Reaching over the back, he plugged the radio in and set it on the end table. He moved the couch back into place and sat down again. Then he turned the clock radio on its side. "See this little button here?"

Banyon moved closer to get a better look. It was a tiny button next to the volume control. "Okay, I see it. Why? What is it?"

Kline pushed the button and a small green light lit up on the top of the radio. "This, my friend, guarantees our privacy this evening."

Banyon was still confused. "What the hell are you talking about? What is this thing?"

"We know there aren't any more listening devices in your home but there are technologies that allow someone - say, outside in a car or some other vehicle - to actually hear what's being said here inside your house. This little gizmo somehow scrambles every sound within the house, making any noises virtually impossible to define or to be recognized by any kind of audio surveillance equipment."

Banyon gave a laugh. "You gotta be kidding me. Are you serious?"

"I don't think Mr. Crown is one for playing practical jokes," Kline replied.

Just as Angela was coming down the stairs from the bedroom the doorbell rang. She greeted Kline as she passed through the living room. "You guys stay put. I'll get it." When she opened the door she was greeted by an unfamiliar face.

"Good evening, Miss. I am Alec Rajani."

Angela smiled and ushered him in. "Professor Rajani! We've heard a lot about you. I'm Angela. Zeke and Alan are in the living room. Come in and make yourself at home."

Banyon got up and introduced himself. "Professor Rajani! Thank you for coming! I'm Zeke Banyon."

Rajani smiled. "Alec, please. Call me Alec."

"All right. Alec it is, then. Glad you could make it, Alec. Have a seat. You know Alan, of course."

Kline sat forward. "Hello Alec. Good to see you."

"Well," Angela said, "while we're waiting for Miriam, can I get you boys some coffee?"

After the coffee was served the four of them got acquainted and engaged in small talk for the next half hour. Banyon was just about to say he hoped Miriam hadn't decided to back out when the doorbell chimed. He got up to answer it.

The stunning young woman at the door smiled and shifted her

briefcase from one hand to the other. "Mr. Banyon, I presume?"

"That's me," Banyon said, shaking her hand. "And you must be Miriam."

"Yes. I'm sorry I'm late. I…"

"No problem! We were just having coffee and getting acquainted with Professor Rajani. Come in, please. Can I take your coat?"

"Yes, thank you." The removal of her coat revealed an outfit that was a little dressier than this casual occasion called for.

Banyon addressed the others as he led her into the living room. "Everyone, this is Miriam Flamel."

Suddenly Angela felt a little underdressed in her simple beige sweater and Levis. Miriam Flamel's neatly pleated black bellbottom slacks accentuated her long legs that were made to appear even longer with the assistance of a pair of stylish high-heeled black leather boots. Her red blouse had a wide cut neckline revealing more bare shoulder than Angela thought was really necessary. There was no doubt about it. This was one attractive woman. *Jesus Christ*, Angela thought to herself. *This is the goth chick Kline described back at the cabin? I guess he was right about the transformation. That alchemy stuff must have something going for it. Shit.* "Welcome to our home, Miriam. I'm Angela." She paused for a moment and added, "Zeke and I are engaged." She immediately wished she hadn't said that. *Crap. That sounded stupid.* "Can I get you some coffee?"

"That would be great," Miriam said, taking a seat next to Kline.

As Angela headed for the kitchen she glanced over at Banyon. Either he was pretending not to be impressed with the young lady's appearance or he had suddenly gone completely blind. After a few moments she returned to the living room with Miriam's coffee and sat in the chair next to Banyon.

After a few more minutes of small talk Banyon addressed the group.

"Well, okay then," he said. "I guess we should get down to the business at hand. I know Alan has told you most of the story. I know it all sounds too weird to be true but since you both showed up here tonight I guess you must be at least somewhat convinced that I'm not totally off my rocker. But just to help add some credibility to the story I want to show you something. If you'll all just follow me into the dining room."

The dining room table was normally littered with bills and newspapers and magazines and anything else that somehow never seemed to get put away. Tonight, however, it had been cleared off and turned into a museum display.

As they entered the dining room Banyon switched on the chandelier above the table. The table was covered with a burgundy tablecloth where the priceless artifacts - the scroll, the loculus, and the mysterious golden ankh – were displayed in all their glory.

Miriam was the first to respond. "Oh...my...god. So it's true."

Rajani was equally stunned. "I am not believing what I am seeing."

The ankh is what really caught Rajani's attention. It was just as Kline had described. He gestured toward it and looked at Banyon. "May I?"

Banyon nodded and picked up the ankh. He held it out to Rajani. "Are you ready for this?" he asked with a grin.

"Oh yes," Rajani said. "I have been waiting for this moment." He took the ankh in his hands and held it tightly, concentrating, trying to feel the vibration that Kline had told him about. "I am not sure I can feel anything."

"Hold it gently against the side of your face," Angela suggested.

Rajani did so but was still uncertain. "I... I am not sure. Is it possible that we could perform the experiment with the water? I am very much wishing to see that."

Miriam held out her hand. "I'd like to see if I can feel the vibration. May I?"

Rajani handed the ankh to her. She held it to her cheek and concentrated. In a moment her eyes lit up. "Oh my god!" She quickly took it away from her face and looked at it. Then she put it back against her cheek. "What the hell is this? I can feel it!"

Rajani was anxious. "The water. Can we...?"

Banyon grinned. "You bet. We knew you would want to see that so we prepared everything. Angela, can you bring in the equipment?"

They conducted the experiment in the same manner as they had done at Kline's cabin. But this time Banyon had constructed a special jig that consisted of an upside down L-shaped piece of wood attached to a wooded base. Banyon inserted the string through the loop of the ankh and tied the ends of the string together. Then he placed the glass of water on the base of the jig and looped the string over the horizontal bar of the upside down L. Next, he lowered the tethered ankh into the water. The length of the string was just enough to allow the ankh to be suspended freely in the water without quite touching the bottom of the glass.

Rajani watched closely as the water began to vibrate, forming tiny ripples across the water's surface. "This is not right," he said, sounding a bit puzzled.

"What do you mean it's not right?" Banyon asked.

Rajani adjusted his bifocals against his nose and leaned over the table. With his face right up to the glass of water, he peered intently at the phenomenon. "Of course I cannot be certain," he said. "The ripple effect is moving so quickly it is difficult to tell for sure, but..." He left the sentence hanging as he continued to stare at the movement of the water.

"But what?" Angela asked.

Rajani straightened up and removed his glasses. "It appears that the shape of the ripples across the surface of the water is not in the form of concentric circles as one would be expecting."

Banyon leaned in to see for himself. "Hmm... You might be right. It's almost like..."

"Spirals," Rajani said.

Banyon nodded. "Yes, spirals. I think you might be right."

One by one the others moved in for a close examination of the tiny, hair-thin ripples moving rapidly through the water.

"That's not normal?" Angela asked.

Rajani shook his head. "No. I am thinking not. And I cannot be certain but I am thinking these spirals may be reflecting something very special."

Banyon was intrigued. "Special?"

"Yes," Rajani said. "The phi proportion. The so called Golden Mean."

The terms *phi* and *Golden Mean* rang a bell in the back of Banyon's mind but he couldn't remember why. He looked confused. "Phi proportion? Golden Mean? I don't understand. What are you talking about?"

Miriam's eyes lit up at the mention of the Golden Mean. "I'm familiar with those terms," she said.

"Care to enlighten us?" Banyon begged.

Miriam opened her briefcase and took out a sheet of blank paper and a pencil and sat down at the table. She drew a square and proceeded to demonstrate how, with a few simple steps, the square could be transformed into a rectangle. She attempted a brief explanation. "The dimensions of this rectangle, in relation to the original square, yields a proportional measurement known as *phi*. In terms of numbers, the *phi* proportion produces what is called a transcendental number."

Banyon groaned. This was worse than trying to understand Angela's explanation of music theory. "What the hell is a transcendental number, if you don't mind me asking?"

Miriam smiled. "That's a number that never ends. When this particular proportion is calculated it looks like this."

She wrote a series of numbers followed by a series of dots:

1.6180339.....

"It goes on forever, actually" she explained. "I just can't remember where it goes beyond the 9. But, generally it's just simplified as 1.618."

Those numbers, thought Banyon. *I know those numbers. But from where? How?*

Rajani seemed impressed. "Yes," he said. "This is all correct. And from this rectangle one can produce the Golden Mean Spiral."

Rajani took the pencil and proceeded to trace out an approximation of the *phi* spiral curve within the confines of the rectangle.

Banyon was amused how the shape of the *phi* spiral resembled the shape of the number 9. Then it hit him. "Oh man!" he said. "Wait a minute! Wait just a minute!" He left the room for a moment and returned with his briefcase. He pulled out a copy of the huge list of phrases that came to him at Kline's cabin. "Yes!" he said excitedly. "Look here!"

He pointed out the relevant phrases that, up until now, seemed to make no sense at all:

ONE POINT SIX ONE EIGHT = 243

THE PHI PROPORTION OF ONE POINT SIX ONE EIGHT = 486

486 / 3 = 162 = THE TONE SPIRAL
= THE THREE TONES = THE TIME PORTAL

THE GOLDEN MEAN SPIRAL = 198
= THE MUSICAL SCALE OF GOD

Miriam was excited to see this. Kline had told her about Banyon's ability to somehow manifest seemingly meaningful phrases with number values that seemed to correspond to other related phrases. She was fascinated because she, too, had experimented with the same concept and had achieved some tantalizing results. She was about to tell Banyon about her work in this area but he jumped in ahead of her.

"Now I see how these phrases about *phi* and spirals and all that stuff fit into the picture!" Then he laughed at himself. "Well, okay, I don't *exactly* understand how it fits but at least it doesn't seem so completely out of place." He looked over at Miriam. "What else do we know about this *phi* stuff?"

The question set both Miriam and Rajani off on a thirty-minute discourse on *phi*.

Banyon found it fascinating although he couldn't say he truly understood most of it. "And this all means what, exactly?" he asked. "Can we get to a bottom line here? Maybe come up with exactly how this works into our big picture?" Then he looked at Miriam. "And how is it that a student of alchemy happens to know so much about this *phi* stuff, anyway?"

"Well," Miriam began, " it might seem like quite a stretch at first but when I read somewhere that the *phi* proportion is found everywhere in the formation of organic matter, living things, I just had a gut feeling that there might be some connection because alchemy does deal with a whole philosophy of life."

Banyon looked surprised. "This proportion is found in all living things? How? What do you mean?"

Citing the growth pattern of leaves on a plant as an example, Miriam explained that the positioning of the leaves is such that their growth nodes follow a spiral path along the length of the stem. Furthermore, she said, even the human body contains many instances of the *phi* proportion such as in the positioning of the finger bones in relation to one another.

"And here's my favorite example," she added, reaching into her briefcase. She pulled out a photograph of a large seashell. She put it on the table and traced the spiral lines of the shell with her finger. "This is a Torus shell. It's a beautiful example of a *phi* spiral in nature. But I have something else to show you."

She reached into her briefcase and pulled out a notebook. After thumbing through a few pages she found what she was looking for and handed it to Banyon. He was shocked to see what she had written:

PHI IS THE KEY = 135

PHI SPIRAL = 108 = GEOMETRY = PHI ETERNAL

GEOMETRY OF THE PHI SPIRAL = 270
= PHI ETERNAL WITHIN THE BODY

THE SPIRAL PATH = 153 = THE GOLDEN RATIO

THE PHI SPIRAL IS THE PATH OF WISDOM = 351

THE MUSICAL PHI = 144

"I've been experimenting with the English gematria too," she beamed.

Oh swell, Angela groaned to herself. *Attractive, intelligent, and she's into the number stuff. Can there be anything else?*

Banyon couldn't believe his eyes. "How long have you been doing this? Do you have more?"

"Not long. A month or so, maybe. Yes, I have more. It's all in that notebook. Just go through the pages. You'll see."

Banyon's eyes narrowed as he studied her work. Angela, reluctantly, read over his shoulder and was also stunned by many of the phrases and familiar numbers.

"Look," Angela said, pointing to the phrase, THE MUSICAL PHI = 144.

"Yeah," Banyon said. "We know that number, don't we?"

Angela nodded. "And then look here." She referred him back to his own download of phrases from that day at the cabin. She pointed out one in particular:

THE GOLDEN MEAN SPIRAL = 198 = THE MUSICAL SCALE OF GOD

Clearly there was a strong correlation between Miriam's phrase, THE MUSICAL PHI, and Banyon's phrase, THE MUSICAL SCALE

OF GOD. At this point they had no idea what it might mean but they did notice 144+198=342, the reverse of 243 which was the gematria of the phrase, ONE POINT SIX ONE EIGHT.

Then, looking at the Ezekiel Code list, Angela noticed something else:

REVERSE THE NUMBER = 198
REVERSE DIRECTION = 198

Miriam's eyes widened at the sight of the list of phrases and numbers on the paper Angela was holding. "So this is the famous Ezekiel Code that Alan told me about?"

Angela nodded. "Yes. Well, it's a printout of the phrases that are on the original parchment. There was no rhyme or reason to the order in which they appeared on the parchment. After studying them I suggested we reorganize them into groups according to the gematric value." She mentally patted herself on the back for using the term, *gematric value*.

"And where is the original?" Miriam asked. "I'd love to see it."

"Of course," Banyon obliged her. He left the room and went upstairs to retrieve the original parchment from the safe. When he returned a few minutes later he added it to the display on the dining room table.

Miriam was fascinated. "God, I love stuff like this!" she said. She studied the original and compared it with the restructured copy and then pointed out even more instances where the numbers in her own list of phrases matched some of those in the Ezekiel Code list.

Comparing the gematria from the rest of the work in Miriam's notebook with that of the Ezekiel Code list and the *Cabin Download*, as they had come to call it, provided several minutes of excited conversation and a stimulating exchange of ideas.

Rajani found it all to be rather interesting or, perhaps, *amusing* would be a more accurate way of putting it. But, from his scientific perspective, he couldn't help injecting some rational skepticism. "Is it not more likely that it is all simple coincidence?"

Kline, of course, quickly interjected his favorite mantra. "Ah," he said, "it's like I always say. There's no such thing as mere coincidence!"

"It may seem like mere coincidence," Miriam was quick to add, "but it's really synchronicity."

She explained synchronicity for Rajani's benefit and carried her argument further. "From my studies," she said, "I've concluded that consciousness is the primary ingredient in the synchronicity phenomenon. In some way, the entire universe is conscious, albeit a consciousness that surpasses our current understanding of just what consciousness is. In fact, as far as I know, no one yet knows just exactly what consciousness is. For all we know, it may even be a technology of some kind."

Banyon leaned over to Angela and whispered, "She sounds like Paretti."

The word *technology* captured Rajani's attention. "Technology?"

"Well," Miriam continued, "not in the Newtonian mechanical or hardware sense as we generally think of technology but…"

"Ah," Rajani said. "I know where you are going now. You would be speaking in a quantum mechanical sense. Yes, yes, I see."

"Exactly," Miriam said. "I think what's happening here is that we – that is, the five of us here in this room – are locked inside a sort of synchronistic bubble. Metaphorically speaking, that is. The universe is a sea of consciousness filled with countless bubbles of synchronicity all interconnected. And the five of us happen to be joined together inside the same bubble. Actually, saying that we just happen to be here together, as if it's nothing more than a random accident, isn't the case at all. At least not the way I see it. At some level, beyond the sea of consciousness, there is some sort of programming going on…"

Angela leaned over and whispered back to Banyon, "Yeah, she does sound like Paretti. But Paretti's probably not as attractive."

Banyon gave her a puzzled glance. *What?*

Miriam continued. "…and we've been guided by that program into this particular bubble for a reason." She looked around at the faces of her companions and wondered if anyone was comprehending what she was trying to say.

Rajani was nodding his head as if he was understanding it on the one hand but still perplexed on the other. "I am getting the gist of what you are saying but I have to be wondering how you come to these ideas. I understand you are a student of alchemy, yes?"

Miriam nodded. "A student of the *history* of alchemy, mostly."

"Well," Rajani said, "I am confessing I am not knowing too much about alchemy but from what little I do know I cannot follow the connection. How do you get from alchemy to quantum physics and synchronistic bubbles?"

Miriam laughed. "It was those damn numbers," she said, casting a wink in Banyon's direction. She took out a page of her notes and handed it to Rajani. "It's a long story," she said. "My studies of alchemy brought me to understand that it was more than just the idea of the transmutation of base metals into gold. The true goal of alchemy was – or is - to discover the secret of eternal life. Following along this path one quickly comes to the question of consciousness. In my quest to understand the nature of consciousness I was led to consider the nature of intuition and that led me, interestingly enough, to two ancient methods of divination, the Tarot and the Chinese oracle of the *I Ching*. Both of these oracles involve numbers. I became fascinated with the number aspect which led me to yet another ancient method of divination, or in another sense, a method of encoding information."

"Gematria," Banyon said.

Miriam nodded. "Yes, exactly. Gematria. But not knowing how to read either Greek or Hebrew I just decided to start experimenting with applying that idea to English. It wasn't long before I began to notice some astonishing synchronicities between certain phrases with matching alphanumeric values. As you can see there on that paper I handed you, certain concepts began to fall into corresponding groups. Alchemy, numbers, consciousness, and transmutation, to be specific. And somehow that whole ball of wax is intimately connected to one specific number."

Banyon chuckled. "Let me guess. Nine."

Miriam looked surprised. "So you know?"

Angela grinned and lit a cigarette. "Boy, do we know!"

"Well, don't hold out on me," Miriam said, excitedly. "I'm all ears."

Yeah, right, Angela thought to herself. *All legs is more like it.*

Banyon took the cue and launched into an hour-long explanation of how the number nine had played such a large part in their long journey beginning with the odd incident with the clock on the wall the day Angela walked into his office to apply for a job. As he talked, he placed sheet after sheet of all their notes on the table for Miriam and Rajani to examine. Miriam was mesmerized by the barrage of information. She could barely contain her excitement. Everything Banyon was showing her was a validation of her own ideas. Rajani, too, was intrigued but, not having had the personal experiences with the *nine thing*, as Banyon kept calling it, he felt a bit like an outsider. It was all so irrational to his scientifically trained mind. Still, he had to admit to himself, there was something strangely compelling about it.

Miriam shook her head and drew a deep breath. "Wow," she said. "This is all so much more than I could ever have imagined. But I still don't understand what my role here is supposed to be. I mean, how can I help? What is it I'm supposed to do?"

"Well," Banyon said, almost apologetically, "I wish I could tell you. The truth is, I don't really know. The good professor here" he nodded toward Kline, "thought it would be a good idea to bring you in and, at the time, it seemed like the right thing to do. And, having heard your story, I still think it was the right thing to do."

"Okay," Miriam said. "But why?"

Banyon sat back and shook his head. "I don't know. But I'm sure we'll find out. For now I think it's enough that you're just here. Like you said, at some level the program has been set into motion and we've all ended up in this cozy little synchronistic bubble."

Angela winced. *Oh puh-lease*, she thought to herself.

A knowing grin crossed Miriam's face. "I can dig that," she said. Then she turned to Rajani. "We haven't heard much from you. What's your role in all this?"

Rajani explained that he'd been ambushed by his friend, professor Kline, and was basically cajoled into joining the group. Miriam was fascinated to learn of his private research into acoustic levitation and, as synchronicity would have it, she happened to be quite familiar with the stories about the Vimanas, the flying vehicles of ancient Vedic tradition.

"So," Miriam said, "have you actually succeeded in producing a levitation effect?"

Rajani nodded. "I have had some success, yes. But only with very small objects. A paperclip, for example. And the results were nearly immeasurable. You see, there are..."

Miriam laughed. "A paperclip?" She immediately hoped she hadn't sounded condescending. It just struck her as amusing.

Rajani took it in good stride. "Yes. Well, it is a very complicated procedure," he explained. "My theory, I am convinced, is stone hard. But..."

Kline interrupted with a chuckle. "Rock solid, I think you mean."

"Yes, thank you," Rajani replied. "The problem is, I am only one person working alone and I need equipment that I cannot afford."

"Great," Banyon said. "We need to be able to levitate a large object off the bottom of the ocean and the most we can do is raise a paperclip a micro-measurement off a tabletop?"

"Maybe," Angela suggested, "that's where our tones come in. Somehow that information needs to be integrated into Alec's theory."

"Yes," Rajani said, "Alan told me a little about these tones you are speaking of. I am interested in knowing more about this."

Banyon glanced over at Angela and nodded. She took the cue and explained to Rajani about the tones, how the idea came about, how the numbers fit into the picture, and she described their conception of the huge ring-shaped structure that would support the sound devices which would generate these tones.

Rajani listened intently, struggling to follow what Angela was saying while at the same time running a mental inventory of his own hypotheses and trying to figure out how this new information might correlate with his theoretical propositions. All of that was problematical enough let alone the idea of actually building the structure for supporting the sound devices. That was an engineering problem completely outside his area of expertise. In the end he was simply not sure about any of it. He conceded there were some interesting possibilities but again he stressed the problem of funding, the lack of equipment, not to mention the time crunch. They had less than three months to make it work… if it was going to work at all. It seemed impossible.

Banyon let out a hopeless sigh. Then he had a thought. *The Nine.* He looked at Kline. "Can we get some assistance?"

Kline lit his pipe and shrugged. He knew what Banyon was thinking. "At this point in the game…" he paused and took a couple draws on the pipe to get it going, "…I'd say it's a good possibility."

"How soon can you find out?"

"Tomorrow."

Rajani looked confused. "Assistance?"

Kline grinned. "My friend," he said, "you may be closer to realizing your dream than you can imagine."

"Well," Banyon said, "while you're at it, see if you can make *my* dream come true, too. Like some way of actually getting us to that location in the Antarctic Sea would be good."

Kline nodded. "I'll see what I can do."

~86~

A lone in his apartment, bags packed and ready to go, Montebeau sat motionless, distraught, waiting for a phone call as he watched the news on television:

'... *police are not releasing any details about the shooting of a Jesuit priest found dead in his home last night. We have learned from other sources, however, that this same priest, Frank Romano, was a victim in a bizarre incident that took place at Queen City University some months ago. You may remember that case in which three priests were apparently assailed by a group of unidentified men wearing black hoods. A janitor at the university found the priests tied to the wall in a storage room. No one was hurt in the incident and the assailants – whose identifications remain a mystery – were assumed to have been members of some sort of cult. Police will not say whether the two incidents are related. They did tell us that they have no suspects at this point but an intensive investigation is underway. In other news, Wall Street today took a sharp...*'

The phone rang. Montebeau picked it up. "Yes, sir," he said. "Yes, I've booked a flight out for tonight. I emailed you the flight number and the estimated time of arrival in Rome. Yes, General. Please know I'm grateful for... what? No, of course. I understand. Yes. Goodbye."

~87~

When Montebeau arrived in Rome he was immediately escorted to the office of the Jesuit General for a private meeting. After the shooting incident at Romano's home, Montebeau decided his only chance was to ask DuPont for protection. DuPont agreed to help in exchange for everything Montebeau knew about Banyon's progress. The meeting, however, was short lived. Montebeau had nothing to deliver that DuPont didn't already know.

"That's it?" DuPont said. "That's all you have?"

Montebeau shifted uneasily in his chair. "Yes, but..."

DuPont's face turned red. He slammed his fist on the desk. "You've wasted my time! You have nothing!"

"But..." Montebeau started.

DuPont threw up a hand to silence the young priest. Montebeau bit his tongue. He knew better than to attempt an argument with the Jesuit General.

DuPont turned to the sentry who had been standing silently by the door. "Take him out of here," he commanded. "Now!"

The sentry walked over to Montebeau and grabbed him by the arm. Montebeau wrenched himself away and straightened his jacket. "I can walk," he said with a glare of indignation. As he left the room and headed down the long hall with the sentry just two steps behind him he wondered what would happen now. Maybe tomorrow the General would be in a more forgiving mood. One could only hope.

Back in his office, DuPont was making a decision. He could send Montebeau back to the states and let the police take care of him. On the other hand, he was well aware of Montebeau's reputation for having a loose tongue. He might spill his guts to the police if they arrested him. Of course it wasn't likely that a lot of what he had to say would be believed. To the uninitiated the story would seem like the ravings of a crackpot. Still, it wasn't worth taking the chance. He called another sentry into the room and instructed him on what needed to be done.

Alone in his hotel room, Montebeau was desperately trying to figure out some way to regain the good graces of the General. Later that night he fell asleep and dreamed Romano had returned from the grave and was trying to strangle him. "Christ!" Montabeau yelled. His own voice woke him up. Choking, struggling, coughing, he opened his eyes in horror. It was more than just a dream. He caught a glimpse of an unfamiliar face at the end of two black-sleeved arms that were pinning him down. The muscular hands of the attacker were wrapped tightly around Montabeau's neck, the thumbs squeezing into the nape of his throat. Suddenly, Montabeau didn't care. He stopped struggling. Nothing seemed to matter because something else was happening. *What is this?* he wondered as he sank deeper and deeper into an unfamiliar darkness. Then, in a final moment of consciousness, he understood. In a moment it was over.

Minutes later the sentry returned to the office of the Jesuit General. "It's done," he reported.

DuPont nodded without any noticeable expression on his face. He motioned for the sentry to leave and then poured himself a brandy before retiring for the night.

~88~

It was another two weeks before everyone's schedules allowed for them all to come together for the next meeting. Finally on a Friday evening they met once again at Banyon's home. Miriam brought a bottle of chardonnay for the occasion. Not to be outdone, Angela decided to pull out the bottle of $75 Tenuta di Gianni Tuscan Merlot. After all, this was war. Banyon, blissfully unaware that he was in the middle of a battle zone, thought it was a great idea and proceeded to order a couple of pizzas from Mario's.

When everyone was settled in the living room Banyon made an

announcement. "Listen up, everybody. Alan has some interesting information to share with us tonight." He nodded toward Kline.

"Indeed I do," Kline said. He paused a moment to light his pipe. "Remember I said I would contact the Nine - Nathan Crown, specifically - to see if we could get some help." He looked over at Rajani. "Alec, my friend, your life is about to change."

Rajani was puzzled. "I am sorry?"

Kline grinned. "Your concerns about the lack of equipment and funding for your continued research and development of the acoustic levitation process are about to be taken care of. Mr. Crown, besides being the current head of the Nine, is also the owner of one of the biggest companies in the high-tech industry. As such, he is in the process of not only making available to you the knowledge and assistance of his top acoustic engineer but within a week you will have access to a huge private laboratory and all the funding you will need to accomplish the task."

Rajani's eyes narrowed. "Alan, again you are stretching my leg. Yes?"

Kline chuckled. "No, my friend, I'm not pulling your leg at all. But there is just one thing. It means you'll have to resign your position at the college. The project will require a full-time commitment if we're to have any hope of making this happen in the short amount of time we have left."

Rajani was both shocked and excited by the news. Kline explained that Crown would handle everything with the college administration as far as Rajani's resignation was concerned.

The news brought a spontaneous round of applause from the rest of the group.

"Hold on!" Banyon said. "There's more. Professor?"

Kline smiled. "Well, as you know, our fearless leader here..." he nodded toward Banyon. "...the Chosen One..."

"Yeah, yeah," Banyon said, rolling his eyes. The inauspicious title had not ceased to be an embarrassment to him. "Just get on with it, please."

"All right," Kline continued. "As you know, Zeke has been plagued with a number of seemingly insurmountable concerns about this whole mission for months now. And one of the biggest of those concerns was how the heck are we going to get ourselves and that huge proposed sound-generating device down to the location in the Antarctic Sea. I brought the matter up with Crown and he said he would take care of it."

"What did that mean, exactly?" Miriam asked.

"Unfortunately I can't tell you any more than that because that's all he told me. I pressed him for more information but he just said he was not at liberty to discuss it until he had a chance to meet with someone."

"Someone?" Miriam asked. "Who?"

"Mr. Crown wouldn't say. But I got the impression it was someone at a very high level."

"High level of what?" Angela asked.

Kline shook his head. "Your guess is as good as mine."

"So!" Banyon said, ignoring the unanswered questions. "Things are looking up! I say drinks on the house! Who's with me?"

Angela brought out the two bottles of wine and the conversation took off in a dozen different directions. As was so often the case, there seemed to be more questions than answers. Banyon was relieved that at least the transportation question had been answered even though the answer, if it could be called that, lacked any specifics. Just the fact that Crown had said he would take care of it was good enough for now. It took a great load off Banyon's shoulders. The thing that was puzzling him more and more lately was the weird download phenomenon that he seemed to have developed an odd knack for. The problem was, it didn't seem to be something over which he had any control. More often than not it just seemed to... happen. How was he doing it? Where were all those phrases and numbers coming from? What was the mechanism behind it? He decided to bring it up in the midst of the current buzz of conversation, not really expecting anyone to come up with the answer but it just felt good to get it out. He was surprised, however, when Miriam actually offered up a rather compelling theory.

"I wasn't really prepared to talk about this tonight," she said. "But now that you bring it up I may have stumbled into an answer."

"No kidding?" Banyon said. "Well, it's really been bugging me lately and to tell you the truth I don't have a clue. So I'm open to anything. What have you got?"

Miram took a sip of her chardonnay and set the glass back on the coffee table. "Well," she began, "ever since our first meeting a couple weeks ago I've been doing a lot of research into this 2012 Mayan prophecy thing." She took another sip of wine and thought for a moment. "Okay, let me see if I can organize my thoughts here. It was kind of a domino effect. One thing leading to another. You know how that goes."

Banyon glanced over at Angela. "Oh yes. We know how that goes, don't we, babe?"

Angela grinned.

"Well then," Miriam continued, "you'll understand if I seem to ramble here. I was really curious about the Mayan system of measuring time. It's pretty complicated. At least it was to me. I suspect it would be complicated for anyone as unfamiliar with the ancient Mayan culture as I am. But I learned that they measured time in units of great cycles. Cycles within cycles, it seemed to me, if I understood it correctly. One of these units of time is called a baktun and one of the time cycles consists of thirteen of these baktuns. The number thirteen, by the way, was very important to them in various ways and for various reasons, most of which I haven't quite figured out yet. But that number stood out for me because in my own explorations of these alphanumerics – this English gematria stuff – I had discovered the word *thirteen* has a gematria value of 99 which, I don't need to tell you, reduces…"

"…to nine," Banyon jumped in.

"Exactly," Miriam nodded. "Well anyway – and I'll try to keep this as simple as I can - apparently one baktun consists of twenty katuns. A katun is just another time unit. Now at some point I went to the internet to find any other information that might help me get a better handle on this Mayan calendar concept and I landed on a website where a researcher had made a rather intriguing discovery. He had made a connection between – are you ready for this? – between the Mayan 13-baktun cycle and the 13-step pyramid symbol on the Great Seal of the United States. You know, that symbol on the dollar bill. Anybody have one handy?"

Banyon fished one out of his front pocket and unfolded it.

"Great," Miriam said. "Notice at the bottom of the pyramid, the first step, or the first layer – whatever you want to call it – there are some Roman numerals."

Banyon nodded and passed the bill around for everyone to see.

"Of course," Kline said. "It's 1776, the date of the founding of our country. And the eye inside the floating capstone represents the Illuminati."

"You're right about the date," Miriam said. "And you're right about the eye in the capstone, too. At least partially. There's more to it but hang on. I'll get to that in a minute. Let's stick with the date for right now." She paused for a moment and took another sip of wine. "Now if we think of each of the thirteen steps of the pyramid as representing each of the thirteen baktuns in the Mayan units of time – and if each baktun consists of twenty katuns, which it does – then each step of the pyramid could feasibly be interpreted as representing twenty years. This is a lot easier to grasp if you could see the illustration that I saw on the website. But here's the deal. Using this scheme of twenty years per step -beginning with 1776 at the bottom – it turns out that the top step – the thirteenth step – ends at the year 2012!"

"Hmm…" Angela said with a tone of skepticism. "I see how that works out but isn't it a bit of a stretch to associate the Mayan calendar units with the image on the Great Seal of the United States? The two things seem so… disparate." She mentally patted herself on the back for once again coming up with a sixty-four-dollar word.

"You would think so," Miriam said. "But in a strange way it does all come together."

"And how is it that all of this has anything to do with my downloading information?" Banyon asked, completely confused at this point.

Miriam smiled. "Like I said, one thing leads to another. Just hang in there with me. You'll see."

Banyon shrugged and leaned back. "Okay, sorry. Please go on."

"Okay. Well one thing we already know is that 2012 has a lot to do with what we're involved in, right? I mean, according to what you've told me, that's really what this whole thing is about. The Hiram prophecy and all of that. But now, more to the point – at least when it comes to you and your strange download phenomenon – we have to turn our attention to the eye in the capstone. Like Alan said just a minute ago, it represents the Illuminati. But think about that word. *Illuminati*. What does it suggest?"

"The Enlightened ones," Banyon said. "It suggests the Illuminati are those who have attained a high degree of enlightened knowledge. Whether for good or for evil, I guess is a matter of opinion."

"That's right," Miriam agreed. "But in my research I found there are many interpretations of what that eye represents. The Illuminati, as a secret society, is just one interpretation. But when you take into account what you just said - that the word *Illuminati* suggests enlightened knowledge - we might ask ourselves where did that knowledge come from? How did they acquire it? This leads us to another interpretation of that eye in the capstone. And this, I think, is key. It's a representation of what is known as the *Third Eye*."

Banyon shook his head. "And what, pray tell, is the third eye?"

"Ah," Rajani said. "Yes, in my native India it is represented by a red dot painted in the center of one's forehead. The mystical third eye."

"But," Angela said, "I thought it was only a cosmetic decoration that the Indian women wore as a mark of beauty or something like that."

Rajani smiled. "It is that also. In that case it is called a *bindi*. There is an old Hindu proverb. *The beauty of a woman is multiplied a thousand times when she wears a bindi.*"

"Yes," Miriam said. "And it's the notion of the third eye, rather than the cosmetic bindi, that we're interested in here."

"Okay," Banyon said, "but what the heck is it? What does it mean?"

"Well," Miriam explained, "Helen Blavatsky – the founder of Theosophy – said the third eye is the seat of the highest and most divine consciousness of the human being. The critical thing to know about this is that humans, and animals too, actually have an organ located in the base of the brain that corresponds with this concept of the third eye. It's called the pineal gland."

"I've heard of that, I think," Banyon said. "Isn't that supposed to be some kind of a little organ that evolution has rendered pretty much useless? Isn't it something that just sort of sits there but doesn't really do anything anymore?"

Miriam laughed. "So the biologists used to think. But a lot of research has been done in recent years that has revealed some remarkable information about that mysterious little organ which, by the way, is only about the size of a peanut. Those of a more esoteric bent say its function is associated with clairvoyance, intuition and various other psychic abilities. Now get this. This is leading to your question about how those downloads of yours work. Scientists have discovered that under certain conditions the pineal gland produces a natural psychedelic substance called dimethyltryptamine, or DMT for short. Now it turns out that DMT is the active substance in a plant that the Mayan shamans ingested. And some researchers say that those shamans, under the influence of that psychotropic plant, were able to *receive...*" she wiggled two fingers of each hand to indicate quotation marks on the word, *receive.* "...the information that allowed them to create one of their culture's most incredible artifacts. That thing we call the Mayan calendar." She paused a moment and looked at Banyon. "Do you see where I'm going with this?"

Banyon squinted one eye. "Maybe. I'm not sure. But go on. It's getting a little weird but it is interesting."

"Well," Miriam said, "it gets weirder. Back in the 1970s, I think it was, a couple of brothers – well-known for their controversial research into psychedelic substances and altered states of consciousness – partook of this particular plant and, under the influence, devised a complex theory of time in which the year twenty-twelve was a key factor. Now talk about weird coincidences..." She shot a wink in Kline's direction, knowing about his firm belief that nothing is mere coincidence. "...it turns out that neither of the two brothers knew anything about the Mayan calendar and therefore had no idea that the year 2012 played an important role in the Mayan tradition. And remember, this is the same plant that the Mayans used in their shamanic rituals."

Banyon shook his head. "I'm still not quite sure where you're going with this. How does this relate to my downloads of information?"

Miriam nodded. "I know. I'm getting to it." She took a deep breath and continued. "Here's the thing. Scientists, doing experiments under controlled conditions, have discovered certain dosages of DMT can cause people to have all sorts of strange experiences. Things like out-of-body experiences, religious visions, and even experiences that mimic the alien abduction phenomenon. You guys are familiar with that, right? Okay, well, some researchers believe that DMT opens up a portal to other realms of consciousness, other dimensions of time and space. And here's a real kicker. Recent research has shown that changes in the earth's geomagnetic field can be a factor in stimulating the pineal gland. Now get this." She leaned forward in her chair to emphasize the next point. "The earth's magnetic field has shifted in the past. It apparently happens at fairly regular intervals of something like every hundred thousand years as I recall. And scientists say we're overdue for another one. In fact – and this is a key point – there is some measurable evidence that the earth is experiencing the beginnings of that magnetic shift right now as we speak. So I'm thinking what may be happening is that some people's pineal glands may be more sensitive than those of other people." She looked directly at Banyon. "You see what I'm saying? This might be exactly what's happening with you! Those moments when the downloads occur could be caused by a sudden release of DMT from your pineal gland. Even though the current changes in the earth's magnetic field are subtle right now, you may be hyper-sensitive to it and don't even realize it. It could be the trigger that is activating your pineal gland and opening your shamanic third eye."

Angela jumped in. "So, virtually creating a portal, if you want to call it that, through which the information is being transmitted directly into his brain?"

"That's the idea, yes," Miriam said. "I think that's what's happening."

"But," Angela wondered, "what is the source of that information? Where is it coming from?"

The only answer that made any sense at all seemed to center on what Banyon and Angela had already talked about months ago. The source must be something akin to the ideas at the core of those movies like The Matrix and The Thirteenth Floor. It was all being generated from some sort of a programmed technology.

Baynon threw up his hands. "Whoa! Hang on a second! I'm not sure I'm ready for this. And if what you say is true, isn't there some way to control it? I mean, the way it is now, it just happens out of the blue. What if I don't want it to happen?"

"Actually, yes," Rajani interjected. "There is a way to control it. But before it can be controlled it must be fully awakened. I am not having such knowledge but there are people who know these things and can teach you."

Miriam nodded. "What Alec says is correct. But from what I understand, having one's third eye fully awakened is a little like winning the jackpot in a Powerball lottery."

Banyon shook his head. "Come again? That's a bad thing?"

"Well," Miriam explained, "it seems like a good thing at first. But if you look at the statistics you'll see that most of the people who become super rich overnight from winning the lottery end up with more problems than they had before. Half of them end up broke and bankrupt."

"How can that be?" Banyon asked.

"I think what she's saying," Kline offered, "is that money, especially that much money, is very powerful stuff. If you don't know how to control it, it can take over and control you in ways that you never could have imagined."

Banyon was silent for a moment as the implications of it all slowly began to sink in. On the one hand, if Miriam was right, it would be good to have control over this thing. On the other hand, if gaining control over it meant that it's power and full potential had to be fully awakened first, that was just a little too scary to think about. *Christ, if it's not one damn thing it's another.* "I don't know," he said shaking his head. "I've had some weird stuff happen to me over the past few months but this...this is really getting into some strange shit, excuse my language."

The language, out of character for Banyon, brought a round of sympathetic half-grins and nodding of heads from the others. He leaned back in his chair and cast a glance at Angela who could only shake her head as if to say *I don't know what to tell you.* Then he turned to Miriam. "I just don't think I'm ready for this!" he said. "Besides, where would we find someone who could teach me what I'd need to know about this third eye awakening business, anyway? Do you know of anyone?"

Miriam shook her head and conceded that she didn't know any such person. Banyon scanned the faces of the others for an answer to the same question and got the same response. Even Professor Kline – who always seemed to know the right person for just about anything – even he was at a loss. Banyon found that almost hard to believe.

Then Rajani offered a bit of wisdom. "In my old country," he spoke quietly with a tone of great sincerity, "it is said that when the student is ready the teacher will appear."

Banyon sighed. "Well, I'll tell you what," he said, not at all comfortable with the whole idea, "if there's a knock on the door in the next few minutes you can tell the teacher he's arrived too soon." He started to chuckle at his own sarcasm when they all heard a knock at the door. It jolted Banyon half out of his chair. He spun around. "What the...?"

Everyone froze in stunned silence.

Finally, cautiously, Angela moved to the window where she could get a clear view of the front porch. Then she went to the door and opened it. In a moment she turned to the others. "It's the pizza guy," she said, grinning. "Should I ask him if he knows anything about awakening the third eye?"

A round of laughter filled the living room.

Even Banyon couldn't suppress a sheepish grin. "Pay the man and let's eat," he said. "I may have a third eye but I only have one stomach and it's starving."

The following week did, indeed, bring a change to Alec Rajani's usual routine. He suddenly found himself out of the teaching business and fully involved in furthering his research and development of acoustic levitation. Nathan Crown had made good on his word, providing Rajani with a well-equipped research facility located just a few miles north of Seattle. It was a large warehouse in a relatively remote area of a neighboring county. His partner, and soon to be very close collaborator in this venture, was a brilliant young engineer named Bud "Buzzy" Webster. Webster had been under contract with Crown Technology Systems for the past ten years. His nickname, Buzzy, was given to him by his father because, as a youngster, Bud was always buzzing around the house looking for something to occupy his time and challenge his mind. His insatiable need for *something to do* drove his poor mother crazy. When he turned 13 he told his friends to stop calling him Buzzy. It sounded stupid. He now preferred the shortened version, Buzz. That was a cool name. Buzz finished high school a year early and went on to study at Massachusetts Institute of Technology where he earned his Ph.D. and was hailed as a budding genius in the field of engineering. When he went to work for Nathan Crown at CTS his fellow employees latched onto his nickname and expanded it to "Busy Buzzy" because he was constantly multitasking on more projects at one time than most people would even dare think about. He was the first to arrive in the morning, the last to leave at night, and rarely did he take breaks to chitchat with the others. Not being the chatty type, it was a little difficult to get to know him. But after several years of working on highly classified projects at CTS, Crown knew at least three things about Buzz Webster. He was incredibly intelligent, he had a lot of unconventional ideas that, more often than not, turned out to be valuable contributions despite whatever doubts his colleagues may have voiced and, last but not least, he could be trusted.

When Webster was informed of his new assignment he was excited and couldn't wait to get started. The one thing he wasn't told was the reason for this project. But Buzz Webster was used to that. He'd participated in many classified projects without knowing the final application of his work. That was just the nature of working on classified projects. He didn't care as long as it was challenging and kept him busy.

Rajani and Buzz hit it off like two peas in the proverbial pod. Buzz was fascinated with Rajani's work on the theory of acoustic levitation and brought a few crucial components of his own to add to the collaboration. He was puzzled about the various tonal frequencies that Rajani insisted on integrating into the theoretical framework. He asked where these numbers came from but Rajani would only say it was classified. That seemed to be enough to satisfy Buzz. He didn't particularly care, really, where the numbers came from. He only cared whether or not they contributed to the process.

Day after day, night after night, they worked out the complex mathematics, testing and retesting Rajani's hypotheses, rejecting some, retaining a few and modifying others. They even managed to decipher some of the strange theories available in the few works left behind by Edward Leedskalnin, the builder of the mysterious Coral Castle. After just two weeks they cobbled together a theory they were certain would prove successful. By the end of the third week they had constructed a scale model of the ring-shaped tone-generating device. By the end of the fourth week they had a breakthrough. And a disaster.

~90~

Early Friday evening Banyon and Angela were getting ready for another meeting with their team when the phone rang. Banyon picked it up. It was Rajani.

"Hey! Alec! How are things going? You'll be here tonight, right?" After a moment Banyon staggered backwards. "*What!*"

Angela had just stepped into the living room and was startled by Banyon's sudden outburst. "What is it?" she asked. "What's happened?"

Banyon didn't hear her. He was listening intently to Rajani. "What do you mean *destroyed? When? How?*"

Angela sat down, staring at Banyon. She couldn't imagine what Rajani could be telling him. From the look on Banyon's face she wasn't sure she wanted to know.

"Jesus," Banyon said, continuing his conversation with Rajani. "But you're okay? And Buzz Webster? Thank God. How soon can you be here? The others will be here any minute. All right. Yes." Banyon hung up the phone and looked at Angela. "I can't believe it," he said, sitting down next to her.

She could see he was in shock. "What is it?"

"Someone broke into the lab and destroyed everything!"

Angela's eyes widened. "What!"

"All the equipment was smashed. Alec said the place was a disaster. Stuff scattered all over the place. And get this. The scale model of the donut was gone."

A puzzled look flashed across Angela's face. *The donut?* It took her a second to remember Banyon had come to refer to the tone-generating device as *the donut* ever since Professor Kline had used the term back at his cabin on the lake."Are they sure it was taken? Maybe it was smashed apart like the rest of the equipment."

Banyon shook his head. "No. Alec said they went through everything. There was no sign of it. No pieces of it. Nothing."

"When did this happen?"

Banyon reached for a cigarette and began pacing the floor. "Last night. Apparently Alec and Buzz left the lab around midnight. They didn't return until late this afternoon. That's when they found it. They've been going through the stuff to see what could be salvaged."

"And?"

"He didn't really say. He just said there was some good news mixed with the bad. He'll fill us in when he gets here."

Their conversation was interrupted by a knock at the door. Banyon put out his cigarette and looked at his watch. "Must be Alan or Miriam." He went to the door and opened it to find Miriam and Kline together.

"We were in the neighborhood and thought we'd drop in," Kline joked. "Alec here yet? Can't wait to hear what progress they've made."

"Come in," Banyon said. "Let me take your coats."

Kline could tell from the tone of Banyon's voice that something was up. "Something wrong?" he asked as they took a seat in the living room.

Banyon relayed the disturbing news. "So that's all I know. Alec should be here soon. He'll fill us in. But he did say there was some good news too. We'll just have to wait until he gets here."

"This is unbelievable!" Miriam said. "Any idea who did it?"

"I have a good guess," Kline said, clearly angry but not entirely surprised.

"Illuminati," Banyon guessed.

Kline nodded. "Via their trained Jesuit attack dogs. They're not giving up and they're getting desperate. They can't have gotten any information from our meetings here. We took care of that by removing the bugs and installing that signal-blocking device."

"Maybe it's not working," Angela suggested. "The device, I mean. Ever think of that?"

Kline shook his head. "Crown has had a man check it once a week, remotely from outside. It's working fine."

Banyon looked concerned. "Someone's been checking it? Who? Why didn't you mention it before?"

Kline shrugged. "Didn't seem necessary. I don't know who it was."

"What if this person is lying to Crown?" Angela asked. "What if he's..."

"Yeah," Banyon interrupted, knowing what she was thinking. "What if he's a damned spy? What if somehow he... they... whoever... somehow disabled the device and they're just telling Crown that it's working fine? Meanwhile, they're recording all of our conversations!"

Kline took a moment to consider the idea. "I suppose it's..." Then he shook his head and reconsidered. "No. No. I just can't imagine Nathan Crown could be duped like that."

Everyone wanted to share Kline's optimism but there was no way to be sure. How else could the Jesuits have found out about the lab?

"Maybe Alec and Buzz were followed," Kline suggested.

Banyon was becoming anxious. He reached for a cigarette. The possibility that their conversations were being monitored was putting him on edge. He turned to Kline. "Maybe we should move our meeting to another location."

Kline shook his head. "I really don't think it's necessary. The only way anyone could be listening to us – given that the house has been swept clean – would be with one of those surveillance rigs set up in a vehicle, a van or something. They don't have a long range. They'd have to be parked right outside the house."

"We could keep watch," Angela said. "There's a clear view of the street from the front window."

Banyon considered what she said. It seemed like a major inconvenience and the idea irritated him. But maybe she was right. "All right," he said with some resignation.

He got up and went to the window just as an unfamiliar car drove up and parked across the street from the house. The headlights went out and nothing happened for several moments. He was about to call Kline to the window when a man wearing a dark trench coat emerged from the car. The man walked around to the back of the vehicle and removed something from the trunk. Banyon beckoned for Kline. "Alan, come here, quick."

Kline got up and joined Banyon at the window.

Banyon nodded toward the street. "Check this out."

Kline squinted into the darkness and leaned closer to the window for a better look. In a moment the stranger began to move toward the house. Kline backed up and gave a laugh, patting Banyon on the back. "It's Rajani," he grinned. "You better get the door."

Banyon looked again. Kline was right. It was Rajani carrying a briefcase.

Rajani looked up, saw Banyon in the window, and waved.

I'm an idiot, Banyon thought to himself. He turned back to Kline. "Okay," he said with a sheepish grin. "So I'm a little paranoid. So sue me."

Kline smiled and returned to the living room. "Relax," he said, reassuring the others. "It's just Alec."

Banyon heard their collective sigh of relief mixed with a little nervous laughter as he went to the door to greet Rajani.

Rajani's demeanor was solemn. Clearly he was still distraught and shaken from the catastrophe at the lab. He settled himself in the living room and immediately informed everyone of the situation.

"It is terrible," he said, shaking his head. He ran his fingers through his silky black hair. "Nothing could be salvaged. All the equipment was destroyed." He opened his briefcase, took out a digital camera and switched it on. Images of the damaged equipment appeared on the small viewscreen. He passed it around so everyone could have a look. Clearly, a tremendous amount of violence had been unleashed inside the lab. It looked like a battle zone.

Miriam couldn't believe what she was seeing. "Attack dogs is right," she muttered.

Rajani looked confused. "I do not think dogs could have done this."

Kline smiled. "Just an expression, my friend." He explained to Rajani what he told the others about the Illuminati.

Rajani was quick to understand. "They should be on a short leash with a choking collar."

Banyon was still studying the photos. "Jesus," he said. "It's worse than I imagined. And I suppose they got all the data you had on the computers."

Rajani looked up. The comment brought a smile to his face. "That is part of the good news," he said. "There was almost nothing on the lab computers that will do anyone any good. All the crucial data is on disks and on our laptops. All of which we took home every night."

Banyon's expression turned hopeful. It was the best news he'd heard all evening. "Excellent! That's great. But what about the donut? The scale model. You said it looked like they must have taken it."

Again Rajani smiled. He reached into his briefcase and unrolled a large schematic diagram of the tone-generating device, the *donut*. "Without this," he said, " and without the data on our computers, they will know nothing. It will be useless."

"Oh man," Banyon said, feeling even more relieved. "When you said there was good news you weren't kidding."

"I am not one to be stretching your leg," Rajani said. "But that is not the only good news. I have something to show you." He reached into his briefcase and pulled out his laptop and a DVD. Setting the laptop on the coffee table, he powered it up and inserted the disk. He motioned for everyone to gather around so they could all see the screen. After a few seconds the video started up. The scene showed Rajani and Buzz in the lab, standing behind a large white table. Each of the two men introduced themselves by name and Rajani recited the time and date of the recording. Looking directly into the camera, Rajani spoke again:

"This is a demonstration of our first successful levitation experiment."

About five feet above the table the scale model of the donut hung suspended from cables like some sort of weird chandelier. On the table, directly beneath the donut, was a shiny steel marble about the size of a golf ball. Buzz turned away from the camera for a moment to make an adjustment to a computer monitor and the screen lit up displaying a frequency wave grid. Rajani was holding a remote control device. Buzz faced the camera again and nodded to Rajani. *"Ready,"* he said. Rajani pushed a power button on the remote control and a low hum could be heard. Then Rajani began tapping another button on the remote control. The frequency curve on the grid began to oscillate in small increments. In a moment a string of numbers began rolling across the screen. Suddenly, slowly, the steel ball began to levitate.

Banyon and the others gasped in astonishment as they gathered closer for a better look. They watched, transfixed, as Rajani continued to tap the button on the remote. The steel ball continued to rise slowly, steadily, until it reached a height of about three feet off the surface of the table.

"Holy Lord Jesus," Banyon whispered. He turned to Rajani. "You've done it! I can't believe it!"

A spontaneous round of applause went up from everyone in the room.

"Fantastic!" Kline said. "Utterly fantastic. But there was no sound, no tones. Why didn't we hear the tones?"

"I wondered about that, too," Angela said. "I thought you were using the tones that we came up with. But this seemed to be completely silent. I don't understand."

Rajani smiled. "We were able to incorporate an experimental technology that directs the sound waves along a highly focused laser-like beam. Literally, a beam of sound. Or, in this case, seventy-six of them."

"So we were right about the number of sound devices!" Angela said.

Rajani nodded. "Yes. Our scale model was complete with seventy-six miniature transducers."

"But," Kline said, "I still don't understand why we couldn't hear the tones that were being generated."

"It is complicated technology," Rajani answered, "but I will try to answer in a simple way." He pointed at Banyon's stereo system on a shelf across the room. "If you turn on that radio we will all hear the sound of the music. If I am in the kitchen and you are in the dining room it will make no difference. Both of us will hear the sound coming from the radio. That is because we are listening to omnidirectional sound."

Miriam shook her head. "Omnidirectional?"

"Yes," Rajani explained. "Think of this. If you throw a pebble into a pool of water it creates a series of concentric circles moving outward from the center, spreading wider and wider. The movement of the ripples is not just in one direction. It is in every direction. The movement is omnidirectional. Do you see? Under normal conditions, sound waves move in the same manner. We realized, early in our experimental phase, that this could be a problem. If we used any sort of standard tone-generating devices, the sound would spread out. If the combination of frequencies being generated actually resulted in a levitation effect then, theoretically, everything within the range of the sound waves would be levitated. Clearly, this could present a problem!"

"I get it," Kline said. "So you devised this method of condensing the sound waves into beams that could be directed at a specific target?"

Rajani nodded. "Well, yes it is something like that. But we did not invent the technology. We borrowed it, you might wish to say."

"Borrowed it?" Banyon asked. "What do you mean, you borrowed it?"

"Some experiments with directional sound have been underway at MIT," Rajani explained.

"Ah, the Massachusetts Institute of Technology," Kline said. "Buzz Webster's *alma-mater*."

Rajani nodded. "Yes. He contacted some people he knew and they pointed him to some technical papers that had been published recently. From these papers we were able to learn enough to duplicate the technology. And the reason you cannot hear the tones is because the frequencies have been raised beyond the range of human hearing."

"But," Angela said, "I thought you just told us you used the tonal frequencies that we gave you."

Rajani nodded. "Yes, that is correct. We did. But we raised them in harmonic increments."

Banyon shook his head. "I think I'm getting lost in all this tech talk. I don't care how you did it," he laughed. "I'm just amazed and thankful that you managed to do it at all! And in such a short amount of time! It's unbelievable." Then he gave Rajani a quizzical look. "I'm assuming the full-sized donut will be able to levitate more than just a steel ball off a table top, right?"

Rajani smiled. "We are reasonably certain."

"Reasonably?" Banyon said.

"Well," Rajani confessed, "there are still a few insects in the system."

"Bugs," Kline said. "Bugs in the system."

Rajani nodded. "Exactly. We need to carry out several more experiments before we can be absolutely certain. But now..."

"But now you can't because the equipment is gone," Banyon said.

Rajani slumped forward. The confidence that radiated from him just moments ago had faded. "Yes. It is true. We can do nothing now."

"I'm assuming Crown has been alerted to the situation, right?" Banyon asked.

"We hope so," Rajani said. "Buzz contacted Crown Technology Systems immediately and left a message for him."

Banyon turned to Kline. "Alan, can you get in touch with Crown directly, tomorrow morning? We need to know if he can replace everything that was destroyed. Explain to him what happened. Tell him we will need some sort of round-the-clock security at the facility. Video surveillance. Armed guards. The works."

Kline agreed. "Absolutely. First thing in the morning."

Angela let out a deep sigh. "Well, what's done is done. I'm sure Mr. Crown has no intention of letting this hold things up."

Kline packed some tobacco into his pipe. "It will all be taken care of, no doubt." He lit his pipe and turned to Rajani. "You realize, of course, this technology will revolutionize the world. Actual levitation in a practical sense? My god! Can you imagine the applications for this? You'll be famous!"

"Well," Rajani reminded him, "we did not actually invent the directional sound technology. We only borrowed from what was already known. And acoustic levitation experiments have been conducted by a number of people for a long time now."

Kline nodded. "That may be true but you're the first to integrate both technologies into one working system. This is an outstanding achievement, my friend! You'll go down in history, you and Buzz Webster."

"Yes," Banyon said, dryly. "If there's a history left to go down into."

"Ah," Kline said. "But that's *your* job, remember? The Chosen One? You're here to save the future so there will be a history for all of this to go down into." Then he gave a laugh. "I'm not sure that made any sense but you know what I mean."

"Which brings up a question that occurred to me the other day," Miriam said. "This whole thing is predicated on the idea that a comet is heading toward earth, right? And supposedly it's due to arrive very soon, right?"

Banyon nodded. "Too soon, as far as I'm concerned. But yes, that's the whole idea. Why?"

"Well, don't you think if that were true, the comet would have been detected by now? Doesn't it seem like astronomers would have seen it? Or what about NASA with all their satellites – the Hubble telescope and all that. You know what I mean?"

The question drew a stunned silence from the group. It was such an obvious question yet it hadn't occurred to anyone until this moment.

Since it was Miriam who came up with the question she was assigned the task of doing the research and coming up with an answer.

Better be a good one, Banyon thought to himself. *The damn thing better be out there and it better be heading straight for us.* For a moment he reprimanded himself for the thought. It was selfish, and he knew it. He just didn't want everything they'd gone through to have been for nothing. On the other hand, if there was no impending doom from a comet impact – or from anything else for that matter – he could forget about it all and resume some sort of a normal life. Marry Angela. Have a couple kids. Watch TV. *Is that too much to ask?*

~91~

A lone in his office at the Jesuit headquarters in Rome, General DuPont paced the floor, mentally going over everything he knew about Banyon's progress. He was reasonably certain he now knew enough to piece together an accurate picture of the situation at this point. Most importantly he knew the location of the object under the Antarctic sea. He'd also learned that Banyon was troubled about how to actually get to the object and how to bring it to the surface. *How, indeed*, thought DuPont. It seemed impossible.

The next day the scale model of Banyon's *donut* was delivered to DuPont's office. He made a few phone calls and assembled a group of experts from various fields of science to examine the strange device. Through a process of reverse engineering, literally taking the thing apart piece by piece, analyzing each component to assess it's function, they were only able to determine one thing for certain. They knew it was a device for producing directed sound. As to it's intended purpose, they could only guess but they were relatively confident that their guess was correct. It had to be an attempt to build a levitation device. It was a strange notion but, according to their analysis, it was the only thing that made sense.

The idea hit DuPont like a lightening bolt. *So that's it! That's how he's going to do it!*

He called a meeting of his experts to find out if they could operate the device. His idea was exactly the same as the plan Romano and his group had conjured up. The only difference was DuPont had the resources to actually pull it off. He would organize an expedition, beat Banyon to the location, and raise the object himself. But the report he got from his own team of experts was not what he wanted to hear.

They explained that the device was useless without more information. They needed the computer data. But after the hatchet job his men did on Banyon's research facility he knew that obtaining the necessary data now would be much more difficult if not impossible.

DuPont knew that Nathan Crown was aiding Banyon's mission. Crown would establish such tight security that it would be impossible to penetrate. The situation required a new strategy. There seemed to be only one option. Let Banyon do all the work. Let him raise the object himself. Then, at the strategic moment, swoop in like the pirates of old with an armada of heavily armed gunships and take possession of the prize. *No doubt*, DuPont surmised, *Crown will make sure Banyon's ship is armed also. But there seems to be no other option. If it turns into a war then so be it.*

He could feel the adrenaline race through his body. He was a warrior, his orders were clear, and his own destiny was at hand. But he needed to know when Banyon was planning to make his move. Timing was everything. *But how?* he wondered. *How can I find out?* There had to be a way.

Acquiring further information of any kind now seemed more difficult than ever. Banyon was getting smart and Crown was blocking surveillance at every turn. He thought about dispatching someone to infiltrate Banyon's group. But the more he thought about it the less he liked the idea. It could be too risky. *There must be a better way. Something simpler. A back door to the information.* He went to his desk and pulled out the dossier he'd been keeping on Banyon from the beginning. He flipped through the pages of data, all the information he'd gathered about Banyon and Angela and everyone they'd come into contact with over the past several months. "There's got to be something," he muttered to himself. "Something that..." Suddenly he stopped turning the pages as a name jumped out at him. It was the name of Banyon's old friend, Father Daniel Caldwell. DuPont's eyes narrowed in on the name and a slow grin stretched across his leathered face. "Yes, dear old Father Caldwell. You will do nicely."

~92~

Banyon shot straight up in bed, eyes wide open. *What the...?* He glanced at the clock. It was just after 2 a.m. He turned to Angela. She was sleeping soundly. He wanted to wake her up and tell her about his strange dream. *It was a dream, wasn't it?* He looked around the darkened room trying to identify the shadows. There was nothing unusual to be seen, only the silhouettes of familiar objects: the dresser, the television, the swivel chair in the corner. *Of course it was a dream.* He tried to remember the details. There wasn't much. The dream was short but intense. There was a pillar of light. He remembered that much. *Wait a minute...* He was reluctant to accept what he now remembered. *It talked to me.* Then he laughed to himself.

Yeah, right. Visions of Moses talking to the burning bush flitted through his mind. *Okay, so what the hell did it say?* He strained to remember but the harder he tried the faster it faded. He shook his head and let out a sigh. It was gone. There was no point trying to recall any further. He slumped back onto the pillow, closed his eyes and drifted back to sleep. Then it all came rushing back. His eyes snapped open *The teacher! It said it was the teacher! It said I was ready! Ready for what? What the hell did that mean?*

When morning came, Angela was up first as usual. He found her at the kitchen table sipping coffee.

"You look terrible," she said. "Didn't sleep well?"

Banyon ran his fingers through his hair and sat down across from her. "I had the weirdest dream."

Angela rolled her eyes. "Oh no. Not again." She got up to pour him a cup of coffee. "The antenna?" She set the coffee in front of him and sat down.

"Thanks. No, not the antenna. This was totally different." He told her about the pillar of light and what it said to him.

She stared at him for a moment. "Okay, wait. Back up. You talked to a pillar of light?"

He shook his head. "No. It talked to me."

"A pillar of light talked to you."

"Yeah. Well, not exactly talked to me. It wasn't like I heard a voice coming from it. It was more like... I don't know. It was communicating with me. Transmitting thoughts into my head."

"And it said what?"

"It said it was the teacher and that I was ready."

Angela thought for a second then looked at him. "What was it Alec said? Remember? When the student is ready the teacher will appear?"

Banyon looked at her, surprised. "Wow, yes, I remember. It's when I was wondering if there was a way to control the activation of the Third Eye. But come on," he laughed. "Are you serious?"

"Hey, I don't know. It was your dream. What do you think?"

Banyon lit up a cigarette and ran his hand through his hair again. "I don't know. I just know it was really intense. I can't describe it. Just... just strange."

"Hmm... So that was all? It just said it was the teacher and that you were ready? It didn't tell you anything else?"

Banyon shook his head. "I think that was it. At least I don't remember anything else. I just remember it startled me so much I woke up."

Angela swirled the coffee around in her cup. "A pillar of light. Seems symbolic. A dream symbol of some kind."

"Yeah, maybe. But a symbol of what?"

It was a good question. The surprising answer was on its way. But they would have to wait.

~93~

Over the next several days the pace of things ratcheted up another notch.

Nathan Crown replaced all of the damaged equipment in the lab and implemented a tight security system complete with video cameras and armed guards on duty around the clock. Alec Rajani and Buzz Webster reconstructed the scale model of Banyon's donut - the levitation device - and immediately set to work exterminating the few bugs remaining in the system. In the meantime, Crown was assembling a team of scientists and engineers whose task was to begin construction of the full-scale version of the levitation device as soon as Rajani and Webster gave the word.

Miriam spent several days trying to accomplish her assignment of finding out whether or not it was possible for a comet to be in a direct line of impact with the earth and yet somehow remain virtually undetected until it was too late to do anything about it. Her persistence paid off. She finally made contact with an astronomer who said such a scenario was highly unlikely but marginally feasible. He went into a long and technical explanation that left Miriam wondering if the man was even speaking English. The technical jargon was nearly incomprehensible to her untrained ears. Something about the trajectory of the comet in relation to the relative positions of the earth and the sun. The gist of it was that if all the variables were just so, it was possible the sun could hinder any discovery of the comet until it was so close that there would be no time to plan any sort of intervention.

"But," the astronomer said, "the odds of such a thing happening are millions to one. I wouldn't worry about it, that's for sure."

Miriam thanked the astronomer for his time and as she left his office she found herself a little more worried than when she went in.

By the time of the next meeting at Banyon's house, Banyon had two more dreams of *The Teacher*. All three dreams were exactly the same. Nothing changed and, as far as he could remember, *The Teacher* wasn't teaching him anything. Banyon was baffled.

In New York, Father Caldwell was beginning work on a novel he'd been formulating in his head for years. Finally he was putting the words to paper, blissfully unaware of the visit he would be receiving from an unwanted guest. Just when that guest would arrive had not yet been determined. DuPont was still deciding. He needed a little more information before he made his move. The timing had to be right.

~94~

E veryone managed to arrive at Banyon's house at the same time, or at least within a minute or two of each other. Banyon was excited. He couldn't wait to find out how things were coming with the *donut* and whether or not Miriam had been able to find any answers to the comet question.

Angela served coffee and a desert she had spent the afternoon preparing.

"Oh, man," Miriam beamed after the first taste of the treat. "This is totally delicious!" She turned to Angela. "What is this?"

The comment caught Angela off guard. *Hmm...*she thought, skeptically, *I wonder what she wants?* "Oh! Thank you. It's a zucchini bread. My mother's recipe."

Miriam smiled. "Please tell me it's not a family secret. I'd love to have the recipe."

"No secret," Angela said. *I knew she wanted something.* "I'll make a copy of the recipe for you."

"Great! Tell you what. I'll trade you for it. I have a recipe for an Irish cream cheesecake to die for. You'll love it."

Angela was taken aback. "Really?" *Maybe I've misjudged the girl.* "That sounds terrific. Thanks, I'd like that."

"Um," Banyon interrupted, "if you guys are done talking about food, we have a world to save."

The two ladies exchanged glances and grinned.

"Or do we?" Banyon continued, turning to Miriam. "What were you able to find out? Could a comet be heading for us without anybody knowing about it?"

Miriam took a sip of coffee and shifted into a more serious mode. She explained to the group what she'd learned from the astronomer.

"So, it's possible?" Banyon asked. "Is that what he was saying?"

Miriam nodded. "But unlikely, according to him. A million-to-one chance is what he told me."

"Well," Kline said, stepping into the conversation, "knowing what we know – as strange as it all might be – I'd say we should treat that one-in-a-million possibility as a firm probability. I mean look. Destiny is playing poker with us here. The unseen comet is the ace up its sleeve." He looked around at the faces in the group. "Do we all agree?"

The question didn't need to be asked, really. No one was taking any part of the situation lightly. None of them were in denial about what was at stake. Still, it was difficult to maintain the constant weight of the dire scenario that lay ahead. The human mind prefers to lighten such a load but Kline's words did bring the gravity of the situation into focus.

Angela spoke up. "I think the fact that we're all gathered here answers the question."

Everyone nodded in agreement.

Banyon didn't know if he was happy about what the astronomer said or not. Part of him hoped the news would have been different. Absolutely no possible way in God's great universe could such a thing ever be possible. *Just no way, no how.* On the other hand he wasn't at all surprised. It had all been coming to this. Deep inside he knew it. There was no way to deny it. "Well," he said, "there you go. So now we know. Set's on his way and he's hiding behind ol' Sol." He paused for a moment then spoke with more than a hint of sarcasm in his voice. "And the Chosen One here gets to try and derail him from his appointed mission. Are we having fun yet?"

His words brought silence from the group. There really was nothing to say. Suddenly he felt a twinge of guilt. "I'm sorry," he said. "I guess I got a little self-absorbed for a minute. I know I'm not alone in this. I know you're all knee deep in it with me."

Kline tapped the tobacco out of his pipe into an ashtray. "I think we all have some idea how you feel," he said. "We're all on this journey with you. I know I'm committed to seeing it through and I don't see anyone getting up and walking out."

Banyon smiled. "Thanks. I wouldn't blame any of you if you did."

Miriam gave a chuckle. "Like I would miss this for the world."

Feeling a little uncomfortable, Banyon turned to Rajani in hopes of steering the conversation in a different direction. "So, Alec, everything is back up and running, I understand. How's the work coming along?"

"Yes." Rajani answered. "The equipment has been replaced and the facility is very secure now." Then he grinned, looking down and shaking his head.

"What is it?" Banyon asked.

Rajani looked up. "Professor Kline spoke of destiny. I do not know if that is what it was or not but it turned out that having to reconstruct the model of the levitation device solved a couple of the problems we were having with the first model. It is possible it would have taken much longer to discover the solutions if it had not been for the fact that we had to scratch it from the beginning."

Banyon looked puzzled. "Scratch it?"

Kline grinned. "Begin again from scratch."

"Yes," Rajani said. "Exactly."

"Ah," Banyon said with a smile. "So what, exactly, was the problem? From what we saw in the video it seemed to be working fine."

Rajani considered how to answer. The problem was complex and he knew Banyon wouldn't understand the technical aspects of it. Finally he decided to make it very simple. "Yes, this is true. We were able to accomplish the levitation effect. The problem, simply put, was that the effect could not be sustained for longer than two or three minutes. As you can imagine, that would not be enough time to accomplish the task."

"You're right about that," Banyon agreed. "So the problem is fixed?"

"Yes, that has been corrected."

Banyon looked hopeful. "So it's ready? We can contact Crown and have him begin construction on the real thing?"

"Not quite, but very close. There is still one more problem. But we are working on it."

Banyon's hopeful look faded. "What is it? Will it take long? We're running out of time."

Rajani's posture slumped. "I know," he said. His tone was apologetic. "We are doing the best we can. It is a problem with the frequency synchronization."

Banyon, of course, had no idea what Rajani was talking about. "Frequency synchronization?"

Rajani searched for an easy explanation. "As you saw in the video, the device works. What you did not see were the six or seven attempts where the device failed to function. The problem is, it does not work with one hundred percent consistency. It is mostly a program glitch. Computer code. I am sure we can fix it once we understand where the error is." He paused for a moment and shrugged. "We are working on it."

Banyon's lips tightened. He took in a deep breath and let it go. He knew Rajani and Buzz were doing the best they could. What they had accomplished – despite the few flaws - was nothing short of a technological miracle. He knew that, too. Still, he was growing more anxious with each passing day. The walls of time were closing in around him. Then he flashed back to the beginning of it all. The morning after he and Angela had spent their first intimate night together. She was feeling anxious, unsure that they'd done the right thing, that maybe they were moving too fast. He responded with a comment that was completely out of character for him at the time but it was intended to lighten the situation and ease her anxiety. *Let's just go with the flow, baby!* It turned out to be good advice then and it was probably the best advice now. His somber expression gave way to an embarrassed grin. He gave a little self-admonishing laugh and looked at Rajani. "You know what?" he said. "You guys are doing an unbelievable job. Let's just go with the flow, baby. We can only do what we can do. Right?"

A wide smile flashed across Rajani's face. "That is true," he said. "I am liking that expression. Go with the flow. I understand this. In my native India we speak of Prana, the life force that flows through everything. I am thinking we are reading the same page."

Banyon grinned and exchanged a glance with Kline. *We're on the same page. I got it.* "Prana?" Banyon asked, turning back to Rajani. "That's a new one on me."

Rajani nodded. "Yes. It is thought to be the original creative force."

"I see. Pretty mystical stuff coming from a professor of physics."

Rajani gave a laugh. "Perhaps not so far from physics as you might think. Especially if we are talking physics in the quantum sense."

Banyon nodded. "You're right. I stand corrected on that one. From what I've learned over the past few months, some of the latest ideas in science seem to be just catching up with a lot of the ancient teachings. Life is weird," he said, shaking his head. "Freakin' weird."

"What did Einstein say?" Rajani asked. "Something about the universe not only being stranger than we imagine but even stranger than we are *capable* of imagining?"

Angela laughed. "Sounds familiar. I think we've had this conversation before, somewhere along the way."

"Yeah, well," Banyon said, "speaking of strange, I've been having a bit of strangeness of my own lately. I don't understand it, and I don't want you all to think I'm crazy, but I thought I'd mention it because it might have something to do with what Alec said at our last meeting."

Rajani sat forward. "Something I said?"

"Yes. Remember our conversation about the concept of the third eye? And I wondered if there was anyone who could teach me how to control it, activate it at will and turn it off at will? And you said something like *when the student is ready the teacher will appear.* Remember that?"

Ranani nodded, not really sure where Banyon was going with this. "You have met a teacher?"

"Well, sort of. Maybe. I don't know." He lit a cigarette and went on to describe the dreams he'd been having about the pillar of light, The Teacher. It only brought a blank stare from Rajani but Miriam nearly choked on her zucchini bread.

"Wait a second," she said, grabbing a quick swallow of coffee. She was clearly fascinated by what Banyon had just described. "If this is what I think it is we're talking about something…" she searched for the right word, "…well, extraordinary, to say the least!"

Her sudden burst of enthusiasm caught Banyon by surprise. "Really?" he said. "This means something to you? You know something about this?"

"Yes, I think so!" Her eyes lit up. This was her territory. "Do you remember I told you about my father's collection of old books on alchemy?"

Banyon nodded.

"One of them," she continued, "was called *Alchemy of Light, The Secrets of Spiritual Transmutation*. I remember reading in it about something like what you described. A phenomenon of being visited by a conscious pillar of light in dreams. It's been known to occur to only a handful of high initiates of the alchemical mysteries but it's very rare. The pillar of light is actually the dreamer's higher self that comes to impart knowledge."

Banyon gave a puzzled look. "Knowledge?"

"Knowledge that the dreamer needs to know. Knowledge that he, or she, probably would not be likely to get by any other means."

Banyon squeezed his eyes shut for a moment and shook his head like a wet dog shaking off the water. If Miriam was even half right this was even stranger than he could have imagined. *Einstein was right*, he mused to himself. "My higher self?" he asked. He was not familiar with the term.

Miriam nodded. "Yes. The higher self, the soul, you might say. The real you beyond the physical illusion of you."

Banyon was straining to understand. *Einstein had no idea how right he was.* "Say again? The physical illusion of me? Seems like the dream would be the illusion."

"Ah, yes," Rajani interjected. "I am familiar with this too. In the sacred teachings of the Hindu masters it is called Maya. It means illusion. Everything of the physical realm is an illusion."

Banyon shook his head. "I don't get it."

Rajani tried to reach back into his memory of things he was taught as a youngster growing up in India. "In the ancient Vedic text, the *Srimad Bhagavatam*, the material world is compared to a cloud. The cloud seems real. It seems to have substance. It even seems to have function. It delivers rain which nourishes the plants. But the cloud soon dissipates and fades into nothingness. It is Maya. It is not lasting. But the sky, in which the cloud appears, lasts forever. The wise man fixes his attention on the sky, not the cloud."

Banyon was again surprised. "More mysticism from our group's scientist! I'm impressed, really."

Angela moved into the conversation. "I can see where that idea actually fits with the quantum physics." She turned to Banyon. "You remember. We've sort of talked about this before, back when we first read some of the information on Paretti's website. That idea about the holographic nature of the universe. The idea that it may, in fact, all be nothing more than some sort of a holographic image. So, basically... an illusion."

Banyon nodded. "You're right. I remember. It's just hard to get my head wrapped around that idea." He turned back to Miriam. "So, you were saying the pillar of light is my higher self? But it communicated with me. So, basically, you're telling me I was talking to myself. Is that what you're saying?"

"Well, yes, in a sense. The higher self is the soul and our soul is our higher consciousness. It's all wrapped up into one, yet existing on different planes of reality, different dimensions, but all interconnected. The way it works is like this - at least according to the book I was telling you about - your soul, your higher consciousness, communicates with your lower consciousness using symbols. This pillar of light is a symbol, a representation of your higher self. Sometimes this communication through symbology can occur while you're awake but more often it occurs during the dream state. Now here's what caught my attention when you were describing your experience." She sat forward, energized and excited to reveal the next clue. "The book teaches that not all images in the dream state are symbols in the greater sense that we're talking about here. The way you tell the difference, the way the soul-level symbol identifies itself to you, is by appearing in three separate dreams. And each appearance of the symbol, each element and action in the dream, each dream in its entirety, must be exactly the same. If there is no variation from one dream to the next then you know that's the higher consciousness signaling to you to pay attention because it has something to tell you!" She paused and waited for Banyon to respond but he was just staring blankly at the floor, shaking his head. He seemed lost in thought. "So," she prompted him, "what do you think?"

He lifted his eyes with a bemused look on his face. "What do I think?" He gave a little chuckle. "I think my dear old Catholic mother – God rest her higher self - is rolling over in her grave. That's what I think."

A frustrated look crossed Miriam's face. She was certain she was right about this but apparently he wasn't quite buying it. She needed something to convince him. Then she remembered. She pulled a pen and a small note pad from her purse and wrote something down. She ripped the paper from the spiral binding of the pad, folded it in half, and leaned over, handing it to Banyon.

"What's this?" he asked, stretching across the coffee table to retrieve the paper from her hand.

"Just a little something to help convince you that the information from my father's old book might actually hold a message for you. Go ahead. Look at it."

Banyon unfolded the paper and looked at the writing:

ALCHEMY OF LIGHT = 144

His head jerked back as if he'd been socked in the chin. "That's the title of... Are you sure this is right?"

"I thought that would get your attention. You can calculate it for yourself. The light number, 144 – the number that has played such a huge part in your incredible journey to this point - is encoded right into the title of my father's old book. The same book where I got the information that I've just been telling you about. Go ahead. Show it to Alan. You know what he'll say."

Banyon handed it over to Kline and knew exactly what he'd say. *There's no such thing as coincidence.* And from his own experiences, Banyon had to agree. This had to be more than a mere coincidence. "But how did you know?" he asked, somewhat stunned. "You didn't just now pull this out of thin air. Or did you?" He started to wonder if she had a bit of the same weird gift that he had.

"No. Remember I told you I'd done a little exploring of this English gematria stuff myself?"

Banyon nodded. "Yes, I remember."

"Well, several months ago, when I was just beginning to get interested in the idea of an English gematria I was experimenting with all kinds of words and phrases. That book was sitting prominently on the shelf beside my desk and something about the title just said *try me.* So I did and when it turned out to be 144 I made a note of it only because I noticed it was a harmonic of the number, 144,000, from the book of Revelation. Even though I never explored that relationship any further, for some reason it stuck in the back of my mind." She smiled and gave a shrug. "I guess maybe now I know why."

Rajani reached over and put a hand on Banyon's arm. "When I was a boy my father used to tell me about things such as this. From what I have heard here tonight I think he would say you are about to receive a few lessons."

Banyon sat back and exhaled deeply. A heavy wave of emotional exhaustion rolled through his body. "Well, that's great," he said with all the enthusiasm of a man who'd just run a mile to catch a bus only to find out the bus-stop had been moved another mile and a half down the road. Slumped in the chair, he had only one comment. "I can hardly wait."

~95~

It was just after midday in Rome. General DuPont's office was dimly lit from the few shafts of sunlight filtering in through the drawn shades. He liked it that way. Too much light bothered him. He was working at his desk when his train of thought was derailed by a knock at the door. Annoyed by the interruption, he responded. "Yes,

yes. Come in."

A young Jesuit, Vincent Bertolli, walked into the darkened room. Barely twenty-five years old, Bertolli was at the lower level of the heirarchy and had only recently been assigned to work as an accountant at the Headquarters. But he was ambitious, very ambitious, which is why he was not particularly popular with some of his young Jesuit Brothers. And, unlike the vast majority of his Jesuit Brothers, he was aware that something was going on in the upper echelons of the Order. He didn't know exactly what it was but, having once overheard Montebeau's side of a telephone conversation, he knew it was something big, something concerning an end-times prophecy, and he wanted in on it. He now approached DuPont and stood before the General's big oak desk.

DuPont looked up. "Yes? What is it?"

"Sorry to bother you, sir. My name is Bertolli. Vincent Bertolli."

"So what can I do for you Bertolli? It better be important."

"Sir, as you may have heard, a few of us with an interest in end-times prophecy have organized an informal discussion group. We meet once a month. Nothing seriously academic but..."

"No, I didn't know. Not that it matters. Why are you telling me this? I'm very busy."

"Something came up the other night. Some information. I thought you might be interested."

"What kind of information?"

"During our last group meeting one of the men mentioned he'd read that book called *The Bible Code* and he wondered if anyone else in the group had read it."

"Drosnin's book. What about it?"

"It led to a discussion about the computer software programs that enables anyone to explore the Torah for encoded information."

DuPont was becoming impatient. "Yes? And...?"

"So we checked the internet to see what we might find. There were several websites where people have posted what they've found in the Torah by using these software programs. Here's one I thought you might find interesting." He handed DuPont a printout of the posted message.

DuPont impatiently snatched the paper from Bertolli's hand, not expecting to be particularly impressed by whatever was on it. He read the message. Then he reached for his glasses and read it again. It was the apparent warning of a comet impact due to occur August 3, 2006. If the proverbial light bulb that flashed above his head had been real, the darkened room would have lit up like a flash-bomb. But he pursed his lips and feigned disinterest. Folding the paper in half he let it slip, quite observably, into the wastebasket beside his desk. He looked up at Bertolli. The young man's face seemed to register a complete lack of expression. *Poker face*, thought DuPont. *Hate that. Can't ever tell what they're thinking.* "Thank you…uh, Bertolli, is it?"

"Yes, sir. Vincent Bertolli. Sorry to have bothered you. I just thought…"

DuPont stood up and removed his glasses. "That's all right, my son. It's an intriguing idea, this comet prediction. But you know what they say about the so-called Bible Code. You can find the same sort of stuff in *Moby Dick* or *War And Peace*. Hell, you could probably find it in the telephone directory if you looked hard enough."

The young Jesuit still displayed no expression. He seemed eerily unemotional. "Yes, sir. So I've heard. If you'll excuse me then, I'll take my leave."

DuPont acknowleged the request with a nod. Bertolli turned and moved toward the door. DuPont sat down again, anxious for the young man to leave so he could read the message again.

Half way out the door Betrolli turned back to DuPont. "Just so you know…" He paused. "The comet prediction?"

"Yes?"

"I ran the program on *Moby Dick*. It wasn't there."

DuPont thought he noticed a grin start to form at the corner of Bertolli's mouth but the young man was out the door and gone before he could be sure. It didn't matter. He leaned over and fished the folded paper out from the wastebasket.

DuPont was keenly aware of the Hiram prophecy, a key motivation behind Banyon's quest. He knew the prophecy spoke of some unspecified global disaster that, if left unchecked, would prevent the human race from experiencing a major evolutionary shift in consciousness and the beginning of a New World Order. Not just any New World Order. *The* New World Order. *Novus Ordo Seclorum*, The New Order of The Ages, an age of wonder and unimaginable power as specified on the Great Seal of the lowly American one-dollar bill. It was a power that the Illuminati believed they were destined to control.

The key to controlling that power was the object now buried at the bottom of the Antarctic sea, waiting to be released. An object the Order of the Illuminati was determined to possess at any cost. DuPont's mind raced. *Could this comet be the unspecified cataclysmic event predicted by the Hiram Prophecy? Does Banyon know about this? Could he be working against the timeline now set into motion by this Bible Code prediction? Is the third of August his target date?* He checked his calendar. *That's less than a month away! He'll need to raise the object prior to that date in order to be ready to activate it at the crucial time.* DuPont read the Bible Code prediction once more. *August third. This must be it.* But he needed to know for sure. Finally the time had come to activate his plan. *Father Caldwell,* he smiled to himself, *you'll be receiving your uninvited guest very soon.*

~96~

A ngela was awakened in the middle of the night to the sound of Banyon's voice. He was mumbling something in his sleep. She wasn't sure but it sounded like he was repeating the word *nine* over and over again. She gave him a gentle nudge. He became quiet but he didn't wake up. She looked at him and smiled. *Poor guy,* she thought. *It must be really getting to him.* She rolled over and was nearly asleep when he started repeating the word again. *Okay,* she thought*, this is getting annoying.* She gave him another nudge, a little harder this time, intended to awaken him. He stopped repeating the word but he didn't wake up. She was just about to try again when he started the repetition once more. This time she put her hand on his shoulder and gently jostled him. "Zeke," she said in a forceful whisper. "Zeke. Honey. Wake up." Again he stopped the odd chanting but he would not wake up. She tried again. "Zeke!" she said in a full voice.

His eyes opened slowly. "Wh-what's wrong?" he droned.

"I'm sorry to wake you. You were talking in your sleep. It woke me up."

He looked confused for a moment. "I was? What was I saying?"

"It sounded like the word *nine*. You kept repeating it."

His eyes were heavy and the sound of her voice seemed distant. "Mmm..." he muttered softly. "Sorry. I think I was... dreaming or something."

She chuckled. "Or something? What does that mean?"

He was drifting back into sleep again. "I don't...know. The teacher. I'm...tired. Can we talk about it...in the..." His voice trailed off and he was gone.

The next morning Banyon came down the stairs and found Angela brewing a fresh pot of coffee.

"So," she said, pouring him a cup, "do you remember talking in your sleep last night?"

He sat down and lit a cigarette. "Me? No. What do you mean?"

She told him what happened and how she tried to wake him up.

He sipped his coffee and shook his head. "Nine?"

"Yeah. You kept repeating it over and over."

He laughed. "No I didn't."

"Yes you did. Over and over. I finally got you to wake up for a minute and you said something about the teacher. Then you just fell asleep again. You don't remember any of it?"

He ran his fingers through his hair and thought for a moment. "Yeah, kinda. Now that you mention it. I do vaguely remember that pillar of light again. But nothing specific. I wish I could remember that *nine* thing you're talking about."

"Too bad I didn't have a tape recorder," she said, reaching for a cigarette.

Banyon nodded. "Yeah." Then he looked at her. "Hey, you know what? That's a good idea. I have a little tape recorder. It's in a box with some other stuff in the closet. We should get it and keep it on your nightstand."

Angela got up and poured herself another cup of coffee. "Why?" she teased. "You plan on making a habit of this?"

"You never know," he teased her.

She set her coffee on the table and moved around behind him. Massaging his shoulders, she leaned down and whispered in his ear. "If you do, you can start sleeping on the couch."

He could feel her warm breath against the side of his neck. *Not in this lifetime*, he grinned to himself. He turned and kissed her gently on the lips. "We'll see about that."

~97~

The next night, as if on cue, it happened again. Angela moaned, groggily, and rolled over to give Banyon a nudge with her arm. Then she remembered their idea. She turned back to the nightstand and fumbled around in the dark for the tape recorder. Before going to sleep that night she made a mental note to memorize the series of switches on the recorder. That way she would know which one to push to record and she wouldn't have to turn on the light and risk waking Banyon. But now, still not fully awake, her memory failed her. *Was it the first button on the left or the first button on the right? I did put the tape in, didn't I? I must have. Sure I did.* Like trying to read Braile, she ran her finger along the row of switches. *Which damn button is it?* Realizing she was wasting time she decided she had no choice but to turn the light on. Reaching up and turning on the lamp, she glanced over her shoulder to check on Banyon. He was still asleep, still repeating the number. *All right*, she thought to herself. Now she could see which button to push. It was the second one from the left. She pressed it and held the recorder a few inches from Banyon's mouth. He was droning the same repetition of the word *nine* just as he'd done the night before.

After a few minutes her eyelids grew heavy. Banyon's monotone drone was almost hypnotic. The *nines* seemed to run together, one morphing into the next, as if the ending *n* sound of the word *nine* became the beginning *n* sound of the next *nine* with no breaks between them. The tone of his voice was deep, relaxed, and resonant. She could almost feel the vibration. A chill rushed through her body. It was eerie and all too surreal.

Soon her eyes began to close, involuntarily, and she started to lose her grip on the tape recorder. In a moment the recorder slipped from her hand and dropped onto Banyon's chest. Her eyes snapped open. She gasped. Realizing what had happened, she was surprised that Banyon remained in a deep sleep as if he'd felt nothing. He continued to repeat the word like a strange kind of chant. After a few moments he stopped. Angela listened. He was quiet now. The chanting was apparently over. She switched the recorder off, set it on the nightstand, and turned out the light.

She retreated back to her pillow, dazed by the experience, and wondered if she should try to awaken him. But he seemed to be resting peacefully. She decided to let him sleep. In a few moments she, too, drifted off.

She found herself walking into the darkened chapel at Rennes le Chateau, staring at the hideous statue of the demon, Asmodeus, bent and disfigured under the heavy weight of the baptismal font balanced on the back of his shoulders. She noticed the font was filled to the brim with water. Cautiously, she approached the demon. Closer…Closer... Reaching up, she touched the water with the tip of her finger, causing a series of concentric circles to begin rippling across the surface of the water. Then the circles morphed into spirals. Immediately, the chapel became flooded with light.

Startled, she opened her eyes. The sun was filtering in through the curtains of their bedroom window. It was morning.

She rubbed the sleep from her eyes and turned to see if Banyon was still asleep. She was surprised to find him missing. The bed-covers were thrown back and his side of the bed was empty. He was almost never up before her. Something must be wrong. She started to get out of bed when she noticed the tape recorder was also missing. She threw on her robe and hurried down the stairs.

"Zeke?" she called out.

"Yeah. In here." His voice was coming from the kitchen.

She found him sitting at the kitchen table staring at the tape recorder. He looked up at her. "Did you hear this?" he asked. "This is freakin' weird."

She pulled a chair back from the table and sat down. "Oh, yes," she said, brushing the hair back from her eyes. "I heard it all right. I mean not the tape. I heard it straight from the horse's mouth. So to speak."

"Hmm... did you notice there seemed to be a pattern to the repetition of the word?"

"The word *nine* that you kept repeating?"

He nodded. "Yes. Listen." He pushed the play button. The entire duration of the droning was only about three minutes. When it was finished he hit the rewind button and ran it back to the beginning. "Did you catch that? There's a pattern to the repetition."

"I don't know. Play it again."

Banyon hit the play button and they listened again. This time he counted aloud each intonation of the word. He was right. There was a pattern. The word *nine* was intoned in a triplet pattern of repetitions. The first was a repetition of what seemed like one long four-syllable word: *NineNineNineNine*. Then a short pause with a deep inhale of breath followed by a long nine-syllable intonation: *NineNineNineNineNineNineNineNineNine*. This was followed by another short pause for a deep intake of breath. Then a five-syllable intonation: *NineNineNineNineNine*. Another pause and a breath and then the pattern started all over again. The entire triplet pattern was repeated a total of nine times and then it was over.

Angela took a sip of coffee and thought for a moment. "You know what that sounds like, don't you?"

"Like I've finally gone over the edge?"

"Well, I mean besides that."

"Thanks for your support."

"It sounds like a mantra."

"A mantra?" Banyon asked. "I've heard the term but I don't know much about it."

"I know a little. A mantra is a kind of chant. Certain words or sounds are repeated over and over to help create a meditative state of consciousness. I think the practice comes from India. Remember when the Beatles went to India to study with that Maharishi guy?"

"Oh yeah. I think George Harrison went first and then the others sort of tagged along."

"Well, anyway, I think each one of them was given a mantra to use in their practice of transcendental meditation."

Banyon nodded. "Oh yeah. Seems like I remember something about that."

"You should give Alec a call. I bet he can tell you more than I can."

"Good idea." He checked his watch. "He's probably at the lab."

Banyon called Rajani and, as Angela had guessed, he did have some interesting information. He told Banyon that a mantra was a system of sounds designed to produce certain tonal frequencies. The mantra, he explained, was chanted in a specific formula of repetitions. Some mantras were designed for healing and some were designed especially for helping the meditator to access his innermost being, his higher consciousness. Generally the student or initiate receives his own personal mantra from his teacher, his personal guru. Rajani had never personally engaged in the practice but, since the concept had been around in his native culture for some 35,000 years, he was quite familiar with it. His own father, as a young man, once spent a year studying with a master Vedic astrologer who had become quite revered in their local area at the time. The Master had given Rajani's father a Sanskrit mantra designed especially for him. It was to be chanted in a sequence of 54 repetitions. According to Rajani, his father would never reveal the mantra to anyone.

"Not even to you?" Banyon asked.

"No. Not even me. But in time he gave up the practice."

"Why? It didn't work as advertised?"

"On the contrary. It worked too well."

"I don't understand."

"My father would practice his meditations alone on a hilltop near his home. Many times he had done this and each time the mantra would take him a little deeper into a peaceful state of consciousness. Then one day it caused him to experience a vision so powerful that it frightened him."

"Did he say what it was?"

"He would not say. Only that it made him realize he was not ready to go further."

"Hmm…interesting."

Rajani became curious. "May I ask why you are wanting to

know this?"

"Well..." Banyon hesitated. "Just more weirdness. I'll tell you more about it at our next meeting. By the way, how are things going? I hope you and Buzz are making some progress."

"Very much, yes. We have identified two of the sequence glitches in the computer code. Buzz was working all night on it. He has gone home now to get some sleep and I am continuing the work now."

Banyon was excited by the good news. "Yes!" he shouted, pumping a fist into the air. "So that's it? It's ready?"

Rajani hadn't anticipated such an enthusiastic response. The situation with the computer code still presented a challenge. They had only managed to find two of the problems and that was just by some stroke of good luck. They suspected there may be at least two more botched sequences but so far the same stroke of luck had not seen fit to strike twice. He was confident they would solve the problem sooner or later but he had no way of knowing when that would be and he didn't want to put a damper on Banyon's hope. "Well, it is not ready yet," he replied. "But close!"

"How close?"

Rajani was feeling the pressure. "Oh!" he said, thinking quickly. "It looks like Buzz is trying to call me on the other line. I better get it."

Banyon bought the distraction and quickly closed the conversation with a quick word of thanks for the mantra information and he requested to be notified the moment they solved the computer code problem.

After telling Angela what Rajani said, she got up and poured herself another cup of coffee. "You know," she said, returning to the table, "I just had an idea."

"Oh-oh."

"No, listen. If this thing is a mantra – and I'm betting it is – why don't you try it out while you're awake. You know. Just to see what happens."

Banyon shook his head. "Uh-uh. I don't think so."

"Why not? What's the worst that could happen?"

"Are you kidding? Remember what Rajani said happened to his father?"

"Yes but..."

"But what?"

"You're not Rajani's father. You're the…"

Banyon put a hand up. "Don't say it."

Angela leaned forward. "The Chosen One."

"I said don't say it."

Angela let out a sigh of frustration. "You've been given a mantra, for crying out loud. I mean, think about it. Why would it have been given to you if you're not supposed to use it? Come on. You know as well as I do that's what this is all about."

Banyon got up and began pacing the floor. The more he tried to deny it the more he knew she was right. *Christ*, he thought to himself, *is there no end to it?* Finally he stopped pacing and threw up his hands. "All right" he said, relenting to the obvious. "You win. But I ain't wearing no turban and I hate the smell of incense."

Angela laughed. "Who said anything about turbans and incense?"

"Nobody. I'm just setting the ground rules."

The warm ambiance of the bedroom in Banyon's home made it the best choice for a space in which to launch the first meditation experiment. Turbans and incense were out of the picture but candles, by mutual agreement, seemed like a good idea. The subject of music came up. Would it be a good idea to have some sort of music playing softly in the background? Banyon wasn't sure.

"Like what kind of music?" he asked.

"I think I know," Angela said. "When we were studying the Aboriginal peoples of Australia the professor brought in a CD of Didjeridoo music indigenous to the Aboriginal culture."

Banyon chuckled. "A CD of Didjeri-what?"

"Didjeridoo."

"What the hell is Didjeridoo?"

"A Didjeridoo is a really strange instrument and it makes really weird sounds. You could hardly call it music. At least not in the sense that we think of music. The professor brought one in to show us. It's a long, hollowed out branch from a eucalyptus tree. I guess the natives just go through the woods looking for these dried out, hollow branches. I remember the professor saying they're hollowed out by white ants that burrow in and make nests inside the branch. That kinda creeped me out. Anyway, the one he brought in was about five or six feet long. Seems like it was about two or three inches in diameter."

"So how do you play it?"

"You blow into one end and vibrate your lips to make the sound. The tighter you purse your lips the higher the sound. Except a high tone on a Didjeridoo isn't at all what you'd think of as a high note. All the tones are really deep and resonant. It can literally vibrate the walls of a room. You can feel it through your entire body. Very strange but really kind of cool."

"Sounds weird. But other than tracking down your professor, where would we get a CD of something like that?"

"Silver Platters."

"That place down by the mall?"

"Yup. They've got everything. If it's on CD, they've got it."

Banyon shrugged. "Okay. I'm game."

After breakfast they drove to Silver Platters and found exactly what they were looking for. There were several titles to choose from but one was just too good to be ignored. It was appropriately titled, *Meditations.*

Angela's face lit up. "Perfect!" she beamed.

Banyon let out a sigh. *What have I gotten myself into now?*

~99~

That evening, just after sundown, Angela helped Banyon prepare the room for his meditation experiment. They had no idea what they were doing, or if there was any sort of protocol for setting up a meditation room, so they resorted to their intuition. Banyon felt uncomfortable sitting on the floor so he opted for the relative comfort of one of the kitchen chairs. They brought it upstairs and decided he should sit facing the window. It just seemed like a good idea even though the drapes would be drawn. The pastel peach color of the drapes made a satisfying backdrop for the glow of the nine candles placed on the small decorative table positioned in its usual place in front of the window.

Banyon sat down on the chair and shook his head. "I can't believe we're doing this."

"Well, we are," Angela said. "Are you comfortable?"

Banyon shifted slightly in the chair. "Yeah. I guess." *Not really.*

"Oh!" Angela blurted. "Wait a second."

He turned his head to look at her but she had vanished into the hall outside the room. A moment later she returned with the tape recorder. She placed it on the floor next to his chair.

"Seemed like it might be a good idea," she said. "You never know."

"Yeah. Okay." *Whatever.*

"So, are you ready?" she asked.

"I suppose so. Let's get on with it."

Angela leaned over and gave him a light kiss on the cheek. "Bon voyage," she whispered in his ear.

"Thanks," he said. "I'll write when I get there."

Angela went over to the stereo by the bed and slipped the *Meditations* CD into the slot. "You're on your own, captain. I'll be downstairs."

She pushed the play button on the CD player, turned out the lights and closed the door.

~100~

A lone now, Banyon sat staring at the glow of the nine candles flickering in front of him. He watched their animated light dance around and between the shadowed folds of the drapes. He drew in a deep breath and let it out slowly.

In the silent stillness of the room he began to detect the incredibly low resonant drone of the Didgeridoo. Barely audible at first, the tone gradually grew in volume producing strange, haunting, undulating waves of overtones. Then overtones within overtones, weaving in and out and around each other, filling the room with a swirling ocean of etheric sound. It was haunting, mesmerizing, like nothing he'd ever heard before. With the strange droning tones vibrating every molecule in the room and the dancing light of the candles flickering before his eyes he was nearly hypnotized before he even began his chant. Suddenly he remembered the tape recorder. He leaned down, switched it on, and returned to his upright position. *Okay*, he thought to himself, *let's get on with it.*

Staring into the candlelight he began to chant the mantra in the pattern as he'd heard it on the tape that morning. On the third cycle of the repetition his eyelids grew heavy. By the time he was on the sixth cycle of the repetition his eyes were closed and he began to feel a tingling sensation at his fingertips.

As he began the ninth cycle the tingling sensation moved up into his limbs and he felt an odd lightness to his entire being. For a moment he was floating. Slowly the tingling that had spread throughout his limbs began to coalesce into a single location at the base of his spine. It felt warm. Then he could feel it begin to rise up through his body.

By the time he finished the ninth cycle of the mantra, this ball of vibrating energy ended its gradual ascent up his spine and was now firmly seated at the front of his skull. He could feel its warmth directly between his eyes.

It seemed as if his entire being was thoroughly absorbed in this experience, yet some part of his consciousness, like a separate entity, was objectively observing all of it and marveling at what was happening. The sensation was intense and invigorating. Then came a brilliant, blinding flash that he would later describe as nothing short of an orgasm of white light. Then suddenly it was over, like someone had grabbed the remote and turned off the TV.

The abrupt shift of consciousness startled him. His eyes flinched open. He looked around, stunned. *Je-sus Christ! That was friggin' amazing!* Then – like a kid who just got off a thrill ride at Disneyland – he wanted to go again.

He checked his watch. The entire experience had taken only a few minutes. Yet, while it was happening, it seemed timeless.

Anxious to try it again, he concentrated on calming himself. He focused his attention on the candlelight and let the droning tones of the Didjeridoo fill every fiber of his body. He began the first repetition of the mantra. Again, by the sixth cycle of the repetition his eyes were closed and the tingling sensation started the same as before. When he reached the ninth cycle the energy once more coalesced into a vibrating ball at the base of his spine, moving gradually upward, eventually settling at the front of his skull at a point directly between his eyes. But this time it was even stronger, more vital, more vibrant, more intense. He knew what was next. He waited, anticipating the orgasmic flash to explode at any moment. But something entirely different happened. Something completely unexpected. He'd heard about such things but he never thought it would happen to him.

He was out of his body.

~101~

Out of Body Experience or OBE. Banyon had read about the phenomenon in *Science Today*. The article recounted the reports from hospital patients who claimed they left their bodies while undergoing surgical operations. One woman, among many others, reportedly hovered over the operating table, looking down on her own body as the surgeons worked on her. Another patient even claimed to have left the operating room in his etheric body and wandered around the hospital invisible to the nurses or to anyone else. After he returned to his body and was taken from the operating room, he was able to accurately describe the operation as well as the comments made by the surgeons while he, the patient, had been sedated and unconscious. Stranger still, others who had taken little invisible jaunts through the halls of the hospital, while in their etheric bodies, could accurately repeat conversations they'd overheard between and amongst people in the hall. One man, Banyon recalled, even described an item that he saw on the top of a locker in the operating room. No one had known the item was up there. The top of the locker was only about six inches from the ceiling, so the item was out of view. The only possible way to see the item was to be standing on a ladder... or floating on the ceiling. When one of the hospital staff did get a ladder, he found the item exactly where the patient said it was and it was exactly as the patient had described it in every detail. But - the *Science Today* article explained - not all OBEs are induced by the trauma of surgery or an injury from an accident. Some occur spontaneously during sleep. Others have reportedly occurred during deep meditation. Banyon had just joined that club.

Now he was utterly stunned to discover himself standing by the bed looking across the room at his own body, eyes shut, sitting in the chair. Then, as he was standing there in a stupor trying to come to grips with what he was experiencing, he received another jolt. Without warning, the Pillar of Light appeared in the room.

Startled by the sudden appearance of this apparition, he found himself thrust back into his body as if he'd been sucked into a vacuum cleaner.

His eyes snapped open. Back in full consciousness, he looked around the room to get his bearings, trying to shake off the affects of the trance. His head was swimming but he was exhilarated. "Whoa!" he whispered loudly. Excited, he jumped up from the chair, anxious to run downstairs and tell Angela. But when he got to his feet his knees buckled. He fell backward into the nightstand knocking over the lamp. It crashed to the floor and he fell to his knees with a thud. Angela heard the sound and came running up the stairs. She threw open the door, flipped on the light switch and rushed into the room. She found Banyon struggling to get to his feet.

"Zeke!" she shouted, rushing to help him. "Are you all right? What happened?"

"Yes, I... I'm all right."

Angela set him on the edge of the bed and brushed the hair away from his face. She looked into his eyes. "Are you sure? You look like you've seen a ghost."

Banyon laughed, shaking his head. "The Teacher appeared. The pillar of light. It was..." he took a deep breath and tried to calm his pounding pulse, "...oh, man, Angela. It was amazing!"

Satisfied that he was all right, she brought him a glass of water and he told her everything.

"Then, when I came to," he explained, "I started to get up but I lost my balance and fell against the nightstand."

Angela sat on the bed next to him. "You saw the Teacher?"

"Yes!"

"Did it talk to you? Did it say anything?"

Banyon shook his head. "It never talks. It just... communicates."

"Well, so did it *communicate* anything?"

"No. At least I don't think so. It scared me, actually. I mean it startled me and suddenly I was sucked back into my body. God, it was incredible! I can't describe it!"

After they talked about it for a few minutes he was anxious to try it again.

"What!" Angela cried. "Are you kidding? Now?" She shook her head. "I'm not sure that's such a good idea."

Banyon insisted. "This is a huge breakthrough! I'm going to do it again. Right now. I know what to expect this time. I want to communicate with the light. But I'd like you to be here. Stay in the room with me. Would you? Please?"

Realizing there was no point arguing with him, she reluctantly agreed. Taking his hand, she looked at him with a sigh of total exasperation. "Okay," she said. "Just do me one favor."

"What's that?"

"Don't break the other lamp."

~102~

Angela inserted a fresh cassette into the tape recorder and set it to record. Then she turned out the light and decided to remain standing by the door, close to the light switch, in case she needed to turn it on again in a hurry.

Seated in the meditation chair, Banyon was now confident about what he was doing. Angela's confidence, on the other hand, was not quite at the same level. He could feel her anxiety from across the room as she stood behind him in the dark by the door.

"Don't worry," he said in his best Arnold Schwarzenegger voice, mimicking the character from the *Terminator* movie. "Ah'll be bok."

Angela rolled her eyes. "Can we just get on with it, please?"

Banyon straightened himself in the chair, inhaled deeply and let it go slowly. Staring into the glow of the candlelight as it danced seductively on the folds of the curtain before him, he began intoning the mantra.

By the third cycle of the repetition Angela was becoming more relaxed. The tension began to leave her body and she leaned back against the door. Soon she felt the deep warm drone of Banyon's voice literally absorbing into every fiber of her being. Several times she had to shake her head to keep her eyes from closing. Suddenly she realized Banyon had stopped chanting the mantra. The only sound in the room was the haunting reverberations of the didjeridoo.

Banyon had concluded the ninth cycle of repetitions. The familiar ball of energy ascended from the base of his spine upward through his body, culminating at the point between his eyes. His body quaked involuntarily from the rush and suddenly, as he had anticipated, he was outside his body. Even though it was exactly what he'd expected, he was still awed by the experience. His etheric body turned to look at Angela whose attention was still focused on his physical body sitting in the chair. Obviously she was not aware of his etheric presence in the room. He was about to move toward her - to see if she would have any reaction at all, any sign of a response if he attempted to touch her – but he was distracted by his own feeling of another presence approaching. He looked around but saw nothing. Then it appeared.

Manifesting before him, a million tiny particles of refracting, swirling lights coalesced into a single vertical column reaching the entire height of the ceiling. Now he was face to face – such as it were - with the Pillar of Light, the Teacher.

On the one hand, it was exactly what he'd expected. What he hadn't expected was the feeling of reverence that now overwhelmed him as he stood in the presence of what he knew was his own higher self. If he'd ever felt humbled by anything in his entire life this was one of those times. He stood, staring at the brilliant apparition, wondering what he should do next. He glanced over at Angela. She was still watching his physical body. Clearly, she was oblivious to the phenomenon taking place right there in the same room yet separated by the veil of another dimension. He turned back to the Pillar of Light and decided to attempt communication.

"How is this happening?" he asked.

The brilliant glow of the light seemed to pulse brighter in response and Banyon heard the reply inside his own head. *The shape of the number nine is phi spiral geometry. The golden mean spiral is the curve of the universe.*

Banyon was confused. "I don't understand. What does that mean? How is this happening?

The light pulsed again. *The vibration of the number nine is the key.*

Banyon could only surmise that this answer was some sort of a reference to the vibratory frequency of the mantra. He wanted to press for a clearer answer but felt strangely intimidated and oddly ashamed of what he perceived as his own ignorance. Gazing into the brilliance of the apparition before him he found it hard to imagine that this awesome spectacle was, in any way, somehow part of himself. But he needed to know. "What are you?" he asked.

The light pulsed. *I am the light of your soul.*

The answer – although it came from the light – seemed to originate from somewhere deep within himself. "And what am I?" he asked.

The light pulsed. *You are the Chosen One.*

Suddenly he remembered why this was all happening and he knew the question he should be asking.

He flashed back to the meeting with his friends when he voiced his concern about the nature of what he called the *downloads* and his desire to be able to control it. That was when he learned from Miriam about the pineal gland. The pineal gland was known to be sensitive to fluctuations in electromagnetic energy and, according to Miriam, some people – himself, for example – were hypersensitive to even the smallest of such fluctuations This caused the pineal gland to become involuntarily and sporadically activated. The pineal gland was associated with the mystical concept of the Third Eye. This Third Eye was believed to function as a portal into other dimensions of consciousness. Shamans believed it to be the primary access route to one's own spiritual essence. Miriam thought it could be the source of his *download* phenomenon. Rajani then told him it was possible to gain control over one's Third Eye but first it had to be fully awakened. Now, standing there in his etheric body, Banyon was convinced that the exercise of the mantra must have been for the purpose of fully awakening his Third Eye and apparently it had fulfilled its purpose. The question to ask now was how to implement some degree of control over the Third Eye. How to manipulate it at will for whatever purpose he might want, or need. He stared into the swirling column of light and posed the question.

Immediately the light pulsed. *To achieve control of the Third Eye, chant the mantra in reverse.*

Then the Pillar of Light began to transform. It's brilliance started to fade slowly as it retreated back into the swirling mist of shimmering particles as when it first appeared. In a moment it was gone.

Banyon felt as if he'd been drained of energy. He looked over at Angela and longed to touch her, to feel her. Instantly, with that one thought, he was catapulted back into his physical body. He opened his eyes and - remembering what happened the last time he tried to stand up - he simply raised a hand to beckon Angela. "I'm back," he said, too exhausted to attempt another Schwarzenegger impersonation.

Angela was relieved to hear his voice. She came to his side and steadied him as he stood up. He sat on the edge of the bed then lifted his legs up and collapsed onto the pillow. She brought him a glass of water. "How do you feel?" she asked.

He sat up and took a sip. "You know what?" he grinned. "I don't think I know. I've just had the most amazing experience of my entire life. I communicated with the Teacher!"

Angela looked surprised.

"What's the matter?" he asked.

"Well… it's just that I sort of thought nothing had happened. After you finished chanting the mantra I kept waiting for something to happen. But you just sat there. I never heard you say anything until you signaled me and said you were back."

Banyon looked puzzled. "Really? Nothing at all?"

Angela shook her head. "No, nothing."

It made sense once he thought about it. "Must be because I was outside my body. I knew you couldn't see me."

"Oh, I could see you all right. You never left the chair."

"No, I mean I had another out of body experience. You couldn't see my etheric body but I could see you." He went on to tell her about the entire experience, describing the appearance of the Pillar of Light and the conversation he'd had with it.

"But what, exactly, did it tell you?" she asked. 'Can you remember any of it?'

"It's a little fuzzy. I remember asking how the whole phenomenon was happening. It communicated an answer but it was pretty cryptic. Something about the phi spiral and geometry I think. And vibration. Something about vibration. Oh! And the number nine! I remember that. Something about the vibration of the number nine."

"That's it? That's all you can remember?"

Banyon thought for a moment. "No, there was more. I think there was something about... yes! About the Third Eye and how to control it! That's what the whole thing was about!"

"So tell me!" she said, excitedly. "How's it work? What do you have to do?"

"Well," he started, "it was... it had something to do with..." He suddenly realized he couldn't remember the details of the conversation. "Dammit!" he cursed. "It's all fading like a damn dream!"

Angela moved closer and put an arm around his shoulders. She could feel his frustration but didn't know quite what to say. "Well," she tried to soothe him, "maybe it'll come to you later. You should relax now. Get some sleep. We can talk about it in the morning."

Mentally exhausted, he lay back on the bed and let out a deep, exasperating sigh. "Yeah, okay" he finally relented. "Maybe you're right."

Angela walked over and dowsed the candles. "I'll go downstairs and turn off the lights," she said. "Why don't you get into bed. I'll come back up in a few minutes."

After she left the room he changed out of his clothes and climbed into bed. Tired and discouraged, he rested quietly, looking at the chair across the room. Then his gaze fell to the tape recorder still on the floor. He stared at it for several minutes, wondering, wishing. *No, if Angela didn't hear anything then there wouldn't be anything on the tape either.* But he couldn't take his eyes away from it. *Oh, hell!* He yanked the covers off and rolled out of bed to retrieve the tape recorder. Sitting on the edge of the bed, he rewound the tape and played it back. Listening to himself chant the mantra was a little embarrassing. *Freakin' weird*, he thought to himself. *My poor mother must really be rolling over in her grave by now.* He listened all the way through the entire cycle of repetitions and then there was only silence. Like Angela said, nothing could be heard but the droning of the didjeridoo in the background. He was about to push the stop button when suddenly he heard his own voice again. *What the...?* He turned up the volume and listened. It was his voice all right, but it sounded strange. Tinny. His recorded voice was asking, *How is this happening?* Then more silence. The next thing he heard caused him to jump. He dropped the tape recorder like a hot coal. "Angela!" he shouted. "Angela! Come here!"

~103~

N ot only was it Banyon's voice they heard *asking* the questions but to their amazement – and after listening to the tape several times - both he and Angela were convinced it was his voice they heard *answering* the questions! Even though both voices exhibited the same odd tonal distortion – almost as if they'd been recorded inside a tin can - they were definitely Banyon's voice.

He looked at Angela. "I don't get it. You said you never heard another word from me after I finished repeating the mantra, right?"

She nodded. "Right. Nothing."

"Then how did it get recorded? And what the hell was I doing? Talking to myself and then answering myself?"

"Well," she said, trying to think rationally, "Miriam and Rajani did say that this so called Teacher, this Pillar of Light, is really a manifestation of your own higher self. So, in essence, yes, I guess you could say you were talking to yourself."

"Great. They put people in rubber rooms for that, don't they?"

Angela laughed. "Don't worry. I won't tell anyone. But it is pretty weird."

The question of how the tape recorder could have picked up his conversation with the Teacher – his so-called higher self - remained a mystery. The upside was that now his inability to remember the details of the conversation was no longer an issue. It was all on tape.

As he listened now, focusing on the content of that conversation, the Teacher's answers to the questions were triggering a familiar gut feeling. "Run it back again," he instructed.

She hit the rewind and played it again. She could see his wheels spinning. "What?" she asked.

He got up and went into the other room for a moment. He returned to the bedroom with a notepad and his calculator. "Run it again," he said. "But stop it after each of the answers so I can write it down."

He began calculating the gematria values of each separate answer. When he finished he looked up at Angela. "You're not going to believe this!" he said, handing the notepad over to her.

Angela looked at the results:

THE SHAPE OF THE NUMBER NINE IS PHI SPIRAL GEOMETRY = 495

THE GOLDEN MEAN SPIRAL IS THE CURVE OF THE UNIVERSE = 495

THE VIBRATION OF THE NUMBER NINE IS THE KEY = 414
I AM THE LIGHT OF YOUR SOUL = 279

YOU ARE THE CHOSEN ONE = 216

TO ACHIEVE CONTROL OF THE THIRD EYE CHANT THE MANTRA IN REVERSE = 594

"Nines!" Angela said. "Every one of them reduces to a nine!"

"Not only that," Banyon added, "but check out the value of those first two phrases. Notice anything familiar?"

It took a moment to come to her. Then her eyes lit up. "Oh, wow! Four-nine-five! It's the repetition sequence of the mantra! *Four* nines, *nine* nines, *five* nines!"

"Right. Now look at the last one. That's the answer to my question about how to control the Third Eye."

Angela glanced at the writing on the notepad and nodded. "Yes," she said, looking back at him. "Same as the others. Four-nine-five. That's really..."

He interrupted her. "No. Look again."

She looked again. "Oh," she said, realizing her mistake. Then her eyes widened as she realized what she was seeing. "Oh! Oh, wow! It's exactly the reverse! It's not four-nine-five. It's five-nine-four! That's remarkable!"

It was indeed remarkable as Angela realized that the phrase instructing Banyon to chant the mantra in *reverse* had a gematria value matching the *reverse order* of the repetition sequence itself!

"This is too weird," she said, shaking her head. "I mean, not only were you talking to yourself but you were answering yourself in gematria-structured language! How the hell do you do that?"

Banyon raised an eyebrow. "Hey, don't ask me. I have no idea."

Angela turned back to the notepad and read the phrase about the vibration of the number nine being the key. "What question was this the answer to?"

"That was when I asked for clarification of how it was all happening. I wanted to know how I got there in that space, in that... dimension or whatever it was."

She handed the notepad back to him. "Did you notice the number from that answer?"

Banyon looked at it.. "Hmm... of course. Wouldn't you know it? Four-hundred-fourteen. The exact diameter of the donut." He shook his head and ran his fingers through his hair. "It's all very clever but why the hell does it all have to be so damned cryptic? Why can't I ever just get a straight answer to anything?"

Angela shrugged. "Maybe it's because the reality behind all of this just doesn't translate into straight answers. I don't know."

"Maybe you're right. I don't know either. But I would like to know more about that reverse mantra thing. It would have been nice if I'd been given at least some hint as to what that would do. I mean as far as giving me control over this Third Eye business."

"Well, I guess there's only one way you're going to find out."

He knew she was right. The only way was to try it and see what would happen. But it would have to wait. His eyes were getting heavy. "I'm exhausted," he complained. "Right now I just want to get some sleep."

The words had barely left his mouth when the phone rang. He looked at his watch. It was almost 11 p.m. "Who the hell would be calling us at this time of night?"

~104~

Zeke!"

It was Rajani's voice on the other end of the line. He was either upset or euphoric. Banyon wasn't sure which.

"Alec? Is that you? It's nearly eleven at night! Is something wrong?"

"I know it is late," Rajani said, apologetically, "but I wanted you to know right away!"

Banyon looked puzzled. "Know what?"

"We have been working all night on the levitation device trying to correct the errors in the computer code and..."

Banyon interrupted. "Oh no," he groaned. "Don't tell me. Let me guess. Another delay."

"No, my friend! We did it! It is ready!"

Banyon's legs nearly gave out. He stumbled two steps backward and sat on the edge of the bed. "I'm sorry," he said. "Could you repeat that?"

"Yes, it is true! I thought you would want to know right away. We just ran the final test! It is working like a charm bracelet!"

"A what?" Banyon asked. Then he laughed. "Oh! Of course! Like a charm!"

"Exactly! Yes!"

"So you're telling me we have a perfectly functioning scale model prototype of the sound generating device? The donut? The levitation machine? Is that right?"

"That is what I am telling you! Yes!"

A grin stretched across Banyon's face. "This is terrific news, Alec! You guys are geniuses! Now we need to get it to Nathan Crown so he can begin manufacturing the real thing. I'll contact him first thing in the morning. Man, I can't believe it! We should all get together for a celebration Friday evening. You can make it, can't you?"

"Yes, of course!"

"Great! We'll see you then!"

Banyon hung up the phone and turned to Angela. "Can you believe it?" he said, grinning from ear to ear. "The donut's out of the oven!"

Angela gave a laugh. "All right! Rock 'n' roll!"

Standing in front of him she raised a hand for a high-five but he grabbed her hand and pulled her onto the bed. She faked a bit of a struggle as he wrestled his way on top of her.

"I thought you were exhausted," she said, coyly, gazing up into his deep brown eyes.

"That was then," he purred, gently kissing the nape of her neck. He breathed in the sweet subtle scent of her perfume. "This is now."

She pretended to look concerned. "Hmm... Well, if you're sure the Teacher won't mind."

He raised up a bit and looked at her. "I *am* the Teacher, baby."

She smiled. "Oh! That's right! Well, in that case... I'm ready for a lesson. Why don't you let me change into my school clothes," she said, wriggling out from under him, "and I'll bring you an apple." She got up and flashed him a flirty look. "Or something."

He watched her disappear into the bathroom. "Bribing the teacher!" he called after her. "It'll get you everywhere!"

The next morning, after the most restful night's sleep he'd had in a long while, Banyon contacted Crown. The method of contact involved the same procedure that was assigned to Kline. He dialed the number. A receptionist answered. Banyon stated his name and requested to speak with Nathan Crown. As per the protocol, the receptionist said Crown was unavailable. Then she connected Banyon to Crown's voice mail. Banyon left a message, stating his name and phone number. Within five minutes Crown returned the call on a secure line. The conversation was brief and to the point.

"It's ready," Banyon said.

"Excellent," Crown replied. "I'll have someone pick it up right away. We'll need all of the necessary computer files of course. As soon as we review the technical data we'll begin construction of the full-scale device immediately."

"Where will the work be done?" Banyon asked.

There was a slight pause. "I would tell you if I could, and I will when I can. For now just be assured it is a secure facility. That's all I can tell you at the moment."

"But..."

"Please understand, Zeke. Even I am bound by some restrictions in this matter. It's a clearance issue. National security."

The phrase took Banyon by surprise. "National security? Government? But I thought..."

"Only indirectly. Don't be concerned. Everything is under control and you'll be informed as soon as possible. You have my word."

"But..."

"Please. I must go. There's no time to lose. I'll be in contact. And Zeke..."

Banyon gave a resigned sigh. "Yes?"

"Stay well. The future of humankind will soon be in your hands."

~105~

Miriam was the last to arrive at Banyon's house Friday evening but only by a few minutes. He ushered her into the living room where Rajani and Professor Kline were already seated. She took a seat on the couch next to Kline as Angela poured everyone a glass of wine. Several bowls of nuts and chips were placed conveniently around the room and a large red platter of cheeses and cold cuts made a festive centerpiece for the coffee table.

Miriam leaned over and whispered to Kline. "Why do I get the feeling something's up?"

Kline shook his head. "Something's up all right," he whispered back. "I don't know what, but I'm guessing maybe Alec knows something. He seems unusually quiet."

Standing in the midst of them, Banyon reached down and picked up his glass of wine. "Well, my friends, tonight we celebrate a huge milestone."

The announcement was met with silent anticipation and a variety of curious expressions.

"I won't keep you in suspense." He turned to face Rajani directly, smiled broadly, and raised his glass. "Let's drink a toast to our resident genius, Alec Rajani. Ladies and gentlemen..." he paused for dramatic effect, "...we have a fully functional scale model levitation device!"

It was the news they'd all been waiting for. The group exploded in a round of applause and cheers.

"Speech!" Kline called out.

"Stand up and soak it in, Alec!" Banyon said, grinning.

Rajani, bashful and unaccustomed to such attention, was finally coaxed onto his feet.

"Well," he began, "first I should say I could not have accomplished the job without the help of Buzz Webster. I feel he was the real genius in this project. I am only sorry he could not be here tonight."

"Such modesty!" Banyon said, laughing. "But you're right. Webster's contribution was invaluable. I would have liked for him to join us in this celebration but, as you're all aware, the agreement was that he would only know what he was working on but not what it was going to be used for. That was the arrangement set into place by Nathan Crown. Everyone agreed to it and Buzz, himself, had no problem with it. He'd worked on a lot of top-secret projects, so he was used to that sort of need-to-know arrangement."

Rajani nodded. "Yes, that is true. In fact Crown already has him assigned to some new top-secret project somewhere in Nevada. He left this morning."

"Well, there ya go," Banyon said.

Nevada? Kline thought to himself. *Top-secret project?* "Wait a second," he said, turning to Rajani. "You did say Nevada, didn't you?"

Rajani nodded.

"Did he happen to say *where* in Nevada?"

Rajani thought for moment then shook his head. "I can't remember. Something about a lake, I think."

Angela chuckled. "Nevada has lakes? My impression has always been that it's all gambling casinos and scorching desert."

"Yes," Kline said. "But there are a few lakes too. And I'll bet the one Webster has been sent to is the one without any water."

"What do you mean without any water?" Miriam asked.

Kline sat forward. "I'm talking about the dry lake bed called Groom Lake, otherwise known as the infamous Area 51.

"What the heck is Area 51?" Banyon asked.

Kline explained that Area 51 was an ultra top-secret military base about 90 miles north of Las Vegas. Until recently, he told them, the government denied its existence although it has been there and fully operational since 1954.

"That long ago?" Angela asked.

"Yes. The government took over the location when they needed an obscure out-of-sight-out-of-mind place to develop the U-2 spy plane during the Cold War. Since then it's been used to develop god-knows-what in terms of flying machines."

Banyon was captivated. "Flying machines? What – you mean like really exotic stuff?"

Kline nodded. "That would be a good word for it, yes. And that's just *our* stuff."

Banyon drew a blank. "What do you mean *our* stuff?"

"I mean *our* stuff." Kline emphasized. "U.S. government."

"So are you saying...?"

"The fact is," Kline went on, "Area 51 has been a hot spot for UFO sightings for years. Use to be you could get a halfway decent view of the place from a high vantage point, a small mountainous outcropping near by. People would trek up there with binoculars and cameras to get a good look at the strange glowing objects that would appear in the airspace over the base."

"Glowing objects?"

Kline nodded. "According to reports, sometimes these objects would just rise up from ground level and hover for a while and then go back down. Others would perform amazing aerial maneuvers that no conventional aircraft could ever possibly match. There's videotape. I've seen some of it."

"Wow!" Angela exclaimed. "Let's go! I want to see this!"

Kline laughed. "Too late I'm afraid. Or so I've heard anyway. They say the government has widened the perimeter of the restricted area and confiscated the land where those vantage points are located. I think there's still one outside the restricted area but it's a good twelve miles or more from the base. If you try to get any closer you'll be met by the Cammo Dudes carrying automatic weapons."

Miriam laughed. "Cammo Dudes?"

"That's what people have come to call them," Kline explained. "You know. Men in full camouflage outfits. Automatic rifles. Night-vision goggles. The whole works. Odd thing, though. Their uniforms don't seem to exactly match the official government issue and they don't have any sort of identifying insignias. They might be a private security force of some kind. Nobody knows for sure. But they do mean business. People have been fired upon by these guys."

Banyon poured himself another glass of wine. "So you think that's where our friend Buzz was sent? This Area-51?"

"Not only that," Kline said, pressing some tobacco into his pipe, "but how much do you want to bet that's where your prototype levitation device is right now?"

Banyon's eyes widened as he suddenly remembered what Crown had told him. The place where the levitation device would be built was a secure facility and, although Crown was evasive about the details, he did infer some sort of government connection.

"Jesus," Banyon said. "Yes. Judging from Crown's guarded comments when I asked him where the device would be built, I think you may be right on the money!"

Miriam looked puzzled. "But I don't get it," she said. "How is Nathan Crown connected with the government?"

Kline was quick to answer. "Simple really. Through his company, Crown Technology Systems. They get government contracts related to classified projects all the time."

"Right," Banyon said, mentally connecting the dots. "So it makes sense that he could have access to such a facility."

Given what they'd just learned about Area 51 from Kline, this was just one more amazing and totally surprising turn of events.

"Unbelievable," Banyon said, shaking his head.

"Speaking of unbelievable," Angela added, "aren't you going to tell them the other reason for the celebration?"

Banyon looked at her. "What? Oh! Yes, well..." Suddenly he wasn't sure where to begin.

"What is it?" Miriam asked.

Banyon took a sip of his wine and decided to just come out and say it. "Well," he began, setting his glass on the table, "I had a conversation with the Teacher. And this time it wasn't in a dream."

Rajani sat forward. He was intrigued. "A conversation? You actually spoke with the entity you told us about before?"

"That's what I'm saying," Banyon replied. He went on to describe every detail of the experience.

"God, how exciting is that?" Miriam beamed.

"Extraordinary," said Kline.

"Yes, but there's more," Banyon continued. "Wait'll you see this."

He showed them the paper with the gematria values of the answers to his questions. Miriam, Rajani, and Kline were astonished. Then, to make sure they understood just how astonishing it was, Banyon pointed out what for him was the most amazing part of it:

TO ACHIEVE CONTROL OF THE THIRD EYE CHANT THE MANTRA IN REVERSE = 594

"Check it out," Banyon encouraged them. "Do you see it? The gematria value of five-nine-four is the exact reverse of the mantra sequence which is four-nine-five! The gematria value produced by the phrasing of the answer corresponds exactly to the meaning inherent within the answer itself!"

The response from the group was silent bewilderment as the odds of such a thing happening by mere chance slowly sank in. One by one the eyebrows began to rise.

"But here's the really weird part," Banyon said. He reached for the tape recorder. "The whole thing is on tape!"

"What's weird about that?" Miriam asked.

"What's weird about it," Banyon explained, "is that Angela was right there in the room at the time and she heard nothing! Nada!"

Angela joined in. "It's true," she said. "After he finished the mantra he didn't speak another word out loud until minutes later when he came out of the trance and told me he was back. During those minutes when he wasn't talking – at least not in his physical voice – the only sound in the room was the sound of the didjeridoo from the CD player."

"Here," Banyon said. "I'll play it for you. Listen to the strange tone of my voice. It sounds slightly distorted like it was recorded inside a bucket or something. And remember, the voice you hear *answering* the questions is also my own voice! You'll be able to tell right away."

After playing the tape Banyon looked around at his guests. He was amused by the bewildered looks on their faces. "So," he said, "did I tell you it was weird or what? I mean not just the strange audio quality of the voices but how did it get on the tape when Angela heard nothing at all?"

"Wait a second," Miriam said. "There is one possible explanation."

Banyon looked surprised. "And that would be...?"

"Have you ever heard of EVP? Electronic Voice Phenomenon?"

Banyon shook his head. He was not familiar with the phenomenon. He looked around at the others. None of them had heard of it.

"It's a strange phenomenon that was first noticed by Nikola Tesla way back in the early nineteen-hundreds," Miriam explained.

"Nikola Tesla," Banyon said. "I read an article about him. He was an electronics genius. He's the one who came up with the concept of alternating current that basically powers virtually every electrical gadget we have today."

Miriam nodded. "Exactly. And he was the inventor of a lot of things that he never got credit for. Like the radio for example. People still think that was the brainchild of Marconi. But Tesla was the first to come up with it. And that brings me to my point. Tesla claimed he occasionally heard strange voices coming through the radio on frequencies that were not being used to broadcast anything. After a while even Edison got into it."

"Edison?" Angela asked. "Thomas Edison?

Miriam nodded. "Right. Edison was obsessed with building an electronic device especially for receiving what he called *spirit voices* on specific frequency ranges. But the real breakthrough came in the mid-fifties when a Catholic priest - Father Pellegrino-something – was recording Gregorian chants on one of those early recording devices, sort of like a cylinder with wire coiled around it. When he listened to the recording he heard the unmistakable voice of his father speaking to him. The shocking thing about it was that his father was no longer alive when the recording was made."

"What!" Rajani said, skeptically. "How is that possible? There would be no physics to explain such a thing."

Miriam shrugged. "I don't know. All I know is what I've read. But it didn't stop with the priest. Over the years more and more people began experimenting with the phenomenon. As the recording technology improved so did the results of the experiments. Some of the research has even been monitored and reviewed by mainstream academics. But they can't explain the phenomenon. On the other hand they can't deny that it's a real thing. It actually does happen."

"Well," Banyon said, "Somebody must at least have come up with a theory. Right?"

Miriam nodded. "They have. The conventional theory is that these are the voices of the dead. You know. Spirit voices. Another theory is that the voices are bleeding through into this dimension of reality from a parallel dimension that lies just beyond the veil of our perception. Anyway, whatever the source might be, there are literally hundreds of thousands of these EVP recordings now since so many people have worked at it over the years."

"That's just spooky," Angela said, only half joking.

"Yes, but what's interesting here," Miriam continued, "is that odd tonal quality of the voices on your tape. That weird tinny sound. It's like that in all of the recordings of this type."

Banyon found Miriam's explanation to be incredibly intriguing. "So you think this is what happened during my out-of-body experience? When I was in the deep meditative state?"

Miriam nodded. "It's the only thing that makes any sense."

"Makes any sense!" Banyon laughed. "I don't know if it makes any sense or not but I have to admit it is a damned interesting theory."

Rajani spoke up. "What I am wondering," he said, turning to Banyon, "is when you will be trying the *reverse* mantra? Were you not told this is necessary in order to learn control of the Third Eye?"

"Yes, that's what I was told. I'm going to attempt it tomorrow. I've been putting it off because…" He paused. "Well, the truth is I'm a little nervous about attempting it."

"But why?" Rajani asked.

Banyon shrugged. "I don't know. I just have this gut feeling that it might be somehow more intense than I'm ready to take on. That reversed gematria value was so… I don't know… extraordinary."

"Yes, I agree," Rajani said. "I think there might be an important lesson in the store for you."

Kline grinned and mentally corrected Rajani's comment. *In store for you.* "Yes, Zeke," he joked, "what's the going price for an important lesson from the store these days?"

Banyon grunted and gave a sarcastic laugh. "My sanity, apparently. Which may be in short supply before this is all over."

~106~

Banyon's experiment with the reverse mantra began with a sensation he later likened to being turned into Jell-o, forced into a funnel and suddenly spewed out the other end. It wasn't uncomfortable and, in fact, he found it energizing in an oddly erotic way. The only part of the experience that was in any way similar to his previous excursions was that he was once again out of his body. He fully expected to be confronted with the Teacher, the Pillar of Light, but such was not the case. Instead, he seemed to be enveloped in a darkness that was almost palpable. He felt as though he was wrapped in a cloak of intimacy that was at once unlike anything he'd ever experienced and yet, in some strange way, overwhelmingly familiar.

As he became slowly accustomed to this environment he had the sudden intuitive realization that he was literally wandering around inside the recesses of his own consciousness. He was inside his own essence. *This is me*, he thought, with a sense of reverence. *I'm... I'm inside myself!*

Soon waves of information began to flow through him, answers to questions he hadn't even asked. He remembered Rajani telling him he may be in for an important lesson so he tried to focus his attention on the information. Some of it came and went so fast he couldn't capture it. But some of it seemed to slow down, almost as if it was intentionally waiting for him to grasp it and store it like an imprint upon his memory. Then a vision began to form.

Particles of light appeared out of nowhere and started to coalesce into a geometric shape. The image was a star tetrahedron, two interlocking 3-D triangular shapes. He instantly recognized it as the merkaba just as Professor Kline had described it during their conversation at the lake house over a month ago. He remembered the word *merkaba* had appeared in the huge download of phrases that day. Now, somehow, he was able to recall the exact phrases as they appeared in the download:

THE INNER MERKABA = 144 = INTERNAL MERKABA = THE HOLY MERKABA = THE PERFECT BALANCE

That moment at the lake was the first time Banyon had ever heard of a merkaba and Kline had to explain the concept to him. At the time they had no idea what significance it could have for them. Now here it was again, but this time in visual form. And still Banyon didn't know why. He was about to plead for guidance when another thought wave came bursting in with a powerful urgency: *Remember this image!*

Then without warning everything went black. He was instantly sucked back through the funnel and then, like a slingshot, he was thrust back into his body.

The jolt of the sudden return left him stunned. For a few moments he sat motionless trying to reorient himself to the familiar confines of his own bedroom. Finally he stood up and made his way down the stairs to find Angela.

"Hey," she said, walking over to meet him at the foot of the stairs. "How'd it go? Are you all right?"

He brushed his hair back out of his eyes. "Yeah, but Jesus H. Christ! What a trip!"

She led him into the living room and had him sit on the couch. "I was just going to fix some iced tea," she said. "You want some?"

He slipped his shoes off and put his feet up on the coffee table. "That'd be good. Thanks."

She disappeared into the kitchen and returned in a few minutes. "So," she said, handing him the drink, "tell me about it. What happened?"

He described the experience to her as well as he could although it was difficult to find the right words to convey some of the strange sensations. She listened intently, trying to imagine what it must have been like.

"So what did you learn about control of the third eye?" she asked. "Isn't that what it was all supposed to be about?"

He nodded. "Information came to me like waves of thought. It was a strange sensation. Some of it came so fast it seemed to pass right through me before I could comprehend what the hell it was. But some of it I got."

"Like what?"

"Like the more I do this reverse mantra thing the more control I will have over this Third Eye business. I understood that with enough practice it would become easier and easier for me to actually communicate with the Teacher – my higher self – even during times of normal consciousness!" He shook his head at the thought. "Wouldn't that be a trip?"

"You mean without having to chant the mantra?"

"Yes and no. I'd have to chant the mantra but not necessarily out loud. Eventually I should be able to simply do it silently in my head and it would work. At least that's the way I understood it. I learned that I'd actually be able to control those information downloads that just seem to happen whenever they feel like it."

Angela nodded. "I remember that's what you were hoping to be able to do."

"Yeah, right. But…" He stopped and took a sip of his iced tea.

"But…?" Angela prompted.

"Well, it came with a warning."

Angela looked concerned. "A warning? What kind of a warning?"

"I was told it might not be a wise thing to stop any of those spontaneous downloads because they're being transmitted from my higher self for a reason. Any interference or attempts to block the information could seriously jeopardize the entire mission. It's all part of a plan that's been set into motion. Basically, if I gained that kind of control – and apparently I can, with enough practice – I'd also have to shoulder the burden of that responsibility.

Angela sank back into the couch and considered what he was saying. "Assured mutual destruction," she muttered.

"What?"

"Like the Cold War. Russia had nukes, we had nukes. Either one pushes the button and everybody loses. Maybe you should forget about the idea of being able to have control of the Third Eye."

Banyon lit a cigarette and shook his head. "Not an option."

She looked puzzled. "What do you mean?"

"That vision I had."

"The merkaba?"

"Yeah. And when the words, *remember this image*, came flowing into me it was underscored with an intensity that I can't describe. Seriously. We're talking intense!"

"I don't understand. What's the merkaba image have to do with you acquiring the ability to control something with the power of your Third Eye?"

"I had a strong intuitive feeling – no, not a feeling – a knowing, that the ability to control the power of my Third Eye was somehow crucially connected with this merkaba image. Somehow the two go hand in hand. I don't know how. I don't know why." He gave an exasperated shrug and looked at her. "I just know that's the way it is."

They sat next to each other in silence for a few minutes trying to take it all in. Finally Angela leaned over and rested her head against his shoulder.

"Remember when we were normal?" she said.

"Normal?" He gave a laugh. "My last day of normal was the day before you walked into my office looking for a job. It was all downhill after that."

"Hmm…" she purred. "So it's all my fault.

He grinned. "Pretty much, yeah."

That night Banyon dreamed he was standing before a huge star-tetrahedron merkaba. He approached it slowly, studying it carefully from every angle. The top of it seemed to tower over him by several feet. He began to chant the reverse mantra silently and the upward-pointed section of the merkaba started to spin clockwise. At first he was excited, elated by the success of his effort. But something was wrong. The other section, the tetrahedron that pointed downward, should have been spinning in the opposite direction. But it would not move! He chanted the reverse mantra again, activating as much control over the power of his Third Eye as possible. Still the lower portion of the merkaba remained static, motionless. He became frightened, overwhelmed with frustration. Somehow he knew this merkaba - this huge star-tetrahedron - was somehow key to the success of the entire mission. Unless he could find the power to activate both sections of this strange machine the mission would fail. Set, the fiery dragon, the blazing comet, would prevail in all of its destructive glory. *Why?* Banyon yelled. Nearly in tears he realized whatever was missing – whatever was required to make the merkaba fully functional – was not within him. *Must I fail?* he cried out. Suddenly the scene changed.

He found himself looking at a swirling mass of alphabetic letters churning, weaving, chaotically in mid-air. Again he recited the reverse mantra in an attempt to use the power of his Third Eye to control the letters, to bring some order to the chaos. A tingling energy sensation vibrated at the front of his skull. He focused his attention on the swirling letters and they began to move ever more slowly, shifting around, moving with some pattern of intent, forming into syllables and finally into complete words:

ANTICLOCKWISE
ANGELA ANN MARTIN
REVERSE DIRECTION
THE KEY IS IN HER NAME

Angela was awakened by the sound of Banyon rustling through the drawer of his nightstand.

"What're you doing?" she asked, rubbing her eyes. She looked at the clock. "It's the middle of the night."

"Looking for my calculator."

She sat up and turned on the light. "What for?"

"I just had the strangest dream. Note pad."

"What?"

"Where's my note pad? I need to write something down before I forget it."

"Bottom drawer. What was it?"

Banyon got back on the bed and jotted down the words that he saw in his dream. "Just a second," he said, tapping away on his calculator. "Let me get this down." When he finished he showed it to her:

ANTICLOCKWISE = 144
= ANGELA ANN MARTIN

REVERSE DIRECTION = 189
= THE KEY IS IN HER NAME

She looked at it and shook her head. "What is it?"

Banyon told her about the dream, the merkaba, the swirling letters. She was puzzled. "I don't understand. What's it all mean?"

"I don't know for sure," he confessed, setting the notepad and calculator aside. Then he turned and looked at her. "But somehow you hold the key to the success of the entire mission."

It was a surprising and shocking statement. "Me?" she exclaimed, taken aback. "What do you mean, me? What can *I* do?"

He shook his head. "I don't know exactly. But I have a feeling we'll find out soon enough."

~107~

B anyon began practicing the reverse mantra routinely twice a day and it became easier with each attempt. Nothing earthshaking happened during the first few sessions but somehow – even though he couldn't put his finger on it - he felt the experience was strengthening his ability to control the power of his Third Eye.

On the third day the Pillar of Light appeared with a message, an urgent message that seemed completely at odds with what he and the others had assumed should be done with the Capstone when they retrieved it from its ancient resting place at the bottom of the Antarctic sea. He and Angela, along with Professor Kline, had assumed the Capstone would have to be transported to Egypt and placed atop the Great Pyramid in order for it to become activated and create the time shift to save the world from the comet impact. Apparently they were wrong.

Now, from his vantage point outside his body, his attention was suddenly drawn to a movement in the room. Angela had just opened the door and was walking toward his physical body that was sitting in the chair by the window. They had agreed she would not disturb him during these sessions except for an emergency. He could tell by the look on her face that something was up. Immediately he returned to his body and resumed full consciousness. Angela apologized for the interruption.

"Of course," he said, assuring her it was okay. "What is it?"

"You got a call from Nathan Crown. I figured you would want to know."

Banyon wasted no time returning the call via the established communication protocol: he called Crown's company, told the receptionist who he was and that he was returning a call from Nathan Crown. As expected, she replied that Mr. Crown was not available. Banyon hung up, and a few minutes later Crown called back on a secure line.

"I have something I know you're anxious to hear," Crown said. "I've been given permission to tell you about the transportation vehicle we'll be using to get to the appointed site in the Antarctic."

"Let me guess," Banyon said. "A nuclear powered aircraft carrier. That'd be big enough. Those carriers are like floating cities."

Crown chuckled. "Not an aircraft carrier. But it's huge and it can float, too. In the air."

Banyon was stumped. "In the air?"

"Your friend Professor Kline has actually seen one of these marvelous craft. But of course, like other civilians who have seen one on occasion, he didn't know exactly what it was."

Banyon thought back to an early conversation with Kline the first or second time they'd met. Kline told them about the one time he saw a UFO. "The black triangle?" he asked incredulously.

"That's it. The craft was developed under the code name Project Deep Black. I can tell you now because the code name has been changed. Actually there are three of these vehicles currently in operation. The one we will be using is called the Delta-3. It's the largest of the three. Four-hundred-fifty feet to a side. Total circumference, thirteen-hundred and fifty feet."

Banyon was astounded. "Four-hundred-fifty feet! That's bigger than a football field! What the hell powers this thing?"

"That I can't tell you. I don't know myself, exactly. But I know it's something exotic and has something to do with manipulating the earth's gravitational field."

Antigravity? Banyon could hardly believe what he was hearing. "Where in the world do they keep these things?"

"That I'm afraid I'm not at liberty to disclose."

Area-51, Banyon thought to himself. "It wouldn't happen to be a secret facility located on a dry lake bed in the Nevada desert, would it?"

There was a long pause.

"You know about that?" Crown asked, cautiously.

"Am I right?"

"I can't say."

"Can't, or won't?"

Crown abruptly changed the subject. "You'll be happy to know construction of the levitation device has begun. I've put together a team of the top people in their respective fields. Structural engineers, acoustic engineers, electronics technicians, computer programmers, the works."

"That's great," Banyon said, realizing it was futile to pursue the Area-51 question. "But I'm worried about the timing. How long will it take to complete the project?"

"Best estimate – at least at this point – six weeks."

"Six weeks!" Banyon did a quick calculation in his head. "But that takes us right up to about the end of July! According to the Bible Code the date of the comet impact is the third of August! What if your team runs into trouble?"

Crown spoke calmly. "Pray that they don't."

"Jesus Christ."

"That's a good start."

"Not funny."

"Not meant to be. Listen, I understand only too well what we're up against here. I've worked out a timetable and, assuming all goes as planned, we're scheduled to complete the levitation device by the thirty-first of July at the very latest. The device will be immediately loaded onto the Delta-3 and we'll depart for the rendezvous point on the first of August. We'll be set up and operational by midnight, on the second of August. Getting us there in time is my responsibility in this mission. The rest will be up to you."

The first of August? "Jesus!" Banyon exclaimed. "Could we cut it any closer, for God's sake?"

"I'm open to suggestions."

Banyon had no response. He knew there was nothing more that could be done. The timing sucked. That's all there was to it.

"Now," Crown said, "just to keep you updated, there's one more thing you should know."

Banyon hesitated and drew a breath. "What is it?"

"We're anticipating some resistance from the Minister of Antiquities at Giza concerning the placement of the Capstone atop the Great Pyramid. The whole idea is not going to sit well with him. It will be difficult to convince him that any of this is real. There are political and cultural..."

"Unbelievable!" Banyon interrupted. "Now I've got an update for *you*!"

Crown was caught off guard. "Excuse me?"

Banyon brought Crown up to date on what had transpired at their group meetings and quickly moved to the most important subject of the moment. He described his work with the mantras and the Pillar of Light, the Teacher. As he heard himself talking it suddenly seemed completely insane, like the ramblings of a madman. But he went on, knowing he really had no choice. "Then just this afternoon," he continued, "moments before you called, I was in the trance state and the information that was coming to me was an urgent message. The bottom line was that we are, under no circumstances, supposed to transport the Capstone to Egypt. The Capstone is not to be placed atop the Great Pyramid. We just assumed that's what was supposed to be done with it. It was the only thing that made any sense at the time. But we were wrong."

"Wrong?" Crown questioned. "But..."

"That's all I was able to find out. It seemed like I was about to receive more information but Angela interrupted my session to let me know you called."

"Hmm... bad timing. I'm sorry."

"Not your fault. You had no way of knowing."

"Will you be able to learn more?"

"I think so. I hope so."

"When?"

"I'll try again this evening."

"Let me know what you find out as soon as possible."

After his conversation with Crown, Banyon was excited to relay the news to Angela. She found the information about not moving the

Capstone to the Great Pyramid to be an amazing turn of events but the news about their mode of transportation completely stunned her. Her jaw dropped. "What!" she said excitedly. "The black triangle craft? The same thing Kline told us about? We're going to be on it? Are you kidding me?"

"That's what Crown told me."

It took a minute for that to really sink in. "That's unbelievable," she mused. "I mean, think about it. That must be an ultra top-secret project! How the heck did he manage that?"

Banyon shook his head. "His connections must run deeper than we can imagine."

That evening, in trance, Banyon did indeed learn more about the mystery behind the missing capstone. The Great Pyramid, the Teacher informed him, never did have a capstone. The top of the pyramid - a flat square surface of 44 x 44 feet – functioned as an altar for ceremonial purposes as well as a platform providing a clear arc of 360 degrees for the ancient astronomers to work out the movements of the stars. The Great Pyramid would, however, be crowned with the Capstone in the near future if – and only if – Banyon succeeded in his mission. The crowning ceremony would take place on the Winter solstice of the year 2012. As monumental as this event would be it was merely a precursor to an even more remarkable event to follow. When Banyon asked what that event would be he was told he would know the answer when the time was right - and only if he successfully completed his current mission.

"But," Banyon protested, "if we're not supposed to transport the Capstone to the top of the Great Pyramid until 2012 then how are we to proceed with the activation process?"

It must remain at its current latitude and longitude, the Teacher replied.

Banyon was confused. "What? But I thought we were supposed to raise it from the ocean floor!"

Exactly so.

"But then what?"

You will know what to do.

"But…"

Before he could articulate the question the Pillar of Light began to fade. In a moment it was gone and Banyon could feel himself being drawn back into his body.

Suddenly he was fully conscious, sitting in the chair in his bedroom, shaking his head. *Just once in a while a straight answer would be nice*, he complained to himself.

"Zeke?"

It was Angela's voice.

Banyon spun around. "You startled me! What is it?"

"Sorry," she apologized. "Didn't mean to. You've got another phone call."

He looked surprised. "Crown again?"

"No," she smiled. "An old friend."

~108~

Z eke?"

It was Father Caldwell's voice on the other end of the line.

"Caldwell! Man, I'm glad you called! How the hell are you? I've been meaning to call you for so long. So much has happened! Wait'll you hear what's been going on!"

"I... I'm, uh..." Caldwell stuttered.

"You all right?"

DuPont's hitman shoved the barrel of the pistol deeper into Caldwell's ribs.

Caldwell winced. "Yes. Yes, I'm... fine. Just a bit of a cold... I guess."

"Sounds like you're on a speaker phone."

"Um, yes. Just got it. I'm, uh, trying it out. So tell me what's been going on. I take it you've been making progress."

Banyon laughed. "That's an understatement! Man, I'm not sure where to begin. So much has happened. We're damn near ready!"

The hitman recorded the entire conversation as Banyon gave Caldwell the condensed version of all that had transpired since the last time they'd talked. He was just about to mention the amazing mode of transportation that was going to be employed for the mission when Caldwell interrupted.

"That's all just... incredible," Caldwell said, trying to sound as calm as possible with a gun in his side. The hitman prompted Caldwell to get to the most important piece of information. "So... um... when are you... um, planning to go? Soon, I suspect, huh?"

"Not soon enough as far as I'm concerned," Banyon answered. "As it stands now, the plan is to leave here on the first of August! I hate cutting it that short. You know what I mean? But there's nothing that can be done about it. And don't think for a minute that I've forgotten about you, my old friend. I remember you said you wanted to be part of the team and as far as Angela and I are concerned you've always been part of the team. So you're coming with us. At least I'm assuming you still want to, right?"

"More than you know," Caldwell said almost under his breath.

"Well, listen." Banyon said, "Why don't I call you tomorrow and we can talk about getting you out here. You know you can stay here at my place and..."

"That'll be...um...fine," Caldwell stuttered, responding to another impatient jab in the ribs.

"Well, great then! I'll call you tomorrow. Say around noon or so? East coast time?"

"Yes, fine, around noon." Caldwell paused, then spoke again. "Zeke?"

"Yeah?"

"If by some chance I can't make it..."

Banyon gave a laugh. "What are you talking about?"

Caldwell felt the cold steel of the gun now press against the back of his head. "Nothing..." he muttered.

Banyon chuckled. "Damn right, nothing. You're coming with us come hell or high water! I'll call you tomorrow. Get some rest and take care of that cold."

Before Caldwell could say another word, the hitman grabbed the phone and hung it up. He quickly and expertly tied Caldwell to a chair and waited for further instructions from his employer, the Jesuit General.

~109~

I'll bet he was excited, huh?" Angela said, handing Banyon a cup of coffee.

Banyon hung the phone up slowly with a perplexed look on his face. "What? Oh. Yeah. Sort of."

"What do you mean, sort of? Something wrong?"

He took the cup of coffee and they moved into the kitchen.

"I don't know. I guess not. He wasn't feeling well. Said he had a cold or something. But it was kind of odd."

Angela sat down at the kitchen table. "What was odd?"

Leaning against the kitchen counter, Banyon stared at his coffee then he looked at Angela. "He didn't even say goodbye. He just hung up the phone."

"Hmm… Well, maybe he was just overwhelmed by the whole thing. He must have been pretty excited, right? You told him everything?"

"Yeah. Pretty much. I didn't want to keep him too long because I could tell he wasn't feeling so good. So I just gave him the headline version of what all's been going on. I figured I'd fill him in on the details tomorrow. I told him I'd call him around noon, his time."

"Good. Maybe he'll be feeling better."

Banyon nodded. "Yeah. Well, right now I have to call Crown. You won't believe what I just learned during my last session."

Angela sat forward. "What is it?"

He explained to her about the altar at the top of the Great Pyramid.

The information surprised her. "So the pyramid was built that way on purpose? Flat on the top and used as a ceremonial altar?"

"And for the astronomers to study the movements of the stars. Celestial mechanics. That's what I was told."

Angela shook her head, trying to bring this changing picture into focus. "And what about the Capstone? The object under the sea that we're going after?"

Banyon nodded. "I was told we *are* supposed to raise it up but it needs to remain positioned right there at it's current latitude and longitude for some reason."

"So it's supposed to be activated right there?"

Banyon shrugged. "Apparently."

Angela thought about it for a minute. Suddenly she had an idea. "Wait a second," she said.

Banyon could see her wheels turning. "What is it?"

"What you're telling me just might make some sense."

Banyon gave a laugh. "Yeah? Okay. Clue me in, Sherlock. What are you thinking?"

"Remember Paretti's information about that guy, Bruce Cathie?"

"Sure. But..." Suddenly his eyes lit up. "Wait a second. Yes! That's when we did an internet search for more information about Cathie's research and we found that picture of what they called the Eltanin Antenna! Now we know it's actually part of the Capstone!"

"Right. And we found out Cathie had discovered what?" Angela prompted him.

"Some kind of a magnetic grid that covered the earth. Magnetic grid! I know where you're going with this!"

Angela nodded with a grin. "Yup. Cathie said the Eltanin Antenna served as the zero point for the grid he discovered. So I'm thinking that has something to do with the reason for leaving the Capstone positioned at that exact latitude and longitude after we raise it up. It has something to do with the energy field at that particular and precise location."

Banyon lit a cigarette and began pacing the floor, putting the pieces together. "Yes, I bet you're right on the money. And it also fits into the whole thing about this Third Eye business and Miriam's theory about my apparent hyper-sensitivity – or, rather, my pineal gland's hyper-sensitivity - to electro-magnetic fluctuations!" He stopped pacing and looked at her. "Remember that dream I had a few nights ago? In the dream I was using the power of my Third Eye to activate the Capstone! I can't believe it! Now it all makes sense! Jesus! This is amazing! Wait'll I tell Caldwell! He's just gonna die!"

At that moment, in Caldwell's apartment, the hitman was making a call. He spoke in low tones. "Yeah, I got it all on tape. Right. What? Are you sure? All right. Consider it done."

The hitman hung up the phone and moved toward Caldwell.

Caldwell, still tied securely to the chair, uttered a quick prayer. Something about the shadow of death.

Without hesitation, the hitman shoved the barrel of the revolver into Caldwell's mouth. Caldwell tried to struggle but it was pointless. The hitman pulled the trigger and winced as the blood spattered against the wall. He cut the cord that bound Caldwell to the chair and dropped it into his jacket pocket. Next, he wrapped Caldwell's dead hand around the butt of the gun, then let the gun fall to the floor. Caldwell's body slumped forward then crumpled to the floor next to the suicide weapon. The hitman stood for a moment, analyzing the scene. Satisfied, he walked out of the apartment, removed his gloves, and disappeared into the New York night.

~110~

Banyon called Crown and gave him the rundown on what he'd learned about the Great Pyramid, the Capstone, and the astonishing information about how it will indeed need to be placed atop the Great Pyramid but not until the winter solstice of 2012. Crown was relieved to know he wouldn't have to engage in complicated dialog with any part of the Egyptian government regarding access to the Great Pyramid, at least for now.

Banyon did voice a concern about how to keep the Capstone at the required geo-positioning long enough to do whatever needed to be done. Since no one knew exactly what would transpire during or after the activation, they had no way of knowing how long they would have to remain fixed at that position. But Crown relieved Banyon of any such concern. He informed Banyon that the hovering capability of the Delta-3 was virtually limitless in terms of duration. Once the Capstone was levitated into the hangar bay of the Delta-3 they would simply hover at that position as long as necessary.

"Just one question," Crown said. "What do we do with the Capstone after..." he paused mid-sentence, realizing there might not be an *after*. "...after whatever happens...happens? I mean - assuming a successful mission - do we lower it back into the ocean? What?"

"Jesus," Banyon replied. "It never occurred to me. I have no idea."

"Well, it might be a good idea to find out, don't you think? We don't want to be stuck hovering over the Antarctic Ocean for the next six years."

Banyon acknowledged the point and promised to make an attempt at getting an answer.

After their conversation Banyon suddenly felt the lateness of the hour. He was exhausted and decided to get some sleep. He could have another go at it in the morning. Assuming he could learn the answer to Crown's question, he would call Crown immediately and then, as promised, he would call his old friend, Father Caldwell for a long overdue conversation.

~111~

B anyon learned two things during his next session with the Teacher. First he learned that the answer to Crown's question was simple enough. After the Capstone had done whatever it was going to do it was to be housed in a secure facility until December, 2012. Nathan Crown, Banyon was told, would know how to make that happen. *Fine with me*, Banyon thought. *The less I have to worry about the better.*

The other thing he learned was something else altogether. He was right about the Capstone being a device that could cause a shift in the space-time continuum. He'd been certain about that all along based on the revelation that came to him back at Kline's cabin on the lake. What he hadn't been sure of was just exactly what that meant. What, exactly would happen when the Capstone was activated? The answer should not have shocked him – he knew that – but it did. It sent his head reeling. Even though he couldn't comprehend it thoroughly, he understood that at the moment of activation an unbelievable and completely extraordinary series of events would occur. These events somehow involved the *many-universes* theory merged with the *holographic universe* hypothesis. It was all very similar to ideas that others had stumbled onto, primarily a handful of quantum physicists and even independent alternative researchers outside academia, people like their early contact source, Vince Paretti. But for all of them – scientists and non-scientists alike - it was still conjecture, a remotely feasible possibility. For Banyon, however, it was now more than that. It was a reality about to happen. And, like most of the other truly important aspects of this whole strange journey, it was keyed to the code number 144. That realization came to him now as he recalled something from Paretti's work:

MULTIVERSE = 144

When he came out of trance he stood up, dazed. His head was swimming. He stumbled across the bedroom toward the door. *I gotta tell Angela.* But as he reached for the door the dizziness overwhelmed him. His legs wobbled and his vision began to blur. Suddenly his eyes rolled back in his head, darkness caved in around him, and he collapsed, unconscious, onto the floor.

~112~

Angela was in the kitchen when she heard the thump.

"Zeke?" she shouted, moving quickly to the staircase. "You okay?"

When she didn't get a response she ran up the stairs and tried to open the door but it was blocked. "Zeke?"

Again no response. She put her shoulder to the door and managed to push it open just far enough to peek inside. She let out a gasp when she saw Banyon's hand laying palm up at her feet.

"Zeke!"

She pushed against the door, opening it another few inches, and squeezed into the room.

He was lying face down, his body blocking the door. She knelt beside him and struggled to turn him over onto his back. His body was heavy and seemed lifeless. She couldn't tell if he was breathing.

"Oh my god!" she cried.

With a final heave she rolled him over. His chest was moving. He was live.

"Zeke?"

No response.

"Zeke! Come on!"

No response.

When it was clear that he was not going to respond she ran to the phone and dialed 911.

~113~

At the hospital, Angela paced nervously back and forth across the waiting room floor. Hospitals made her feel uncomfortable even if she wasn't a patient. She'd always felt that way. She didn't know why. Now she was more than uncomfortable. She was scared. She glanced up at the clock. It was nearly 4:30 in the afternoon. *Over an hour! What's taking them so long?*

"Miss Martin? Angela Martin?"

Angela spun around. "Yes?"

"I'm Doctor Heron. I've been examining your fiancé."

Angela stepped forward. "Is he going to be all right?"

"Please," the doctor said, gesturing toward a chair. "Have a seat."

Angela hesitated then sat down. Doctor Heron took a seat facing her and informed her that Banyon was in a coma.

She stared at the doctor. Heron. The name fit. His large hooked nose looked like a bird's beak and seemed artificially attached to his thinly chiseled face. His oversized horn-rimmed glasses were much too wide for his face and the thick lenses magnified greatly the true size of his moist gray eyes. *In a coma?* She heard the doctor's words but they didn't make sense. "I'm sorry. What did you say?"

The doctor repeated the diagnosis. Banyon was in a comatose state. That was the bad news. The good news was that, although Banyon remained unconscious, his body was responding to pain stimuli. A needle poke on the foot, a pinch on the arm, and other simple tests all resulted in immediate and appropriate physiological reactions. A lack of physical reaction to such stimuli would indicate a very deep comatose level, the kind from which patients often never recover. Banyon's condition, by comparison, was more hopeful.

Angela shook her head. "I don't understand. What does that mean? How long will this last? Will he be okay?"

"We need to run some more tests. But I can tell you that in cases like this the patient could regain conscious in as short a time as just a few hours. On the other hand, it could be days. Possibly even weeks. It's impossible to say for sure. There's simply no way to know. But it would help if you'd be willing to answer some questions."

Angela couldn't believe what she was hearing. *How can this be happening?*

"Would you mind stepping into my office?"

Angela shook her head, dazed, trying to process the information. The doctor's voice seemed far off in the distance. "I'm sorry. What?"

"I'd like to ask you some questions about Mr. Banyon to see if we can give his condition a position on the Glascow Coma Scale."

"The what?"

The doctor stood up. "This way, if you would, please. I'll explain it to you in my office."

Doctor Heron explained that the Glascow Coma Scale was a system of examination that served as an indicator of the severity of the patient's condition. In addition to the actual physical exam, blood work, and other procedures, there are a number of questions that can be asked of a family member or anyone who knows the patient intimately. The Glascow Scale, he told her, is based on a point system. The results of these various procedures produce a range of points on the scale. Three points is the minimum and indicates an extremely deep coma with little chance of recovery. The highest number of points, indicating an extremely mild case, is fifteen. Most patients, he told her, fall somewhere in the middle.

"Like I said," the doctor continued, "we need to run more tests, including an MRI. But whatever you can tell me, added to what we have already observed, will help me give you a better idea of what we may be facing here."

Angela agreed to tell him whatever she could.

After asking a few questions about Banyon's general health and activities, he asked if she knew what Banyon was doing just prior to his collapse. She hesitated for a moment, not sure how to respond.

"Well," she said, "actually he was meditating."

Heron slid his glasses part way down his beak and peered over the rims. "Meditating?"

"Yes. Um… sort of a transcendental type of meditation. He's sort of… um… self taught, I guess you would say."

The doctor seemed amused.

"What?" Angela asked.

"Well," Heron smiled, "it's just rather paradoxical. Transcendental meditation is actually what some coma survivors use as part of their recovery therapy. I don't think it could have been the *cause* of the coma."

"Well, you asked me what he was doing. That's what he was doing."

The doctor rubbed his chin and wrote something on his chart. "Interesting. But I'm guessing the coma was more likely caused by the blow to his head. Probably when he fell. But I am interested in what you were telling me. How long has he been practicing this meditation technique?"

"I don't know. A couple of weeks maybe. But he's able to go pretty deep into trance."

The doctor looked surprised. "A couple of weeks? That's all? And he achieves a deep trance state?"

"I know it seems unusual but..." She stopped herself from saying any more as it dawned on her that this line of questioning could lead to her revealing more information than she should let out. She was torn. If the information could help Banyon then how could she not tell what she knew?

"Has he ever described these deep trance states to you? I mean has he ever claimed to have had visions? Anything of that sort?"

Angela took a deep breath and told the doctor about the Pillar of Light and the Teacher that Banyon understood to be his higher self. Noticing the skeptical expression on the doctor's face, she stopped short of mentioning anything about the pineal gland and a Third Eye. *Yeah, like that'd go over real well*, she thought.

The doctor continued jotting notes on his chart. "And you say he actually has conversations with this... this pillar of light? This teacher?"

Angela nodded.

The doctor jotted more notes. "Has he ever had any sort of unusual visions or claimed to hear disembodied voices – or anything of that sort - during times of *normal* consciousness that you know of?"

Angela thought about the information download phenomenon and the sudden revelation at Kline's cabin concerning the Capstone and it's purpose. This wasn't exactly the same as hearing voices or seeing visions. But there *were* the strange dreams with images of the Eltanin

Antenna and the merkaba. *Does that count?* she wondered. But something told her it was better left unsaid. "Well, sort of," she shrugged, faking a tone of indifference. "Maybe once or twice. Nothing specific. I don't remember exactly what it was. I just brushed it off as a fanciful daydream."

She watched as the doctor made more notations on his chart. Then she added, "Zeke's really just a very normal guy, actually."

The doctor studied his notes for a minute and then looked at Angela. "Are you familiar with a medical condition known as temporal lobe epilepsy?"

She'd never heard of it but it didn't sound good. She shook her head. "No. Why? What is it?"

Heron explained that it was a neurological disorder often causing people so afflicted to have what they truly believe are religious experiences.

Angela shifted in her chair. She wanted a cigarette. "Religious experiences?"

Heron nodded, observing her reaction. "Yes, you know, hearing the voice of God, seeing visions of everything from Buddha to the Virgin Mary to Jesus Christ himself. Sometimes the patient even claims to have out-of-body experiences. We believe it may even be the cause of the so-called alien abduction experience. You may have heard of it."

Angela was becoming increasingly uncomfortable.

The doctor smiled. "But it's all just hallucination."

"Hallucination?"

"Yes. Audio hallucinations. Visual hallucinations. None of it is real, obviously."

Angela nodded. "Obviously." Then she asked, "Are you suggesting Zeke is suffering from this... this..."

The doctor leaned back in his chair and put the chart aside. "Temporal lobe epilepsy. Well, I can't say for sure. Like I said, we'll know more after a thorough examination."

Angela shuddered. *Could it be true?* It seemed impossible that all of Banyon's experiences could have been nothing more than hallucinations. "Can I see him?"

Heron stood up and moved out from behind his desk. "Of course. For a few minutes."

Angela followed the doctor down a long corridor to the neurology wing of the hospital. He stopped at room N-108. The number didn't escape Angela's attention. *Hallucination my ass.*

"Here we are," Heron said, opening the door. He walked in ahead of her and checked the chart at the foot of Banyon's bed. Then he looked at Angela. "Five minutes," he said, moving toward the door. "I'll leave you alone now. We'll call you with any further updates on his condition."

Angela thanked him and turned to look at Banyon. He was lying peacefully under the crisp white sheets. His sleeping body was connected to all the tubes and wires and monitoring devices she'd seen in a dozen hospital dramas on TV. She pulled up a chair and sat beside him. Her eyes welled up. "Hey, Chosen One," she whispered "It's me." She reached out and held his warm but otherwise lifeless hand. "God damn it, Zeke," she said softly as the tears flowed freely. "You better not leave me."

~114~

Angela returned home from the hospital, tired and emotionally spent. Sitting alone on the couch, the house seemed somehow larger and disturbingly quiet. Almost morbidly so. It was a familiar feeling. She'd felt it before when her husband passed away. She shuddered and swallowed hard. *That was then, this is now,* she reminded herself, shaking off the painful memory. *Zeke's not dead, for crying out loud. He'll be all right. The doctor as much as said so.*

An hour passed before she knew it and she had chain-smoked four cigarettes without realizing it. *All right,* she scolded herself, *I've got to do something. I can't just sit here. I'd better call Alan.*

Kline was predictably shocked by the news but disagreed with the doctor's suggestion that Banyon might be suffering from temporal lobe epilepsy.

"Ridiculous," he said. "You don't believe that for a minute, do you?"

Angela hesitated. "No, I guess not."

"You *guess* not? Angela, come on! Think about it! Temporal lobe epilepsy doesn't make physical items magically appear! The gold box, the scroll, the ankh. They're all right there in your own home! They're real!"

"I know. I know. You're right."

"Well, then..."

"It's just that..."

"It's just that nothing," Kline came back at her. Then, reminding himself of her situation and her state of mind, he backed off. "Forgive me," he said. "I didn't mean to jump on you. Are you all right?"

"I guess so, yes. I'll be fine."

"Do you want me to come over? Are you all okay alone?"

"No, that's okay. Really. I'll be fine."

"You're sure."

"Yes."

"All right. Well, I better get hold of Crown right away and let him know what's happened. In the meantime you should call Miriam and Rajani. Set up a meeting. I think we should all get together as soon as possible."

~115~

The next morning, having received the news from Kline, Crown convened an emergency meeting of the Nine to inform them of the situation. The tone of the meeting was somber. The news generated grave concern not just for Banyon but for the future of the entire mission. Nothing less than the survival of the planet was at stake.

"Six weeks," said one of the Nine. "That's all we have. Six weeks!"

"What can we do?" asked another. "It seems the situation is completely out of our hands and time is running out."

"For the most part, yes," Crown agreed. "But not entirely. You'll notice we have one empty seat at the table. One of our members is not with us today."

"Doctor Nazarovich," said one of the other members. "He's still in Russia?"

"He is, yes," Crown advised them.

Dimitri Petrov Nazarovich was not only a senior member of the Brotheood of the Nine Pillars. He was also Chief neurosurgeon at the Polivanov Neurological Research Institute in St. Petersburg, Russia and he was preparing to receive a very important patient.

"The hospital in Seattle agreed to such a transfer?" one of the Nine asked with great surprise.

Crown shrugged. "I pulled some strings."

"How soon?" asked another.

Crown looked at his watch. "In less than two hours Banyon's body will be on a plane to Saint Petersburg."

"But why?" asked one of the Nine. "What can be done for him there that can't be done here?"

"Perhaps nothing," Crown conceded. "It's more of a security precaution than anything else. The facility in Seattle is too vulnerable to a possible intrusion by the enemy. I don't want to take any chances. The situation is bad enough as it is. Besides, Nazarovich is the top neurosurgeon in the world. The *Chosen One* will be in the best possible hands. If and when he recovers he'll be returned here immediately. That's all we can do."

Angela arrived at the hospital at noon, intending to spend a few minutes with Banyon. The nurse at the front desk, however, informed her that he was no longer in the hospital's care.

Angela's eyes narrowed as she glared at the nurse. "What the hell do you mean he's no longer in the hospital's care? What are you talking about? Where is he? I want to see him! Now!"

The young nurse, innocently unaware of the details of the situation, was shaken by Angela's outburst. "I'm sorry ma'am. I only know..."

Angela was furious. She flew into a rage. Leaning over the counter, she grabbed the nurse's sleeve. "I want to see Doctor Heron! You get him for me, right now!"

"I... I'm sorry..." the nurse stammered. "Doctor Heron is not here today. He's..."

"Angela!" A familiar voice shouted from somewhere behind.

Angela spun around. It was Kline. He'd just entered the hospital and was moving quickly down the hall. He seemed out of breath.

Angela looked confused. "Alan! What are you doing here?"

Kline caught up with her and paused to catch his breath. "I tried to phone you but you weren't home. I guessed you were probably on your way here to see Zeke. I was hoping to catch you before you got here so I could tell you..."

Angela reached out and grabbed him by both arms. "Tell me *what*?" she demanded. "What's happening? Where's Zeke? What have they done with him?"

"Please," Kline said, trying to calm her fears. "Don't worry. He's all right. Come outside so we can talk."

They found a bench outside and took a seat.

When Angela learned from Kline what had transpired without her knowledge or consent she was furious. "Saint Petersburg!" she shouted. "What the fuck are you talking about? Why wasn't I told about this?"

It took some doing but Kline finally managed to get her calmed down enough to grasp what he was trying to tell her.

"So," he explained, "Crown wanted to make sure everything was in place to carry out the plan before he called me and asked me to call you. I called you as soon as I could but you were already gone. I figured you were on your way to the hospital so I got here as fast as I could."

Angela closed her eyes and drew a deep breath. "Okay. All right," she relented. Her hands were still shaking as she fumbled through her purse and pulled out a cigarette.

Kline produced a lighter, gave it a flick, and lit it for her.

"Thanks," she muttered softly. She stood up and paced around in a circle. Finally she stopped and looked at Kline. Her rage had subsided and turned into resignation. Her eyes glistened as she fought back the tears. "So," she pleaded, "what do we do now?"

Kline shook his head slowly and shrugged. At this point he was as much in the dark as she was. There was only one answer he could give her. "We wait."

~116~

DuPont noticed a small cobweb had started to form on the upper right corner of the ornate goldwork that so elegantly framed his own life-sized self-portrait. It hung prominently on the richly dark paneled wall exactly opposite from his desk so he could admire it easily from the comfort of his large, contoured leather chair. The painting was a work he had commissioned just two years ago by Gianni Valerio, an artist highly regarded for his mastery of the Renaissance style. DuPont's deep-set eyes, the crevasses that crisscrossed his face like the cracks in a parched desert floor and the thick black hair - white at the temples - all presented a formidable countenance and these physical features were aptly portrayed. But Valerio had also somehow captured several facets of DuPont's personality in the remarkable painting, including what most people interpreted as his legendary arrogance. DuPont interpreted it as his stalwart confidence.

He got up from his desk, opened a small cabinet and retrieved a feather duster. Just as he was about to snag the cobweb, the phone rang. Annoyed by the interference, he walked back to his desk and answered it. "DuPont," he grumbled.

A man's voice with a thick British accent was on the other end of the line.

"I have some good news for you, DuPont."

It was Mr. York, the Illuminati representative that had been DuPont's only contact with the Illuminati from the beginning.

Mr. York seemed to not have a first name and DuPont was never sure that York was the man's real surname. He suspected not. But it didn't matter. Whatever the man's name was, he was positioned at a considerably high level on the proverbial Illuminati pyramid.

DuPont walked around his desk and slid back into the comfortable contour of his leather chair. "Hello, Mr. York. Good to hear from you. What is the news?"

The news was remarkable. Almost unbelievable. But DuPont was not surprised. Given the deep pockets of the Illuminati and the length of their innumerable tentacles, they could reach into back rooms and private offices that most people didn't even know existed.

York informed DuPont that the mode of transport for their rendezvous with destiny in the Antarctic Ocean had been obtained. By sheer providence it happened that the final sea trials of Italy's newest aircraft carrier, the *Cavour*, was scheduled to take place during the last week in July and the first week in August. The Italian Navy had been *persuaded* – "quote, unquote," York added – to assist them under a quickly conceived and covertly implemented top-secret project. A skeleton crew of highly trained personnel – each with a security clearance – would operate the ship with a full arsenal of weapons including two attack helicopters.

"Why am I not surprised," DuPont said. "That is extraordinary news. But now I'm afraid I have news that is not so good. Banyon had some sort of an accident and is currently in a coma under the watchful eye of a Doctor Nazarovich at the Polivanov Neurological Research Institute in St. Petersburg."

York was genuinely surprised yet at the same time his voice betrayed an unexpected tone of indifference. "Well," he replied, "isn't that interesting. A coma, eh? What the hell is he doing in Russia? What's his prognosis?"

"I wasn't able to get any more information," DuPont said. "Security is tight."

"Well, it doesn't matter. Banyon or no Banyon, nothing will keep the Nine from going ahead with the retrieval mission. The only thing that matters is that we gain possession of the Capstone as soon as it is raised and secured aboard their vessel – whatever that might be. Probably a barge. Maybe a large cargo ship. Even if they're armed – which we assume is likely – they won't put up much of a fight when they're confronted with the full arsenal of the *Cavour*. Resistance, as they say, would be futile."

DuPont sat up in his chair. "Aren't you forgetting something?" he asked, pointedly.

"What do you mean?"

"You seem to have forgotten that Banyon is the only one who can activate the Capstone! And from the information I received just a few days ago, the Capstone must be activated right then and there – at that precise location – to prevent the comet from impacting the earth! What if Banyon doesn't recover from the coma in time? Or at all, for that matter! The prophecy says…"

York laughed smugly. "I guess the time has come to let you in on the truth."

DuPont was taken aback. "The truth? What do you mean the *truth*? The truth about what?"

"The truth is we don't believe that part of the prophecy. We never did. There is no comet. It's a myth. A fairytale. All we're concerned with is the Capstone. It's our destiny. It will fulfill the promise depicted in our symbol emblazoned on the American dollar bill. The all-seeing eye in the triangle, the Capstone above the pyramid."

"What are you saying?"

"It's the symbol of the ultimate power that will be ours when we possess the Capstone. It's really as simple as that."

"But the Capstone – the *real* Capstone - is… it's…"

"It's not exactly what you think it is," York interrupted. "We believe it is a suppository of knowledge. Knowledge beyond our current comprehension. The secrets of the Universe. If knowledge is power – and it is – then we will have the ultimate knowledge, the ultimate power. Like I said, it's really as simple as that." His voice was cold as steel. "Banyon or no Banyon, it doesn't matter. What matters is that we will finally get what is destined to be ours. Total control of the planet. The New World Order."

"But…" DuPont protested, "…what if you're wrong about the prophecy – about the comet? Then what? There'll be no planet left to control! The Capstone won't do you much good then, will it!"

York was becoming annoyed by DuPont's persistence. "Perhaps I didn't make myself clear. There is no comet. That part of the prophecy is a fallacy. A lie. The future of the earth will soon be in *our* hands! Not in the hands of Mr. Banyon! And certainly not in the hands of the Nine! Their time is over. Our time has come!"

"But," DuPont fired back, "if Banyon does survive and he is there when the Capstone is raised, are you telling me you won't even allow him to perform the activation? That's insane! If you're wrong about that part of the prophecy then you'd be making a tragic mistake!"

York chuckled patronizingly. "You're an old fool, DuPont. Just do what you're told. So far you've performed admirably. You've served us well. Don't change course now. Trust me. You'll be rewarded beyond your wildest dreams."

With those final words Mr. York abruptly ended the call and left Dupont in a state of anger and confusion. Was it possible that York was right? Could that part of the prophecy be nothing more than a mythological tale? A fabrication mistakenly – or even intentionally, for some reason – tacked onto the original prophecy of the coming of the *Chosen One*? Was Banyon's singular purpose in all of this nothing more than to raise the Capstone from its watery grave only to pass it into the hands of the Illuminati? Was this truly nothing more than the way in which their manifest destiny would come to pass?

DuPont had no problem with the idea of the Illuminati's plans for global control, a One-World Government under the flag of their New World Order. He'd been expecting it all along. He never doubted they would eventually achieve that goal. He'd been promised an important position in this new governing body from the beginning. It was to be his reward for his covert service to them. But all of this was supposed to happen *after* the earth was saved from its otherwise inevitable collision with the destroyer comet! *That* was supposed to be the true purpose – the ultimate mission – of the *Chosen One*!

DuPont got up from his chair behind the desk and began pacing the confines of his office. Then he stopped for a moment and turned to look at his self-portrait. The face in the portrait was stoic, assured, confident. Until this very moment the painting had been an accurate portrayal of the man who had risen up through the ranks of his Order like a shooting star, always on course, never wavering, never for one minute doubtful about what he was doing or where he was going. Now he wasn't so sure.

He stood glaring up into the eyes of the man in the portrait and shouted in frustration. "The truth! I want the truth, God damn it!"

But the portrait only stared back at him, its frozen confidence now oddly surreal, unfamiliar, condescending.

He turned away, frustrated. He had no way of knowing what the truth was. He could only hope York was right – that there was no comet, no imminent threat of total global annihilation. But deep down in his gut he was afraid York was wrong. And the horrifying fact of the dilemma was that he could do nothing about it.

He wandered back to his desk and sat, slumped in his leather chair, chasing his own thoughts around and around in his head. It suddenly occurred to him how easy it had been for him to send others to their death in his obsessive drive to serve the Illuminati. Now he prayed the Illuminati were not about to send him to his own death – along with the rest of the world that he normally seemed to care little about.

As a kaleidoscope of thoughts whirled through his head his mind unexpectedly conjured up a dusty half-forgotten memory from his childhood. He and his best friend, Tony Miller, couldn't have been more than six or seven years old at the time. They were playing with Tony's new red wagon in the vacant lot down the street when Tony tripped and fell, striking his head on the sharp edge of a large rock. The blood began to flow from the wound. *Tony! Come on! Get up!* But Tony didn't move. Realizing something was terribly wrong DuPont managed to lift Tony into the wagon. He ran, pulling the wagon as fast as he could to Tony's house, three blocks away. It was an act that literally aided in saving Tony's life. Several days later, when Tony returned home from the hospital, Tony's father put his arms around DuPont and thanked him for having helped save his son's life. *You're a darn fine young man, Bernard*, he said to DuPont. *You'll grow up to do great things, I have no doubt.* DuPont swelled with pride. *Thanks, Mister Miller! Maybe I'll become a fireman or maybe a doctor and save lots of people's lives!*

As the vision of the recollection faded, a ray of pale orange light from the setting sun popped in through the window and crept along the dark paneled wall. He followed it with his eyes as it eventually passed over the golden crucifix that hung next to his self-portrait. He looked at the holy symbol for a moment and then turned away. Staring at the floor he shook his head and wondered silently to himself. *What have I become?*

~117~

Aside from Angela, herself, Professor Kline was the only member of Banyon's group that was aware of Banyon's current situation. Angela decided to call for an emergency meeting to inform the others. They met at Banyon's home as usual.

Miriam and Rajani were visibly shaken by the news. The situation presented them with a range of disturbing and conflicting emotions. Their good friend – the warm and gentle man who had entered into and dramatically changed their lives - was in a critical condition from which he might never recover. At the same time, the mission – and therefore, their own lives, as well as the rest of the unsuspecting world - were in equal jeopardy. If the entire human population of the planet were to be wiped out from the impact of the comet then the reality was that Banyon's recovery – as much as it pained them to admit it – was a moot point. Everything – including Banyon - would be gone.

But Miriam tried to stay focused. In an act of genuine compassion, recognizing the depth of Angela's distress, she reached over and laid a gentle hand on Angela's arm. "Angela," she said, softly, "I'd be happy to stay here with you for a few days if you'd like. Anything I can do..."

Given the history of tension that Angela had sensed between Miriam and herself – perhaps foolishly and mistakenly, as she now realized – she was surprised and moved by the offer but she gracefully declined. "Thank you, but I'll be all right," she said, tearfully. She struggled to hold back the tears and tried to sound confident. "I know you're all as close as the phone if I need you."

Several minutes of silence passed uncomfortably. Professor Kline fiddled with his old leather tobacco pouch, his short stout fingers mindlessly kneading it like it was a hunk of dough. Each member of the group was absorbed in their own private thoughts, a mix of confusion, desperation, and a thin thread of hope.

Then, in a moment of clarity, Angela had an alarming thought. *Was this the meaning of the vision in Zeke's most recent dream? He said the dream indicated that I would have an important role in activating the Capstone!* "Oh my god!" she said, sitting bolt upright in her chair.

The others were startled by her sudden outburst.

Kline dropped his pouch and looked up. "Jesus, Angela, what is it?"

She told them about Banyon's dream and struggled to recall exactly what it was he had told her. "I think he said somehow I hold the key to the success of the entire mission!"

Kline looked puzzled, as did everyone else. "What did he mean?"

Angela shook her head and tried to think. "All I can remember is that it had something to do with my name. Something about activating the Capstone, I think! I didn't know what that meant and neither did Zeke. He just said we'd probably find out soon enough. That was all, really. We didn't talk about it anymore."

"I don't understand," Miriam said. "Are you saying that if Zeke…" she paused a moment and lowered her eyes. She wanted to choose her words carefully so as not to sound insensitive. She looked up again. "Are you saying if Zeke doesn't recover, that somehow you can activate the Capstone yourself? You know how to do that?"

Angela was now the focus of attention for an entirely new reason. They were all wondering the same thing: Was there a chance? Could she activate the Capstone?

"No!" Angela said. "I mean, yes." She shook her head in frustration. "What I mean is, it seemed as if that was the idea, yes. But Zeke didn't know for sure and he never had a chance to find out more!"

Miriam thought for a moment and then had an idea. "You say it had something to do with your name?"

"Yes," Angela nodded. "But…"

"I bet it has something to do with the alphanumeric value of your name," Miriam suggested. "Do you know what it is?"

"Yes. It's one-forty-four."

"Of course," Miriam nodded with a knowing smile. "I should have guessed. Well, that number has played such an important part in so many ways I wouldn't be at all surprised if it's a clue to your part in the activation process."

"I wouldn't be surprised either," Angela replied. "But how?"

It was a good question but Miriam had to confess she had no answer. She was just reaching for anything hoping something might trigger an idea.

Kline stepped into the conversation. "As I understand it," he said, adjusting his glasses, "Zeke's ability to activate the Capstone is all dependent upon his ability to exercise the power of his Third Eye. Isn't that right?"

Angela nodded.

"And his ability to exercise that power has come from those – what does he call them? – reverse mantra trance sessions. Right?"

"Yes," Angela said cautiously, not quite sure where Kline was going with this.

"Well," the professor continued, "is it possible that you could learn to access the power of your own Third Eye by chanting Zeke's reverse mantra?"

Angela looked puzzled. "I don't know. It never crossed my mind."

"I can tell you now, it would not work," Rajani interjected. "That mantra was created for Zeke and for Zeke only. A mantra like that is specifically tailored to an individual's own vibrational frequency. It is a very special gift and will do nothing for anyone except the one for whom it was created."

Kline sat back and accepted Rajani's comment, realizing Rajani was much more knowledgeable on the subject than anyone else in the room.

As the discussion about Angela's mysterious key role wore on, they realized they were getting nowhere. Further speculation seemed pointless without more information and the only source for such information, so far, had been the Teacher. And the only access to the Teacher was directly through Banyon. And Banyon – in some strange but apparently very real sense – *was* the Teacher. It was a closed circle with no way in except through Banyon himself.

Everything hung in the balance now and only the Chosen One could tip that balance in their favor. They had no choice but to wait and pray to whatever higher power was running this strange and unpredictable show.

~118~

Doctor Nazarovich called Angela every afternoon to keep her apprised of Banyon's condition. But the news was not good. The days passed with no sign of improvement. A week went by. Two weeks. Three. Four. And still nothing. The thin thread of hope that they were all clinging to was being stretched to the limit. *Perhaps,* Angela thought to herself on yet another sleepless night, *perhaps that higher power had abandoned them. Or maybe there was no higher power at all.* Suddenly the phone rang. Angela's heart jumped. *The doctor!*

She threw back the covers, turned on the light and reached for the phone but she stopped just short of picking it up. She turned cold, her body froze like a marble statue. Never before had the doctor called in the middle of the night. *Why now?* She almost didn't want to know the answer.

~119~

Bolstered by hope on the one hand but filled with an anxious trepidation on the other, Angela stared at the phone. Nervously, she picked it up and cleared her throat. "Hello?"

"Miss Martin?"

Angela immediately recognized the deep, rich voice of Dr. Nazarovich. His command of the English language was nearly flawless despite the heaviness of his native Russian accent.

Angela swallowed hard. "Yes."

"Miss Martin, I have good news."

Angela gasped so deeply she couldn't respond. A torrent of emotions rushed through her body. Her eyes welled up.

The doctor continued. "Mr. Banyon awoke from his coma about two hours ago."

"Is he all right?" she asked, with reserved excitement. "Can I talk to him?"

"Yes, he is well. Remarkably so, I might add. As you can imagine, however, he was quite disoriented and confused. I explained the situation to him, told him where he was and why he was here. It took him a while to comprehend what I was saying but eventually he seemed to understand."

Angela wiped the tears from her face. "Can I talk to him?"

"I'm afraid not at the moment. He is sleeping now."

"But he's all right, yes?"

"He is, indeed. His condition is amazingly stable. I have never seen anything quite like it."

A series of tests, the doctor told her, had revealed absolutely no brain damage. In fact Banyon's physical condition showed none of the usual signs of having been in a comatose state for nearly five weeks. Nazarovich used the word 'miraculous' at least twice in the few minutes he spent describing the situation to her.

Under normal circumstances, he told her, the patient would have to remain in the hospital for some period of time to regain strength and to undergo more tests. But he knew these circumstances were far from ordinary in nearly every way imaginable. Banyon would be released within the next twenty-four hours. A private jet was ready and waiting to take him home.

Nazarovich, being one of the oldest members of the Nine, understood the situation only too well. The Great Dragon was coming. There was no time to lose.

Part 3: Countdown

~120~

Sunday, July 30, 2006

B anyon's plane landed at the Boeing airfield in Everett, just a few miles north of Seattle, where he was immediately shuttled into a limousine, provided courtesy of Nathan Crown.

When the limo pulled up to the house, Angela rushed out to greet him. With tears streaming down her face she crushed him up against the side of the car and they locked in an emotional embrace. The driver smiled and patiently waited for the lovebirds to step free of his vehicle. After a full minute he finally rolled down the window and leaned out.

"Will that be all, Mr. Banyon?"

Banyon grinned, embarrassed, and stepped away from the car with Angela still clinging to him. "Yes, thank you," he said. "And thank Mr. Crown for me too, will you?"

The driver smiled. "You can thank him yourself in just a few minutes."

Banyon looked surprised. "He's coming here?"

The driver shook his head."Expect a phone call." Then he pushed a button on the console, the window rolled up and he drove away.

Banyon turned to Angela as if he was just now seeing her for the very first time. He drew her close for another long kiss. Then, as he wiped a tear from her cheek, his own emotions welled up and it was Angela's turn to brush his tears away.

"What are the neighbors going to think?" he chuckled. "Let's go inside. We've got some catching up to do."

The phone rang the moment they walked into the house. Banyon was visibly perturbed by the intrusion. He shook his head. "Of course," he muttered. "No rest for the wicked."

It was a phrase his mother had often used when she was cleaning house which, when he thought about it, seemed to have been most of the time. Still, as a child, he could never understand why she said that. *You're not wicked, mom,* he would say. *You're a lot nicer than Bobby Hoagland's mom!* Of course the fact that Bobby Hoagland's dad abandoned the family and left Mrs. Hoagland to raise four kids on her own may have had something to do with Mrs. Hoagland's unpleasant demeanor and frightfully short temper. But little Zeke Banyon was too young at the time to put all that together.

Angela was still clinging to his arm. "The driver said Crown would call," she sighed. "Must be him. I guess you better get it."

Banyon plopped himself down on the couch and took the call.

Crown's voice was exuberant. "So the Chosen One returns!"

Banyon smiled. "Yes, and I want to thank you for everything. That doctor... Nazarovich? He was..."

"He's one of us," Crown said. "I knew you'd be in the best of hands. How are you doing?"

"Well, to tell you the truth, my head is still spinning."

There was a brief pause before Crown replied. "I hope you mean that figuratively."

"What? Oh! Yes, I didn't mean it literally. No, I'm fine, really. I just mean the whole episode has been a bit disorienting. I just now got in the house. Angela and I haven't even had a chance to talk."

"I understand. And I won't keep you. I just wanted to welcome you home and tell you the good news."

Banyon sat up. "I'm listening."

"Construction of the levitation device is completed. It's ready."

The news sent a chill up Banyon's spine. "God, I can't believe it! That's great! So what do we do now?"

"Well, for right now, you just get some rest. I'll contact you in two days with a full itinerary. There's been a slight change in the original plans."

"Itinerary? Change?"

"Yes. We'll be departing from..." he paused. He still didn't have permission to reveal where they would be departing from. "...from the location where the levitation device is located on Wednesday, August the second instead of Tuesday the first."

Banyon's back stiffened. "Jesus!" he fired back. "Are you serious? *Why,* for God's sake? The original plan was cutting it too close for comfort as it was! Now this!"

"I know. I know. It can't be helped. Believe me."

"Can't be helped? What the hell is the problem?"

"Red tape, to put it simply. Something about security clearances and the Delta-3. That's all I was told and that's all I can tell you."

Banyon was incredulous. "Are you kidding me? Red tape? We're talking about trying to avoid a global catastrophe here, for Christ's sake!"

"Zeke, listen to me. There is nothing I can do. Believe it or not there are some things beyond my control. This is one of them."

Banyon sank back into the couch, exasperated. He let out a long sigh. "All right," he said, reluctantly. "I'm sorry. I just..."

"No apology is necessary, my friend. Like I said, I'll call you in two days with more information. Until then you just get your rest. You'll need it. The future of the entire human race will soon be in your hands."

Banyon shuddered. "Thanks for reminding me. I can hardly wait." He hung up the phone and lit a cigarette.

Angela walked over and sat next to him.

"What'd he say?" she asked. "You look worried."

He took her hand and gave a tender squeeze.

"Well," he said, "the good news is the donut – the levitation device – is ready to go. The bad news is our departure for the Antarctic has been delayed by a day. We're not leaving now until Wednesday!"

Angela looked shocked. "Wednesday? That's..."

"Yeah, the second of August. Three days from now."

"But..."

Banyon shook his head. "Crown says it can't be helped. Something about red tape. If you can believe that. He said he'd call us in two days with more information. Our itinerary, as he put it. In the meantime we should call Kline and the others to let them know what's..." He stopped short as a pre-coma memory came flooding into his brain.. "Oh, Jesus!" he blurted.

Angela jumped. "What's the matter?"

"Caldwell! I was supposed to call him! Remember? I talked to him briefly, earlier on the same day I fell after the meditation session. I told him I'd call him the next day around noon to arrange for him to come here so he could join the rest of the group!"

Angela nodded. "Right. I remember."

A troubled look crossed Banyon's face. He turned to Angela. "And he didn't call you?" he asked her. "Like the next day? You never heard from him?"

Angela shook her head. "No. I mean, I hate to admit it, but with all that happened to you I didn't even think about it. I just..."

"That's not right. He would have called when he didn't hear from me. I know he would have. It's been weeks now. It doesn't make sense."

Angela agreed. She nodded toward the phone. "You better call him now."

Banyon grabbed the phone and dialed the number but got a recording:

The number you have dialed has been disconnected or is no longer in service.

"What the..." he muttered. *Maybe I dialed wrong.* He tried calling again but got the same recording. He stared at Angela. "His number's been disconnected."

"What?"

"Something's wrong. I can feel it." Then he remembered back to the last conversation he'd had with Caldwell. "Something seemed odd when I talked to him. I asked him if he was all right and he said he just had a cold. But then he said... what was it? He made some comment about if for some reason he couldn't make it... couldn't come here to be with us." Then the worst possible thought crossed Banyon's mind. "Jesus," he said, "do you think he was sicker than he let on? What if he's... What if it was more than just a cold? But then, why wouldn't he just tell me about it?"

"Knowing him," Angela said, "and with all that was going on here, he probably figured you had enough on your mind and didn't want you to be worrying about him."

Banyon rolled that around in his mind for a minute. It made sense. Maybe that was it. Still, there was the fact that several weeks had passed. There could only be one reason he never called. The thought of his good friend dying was more than he could bear but he had to find out the truth. *But how?*

He didn't know any of Caldwell's relatives. The only connection he could think of was the college where Caldwell had been teaching part time. *I'll start there.*

He made the call and learned the crushing truth. His friend was dead.

"But... how?" he asked the college administrator. "What happened? Was it a heart attack?"

"Are you a relative?" the administrator inquired.

"No," Banyon explained. "Father Caldwell and I were good friends of many years. I've been... well, out of touch for a while. But I'd like to know what happened."

Caldwell, the college administrator explained, had been on sabbatical and was working on a novel. One of Caldwell's favorite students – a young lady named Shelly Preston - had called Caldwell at his home to see if she could solicit his help with a paper she was writing. It was an arrangement she and Caldwell had made just prior to taking his sabbatical. But when he didn't answer the phone she left a message asking him to please return the call. But of course he never did.

"When was this?" Banyon asked.

"Must have been four weeks ago," the administrator replied. "Maybe five."

That caught Banyon's attention. "Can you be more precise? Do you have the date?"

"Let me see. Can you hang on for a moment?"

Banyon waited.

The administrator returned to the phone. "That would have been on a Monday," he informed Banyon, "Monday, the twenty-sixth of June."

The twenty-sixth? Banyon got up and carried the phone with him into the kitchen. Checking the calendar on the wall, he flipped the page back to June. "Jesus," he muttered under his breath.

"What's that?" the administrator asked.

"Nothing. Please go on. What more can you tell me?"

"Well, the student, Miss Preston, tried to call him several more times over the next couple of days. She left a message each time but Father Caldwell never returned any of her calls."

Banyon's legs felt week. His stomach churned. He sat down at the kitchen table and listened as the administrator laid out the rest of the story. Or, at least, the version he knew.

"Miss Preston," the administrator continued, "couldn't understand why he wasn't returning her calls so she drove to his apartment hoping, of course, to find him home. But when she got there she found the door slightly ajar. She called his name but there was no reply. So she opened the door and found him lying on the floor in a pool of blood."

"What!" Banyon cried. "How? What happened?"

"The official report was suicide."

Banyon was shocked. "What! Suicide? That's not possible! Caldwell had no reason to…"

"You might want to talk with Detective Devlin. He's the one who handled the case. Perhaps he can tell you more."

"Devlin?" Banyon asked. "How can I get in touch with him?"

"I can ask him to call you."

Banyon agreed, gave the administrator his number, and walked back into the living room. He was just about to tell Angela what he'd learned when the phone rang. It was Detective Devlin of the N.Y.P.D. He sounded much younger than Banyon had for some reason anticipated and his demeanor seemed less than friendly, almost as if he was irritated by having to make the call. He wanted to know why Banyon was so interested in the case. Banyon explained his long-term friendship with Caldwell.

"I just want to know what happened," Banyon said.

"Suicide," Devlin answered. "Cut and dried."

Banyon protested that such a thing made no sense. It just wasn't possible. But the detective insisted, saying there was no sign of forced entry, no sign of a struggle, no sign of fingerprints, other than Caldwell's and those of that student, Shelly Preston. Her fingerprints were on the door. But she had been fully interrogated and was found completely innocent. She had nothing to do with any of it.

"And Caldwell's own fingerprints were on the gun," the detective added with emphasis. "Open and shut case. Nothin' else I can tell ya." After a pause he added, "Unless, of course, *you* have something to tell me that we don't know."

Banyon had plenty to tell the detective as all the jigsaw pieces of the story suddenly snapped together in his mind, forming a more accurate picture of what must have really happened. "Goddam Jesuits!" he blurted out.

The detective was caught by surprise. "Say again?"

Banyon bit his tongue. "Nothing," he said, lowering the tone of his voice. "Nothing. I'm just... I'm just upset by the news. Thank you for the information, detective. I appreciate it."

"Yeah, well, sorry about your friend," Devlin said, sounding uncharacteristically sympathetic. Then, back into character, he added, "What is it they say? Life's a bitch and then you die?"

Banyon winced and fired back. "You've got a hell of a bedside manner, detective." Then he slammed the phone down and took a deep breath. *Christ Almighty*, he thought to himself. *They killed him. My best friend. The fucking Jesuits killed him! But why?*

Distraught and exhausted, he sat with Angela and told her everything he'd learned from the college administrator and the detective. A deep sadness settled into her heart as she listened to Banyon tell the story. In just the short time she'd known Caldwell during their trip to France she'd become enamored of his warmth and *Old World* charm.

"But why?" she asked. "Why would they kill him?"

Banyon nodded. "Exactly my question," he said. "It doesn't make sense. But nothing else would make sense either. Caldwell didn't have an enemy in the world. At least not that I know of. It had to be the Jesuits, or the goddam Illuminati or whoever else is out there trying to stop what we're doing. But why Father Caldwell? I just don't get it."

Angela puzzled over it for a moment. Then she had an idea. It was such a strange idea that she was almost tempted to not even suggest it. But at this point in the journey it seemed nothing was apparently too strange to at least be opened up for consideration. "This might sound weird," she said, cautiously, "but there might be a way to find out."

Banyon whipped around and shot her a puzzled look. "How?"

"The Teacher."

The Teacher? He stared at her for a moment until the idea sunk in. "You know what? You just might be on to something."

"Do you think you're up to it?"

"I think so. Besides, I need to know if I can still do it."

"All right," she said, looking him squarely in the eyes. "But this time I'm going to be in the room with you. We don't have another five weeks for you to spend in a coma."

"You're the boss," he said. "Let's go."

As he walked into the bedroom he saw the meditation chair still sitting in front of the window. He hesitated, then approached it slowly.

Angela sat on the bed, watching him.

He ran his hand across the back of the chair like stroking a wild beast before climbing onto it. He took a deep breath and sat down. The instant his body made full contact with the chair he recognized a familiar feeling come over him. *Like riding a bicycle*, he thought to himself. He glanced over at Angela.

"I'll be back," he said, deciding to leave out the Schwarzenegger accent.

"I'm counting on it," Angela smiled.

Banyon inhaled deeply and began to chant the mantra. In a few minutes he was in trance and out of his body.

The transition was smoother than ever before. Either someone or some*thing* was helping him or he'd attained a mastery that even he had not realized. Or, he wondered, did it have something to do with the coma? *Some sort of a residual effect? But the coma incident was an accident. Wasn't it?* Before he could think about it any further he saw the familiar Pillar of Light beginning to form. He felt the same sense of awe that had filled him each time the Teacher appeared. Banyon started to ask about Caldwell but the Teacher apparently already knew the question as a three-dimensional holographic image began to form within the Pillar of Light.

As Banyon stared into the light the image slowly came into focus. He gasped. He recognized what he was seeing. It was Caldwell's apartment.

Suddenly the light completely engulfed him and he found himself inside Caldwell's living room! There came a knock at Caldwell's door. Caldwell went to the door and opened it. The man at the door was dressed as a priest. The man said something to Caldwell and Caldwell let him in. Suddenly the man produced a pistol and forced Caldwell back into the room. Then the gunman ordered Caldwell to call Banyon. Now Banyon watched, horrified and helpless, as the entire scene unfolded before his eyes. The phone conversation...the gunman constantly jabbing the gun into Caldwell's ribs, prompting him to ask the pertinent question...

"So... um..." Caldwell stuttered into the phone, *"when are you... um, planning to go? Soon, I suspect, huh?"*

Banyon now recalled those words only too clearly. *So that was it!*

They wanted to know our departure date! Son of a bitch! When the conversation ended, he watched as the gunman pulled Caldwell up off the couch and shoved him into a straight-backed chair and tied him securely to it. Banyon froze as the gunman forced the barrel of the pistol into Caldwell's mouth. Mercifully, the Teacher ended the vision before the final moment of bloodshed. Still, the deafening sound of the gunfire managed to ring out, resonating horrendously through Banyon's soul. The shock of it sent his etheric body into a spin and released him from the trance. Instantly, his eyes snapped open and he sat there panting, emotionally spent, gasping for air.

Angela rushed to his side and helped him over to the bed. His entire body was shaking. She laid him down and knelt beside him and gently wiped the sweat from his forehead.

"Jesus," she said. "Once again, you look like you've just seen a ghost."

He stared at her and nodded slowly. "I did."

Later, when he told Angela what really happened to Caldwell, she was sickened and angry. His death caused her a deep sadness but now, knowing how it happened, she couldn't hold back the tears. Banyon's homecoming was not turning out to be quite as she had imagined. First, the added pressure from the news of the delay in their departure was bad enough. Then finding out Caldwell was dead cast an even darker shadow on the day. And now this.

Curled up on the couch, they consoled each other as best they could. Finally, Angela sat up and tried to pull herself together.

"We need to call Alan and the others," she said.

Banyon nodded. "Yeah, you're right. Let's get everyone together. We should set up a meeting for tomorrow night."

Angela made the calls and they spent the rest of the day thinking back over the events of the past several months. The more they talked the more bizarre the whole thing sounded.

"Nobody in their right mind would believe any of this," he said in all seriousness. Then he started to chuckle. His chuckle turned to laughter and he laughed until he cried. Literally. The dam broke wide open as all the pent up stress and emotions flowed out.

Later that night they made love like it was the first time.

~121~

Monday, July 31, 2006 – 7:29 a.m.

Banyon opened the lid of the precious gold box and stared in shock.

"The ankh!" he cried. "It's gone!" Suddenly he heard a noise behind him. But before he could turn around the cold steel of a pistol barrel gently met the back of his head. He froze. "What the…?"

"Don't turn around," a man's voice calmly commanded. "What did you think? That we'd let you keep the key to the Capstone?" The alarming words were followed by a sinister deep-throated laugh.

Banyon's hands shook. "Where… where's Angela?"

"Angela? Well…" the man paused. "Let's just say she's in a much better place now."

Bayon's eyes widened. His pulse raced. His face turned red. Nothing else mattered now. "You son of a bitch!" he yelled, spinning around in a rage.

The ferocious shout from Banyon's voice and his violent move awakened Angela from a sound sleep.

"Jesus Christ!" she shrieked, rolling out of the way just in time to avoid being crushed by the swift thrust of Banyon's closed fist. She leaped from the bed, catching her breath, trying to make sense of the moment. Then, realizing he was having a bad dream, she leaned in cautiously and grabbed his arm. "Zeke! Wake up! You're dreaming!"

He opened his eyes and stared at her, confused. He was sweating. "Angela! You're all right!"

"Of course I'm all right. You were having a…"

"The ankh!" he interrupted. He threw the covers off and sat straight up.

"What about it? You were dreaming!" she said, trying to calm him.

He looked at her and then looked around the room. "What?"

"A dream," she repeated. "You nearly knocked my block off, for crying out loud."

He shook his head to clear the cobwebs then fell back against the pillow, exhausted and somewhat relieved. But snapshots of the dream kept flashing through his mind. He shot up again and jumped out of bed. Throwing on his robe, he headed out of the room.

Angela put on her robe and followed after him. "Where are you going?" she asked.

In the spare room across the hall, Banyon opened the safe and took out the gold box. He sat on the floor with the box in his lap and quickly manipulated the double-ring fastener. Cautiously, he lifted the lid and let out a weighty sigh of relief.

"It's still here," he said, running his fingers over the ancient artifact. Then he looked up at Angela. Her hair was tousled as if she'd been through a windstorm and her robe was hanging off one shoulder. She looked like a disheveled angel. He smiled. "And *you're* still here."

Looking down at him, she shrugged. "Where else would I be?"

"In a much better place," he muttered.

"Huh?"

He stood up and put the gold box back in the safe. Then he turned to Angela and drew her close. He brushed a wisp of hair back from her face and kissed her on the nose. "Never mind," he said. "You're here. That's all that matters."

7:47 p.m.

Banyon greeted Miriam at the door.

"Great to see you!" he said, smiling.

"No," she beamed. "Great to see *you!*" She reached out and gave his hand a friendly but affectionate squeeze. "You gave us all quite a scare," she scolded him.

He took her coat and hung it in the closet. "Gave myself a pretty good scare," he joked.

She could hear voices coming from the living room. "Am I late?" she asked.

"No, come on in. The others just got here a few minutes ago."

When everyone was settled with a drink in their hands Banyon gave them the rundown on all the latest news, the good and the bad. They were all shocked to hear about Father Caldwell. The circumstances of his death underscored the true gravity of the situation. Not that any of them needed to be reminded. Miriam confessed that the creeping approach of the appointed hour was pushing her anxiety level to the limit. Alan and Alec also admitted to feeling increasingly apprehensive, even fearful, of what was coming.

The conversation veered off in several directions, everyone trying to keep it as light as possible given the enormity of the mission they were about to undertake.

"So," Kline said, "today is Monday and we'll be leaving on Wednesday?"

Banyon nodded. "Yes. Crown will call me tomorrow with the particulars."

"Do you know yet exactly where we'll be going?" Miriam asked. "And how we're going to get there? Where ever *there* is?"

Banyon took a drink and set the glass on the coffee table. "Crown was still reluctant to tell me where we'll be going but I think Alan was right. I think we're going to Area-51. No doubt we'll be taking a plane."

"What plane?" Miriam asked. "I don't think you can just go down to the Sea-Tac airport and ask for a ticket to Area-51."

"I don't know," Banyon said. "As soon as I find out from Crown, I'll call each of you and let you know."

"Well, I know one thing," Miriam said. "I've been monitoring the NASA website and several credible astronomy websites and no one is reporting any comets heading for earth."

"But," Banyon countered, "we knew that was going to be the case. Right?" He scanned each of his guests for signs of agreement. He turned again to Miriam. "Are you beginning to doubt the whole thing?"

Miriam didn't respond one way or the other.

"Look, gang," Banyon said, "if anyone has any doubts or wants to drop out then I guess now's the time."

There was an awkward moment of silence before Kline spoke up. "I'm in," he said, holding up his glass. "Always been in. Gonna stay in."

Rajani followed. "I am in it too," he said, raising his glass. "I designed your donut! You think I would not see it work?"

All eyes were on Miriam now. Tapping her fingernails on her glass, she looked at each of them for a long moment. "I still don't really know why I'm even part of this group," she said. "I don't feel like I've contributed much. But for some reason fate has seen fit to stick me with you guys." Almost reluctantly she raised her glass. "I'll go along for the ride."

"All right, then!" Banyon said, grinning. He and Angela raised their glasses along with everyone else. "A toast! Let us boldly go where no one has gone before!"

It was a corny thing to say and he knew it the moment it rolled off his tongue. Everyone groaned. Angela rolled her eyes. It was borderline embarrassing. Still, somehow it seemed amusingly appropriate. Captain Kirk would have been proud.

~122~

Tuesday, August 1, 2006 – 12:06 p.m.

B anyon sat by the phone filling the ashtray with one spent cigarette after another as he waited for word from Nathan Crown. He looked at his watch for the third time.

"Don't worry," Angela said, bringing him a cup of coffee. "He'll call."

"He said he'd call at noon," Banyon complained, crushing out another cigarette. "It's six minutes after."

Angela shook her head and started to say something when the phone rang. "What'd I tell you?"

Banyon picked it up. "Hello! Nathan?"

"Yes. Good afternoon, Zeke. How are you doing?"

"All right, I guess. Just getting a little nervous about the whole thing."

"Angela and the others?"

"Angela's probably holding up better than I am. But everyone is ready to go."

Crown was calling from the secluded meeting room of The Nine. The other eight members were seated around the large round conference table listening to the conversation on the speakerphone.

"Excellent," Crown replied. He got up from the table and turned to the large bay window behind him. The great Bearing Sea that stretched endlessly before him seemed less gray than usual, reflecting a bit of the blue from a cloudless sky. "Now here's the plan."

Crown instructed Banyon to call the others in his group and tell them to be ready by 11:30 tomorrow morning. Everyone, including Banyon and Angela, would be picked up at their homes by taxi – Blue Cab Company - and shuttled to the Boeing facility in Everett.

"Gees," Banyon said. "I thought at least we'd get limo service."

Crown groaned. "We want to attract as little attention as possible."

"Just joking."

"Good to see you haven't lost your sense of humor," Crown replied.

"Yeah, well my humor is about all I have left since my sanity has apparently completely abandoned me."

"You'll be all right," Crown tried to assure him. "Trust me. Everything is under control."

"If you say so."

"Now," Crown continued, "the drivers of each of the cabs are – well let's just say they're my people. They can be trusted. So no worries there."

"Your people?" Banyon asked, surprised. "You mean members of the Nine?"

"No," Crown chuckled. "They're not members of the Brotherhood. They just sort of work for me."

"You have cab drivers that work for you?"

Crown was becoming annoyed with Banyon's trivial questions. "They're not actually cab drivers, per se. They have, shall we say, other occupations. We'll leave it at that."

Banyon couldn't help wondering how Crown managed to get Blue Cab Company – the biggest and oldest taxi service in the entire Puget Sound area - to loan out their cars, especially to people who weren't really taxi drivers. But he decided not to push it.

"When you arrive at the airfield," Crown continued, "you'll be met at the gate by a man who will introduce himself as Captain Frisk. He'll be your pilot. You'll be taking a private jet to the next rendezvous point."

"Which is where?" Banyon asked, thinking maybe he'd finally learn for sure whether they were really heading to Area-51 as Kline had suspected.

"You'll find out when you get there."

Banyon winced. *I should have known.* "And what about you?"

"Me?"

"Yes. I mean I was just wondering. Will we finally get to meet the mysterious Nathan Crown?"

Crown gave a friendly laugh. "Just be ready to leave tomorrow. Oh, and one more thing."

"What's that?"

"No cameras or recording equipment of any kind. Be sure to tell the others."

"What! You gotta be kidding. Without photos or video we'll have no way of documenting the mission!"

"Exactly."

"But…"

"I'm sorry. That's the way it has to be."

Crown hung up the phone and resumed his position at the conference table. "Well, gentlemen," he addressed the eight men, "at long last the prophecy is about to be fulfilled."

"And what about the Jesuits?" one of the men asked.

The aged lines in Crown's face converged into a look of concern. "I'm afraid an impenetrable wall of security has gone up around the office of the Jesuit General. All we know is what we learned from the Chosen One. DuPont's small but persistent rogue faction of the Jesuits will be there. We know that. What we don't know is how they will get there and exactly what their plan of attack will be."

"But the Delta-3…" the man started.

"Yes," Crown assured him. "We will have that advantage."

~123~

Wednesday, August 2, 2006 – 9:00 a.m.

T he morning sun shone brightly through Banyon's kitchen window. Angela was on her second cup of coffee at the kitchen table when Banyon came down the stairs.

"In here," she said.

Banyon, still in his robe, poured himself a cup and joined her at the table.

"Sleep okay?" she asked.

He shook his head slowly. "Hardly at all," he moaned. "The last couple of hours I guess. But not much more than that. You?

"Same here. I kept waking up about every half hour it seemed."

Banyon nodded. "I don't think I ever got out of REM sleep." He took a sip of coffee and lit a cigarette. "I couldn't stop dreaming."

Angela looked at him across the table. His dreams had so often been sources of vital information. "Anything significant? Messages? The Pillar of Light?"

"Linda Shoemaker. I dreamed about Linda Shoemaker."

"Who?"

"A little girl that lived in my neighborhood where I grew up. When I was a kid I found a little tree frog. When I showed it to her it jumped out of my hand and scared her. She jumped and accidentally stepped on it and killed it."

Angela looked at him quizzically. "You mean that really happened or it just happened in your dream?"

"No. It really happened. In her backyard."

"But what was the dream about?"

"I can't remember."

"You can't remember?" She shook her head. "Then why are we talking about this? We're about to be picked up by a taxi and taken to an airfield where we'll be flown to god-knows-where to board something called the Delta-3 so we can head for the Antarctic Ocean to save the world and you're telling me about a tree frog? Hello?"

Banyon chuckled. "I don't know. I'm just babbling." Then he looked at her seriously. "To tell you the truth, I'm scared. I feel like I'm being swept along in the current of some swift moving river and I have no control over where I'm going or what's going to happen."

Angela didn't quite know how to respond. She was feeling her own pangs of anxiety but she was trying not to show it. She couldn't imagine how it must feel to be in his shoes. All she had to do was go along for the ride. He was the one who had to fulfill an ancient prophecy and save the planet. It wasn't just a frightening concept. It was completely insane by any normal standards. And yet in less than two and a half hours a taxi was coming to take them away on the first of the final steps into the heart of that insanity. When she took the job as his assistant at the homeless shelter she could never have imagined it would lead to this. But through it all she had been his support. She knew that was still her role now. She got up and walked around to his side of the table and massaged his shoulders.

"If Nathan Crown said everything is under control then I'm sure it is," she said, feigning a tone of total confidence. "Besides, think about it. Think about everything that has happened up to this point. Step by step, everything has fallen into place. Even when it didn't seem like it would, somehow it did. You know what I mean? Why should it change now? This is your destiny." Then she leaned down and whispered in his ear. "You're not a little tree frog, Zeke. Nobody's going to step on you. You're the..."

"The Chosen One," he grumbled. "I know. I know."

"Damn straight," she said, giving his shoulders a final forceful squeeze. "Now let's get you dressed. You can't go around saving the world in your bathrobe."

~124~

Same day, later that morning – 11:32 a.m.

The four Blue Cabs arrived at the airfield almost simultaneously. The cab carrying Banyon and Angela was the first to arrive followed by Kline's cab a few moments later. Then came the cabs carrying Miriam and Rajani. The drivers of each cab instructed their passengers to remain seated in the car until they entered the gated area.

The guards at the gate apparently had orders to let the cabs pass through with no questions asked. They were not even stopped for an ID check. Unbeknownst to the passengers, the only ID that was needed was the special sticker temporarily attached to the lower corner of the windshield of each cab.

Once inside the gate the passengers got out of the cabs and the cabs drove away.

Miram and Rajani walked over to join Banyon and Angela. Banyon was the only one with a suitcase. It contained the gold box with the ankh, the laptop computer with all the information they'd gathered over the course of their long strange journey, a copy of the scroll and, lastly, Densmore's book. Banyon didn't know why he brought the book other than the fact that it was in the pages of that book where they first learned about the legend of the lost scroll of Ezekiel and the prophecy they were now about to fulfill. It just seemed like bringing it along was the right thing to do.

"Well," Banyon said, "here we are." He didn't know what else to say to any of them. He felt awkward, knowing they were all there because of him and suddenly he felt strangely guilty about that. He didn't know why. Any one of them could have opted out at any time but they didn't. *I should be thanking them, is what I should be doing.* He was about to do just that when a white mini-van drove up behind them and stopped. The door on the passenger side opened and a man got out. Dressed in a short-sleeved Hawaiian print shirt and khaki pants, he looked to be about thirty years of age. He walked briskly up to the group. Raising his aviator-styled sunglasses to his forehead he seemed to be sizing them up, one by one.

"So," he smiled, "you must be my passengers. And one of you must be Mr. Banyon, I presume?"

"That would be me," Banyon said, stepping forward to offer his hand. *Thank God he didn't call me the Chosen One.* "And you must be Captain Frisk?"

"At your service," Frisk said, returning a firm handshake. Then he motioned toward the mini-van. "If you'll all just climb inside we'll be on our way."

"Where to?" Banyon asked.

"The plane," Frisk answered. "She's being fueled up right now. We're scheduled for take-off in..." he checked his watch, "...just about fifteen minutes."

Banyon saw another opening for his big question. "And I don't suppose you can tell us exactly where it is we'll be going, can you?"

Frisk grinned. "Nope."

"Figured," Banyon groaned, climbing into the mini-van. "But won't the location be obvious to us even as we begin our approach? Or at least when we land?"

Frisk climbed in behind the wheel. "Doubt it," he said, putting the vehicle into gear. The tires gave a short screech on the hot pavement and they were on their way.

Kline shot Banyon a knowing nod and a wink and silently mouthed the words: *Area Fifty-One.*

Within a few minutes they arrived at the private jet and were quickly ushered to their seats. The captain made sure everyone was comfortable then he moved forward and disappeared into the cockpit. He closed the door behind him, leaving the cockpit sealed off from the passenger section. The engines started up and the plane taxied down the runway.

Inside the cockpit the pilot pushed a button and the windows in the passenger section were suddenly blocked by panels that slid into position preventing any possibility of a view to the outside world.

Startled by the unexpected action, everyone panicked. Banyon tried to force the panel on his window to slide back but there was no way to manipulate it. Then Frisk's voice came over the intercom.

"Don't be alarmed," Frisk said. "It's a security measure."

Banyon sat back and looked at Kline across the aisle. "So that's why Frisk was so sure we wouldn't be able to tell where we were going. He's the only one with a view."

Kline nodded. "Area Fifty-One," he said, leaning back in his seat. "I just know it."

~125~

Later the same day - 2:33 p.m.

T he slight jolt of the jet's tires touching down on the landing strip awakened Banyon from a deep sleep. He couldn't believe he'd dozed off but he realized it was probably due to the lack of sleep the night before. He looked around and found the others were wide awake.

"Apparently we're here," Angela said. "Where ever *here* is."

The window panels still blocked their view but they could tell the plane was in motion, slowly moving down the runway. After what seemed like several minutes it finally came to a full stop. Then it began moving again. Banyon thought he detected a slight change in the movement as if the plane was turning to the left. In a moment it felt as if it might be turning again, this time to the right.

"What the hell is going on?" he wondered aloud.

Then the plane came to a complete stop once more. The engines were cut and there was a dead silence.

Miriam shivered. "I have to get out of here. I feel like I'm trapped in a tomb."

She was half way out of her seat when the plane suddenly lurched downward as if it had dropped a couple inches to a hard surface. The jolt caused her to lose her balance and she fell back into her seat. "Jesus!" she cried in a startled voice. "What the hell was that?"

Banyon put a finger to his lips. "Shhh! Listen. What's that sound?"

"It is coming from outside the plane," Rajani said, listening carefully.

"What is it?" Kline asked.

Rajani cocked his head, trying to zero in on it. "I am thinking it sounds like the hum of an electrical motor of some kind. Something...large."

Then the hum became a vaguely familiar whine and the plane seemed to be vibrating just slightly as if it were in some kind of motion again. But the whining sound was not coming from the plane itself. It was definitely coming from somewhere outside.

"It sounds like..." Rajani said, pausing to listen again. "It sounds like an elevator."

Banyon unlatched his safety belt and stood up. "All right, that's it. I've had enough of this. I'm getting the captain."

He started to make his way down the aisle toward the front of the plane when the cockpit door opened and Captain Frisk appeared, smiling. "Everyone enjoy the flight?" he asked.

"Oh yes," Miriam replied. "The scenic view was lovely."

Frisk shrugged. "Sorry about that. Just following orders."

A loud buzzer sounded somewhere outside and the slight vibration stopped. Frisk reached up and pushed a button. The door slid open and he gestured for them to exit the plane.

"Ninth floor," he said, with a wave of the hand as his passengers filed past. "Housewares, furniture, tools..." he paused as Miriam brushed by him. "...lingerie."

Standing outside the plane, they found themselves enclosed by smooth white concrete walls in a huge, but otherwise rather nondescript, well-lighted space with no windows.

"What do you mean, ninth floor?" Banyon demanded. "Are you telling me we're up in a building of some sort?"

Frisk gave a laugh. "Not up, Mr. Banyon. Down."

Banyon looked puzzled. "Down? You mean...?"

"We're now at level nine, below the ground," Frisk said. "Directly beneath hangar 18, actually."

Kline's eyes lit up. "Hangar 18? You mean *the* hangar 18 where the alien bodies from the Roswell crash were kept?" Then he added, "According to legend, I mean."

Frisk grinned. "No, that hangar 18 is at Area-51. Besides, you don't believe all that alien stuff, do you?"

"Well, I…" Kline started. "You mean we're not at Area-51?"

"Afraid not. Sorry to disappoint you. But welcome to Area-27."

Kline looked confused. "Area-27? Never heard of it."

"Of course not," came the reply from a man walking toward them. He was a tall, older gentleman, tanned, with thick white hair, dressed in a dark suit, white shirt, open at the neck, no tie. "You never heard of it because it doesn't exist. It doesn't exist and you're not here. None of us are here. That's pretty much the way it works."

Banyon and Kline exchanged glances. They recognized the man's voice.

Frisk stepped aside as the man approached the group. He walked directly up to Banyon and extended his hand. "Nathan Crown," he said, introducing himself.

Banyon firmly grasped Crown's hand and swallowed hard. "Glad to finally meet you, Mr. Crown. I'm Zeke Banyon."

"Indeed you are," Crown said, still gripping Banyon's hand. "Indeed you are."

Crown seemed almost mesmerized as he stood staring into the face of the Chosen One. This was the man who had come to save the world, to fulfill an ancient prophecy; a prophecy that some – even some of the Nine – had begun to doubt. This was a moment Crown had anticipated for years. He was not one of those who ever doubted it would happen.

After absorbing the moment, Crown released Banyon's hand and turned to greet the rest of the group. Each of them held a special significance for Crown. Angela, of course, had been Banyon's constant support, providing much of the intuition that guided the Chosen One along the way. Professor Kline's role had been equally invaluable, even to the point of risking his own life. Miriam, even though still unconvinced of her own importance to the group, had provided subtle pieces of information that were necessary to help bring the puzzle together. And then there was Alec Rajani, without whose technical genius and pure persistence in the face of so many setbacks, this mission could not have gone forward.

"If you'll all follow me," Crown said, "there's something I think you'd like to see."

He led the way across the huge expanse of the enclosed space until they reached the only door in the place. He leaned forward and placed his forehead against a retinal scanner. The computer screen on the security panel displayed his name and a series of numbers. Then he placed his hand on another panel and the door slid open. Once they all passed through the door it closed behind them.

3:10 p.m.

They now found themselves inside what appeared to be a subway tunnel with a track that obviously accommodated a rail vehicle of some kind. Crown pushed a button on a control panel attached to the wall. In a moment a small railcar came zooming down the track from behind. It stopped precisely where they were standing.

The car was about eight feet long, tubular, maybe five feet in diameter, shaped like a big snub-nosed bullet. The bottom half was white and the top was transparent. The whole thing appeared to be molded out of fiberglass. Banyon noticed a small logo toward the back of the lower half of the car. The logo was a simple blue oval with a white horizontal line running through the center of it. Next to the logo was the word, *PodCraft.* Below that, in small block letters, it read: *Crown Technology Systems, Inc.* Banyon smiled. *Of course. Why am I not surprised?*

Crown reached out and merely touched the transparent top of the vehicle which caused the top to swing upward. Simultaneously, the bottom section dropped down, revealing three pair of well-worn vinyl covered bucket seats situated side-by-side, facing forward. He climbed in first and took a seat up front. "Please," he said, gesturing for the others to follow suit. "Find a seat and buckle up."

When everyone was seated, the top and bottom sections closed around them, encapsulating them securely inside the vehicle.

"Computer on," Crown said. At the command of his voice, the computer screen in front of him lit up. Then the computer spoke in a pleasant female voice.

"*Destination please.*"

"Sector seven, vertical transport station," Crown said.

Immediately the *PodCraft* began to glide swiftly along the track. The ride was completely free of any vibration, like gliding on air, and it was totally silent.

Rajani was impressed and curious. "May I ask what is the power source for this vehicle, Mr. Crown?"

Crown smiled. "It's a magnetic propulsion system. Nice ride, eh?"

"Wouldn't happen to be reverse engineered from alien technology would it?" Kline asked.

Crown gave a chuckle. "Some things we actually come up with on our own, Alan."

If it weren't for the fact that the walls of the tunnel were zipping by in a blur as the car flew along the track, they wouldn't have known they were now traveling at a speed of nearly 75 miles per hour. At that speed, there wasn't much time for further conversation as the *PodCraft* was about to reach its destination in a matter of just a few more seconds. In less than two minutes they had covered a distance of two miles underground.

When the *PodCraft* finally slowed to a stop the top and bottom portions opened automatically. Crown stood up and stepped out, motioning for the others to do the same.

3:20 p.m.

Their new surroundings didn't look any different from the place they left just a few minutes ago.

"Where the hell are we?" Banyon asked.

"This way," Crown said, heading toward a large door. This time he pulled a card from his shirt pocket and inserted it into a slot beside the door. The door opened into an elevator. "After you," he said.

The elevator, too, was equipped with voice-command technology.

"*Voice Identification, please*," the computer demanded.

"Nathan Crown."

The sound of Crown's voice activated a short series of electronic tones.

"*Identification confirmed,*" the computer said. "*Destination, please.*"

"Level three," Crown replied.

The elevator began its ascent although there was no sensation of movement whatsoever. The only indication that they were, in fact, going anywhere was the digital indicator on the panel above the door.

In a moment the door opened and they stepped out into a huge enclosed area at least the size of two football fields. And hovering a foot off the floor, directly in front of them, was a sight that literally took the group's breath away in one collective gasp.

Banyon's jaw dropped. "Holy mother of…" he said, barely able to choke the words out.

The five of them stood in awe, staring, speechless, trying to comprehend what they were seeing.

Kline knew exactly what it was. He'd seen it before but only from a distance when it was high in the night sky. UFO buffs referred to it as the Black Triangle UFO.

"There she is," Crown said, proudly. "The Delta-3."

The giant craft was exactly 450 feet to a side and 72 feet from top to bottom. It was divided into two levels. The lower level was 54 feet from deck to overhead. It could function as a hangar bay for carrying various types of aircraft or as a cargo bay for transporting just about anything that would fit. The upper level housed the control room, several research facilities, living quarters and even a recreation area.

Banyon looked puzzled. "May I ask how the hell this thing gets out of here? I mean, we are three levels underground, aren't we?"

Crown nodded and pointed upward. "Simple," he said. "See the ceiling?"

Banyon cranked his head and looked up. The ceiling height was at least 90 feet. "Yes, of course I see it."

"See that partition in the middle that runs the entire length?"

"Yes."

"That entire overhead structure is built in two sections. The whole thing retracts, opens up into the level above us. Level Two. Then the Level Two ceiling opens up into Level One. Level One opens up into the great outdoors. Then up, up, and away we go!"

Banyon's only response was to shake his head in a state of wonder.

Angela was still bewildered by the size of the craft itself. She couldn't believe what she was seeing. Up to this point the Delta-3 had just been a name, a vague image in her mind. She could never have imagined anything like what she was looking at now. "We're going on that?" she asked with some hesitation.

Crown gave a laugh. "Yes, ma'am. In fact we're going aboard right now if you'll follow me."

"Now?" Angela asked.

"Well, in a few minutes," Crown said. "First there's something I think you'll all want to see. Especially Mr. Rajani."

Alec's eyes lit up. "The levitation device?"

Crown was already walking quickly toward the craft. "Come on," he said.

They hurried to catch up with him.

When they reached the craft – which was suspended in mid-air about three feet off the floor - Crown knelt down on one knee and pointed at the underside of the craft. He beckoned the others to crouch down and have a look. "There it is," he said. "The levitation device."

The miraculous device – Banyon's donut, 414 feet in diameter – was attached to the bottom of the Delta-3.

Crown watched their faces. "You look surprised."

"Well," Rajani said, "I guess I assumed it would be inside the craft. It is difficult to see under here but it seems to be a little different than the original scale model that we built."

Crown stood up. "You're right. It is a bit different in physical design but the working concept is exact to your specifications. As you know, it was the diameter of the device that was crucial to the function. That didn't change. Your partner Buzz Webster slightly modified the outer construction of the device when he learned it would have to be attached to the bottom of the craft. So the device is a little flatter, but precisely the correct dimensions where it counts."

Alec stood up now, as did the others. "I am wishing I could get a better look at it," he said. "Very difficult to see under there."

Crown grinned. "And so you shall. We can get a better view from inside the craft."

The comment puzzled everyone.

"From *inside* the craft?" Alec asked. "But how can we see it from *inside* the craft?"

"Come with me," Crown beckoned. "I'll show you what I'm talking about." He turned to Miriam. "You will especially find this interesting."

A portable boarding ramp on wheels had already been moved into position providing access to the entry hatch on the side of the craft. The interior of the craft's lower level was only dimly lit as they entered. It gave the feeling of walking into an enormous and virtually empty cavern. But when Crown touched a control panel next to the hatch the place lit up like Monday morning at a Wal-Mart. Now they could see more of the detail of their surroundings. The perimeter of the huge space – the *bay*, as Crown called it - was lined with workstations, flat-panel computer screens, and enough high-tech gadgetry to make Rajani think he'd finally attained a state of pure nirvana.

"Incredible," Rajani said, looking around like the proverbial kid in a candy store. "But the levitation device. How can we see it?"

Crown led the group about a hundred feet out toward the middle area of the great bay. "If you will all wait here a moment, I will demonstrate." He turned and walked to one of the workstation cubicles. A young technician was in the cubicle sitting at a control panel. He was dressed in a dark gray uniform that carried a black triangle patch on the shirt pocket. The black triangle patch had a red dot at each corner and a red *D3* in the center.

Crown spoke to the young man. "John, I would like to demonstrate the deck conversion for our passengers."

The young man looked up. "Very well, sir. Just give the word."

Crown rejoined the group out in the middle of the bay. "Now," he said, "if you will please observe the deck beneath your feet you will see something quite remarkable."

Puzzled, but going along with Crown's seemingly odd request, they all cast their eyes downward.

The surface of the deck was probably some kind of a high-tech industrial polymer, Banyon thought. It was a deep blue color, highly polished, almost glasslike yet not at all slippery to walk on. Other than that it seemed quite unremarkable.

"All right John!" Crown addressed the technician. "Let's see it!"

Almost instantly the deep blue color of the deck material began to change, becoming lighter around the central area where they were standing. The lighter color began to spread rapidly outward in all directions toward the perimeters of the interior. The blue hue was fading but the lightness that was replacing it was not increasingly lighter shades of white as it first appeared. The blue hue was actually giving way to complete transparency. In just a matter of seconds the deck beneath their feet was as transparent as a sheet of glass. The effect was utterly mind boggling.

"And there's your levitation device!" Crown said, with a 360-degree gesture.

Sure enough, as Crown had promised, they had a clear, unobstructed view of the levitation device right under their feet. It was unbelievable.

Awestruck, Rajani moved to where he could stand directly over one section of the device and began to follow along its circumference. With every step he marveled at the achievement, his handiwork, transformed into this huge piece of technology. "Incredible," he muttered under his breath.

Out in the middle of the deck, the others were still stunned by the magical display.

"What in the world? Banyon started. "How did that happen? What the hell was that, anyway?"

Crown gave a laugh. "That's something, isn't it?"

"Yes," Banyon replied. "It was something all right. But what?"

"That, my friends," Crown informed them, "was ATOMS."

Banyon shook his head. "I beg your pardon? Atoms?"

Crown turned to Miriam, as he wanted to see the look on her face when he explained. "It's an acronym," he said. "Alchemical Transmutation Of Molecular Structure. ATOMS."

Miriam's eyes grew wide. Her expression was one of astonishment. "Are you...?" she started, then backed off. "No, you're not serious."

Crown's response was simply a tilt of the head and a look that said *would I kid you about a thing like that?*

"My god," Miriam said, putting a hand to her mouth. "You are serious, aren't you?"

"As a heart attack," Crown said, smiling.

"I need to know how this was done!" Miriam exclaimed. "How did you develop this? *Who* developed this?"

Crown raised a hand. "All in good time, my dear. I promise you'll have a chance to learn all about it when the time is right."

"And when will that be?" she asked.

"Patience, Ms. Flamel. You'll have your answers in due time, I assure you."

While Crown and Miriam talked, Banyon was walking around examining what he could see through the transparent deck. "I don't see any kind of support structure under the craft," he said, addressing Crown. "It looks like it's just floating in the air. How can that be?"

"Anti-gravity technology," Crown said. "Don't ask me how it works. I don't have the slightest idea."

"If you did know how it works," Kline prodded, "would you tell us?"

"I might. But of course then…"

"Then you'd have to kill us," Kline said. "I know the routine."

Crown laughed.

"I don't get it," Banyon said. "This whole place – this Area-27, or where ever the hell we are – I presume it's owned by the government, right? And operated by the military? But I thought not even the government knew anything about our mission. So how can it be that we're even here? Not to mention having access to this craft! I just don't get it."

"Well," Crown said, "you're right about one thing. It is operated by the military. That is, a certain special faction of the military. But it's not owned by the government."

Banyon was lost. "What? How can that be? I don't understand."

Crown paused a moment, trying to figure out how to explain it without revealing more than he should. "Put it this way," he said finally. "And," he inserted parenthetically, "trust me, you'll just have to take my word on this – there are levels of power above the government of the United States. Above the governments of all the nations, actually."

Banyon nodded. "So we were informed by our friend Professor Kline, here, some months ago. But if the U.S. military is running the place, then how…" he paused, trying to think of how to frame the question. "How is it that not even the President knows about our mission? Does he even know about the Delta-3? Does he even know about this place where we are right now? His own military is running the place, for crying out loud! He must know! How could he not?"

Crown shook his head. "Ever hear of the Black Budget?"

"The what?"

"The Black Budget. Every year Congress approves billions of dollars to be funneled into what are known as Black Budget projects. Top-secret research and development programs, weapons development, and that sort of thing. They approve these funds without even knowing exactly where the money is going or exactly what it will be used for. They don't know and the President doesn't know. And nobody asks. Why doesn't anyone ask? Because, frankly, they wouldn't know *who* to ask. And if they did know who to ask, they know they wouldn't get an answer."

Banyon looked Crown square in the eyes. "Would *you* know who to ask? Are you... one of them?"

Crown breathed a deep sigh. "My friend," he said, smiling, "you give me too much credit." Then he looked at his watch. "We don't have much time. We take off for our primary destination in just over an hour. If you'll all come with me, I want to introduce you to a few people who will be coming with us." He turned and began quickly walking toward an escalator near the entry hatch.

Banyon wasn't satisfied with Crown's answer. He'd really like to know who the hell was running things behind the scenes. But the realization that they would be taking off for their primary destination in just over an hour quickly brought him back to the urgency of the mission at hand. Suddenly he realized it didn't matter who was running what. He had a date with destiny and the clock – quite literally – was ticking.

4:01 p.m.

The escalator took them to the upper level of the craft where Crown led them to a combination conference room and lounge. Inside the room Crown introduced them to the four men and one woman who would be going along on the mission. The young technician who helped Crown with the demonstration on the lower deck was present. Each of them wore an identical uniform with the Delta-3 patch.

"This is our crew," Crown said. "John Mitchell here is our primary technician. There isn't much, if anything, he doesn't know about this craft. For all intents and purposes, he'll pretty much be our pilot even though the craft will virtually be piloting itself since the coordinates have already been programmed into the navigational system. Paul Hanson, here, is our meteorologist. Always a good idea to know what the weather is doing. Patricia Hart, electronics and communications specialist. Robert Pershing, astrophysics. And last but not least, Michael Brock, our resident generalist without a single academic degree to his name. But I'll be damned if he doesn't know a little something about almost everything. Just don't ask him the date of his wedding anniversary. He never gets that right."

The joke brought a round of laughs from the rest of the crew.

Crown turned to Banyon and his group. "I'm going to leave you all here to get acquainted with the crew while I attend to a few things back up there on the ground. Make yourselves comfortable. There's plenty of food and beverages in the refrigerator. And feel free to discuss anything about the mission with our Delta-3 crew. They're all hand-picked by me and they all have security clearances several grades above top-secret. Which basically means you can tell them anything you want but there's a whole hell of lot of stuff *they* can't tell *you*."

With another round of laughs, Crown turned and left the room.

Banyon checked his watch. It was 4:30. In just one hour the ceiling structures of levels 3, 2, and 1 would open up and the final leg of their long, strange journey would begin.

~126~

5:05 p.m.

C rown returned to the conference lounge with a confident look. "Everything is in order," he said "We're set to depart in twenty five minutes." Then, beckoning to Banyon and the group to follow him, they went back down to the entrance level of the craft.

"Where are we going?" Banyon asked when they reached the bottom of the escalator.

Crown pointed to a location at the far end of the large and virtually empty bay. "The door with the red light above it," he said. "That will be your private quarters where all of you will stay during the flight."

Crown led them over to a white, military style Jeep that was parked near the landing of the escalator. "No sense walking when we can ride," he said. "Hop in."

As they traveled across the deck - which had returned to its original dark, almost Navy Blue color - Banyon suddenly realized no one had explained just how they were going to get the Capstone into the craft.

"Another question," Banyon said.

"Yes?" Crown replied, shifting the Jeep into second gear.

"Assuming the levitation device actually works, and we manage to raise the Capstone out of the water, how the heck do you plan on getting it *inside* the craft?"

Crown smiled. "Sorry, I guess I forgot to explain that part of the operation. The central portion of the deck retracts. That will create an opening – virtually a big square hole – up to a hundred feet per side. When the Capstone reaches the level of the levitation device beneath the craft we'll lower steel cables from the overhead. They've been specially designed to attach to the bottom of the Capstone and raise it the rest of the way into the craft to a point just above deck level. Then the opening in the deck will close and the Capstone will be lowered down onto it."

Banyon raised an eyebrow. "Good old fashioned steel cables, huh?" Then he gave a laugh. "Pretty low tech for such a high tech operation."

"Well," Crown replied, "they're not exactly steel cables the way you're probably thinking of them. More like robotic arms, I guess you might say. You'll see what I mean when the time comes."

Arriving at the door with the red light above it, they piled out of the Jeep. Crown opened the door to the room and ushered them in.

As they entered, everyone was quite surprised by what they saw. It looked like a large, comfortable hotel lobby complete with vending machines for soft drinks, sandwiches and snack foods, a 52-inch flat panel TV on the wall, glass-encased book shelves, and six black leather swivel-recliners situated around an octagonal-shaped glass-and-chrome coffee table. Sitting on the coffee table were six flat-screen monitors, one facing each recliner.

"Please," Crown said, "have a chair and fasten your seat belts. Not that you'll probably need them. When this baby takes off, you won't even know you're moving. It's just a precaution. I'll be on the upper level in the control room but we'll be in constant two-way communication via the monitors you see here facing each recliner." He paused and checked his watch. It was 5:19. "They're waiting for me in the control room. Any questions?"

Angela spoke up. "Yes. How long will it take us to get there?"

"About an hour and a half."

"Jesus!" Banyon blurted. "Just an hour and a half to get from here all the way to the Antarctic? How fast are we going to be traveling in this thing anyway?"

Crown thought for a moment and then grinned. "Pretty damned fast."

He turned to leave but stopped momentarily at the door. He turned back and looked at Banyon. "Are you doing all right? Anything I can get for you? Anything you need?"

Banyon shook his head. "No, thanks. I'm all right. I should be nervous as hell, I know. But for some reason I'm not. Must be the inner calm before the storm. I don't know."

Angela reached over from the chair next to Banyon and put her hand on his arm.

Crown nodded. "You couldn't possibly be in better company," he said to Banyon. "Everything's going to be fine. This has been a long time coming."

Then he left the five passengers and headed quickly for the control room. Five minutes later he appeared on each of the monitors in front of them.

"Stand by," he said. "Watch the upper left portion of your screen."

A view of the ceiling of Level-3, outside the craft, appeared in the corner of the monitor. Then they heard the voice of the technician, John Mitchell.

"Activating the overhead retraction sequence," Mitchell said. "Go Three."

The overhead began to part at the center mark just as Crown had described. Within a few moments it was completely open, revealing a clear view to the ceiling of Level-2 far above them.

Again they heard Mitchell's voice. "Go Two," he said.

The overhead of Level-2 began to part in the same manner. In just a matter of a few moments it, too, was wide open and they could see all the way to the ceiling of Level-1.

"And go One," Mitchell said, finalizing the sequence.

The final overhead began to open, revealing a sliver of brilliant blue sky. Slowly the sliver of blue grew wider... wider... until finally it appeared like a big blue square hundreds of feet above them. Then all was quiet for several minutes.

Banyon turned to look at Angela. Her eyes were glued to the screen in front of her. He glanced around at the others. They, too, were focused on the monitors but Miriam felt Banyon's glance. She looked up, briefly, and gave an abbreviated smile that vanished as quickly as it appeared. Then she turned back to the screen. Clearly she was as nervous as the rest of them.

5:30 p.m.
"Stand by for vertical lift," came Mitchell's voice again.

Banyon and the others instinctively gripped the arms of their chairs and waited, holding their breath. They noticed the perimeter of the Level-3 opening slowly moving outward toward the edge of the screen until it vanished from view. The vertical lift was underway. They were moving but there was no sensation of movement at all. The Level-2 opening grew larger until it, too, was out of the screen's viewing area. Then Level-1 disappeared as well and the square patch of blue sky grew ever larger. In a moment there was nothing but blue.

"I am not believing this is happening," Rajani said, still needlessly but instinctively squeezing the arm of his recliner.

"It's happening all right," Kline replied. "As unbelievable as it seems, it sure as hell is happening."

Banyon closed his eyes. He was nine years old riding in the back seat of the family car on a summer road trip. They were on an endless stretch of highway in the middle of nowhere and there was only a quarter of a tank of gas left in the car.

"Let's hope we hit a gas station pretty damn quick," his father said.

Young Zeke Banyon scooted forward, hanging his arms over the front seat. "Why, dad?"

"Because the last gas station we passed must be at least a hundred miles behind us by now. We've passed the point of no return."

The point of no return? It sounded ominous. "What's the point of no return, dad?

His father glanced at him in the rearview mirror. "It means there's no turning back now. We just have to keep going and hope for the best."

Banyon opened his eyes and gazed at the endless blue sky on the screen in front of him. *You're right about that, dad. God help me, you're right about that.*

~127~

7:00 p.m.

B anyon was getting impatient. He looked at his watch. *Been an hour and a half since we took off. If this thing flies so damn fast how come we're not there yet?*

A moment later the door opened. Crown stepped in and closed the door behind him. He didn't really need to say anything. The look on his face said it all. They had arrived at their destination. "Come on," he said. "You'll want to see this."

Then, as he was about to open the door, he stopped. "Now, don't be alarmed when you walk out of here," he said. "The ATOMS converter has been activated. The deck is in a grade-2 transparent mode. You'll be looking at the Antarctic Sea about three hundred feet directly below us."

Banyon looked puzzled. "Grade-2?"

Crown nodded. "There are three grades of transparency. What you saw during the demonstration was grade-3, complete transparency. Very difficult for the mind to adjust to the illusion of walking on air when you're hovering above a moving surface like a body of water. The grade-2 mode is easier to adjust to. More translucent than transparent with a light blue grid pattern running through it. But you can still see through it so it can still produce a bit of vertigo if you're not prepared."

He opened the door and stepped out, waiting for the others to follow.

Banyon was the first of the group to emerge from the doorway. He stopped mid-step at the threshold. "Holy sh...!" he gasped, immediately withdrawing back into the room. He grabbed onto the doorframe to steady his balance. Looking down through the translucent deck, the levitation device was clearly visible on the underside of the craft and he could see the foreboding dark choppy waters below. Then, regaining his composure, and seeing that Crown was standing securely on the deck, he cautiously ventured out. The others followed with the same feeling of apprehension in their first few steps.

Miriam was wide-eyed. "Oh – my – god," she whispered as she scanned the view beneath her feet. "That is incredible! Unbelievable!" Then she looked up at Banyon standing beside her and suddenly it all seemed remarkably familiar. *I've been here before!* She thought to herself. *I've seen this! No, wait. I dreamed it! Oh my god!* She remembered back when she was just seventeen years old. Her father had passed away and she was reading one of his old books on alchemy. She'd fallen asleep with the book in her hands and dreamed about standing on a floor of glass with a dark-haired man standing next to her. She had awakened with a start, wondering what the heck the dream could mean. She recalled now how it seemed to portend major changes to come into her life. Now, after all these years, it made sense. *There is a reason I'm here!* She still didn't know exactly what the reason was but at last she felt confident that there was some purpose for her being part of this extraordinary experience. She wanted to tell Banyon about the dream, about this amazing realization, but she didn't get the chance. Banyon had already left her side and had moved over next to Nathan Crown.

"And the Capstone?" Banyon said to Crown. "It's directly below us right now? This is the spot?"

"This is it," Crown said. "According to the coordinates you provided. This is the precise location of the Eltanin Antenna. The Capstone."

The Eltanin Antenna, Banyon thought to himself. It seemed like such a long time since he'd heard anyone refer to it by that name.

"No time to waste," Crown advised. "I want to take Alec up to the control room. He can help us run some last minute checks on the levitator system. The rest of you can wait here in the bay or back in your quarters. We won't be long."

Rajani and Crown stepped into the white Jeep and headed out across the bay toward the escalator.

As they drove away, Banyon remained motionless, staring down at the churning waters below the craft.

Angela slipped her arm through his and looked up at him. "Are you okay?" she asked.

"What? Oh, yeah. Just… I don't know. It all seems so unreal. Part of me is having a hard time believing any of this is really happening."

Then Angela noticed his expression of wonder turn to something more somber. "What is it?" she asked.

He tried to shake it off. "I was just thinking about Caldwell. He should be here. He wanted so badly to be here."

Angela squeezed his hand. "Maybe he is. Somehow."

Banyon tried to smile. "Yeah. Maybe."

Kline walked over and put a hand on Banyon's shoulder. "Probably wouldn't be a bad idea if we all went back to the room," he suggested. "You should be getting as much rest as possible before Alec and Crown get back."

Banyon agreed and they headed back to their quarters. When they reached the door they noticed Miriam was still standing out in the bay staring through the translucent deck. She seemed preoccupied with something.

"Miriam!" Banyon called. "You coming?"

She looked up. "What? Oh, yes. Sorry." She walked over and joined the others.

Banyon looked at her. "Something wrong?"

"No," she said. "Not really. I was just having one of those deja-vu moments."

"Deja-vu? What do you mean?"

She wanted to tell him but the timing didn't seem right. There was too much to do and the others were waiting. "Nothing," she said. "I'll tell you some other time."

Back in their quarters Banyon and the others resumed their original seating and waited for Crown to return.

Banyon leaned back in the comfort of his recliner and closed his eyes. In his mind he silently rehearsed his role in the scenario that he knew was about to take place. He imagined the Capstone sitting on the deck. He tried to imagine what it would look like. Then he remembered the golden ankh. He'd brought it along because he knew it was needed to activate the Capstone. *But what the hell am I supposed to do with it? Wave it around like a goddam magic wand?* The very idea seemed absurd. All he could do was have faith that he would be guided by his higher self when the time came. Suddenly he

recalled the vision he'd had of the huge merkaba and the voice telling him to remember that image. *Why? What does a merkaba have to do with any of this? Will the Capstone turn into a merkaba? How could that be? I don't understand!* When he had the vision, he now recalled, he had tried to make the two portions of the merkaba spin in opposite directions by chanting the reverse mantra. But he was only able to make the upper portion spin. He remembered being frustrated and frightened that he would fail in the mission if he couldn't get both portions of the merkaba to spin. Then he remembered the vision changed to a mass of swirling letters and the letters formed into words:
ANTICLOCKWISE
ANGELA ANN MARTIN
REVERSE DIRECTION
THE KEY IS IN HER NAME
He remembered calculating the alphanumeric values of those phrases:
ANTICLOCKWISE = 144 = ANGELA ANN MARTIN
REVERSE DIRECTION = 189 = THE KEY IS IN HER NAME
Once again he was frustrated and confused by the information. A stifling anxiety was setting in on top of the pressure to succeed in this mission. There were questions to which he still had no answers and the minutes were swiftly ticking away.

8:35 p.m.
The door to their quarters opened suddenly and Crown entered the room. "We have company," he said. "The enemy has arrived."

~128~

8:45 p.m.

O n the bridge of the Italian aircraft carrier, in the twilight of the approaching night, DuPont stood motionless and silent for several minutes, eyes raised upward, staring in complete disbelief at the strange dark triangular spectacle hovering overhead.

Inside the Delta-3 Crown issued an order and suddenly the Cavour and the surrounding waters were awash in a flood of light beaming down from several points around the perimeter of the triangular craft.

DuPont's jaw dropped. "What the...?" Shielding his eyes from the intense floodlights he bellowed out to Luis Barone, his second in command. "Barone! Tell me what the hell I'm looking at!"

Barone moved quickly to join DuPont at the window of the bridge. He looked up. Shaken by the sight, he swallowed hard and crossed himself. "Mother of God," he muttered. "I'd heard rumors but I didn't think..."

DuPont shot him a demanding look. "Rumors! Rumors of what? What the hell is that thing?"

"I heard the American military had been developing an anti-gravity propulsion system for a large triangular aircraft. A report came across my desk two years ago but it didn't seem credible. I filed it away and never gave it a second thought." He shook his head and looked up again at the craft. "My God. We don't stand a chance."

DuPont scowled. "What do you mean?"

"We have no idea what sort of exotic weapons systems that monster might be carrying. Could be anything. If they've got a PBW we might as well turn around now and get the hell out of here."

"PBW?"

"Particle beam weapon. Fires a beam of atomic particles at the speed of light. The speed of light! The resulting kinetic reaction..." he stopped mid-sentence searching for the words to accurately describe the immense power that would be unleashed upon a target. "Well, I can tell you if it hit our ship there would be nothing left of us. Nothing! And we'd never see it coming."

DuPont's jaw tightened. He shook his head. "No. I don't believe it. No one has developed anything of the sort. Science fiction, Barone. You've been reading too much science fiction."

Barone nodded. "Maybe." Then he turned, facing DuPont directly. "On the other hand," he point upward toward the Delta-3 looming over them, "we're standing here looking at an airship with antigravitic capability." He paused to let that sink in. Then he asked, pointedly "Do you really want to take the chance?"

~129~

9:15 p.m.

Looking down through the transparent deck of the Delta-3 Banyon did a double take. "Jesus! An aircraft carrier! How the hell did the Jesuits manage to get hold of an aircraft carrier?"

"Not just any aircraft carrier," Crown informed him. "That's the Cavour. Italy's latest high-tech contribution to the world of warfare."

Banyon's brow furrowed. His eyes focused in on the spectacle. "Look at the guns on that thing!"

Kline tapped Banyon on the shoulder and pointed. "Check out the helicopters. Nasty looking buggers."

"Mangusta A-129s," Crown said. "Air-to-air missile capacity. Off-axis canon. You name it. They're capable of some serious damage."

Banyon looked at Crown. "How do you know so much about that ship? Did you know it was coming?"

"No. I had no idea. When we saw it heading toward us I had Jacobson pull it up on the computer. We have a data bank with a file on every known military warship, ground unit, aircraft, and so on, that currently exists on the planet."

Banyon looked worried. "Do you think they actually plan on using any of that fire power?"

"Well, I'm sure they expected we'd be on an ocean-going vessel of some kind. They were probably planning on somehow capturing the Capstone once we raised it up. Then I suppose the plan was to transfer it to their own ship."

Banyon nodded. "That was my guess, too."

"Then blow us out of the water." Crown added, parenthetically.

"That part hadn't crossed my mind," Banyon replied.

Crown gave a shrug. "Whatever they were planning, I suspect they're having second thoughts now that they've seen what they're up against."

"Just what are they up against?" Banyon asked. "I never thought to ask you about any sort of weapons or defensive capability. We do have something like that don't we?"

Crown grinned. "You mean other than the particle beam weapon system?"

Banyon looked stunned. "Particle beam weapon system! I've read about that but it's still in the development stage. Nobody has one."

Crown chuckled. "Oh, somebody has one."

Banyon gave him a skeptical look. "You're telling me the Delta-3 is equipped with such a weapon?"

"Not just that. We also have an electromagnetic pulse beam system. We'll use that first if we have to."

"And that will do what?"

"It'll disable every bit of electronic equipment aboard the Cavour, thus rendering the entire ship helpless."

The conversation was interrupted by a ringtone coming from Crown's cell phone. He drew it out from his pocket and flipped it open. "Crown here. What is it?" His expression changed suddenly. "What? We'll be right up!" He grabbed Banyon by the arm and motioned for everyone to climb into the Jeep. "Come on," he said. "Something's happened."

~130~

The door to the control room slid open. Crown and the others rushed in. Patricia Hart, the communications specialist, met them with a look of intense concern as they entered. She locked eyes with Crown.

"What is it, Patricia?" Crown asked.

Patricia Hart, now a civilian, had served four years in the Army, including a tour of duty in war torn Afganistan. She was not given to bouts of panic but the news she'd just received had brought her to the edge. "I've been monitoring NASA's internal communications and..."

"Yes," Crown said, impatiently. "What is it?"

"They've just confirmed a comet sighting. It's heading directly toward earth." She swallowed hard and tried to remain calm. "Two and a half hours to impact."

Banyon, the one person who should have registered the least amount of surprise, suddenly felt dizzy. His head began to swim. "Oh Jesus," he muttered.

Angela held his arm and steadied him.

He gripped her hand.

Crown ran his fingers through his thick silver hair. He looked at Patricia. "Have they gone public with this?"

"No, not yet. There seems to be some confusion, some disagreement about whether or not they should make a public announcement."

Pershing, the astrophysicist, stood up. "Doesn't matter," he said, shaking his head. "I just did a quick Google search. The news is out. It's all over the net." Then he turned to face Banyon. "Mr. Banyon, I sure as hell hope you can do what they tell me you're here to do. I have a wife and two little girls waiting for me at home. You know what I'm saying?"

Banyon was speechless and could only stare back at the man. The true gravity of the moment now weighed down on him.

Crown stepped to the middle of the room and addressed the crew.

"All right, people," he commanded. "The clock is ticking. You all know what to do. Let's get the levitation device fired up. Zeke, Angela, Alan, Miriam, come with me." He turned to Rajani. "Alec, I'm guessing you'll want to stay here and observe how the fruit of your labors is put into action, yes?"

Rajani's grin was ear-to-ear. "Yes! I could not be dragged away with the wild horses!"

"And where are *we* going?" Banyon asked.

"I'll take you back down to your quarters on the hangar bay," Crown answered as he opened the door for them. "It's time for you to get ready."

~131~

9:43 p.m.

Aboard the Cavour, DuPont paced back and forth alone in his private quarters. His mind was cluttered with confusion about how to proceed. The presence of the strange triangular airship was a complete surprise and Barone's description of its superior weapons systems put everything in a different perspective. He'd expected Banyon and the Nine to show up in an ocean-going vessel of some sort and his plan to overtake their vessel and commandeer the Capstone now seemed simplistic and out of the question. The Delta-3 was a formidable monster hovering low in the night sky, boldly, mockingly.

DuPont was aggravated with himself, angry for having underestimated Crown's resourcefulness. *But how could I have known? How could I?* Then his anger turned to the mysterious Mr. York, the Illuminati representative who had been his only contact with the Illuminati throughout his entire career as the Jesuit General. *York should have known! The Illuminati should have known! How could they not?* Then he was struck by a sobering thought. *Maybe they did know but were powerless to do anything about it! Jesus! Did they knowingly send me on a suicide mission? But why? It doesn't make sense! Or were they simply hoping against hope that by some miracle I might succeed and deliver their long awaited prize as planned?* His thoughts were interrupted by the buzz of the phone on his desk. Angrily, he picked it up. "Yes!" he bellowed. "What is it?"

He stood frozen as he listened to Barone relay the shocking news. A comet had been spotted heading directly toward the earth. The estimated time of impact was less than two and a half hours. DuPont couldn't believe what he was hearing."What! Are you sure? Mother of..." He slammed the phone down.

Everything was turning upside down. The game had suddenly changed. The comet was real. *The Illuminati had been wrong about that, too! Maybe they aren't as illumined as they'd like one to believe!*

Stunned by the abrupt turn of events, his head began to swim. He sat down behind the desk and struggled to understand what was happening. His confusion turned to a disturbing realization as the bigger picture began to shift. The promised position of power had been his obsession, his single-minded goal, indeed – as he truly believed - his destiny. All these years he'd done everything they'd instructed him to do. The time for the payoff had finally arrived. Was it now, suddenly, not to be? Was he now to be deprived of his rightful place in the New World Order? The very idea ignited a fuse to an emotion more deeply embedded than anything he'd ever felt before. This alien emotion - writhing and twisting like an ancient serpent awakening inside him – began to breathe fire into the pit of his stomach. The fire raged until his anger exploded leaving his soul enshrouded in darkness. A tiny sliver of light tried, fleetingly, heroically, to squeeze into the darkness in the form of a final rational thought. *The thing to do now*, the light whispered, even as its fragile life was being choked out - *is to let it all go, let Banyon activate the Capstone and prevent the destruction that is about to be unleashed upon the earth.* But that momentary glimmer of light – the last hope for life on the planet – was quickly extinguished. With a fierce burst of energy, DuPont shot up from his chair. The chair went flying back and slammed against the wall. "To hell with it!" he shouted. "To hell with all of it!" He reached into the drawer of the desk and pulled out a semi-automatic handgun, slammed a full clip into place, dropped another clip into his jacket pocket, and headed for the bridge, the main control room of the Cavour.

~132~

10:00 p.m. – 2 Hours To Impact

Rajani could barely hold back his excitement as he watched the technician enter a sequence of codes into the levitator's computer system. Then one of the screens displayed a bank of columns with flashing colors cascading up and down each column.

"Each of those columns represents one of the seventy-six tone generators located around the perimeter of the levitation device," the technician explained. "Every frequency generates its own unique color. It'll take about fifteen minutes for the frequency modulators to synch up. When they do, all the colors will line up to match that preset color bar you see across the top of the screen."

"And then what?" Rajani asked.

"And then," the tech replied, pointing to a single red button in the middle of a small gray panel next to his keyboard, "someone needs to press that button."

Rajani looked puzzled. "Someone?"

"Well," the tech shrugged, "I could do it myself but I thought you might like to have the honor. Seeing as how this is your baby and all."

Rajani nervously accepted the offer. He grew more anxious with each passing minute as he watched the cascading columns of colored lights and waited for them to synch up with the color bar at the top of the screen. He checked his watch. Less than two hours to impact and only four minutes had passed since the tech had entered the code sequence. It was taking forever. Beads of perspiration began forming on his brow.

Suddenly one of the cascading columns turned a solid bright red and stopped flashing. The color matched perfectly with the red square above it. Another 75 to go. Another minute passed. The lights in the remaining 75 columns continued to cascade rapidly from top to bottom like digital rainbow-colored waterfalls. Then another column stabilized. Its green color matched the shade of green in the color bar above it. Then two more columns stabilized. Then another and another. The process was accelerating rapidly. Rajani checked his watch again. They were seven minutes into the sequence.

One hour and fifty-three minutes to impact and there was still much to do. The Capstone still needed to be raised up from the bottom of the sea and brought securely into the hangar bay of the craft. No one knew for sure how long that would actually take. Then, once inside the craft, Banyon had to activate the Capstone to make it do whatever it was going to do to prevent the comet from destroying the earth. No one, including Banyon, had any idea how long that would take either. No one could even be certain that Banyon was actually capable of pulling off this unprecedented miracle. No one except, perhaps, Nathan Crown.

The columns of cascading lights continued to stabilize in rapid succession. Thirty-three of them now. Thirty-four. Thirty-five. Thirty-six. Thirty-seven...

Aboard the Cavour, with gun in hand, DuPont scurried up the ladder to the next deck. He ducked through a hatch and moved quickly down the passageway toward his own newly fabricated and insanely conceived destiny.

Rajani's eyes were glued to the instrument panel in front of him. Forty columns of lights were now stabilized. Forty-one. Forty-two. Forty-three...

Barone and two of the Cavour's officers were in the middle of an intense discussion about their current situation. They were about to hatch a plan to subdue DuPont and turn the ship around when DuPont burst in through the door and slammed it shut. With an intense and determined look on his face he pointed the gun and motioned for the three men to move back up against the wall.

"DuPont!" Barone cried out. "What the hell...?"

"New plan," DuPont said, waving the gun from one man to the other. Then he pointed it directly at Barone. "I want those two helicopters armed and ready and in the air immediately!"

Barone shook his head as if he hadn't heard right. "What?"

DuPont waved the gun. "You heard me!"

"What are you talking about? Are you crazy? Do you know what will happen to us if we do that? What the hell do you think you're doing?"

An odd grin crossed DuPont's face. "We're taking out the levitation device! That's what we're doing!"

"That's crazy!" Barone argued. "It's suicide! I won't give the order! We should just turn the ship around now and go back home!"

DuPont laughed. "It's all over now anyway! In less than an hour and a half that comet is going to hit and there won't be any home left to go back to!"

"But if the prophecy is right," Barone said, nervously eyeing DuPont's trigger finger, "Banyon has the ability to prevent the catastrophe by somehow activating the Capstone! You know that! I say let him do what he came here to do, for Christ's sake!"

DuPont's patience was running out. The Capstone had been the key to the only future he was interested in. But that future now seemed doomed and if he couldn't have the Capstone then no one could have it. It was that simple in his crazed state of mind and nobody was going to talk him out of it. "Give the order now!" he demanded. "Or so help me God I'll kill you where you stand and give the order myself!"

Seventy-one columns of cascading lights were now stabilized. Six more to go. In a few moments an unprecedented technological miracle would take place.

Banyon, Angela, Crown and the others were standing behind the safety line at the perimeter of the crystal clear hangar deck waiting with heightened anticipation. Gazing down through the deck they would soon witness the resurrection of the mysterious ancient artifact as it rose from it's watery grave.

Up in the control room Rajani's gaze shifted back and forth from the computer screen to the red button, from the red button to the computer screen.

Seventy-two columns stabilized. Seventy-three...

He checked his watch. They were fourteen minutes into the synchronization sequence. The technician had been right on the money.

Seventy-four. Seventy-five.

One more to go.

Rajani positioned his hand over the red button.

Seventy-six.

The tech gave Rajani the go-ahead nod.

Suddenly Crown's voice bellowed over the intercom. "Hold it!" he yelled.

Startled and confused, Rajani pulled his hand back. "Am I not supposed to press the button?"

"We've got company!" Crown said. "And they don't look friendly!"

Everyone's eyes turned toward the monitor on the wall. The two Mangusta helicopters had lifted off the flight deck of the carrier and were heading toward the Delta-3.

"Idiots!" Crown chuckled.

Banyon looked shocked. It hardly seemed like a laughing matter.

Crown adjusted his headset and issued an order to Mitchell up in the control room. "Shut 'em down, Mitchell!"

Mitchell turned to his console. "Yes sir!" He quickly typed a code into the computer and hit the return button. A series of numbers flashed across his monitor. "In four...three...two...one..."

Suddenly the helicopters appeared to be out of control, losing altitude quickly.

With a bird's-eye view through the translucent deck, Banyon and the others watched the drama unfold as one of the choppers took a nose dive into the churning, icy, dark waters of the Antarctic Sea. The other chopper was in a spinning free-fall heading straight for the Cavour. It crashed onto the flight deck, exploding in a burst of flame, sending a ball of fire a hundred feet into the night sky. In a startled reaction, Banyon and his group nearly fell backward, shielding their eyes from the intensity of the flash.

Crown, seemingly unmoved, nodded approvingly. "If you detect any more suspicious activity from our neighbors down there," he said to Mitchell, "shut down their entire ship."

"Yes, sir!" Mitchell acknowledged.

Rajani had hardly moved, nearly petrified by the whole ordeal. Then he heard Crown addressing him over the intercom.

"Alec?"

"Y-yes, Mr. Crown. I am still here!"

"Well," Crown grinned, "what are you waiting for? Push the damn button!"

"Now?"

Crown shook his head and glanced at his watch. It was 10:32 p.m. One hour and twenty-eight minutes to impact. "Yes, Alec. Now would be good!"

Alec wiped his sweaty palm on the side of his pants and pushed the red button.

For a moment nothing seemed to happen. Nothing out of the ordinary could be felt. No unusual sounds. Nothing. Then... something.

Gazing down through the transparent deck, Banyon tilted his head and rubbed his eyes as if he couldn't believe what he was seeing. "Oh... my... god," he muttered.

The others, Crown included, gathered around in silent witness to what was happening below them.

~133~

10:35 p.m.
1 Hour, 25 Minutes To Impact.

Even from his vantage point high up on the bridge of the Cavour, DuPont was unaware of the phenomenon that was occurring in the water just a few hundred yards out from the ship's port bow, directly below the Delta-3. Distracted by the frenzied activity on the carrier's flight deck, DuPont was focused on the emergency crew battling the billowing black smoke and the intense heat as they struggled to subdue the blazing inferno. Burning hunks of the crashed helicopter were scattered everywhere. The scene was chaotic.

"I told you!" Barone screamed at DuPont. "Look what you've done!"

"Done?" DuPont said, with an unnerving calmness. "Oh, no, I'm not done yet."

Barone's eyes narrowed as he backed away from the man he now knew was completely mad. He realized he had to do something and he had to do it quickly. He was bigger than DuPont. He had at least twenty pounds advantage. *I could take him*, he thought, sizing up the situation. But the weapon still in DuPont's hand made him think twice. Still, he felt he had no choice. He knew DuPont's next move would be to order one of the Cavour's weapons systems into operation to destroy the Capstone as it came up out of the water. *I can't let that happen!*

In a sudden desperate move, Barone lunged at DuPont, slamming him against the bulkhead. DuPont lost his grip on the gun and it fell to the floor. Barone kicked it across the room, losing his balance in the process and he dropped hard to his knees. Undaunted, he quickly scrambled toward the gun. Just as he was about to reach it DuPont grabbed him from behind and pulled him back. Barone took a swing at DuPont but DuPont ducked the punch and – in a single motion – managed a back-swing with his elbow, landing a swift blow to the back of Barone's head. Barone toppled forward. DuPont took advantage of the moment, hurled himself across the floor and scooped up the gun. Barone spun around and started toward him but froze as DuPont got to his feet, raised the gun and fired. The bullet hit Barone square in the chest with a force that knocked him back against the wall. His eyes glazed over and his body grew limp. He stared blankly at DuPont and struggled to breathe as he uttered a final curse. "Even God...will not...forgive...you." Then with a groan he collapsed to the floor.

But the dying man's words fell on deaf ears as something outside grabbed DuPont's attention. A gust of wind parted the towering veil of smoke from the burning chopper. Through the cleared portal DuPont noticed something strange about the water directly below the hovering triangular craft. Puzzled, he moved to the window for a better look.

"What the...?"

When he realized what was happening, he knew he had to act quickly.

~134~

10:45 p.m.
1 Hour, 15 Minutes To Impact

Somehow the tonal frequencies produced by the levitation device were causing a localized section of the furiously rough waters below them to become still, almost tranquil. The floodlights around the perimeter of the Delta-3 lit up the area below the craft as if it was the middle of the day. The choppy, white-capped surface of the water gradually became as calm as the lake outside Kline's cabin on a lazy, summer evening. It was surreal. The affected area seemed to spread out into a circle roughly the same size as the diameter of the levitation device.

As Banyon and the others continued to peer down through the transparent hangar deck of the Delta-3, the phenomenon they were witnessing left them nearly speechless.

Miriam finally managed a comment. "That's just freakin' weird," she said, shaking her head in awe.

The comment seemed at once simplistic – almost comical – and yet completely appropriate.

Even Professor Kline nodded in agreement. "Freakin' weird is right," he echoed.

Mitchell's voice came over the intercom. "Phase-one completed," he said. "Frequencies locked. Initiating phase-two. Stand by."

A chill ran through Banyon's entire body. "Oh, God," he murmured. He and Angela locked eyes. She was about to say something when Mitchell's voice broke in.

"Phase-two activated," he announced. "Banyon's donut is up and running."

Crown put a hand on Banyon's shoulder. "This is it," he said with a smile. "Resurrection time."

With a sense of heightened anticipation – the likes of which none of them had ever experienced before – they watched and waited in silence for something to happen.

Five minutes passed with no sign of anything rising up out of the water. Six minutes. Seven. Still nothing. Eight. Nine.

Banyon gave a nervous laugh. "Well, that's it. Can we all just go home now?"

"Wait!" Miriam said in a loud whisper. "Look!"

~135~
11:11 p.m.
49 Minutes To Impact

A hint of a dark shadow seemed to be forming deep beneath the surface of the eerily still water. It was impossible to make out any kind of shape. It was just an amorphous darkness that seemed to be getting bigger. As they watched in awe, the shadow grew larger, darker, more defined.

The glassy still surface of the water began to stir. Ripples began to form. The shadow grew larger with each passing moment. More movement in the water. Then something, an object, pierced the surface and Banyon's heart jumped to his throat. It was the rod with the six crossbars that plagued him in the dreams so many months ago. *The Eltanin antenna!* A rush of adrenaline surged through his veins. He knew what was coming.

In the next moment a gigantic golden object - to which the antenna was attached - suddenly gushed up through the surface of the sea with the force of a volcanic eruption! The waters churned and tossed and the waves rolled outward from the great object as it emerged from its ancient tomb!

"Holy Jesus Christ!" Banyon cried. "That's it! The capstone!"

Angela grabbed Banyon's arm and held tight as an upwelling of emotion surged through her body. Her moist eyes glistened.

As the colossal pyramid-shaped object broke free of the water it continued to rise slowly upward into the air, drawn like a magnet toward the levitator.

Crown adjusted his headset. "Open the deck, Mitchell!" he ordered. "Let's get 'er inside!"

Mitchell acknowledged the command and within seconds the great center portion of the hangar deck began to open. Then Mitchell heard a gasp of panic come from Patricia Hart at the console behind him. He spun around in his chair. "What is it?"

~136~
11:20 p.m.
40 Minutes To Impact

L ook!" Patricia said, directing Mitchell's attention to the two points flashing on the animated schematic. She had been able to upload a complete schematic of the entire weapons systems of the Cavour. With that at her disposal, and the Delta-3's unprecedented top-secret monitoring and detection capabilities, she was able to lock in on the electronic control systems for all the weapons aboard the carrier. Any suspicious activity would immediately be isolated and identified – which is precisely what happened. Two of the Cavour's 8-cell, surface-to-air missile systems were showing activity. "They're preparing to launch!"

"What? Holy sh...!" Mitchell swung back around to his own console. "Mr. Crown! The Cavour is about to launch an array of warheads! The target appears to be the Capstone!"

Crown reeled. "What! My God!" He was momentarily dazed by the announcement. *Has DuPont gone completely insane?* "Shut them down, Mitch! Now!"

"I'm on it!" Mitchell acknowledged. Then, a moment later, he reported back."Something's wrong! They've initiated some sort of a protective override on the launch system! I can't jam it!"

"Jesus!" Crown hissed.

Banyon and the others saw a look of fear in Crown's eyes. They'd been convinced that he was immune to that particular emotion. Yet there it was.

Knowing it may be only mere seconds before the missiles would launch and destroy the Capstone, blowing it to Kingdom Come, Crown was desperate. His mind raced, trying to sort through his options. But he knew there was only one that made any sense. The PBW, Particle Beam Weapon. He didn't want to use it. There would be nothing left of the Cavour but a cloud of smoke and a mile of scattered debris. DuPont aside, there were a lot of otherwise innocent people, the crew, aboard the Cavour. *But what choice do I have?* "Damn it!" He was about to give the one order that he most desperately wanted to avoid when Mitchell broke in.

"I've got it!" Mitchell shouted. "I tweaked their system!"

Crown's eyes lit up. "What?"

"I overrode their override!" Mitchell laughed.

The collective sigh of relief from everyone aboard the Delta-3 was palpable.

Inside one of the launch stations aboard the Cavour, DuPont staggered forward and fell, face down, onto the floor with the six-inch blade of an Italian-made stiletto embedded firmly between his shoulders.

Barone, barely alive - weak from the bullet he'd taken to the chest several minutes earlier - stood wavering over the body. "But God...might...forgive...me," he stammered with his last breath before falling, lifeless, onto the cold, hard floor.The two bloody corpses now lay side by side. Barone, in his final moment of life, had accomplished what, for years, so many others had wished for. The Jesuit General was dead.

~137~

11:25 p.m.
35 Minutes To Impact

The hands of the clock were moving swiftly as the huge golden capstone continued to inch its way upward. The fate of the earth was just minutes away.

Within moments the strange antenna at the top of the Capstone peaked through the huge opening in the deck. Banyon stood wide-eyed, marveling at the object that was at once so alien and yet so intimately familiar.

As he watched it rising up into the hangar bay he shivered, overcome with a peculiar feeling. Whatever residue of doubt - whatever lack of self-confidence that may have haunted him before - was gone in an instantaneous and profound shift of consciousness. He was the Chosen One. He knew it. He was ready.

Then the tip of the Capstone made its appearance. The levitation device had done its job. Now it was time for a mechanical assist to lift the giant Capstone all the way into the craft.

On Crown's command, four strategically placed robotic arm-like structures swung down from the overhead. Simultaneously, each arm lengthened in sections, one section telescoping out of the other – until they reached the bottom of the Capstone that was still about twenty feet below the underside of the craft.

Mitchell, operating the arms remotely from the control room, quickly maneuvered them into position. When each arm was directly aligned with each of the four corners of the base of the Capstone they latched onto the ancient object and began lifting it upward into the craft.

When the Capstone was fully inside the bay, Mitchell closed the opening in the deck and deactivated the transparent mode. In the next moment the arms lowered the Capstone gently onto the deck, released their hold, and then retreated upward into the shadows, back to their positions high up on the overhead.

Crown checked his watch. That final part of the operation had taken just over six minutes. He looked at Banyon. "Well," he said, with just a hint of uncharacteristic anxiety, "it's showtime."

~138~
11:31 p.m.
29 Minutes To Impact

The huge, towering Capstone – that ancient and mysterious monument - now stood before them, silent and majestic like a gleaming mountain of gold. It seemed out of place, out of time. But it was exactly the right place at exactly the right time and Banyon had not one minute of that time to spare.

While everyone else stood silent, awestruck, gazing at the magnificent structure, Banyon disappeared into the room with the red light above the door and returned in a moment with the golden ankh in his hands. He paused for a moment to take a deep breath. Then he moved toward the capstone as the others moved back.

He approached the great object slowly with the stealthy curiosity of a cat checking out some new and unfamiliar thing that suddenly appeared inside the bounds of its personal territory. The ankh felt cool and smooth in his hand and he could feel the tingle of its subtle vibration against his sweating palm. His anxiety was building. The pressure was on. *Third Eye don't fail me now because I have no idea what the hell I'm supposed to do.*

He walked along the perimeter of the base of the Capstone, exploring it, looking for something, anything that might provide a clue. Then he stopped. *What was that?* He thought he felt the ankh's vibration increase momentarily and then subside. He backed up, retracing his footsteps. *There!* He stood still. *It did it again!* The intensity of the vibration increased and then faded. He took one step forward and the vibration increased. He stopped in his tracks. The vibration held and didn't fade. The ankh seemed to be reacting to something much like the metal detector he and his dad used to locate coins and other hidden metal trinkets in the lawn at the park or under the sand at the beach. *But what's causing this?* He visually scanned the surface of the Capstone, looking for whatever might be causing the phenomenon. Then he saw something about knee level. He knelt down for a closer look.

There was a small round hole about an inch in diameter in the side of the Capstone. The ankh was responding now even stronger as he got closer to the hole. Then a memory of something flashed through his mind. He recalled two of the phrases with identical alphanumeric values that came to him in the download back at Professor Kline's cabin:

ACTIVATE THE CAPSTONE

THE GOLD ANKH IS THE KEY

All along he'd assumed the words, THE KEY, were being used metaphorically - not literally - implying that the ankh was of *key* importance. But now, as he looked down at the ankh in his hand, then at the hole in the Capstone, it suddenly made perfect sense. *The key! The keyhole!* He realized it wasn't a metaphor after all. It was exactly what the phrase said it was. His face bristled with excitement. He looked up and over at Angela. She was standing with the others several feet back. "It's a damn key!" he shouted to her, holding up the ankh.

Angela shook her head. "What?"

Banyon stood up and motioned for everyone to back up. "I don't know what this is going to do!" he shouted. "Get ready!"

With confused looks on their faces, Angela, Miriam, Rajani, Kline and Crown all moved back behind the safety line near the bulkhead. The other crew members, who had now gathered to watch, did the same.

Banyon knelt down in front of the small hole. Cautiously, slowly, he inserted the tip of the long stem of the ankh into the opening. It fit snuggly but smoothly. He was about to push it in a little further when instantly, as if by some enormously strong magnetic pull, it was jerked from his grasp. With a resounding *thunk!* the stem of the ankh was sucked all the way into the hole right up to the ankh's crossbar.

Startled, Banyon lost his balance and fell backward. Angela started toward him, concerned that maybe he'd been shocked or injured. He looked up and saw her approaching and waved her off. "I'm all right!" he yelled. "Get back!"

She stopped, not sure if he was really okay or not. She started toward him again but Crown stepped forward and grabbed her gently by the arm. "It looks like he's okay," he assured her. "Come on back."

Reluctantly, she returned to the group behind the yellow safety line.

Banyon got to his feet, brushed himself off, and knelt down again in front of the ankh that was buried up to its crossbar in the side of the Capstone. *Okay, what do I do now?* Then he was struck by the obvious. *It's a key, you idiot! What do you do with a key when it's in the keyhole? You turn it!* He grabbed hold of the looped part of the ankh and gave it a cautiously experimental twist. It was snug but it moved smoothly with just a hint of resistance as if it was actually engaged with some mechanism inside the Capstone. He tried it again. This time the resistance gave way to a click. He gave it another twist and heard another click. *The damned thing's a big friggin' wind-up toy!* Again, and then a third click. A fourth. A fifth. He kept turning the key. After the ninth click the key had been turned a complete 360 degrees and wouldn't turn any more. *Nine,* he thought. *Of course. Now what?* No sooner had he posed the question than he got his answer. A very low hum began resonating from deep within the Capstone. The ankh popped out of the hole and dropped to the floor. He grabbed it up and scrambled to his feet and quickly backed away.

The hum grew stronger. It wasn't loud so much as it was just more intense, causing a vibration that everyone could feel pulsing through the deck beneath their feet.

With some trepidation, Banyon continued backing away, unsure of what was happening. He quickly turned and hurried to join the group behind the safety line. Angela reached out, grabbed his arm, and drew him close.

Crown checked his watch. It was 11:42 p.m. "Eighteen minutes," he said, dryly. "Something better happen soon."

"I don't know what else I…" Banyon started, but he was cut short by a loud gasp from Miriam.

"Look!" she said, pointing upward toward the top of the Capstone.

Everyone lifted their eyes to see what she was pointing at. Crown had gotten his wish. Something was indeed happening.

~139~
11:43 p.m
17 Minutes To Impact

B anyon and the others watched as each triangular side of the Capstone began to separate, opening outward from the center. Hinged at the base, the sides - like separate walls - continued their slow descent, each one lowering like a huge drawbridge at the entrance to a castle.

The strange antenna-like object at the top remained upright. As the opening grew wider they could see that the antenna extended further down into the interior of the Capstone, apparently anchored at the base of the great structure.

"What the hell is happening?" Miriam whispered.

No one had an answer. They could only watch in wonder as the sides continued to open slowly. Then a glimmer of light reflected off something inside the Capstone.

"Look!" Banyon said. "What is that?"

As the space between the walls grew wider they could see the Capstone was housing something inside, something shiny, glass-like, round, huge, spherical.

Finally what had been the great Capstone just moments ago was now transformed, its triangular sides now spread out flat on the deck like a huge four-pointed star. And sitting in the center of that star was an object so extraordinary, so alien and yet so breathtakingly beautiful, it stunned the senses and stirred the deepest of emotions.

"My god," Angela muttered, wiping away a tear.

Banyon's eyes welled up. He knew what he was looking at. He'd seen it in a vision during meditation. He wanted to speak, to say something, anything, but no words came out. Mesmerized by the sight, he let go of Angela's hand and began moving slowly toward the wondrous object.

~140~

11:46 p.m

14 Minutes To Impact

Sitting majestically at the center of the Capstone base, this was the merkaba, the final element, the last piece of the puzzle in the big picture.

It was a huge crystal sphere - nine feet in diameter, exactly - gleaming with a dazzling brilliance under the bright lights overhead. The antenna - now clearly seen as some 30 feet from top to bottom - was sticking straight up out of the top of the sphere.

Inside the sphere were two conjoined crystalline tetrahedrons, one pointed upward, the other pointed downward, exactly as Professor Kline had described the concept back at the cabin and exactly the way it had appeared in Banyon's vision. The antenna appeared to pass directly down through the central axis of the conjoined tetrahedrons, reaching all the way down to the bottom of the sphere.

Banyon stood alone now before the strange crystal globe. Suddenly his previous trance vision of the merkaba came rushing into his head in astonishing detail. He recalled the particles of light appearing and coalescing into the shape of a star tetrahedron, exactly the same geometric configuration that he was looking at now as it was situated inside the crystal sphere. He remembered the urgent message impressed upon him by the Teacher, his own higher self: *Remember this image!* At the time he didn't understand the message. It made no sense. Now it was all coming together. Then he remembered the dream he'd had that same night. In the dream he'd done exactly what he was doing now, this very moment. He dreamed he was standing before a huge star tetrahedron, staring at it. Marveling at it. Then, in the dream, he began to silently chant the reverse mantra and, magically, the upward-pointing tetrahedron started to spin.

Now he shook the dream out of his head and brought himself fully back into the present moment. He checked his watch. *Jesus!* There wasn't a second to lose. He knew what he had to do even though he still didn't have a clue as to how any of this was going to save the world from the comet that was, at that very moment, heading toward the outer layer of the earth's atmosphere. If ever there was a moment for prayer, this was it. *God,* he prayed, *if you're out there, I could use a little help here.*

~141~

11:51 p.m.
9 Minutes To Impact

Banyon closed his eyes and drew a deep breath. Letting it out slowly, a strange energy seemed to envelope his entire being. Silently he began to chant the reverse mantra.

Several feet away, standing with the others behind the yellow line, Angela could see Banyon's face. She recognized the subtle change in his expression. "This is it," she whispered to the others. "He's going into trance."

Miriam moved next to Angela and gently held her hand. Side by side they watched the Chosen One attempting to create a miracle that none of them really understood but which all of them prayed would happen.

As Banyon completed the fourth cycle of the mantra the miraculous began to occur. The upward-pointing portion of the crystalline star tetrahedron, the male aspect, started to rotate, slowly, clockwise. As he completed the fifth cycle the rotation picked up speed. By the time he finished the ninth and final cycle of the mantra the upward-pointing portion of the merkaba was spinning so fast that its appearance was nothing more than a crystal blur.

Nathan Crown, always confident and in control of his emotions, noted that his own nerves were on the edge. He glanced at his watch and swallowed hard. *Five minutes to midnight! Cutting it a little close, Zeke!*

Banyon was now outside his body observing the phenomenon with an intense rush of exhilaration. *It's working!* Then his exhilaration turned to panic. The downward-pointing section of the merkaba, the female aspect, was not rotating. He knew it should be turning counter-clockwise to complete the energy field. *What am I doing wrong?* He ran through the mantra cycle once more with no effect. A sense of terror began to interrupt his concentration, nearly breaking his trance. For a moment he felt the familiar tug of wanting to merge back into his physical body but he dared not let go for fear that the merkaba would wind down completely. Then to his surprise - and not a second too soon - the pillar of light appeared and he heard the voice of the Teacher.

Remember the dream, the voice said, calmly.

For a moment Banyon wasn't sure what dream he was supposed to remember. Then it hit him. The dream he'd recalled just a few minutes ago! This same thing had happened in the dream! *What was it?* He relaxed and let it come to him.

In the dream the lower portion of the merkaba was static, not turning at all. Afraid and unsure of what to do he feared he would fail in his mission. Now he remembered more. He remembered the scene shifted and he found himself looking at a swirling mass of alphabetic letters moving around chaotically in mid-air. He remembered he then

chanted the reverse mantra in an attempt to use the power of his Third
Eye to control the letters. The effort worked and soon the letters were
shifting around, forming into syllables and finally into complete
words:

ANTICLOCKWISE
ANGELA ANN MARTIN
REVERSE DIRECTION
THE KEY IS IN HER NAME

Now, with less than three minutes to go, the pillar of light vanished
as suddenly as it had appeared and the dream memory faded. As he
reentered the present moment he remembered something else. *After
having the dream I calculated the values of those phrases! They were
intentional alphanumeric equations!*

ANTICLOCKWISE = 144 = ANGELA ANN MARTIN

REVERSE DIRECTION = 189 = THE KEY IS IN HER NAME

Suddenly it all came together. He knew why Angela had been the
only person to apply for the job back at the shelter. He knew now that
his name and her name having the same alphanumeric value of 144
wasn't just a coincidence. The number 144, they learned, is the *light
number*. Two times 144 is 288, the *double light number*. The merkaba
is known as a vehicle of light, a vehicle with the power to carry a
person across parallel dimensions throughout the *multiverse*! That
realization triggered another memory:

MULTIVERSE = 144

What he didn't realize at that very moment was that he now had
precisely 144 seconds to save the world. What he did realize, however,
was that he now knew exactly how to do it. He needed Angela.
Together they would complete the circuit. There was just one problem.
He was outside his body and she was inside hers. There was no way
for the two of them to communicate. He knew if he reentered his body
it would bring him out of the trance and his connection to the merkaba
might be broken. *The spinning portion of the star tetrahedron might
come to a stop!* He felt he couldn't take that chance. There wouldn't

be enough time to get Angela and then cycle through the entire mantra again to get back into trance to start the entire process all over. He was being torn apart by the indecision and the last few grains of sand in the hourglass were about to slip into oblivion. His time – everyone's time - was nearly up. *Jesus! What the hell can I do?*

~142~
11:58 p.m.
2 Minutes To Impact

Banyon knew he had to do something – *anything*! He moved quickly, in his etheric body, toward Angela. Standing directly in front of her now, he spoke her name but she didn't respond. Like the others, she was staring at his physical body that was standing motionless before the merkaba sphere out in the middle of the hangar bay. He could see the anguish and the fading hope in the faces of his friends, his companions who had devoted the last months of their lives to his strange mission. Even the face of the ever-confident Nathan Crown seemed to be straining to hold on to some last thread of hope. There had to be some way to make this work. Some way to communicate with Angela. Looking into her eyes he saw her tears welling up.

"Angela!" he shouted.

But she heard nothing and the tears were about to flow over. She looked down at her hand, at the engagement ring on her finger, and cried.

~143~

11:59:30 p.m.
1 Minute, 30 Seconds To Impact

In a final desperate attempt Banyon moved his etheric body around behind Angela. If he could somehow merge with her, he reasoned, maybe she could hear him or in some way sense his presence. It struck him as a dangerous thing to try. He had no idea what it might do to her but in these final moments there was nothing left to lose.

He moved his etheric body forward, directly into her physical space. A sudden jolt of energy surged through both of them.

Angela's body jerked and she felt a warmth radiating through her from the inside out.

As the energy surge within each of them diminished, he spoke her name. "Angela?"

Her eyes opened wide. She didn't hear him but she sensed his presence. *Zeke?*

"Angela! I need you to help me!"

Again she didn't hear him but she felt an overwhelming sense of urgency rush through her body. She knew he needed her. With a sudden, instinctive lunge, she broke away from Miriam's hand and tore out across the deck, racing toward Banyon's physical body.

Miriam, shocked by the sudden move, started out after her then stopped and shouted. "Angela! Wait! What are you doing?"

On the run, and without even bothering to look back, Angela shouted, "I don't know!"

~144~

11:59 p.m.
1 Minute To Impact

Banyon's etheric body remained merged within Angela's physical form as she raced across the deck. When she reached his physical body, she stood beside him, awed by the gleaming spectacle of the huge crystalline sphere now before her eyes. At the same time she was confused about what she was doing there.

"Angela," Banyon said, "grab hold of my hand!"

Bewildered and completely mystified by her own behavior, she instinctively grabbed the hand of Banyon's physical body and waited for the next infusion of what she could only surmise was some unexplainable sense of intuition that was guiding her actions. But in the next moment she knew she'd done all she needed to do. The lower portion – the feminine aspect - of the great star tetrahedron began to rotate.

Revolving in a counter-clockwise motion, it continued to gather speed until – like the masculine aspect above it – it became a whirling vortex of light, self-contained within a spinning blur of crystalline energy.

Then, unexpectedly, the light began to spread outward from the spinning vortices and quickly filled the entire sphere. Brilliant lights of various colors – aqua blue, white, gold, shades of lavender and crimson – swirled around and around inside the sphere, blending into and through one another in a breathtaking display of holographic harmony.

Everyone stood transfixed, spellbound by the dazzling sight.

Then the intensity of the colors began to shift to softer, almost pastel hues and the swirling motion of the colors began to subside until there was no movement to them at all. In a matter of a few seconds the colors started to coalesce, shrinking into a single small point of light in the center of the sphere.

Somehow, in the midst of all this wondrous phenomena, Crown had the presence of mind to glance at his watch.

Six seconds to impact...five...four...three...two...

Suddenly a blinding white flash burst forth from the crystalline sphere, filling the entire hangar bay with the brilliance of the sun.

Shaken to the core and shielding their eyes, everyone fell to the deck. Even Banyon dropped to his knees as the disturbance broke his trance and catapulted him back into his physical body. He grabbed Angela and drew her in close. They held tight to each other, holding their breath, waiting for whatever would happen next.

The light had lasted but a brief moment and then, suddenly, it was gone. The spinning motion of the star tetrahedron slowed to a stop.

The sides of the Capstone began to rise, closing up around the crystalline sphere. In just moments the merkaba was once again enclosed within the ancient structure.

Banyon and the others looked around, dazed, confused. Several heartpounding moments later - sensing it was safe to move, and realizing they were still alive - they all staggered cautiously to their feet. Crown, Kline, Rajani, and Miriam hesitated for a moment behind the yellow safety line and then ventured out to the center of the deck to join Banyon and Angela.

Banyon released the breath he'd been holding. He turned to Angela. Her eyes now looked tired, weary, exhausted. "You all right?" he asked.

"Yeah." She shook her head, still dazed from the experience. "I think so. You?"

He wiped the sweat from his brow and checked his watch. It was five minutes past midnight, Friday the 4th. They'd made it. He turned to her with a half grin. "Hey, I just saved the world. I couldn't be better."

Angela cocked her head and, with hands on hips, she gave him *the look*.

"I mean *we*," he responded sheepishly. "*We* saved the world. I'll be damned if I know how. But we did. And just in the nick of time! Jesus! Do you think we could have cut it any closer?"

Crown rested a hand on Banyon's shoulder and gave a congratulatory squeeze. "I wasn't worried for a moment," he said.

"Well, okay," he added with a grin. "Maybe for just a moment."

A hint of the old brightness was returning to Angela's eyes. She leaned in and wrapped her arms around Banyon. Then she reached into the pocket of her Levi's and pulled out a little strip of paper.

"What the hell is that?" Banyon asked.

She looked up at him. "You remember, a few months ago, when we had dinner at that Chinese restaurant and you didn't want to see what was inside your fortune cookie?"

He looked puzzled and thought for a moment. "Yeah, kinda. Why?"

"Well, I kept that fortune cookie and this is what was inside. I've been carrying it with me all this time, waiting for just the right moment."

"No way!" he scoffed. "Let me see that."

She handed him the strip of paper and he read the words printed in faded red ink:

A STITCH IN TIME SAVES NINE

"You gotta be kidding me!" he laughed. "Well, like our friend, Professor Kline, always says..." he paused and winked. In unison, they finished the sentence in harmony.

"There's no such thing as coincidence!"

Epilogue

What Happened:

Just exactly how the earth managed to escape the impact of the Destroyer comet that August night in 2006 remains a mystery to scientists around the world. Even Banyon admits he doesn't really know what happened. But someone knows. Nine someones, to be precise.

The report, authored by Nathan Crown and issued to the members of the Brotherhood of the Nine Pillars – one week after the event - offered a lengthy explanation which included some 270 pages of information pertaining to such exotic concepts as parallel universes, quantum holographic teleportation of light fields and the strange phenomenon of quantum entanglement or, as Einstein once put it, *spooky action at a distance.*

The gist of it was that the comet didn't actually just vanish into thin air at the last second before impact. Not exactly, anyway. The bigger picture – to borrow one of Professor Kline's favorite phrases – was considerably more complex. The energy field created by the merkaba triggered a kind of macrocosmic version of a teleportation phenomenon that scientists today are only beginning to understand at the microcosmic level. In the most rudimentary of terms it will suffice to say that, at the last possible moment before impact – the moment of the blinding flash of light from the merkaba - our earth exchanged places with a duplicate earth existing in a parallel universe. Simply put, where we are now is not where we once were and, in the place where we once were, that other earth is suffering the catastrophic disaster unleashed upon it by the impact of that fiery dragon, Set, the Destroyer comet. That alone was remarkable enough. Perhaps even more remarkable, however, was the fact that the event happened so instantaneously and so smoothly that almost no one on earth actually noticed it. Any residual effects were so minimal that anyone who did notice anything simply shrugged it off and went on with whatever they were doing. It is true that various types of scientific instruments around the world did record an anomaly of some sort but it only served to provide scientists with something new to scratch their heads over.

All of this is a great mystery to most of us for sure. An equally puzzling mystery, however, is how it was that Nathan Crown – not being a quantum physicist himself - knew enough about the particulars of the phenomenon to put it in his detailed report. Who or what was his source for that information? There was a source, to be sure. But that's a story for another time. For now the important thing is that the human race was saved from extinction and, because of that miracle, the promise of even greater things to come - following the winter solstice of December, 2012 – will be fulfilled.

What, exactly, will happen at precisely 11:11, Universal Time, on the winter solstice of 2012? According to Nathan Crown's unidentified source, a sign of some sort will be seen by every man, woman, and child on the planet, no matter if they are asleep or awake. This sign, Crown was told, will trigger a massive upward shift in human consciousness, thus laying the foundation for a brighter future and a truly harmonious world.

We shall see.

The Aftermath:

Immediately following the extraordinary event aboard the Delta-3, the Cavour headed back to its homeport on the Italian coast where the surviving members of the crew were immediately debriefed and were paid extremely well for their silence. None of them, they were instructed, had witnessed anything out of the ordinary. One of them did try to get the story out by taking it to the largest newspaper in Rome. The story, however, was never published and within 24 hours the poor fellow was found dead in the blood soaked sheets of his own bed, his throat cleanly slashed from one side to the other. That *did* make the news. It also made a lasting impression on all of his fellow crewmates.

The office of the Jesuit General was quickly filled – coincidentally enough – by one of DuPont's own cousins who seemed to have magically risen to the occasion from a position of relative obscurity. Then again, nothing in high places is ever what it seems. And, as Professor Kline says, there's no such thing as coincidence.

The Capstone is resting securely in its new surroundings several stories underground in one of those locations the government, of course, insists does not exist. There it will stay - according to Nathan Crown's information - waiting to be transported to the Giza plateau in Egypt. Then - in an unprecedented world event, at 11:11 (UT), December 21, 2012 – it will be lowered onto its final resting place atop the Great Pyramid, officially marking the beginning of a new age of miracles for the human race.

Until Then...

...Miriam Flamel – studying under the tutelage of a master alchemist that she suspects may be one of the Nine - is already in Egypt preparing not only for the great event yet to come but, even more importantly, for the role she will play in the days following that event.

...Alec Rajani was given a key position, with unlimited resources, in the research and development division of Nathan Crown's company. There, he and his old friend, Buzz Webster, are working on a zero-point energy device - a device that will change the world forever - due to be revealed, of course, on New Year's day, 2013.

...Professor Kline doesn't know it yet, but one of the older members of the Nine has become seriously ill and Kline is being considered as a possible candidate for the dying man's replacement. In the mean time the good professor is still teaching sociology at Shorewood Community College and remains close friends with Banyon and Angela.

...Banyon struggles daily to cope with the emotional burden of knowing that he was - indeed *is* - the Chosen One of the ancient prophecy, not to mention the incomprehensible fact that he, along with Angela - who shares the burden – both saved the entire human race from extinction. The stress is compounded by the fact that they can't tell anyone about it. Oh, they could, of course. But who would believe any of it? The truth of the entire mission seems safeguarded by the utter absurdity of the tale. The one saving grace, giving them solace, was the promise from Nathan Crown that, in the very near future, their accomplishment will be recognized and what is now their burden will become their joy. Exactly how that would happen, he didn't say.

Recently, however, a joy of another sort has already brightened their lives. Remember that clever ring-like fastener that Banyon removed from the lid of the gold box? He had the equation *144+144=288* engraved on the inside. It wouldn't mean much to anyone else but the meaning was preciously and eternally etched into Angela's heart. It made a perfect wedding band.

Printed in the United States
221775BV00006B/2/P